Night Sky

CLARE FRANCIS

Night Sky

MACMILLAN

First published 1983 by William Heinemann Ltd

First published by Macmillan Publishers Ltd in Pan Books 1984

This edition published 2001 by Macmillan
an imprint of Macmillan Publishers Ltd
25 Eccleston Place, London SW1W 9NF
Basingstoke and Oxford
Associated companies throughout the world
www.macmillan.com

ISBN 0 333 90468 0

1 3 5 7 9 8 6 4 2

A CIP catalogue record for this book is available from
the British Library.

Typeset by SetSystems Ltd, Saffron Walden, Essex
Printed and bound in Great Britain by
Mackays of Chatham PLC, Chatham, Kent

For my son, Thomas

ACKNOWLEDGEMENTS: My thanks to David Birkin, who navigated motor gunboats on clandestine missions during the war, and who let me study his collection of original charts and log books; to David Beaty and Tony Spooner, who flew Wellingtons and Liberators on U-boat hunting operations and were kind enough to provide me with much useful information; to Patrick Beesly for his help on the U-boat tracking techniques used by the Admiralty during the war; and to Robin Coventry and Sir Brooks Richards for their long and informative letters.

Contents

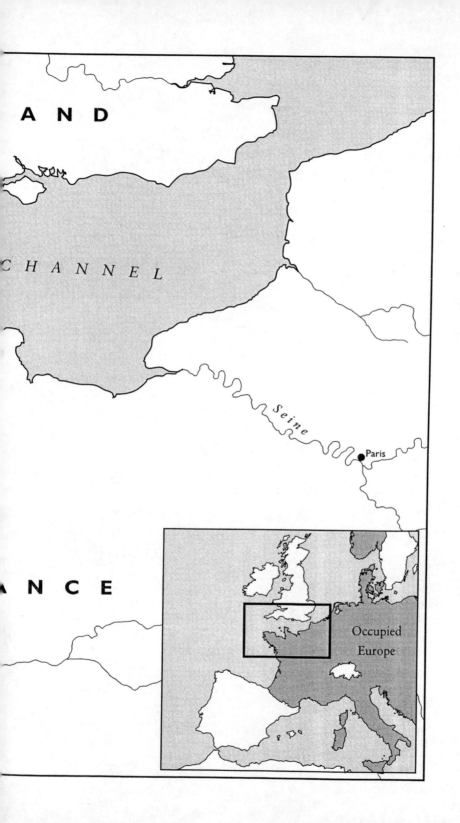

Part One

1935–1939

Chapter 1

———•———

HE WAS IN a tiny dark cupboard, the door locked, the air foul and hot. Outside he could hear voices, sometimes loud and coarse, sometimes low and secretive. He tried to call out but he could make no sound. His body would not move, though nothing held it down. At some point he must have wet the bed, for the sheet underneath him was damp. Then his stomach heaved and without warning a thick trail of vomit streamed out, covering the pillow, clogging his hair. He was desperate to clean up the mess, but there was no water, no cloth, so he tried to mop it up with a corner of the sheet, wretched with the knowledge that this too was a mistake.

He lay back on the bed, shivering despite the heat. Tears of misery rolled down his cheeks and he cried a single '*Maman!*' Then he remembered that he was not allowed to call out, that he must stay silent. The loneliness enveloped him; he wanted to close his eyes and sleep for ever.

There were voices again now: his mother's, steady and light, and a man's, low and furtive. The voices droned on, then rose to a higher pitch. There was a scream, then silence. Suddenly he was in a room and he saw his mother lying motionless on a bed. She was held down by the man, her arms twisted behind her, unable to move. Then she looked up at the man, her lips open, her teeth bared. She did not cry out; instead she smiled. His mother and the man moved in a strange way he did not understand. Then the picture faded.

He was in the cupboard again, unable to breathe, suffocating with the heat. He could hear voices still, but they were more distant now. The despair pressed in on him, crushing and hopeless. But this time he did not cry: he was learning how not to cry. He felt as if he had been alone all his life.

Paul Vasson woke with a start. For an instant he couldn't remember where he was. Then he recognised the familiar outlines of the shabby room and, exhaling slowly, sank back on to the pillow. The voices from the dream murmured on. He listened and realised that they were floating up from the street outside. One, with a thick Provençal accent, he recognised as that of the old concierge next door. He closed his eyes and tried to sleep again. But it was no use. He had been dozing fitfully for less than half an hour and now he was wide awake.

He sat up and swung his legs to the floor. His mouth felt dry, his stomach unsteady. It was the fear. And worse than he'd imagined: stabbing, cold, dragging him down. The nightmare hadn't helped either. The dream was always the same: the small room, the locked door, the suffocating heat. And such detail – so vivid. He remembered the shame of discovery and how, when his mother opened the door, he had wept even before she struck him. Later she had washed and dressed him in clean clothes and then – then she had given him a brief kiss on top of the head.

Or had that one startling kiss happened some other time?

He got up suddenly and, groping for the shutters, let in a small shaft of warm afternoon sunlight. He never let in too much light: it showed up the shabby furniture and the peeling paintwork.

He wondered what the time was – probably about four.

Still too early to go out. He picked up *La Dépêche du Midi* from the floor and flopped back on to the bed. The headlines didn't interest him: half a million unemployed; France protesting against something called the Anglo-German Naval Treaty; increasing numbers of Jewish refugees arriving in France from Germany.

He skipped to the sports pages but couldn't concentrate and threw the newspaper back on to the floor.

God, he was nervous.

He stood up abruptly and walked naked across the room. Taking a clean towel from the dresser, he wrapped it round his waist and poured some water into a tin bowl that stood on the only table. He splashed his face and looked into the small mirror above. Usually he avoided mirrors, they made him uneasy, but today he wanted to be sure he looked normal, *ordinary*. The thin face stared back at him, the eyes small and dark. And frightened. Mustn't show the fear. Dear Lord.

Picking up a razor, he scraped at the soft stubble that sprouted unevenly on his chin. After a while he dropped his hand and, staring into the mirror, swore quietly. His skin, always sallow, had developed a yellow-grey tinge. He shivered and felt his stomach twist with griping pain. He realised with disgust that he must get to the WC and quickly.

He hurried out of the room and made for a door at the far side of the landing. He went in and almost retched. A foul stench rose from the pan and he saw that it was blocked. There was another WC two floors down, but there wasn't enough time. He crouched miserably on the seat, muttering, 'Dear Mother of God!'

The spasms faded at last and, his bowels empty, Vasson got to his feet and stepped quickly on to the landing, gasping for fresh air. He stood for a moment, listening. The house was quiet. Faint street sounds drifted up the stairwell and the murmur of snores floated across the landing. Most of the women were asleep or out, though some might have customers. No-one had seen him.

He went back into his room and was sure of one thing – he would go ahead with what had to be done. There was no going back, no giving up, not if he was to get out of this terrible place.

And he had to get out.

It wasn't just the filth and the disgusting women, it was the humiliation. The *Patron* had put him in charge of this house on purpose, just to humiliate him, he was certain of that. Any cheap *mac* in the *quartier* could have done the job. The women were old, worn-out and pathetic, their only customers drunks or perverts. He loathed the sight of them. The job was an insult.

At first Vasson had thought that the job was a testing ground, that after a short time the *Patron* would ask him into the Business itself. But after six months he realised the move would never come. The *Patron* was purposely excluding him from the real action, purposely keeping him here in this hole. Treating him like rubbish. A very stupid man.

He dressed carefully, choosing old but freshly ironed cotton trousers and a cool white shirt. He hesitated over the choice of shoes: his old ones were badly worn now, while the new ones hidden in their box were tantalisingly smart. They were two-tone black and white in softest Moroccan leather and very expensive. But too risky, he finally decided. The most junior of house-minders did not have money for things like that.

He leant down and unlocked the bottom drawer of the old *commode*. He went through the contents carefully: new suit in pale blue linen, white silk shirt, tie, cotton socks, and a wallet, including identity card, driving licence and seven thousand francs in large notes. He was particularly pleased with the suit: it had been a real bargain. At first Goldrich, the tailor, had pressed him for the full price but Vasson had soon worn him down. Belonging to an organisation did have one advantage: people didn't argue with you. Anyway, Goldrich was a Jew and Jews could always afford to reduce their prices.

The identity papers had taken a lot of finding. But, as Vasson kept reminding himself, they were almost untraceable and therefore worth every bit of the effort. He had gone to Lyons, though it had meant a tedious two-hour train journey. But the further from Marseilles the better. Even if the worst came to the worst and they thought of checking up, Lyons was an unlikely place to go for documents. Anyway, they wouldn't find anything: Vasson had avoided going to the local dealer – even if one existed, which he doubted. Instead he had watched outside the Collège des Sciences Physiques in the Rue de la Trinité until, after two long days, he had finally seen a student who bore a resemblance to himself. The youth's height and colouring were right and Vasson judged his age to be about twenty-one or twenty-two. Vasson himself was twenty-three, but he never thought of himself as young. He had never felt young, even when he was a child.

He had followed the youth back to a tall ugly house on the edge of the town and seen a light come on in a top left-hand window. Vasson had been sick at the thought of what he might have to do next: he loathed the idea of physical violence. But there was little possibility of the student leaving his wallet and identity card lying around in the daytime. Vasson would have to take them while the boy slept, although the risk of discovery – and of having to defend himself – was appalling.

As it was, the whole thing had been ridiculously easy. The side door of the house had been open and then, astonishingly, the student's door too. Vasson's heart had hammered so loudly that the *tête de con* must surely hear, but no, he slept on and it had taken only minutes for

Vasson to find the wallet lying casually on a side table. He
had crept out, sick with excitement, and vomited in the
alleyway beside the house.

The wallet contained an identity card in the name of
Jean-Marie Biolet, aged twenty-two, resident of 17, Rue
Madeleine in the town of St Etienne. Vasson had been
rather disappointed in the photograph: the likeness was
not as good as he'd hoped. But a change of hairstyle and
some glasses would hide the differences. The driving licence
was a real bonus though, and more than made up for the
photograph.

Vasson was immensely pleased with the result of his
three-day excursion. He could easily have bought an
identity card on the Marseilles market, but that would
have been stupid: once the pressure was on, someone,
somewhere, would have talked. As it was the card in the
name of Jean-Marie Biolet could never be linked to Vasson.
The knowledge gave him deep satisfaction. The identity
would mean a complete break with the past. After today
Paul Vasson, born in the Old Quarter of Marseilles, would
cease to exist. The thought gave him a curious thrill.

Vasson examined the last item in the drawer: a leather
money belt. The remaining two hundred thousand francs
should fit into the neat pouches, but he couldn't be sure
until he actually got hold of the money and tried it in
place. He'd asked for large notes, as large as possible, but
they would still take up a lot of space. He would have to
worry about that when the time came.

Vasson locked the drawer again and looked round the
room. He picked up his washing things and put them into
a hold-all with his raincoat and felt hat. He would leave
the rest of his possessions; they would be no loss, no loss
at all.

His eye caught a magazine cutting pinned to the wall
above the bed and he took it down. It was an advertisement
showing a stylised drawing of a car. Vasson examined it

closely as he had a hundred times before. It was a D8SS Delage. The most beautiful, *perfect*, thing in the world.

He had often imagined what it must be like to drive such a thing, to feel it round your body: the leather seats, the throb of the 4-litre engine accelerating to over 160 kilometres an hour, and the shiny newness of the long, smooth body, as sleek as a cat's.

He folded the cutting and put it in his wallet. Soon – by tonight – he would have enough money to buy a D8SS. The thought made him sick with excitement and he almost giggled.

The air was very still, the cooling wind that sometimes wafted up from the harbour had died away and the atmosphere in the room was stifling. It was still a bit early to meet Jojo, but suddenly Vasson had to leave, to get going before he started thinking too much. Thinking was all right when he was making plans: he liked planning. But it was no good now – he kept thinking about what might go wrong.

Anyway it was too late now.

And then he remembered with a jolt that it really *was* too late.

He ran quickly down the stairs and out into the cobbled street, blinking at the harsh afternoon light. The Old Quarter was crowded and he had to push his way through knots of people meandering along the hot narrow alleys. A couple of Arabs walked towards him, their arms around each other, and Vasson cursed as he was forced to step round them. One of the Arabs laughed and brushed his lips across the other's bearded cheek. Bare-footed children were playing in the doorways while their mothers hung washing between the tall crumbling houses and leaned over the latticed balconies, shouting at one another.

Vasson regarded the scene with distaste: it had not changed since he had been a child here twenty years before. The people lived like pigs, squashed together. They had no will to change, no drive to escape. They were happy to exist like this all their wretched lives.

A child came pelting out of a doorway, shouting with laughter, and ran straight under Vasson's feet so that he almost tripped. He swore loudly. The child swerved quickly away and scampered down an alleyway, its feet flying. Vasson watched it angrily, half determined to chase after it. Suddenly the small figure lurched and fell forward onto the cobblestones, its limbs sprawled.

Vasson felt glad: it served the little devil right. The child did not move. Vasson wandered up the alley and looked down at it. He prodded its ribs with his foot. The child slowly lifted its head and turned towards him, its bleeding face crumpled with misery. Vasson stood and watched. The child lowered its head again and began to cry noisily.

There was something despairing about the sobbing shoulders. Tentatively Vasson reached down and touched the child. The child seemed not to notice. He grasped the small body and lifted it to its feet, holding it at arm's length. It was a strange sensation, to be holding a child. He patted the child's cheek rather brusquely. 'All right?'

The child did not answer but continued to cry. Vasson went on one knee and, very slowly, pulled the child towards him, putting an arm round the narrow shoulders. He felt the child stiffen. 'Don't touch me, you bastard!' The small face, so close to his, was ugly with contempt. Vasson got hastily to his feet and choked back his anger. The child ran off, screaming obscenities.

Vasson strode furiously back into the street. The bloody child had tricked him, made a fool of him. Children were no different from anyone else, he thought bitterly; they were out to get you, like the rest.

He turned on to the quay and hurried along the harbour, but went past the street where Jojo lived. Only when he felt calmer did he go back and walk up to Jojo's. He was still half an hour early. He paused, wondering whether to wait in the street or go straight up to the apartment.

It was the thought of Jojo's woman that made him hesitate.

She was a bitch, first class. She made Vasson feel uneasy. She was crafty, clever, like a cat, and, when she wanted to she could make people feel small – especially men who didn't go for her. Not that there were many of those. She was beautiful in a flashy, grotesquely physical sort of way and men made fools of themselves over her. Vasson always went out of his way to avoid her.

Also, she was a whore.

For several minutes Vasson leant against the wall, full of indecision, angry he should be nervous of the wretched woman.

But suddenly he made up his mind and strode into the building, thinking: Christ, what the hell am I worrying about?

Today Jojo's woman was going to be the very least of his problems.

Solange lay on the bed and drew heavily on her cigarette. She noticed that her hands were shaking. She wasn't surprised: she'd never been so angry in her life. Her temper was, she knew, appalling. But it wasn't her fault, it was just the way she was made. It was the mixed blood or something. She liked to think she had some of the gentle qualities of her Cambodian mother, but her father seemed to come out in her every time. He had been half-French, half-Martinican, and his favourite sport was fighting. He'd died in a bar brawl.

Jojo had finally gone too far. She loved him most of the time but at other times she could kill him. This afternoon was one of the times when she could positively strangle him. Why, oh why couldn't he get going and actually *do*

something? All he did was talk – and even then he
backtracked.

There were sounds from the tiny kitchen and she
guessed that Jojo was making some of his beloved black
treacly coffee. She considered whether to go in and have it
out with him again but she knew it would end the same
way as before, with her throwing something. Just half an
hour ago it had been an ashtray – the shards were still
lying on the floor – but as usual Jojo had ignored her.

The row had been about the same old subject: their
future.

They had discussed their plans more times than she
could count. At first Solange had loved going over the
details, it really used to cheer her up. The idea was simple:
as soon as they had saved enough money they were going
to take an apartment off La Canebière – something really
smart with large rooms and a beautiful bathroom – and
live there together, just the two of them. During the day
Solange would see her high-class punters, but strictly by
appointment; she would have a maid-cum-secretary,
dressed in elegant black, to answer the door and the
telephone. Then Jojo and she would have the evenings all
to themselves, they would walk down La Canebière and
look at all the smart shops and visit the top restaurants,
like that La Babayette place where the waiters wore stiff
collars and the *crêpes* were *flambéed* at the table.

It was all going to be wonderful. She just *knew* their
new life would be a success.

Solange had saved nearly all the money, even though it
had meant taking on punters she could normally have
turned over to someone else.

Then Jojo had got cold feet. He had started to mutter
about the problems, always the problems. Solange had the
unpleasant feeling he was just frightened, nervous of the
Patron and how the old man would feel about it. To hell
with it – girls had left the *Patron*'s establishments before

and nothing had happened. Jojo was just a goddam coward.

It was more than she could bear to think of staying on at the Red House. It was a dead-end job: the decent punters didn't dare be seen round the place too often because of its reputation, though they all said they would love to visit her more often. And those who *did* come regularly were rubbish: no finesse, no style at all. Solange admired style.

She deserved better, everyone said so. But she couldn't get out on her own, she had no illusions about that. She needed Jojo to protect her, and she needed him *now*, damn it.

Jojo appeared in the kitchen doorway and she could see that he was still sore with her. He was avoiding her eyes and shuffling his feet like a spoilt child. Suddenly she didn't have the energy to yell at him any more. Her frustration and rage began to evaporate. She went towards him and hugged his back. 'I'm sorry.'

Jojo pulled a face. He enjoyed being a martyr and Solange knew she would have to cajole him into forgiving her, a process which could take two days or more. She thought: The bastard, how he's putting it on. But at the same time she knew she would play the role of repentant sinner to the full, as she always did.

She sighed. 'Am I forgiven?'

Jojo stared out of the window and shrugged, but she could see he was softening.

She smiled brightly. 'Let's go out for a drink. Come on. I'll buy!'

He moved away and she spotted a sheepish look in his eye. She thought: He's feeling guilty about something, he's got something to hide.

He murmured, 'I've got to go out. Vasson's arriving in a while and we're . . . going on a job.'

Solange froze. She knew exactly what that meant. It

meant they were going to deliver a consignment for the *Patron*. The anger came surging back. 'You're mad, bloody mad! You ... You realise that you could go down for *years* if you're caught. And it'll be *you* who gets caught, not the *Patron*! He should do his own dirty work.' Jojo started to move hurriedly round the small apartment, collecting clothing. She followed him, shouting, 'How do you think he gets so rich, eh? I'll tell you – by getting fools like you to move all the stuff around for him. And I suppose it's the hard stuff, *noire*! . . . Eh? Jesus!'

He turned on her. 'Shut up! Do you want everyone to hear?'

In the fraction of silence that followed, she heard a shuffling sound at the apartment door and stared at Jojo, horrified. He had heard it too and reached the door in two strides. He flung it open and she saw him relax. 'Oh, it's you. Come in, for Christ's sake.'

Vasson came through the door and Solange glanced at him furiously. She turned to Jojo, catching his arm as he walked back into the room. She heard herself shouting again. 'You have no brains, none of you. No *idea*! You think you're so clever!' She threw her hands up in a gesture of despair, 'You're mad!'

Jojo turned slowly to face her. He spoke deliberately, his eyes cold. 'Shut up, you nagging cow. You talk crap. Stick to what you're good at.'

Solange stared, aghast. He had never talked to her like that before. He'd always treated her with respect. Suddenly she realised why he'd said it: to impress Vasson. She glared at Vasson with distaste. She didn't like him at the best of times. He was a real little creep, always trying to muscle in. Some people were fooled by his polished airs and his educated accent – the Jesuits had schooled him, so they said – but not she. She had his measure: she recognised him for the shifty little rat he was.

There was something else about him too, though she

couldn't quite put her finger on it; something not quite right, something that made her hackles rise.

She stared at Vasson and saw that he was looking uncomfortable. She thought: Good.

She pulled her mind back to the problem: something had to be done to persuade Jojo to drop this mad idea. She hated pleading with him in front of Vasson, but there was no other way. She whispered gently to him, '*Please*, Jojo. Don't go, don't get mixed up in that side of the business. The *Patron*'s just using you, don't you see that?'

Jojo frowned. 'Look, I do as I'm told and then I have a quiet life, okay? Anyway, it's extra money.' He turned to Vasson and said, 'I'll be with you in a minute.' He pulled off his shirt and, taking a towel, disappeared into the kitchen.

Solange yelled, 'You're bloody mad!' at the closed door, then groaned with exasperation. There was no getting through to the stupid idiot. He would end up in prison for years and she would be stuck in this tomb for ever. She thought: God, what a bloody mess.

She looked at Vasson. He was sitting on a small chair in the corner, lighting a cigarette and pretending not to listen but hearing everything. Solange hesitated. She hated the idea of asking him anything, far less a favour. But – it might just work. She pulled up another chair and sat beside him. 'Look, what do you think about this? I mean, you must agree that it's mad. If you're caught you'll take the time, not the *Patron*.'

He looked down at the floor and for a moment she thought he wouldn't answer. Then his dark eyes darted up to her face, and she was surprised by the intensity of his stare. He said, 'I just do as I'm told, like Jojo.' He smiled, but Solange noticed that his eyes were cold. He went on, 'You see, I'm a new boy around here, and I've got to stay on the right side of the *Patron*, otherwise I'm out.'

His eyes held hers, still smiling. So he was trying some

charm on her, was he? Right, if that was the game, she could play it too.

She moved still nearer and put her hand on his leg. 'You're an intelligent man. You can see it's far too risky.' She gave him a long intense look from under her lashes. It was her favourite weapon and it usually did the trick. But almost immediately she saw that she had made a mistake. A look of alarm had come into his eyes, a look almost of ... for a moment she was puzzled, then she had it: it was *revulsion*. She thought: Ah, so that's it, that's what I couldn't pin down: you're a woman-hater.

She withdrew her hand and stared at him. His smile had vanished and he was watching her coldly. Eventually he said, 'Nothing's risky if you're careful enough. Jojo was right, you should keep to your work and mind your own business.' He had put a small but unmistakable tone of insolence into the word 'work'.

Solange gritted her teeth. He had humiliated her and she thought: One round to you, but not the last!

Jojo came into the room and Solange moved away. One glance at Jojo and she knew he wasn't going to listen to any more arguments. She sat down on her favourite piece of furniture, a little pink *chaise longue*, and thought: To hell with him.

Jojo planted a kiss on her cheek, and said: 'See you later. Don't know when.'

Solange did not reply, but sat stiffly on the *chaise* staring out of the window. She felt the dull ache of anxiety in her heart and she knew she wouldn't stop worrying until Jojo was safely back.

Vasson watched Jojo striding ahead of him and wondered why he was in such a hurry. God forbid that the pick-up was going to be early. That would ruin everything. He had told the Algerian that it would be at ten, and everything had been arranged accordingly. Damn, he would have to make sure.

He put in a couple of loping strides and came up beside Jojo. 'What's the hurry? We've got hours yet. It's only six, you know.'

'Eh?' Jojo slowed up and looked around him, as if realising for the first time where he was. 'Oh. Sorry. I was . . . still thinking . . . you know.'

Vasson was relieved. It was the woman who was on Jojo's mind, not the pick-up. He shivered at the memory of the woman, with her roving hands and her large open mouth. She had no idea of how disgusting she was: the foreign brownish skin was somehow greasy and unclean.

But at least she'd got Jojo in a state and not thinking straight, which should make things easier. He wondered what to ask first. Best to make sure about the time. He said casually, 'It is still on for ten, isn't it?'

'What? . . . Oh, yes, yes. There's no change.'

Vasson gave Jojo a sidelong glance. He was frowning, his eyes on the paving in front of his feet. Vasson decided that some sympathy, some intimate conversation, was needed before it was safe to go on. He touched Jojo's arm and said, 'Look, I'm sure it'll all be all right when you get back. She'll have forgotten why she was angry.'

Gratitude flashed across Jojo's face and Vasson saw that he had been right to bring up the subject. Jojo shook his head. 'Honestly . . . I don't know why she has it in for me sometimes. It's a mystery to me. Trouble is . . .' He looked across with an expression that Vasson couldn't fathom. 'I like having her around.'

They turned a corner and Vasson had to drop behind Jojo to pass two black-scarved women talking in the middle of the street. He considered whether to ask the big question now or leave it till later. Jojo might refuse to answer in such a public place. It might be better to wait until they'd had a couple of pastis and Jojo was more relaxed. On the other hand time would be getting short by then and the right moment might not come up again. Vasson prided himself on judging the right moment.

Suddenly he decided that this was the best moment he would get. It was only fear, he realised, that had held him back.

He came up beside Jojo again, his heart thumping loudly. He swallowed and, leaning towards Jojo, said, 'Look, I've got a bit of a woman problem too. I want to see this girl tonight. She's really hot stuff . . . But, well, she can't get off work until nine and . . . it would mean a lot to see her for just half an hour or so. Is there any chance that I can meet you *there*?'

Jojo looked at him sharply. Vasson put on a rueful, sheepish expression and laughed. 'I know it's stupid, but I'm really mad about her and there's this other guy hanging about. If I don't get to see her tonight, he'll be there like a shot.' He sighed. 'He's got the lot: money, a car, flash clothes. My only hope is to see her and tell her . . .' He trailed off and tried to look lovelorn.

They turned on to the quay and up a small road beside a fish warehouse. This was where the car was kept. Jojo still hadn't answered and Vasson glanced across at him, trying to read his face.

Jojo paused to unlock the garage door. He was frowning. 'I'd have to tell you where the pick-up was and you know the *Patron*'s rules about that.'

Vasson nodded and stroked his chin. 'Yes, of course. I hadn't thought of that.'

Jojo backed the car out. Vasson closed the garage door and got into the passenger seat. The Citroën set off towards the quay, bumping gently over the cobbles.

Jojo lit a cigarette one-handed and said brightly, 'Well, where's it to be? Hamid's? Or shall we go to that new bar just off the Rue Caisserie? There's a place next door that does a really good *cous-cous*.'

Vasson thought: Shit! He's not going to buy it. That meant that Vasson would have to contact the Algerian to arrange a tail and then stay with Jojo all evening, right up until the end. He didn't like that idea at all: it would mean slipping away at the very last moment which would be risky, horribly risky. He felt angry. Christ, he didn't ask much. Just a little confidence, and Jojo, who was meant to be his friend, wasn't even going to give him that!

Jojo was waiting for an answer. Vasson shrugged and said in a tight voice: 'I don't care where the hell we go.'

'Oh, for God's sake, it's that bad, is it? This girl, I mean.'

'Yes, it is.'

Jojo sighed deeply. Eventually he said, 'Okay, okay, you win. But if it ever gets back to the *Patron* that I told you *where* to go, I'll kill you. He's really nervous at the moment. There's a lot of pressure, as you know.'

'Oh?'

'The Algerian. He's trying to move in again. You must have heard.'

'Ah. No, I hadn't.' Vasson enjoyed lying, mainly because he found it so easy. The best thing in the world was to carry a lie through all the way, to build on it, to refine it. He really liked that; it gave him a lot of satisfaction.

Vasson appeared to consider, then said, 'Well, of course, there's no way the *Patron* is going to find out, but ... if you really think there's a problem?'

'No, go on. See her. Just don't let me down, that's all. *Be* there, and on time.'

They stopped at a junction. Jojo turned and said softly, 'Okay, the place is a small store off the Quai de la Rive Neuve. Behind the big warehouse, L'Entrepôt du Midi. It's got Laborde et Fils over the main door. It's in the same street as that night club, La Ronde.'

'Okay, and thanks. Thanks a lot. I'll remember the

favour.' Vasson smiled warmly. He really *was* pleased. Jojo had done him the biggest favour of his life.

'Where to, then?'

'Hamid's. I don't like that new place.' Vasson didn't like the new place because there was only one telephone and it was on the bar itself.

Hamid's was already crowded and the air was thick with smoke and the smell of herbal tobacco. The two men squeezed in at the far end of the counter and ordered Pernod. Vasson didn't attempt to keep the look of triumph off his face. After all, he had every reason to be happy: he was in love, wasn't he?

There was only the phone call left now, and that would be easy. He waited for Jojo to order another round, then made a show of looking at his watch. 'Look, I can get her on the telephone at work now. It'll save me having to go round to meet her.'

Jojo stirred the water into his Pernod. 'Where does she work?'

'La Belle Epoque. It's a dress shop off La Canebière. Very classy.'

'What's her name?'

'Marie-Hélène. Hey, why all the questions? You're not thinking of pinching her, are you?' He gave Jojo a friendly dig in the ribs and leered at him, thinking: This inquisition has got to stop.

Jojo smiled and said, 'No, I've got enough trouble with Solange. She doesn't give me enough time for other women. Anyway, I'm not an educated type like you. I'm not into classy pieces who work in dress shops.'

Vasson took out his wallet and put some money on the bar. 'Here. Have another while I'm phoning.' A drink would keep Jojo busy.

Jojo caught his arm. 'What's that you have there?' He was peering at Vasson's still-open wallet.

Vasson's heart missed a beat and he thought: God, what the hell's he spotted?

Jojo smiled and, taking the wallet, pulled out the newspaper cutting of the Delage. 'That car again, eh? What with girls from La Canebière and cars like this...' He shook his head and flicked the picture with his finger. 'You have expensive tastes. Very expensive.'

Vasson shrugged and smiled casually. 'No harm in dreaming, is there?'

'None at all.' Jojo replaced the cutting and handed the wallet back to Vasson. 'No harm at all. Just as long as you don't try to get it the easy way.' He grinned broadly to soften the words, but Vasson thought: Goddam you, you're treating me like a child too.

He said lightly, 'I know there's no easy way.'

He pocketed the wallet and, moving quickly down the bar, went through a door into the back. Hamid was there. Vasson asked, 'Mind if I use the telephone?'

Hamid looked up. He was a Tunisian Arab who, after twenty years in Marseilles, still wore a jellabah. He indicated the telephone on the desk. 'Salam, my friend. Please, please.'

'It's a private call. Do you mind?'

The old man smiled. 'Of course, of course.' He disappeared into the bar and closed the connecting door.

Vasson thought carefully. There was a second extension in the bar itself, but he would know immediately if anyone listened in because of the noise. It was possible there was another extension upstairs, but doubtful. Hamid was a careful businessman. He wouldn't spend money on luxuries like that.

He raised the receiver and asked for the number he'd been given. There was a long silence and for a moment Vasson was worried in case he'd memorised the wrong number. But then there was a voice on the line, 'Yes?'

'It's me.'

'Have you any news?'

'Yes, ten tonight, at a warehouse named Laborde et Fils, behind L'Entrepôt du Midi, on the other side of the harbour.'

'Got it.'

'And the other address?'

'When you deliver what you owe me.'

There was a silence. 'All right. A briefcase will be delivered to you at the corner of Rue Caisserie and Rue Roger at exactly ten-thirty. Make sure you have that address written on a piece of paper ready to hand to the driver. Goodbye.'

Vasson replaced the receiver. He moved round to the other side of the desk and found a pencil and a piece of clean paper under the piles of till receipts. In block capitals he carefully wrote the address of the heroin processing laboratory that the *Patron* maintained in a quiet suburb on the south side of the city, beyond the hill of Notre-Dame de la Garde. He had delivered some stuff there once. They had told him it was only a safe house, but he had checked on it. He had gone back and watched the place: two men arrived at eight and left at four on the first day. And the second day. And the third. Regular little workers, they were.

He had followed one home. A garrulous neighbour had informed him that the worker was a chemist who used to work for a big pharmaceutical company somewhere. No one was sure where he worked now. Vasson hadn't bothered to check on the second worker: he knew he'd found the laboratory.

He put the piece of paper in his back pocket and went through into the bar. Jojo had obviously been watching the door: as Vasson looked round he found the other man staring at him. Vasson smiled and waved. But something else was expected. Of course: he smacked his hand in the crook of his elbow in the age-old obscene gesture.

Jojo laughed and shouted, 'Lucky devil!'

Yes, thought Vasson, how right you are.

Vasson peered up and down both streets again. Occasionally the headlights of a car came sweeping up the Rue Caisserie, but none of them slowed down. He felt sure it must be after ten-thirty, but without a watch he couldn't be positive. He had left Hamid's just before nine and gone to a strange bar in the north of the Quarter until just before ten. Since then he'd been walking the streets for at least half an hour. He decided a watch was one of the first things he was going to buy with the money. He rather liked the new metal Rolexes: smart yet practical.

He'd never had real money before, but he knew exactly what he was going to do with it. There would be a small rented apartment in the 18th Arrondissement, a D8SS Delage – though he probably wouldn't be able to afford a new one – and a nice little business. A club probably, with high-class girls and some expensive décor. But whatever the business, he would work hard at it and it would be a success. He couldn't understand people who spent wildly instead of investing for the future. There was no way he was going to be caught in *that* trap. Apart from the Delage which would have to be bought for cash, he was going to invest every penny.

There was still no sign of a car. Vasson began to feel nervous. They must come soon; they needed that address.

Suddenly a terrible thought came to him. Suppose . . . suppose they had got the address out of Jojo . . .

He felt sick and groaned. *Of course.* Why hadn't he thought of it before? If Jojo had talked . . . then they wouldn't turn up in a million years. *And they wouldn't bring the money.*

Oh God, please don't let it be true, please.

He leant back against the wall and stared through the darkness at the building opposite. The thought of not having the money was so appalling that he couldn't imagine it. The money was everything . . .

He stayed immobile against the wall, as if by freezing his body he could postpone the moment of truth.

The time must be at least a quarter to eleven.

There was a sudden flash of light and he looked up. A long low car was sliding into the kerb. He stared at it uncomprehendingly.

A car . . . *The car* . . .

Oh dear God, thank you, *thank you*. He stepped forward, half-chuckling, half-crying.

The rear door opened and a voice called, 'Get in!'

Vasson stood by the open door. 'No, I'd rather not.' Through his elation he thought: I'm not going to be caught by that old trick.

The voice said, 'I thought you'd want to count the money.'

Vasson considered. They were right, of course. But it was still too risky to get in; he would take a quick look at the cash and he'd soon know if there was a lot missing. 'No, just hand it over.'

'You have the address ready?'

An old attaché case appeared from inside the car and Vasson crouched on the pavement to open it. In the dim light of the street lamp he saw piles of clean new bank notes. 'They're new! I asked for old!'

'They're straight out of the bank. Clean as a whistle.'

'But how do I know they're not hot?'

'They're not pinched, if that's what you mean.'

Vasson cursed, but he knew he was beaten. He'd have to accept the new notes and like it. He thrust the piece of paper into the car and a hand reached out to close the door. Vasson leapt for the door and held it open. 'Stop!

You promised! You promised to tell me what happened.'
He clung on to the door. No-one was going to close it until
he had an answer.

There was a pause, then the voice said, 'Okay, okay.
We gave the news of the pick-up to our friends at the
commissariat.'

'Why? Why *them*?'

'We owe them a favour. Anyway we want them to get
the odd conviction; it keeps everyone happy.'

So, it was prison for Jojo. He'd got off lightly then.
Vasson was glad: he'd quite liked the guy.

The voice had fallen silent. Vasson prompted. 'Well?
What about the *Patron*?'

'We've already dealt with him. He had ... a little
accident, about half an hour ago. And the laboratory, the
technicians – we'll be taking them over ourselves.' There
was a pause, then the voice said mockingly, 'Does all this
meet with your satisfaction?'

Vasson ignored the sarcasm and grinned, 'Oh yes, oh
yes!'

The car revved up. 'You won't be staying around, will
you? The Algerian doesn't think it'll be very healthy for
you.'

'Don't worry, I'm going on a long trip. To Algeria.'

As the car drove off, Vasson laughed. To Algeria. He
liked that. Very neat.

He walked rapidly, the attaché case swinging in his
hand. God, what a coup! What a strike! Perfect – the
whole thing had gone perfectly.

And it felt so good! *Sweet* – yes! That's how it felt.

He had only one regret: that he hadn't been able to see
the *Patron*'s expression when he realised he'd been out-
manoeuvred. The bastard, that would teach him.

Vasson paused near the house. The place seemed quiet.
If possible he wanted to get to his room without meeting
any of the girls.

He crept up to the doorway and into the hall. No-one. He ran lightly up the stairs to the landing outside his room. He put his ear to the door and listened carefully.

There was no sound; nothing to worry about. Everything was going to be all right.

He put the key into the lock and in that instant he knew that it had all gone dreadfully wrong.

The door was already unlocked.

As it swung open he saw the bottom drawer gaping at him. The lock had been broken. He stared stupidly at it until a slight movement caught his eye.

There was someone in the room.

It was Jojo's woman.

She was staring at him, her eyes wide and angry.

For a moment neither of them moved. Vasson noticed that the woman was panting heavily. Slowly he looked round the room and understood why. The bitch had been through the place. Magazines spilled off the shelves; his new suit lay in a crumpled ball on the floor. The beautiful white silk shirt hung off the side of the bed, a smear of dirt showing grey on its sleeve.

He thought: God, why did she have to *spoil* everything? Why couldn't she have left me *alone*?

Then he saw the money. The thirty thousand francs advance payment lay neatly stacked on top of the chest. Next to it were some papers.

Oh God. The papers.

He closed the door slowly behind him and faced her. 'Why? Why did you come here?'

'You bastard! You shopped Jojo! You bastard!' She started to scream at him.

Vasson thought: Damn, damn. He had to think clearly but it was impossible while she was still yelling. 'Shut up!' he shouted.

Her mouth closed in surprise.

Quickly he said, 'What gave you that idea? That I shopped Jojo?'

'Oh, I *know* you did! My friend told me, my *Inspector* friend.'

'Impossible.'

'Oh he didn't *say* it was you.' She was beginning to scream again. 'But as soon as he told me someone had, I knew it *had* to be you. And what do I find, eh? *All this!*' She picked up the money and shook it at him.

He thought: Perhaps she hasn't seen the papers, perhaps it's all right after all. But then he realised she *must* have, when she took them out of the drawer.

She had seen the papers.

She knew his new name.

He took a step forward and said quietly, 'Give me the money.' She started to move to one side and he saw her glance at the door. God, she was stupid. He took a step sideways and cut her off.

She stared at him defiantly. 'You bastard, take your bloody money!' She threw the notes at him and they fluttered down to the floor.

She's done it again, he thought. Dirtied everything unnecessarily, spoilt it all.

He reached for her and saw the fear leap into her eyes. He would have to be quick otherwise she'd scream. He grabbed at her but she pulled free and ran for the door. Even before she got to it, he knew he would be able to catch her and he felt a surge of power. She was grappling with the handle. He came up behind her and got a hand round first one arm then the other. Then he thought: God, what do I do next?

She was kicking backwards at him and he pulled her closer so that her legs would lose their momentum. She started to yell and he suddenly realised what he would have to do. He put an arm round her throat and as her hand shot up to pull it away, he raised his other arm. After that it was a simple matter to slide his hands on to her neck.

He squeezed and the yelling stopped. Her breathing changed to a series of loud agonising rasps. It was too noisy: he would have to squeeze harder. The noise changed to a gurgle and he thought: That's better. Then she started to fight, writhing her body from side to side and kicking her legs again. It occurred to him that it would be much easier on the floor.

He twisted her round and started to push her down. At the sight of his face she went for his eyes and he felt her nails digging into his skin. Panicking he squeezed harder and she grasped desperately at his hands again. Her eyes began to pop and he stared at them, amazed at the enormous size of the human eye.

He wondered how much longer it would take. He was running out of strength. It was much more difficult than he'd thought: she was so strong. He looked down at her. She was purple now and her tongue was protruding from her mouth. The sight was disgusting and he closed his eyes.

At last he looked again. Her eyes were staring blankly and the obscene tongue was hanging swollen from the mouth. Tentatively he let go. The head lolled back. The body lay still.

He backed away on hands and knees and crouched, crying quietly. God, what a stupid bitch. Why couldn't she leave well enough alone?

His stomach heaved and he lurched to the basin to throw up. Afterwards he dipped a cloth in the water jug and washed his face for a long time.

Eventually he realised it was late. The last night train left in half an hour. He picked up his crumpled clothes from the floor and began to change. By facing towards the basin all the time he could avoid looking at the body. When he had changed he picked the money up from the floor, leaving only one note which was protruding from under the woman's head. He packed the money into the money belt along with the notes from the attaché case. The new identity papers went into his jacket pocket.

At last he was ready. The clothes didn't look too bad, though the shirt was dreadfully creased. He would have it dry-cleaned when he got to Paris.

He looked in the mirror. He looked just the same but he didn't feel it. He would never *feel* the same again. That woman had tainted him with her dirt. It must never happen again. He would make sure of that.

Thank God at least for the money, the sweet, beautiful money. That made him feel clean again.

Chapter 2

IT WAS A CLEAR, cloudless September day. In Plymouth Sound anchored warships were silhouetted black against the sparkling sea and twelve miles away, on the horizon, the tall Eddystone Lighthouse was clearly visible, a dark needle against the pale blue sky. A fresh south-westerly breeze was blowing in from the sea and on the exposed height of Plymouth Hoe it was rather cold. Only a handful of people were braving a stroll along the historic pathways where, according to popular legend, Drake had played his game of bowls.

Julie Lescaux sat on a bench and stared out beyond the breakwater to the wide English Channel. She thought: I could always kill myself.

But she knew she wouldn't. She hadn't the nerve to do something like that. Even at school she'd never had the nerve to do anything daring or risky. When some of the other girls had dressed up to look eighteen and gone dancing in the city, she'd ducked out. They'd called her a goody-goody. And they were right: she had always been – well, anxious to do the right thing.

Julie thought: If only they knew the truth.

It was strange how life changed – and so quickly, without warning. She'd always thought of herself as an ordinary sort of person who would always have an ordinary life. Well, perhaps ordinary sounded a bit dull. Average was better.

Yes, she thought: That's what I am – average.

And yet it was she who was going to be different from all the others. She, the goody-goody. Bad things were half-expected of girls like Maggie Phillips, who had begun pencilling her eyebrows and wearing high heels at sixteen; Maggie who had lots of boyfriends and was considered 'flighty'.

But it hadn't happened to Maggie; it had happened to Julie.

Julie could imagine what people would say. They would use all the stock phrases, all the old clichés.

But there was no way round it. No way round the bald facts.

She was just nineteen and pregnant.

She had got into trouble.

She had been 'easy'.

She had ruined her life.

She tried to imagine what it was like, to have people whispering and sniggering about you, talking behind your back and pointing you out. It would be terrible, she knew, not just for her, but for Mother. Mother would find it unbearable, worse than anything else that could possibly happen. Her mother believed in respect and being able to hold your head up. She set great store by what people thought.

It would be like stabbing her in the back.

Unless Julie got married. But she knew there was no chance of that, none at all.

Her mother . . . Julie had no idea how she was going to tell her. Whichever way she did it, her mother would die of shame and anger and bitterness. She would accuse Julie of ingratitude and disloyalty and selfishness and say she had ruined both their lives. Julie could hear her very words.

The only thing worse would be another interview with Doctor Hargreaves. Julie shrank at the memory. It had been deeply humiliating, much worse than she'd ever imagined. He had called her shameless and ungrateful.

He'd asked her why she'd gone and thrown herself at the first man who'd asked.

She hadn't replied. She'd thought: Perhaps he's right. Perhaps I am shameless, ungrateful.

In the end he had told her he would keep her as a patient, but only out of loyalty to her mother. Then he said – and the words had taken Julie by surprise – that the baby would need to be adopted and that he would arrange it.

She hadn't thought about what would happen to the baby. How strange! The whole fuss was about having a baby, and she hadn't thought about the actual baby, the object of it all. A baby . . . She knew nothing about babies, she'd never even held one. Did she want a baby? Would she love it? She had no idea.

A gust of wind blew across the Hoe and lifted the hem of her frock. She pushed the skirt down again and pulled her coat round her knees. When she looked up she was aware that someone was staring at her. It was a sailor walking slowly towards her. Julie looked quickly away and waited nervously for him to pass.

For an awful moment she thought he was going to stop and try to pick her up. But, after pausing for a moment, he suddenly quickened his step and walked away.

Julie relaxed and sat back on the bench. It would have been surprising if he had tried to pick her up. She rarely had trouble of that kind. She supposed it was because she didn't look the type. She was wearing the white gloves her mother insisted she wore, and a frock at least two inches longer than the current calf-length fashion; not exactly the outfit for a scarlet woman. She didn't *look* easy, *even if she was*. Julie groaned and shut her eyes tightly.

She stood up and began to walk slowly along the Hoe. Easy . . .

But she hadn't been 'easy', far from it. It had only happened twice, and then after days of argument and fierce persuasion. Even when she'd agreed to it, she'd had terrible doubts. She had realised that there should be much more love and tenderness and caring. But Bill had been very clever. He had swept away all her arguments and told her she was being too romantic and that life wasn't like that. He had made her feel very gauche and silly. His favourite word for her was 'immature'. He told her that all the other officers slept with their girlfriends and no-one thought anything of it. He had made her feel like the odd one out. Yes, he had been very clever.

She had held out for a long time, then he had threatened to take another girl to the Summer Ball. It was Mother who had been horrified at the thought of Julie not going. The Summer Ball was the social event of the season. She had forced Julie to write to Bill and make it up.

So she had gone to the Ball and drunk gin, which she had only tried once before, and then wine, which she wasn't used to either. Afterwards Bill had driven her up on to the moors and it had happened for the first time.

It was brief and painful and Julie had wept. He had promised her it would be better the next time. But if anything it had been worse. On the second occasion they had driven on to a remote headland. But this time he didn't say a word, he didn't even kiss her, he just grabbed her and pulled at her clothing. Then he lay on her and hurt her again, except that it lasted much longer and she hated it even more than the first time.

Afterwards she had felt miserable and unclean. It had been so beastly, so ugly. If that was love then she didn't want anything more to do with it. One thing she knew straight away: she would never let Bill do it again.

She had felt wretched for weeks. Her mother had put her unhappiness down to being in love. Poor Mother! She still thought that Bill was marvellous. Bill was everything she wanted for Julie: he was well-spoken, dashing and a gentleman. Mother had never let Julie go out with anyone she considered common. Julie was not allowed to go to the

Golden Dance Hall to meet the non-commissioned ranks like the rest of her school friends did.

The idea of Bill being a gentleman made Julie smile grimly. She had used the risk of pregnancy as a reason for not giving in to him, but he had swept that aside as he swept everything else aside. Nothing, he had assured her, would happen; he would take care of that. A real gentleman, Julie thought bitterly.

A small sailing craft had appeared by Drake's Island and was heading out into the wide expanse of the sound. She thought how pretty it looked, with its white sails and gay red hull. It was skimming over the waves, fast as the wind.

She walked on and for no particular reason thought of her father. Perhaps it was the boat that reminded her.

She remembered his dear gruff voice. He had died when she was twelve and it had broken her heart. She still missed him dreadfully.

Her father would have understood about this. He would have listened and sighed and looked at her with love in his eyes and taken her in his arms and said: Juliette, my Juliette. He would have understood. He would have protected her and found a way for her to survive it all.

Perhaps he would have taken her away . . . Julie stopped abruptly.

She hadn't thought of that. That would be an answer. To go away. But where? She had only a few pounds saved. As a junior secretary she earned just fifteen shillings a week and it was hard to save on that. Anyway, she couldn't stay in her present job: she'd have to leave Plymouth and go to a new area and find a new job, and that wouldn't be easy. And then what? She had few relatives to go to. There was only Aunt Beryl at Ramsgate, and she – well, she was like her mother.

She had never met her father's family in Brittany; her mother had always discouraged any contact with them.

Julie walked down the long flight of steps into Grand Parade and wondered if it was five o'clock yet. She usually went out on Saturday afternoons, either to meet some of the girls for tea at the tea house, or in the old days, to go out for a drive with Bill. She always promised to be back by five-thirty.

Today she had told her mother she was going into town, but nothing more. Her mother had been suspicious and as soon as Julie got back to the house there would be questions. Then the truth would have to come out, and nothing would ever be the same again.

Julie turned into West Street and walked down the hill towards Radley Terrace and her home at Number 34.

As she drew near the bottom of the hill two women came round the corner, walking arm-in-arm. One of them was Maggie Phillips. Julie's first thought was to turn round and get away, but she realised that Maggie had seen her and was waving. It was too late. She made herself walk on.

'Hello, Julie! Well, it's a long time since we saw you round these parts.' Maggie gave a dazzling smile between vermilion lips. She modelled herself on Joan Crawford, down to the padded shoulders and the peep-toe shoes. 'We thought you'd got too grand for us.'

Julie felt herself blushing. 'No, I – I haven't been doing anything special.'

Maggie looked at her enquiringly and said, not unkindly, 'Oh, it's like that is it? No more boyfriend, eh? Oh well, there'll be others.'

Julie gave her a thin smile and nodded.

'What about coming to the Golden tonight then? Joan and I are going, and maybe Phyllis. It'll be fun – they've got a really good American-style band tonight.'

'Thanks . . . it's kind of you but I can't. I . . .'

'Oh come on. It'll be good fun. We'll get a table and sit all demure and ladylike on the side.' She giggled.

Julie shook her head. 'Really, my mother's not keen . . .'

'Your mother doesn't own you, does she? Break loose, my girl, that's what I say! What about next Friday then? Joan and I are going to the Rialto with two nice Navy lads. They can bring along one of their mates. Go on, say you will. It's the new Gable–Crawford movie!'

Julie felt worn down and heard herself say, 'Oh, all right.'

'We'll meet you outside for the early house then. Byeee!'

Julie walked quickly away. She could have kicked herself. Why had she agreed to go to the pictures? She didn't want to go anywhere with anyone, let alone a group of strangers. Why did she always agree to things she later regretted?

She paused at the corner of the street and thought: Yes, that's the problem. I agree to things I don't really want to do. Why? Why *had* she agreed to Maggie's suggestion? To avoid unpleasantness perhaps. But no, there was more to it than that. She had wanted to *please* Maggie. That was the key: she had been anxious to please. Just as she always tried to please her mother. And her employer. *And* Bill. She hated to remember it now, but she had tried to please *him* too.

Julie thought: What a revelation. I live to please other people. And look where it's got me! Into the oldest trap in the world.

As she approached the house she found she was dangerously near to tears. She turned and walked quickly away from the house until she felt more composed. Then she blew her nose and retraced her steps.

It would be time for tea at Number 34, and she mustn't be late.

Julie leant back against the chair and wondered how much longer it would be before she could get to bed. She was desperately tired. The emotion and tears of the last few hours had left her feeling drained and now a small ache at the back of her neck was threatening to become a full-blown headache.

Anyway there was nothing new to say, nothing that hadn't been said already.

Julie rubbed her neck and turned to look out of the window into the twilight. The road outside was lit by the soft glow of the street lamps which cast a pale light into the small front room. Normally Mother would have the curtains drawn and the lamps lit by now. But the ritual had been forgotten and the room seemed eerie and unreal in the gloomy darkness.

There was a loud sniffle and Julie looked back at her mother.

Mrs Lescaux was sitting on a low stool, rocking back and forth. Now and then her body shook with a great sob and her breath came in long shuddering gasps. At other times she moaned and shook her head and put a large wet handkerchief to her eyes.

Julie sighed and wondered what she could say that would help. But there was nothing . . .

Mrs Lescaux blew her nose loudly and raised her head. 'How can you be *sure* he doesn't love you, that's what I want to know.'

'I just know, Mum.' They had been over that one half a dozen times already.

'Well *how* do you know?'

Julie closed her eyes. 'I told you, he's been avoiding me. And . . .'

Mother said impatiently, 'Yes?'

'Well, I saw him with another girl. She seemed much more his sort.'

Mrs Lescaux got wearily to her feet and moved to a chair nearer the window. Julie saw that her eyes were red-rimmed and bloated, and her face mottled with angry red patches. She had never seen her mother look anything but neat and composed before, and it made her feel terrible.

Mother said, 'What do you mean by that? More his sort?'

'I mean . . . she was more his class, Mother.'

'I don't see what that's got to do with it! You're as good as anyone else. As good as *anyone*. No!' She shook her head vehemently. 'That can't have anything to do with it!'

Julie thought that class probably had a lot to do with it, but it was best not to say so. Instead she nodded and said, 'Well, maybe I'm wrong, maybe that didn't make any difference. But the fact is he doesn't love me, Mother.'

'But you can't be sure of that! Perhaps he just never *told* you . . . Anyway, love can grow. Take it from me.'

Julie thought: Oh God, how do I make her understand? She said gently, 'Mother, please believe me when I tell you this. He doesn't love me.'

He had come to the house for tea a couple of times and Mother had gone to a lot of trouble, making cakes and sandwiches and laying everything out properly. But though he had been polite enough, she had sensed a mocking edge to his comments when he thanked her for the tea or admired the china or enquired about her mother's health. Now Julie could see that he must have thought it all rather quaint, the tea parties with the lace doilies, and Mother's refined manner, and the polite conversation.

If I'm right, Julie thought, then I'd rather die than let him know I'm in trouble.

Mrs Lescaux cleared her throat again. 'You must try once more, try to *tell* him at least. He might well ask you to marry him. How can you be certain he won't?'

'Oh, I'm certain, please believe me.'

'I've a good mind to tell him myself. Or his commanding officer. He'll probably be *ordered* to marry you.'

Julie felt a surge of anger. 'Mother, if you so much as

think about doing such a thing I shall never speak to you again!'

'Well! That's a fine way to speak to your own mother! There's a daughter's loyalty for you!' She started sobbing again. 'And after the way you've treated *me*! Bringing such shame on me, such shame!'

'Oh Mother, please don't start all over again. I told you, I'll go away. No-one will ever know.'

'Go away! On what? Where will you go?' Mother shouted angrily.

It was a good question. 'I'm not sure yet. But it would be the best thing, Mum. At least that way no-one will know, and . . . And you can make up some story about me getting a job somewhere else . . .'

Mrs Lescaux dabbed at her eyes again and shook her head. 'Well, if there's no other way . . . But—' She threw her head back, looked up at the ceiling and closed her eyes in a gesture of suffering. 'But . . . goodness knows where the money's to come from. It'll cost, mark my words. I can't send you to Aunt Beryl's, I just couldn't face that. That means a boarding house – dreadfully expensive. And you wouldn't be able to find work, not in your condition!'

'I could go to Brittany.'

'What—?'

'Well, it's out of the way, isn't it? And Dad's people would probably take me in. For a while at least.'

'No—!' Mrs Lescaux looked horrified. 'You've never met them. You don't understand. They're not like us. They're . . .' She sighed with exasperation. 'They're . . . farmworkers . . . fishermen, that sort of thing . . .'

Julie remembered her loving kindly father and thought that, surely, his family couldn't be so different from him. He'd come to Plymouth on a French frigate before the Great War and met Mother at a tea dance in the town. Later he had returned and they had married. He'd worked at the fish market, eventually rising to foreman and wearing a suit that always looked uncomfortable on him. To please Mother, he'd never spoken French or talked about his family – at least within earshot.

With Julie it was different. At bedtime he spoke to her in French, telling her stories about the mythical sea creatures of Breton legend; talking about his family, his childhood and Brittany itself. Sometimes he even spoke Breton, the strange harsh language which was his native tongue.

He had been a good father and she had loved him with all her heart.

'No,' her mother said decisively, 'you can't go there. They wouldn't be very understanding, you know! You must go somewhere else. You could be back four or five weeks after the – event. They might even give you your job back.' She sniffed again. 'Oh, what a muddle, what a muddle!'

Julie frowned. 'Mother, I don't think I could come back. You see – there'd be the baby.'

'What are you talking about? You won't even see it. It'll be taken away straight after the – after the *event*.'

'But I'm not sure . . .' A vivid picture came into Julie's mind, of a tiny baby lying in her arms. The baby was looking uncertain and frightened; it was crying and reaching out for her, for *her*. She hated the thought of someone taking it away and sending it to a strange, anonymous place that she'd never be allowed to see or to know about, a place where – God forbid – it might not be loved. She said, 'Suppose I wanted to keep the baby . . .'

Mrs Lescaux snorted. 'Don't be so silly! It's out of the question! All the girls who – who have this problem have their babies adopted. It's quite normal.'

Julie shook her head. 'But I think I might want to keep the baby very much. I'd never forgive myself if I gave it away.'

'Now I've heard everything! How selfish can you get!

First you get yourself into trouble, then you want to ruin *my* life as well as your own! Really! You young people just don't *care!*'

'Please don't shout, Mother.'

'I'm not shouting!' Mrs Lescaux closed her eyes and blew her nose again. Then she said, more quietly, 'The only way to keep the baby is to marry, don't you understand that!'

Julie felt sick. They were going in circles, nowhere, in circles.

'At least *try* to see him once more. Do just that for me, just that one thing. Is that too much to ask?'

'But I won't tell him. I won't tell him.'

Mrs Lescaux shook her head in exasperation. 'All right, all right. But at least see if he still cares for you. Please, I'm asking you this one thing. *Please.*'

Julie stared angrily at her hands. She hated the thought of trying to see him again. It would be humiliating and shaming and it wouldn't help, she knew it wouldn't. Anyway, what excuse could she find for visiting him? She would rather die than just turn up and ask to see him; he would think that she still liked him, that she was still prepared to go off in the car with him ... The thought made her shudder. 'Mother, I can't just go and see him, not like that, he'll think I have no pride.'

'Well, you didn't, did you—' Mrs Lescaux bit her lip.

Julie stared at her mother and the tears came again. She had cried so much she didn't think she could manage any more. But the tears came nevertheless, rolling effortlessly down her cheeks. She suddenly thought: I can't face any more.

She was tired of crying, tired of arguing. Her head throbbed and her throat ached. All she wanted to do was sleep. She would do anything for that, and for the privacy of her own room.

Wearily she said, 'All right, Mother, you win. I'll try to see him tomorrow.'

The bus lurched into bottom gear and began to climb slowly up the hill behind Millbay Docks. It was only a mile or two to the Naval Dockyard, a journey which would take fifteen minutes at the most. Julie felt a rising panic. She had found only the flimsiest of excuses for going to see Bill and she had the unpleasant feeling that he would see straight through it.

But it was the only pretext she had and it would have to do.

Back in the early summer Bill had taken her to a party aboard a small sailing boat moored in a creek near the dockyard. Late in the evening a few people started to sing sea ballads and everyone stopped to listen. Some of the ballads were mournful, about the cruelty of the sea and the separation of lovers. Julie had been rather taken by them. The evening had been still and utterly peaceful and, though the lights of Plymouth were brightly reflected in the calm water, the city seemed very far away. Julie had looked out beyond Drake's Island to where the water was dark and cold, and she'd thought how romantic it all was. The sea, so vast and cruel, which asked so much of the noble men who sailed on it . . . And the songs, they were so lovely, so sad, with their tales of brave sailors who withstood so much only to drown in the icy water.

Afterwards she told Bill how much she'd loved the songs. Two days later he thrust a book in her hand. It was a pocket edition of *Naval Songs and Ballads*. It was the only present he'd ever given her.

And now she was taking it back.

It was the only excuse she could find for seeing him again.

He would think it strange that she was returning a gift, but she was going to pretend it had been a loan. Then she could thank him for letting her keep it for so long and apologise for not returning it sooner. He wouldn't be fooled for a moment, of course – he had told her it was a gift at the time – but it was the best she could do. And when they met it would at least give her something to talk about.

If they met. He might not be there at all. With a bit of luck he would be out for the day, driving up on to the moors with his new girlfriend for a quiet Sunday lunch.

One thing at least, she hadn't dressed up for him. If he *was* there she didn't want him to think she had spent a lot of time over her appearance. There were no white gloves today, nor a hat. She was wearing a plain blue summer frock with an off-white linen coat. Her long dark hair was drawn back from her face by two combs, but otherwise it was loose and unpinned. It looked as if she were going out on an errand, and that was exactly the impression she wanted to make.

The bus trundled past the main gates of the dockyard and came to a noisy halt in the next street. Julie got out and walked towards the gates of HMS Drake, the shore establishment attached to the dockyard. She was dreading the next part. She would have to ask for him at the gate and admit that no, she wasn't expected, and the men on the gate would look at her knowingly, and smile at each other. She thought: Still more humiliation. It never ends.

She approached the gatehouse and saw that there were three sentries on duty. As she came towards them they turned to stare at her and two of them exchanged glances. She thought: Oh God, this is going to be even worse than I thought.

Suddenly there was a burst of noise.

Julie jumped with fright and spun round. It was the roar

of a car engine. The car itself, a vivid blue Austin 7, rattled past and ground to a halt beside the sentries. A young man was leaning out of the window waving a pass in his hand.

Julie stood stock still and tried to regain her breath. She was shaking with fright.

The young man was looking back at her with a rueful expression. Then his head disappeared into the car and the door was flung open. He leapt out and said, 'I'm terribly sorry, I didn't mean to startle you. I came round the corner rather fast, I'm afraid.' He grinned at her, then looked serious again. 'I say, you're really shaken. I'm so sorry. What an idiot I am.'

Julie shook her head. 'I'm fine. It was rather a shock, that's all.'

'You're sure you're all right then?' He peered at her solicitously and put a hand on her elbow.

'Yes, really.'

'Well . . . if you're sure.' He glanced at the sentries. 'Are you being looked after? I mean, can I find anyone for you?'

'No, no, I . . .' Julie paused and looked carefully at the young man. He was vaguely familiar and she realised she must have met him before at some time. He was dressed in a large shapeless sweater and baggy rust-coloured trousers, and on his head was an old black cap speckled with paint. He looked rather roguish, like a pirate.

He was smiling at her; there was no doubt he was very charming, but Julie wondered if it wasn't laid on. Bill had been charming too, but that had meant nothing, nothing at all.

He was waiting for an answer and she said, 'I was hoping to see a friend, but I think I've missed him . . .' It sounded weak and she trailed off.

'Oh, it's impossible to find anyone on a Sunday. But if you want me to ask . . .?'

She took another look at him. He was watching her

intently, waiting for her reply, his eyes friendly and enquiring. Maybe she'd been wrong: maybe he was everything he seemed, and wasn't the sort to make fun of her. She decided to trust him after all: it would be a lot less embarrassing if he asked about Bill rather than the sentries.

She said, 'Well, perhaps you could ask if Bill Crozier is around.' She looked down, a little flustered, then remembered the book and fumbled in her handbag. 'I wanted to return something he lent me.' She held the book up as if it were a trophy.

'No problem.' He smiled and she noticed the eyes again. 'Look, why don't you hop in the car and we'll go and ask in the wardroom. Someone there might know.'

She nodded and after he had spoken to the sentries they got into the car and drove slowly into the establishment. He laughed. 'We're not allowed to drive fast in here, so you're safe!'

She smiled politely and looked out of the window at the barrack-like buildings.

He negotiated the car round a sharp corner and she could feel him looking at her. He said, 'Didn't you come to that party on my boat? The one where we had the singsong?'

She looked at him blankly. 'Oh, was it your boat? I didn't know.'

'Yes, *Dancer*'s her name.' He laughed again. 'Oh, and my name's Richard Ashley. We were probably introduced, but there were so many people there . . .'

'I'm Juliette Lescaux.'

'Of course!' He lifted both hands off the wheel in an expansive gesture. 'I remember the French name now. *Are* you French in fact?'

Julie thought: God, he knows my name. Perhaps I'm infamous already. Perhaps Bill has been talking about me . . . She glanced across at the young man but his expression hadn't changed, it was still interested and amused. No, she thought, I'm being stupid: he really did remember my name because it's French.

She said, 'Half. I'm half French. My father came from Brittany.'

'Ah, what a fantastic place to come from. I sailed over there last year and had the most wonderful time. The locals were so amazed to see old *Dancer* and me all alone that they couldn't do enough for us.'

Julie looked at him curiously. 'You sailed the boat alone?'

'Oh yes, always do if I can. Nothing to compare with it.'

Julie didn't reply immediately: she was thinking of what would happen if Bill was at the mess. She dragged her mind back to what Richard Ashley had said. 'Isn't it risky, alone? I mean what happens in a storm?' They drew up outside the wardroom. Julie regarded it with horror.

'In a storm?' Ashley was considering her question. 'Oh, I just shorten sail and go below for a sleep.' Leaving the engine running, he got out of the car and stuck his head back through the window. 'Unless I'm about to bump into the land. Then I sail like hell!' He grinned. 'Won't be a tick.' She watched him walk to the door and disappear into the building.

Julie sat still, thankful for the safety of the little blue car. She began to pray that Bill wouldn't be there. The last time they'd met, Bill had made it plain that he didn't want to see her again. Well, he hadn't actually *said* so, not in so many words, but she'd known by the long silences and the way he'd avoided her eyes. Julie put her hands over her face and thought: Please God, don't let him be there.

The door to the wardroom opened and Julie's heart went into her mouth. Richard Ashley came out and closed the door behind him. He was alone. Julie closed her eyes with relief.

Richard slid back into the driver's seat. 'Sorry, no luck, no-one seems to know where he is. But he *is* expected back fairly early this evening.'

'Oh.' Julie wondered what to do next. She didn't want to go home, not yet.

'I say . . .' Richard's face was alight with enthusiasm. 'What about coming down to *Dancer*. I'm doing a bit of work on her today. I could do with someone to help . . . I mean with the sandwich-making and all that. Everything's on board: cheese, bread, you name it. It would be much more fun than working on my own. Then I could bring you back here later.'

'Oh—' The question took Julie by surprise. She had no desire to go home, but on the other hand she didn't know this man . . . she wasn't sure she wanted to spend an afternoon with him. Anyway she wasn't dressed for a boat. She looked down at her flimsy frock and stockinged legs. Climbing about in boats would ruin her stockings and probably dirty her frock too.

Richard followed her look. 'Oh don't worry about your clothes. As long as you don't mind taking your shoes off then the heels won't damage the deck.'

For a moment she looked at him in amazement, wondering how a boat's deck could be so important, then she saw the funny side of it and smiled a little. He looked at her, puzzled, then understanding flashed into his eyes and he laughed. He said, 'You'll have to forgive me. You see, *Dancer*'s the love of my life and, like all good women, she has to be pampered!' Still laughing, he let in the clutch and the car moved off.

They stopped for a moment outside another building while he collected some things from his quarters and then they were through the gates and heading towards the Tamar River. Julie realised they were on their way to the boat, though she hadn't actually said she would go. But she was glad. Why not? She had nothing better to do.

They left the main road and started slowly down a
rough lane towards the water. As the car bumped and
swayed along, Julie asked: 'How did you manage to find
this amazing colour?'

'Sorry?'

The little car was noisy and Julie raised her voice. 'The
car, why is it such a bright blue?'

'Ah! What colour is every *other* Austin 7 in the world?'

'Black. Or sometimes grey. Or a sort of beige.'

'Exactly! Very dreary. That's why I decided to paint this
one blue!' He laughed again. He seemed to laugh most of
the time, and Julie found herself smiling too.

She decided she was glad she had come.

The afternoon was warm and Julie lay on the foredeck
with her face towards the sun. She had taken her stockings
and shoes off in the car and left them on the back seat with
her coat. Richard had lent her a waterproof jacket to put
round her shoulders in the small rowing boat and then,
when they arrived on board *Dancer*, he had found her a
sweater. The sweater was enormous and she probably
looked extraordinary in it, but she didn't mind. Somehow
it didn't seem very important.

She had done very little all day and it had been
wonderful. She had made the sandwiches and boiled up
the kettle for a cup of tea. Then she had lain down here
and let herself be lulled by the lapping of the water and the
gentle movements of the boat.

Eventually she drifted off into a pleasant dreamless
sleep, very different from the long, troubled nights of the
previous week. Only the occasional noise of hammering or
loud humming from the inside of the boat interrupted the
stillness of the day.

When she awoke she guessed it was late afternoon,
about four or five o'clock. She looked up and saw that

Richard was sitting on top of the cabin roof with a mug of tea in his hand, watching her with amusement. He grinned. 'Have a nice sleep?'

'Oh, I'm sorry. I didn't mean to sleep so long. I just seemed to nod off.'

'Yes, it does that to you, the sea.' He put down the mug and said, 'Look, I've finished my carpentry. Well ... I wouldn't say my carpentry was exactly *finished*, but it's as *done* as it ever will be – and it's still standing. So why don't we go for a short sail? Just into the sound and back. Won't take long.' He stood up and made a sweeping gesture with his arm. 'It'll blow the cobwebs away!'

Julie looked at him nervously. She had never been sailing before and the idea didn't appeal to her at all. Yachts looked very unstable – they always seemed to be on the point of tipping over. She also suspected that she was prone to seasickness. Once she and Mother had gone on a steamer trip to Fowey and Julie had felt very peculiar on the way back. Anyway, she knew absolutely nothing about sailing.

He was looking at her expectantly and she said, 'Thank you. It's awfully kind of you to offer but ... well, I've never sailed before.'

'Then it's high time you did!'

'No, really, I ... I get seasick.'

'Don't worry! Most people do – *especially* me. I'm always sick as a dog for the first day or two. But that's out at sea. It'll be fine in the sound, there's not a ripple, not a wave. Honestly, trust me!' He lent down and offered her his hand.

She stared up at him and thought: Yes, I do trust you, it's impossible not to. She took his hand and let him pull her up.

He pushed her gently in the direction of the cockpit and went forward to untie a rope.

She called, 'Where shall I sit? On the seat in the back here?'

He laughed. 'It's called the cockpit, and it's situated in something called the stern! This sharp end up here, this is called the bow. Yes, just sit there, next to the companionway.'

Julie sat down and gripped the piece of wood that ran round the cockpit. She watched him pull up the sails and arrange the ropes. Then he threw a chain off the front of the boat and she realised they were off. For a moment everything flapped and there was the most terrible din. Then he ran back to the cockpit and pulled some more ropes. Suddenly the sails stopped flapping and *Dancer* leapt forward.

For a while the yacht skimmed along quite steadily and Julie began to relax a little. Then the little boat shuddered and the next moment it was tipping over. Julie gripped the side and felt a touch of fear. It seemed to her that there was nothing to stop the boat from going all the way over and turning upside down.

She looked back anxiously and saw that Richard was steering the boat quite happily. He said, 'Isn't this wonderful! There's nothing like a good sail! It's a wonderful day for it, too. A really nice breeze.'

Julie looked towards the bow again. It seemed to her that there was altogether too much wind. The boat was still leaning over at a sharp angle and showed no signs of coming upright again. Julie found it impossible to believe that everything was all right, though Richard obviously thought so. She could not rid herself of the feeling that something unexpected and frightening would happen at any moment.

Dancer sped past Drake's Island and into the open sound. Small wavelets rushed at the boat and *Dancer*'s bow pushed a curtain of fine spray up into the air and back into the cockpit. Julie shivered slightly and wondered how much further they would go. Then Richard leaned forward and loosened some ropes. The boat changed direction and gradually came upright again. Immediately the motion was easier and the waves, instead of rushing at the boat, seemed to be travelling with it.

'That's better, eh? No point in getting wet.' He looked at her with a funny mock frown, and she realised he had changed course for her, to make the sail more enjoyable.

'Thanks. It's better like this.'

'Oh yes, it's always better going with the wind. I only wish the wind always blew from behind. But it never does. Quite the opposite, in fact.' He cast his eyes skyward. 'Sometimes I think there's a heavenly conspiracy to make sure it always comes from ahead.'

'Do you really get seasick?'

'Most certainly. There are two stages to seasickness, so they say, one when you want to die, and the second when you're frightened you're not going to. Well, I go through both! The only remedy is to keep busy, stay on deck as much as possible – and remember it can't last for ever.'

'And do you often go far? To places like Brittany?'

'Whenever I have the time I do. This summer I went to the Scillies. Now the Scillies! They're the most wonderful islands in the world. I spent a whole fortnight there and you wouldn't believe it, but I anchored at a different place every night. Most of the islands are uninhabited. You can walk all day and see nothing but birds.' He said blissfully, 'At one point I didn't see another living soul for four whole days.'

Julie thought: What a strange one you are. All that laughter and charm and you like being on your own.

He went on, 'The Scillies are covered in wrecks, you know, literally hundreds of them. Not surprising really, when you consider where they are, stuck miles out into the sea, just there in the entrance to the English Channel. And they're low, of course; ships can't see them until they're

almost on top of them. Not a good place to find yourself
in bad weather.' He laughed as if such danger were a great
joke and Julie suspected that he would like nothing better
than to be sailing off the Isles of Scilly in a storm.

He started to tell her some stories about the Scillies;
about the famous wrecks and the people who lived there
and the beautiful scenery. As he talked Julie found herself
watching him. He was attractive, there was no doubt about
that, but not in an obvious way. He wasn't good-looking
as Bill had been, and he would probably put on weight
when he was older. But those eyes did light up his face. He
reminded her of a teddy bear, kind and safe and – yes,
cuddly.

She decided that her first impression had been wrong.
His charm was not laid on, it was perfectly natural; it
stemmed from his enormous enthusiasm for everything he
did.

She looked at him and thought: I could have liked you
a lot. *Could have* – she had used the past tense automatically. There would be no boyfriends now: that was all
over.

Anyway, he probably wasn't interested. Why should he
be? There was nothing special about her; Bill had made
that quite plain at their last meeting. Besides – how stupid
of her not to think of it – he probably had a girlfriend
already.

Dancer was sailing quietly into the Cattewater, the
creek that leads to the Barbican – the oldest part of the city
– and to the fishing harbour. Julie was quite enjoying
herself now that there were no waves and hardly any wind.

Richard said, 'Well, best not get into the harbour itself.
We'll probably meet a fishing boat coming out. I'll gybe
her round and we'll head back to the mooring.'

Julie nodded, not having the slightest idea of what
gybing involved. The next moment he shouted, 'Mind your
head,' and there was a great crash. For a second Julie

thought the mast had come down, but then she saw that it was the noise of the sail changing sides. She laughed and put her hand to her chest. 'You might have warned me!'

'Sorry, I forgot you didn't know about sailing. Listen. I'll explain a few of the basics. It's really quite simple. You see, there are just three things to remember. First, always know where the wind's coming from. Second, pull the sail in just enough to stop it flapping. And three, always try to avoid gybing!'

Julie found herself laughing with him. 'Then how do you turn round?'

'Ah, you turn *into* the wind. That's called tacking.'

She shook her head. 'I'm afraid it's all beyond me. In future I'll leave the sailing to you.'

He didn't say anything but stared at her, searching her eyes. She glanced quickly away, angry with herself. He had taken her remark as an indication of interest; he had thought she was staking a claim. Well, she'd have to make it quite clear that she hadn't meant anything of the sort. What a pity. The day had been going so well.

He was talking again and she saw that he was serious now. 'Sailing is a wonderful freedom, you know. You can just set off for who-knows-where whenever you please. I keep *Dancer* stocked up with food and water all the time. Then I can go whenever I have the time.'

'Isn't it enough to be in the Navy?'

'Oh no, it's not the same at all. Being at sea with three hundred other people in a tin ship is . . . well, it's my job. I enjoy it, but it doesn't compare with setting off on your own. I love the excitement, you see, and the challenge of making for a new place, and exploring it. There's nothing like it.'

'But why on your own?'

He thought for a moment. 'Well, I don't always go on my own. I often sail with my father – *Dancer*'s really his boat, not mine. But half the trouble is I haven't met a crew

who wants to do the same kind of sailing as I do. So ...
there's no other solution. You see, I believe you've got to
go out and do what you want to do.'

Julie stared at him. She admired him for his certainty
and his self-assurance. It must be wonderful to be so sure
of what you wanted and to have such confidence in your
ability to succeed. But most of all she admired him for his
ability to make his own decisions. She thought: Why can't
I be like that? Why am I so bad at deciding? It was easier
when you were a man, of course; somehow men had fewer
people to consider. But all the same, she should be able to
do it, to decide things for the best.

As they sailed back across the open sound the wind
increased again and *Dancer* pulled away, cleaving a
straight path through the waves. Julie stared ahead, trying
to enjoy herself but feeling the unhappiness closing in on
her again. The day was almost over. Soon she would have
to decide whether to return to the wardroom and risk the
dreadful humiliation of seeing Bill, or give up and go home
to face her mother. What a choice!

Dancer drifted slowly into the creek and Richard Ashley
sprinted forward to lower the sails. As soon as he'd finished
he ran back and pushed the tiller hard over so that *Dancer*
turned in a neat semicircle. Then he picked up a boathook
and, running forward again, used it to fish a bright red
buoy out of the water. He was breathing hard. He called
back, 'You see, nothing to it! You could learn in no time!'

She smiled. Sailing was as much a mystery to her as it
had been at the beginning of the day. The only thing she
could say was that the experience had been less unpleasant
than she'd thought. But the sea still terrified her. She
decided she had no desire to try it again.

By the time they got back to the bright blue car it was
six o'clock. On the journey back to the officers' quarters
Julie hardly spoke. Then he asked, 'Well, what do you

want to do? Shall we see if Bill's there? Or do you want to give me the book to pass on?'

'I . . . I don't know.'

'Well, shall we see if he's there then?'

Julie was frozen with indecision. Whatever she did would be wrong. And now there was the added complication of this man – he must have guessed what the situation with Bill was: boy gives girl brush-off, girl can't take hint. He must think she was cheap, to be chasing after a man like this.

Suddenly she made up her mind. 'No, I'll go straight home, thanks. The book really isn't important. I can catch a bus outside the dockyard.'

'No, I won't hear of it. The least I can do is to drive you home. Where do you live?'

She told him and leant her head back on the seat, happier than she had been for days. It was lovely to have made a decision, and now she had taken it she knew it was the right one. It would have been dreadful to go cap in hand to a man she didn't love and certainly didn't respect. Bill had made it plain that the affair was over. It was up to her now, to make the *best* of a bad situation.

She would go away and make a fresh start.

She glanced across at Richard Ashley. His face was set in lines of concentration as he negotiated the narrow streets of Plymouth. She was thankful to him. He was right about reaching out for things and leading your own life. If you didn't, it seemed to her that everyone else used you to lead theirs. Her mother meant well, but she had always pushed Julie into doing things *she* wanted her to do. And Bill, he had used her too.

Yes she would definitely go away.

But not to anywhere in England: here there was nowhere to go and no-one to help her. It would have to be France then. The thought was rather frightening. She had never met any of her father's immediate family. All she knew was that her grandparents must be very old by now – perhaps dead even – and that she had an uncle and an aunt. And possibly some cousins, though she wasn't sure about that either.

She would have to tell them she had been married, of course, and that it hadn't worked out. They probably wouldn't believe her, but it wouldn't matter as long as appearances were kept up. She would go out and buy a wedding ring. The thought gave her a curious thrill. She would call herself Mrs something – but not Crozier, that was for sure – no, it would be another name. She would have to think up a good one.

She would need a passport, she hadn't thought of that before. She wasn't sure, but she seemed to remember that when you were under twenty-one you had to have parental permission. That would lead to problems with Mother. Julie sighed at the thought of yet more battles ahead.

'Anything the matter?' He was looking at her, concern on his face.

Julie realised she must have sighed out loud. 'Oh no, nothing. I was just thinking, that's all.'

He nodded and looked back at the road.

The little car drew up outside Number 34 Radley Terrace. Julie had no doubt her mother would be peering through the curtains, but she didn't care. She turned to him. 'Thanks so much. It's been a lovely day. I can't tell you how much I enjoyed it.'

'It was *my* pleasure entirely!' He glanced down at his hands then said, 'Look, it would be super if you could come again some time. Would you like that? I could do with a first mate.'

'Oh, I . . . I'm very honoured to be asked. But, well . . . I'm going away soon, you see. Very soon.'

'Ah!'

He was taken by surprise, she could see that, and she

tried to smooth the moment over. 'I'm going to live with my relatives in France for a while, to work there and learn the language. I've always wanted to go.'

'To Brittany?'

She nodded.

'Well, I hope you have a good time there. I'm sure you will. The Bretons are wonderful people.' He sounded disappointed and a little puzzled. He must think her devious for not having mentioned the trip before.

Julie wished she could explain about having to go, but there was no point in starting explanations she couldn't finish. It was best as it was.

She opened the door and said, 'Goodbye, and thank you again.'

He smiled at her and the kindness was back in his eyes. 'Bye. I hope it all goes well!'

What a nice man you are, she thought.

She closed the door and walked up the path. The sound of the noisy little engine faded down the road. She turned to wave, but the bright blue car was already out of sight round the corner.

She paused at the front door, the key in her hand, and thought: Brittany. Yes, I'll definitely go to Brittany.

It was easy to say now, surprisingly easy . . . but would she ever be able to go through with it?

She thought: I'm going to *have* to.

And she opened the door and went quickly into the house before she changed her mind.

Chapter 3

———

THE BAY OF Lubeck is wide and open. On its southern shore lies the busy port of Travemunde and beyond that, some miles up the broad Trave River, is the city of Lubeck. On the north-western shore of the bay, some twenty miles from Travemunde and well away from prying eyes, is the small harbour of Pelzerhaken. It was here that the German Navy had built one of its principal research establishments, a group of low, ugly buildings surrounded by barbed wire.

On this September day a blustery north-easter was blowing in from the Arctic, bringing a cool foretaste of the winter ahead. Out in the wide bay short steep seas bowled in from the open Baltic, throwing angry white surf on the holiday beaches lining the shore. At the single wharf in Pelzerhaken Harbour the trials ship *Welle* tugged uneasily at her lines as the strong wind pulled at the mass of aerials and strange dish-shaped objects sprouting from her superstructure.

David Freymann shivered and pulled his jacket tighter round his neck. He felt the ship move slightly and hoped that, once they got under way, he wouldn't be seasick. He usually was, even in a rowing boat.

Ellen said he was stupid even to consider coming on this trip because he was bound to disgrace himself. She also said that the only reason he got seasick was because he was overweight and didn't take any exercise. Ellen had a way of implying that everything was somehow David's fault, but he didn't mind. In most ways she was a good wife and she wasn't having an easy time of it at the moment. She complained about being neglected and she was absolutely right. His work was taking up more and more time. He had tried to explain to her how important it was and how much it meant to him, but she didn't understand. That, he thought fondly, was women for you.

He realised with a shock that, come October, they would have been married fifteen years. On their anniversary it would be a good idea to spoil her a bit; he would take her out for a meal in Berlin, to a good restaurant on the Unter den Linden. Fifteen years: he could hardly believe it. Little Cecile must be almost eight. It was strange how the time flew so quickly, yet one remained young inside. He'd be forty-five this year, almost middle-aged.

Still, as long as you achieved something lasting, then age didn't really matter. He looked up at one of the dish-shaped objects above the *Welle*'s bridge. Now *there* was something lasting, something that really mattered. An achievement that any man would be proud of.

David walked across the deck to where Hans Rathenow was standing. Hans had been David's colleague for a year now, ever since they had joined the new Gema Company together. Hans was a good sort: hard-working, straightforward and kind. David liked him a lot. There was a bond of fellowship and camaraderie between them which came from working on the same project. Together they had solved the problem of range measurement. It had been a hard one to crack but somehow David had known they would do it.

Hans inclined his head in the direction of the land. 'The brass are late.'

David laughed. 'That's their privilege.'

'How many are there going to be? Do you know?'

David shook his head.

'Well, I hope there aren't too many, otherwise we'll never be able to deal with all their questions.' Hans liked to have plenty of time to consider questions, so that his answers could be as precise and complete as possible.

The two men watched a lorry bump along the wharf and stop in front of a warehouse. Hans turned and said, 'By the way, have you heard the rumour about Telefunken?' David looked blank and Hans continued, 'Evidently, they're to be given a government contract like ours, but to develop a device for aircraft.'

'Oh.' David frowned and tried to hide his surprise. 'I thought *we* were to do the work on small devices. I . . . I've been working on the programme scheduling.'

'Yes.' Hans gave David a sympathetic glance. 'I know. And I know you are right in your approach. But I fear that Schmidt does not see it your way.'

David stared into the distance, and sighed. Schmidt, head of the research programme and recently appointed Chief Scientist of the Third Reich, had long been a thorn in his side.

David touched the other man's arm. 'I tell you something, my friend – not only am I sure that it is possible to develop small devices for aircraft, but I am certain those devices could be made incredibly powerful. Can you imagine what definition and detail could be achieved by using exceptionally short waves?'

Hans smiled kindly. 'Yes, but David, no valve exists which is remotely capable of such a thing. Where is your power to come from?'

'I have an idea; I believe it could work. It would take less than six months to prove either way. All I need is two people, a bit of space and some resources.' He ran a hand through his hair. 'But this new contract . . . Now Schmidt will have the perfect excuse to refuse me permission. And I've no doubt he *will* refuse.'

Hans nodded solemnly.

The wind gusted across the deck and David stamped his feet to ward off the cold. He said, 'I could offer my services to Telefunken, I suppose. Perhaps they might be prepared to follow my idea in spite of Schmidt.'

'I doubt it, I doubt it very much.' Hans paused, deep in thought. When he finally spoke, it was very quietly and David had to turn his head to hear. 'You must think very carefully about your position, David. I worry about you.'

'What do you mean? Schmidt cannot eat me, you know. He is stupid and arrogant, certainly, but he knows my worth. He won't throw me out or anything. Why should he?'

'It is not Schmidt himself I worry about. It is the . . . the official policy.'

David began to understand. 'My friend, you mean I will be pushed out because I am Jewish?' He smiled and shook his head. 'First, I don't believe this silly campaign will go on. Second, they will never interfere with work like mine; it's too important. They aren't stupid, you know.'

'I hope you're right, but I think you're being too generous. I fear it will get worse, not better.'

David shrugged. The events of the last year had been . . . unfortunate, even – yes – deplorable. The Nuremburg decrees had been a shock. Most Jews had been deprived of their citizenship and intermarriage with Aryans was now forbidden.

Too late for Ellen and me, David thought. They can't *un*marry us after all these years.

There were other things, of course. A number of Jews had been arrested and never seen again. But then the same was happening to others: leftists, intellectuals, trouble-makers. It wasn't *only* the Jews. It was just a question of keeping your nose clean. Keeping out of trouble.

David shook his head. 'No, Hans. I honestly don't think it'll get any worse.' He thought of adding: anyway, not for me. But it sounded too selfish and uncaring, and he kept silent.

A fleet of cars appeared at the end of the wharf and

there was a flurry of activity around the ship as sailors
stood to attention. The two men began to walk slowly
along the deck towards the group already waiting at the
top of the gangway. David could see that Hans was still
frowning and he said softly, 'So the Jews are excluded
from the professions, but that is nothing new. It was the
same before the Great War. Anyway, I am more German
than Jewish. I'm only half Jewish, in fact. I haven't been
inside a synagogue for years, my wife is gentile, my
daughter goes to a nice Christian school. I am no threat!'

'That's not the point,' Hans persisted. 'You are officially
Jewish. You have your scientific status – *at present* – but
you are not safe where you are. Why don't you think about
working in this place?' He indicated the complex of stone
buildings that made up the research establishment.

David stood still, astonished. 'Here? Why?'

'Haven't you heard? The Navy is refusing to throw Jews
out of the service. Old Raeder is defying Hitler. As a naval
scientist you would be safe. Hitler will never take on the
whole Navy: he's too frightened of it.'

David walked on slowly, shaking his head. Hans meant
well, there was no doubt about that, but come and work
here? No, it was impossible. Very little original work was
done in the establishment. He would die of frustration.

The two men joined the rest of the scientific and naval
personnel standing silently in a knot by the rail.

David stroked down his windswept hair and watched
the group which was making its way up the gangway. He
recognised the well-known figure of Grand Admiral
Raeder, Commander-in-Chief of the German Navy, but he
was not certain about the others. He was no expert on
rank or uniforms, but he guessed there were at least five
other admirals in the group. Behind the Grand Admiral
was Schmidt, looking as officious and self-satisfied as ever.
David sighed inwardly. How simple life would be if the
Schmidts of this world were not allowed to poke their

noses into the *real* work. The problem with Schmidt was
that he was not overblessed with brains. He had never
been a good scientist, let alone a great one. Perhaps that
was why he had grabbed an administrative job: it was the
only thing he could do.

David stood back as Schmidt started to introduce the
managers of the Gema Company to the naval officers.
David thought how strange official protocol was, when the
organisers came before the people who actually did the
work. Still, as long as he was allowed to get on with his
project, he didn't really mind who took the glory.

When it was David's turn to come forward he tried to
concentrate on the name and rank of each man as he shook
hands with him but, apart from Raeder, he managed to
memorise only about half of them. After the introductions
one name – Doenitz – stood out in his mind and he tried
to think why. Then he remembered: it had just been
announced that Doenitz was to command the new submarine arm of the Kriegsmarine.

U-boats: now there were vessels in need of a really small
high-definition apparatus. If the opportunity arose it would
be interesting to talk to Doenitz. David looked at the rings
of Doenitz's sleeve to make sure that his rank was indeed
no higher than that of captain. There was a chance, then,
that David would be allowed to talk to him without
Schmidt interrupting. Schmidt did not like anybody talking
to really senior officers without him being present. He said
it was a matter of protecting his scientists from outside
interference, but David knew better. Schmidt just hated
anything going on without his knowledge, particularly
when a scientist had views which differed from his own.

The main group had moved off towards the bridge.
Schmidt was pointing to the bowl apparatus and explaining the reason for its shape, which differed considerably
from that of the earlier prototypes. As Schmidt's voice
droned on David felt the deck vibrate beneath his feet and

saw that the *Welle* was beginning to move gently away from the wharf. The wind was coming in great gusts now; the sea outside must be very rough.

David began to wish he hadn't come. He'd always disliked physical discomfort – as a child he'd been hopeless at sport and rough games – and he had no doubt the *Welle* would toss and roll like a pig.

Schmidt's voice had ceased and everyone moved into the large chart room behind the wheelhouse. David followed and looked for a quiet corner to stand in, but Schmidt impatiently beckoned him forward and directed him to join some junior officers on the outside of the group. The group had formed a circle round a large metal cabinet bolted to the chart room floor. On the top of the cabinet was a circular screen which the senior officers were watching expectantly.

Schmidt cleared his throat and announced, 'It will take us a few moments to get to the open sea, where the device can best be demonstrated. We beg your indulgence, but we assure you that the wait will not be in vain. You will not be disappointed!'

David felt faintly embarrassed at Schmidt's manner. He was making it like a circus performance. The brass were intelligent men; they didn't go in for dramatics.

Suddenly there was a quiet voice at David's elbow. 'We have not met. My name is Fischer, Karl Fischer.' David turned to see a young officer with his hand outstretched.

'Ah, I'm Freymann, David Freymann.' He shook the hand, then said by way of explanation, 'I work on this project. My field is radio ranging.'

Fischer nodded. 'Well, it will be most interesting to see this device working. I had no idea anything like this was being developed. It is really most extraordinary.'

David smiled politely. 'And yourself, are you on the naval staff?'

'No, no.' Fischer shook his head, and David noticed

how even and finely drawn were the younger man's features. The hair was blond, the eyes pale-blue: he supposed this was what the Nazis meant by Aryan. Then he thought: Why on earth did I think that? I'm getting as bad as Hans.

Fischer was saying, 'I have come here with Captain Doenitz. I'm with the First U-boat Flotilla at Kiel, in command of U-13.'

'Ah.' David did not know much about the new submarine arm.

'It is the first operational flotilla. It is a great honour to serve in it.'

'Indeed, indeed. It is wonderful that Germany has submarines again, after all these years.'

Fischer looked at the device humming quietly in the centre of the chart room. 'And this, will it be useful for submarines?'

'Well, at present – in this form – no. As you see the whole thing is too large. Really it is only suitable for use on ships – or on land, of course. It would never fit into submarines or, for that matter, aircraft.'

'I see, I see.' Fischer frowned in concentration. 'And what about being *detected* by such a thing. Could an enemy detect *us* easily? I am thinking particularly of when we are on the surface at night.'

David looked at Fischer with new respect. Here at least was someone who recognised the possibility of an enemy possessing this device, which was more than Schmidt did. He said, 'Well, yes, a surfaced submarine *could* be picked up. But it would be difficult. A submarine is so low in the water – and so much smaller than a ship, of course – that the conditions would have to be perfect for an enemy to see you. I mean, a calm sea and the range between three and five miles. But even if a ship did manage to detect you I imagine there would be plenty of time to dive and get away. A plane . . . now a plane would be a bit more tricky.

If a plane managed to detect you it could be on top of you very quickly.'

'I thought you said it was impossible to construct a device small enough to fit in a plane.'

David shook his head. 'Ah, no. What I said was, *this* device is not suitable for planes. I did not say it was impossible to develop small devices. Quite the opposite.'

Fischer nodded slowly. 'After the demonstration, could we talk again? I know that Captain Doenitz would be most interested in what you have to say.'

'Of course.' David was pleased. It would be an honour to talk to Doenitz.

The *Welle* had begun to pitch gently and David realised they must have reached the open sea. He looked out through one of the chart room's large ports and saw rolling, white-topped waves. He tried to concentrate on the horizon: someone had told him it stopped you from feeling sick.

Schmidt was speaking again. 'As you know we have been working hard on the development of the DT device. Incidentally, I shall continue to call it by its cover name, the DT Apparatus, because secrecy is so important. Originally you may have heard it called the revolving turret device, but more properly it should be called a radio detection and ranging device, or radar for short.' He cleared his throat and paused. Ever theatrical, David thought. Well, perhaps it was justified. It was, after all, a special occasion.

'When we last demonstrated the device, we could not give you great range accuracy. And of course it is not much good if you don't know how far away your opponent is. But now . . .' Schmidt put a hand on the metal cabinet. 'I am glad to say that, by means of a revolutionary new concept, we can give you the range of your enemy to within about a quarter of a nautical mile.'

Schmidt's audience was silent and expectant. For a moment there was no sound except the hum of the device and the vibration of the ship's engines. Then the chief scientist continued, 'We have developed a *pulse* system which sends out a short but powerful radio signal in a single burst. It then waits for the signal to return before sending another. By measuring the time it takes for the signal to get to its target and return, we can measure range with a good degree of accuracy.'

Schmidt raised his voice. 'Furthermore, gentlemen, that range is now improved. You will be able to see land approximately ten miles away, other ships eight miles away, and aircraft as much as fifteen miles away.'

He stepped to one side. 'And now, gentlemen, I invite you to look at the screen, to see for yourselves.'

Admiral Raeder and the senior officers stepped forward and leant over the screen. Schmidt pointed to a piece of coast visible on the port side and then put his finger on to the screen. Comparisons were made and there was a great deal of nodding; the brass were obviously impressed. David felt pleased. Schmidt then ordered the aerial to be rotated and the group examined the echo of a ship which was just visible on the horizon. Raeder summoned more of his colleagues and Schmidt began his explanations afresh.

David was feeling sick. The trick of staring at the horizon had not worked at all. The *Welle* seemed to be rolling and pitching in every direction and each new movement took his stomach by surprise. He edged towards the door in case he had to make a sudden dash for the rail. He realised he should try to be unobtrusive, but he was fast getting to the stage where he didn't care.

Suddenly the sickness welled up. David pulled open the door and heaved over the rail. As soon as his stomach was empty he felt better. The fresh wind helped too; it seemed to blow the cobwebs out of his head. He concentrated on the horizon again. This time the trick seemed to work and the nausea passed. But he decided against going back into the chart room; he wouldn't last five minutes in there.

After a while he became mesmerised by the rise and fall of the waves. At one point he looked down to where the waves growled along the ship's side. But that was a mistake – it brought the nausea back – and he quickly looked up again. Then he tried closing his eyes and found that, despite the sharp wind, he was able to doze where he stood. The sensation was quite pleasant: he felt as if he were floating, gently suspended in water.

'Ahem.' Someone was clearing his throat. For a moment David hoped the sound might go away, but it was repeated. Reluctantly he opened his eyes and turned round.

It was Fischer. Beside him stood the tall, erect figure of Captain Doenitz.

Fischer said, 'Herr Freymann, may I introduce Captain Doenitz? The Captain would be most grateful if you would answer a few of his queries.'

David tried to wake himself up. He smiled thinly and said, 'Of course.'

The captain was frowning in concentration. He had a sharp face with thin lips and protruding ears. But most of all David noticed his eyes, which were small and penetrating, like those of a small animal.

Doenitz spoke slowly, choosing his words carefully. 'I have grasped the principles of the DT device. I understand how it can be used against aircraft and surface vessels *by* surface vessels. But I gather this device will never be suitable for submarines. Is that correct?'

David made an effort to concentrate. 'In its present form, no. It is too large and cumbersome.'

'Can it be made smaller?'

'It is possible, but it means using shorter wavelengths.'

'And this can be done?'

David nodded. 'Work on slightly shorter wavelengths is to start soon, I believe.'

'Slightly—?'

David sighed and looked down. What was he to do? Tell the truth and suffer Schmidt's wrath, or toe the official line?

He brought his eyes back to Doenitz's face. The captain's expression was enquiring but anxious. The answer was obviously important to him.

David thought: Why not? This man deserves to know.

He said, 'Yes, only *slightly* shorter. Investigation into really short wavelengths is not being considered at present. There is a belief that such short wavelengths are impossible to generate – and that they would be *less* efficient rather than *more* efficient. But . . .' David said firmly, 'this is only a belief. It is by no means proved.'

Doenitz was trying to absorb the information. 'But if it *was* possible,' he said slowly, 'it would be useful for us?'

'Not just useful, it would be *revolutionary*!' David talked rapidly, his sickness forgotten. 'You see, first, short waves would make the device very small indeed. It would be no more than the size of – of say a large suitcase standing on its end. Obviously it would fit easily inside a plane or a submarine. That would mean – well, you can imagine! For the Luftwaffe, it would mean they would be able to see enemy planes coming from miles away, even at night. For you, it would mean you could find your enemy and make your attack in the blackest of conditions!'

David always liked to understand the practical applications of his work. So few scientists did, and that, he believed, was a great mistake. It meant you were much slower to appreciate the shortcomings of your inventions – and slower, too, to *foresee* problems.

David paused before going on. So far he had stated facts that were generally accepted – although Schmidt would have a seizure if he knew David had mentioned them. But it was the next part – the most *important* part – that was really David's personal theory. And not only was the theory unproved, but Schmidt was bitterly opposed to it.

David hesitated, then said quickly, 'It would also be revolutionary for a second reason – though I must tell you immediately that I am almost alone in this belief.'

Doenitz nodded and David went on, 'I believe that a valve could be developed to give enormous power on short waves. This would mean that the device would be small *and* immensely powerful. It would give the most incredible definition . . .'

He was not explaining it properly. These men wanted to know what it meant in practical terms. He searched for the right words. 'It would *pick out* each individual object in a group of objects, almost like a photograph. This device here –' he indicated the cabinet in the chart room – 'is useful only for seeing objects against the *sky*, so to speak – for things standing out against a blank background, like an aircraft in the sky or a ship on the horizon. Even then it would be of limited use in a plane because when it is angled down to the land or the sea it cannot pick out individual targets. It gets too many echoes back from the sea or the land for the user to distinguish individual towns or buildings or ships out of the blur.'

David paused to make sure he had been understood. The two men nodded and he went on, 'Now a shortwave device . . . well, it could see like – like a pair of eyes. From the air it could look *downwards* and read the land like a map. It could pick out individual towns, rivers, lakes, and roads; it could identify individual bombing targets; it could see small objects floating on the surface of the sea; it could see a submarine sitting on the water. *Nothing* would be hidden from it.'

Doenitz stared at David in alarm. 'If this is true, it is . . .

very important. But you say that there is doubt about this. You say some people believe such a device would be *less* efficient?'

David spoke carefully. 'There is a school of thought which believes it is impossible to develop the power. But personally I do not. I believe the necessary valve *can* be developed.'

'If there is the slightest chance of it, then—' Doenitz pursed his lips and looked out to sea.

'Of course I would have to do a lot of work on it. And I would need official support . . .'

Doenitz looked at him sharply. 'I have no say in scientific policy. However . . . I shall do what I can.'

David nodded and wondered how much longer he could survive without being sick again. He gave himself a minute, certainly no more. It had been all right while he'd been talking.

Doenitz fixed his dark, penetrating stare on to David and said, 'So a submarine would be particularly vulnerable to a shortwave device?'

'Yes.'

'Do we know if anybody else is working on it? The British, for instance?'

'I'm not sure. I can only say that, as a scientist, I have read nothing – I have heard nothing – to indicate that they have the secret.'

'If they did . . .'

David thought quickly. 'If they did then we could produce a warning device, a detector, to tell a vessel that radar was being operated against them.'

Doenitz's eyes lit up. 'Ah, so there *is* a defence.'

'Yes,' David agreed. 'But we can only develop a detector when we have developed our own technology. No technology, no detector.' David was forced to be brief; he had only a few seconds left.

'I understand. Thank you.' Doenitz inclined his head and for a moment David thought he would continue. But he turned and walked away.

David threw himself across the rail and heaved miserably. Though his stomach was empty, the convulsions went on for several minutes. When he finally looked round the two naval officers had gone.

David laid his head on his arm and closed his eyes. He no longer cared what he looked like; nor did he mind if people were laughing at him. He just wanted to die.

After several minutes he looked up. There was no sign of land. It seemed to him that they were still heading out to sea.

Hilf mir Gott! It was an expression his father often used. His father – dead, and thank God for that. He had been Jewish and proud of it.

'Freymann! Freymann!'

Without bothering to look up David knew it was Schmidt.

'Freymann, I am appalled!' The voice was angry, hissing like a snake. David waved a hand of acknowledgement. Nothing would make him raise his head again.

'I absolutely forbid you to speak to anyone else during this trip. You are absolutely not to be trusted. How dare you! How dare you give people the idea that we don't know what we're doing!' The voice spluttered for a moment, then continued, 'Your lunatic ideas! They are dangerous and stupid and . . . I will speak to you later. In the meantime keep away, just *keep away*!'

David waved a hand again. Schmidt's order suited him perfectly: no more talking and no more questions to answer. If no-one was going to believe him, there was no point anyway.

He was beginning to think Ellen was right: he should never have come.

*

Doenitz excused himself from a discussion on the use of radar in surface warfare and left the chart room. He chose to go out to the starboard side of the ship so as to avoid the scientist, Freymann, who was still wedged firmly against the port rail.

Doenitz walked slowly towards the afterdeck and wondered if there had been any truth in what the odd little man had said. The fellow had been so enthusiastic, so *sure*, that Doenitz had almost been convinced. But then he had talked to Schmidt and Schmidt had been adamant that Freymann was talking nonsense. In fact he had been so vehement Doenitz suspected that there was a great deal of animosity between the two men. Personal differences should not be allowed to interfere with people's judgement. Doenitz never allowed such things to happen among his men. Nor did he let himself be swayed by personal feelings. One's duty was to serve, and to serve to the utmost of one's ability.

But these scientists were different. They seemed to be incapable of working as a team. Still, Doenitz thought, one has to learn to live with these people, irksome though they may be, if one is to benefit from their extraordinary inventions.

He considered whether to bring up the subject of Freymann's theory with the Grand Admiral. But no, he decided, it would not be necessary. Schmidt had promised Doenitz that the theory would be investigated, and finally and conclusively proved or disproved either way.

Besides, Doenitz had more important things to worry about. For years Germany's strength had been severely curtailed by the humiliating Versailles Treaty, but now at last the Anglo-German Naval Agreement had been signed and Germany was allowed to build a navy again.

It was a race against time.

German U-boat development had never really stopped – it had been carried out secretly in Holland since 1922 –

but it would be years, perhaps as many as ten years, before the Kriegsmarine – and particularly the U-boat Arm – would be powerful enough to take on the Royal Navy.

There was a tremendous amount of work to do. It wasn't just a question of building vessels but of development and training . . .

Doenitz had paused at the after rail, but now he turned and started to pace back along the deck. He looked up and saw the figure of Fischer waiting patiently a few yards away. The U-boat Arm needed more men like Fischer, men who served with skill, optimism and enthusiasm.

He beckoned the younger man over and the two of them fell into step. Doenitz said, 'It has been an interesting day, hasn't it?'

'Yes, sir. Most fascinating. This device will obviously be very useful to us.'

'We will see. I don't always believe everything that these things are meant to do. When we've had a chance to try it *on exercise*, then I will believe it!'

'Will we have a fleet exercise soon?'

'In the spring, I expect. And then we will be able to display our tactics for the first time. It is very important that we show the High Command the effectiveness of the wolf pack. They must understand that our success depends on numbers.'

Fischer nodded thoughtfully. 'Yes, sir. I see. Greater numbers . . .' He looked at his new commanding officer with gratitude. 'Thank you for telling me. It makes me realise how important our training programme will be this winter.'

Doenitz nodded. His policy was always to tell his junior officers as much as possible. Above all else he valued trust and loyalty, and he believed that they grew not from aloofness, but from mutual openness and understanding of each other's problems. He intended to be fully involved in the day-to-day activities of his men. Whenever possible he would meet boats when they returned from exercise, he would attend debriefings, he would hear about operational problems first-hand. He did not intend to lose touch with his men, ever.

There were certain things they could not be told, of course. It would be wrong to talk about the power struggles between the Navy and the Luftwaffe, which Goering, as Hitler's favourite, was already winning; it would be wrong too to say how worrying Hitler's ideas about warfare were. Hitler had made a friendly gesture to Britain it was true, and that was the wisest thing to have done, but Doenitz wondered if Hitler appreciated that a war, if it came, would inevitably be fought against Britain. And the only way to beat Britain was to choke off her supplies, to sink all her merchant shipping, to make her slowly but surely starve.

For that they needed U-boats and lots of them.

Doenitz said, 'Yes, we have much to do this winter. As soon as the flotilla is up to strength, we will work up our tactics.' He looked towards Pelzerhaken which was coming up ahead as the *Welle* made for the shelter of the harbour once more. 'The wolf pack will revolutionise warfare at sea. Think of the number of ships that can be sunk by a group of U-boats hunting together; it will be three to four times the total that all U-boats could achieve on their own. Also, I believe that such tactics will take our enemies by surprise.'

Fischer frowned. He was wholeheartedly behind his new captain and just as anxious to prove that these new tactics would work. But he, like everyone else, had heard about the new British invention, Asdic, which used sound waves to detect submarines underwater. The British seemed to think their invention would mean the end of the submarine as an offensive weapon. Tentatively he asked, 'What about Asdic? The British are boasting about it. They seem very confident in it.'

Doenitz stopped and looked at Fischer. 'But it's only effective against *submerged* boats. When we attack, it will be at night on the *surface*. They will have no defence against that. Of course, after an attack they will come after us and then, once we are dived, they will use it against us. But even so, we only have their word for its effectiveness. It's like this radar here; I will believe it when I see it!'

The captain started pacing the deck again and Fischer had to stride out to keep up with him. Doenitz said with emphasis, 'In fact, Asdic has done us a good turn. It has made the British complacent. You know they have fewer submarines than the French? They think submarines will not be important. Well, if war comes, we will prove them wrong.'

'What about the small DT device the scientist was talking about? Will we be getting some for our boats?'

Doenitz shook his head. 'Apparently the little man suffers from over-optimism. He was talking about a really small device, but it seems this will not be possible. If we are lucky we will get something that might just fit into a U-boat. Even then I will want its effectiveness proved.'

Doenitz clasped his hands behind his back and wished the *Welle* would hurry back to her berth. He wanted to return to Kiel as soon as possible. There was so much to do and so little time to do it in.

Fischer went on, 'And the British – they don't have the DT device?'

'No, they don't.' Doenitz almost added: at least that's what we're told. Schmidt had better be right about that, otherwise – well, the consequences hardly bore thinking about.

'That's the main thing anyway,' Fischer said with a smile. 'At least we'll be free to make surprise attacks on the surface.'

'Yes.' And if we don't have that, thought Doenitz, we don't have anything. If, by any dreadful chance, the little scientist was right, if a device could be made to pick out a submarine on the surface in any weather, on the thickest of nights, then his wolf pack strategy would be in ruins.

His boats and his men would be desperately vulnerable.

Like sitting ducks.

The Hamburg–Berlin express lumbered slowly into Lehrter Bahnhof. The squeal of brakes and the hiss of escaping steam woke David up. He stretched his arms and nudged Hans, still snoring in the seat beside him. 'We're here.'

It was late, almost ten o'clock. David couldn't remember what time the last train to Hennigsdorf left, probably about eleven. He should have plenty of time to get to Stettiner Bahnhof and catch it.

Hans was looking at his watch and cursing. 'I must rush. My train leaves in half an hour!'

David followed him on to the platform and said, 'You go ahead. I'm going to see if I can get something to eat.'

Hans laughed. 'What, more?' Then waved and strode off.

David went into the station buffet and ordered bratwurst, sauerkraut, black bread and beer. He was amazed at how hungry he was, even after the substantial dinner he had eaten on the train. One good thing about seasickness – the *only* good thing – was that you felt marvellous afterwards.

Ellen said he ate too much, and she was right. But there would be nothing hot waiting for him when he got home; Ellen liked to eat early and have the kitchen tidied by the time she went to bed at ten.

She was a good wife, Ellen, but she did like her sleep. David had long since realised that she couldn't function without at least nine hours a night. He never disturbed her when he came in late and he always woke her in the mornings with a cup of lemon tea. On Sundays he did not wake her at all, and she often slept until ten or eleven. Then he would take Cecile for a walk, and they would have long talks about how trees grew, and why steam drove trains and what made lightning strike church steeples. She was a bright child and David was immensely proud of her. Her science reports were very good and David secretly hoped she might be a physicist or perhaps a biologist. He never said as much to Ellen, who thought science not only dull but extremely unsuitable for a girl.

It was ten-twenty and David hurriedly finished his meal. The last train might well leave before eleven and it would be stupid to miss it.

Outside the station he waited for a bus to Stettiner Bahnhof. But when none had appeared after five minutes he decided to walk. It would do him good. Anyway the station wasn't far, just ten minutes' walk along Invalidenstrasse. He relaxed again. There was plenty of time. He needn't have worried.

Ellen said he didn't worry enough, and there was some truth in it. Yet he did worry about things that mattered, like Cecile and her education and her happiness. What he couldn't see any point in fretting about was money or the cost of living or politics or any of those things.

When David arrived at Stettiner Bahnhof he discovered he had ten minutes to spare. The last train for Hennigsdorf was due to leave at ten-fifty-five.

He sat on a bench to wait. Somehow he had known he would have plenty of time. He often got a feeling about things. He had a feeling about his shortwave research project. He just knew that somehow, somewhere, it would go ahead. It was just a question of waiting and putting his case before the right people. Whether his talk with Doenitz had helped or not he did not know, but it had certainly stirred things up a bit. Schmidt had been purple with anger. David smiled and thought: Well, it can't do any harm.

The Hennigsdorf train arrived and he got into an empty

compartment. Eventually the train drew out and began its slow journey into the suburbs.

David watched the bright lights of the city pass by and considered his project. The more he thought about it, the more determined he was to get the thing off the ground. They all said the idea was impossible. They said that no valve could ever produce the sort of power he needed. True, nothing existed at the moment – but it *could*. It *would*. He would make one.

The train drew into Hennigsdorf and he got out, turning the matter of the valve over in his mind. He went out of the station and automatically turned left towards home. He walked with his head down, deep in thought. At present there were two kinds of valve, the klystron and the magnetron. If he could take the best qualities of both and combine them ... keep the magnetron but use a closed resonator ...

He was passing a shop and something in the window caught his eye. He looked up. It was a large notice pasted across the window. It said, simply: *Jude*!

David realised it was old Finstein's shoe shop. He stood staring at the window for a long time. He knew this happened in the centre of the city, but here, in Hennigsdorf? This place was so quiet, so safe. Everyone knew each other. Damn it, everyone knew old Finstein.

He walked slowly on, thinking of what Hans had said. He couldn't believe there was really a risk of losing his job. For others, well, he had to admit that it was not a good time to be in business or one of the professions. But the Jews had been through times like this before. As he'd said to Hans, there had been some unpleasantness before the Great War, but it had passed like these things always did. The new laws would make marriages like his and Ellen's illegal. Well, he repeated to himself, they couldn't *un*marry two people who had been married fifteen years. As for Cecile, nothing would happen to her. She was a second generation *Mischlinge*, or mixed-blood. She counted as German. Nothing would ever happen to her or to Ellen. And as for making him leave – well, they were doing that to the poor and to the business people but they would never do that to him. They *needed* him; they knew it and he knew it. There was no more to be said.

He turned into the street where he lived and felt the familiar warmth of anticipation. Whenever he walked up the slight hill under the row of linden trees, he looked forward to the first sight of his small house, so neat and pretty. It gave him a peculiar thrill to think that this was his own small patch.

The house was dark, as he knew it would be, and he opened the door very quietly so as not to wake anybody. He checked that all the doors were locked and then climbed the stairs. He paused on the landing and crept towards the open door of the back bedroom. He looked in and saw Cecile's dark hair spread across the pillow.

He knelt beside the bed and caressed her hair.

He whispered the words he had always whispered, ever since she was a baby. 'I love you, *meine kleine Rosenknospe*, I love you.'

He thought: What a lucky man I am, to have so much – my work, my house, my family. And you, my *Liebling*, most of all, to have you.

And then he whispered out loud, 'I will love you and protect you always. Always.'

Chapter 4

THE TOLLING OF a single bell echoed faintly over the city. Vasson thought: Is it really Sunday? He'd quite forgotten.

Mea culpa! Mea culpa! Lord forgive me, for I have sinned . . .

To hell with it. He hated Sundays.

It was a perfect August day, clear, sunny and not too hot. The sunlight was bright yellow, transforming the drab streets of the *dix-huitième* into brilliant ribbons of light. Vasson screwed up his eyes and walked slowly across the Place du Têrtre. A couple of artists sat doggedly at their easels, painting yet more bad pictures of the Sacré-Cœur. They were probably English or American like most of the so-called artists in this quarter. Vasson had heard that many were packing their bags and disappearing back to their own countries. Apparently the wealthy American tourists had already left their expensive hotels and crowded aboard the transatlantic liners in Cherbourg.

Let them go, Vasson thought. They're no loss to anyone. Life in Montmartre would be just the same without them.

He walked gently towards Pigalle – gently because his head ached and his eyes hurt and he had a stinking hangover. He should have stayed in bed.

On the street corners and in the cafés the news-vendors were doing a roaring trade. It seemed that all the residents of Montmartre wanted a newspaper today and when Vasson tried to buy *Turf,* the only paper he ever bought nowadays, he found it had sold out like all the rest. It was annoying. He was planning to bet on a big race at Longchamps and now he wouldn't be able to study the form.

The world had gone mad; everyone was behaving like a lot of frightened rabbits. So the Germans were going to swallow up the Poles. So what? Vasson couldn't see how that affected France. Poland had nothing to do with France. At least it damned well *shouldn't*.

He emerged on to the Boulevard Rochechouart and walked the last few yards into Place Pigalle. The club was situated in a tiny street leading off the circus. In the harsh light of day the façade looked drab and slightly seedy, but in darkness, when the name was illuminated in scarlet and the doorway open to reveal the softly lit staircase, the effect was inviting and seductive.

Vasson went down the stairs into the darkness of the club, grateful to rest his eyes from the painful sunlight. The floor had been washed and the chairs were upturned on the tables. He walked round the edge of the room to the bar. Without a word the barman poured him a coffee and pushed it across the counter.

Vasson pulled a chair off the nearest table and sat down wearily. He cast a critical eye around the room. He had the feeling that the previous night's takings must have been high. The club had been crowded from ten onwards and most of the customers were big spenders. But ... He sighed. There was so much room for improvement. The takings could be so much better, maybe even *double*, if only—

If only—

He knew exactly what made a successful club. He had analysed the ingredients countless times during the last four years.

There was the music. Now that was the one thing this

club could boast about. Its music was much classier than you generally heard in the small intimate clubs. Instead of an accordion or solitary piano, there was a three-piece band, with piano, bass and drums. And the band was good. They played a few of the new-style swing numbers for those who wanted a wild dance, but for the rest of the time they stuck to slow romantic stuff. Perfect for getting the customers close to the girls and keen to spend their money.

The décor: now that could be much better. It was very out of date, all red plush and gilt. From the look of it nothing had been changed since 1910. Vasson would have liked to see mirrored walls, chromium furniture and a black linoleum floor, the kind of simple sophistication which was all the rage.

But the main problem was the girls. Some of them were distinctly rough-looking even in the near-total darkness of the club. Only the drunkest or blindest customers managed to find them attractive. They should be replaced, and straight away. It was stupid to economise on the girls' wages. Much better to pay more and get top class women who would not only attract the money but be highly skilled at extracting it.

He sighed. This club could be one of the best small places around, if not *the* best.

He downed his coffee and took the cup back to the bar. The barman was washing glasses. Vasson called, 'Hey, how *were* the takings last night? They must have been good.'

The barman eyed Vasson impassively. 'Good enough, I should think.'

'But I mean, a record or what?'

The barman stared and there was a hint of insolence in his expression. Vasson was irritated; the man was being less than co-operative. He said impatiently, 'Look, I need

the information if I'm to run this place properly. That *is*
what I'm meant to be doing, you know, running the place!'
He knew he sounded peevish, but he couldn't help himself.

The barman smirked and shrugged his shoulders.
Vasson wanted to hit him.

Suddenly there was a voice at Vasson's shoulder, so
close that it made him jump. 'Yes, you run the club – but
it's me that runs the money. And don't you forget it.'

Vasson flushed and turned round. It was Birelli. Birelli
was small, fat and bad-tempered. He was wearing a flashy
suit and expensive gold cufflinks. He looked every inch the
proprietor of a small club.

Which was precisely what he was.

Birelli owned three clubs, and this was one of them.

Vasson said nothing. Birelli wanted a reaction and he
bloody well wasn't going to get one.

Birelli took out a cigar and slowly lit it, his beady eyes
watching Vasson through the clouds of smoke. Finally he
said, 'While I'm the owner of this place, I will worry about
the takings, and no-one else.' The little man exhaled and
the stench of garlic hit Vasson's nostrils. Instinctively
Vasson pulled back, but Birelli moved closer and said with
emphasis, 'You would do better to mind your own business
and stick to your job, such as it is. If you go on poking
your nose into things that do not concern you, you'll be
amazed at how quickly you'll be out in the street.'

Vasson shivered. He had the urge to crush the man's
head against the wall. He wanted to chant obscenities at
the pompous self-satisfied little pig, then beat him into
pulp. And to think he had actually put up with this cheap
little crook for more than six months. It was obscene!

Birelli was watching Vasson's reaction with satisfaction,
and Vasson realised the little man knew exactly what was
going through his mind.

Birelli drew breath and said, 'Furthermore, while we're
on the subject of you and your incompetence, I'm tired of

hearing about your grandiose ideas. They are idiotic rubbish; they're not worth anything. You have no idea what makes a club go. You can *spend* money, oh yes! But you have no idea what *makes* money. You think your ideas are so much better than anyone else's. Well, if you're so brilliant why aren't you a tycoon, eh? Why don't you own all the clubs in the area? Eh?'

Vasson gripped the side of the bar and waited. He wanted the heat to go out of his anger so that he could think clearly. He needed to be calm when he decided what to do next.

The coolness came over his body and then he knew.

Very slowly he reached forward. At first Birelli looked bemused, then realisation dawned and he turned white. As Vasson's hands closed round his neck, he screamed and tried to step backwards.

Vasson's hands closed rapidly round the fat neck and he began to shake the man, slowly at first, then rapidly so that the head snapped backwards and forwards like a puppet's. Then he lifted him by the neck, thrust him against a wall and started to smash his head against the hard surface of the red flock wallpaper.

Birelli had been screaming but now, as his head thudded dully into the wall, his breath came in long gasps. Blood began to smear the red flock and his eyes were round and staring like little white eggs.

Vasson found the movement of the head hypnotic as it snapped backwards and forwards; he wondered what it would take to make the head snap right off. He had got into a rhythm now and it was strangely satisfying. He wanted the rhythm and the feeling of satisfaction to continue.

Suddenly an arm encircled Vasson's neck and forced him to let go. Vasson felt an overwhelming disappointment and then, almost immediately, relief. He was sorry that the disgusting little man was going to escape lightly. On the other hand, he was glad he had been stopped. He had forgotten himself, and he didn't like doing that.

The armhold was vice-like and Vasson felt a moment of panic. He should have remembered about the barman. The man was large and powerful: he could hurt people.

Vasson tried to think. It would be a mistake to struggle; better to play dead. He made himself go limp and heard the barman grunt as his arm took the additional weight.

For a second Vasson thought nothing would happen, then there was a sickening blow to his kidney and he screamed.

After what seemed a long time the barman finally loosened his grip and let Vasson slide to the floor.

Vasson lay still for a moment then slid quickly under a table, out of reach. God, the pain! It was terrible, a great stabbing ache in his side. He felt sick.

He heard a sound and looked round. He could see the barman's feet advancing towards the table.

Vasson crouched lower and shouted, 'I've no argument with you, friend. How about laying off, eh?'

There was silence. Vasson crawled out on the other side of the table and got cautiously to his feet.

The barman was hovering, fists clenched. Vasson panted desperately, 'Look, be a good bloke and lay off. You've done me in the back and I'm in bloody agony. You've done your bit, *for Christ's sake.*'

For a moment the barman stared at him, then he hissed, 'Coward!'

Vasson didn't care what the man thought, just as long as there was no more fighting.

The barman advanced again. Vasson retreated quickly towards a wall.

Suddenly there was a loud groan. Both men stopped and looked across at the proprietor. He was slumped untidily on the floor, blood pouring from his head, his face sheet white. Vasson thought with satisfaction: Perhaps I did the sod some real damage after all.

The barman murmured angrily, 'You've half killed him!'

'No!' Vasson said hastily. 'He'll be all right. It's only superficial. Looks worse than it is. Really—' He let out a great moan of pain and clutched his back. The barman stared in surprise. Vasson groaned and started panting. 'God, my back! The *pain*!' The barman was impressed, just as Vasson had intended him to be.

The barman lowered his arms. He was still unhappy but it was obvious the fight was over. Vasson almost smiled with relief.

Birelli was groaning again and the barman shuffled over to take a look at him. Quickly Vasson straightened his jacket and tie and smoothed down his hair. He moved rapidly away from the barman, round the room to the stairway.

The barman spotted him and said, 'Oi! Hold on!'

Vasson poised himself on the bottom step and snapped, 'Just tell the ugly bastard that if he has any silly ideas about getting his own back, I'll tell the cops about the extra activities upstairs! Okay?'

The barman looked angry again and started to move towards him. Vasson sprinted up, three steps at a time, and ran into the street. He didn't stop running until he was across Pigalle and into Montmartre.

'Bastard! Bastard!' He kicked a wall angrily. He wished he'd finished Birelli off, squeezed his neck *tight* until he'd bloody choked! At the same time he hated himself for having lost control.

'God damn it!' He roared on up the street, bumping into people and forcing a woman off the pavement.

He came to a pavement café and threw himself disgustedly on to a chair. He stared blindly across the street still shaking with rage and humiliation.

Later, when the rage had subsided, he walked on, more slowly this time, wondering what the hell he'd done to deserve his luck.

It had been four years now. Four years since the disaster.

Even now he could hardly bear to think about it. He could hardly bear to remember the smell of that lovely, sweet money.

Paris was just as he imagined it would be, except better.

For the first few days he stayed at a good hotel and strolled around, eating at different restaurants and watching the smart ice-cool Parisians as they ate and talked and did their business. He was cautious: he wanted to get a feel for the latest fashions before buying any clothes; and he wanted to be sure that he had found the right neighbourhood in which to rent an apartment. For the moment he was happy to watch and listen and relax; to savour the freedom that money brought. The money: it was like the feeling of hot sunshine on your skin, warm, sensuous, intoxicating.

When he felt ready he slowly began to acquire the trappings of a successful man. First he bought a few really good clothes and some gold cufflinks. Then he began to look for an apartment. It had to be fairly near Pigalle where the club would be, but not too near. Montmartre was impossibly vulgar, so it would have to be the *neuvième*.

It took several days to find what he wanted. The apartment was in a purpose-built block in a quiet street off the Rue de Clichy. It was in need of decoration, but it would do until he was properly established, and then he would go to an even better place in the *huitième*, somewhere off the Champs Elysées.

The only luxury he would allow himself at this stage was the car. He had wanted it so long that he couldn't bear the idea of waiting any longer. He decided, rashly, to have a new one after all. There was a showroom on the Champs Elysées which had Delages and Bugattis in the window. It gave him a curious thrill to walk in and ask for a D8SS, for immediate delivery. The manager himself came out of his office and showed him a car with Falaschi bodywork in green. He liked the body – very much. It was open, with sleek wings which flowed into the running boards and a long, long bonnet.

Perfect – except for the colour. He wanted red, ruby red, with black leather upholstery. The manager was downcast. That could take weeks, maybe months.

Vasson said he would wait for it.

The manager went to the telephone. He returned smiling. It would be only two weeks, after all.

Two weeks. Vasson rather enjoyed the idea of waiting. It would be a sort of sweet agony. It appealed to his sense of Christian guilt. Yes, he would wait for the red one.

He paid a deposit, in cash as usual.

The money was lasting well; the hotel, the month's advance rent for the apartment, the new clothes and the cufflinks had hardly made a dent in it. But the car would, of course. For the deposit he had to dip into the crisp new notes for the first time.

The two weeks passed surprisingly quickly. He busied himself looking at premises around Pigalle. It would take quite a while to set up the club: there were difficulties – permits, licences, access and so on. And he had to be careful; his new identity wouldn't bear detailed examination by the police. Everything must be in order; none of the paperwork must be forgotten. If anything the difficulties made him more determined.

Then at last the two weeks were up and he telephoned the showroom. Yes, the car was there, ready.

It was like Christmas, or a birthday except he'd never known what it was like to get presents before. His heart

started to hammer with excitement as he walked along the
Champs Elysées. He approached from the opposite side of
the avenue, under the trees, and stopped at an intersection
to cross the wide boulevard. He looked across at the
showroom and frowned. He couldn't see a ruby red car
anywhere, either in the window or on the wide pavement
outside. He thought: Damn, it hasn't arrived after all.

He was just about to cross when he saw something that
made him freeze. A man leaning against a tree pretending
to read a newspaper, but actually watching the showroom.

There was another further up the avenue, standing in a
shop doorway, smoking a cigarette.

Oh God.

They were waiting for him.

Sweat started from his forehead and he went quite cold.
For several moments he stood absolutely still.

The man in the doorway threw his cigarette away and
looked up and down the avenue. Vasson turned quickly
away and walked rapidly towards the Etoile. He came to
one of the large pavement cafés and, going to the bar,
asked to use the phone. He called the showroom and said
he was delayed. Were they certain the car was absolutely
ready? There was a slight hesitation, then they had assured
him it was ready, there and waiting. He told them he
wanted to drive it straight off and did they have it parked
right outside? There was a moment's silence, then they told
him yes, it was just outside, ready to go.

Vasson watched the showroom for ten minutes. There
was no red Delage outside and none arrived while he
waited. Instead there was plenty of activity among the men
staked outside. A man came out of the showroom and
spoke first to the man under the tree and then to the one
in the doorway. There was a third Vasson hadn't spotted
before, in another doorway on the other side of the
showroom. After their discussions they looked more

relaxed as if they had been told that the action was off for the moment.

Vasson turned away, sick at heart.

It must have been the money, it could only have been the *money*.

The money must stink to high heaven.

He walked a long way, then went into a café and had a drink. It made him light-headed and he felt slightly hysterical. He had the dreadful desire to cry.

Later he sat in a daze, thinking, thinking hard. At last, late in the evening, he left the café and walked slowly towards the apartment.

He stayed in the apartment for three days, lying on the bed smoking or sometimes pacing up and down, thinking of a way to utilise the money.

There was no way. He had known that straight away, but it took him three days to face it. Then he wept.

He had been so naive it was incredible. How the Algerian must have laughed! How they all must have laughed! They'd probably been wondering how to get rid of that rotten money for years. The Algerian wouldn't have printed it himself, it wasn't his style, but he'd probably bought it cheap for an occasion like this . . .

At one point he thought of revenge, he thought of nailing the Algerian with the money, of doing a deal for perhaps half the two hundred thousand.

But he was frightened. If he went to Marseilles he knew the Algerian would kill him. He wouldn't get within a mile.

He tried to remember how lucky he was not to have been caught. And there was still some money from the down-payment: clean money. But it didn't help. He had been robbed and cheated, and it hurt like hell.

A week later he tried to shift some of the bad money with a bullion dealer. The dealer got the scent of the money

even as it came out of the briefcase: Vasson saw it in his
face. He made a quick exit before the dealer reached a
telephone. It was no better at a small pawnbrokers: the old
Jew handed the money back and yelled, 'Get this rubbish
out of here!'

Vasson realised the money was well known. It must
have been around for years.

Eventually, in desperation, Vasson sold the lot for three
thousand francs to a *pied-noir* who hoped to offload it in
Tangiers.

The good money lasted a year, spent carefully. There
was no club, no car, no security.

He was back where he'd started.

Vasson strode up the steps and steeply-climbing streets
that lead into the heart of Montmartre, and felt the sweat
soaking his back. He walked faster again, pushing his body
harder and harder to ease the pain in his kidney and the
bitterness in his mouth.

Finally he turned into a small dark café and sat near the
window. The group of men sitting at the counter glanced
at him and resumed their conversation. They knew he
never said hello. The waiter brought him a coffee.

He considered ordering a pastis; it might just revive
him. He'd drunk enough the night before. He couldn't
remember exactly how many. Twenty or more. The
memory sickened him, not only because of the hangover
but because the evening had cost him at least a hundred
francs.

Raoul had talked him into going. Well, Raoul could
damn well buy him a pastis.

He closed his eyes and tried to remember what it was
like to feel well. It had been a long time since he'd felt
really well; there had been too much drink and too many

cigarettes. And now the kidney, which was still aching viciously.

Someone sat down at the table. Vasson opened half an eye and saw that it was Raoul. Vasson said, 'Buy me a drink, you *tête de con*.'

'Have you read the news? Have you read the news?' Raoul unfolded his newspaper and started to read avidly.

Vasson waited for a moment, then leant forward and took Raoul's wrist. 'Look, after last night you owe me a goddam drink!'

Raoul looked up impatiently. 'Oh for Christ's sake shut up, will you? I'm reading this.' He flicked his hand across the newspaper. 'This Polish thing . . . it means war, do you realise? We will be at war by the end of the week!'

Vasson controlled his annoyance. Raoul thought he knew so much about world affairs, but he couldn't even run a couple of girls at a profit. 'War? So, maybe there'll be a war. But it's not going to affect us.'

Raoul slowly lowered the newspaper and stared across the table. 'Listen, big-time operator, this is the end of it, as far as I'm concerned. If France is going to war, then I will be there fighting, and you can rot here, hatching your grand plans. Alone.'

Vasson regarded him with contempt. 'Then I'm sorry for you, because I'll be the richer.'

'That's what you've been saying for the last three years – and I'm still counting my *sous*.' Raoul stabbed a finger across the table. 'And so, for that matter, are you!'

Vasson flushed. They'd had an idea to open a club, but it had failed for the usual reason: lack of money. They'd tried to borrow some, even tried to extort some, but it had all come to nothing.

Vasson retorted, 'At least I try, which is more than you do.' Raoul was a lazy swine who'd be quite happy to sit around for ever, earning nothing and drinking himself stupid. Vasson added, 'None of your ideas are worth a *sou*.'

Raoul shrugged; he'd heard it all before. 'There's nothing wrong with my ideas. It's you! You just find problems that aren't there.'

Vasson gave a short laugh. He knew Raoul's ideas all right: bank robbery. The quickest way to get inside, short of stabbing a *flic* and waiting to be arrested. God!

Raoul bought two pastis and plonked them on the table. 'Look, the idea of setting up your stupid club would never have worked anyway. We're small-fry. We could never have set up a big place like that. Hundreds of women indeed! High-class décor!' He shook his head. 'Look, for a start our police contacts just weren't good enough. And then do you think the existing businesses would have made room for you without a fuss? I tell you it would never have worked.'

Vasson watched him coldly. He decided Raoul was simply a very stupid man.

Raoul said tolerantly, 'You know, you should use that learning of yours, and get a good job with prospects. You *do* have an education, don't you, eh? I mean you read books and all that. It's obvious that someone stuffed the knowledge in somewhere. Well, you should use it!'

Vasson stared out of the window. He loathed people referring to his past.

Raoul went on, 'Was it the priests? That gave you the learning, I mean? I knew a lad once who'd started life with nothing – on the scrapheap at five years old, he was – and the priests took him in and stuffed his head full of books and Latin and he ended up a professor, a *professor*! The nephew of my mum's best friend, he was. Very proud, his family, very proud.' He turned to Vasson. 'Was it the priests, then?'

'Shut up,' Vasson snapped.

He downed his pastis and stood up. Raoul looked up in surprise. 'Where are you off to?'

'Away. Somewhere. So I'll say goodbye. I hope you enjoy the army and getting killed. Should be fun.'

'Don't be like that.'

Vasson leant over the table. 'We'll see who's the clever one, and I tell you, it isn't going to be you!'

He strode out of the café and up the street, swearing under his breath. So Raoul wanted out. Fine! Let them all go to hell. He could manage very well on his own.

The room was at the back of a tall, dingy house in the Rue St Vincent. It cost him a few francs a week, so that, after meals and clothes, he could save about one hundred a week. When he had a job.

The idea was to save enough for a lease on a club premises. By any calculations it should take twenty years to buy even the most modest property. Even assuming he had a job. He grimaced: it was pathetic, laughable.

Wearily he climbed the dirty narrow stairs and opened the door of the room. It was dark inside. He felt his way across the window and opened the shutters. Even then there wasn't much light: the window gave onto a narrow opening between tall buildings.

The room was a mess. High-heeled shoes lay scattered on the floor and piles of skirts and dresses were draped over the two chairs. I'll have to get rid of her, Vasson thought. She was a brainless little country girl named Yvette, and she was cluttering up his life. It had been her idea to move in, not his. He should have kicked her out straight away.

He threw some cheap magazines off the bed and lay down. His head ached and his kidney was still hurting badly. He wondered if the damage was serious. Perhaps he should go and see a doctor, except that doctors cost money and he begrudged paying them.

He lit a cigarette and began to think.

No job. No prospects. He'd been through it before. There'd been four, maybe five jobs in the last four years. The story was always the same: they wanted him to work like hell, but they offered him nothing in return. No real share of the action. No opportunity to change or improve things. And then – then came the disagreements. They always blamed him – *him!* – though the problems were their own stupid faults.

He felt cheated. Frustrated. Bitter.

Like he did now. Especially now. Because he hadn't managed to control himself and he'd half killed a man and that frightened him.

But it was the fault of the system. It was the system which was killing him. The fat kings ran the system and they had it sewn up. You didn't have a chance without weight and influence – and that meant money. And you couldn't get the money without the influence.

The system stank.

Christ, he thought, I just go round in bloody circles. And the circle always comes back to money.

Suddenly he was tired. He stubbed out his cigarette and closed his eyes. He liked sleep. He liked the blackness and the peace of it and the way it passed so much of the time.

The dream, when it came, was vivid. He was back in Marseilles, in the Algerian's car. His arms were bound and he was lying on the floor. The Algerian was discussing how he would kill him. But Vasson didn't care because he had the money on the floor next to him. *He had the money.* He knew he'd be all right.

But then he was slipping, down the floor of the car, on to the road. Someone had opened the door. It was his mother. As he fell past her he called to her, but she looked past him at the Algerian and smiled.

There was darkness. He was in the cupboard again. He shouted and yelled, but the door was made of steel and so thick that no-one could hear. Finally, after time which seemed to have lasted for ever, the door was opened. He did not want to come out. But it was one of the priests and refusal was not allowed.

He asked for his mother.

'Your mother is a long way away, Paul.'

'But I want her.'

'Paul, your mother has not yet found the way to the true God. She is – searching for Him. While she searches, she cannot come to you.'

'Searching? Why is she searching?'

'Paul, your mother is a long way away . . .'

No, she was near, he knew she was near. Why did they lie to him? Why did they keep her away?

Maman, maman—

He awoke. Someone was there, in the room.

It was Yvette.

'You all right?' She teetered across to the bed on her high heels and put her heavily made-up face close to his. He closed his eyes in disgust.

'You were muttering away. I thought you were awake, talking to yourself! Sorry, did I actually wake you up?' She was using the little-girl-lost voice she usually kept for fat rich men. It annoyed him.

He said irritably, 'Get out. I want to sleep.'

'Oh, well, don't mind about me. I'll stay quiet as a mouse. You won't even know I'm here.' She began to stroke his forehead.

He brushed her hand away and reached for a cigarette.

'Let me get you a cold drink, eh?' she persisted.

'No. And I've something to tell you. I'm going away.'

She stared at him and then nodded. She wasn't surprised. 'Can I come too?' She knew it was risky to ask, he might fly off the handle like he sometimes did. But she wanted to go with him. She wanted to look after him.

He said, 'No.'

She kicked off her shoes and lay on the bed beside him. She knew exactly how far she could go before he got angry. She put an arm across his waist and moved her head against his.

'I'll miss you terribly.'

'Like hell.'

'I know I don't suit you . . . I mean I'm not attractive to you, and all that. But I'd look after you, you know that.'

Vasson sighed. The sex thing again. It was her only level of understanding. Everything began and ended with sex. She couldn't understand how repulsive she was to him, how he couldn't bear her to touch him.

He sat up suddenly and, pushing past her, stood up. 'I'm off tomorrow, so you'd better find somewhere else.'

'Where are you going?'

'I don't know.'

'What about this war then?'

He glanced at her impatiently. 'What about it?'

'Well, *that* might offer some opportunities, I mean for the two of us.' She was always trying to think of money-making ideas. They were always pathetic, just like her.

He didn't answer, but began to pack his suitcase.

She fluttered valiantly on. 'There'll be shortages, right? And a black-market. Bound to be. That's where the money'll be. In buying things up cheap. You've got enough saved to make a start. It'll be a real money-spinner, you'll see!'

Vasson paused and looked at her. 'And what do you think people will be short of?' he asked.

She thought for a moment, her pencilled eyebrows puckered in concentration. At last she said, 'Oh, stockings, make-up, clothes, things like that . . . Oh and food, I suppose. And I could think of lots more, I'm sure I could—'

Vasson stared out of the window. The silly girl might actually have something. Perhaps there *would* be a war, perhaps it would go on for some time, perhaps there would be plenty of money to be made.

He pushed the last few things into his suitcase. He said abruptly, 'I'm off then.'

'Oh, please . . .!' She started towards him, a pleading expression on her face.

He glanced at her, thinking again how repulsive she was, and turned away to open the door.

She yelled, 'You shit!' But he walked quickly down the stairs and by the time he reached the street he couldn't hear her any more.

He walked rapidly, needing to get away quickly. He thought: It's good to be free again. He would get another room, alone. He would start again.

He stopped for a coffee and a cigarette in a place he hadn't been to before. He thought about the girl's idea. There definitely might be something in it. Luxuries, food, what else had she said – stockings. Yes, and cigarettes would be short too.

A war might be rather a good thing after all.

Chapter 5

THE COAST IS wild and rugged and utterly beautiful. From its border with Normandy to the point where the land turns to face the open Atlantic the North Brittany coast measures little more than a hundred miles as the crow flies. But this means nothing. It is so indented with bays and deep estuaries that its true length is at least twice that distance. Most of this length is impenetrable to anything but the smallest craft – and then only in good weather – for the land is defended by a great barrier of natural hazards.

A thousand storms have shaped the jagged cliffs and eaten into the soft rock, leaving a dense fabric of reefs, islands and islets to seaward. Some of the dangers stand proud and high in the water: great stacks of rock rising like dragon's teeth, or larger islands which lie cowed and barren before the wind. But most of the perils lie near the surface: sharp reefs marked only by breaking water, or islets so low that they are almost invisible. These dangers reach out four, five, sometimes twelve miles from the land.

Then there are the tidal streams. They run very strong along these shores, ripping across rocks and reefs, tearing through the deep channels, and swinging into bays and inlets, making accurate landfall difficult even for the most careful of navigators.

The strongest winds come in winter, blowing storm force from the Atlantic. They send before them armies of waves which curve in towards the shore, gathering speed

until they break on the myriad of rocks and islets in a
cauldron of white foaming surf, then advance, still snapping and roaring, on to the fragile mainland itself.

This coast is no friend to the sailor. Only those familiar
with its dangers dare approach it with impunity; strangers
must rely on good charts and blind faith. At night the
dangers are marked by the powerful lights of tall lighthouses; with the help of leading lights and channel buoys
it is even possible for small fishing craft to navigate one or
two of the estuaries in darkness. But for the most part this
coast does not invite visitors; the great lighthouses serve to
warn rather than welcome.

The wind blows the fine salt mist several miles inland,
so that only the hardiest vegetation can grow there. There
is gorse and heather and thin coarse grass, and the pastures,
such as they are, support only a small number of cattle.
Further inland there are market gardens and fields of wheat
and richer pastures, but even here the land gives grudgingly
and there is none of the lush abundance of Normandy or
Picardy.

Like all wild, windswept places the land is rich with
romantic legend. Except that in Brittany fact and fable are
closely intertwined. The people who have inhabited this
land for centuries are quite alien to their neighbours in the
rest of France. Brittany is French by nationality, but not by
race, language or culture. The proud, tough Bretons are
not Gauls but Celts, and their closest links are with
Cornwall, Wales, and Ireland, whence they came centuries
ago. The Breton language sounds harsh to the French ear
and the names of the rocks and headlands are easier spoken
by a Cornishman than a Frenchman: Beg an Fry, Mean
Nevez, L'Aberwrac'h, Lizen Ven, Pen Ven. You would
even be forgiven for thinking you were in Scotland when
you hear their music, for they play not the accordion, but
the plaintive, mournful bagpipes.

To the great nation of France, Brittany is something of

a backwater, not sufficiently fertile or industrially developed to demand a great deal of attention. For the Bretons, proudly nationalistic and stubbornly independent, their subjugation to the mother country is tolerated with equanimity, and the benefits, if any, absorbed. The idea of freedom has long been forgotten – the land has been fought over often enough as it is – but the people remain independent in spirit.

The land is poor and in places infertile, but the Bretons find it sufficient for their needs; the way of life is simple and austere and not to the taste of the sophisticated French, but for the Bretons this is the only life they know. Many of them live off the sea, and the sea is the harshest life there is.

It was a pleasant day in August and the coast looked almost benign.

The sun had penetrated the morning mist at midday and now in the late afternoon the ragged headlands and narrow estuaries were lit in firm bold colours. The greeny purple of the sparse vegetation showed clearly against the grey and terracotta of the jagged rock formations. The sea itself was a pale grey-blue and unusually calm. There had been no gales for some days and only a slight swell washed around the walls of rock and on to the narrow pebble beaches.

Julie lifted her head and let the soft salt wind caress her face. For a few moments she stood quite still, listening to the gentle murmur of the surf far below, watching the waves ripple across the wideness of the sea. The cries of seabirds echoed faintly on the wind; occasionally one would fly high into the air and she followed it as it glided motionless on the breeze.

Julie closed her eyes, thinking: It's so beautiful and I love it all.

She opened her eyes and looked again. She loved it partly because it *was* beautiful and partly because she was happy here. She loved the peace and the loneliness of it; on a day like this you could walk for hours and never see a living soul. At first the remoteness had seemed strange and unsettling after the close warmth of the city. But slowly she began to appreciate the austerity and rugged beauty of the landscape. Now it seemed so familiar that she might have lived here all her life.

Standing on the headland it was difficult to believe that Plymouth and England lay just a hundred miles across the Channel. It seemed like a thousand. The small house in Radley Terrace belonged to another life, another *person*. That's what she had been then – another person.

Suddenly she remembered she should have counted to twenty by now. Peter must have been hiding for ages. She yelled, 'Twenty! I'm coming!'

She knew exactly where he would be. There were few places to hide on the windswept headland. The heather and gorse grew low and sparse, clinging to the stony soil around the rocky outcrops, and there were no trees. The only object capable of concealing a small boy was a large boulder which stood round and grey against the skyline. There was also a slight dip in the ground where someone could lie still and remain unseen, but Peter preferred a really solid hiding place, so it had to be the boulder.

But it was important to make a proper show of searching. She said in a loud voice, 'My, my! Where *can* he be?' then called, 'Peter, Peter, where are you?' At this point he often gave the game away by calling, 'Whoo-hoo!', a funny cry that always made her laugh. But he had got much cannier recently and had finally realised that keeping quiet was the smart thing to do.

Julie approached the boulder and waited. Sometimes Peter couldn't bear the suspense any longer and jumped out with a loud 'Boo!', but he was being patient today.

For a moment she thought she was mistaken and he wasn't there after all, but then she heard a small giggle. She crept silently up to the boulder and, running quickly round it, pounced on the small person crouching behind. With a shriek he tried to run away but her arms went round the little body and the two of them rolled on to the ground, yelling and giggling.

They wrestled and tickled each other until Julie cried, 'Enough, enough!' She rolled on to her back, panting hard. Peter plonked himself on her stomach and grinned triumphantly.

'I give up. You win, you horrible child!'

Peter bounced with delight, then chanted, 'Again, again. Please let's play it again!'

'In a minute. Give your poor old mum a chance to recover.'

He nodded gravely as he always did and, getting up, wandered off to examine some tiny blue flowers peeping up through the heather. He was always fascinated by tiny things.

He called, 'Mummy.'

'Yes, darling.'

'Shall I pick you some flowers?'

She smiled. 'That would be lovely.'

She watched him as he carefully bent down to search for the stems of the flowers. When he was younger he had yanked them off at the head but she had explained to him why it was better to pick them at the bottom and he had listened with his little head on one side, and then nodded. Now he set about doing the job properly, a frown of concentration on his forehead.

She smiled as she watched him. He was a small boy now, almost three and a half years old, but there was still a lot of the baby in him. Most of the rounded chubbiness had gone and every one of the babyish creases, but he still had a lovely velvety skin, and when his little arms went round her neck and he hugged her tight she loved to feel its softness against her. He still needed plenty of hugs, thank goodness. She couldn't bear to think of him growing up and not wanting them any more. The two of them spent at least two hours a day just talking and reading. Julie looked forward to those hours: to the little body that wriggled into bed in the mornings and snuggled close; to the small fellow who needed a hug when he'd grazed his knee; and to the sleepy bedtime boy who wanted just one more story before falling asleep in her arms.

Her only regret – and it was a big one – was that she had to spend so many hours away from him, working. But that couldn't be helped: they couldn't survive without money.

Sometimes she wanted him to stay just the way he was now, not to grow up and drift away from her. At the same time she was fascinated by his development, the way he picked up new words and slotted them into one of his two vocabularies, French or English, and the way he thought things out for himself. The other night, when he'd been up late, he'd announced that, since the moon was nowhere to be seen, it must have forgotten to put its light on. She had been careful not to laugh – the logic was, after all, irrefutable – and she had nodded seriously instead.

Peter was striding towards her, lifting his feet high in the air to get across the carpet of springy heather. In his preoccupation he forgot to hold the bunch of flowers upright and a few of the tiny blooms were torn away by the ragged branches. When he arrived breathless beside her he looked at the flowers in surprise, puzzled that some should have so mysteriously disappeared. But apparently the loss was not too serious: he thrust his arm out and proudly announced, 'Here's a present, just for you!'

Julie thanked him and got to her feet. 'They're quite

lovely,' she said. 'I'll put them in water when we get back.'
She placed the flowers in a pocket of her cardigan and
glanced at her watch.

It was getting on for four-thirty, time they went back
for tea. They walked up to the path which led inland
towards the village.

'Mummy, hide and seek again? You promised.'

Little demon. He never forgot.

They played two more games, first Julie hiding, then
Peter, and then it really was time to head for home.

They climbed the narrow path which led upwards round
the side of a rocky bluff and along the top of a steep cliff.
Although the cliff was fenced at this point and the drop a
safe distance away, Julie gripped Peter's hand more tightly.
They came to a corner where the path led away from the
cliff and paused.

Peter said, 'Look, a fishing boat!'

Julie turned and followed his gaze. A small boat was
drifting gently a short distance from the shore, its tan sails
hardly filling in the windless lee of the headland. Several
rocks were plainly visible just above the surface on the
seaward side of the vessel. Julie shook her head. The
Bretons were known for their knowledge of this coast, but
all the same . . .

She looked beyond the boat, towards the horizon. At
night she could see the flash of a light from her bedroom
window. Now, squinting her eyes against the sun, she
could make out the form of the lighthouse itself. It was a
tall grey and red structure standing stark and solitary in
the middle of the sea. It marked a plateau of rocks lying
just beneath the surface some miles offshore. She shivered
slightly; the tower seemed lonely and somehow sad.

She turned away. 'Come on, darling.'

They climbed up to the top of the ridge and walked
slowly towards the village, just visible through a dip in the
land. Although the path was fairly level now, Peter was

puffing and panting as he strived to match her step. Presently he began to hang back and Julie wasn't surprised when he said, 'Mummy, please carry me.'

She lifted him over her head and on to her shoulders.

She said, 'I don't promise to take you all the way. You're too heavy, young man!'

It was true: in five minutes or so her shoulders would ache and then she would have to put him down. A man could have done it easily. But there wasn't a man.

She hardly ever thought about Peter's father. It was as if he belonged to another world that had existed a long, long time ago. Her memory of him was completely neutral; she neither hated him nor cared about him. It was almost as if she had never really known him. The only thing she felt, possibly, was gratitude: he had after all given her Peter. But at the same time she never thought of Peter as belonging to him. Peter was hers and hers alone.

She'd adored her son from the start, and it surprised her. In the months before the birth she didn't have much time to think about how she'd feel; she was too busy sorting things out – difficulties mainly. It was only in the last few weeks that she realised she was about to give birth to a *person*, somebody who would rely on her for every-thing. It frightened her, but she was determined to do the right thing, to do her *best*.

Settling in Brittany had been far from easy. Looking back, she wondered how she'd stuck it out. In fact, at one point just after she arrived, she'd nearly given up and gone home to England.

The village was in full view now, a group of grey stone cottages standing out against the pastel grey-greens of the fields. Julie regarded it fondly. She was glad she hadn't given up and run away.

*

As soon as she'd decided on Brittany Julie had written to her uncle and aunt. She didn't know their full address, only the name of the village: Tregasnou. She asked if she could stay with them while she found somewhere to live.

The reply came in two weeks. It was short, stiff and impersonal: they would be expecting her and they had a spare room where she could stay.

The journey lasted three days. She took a ferry from Dover to Calais and then a train to Morlaix. She had to change three times and then wait two hours for a bus from Morlaix to Tregasnou. By the time she walked up the long hill to the small grey house, a heavy suitcase in each hand, she was exhausted.

The farmhouse was typically Breton: it was built of grey stone with a high, pitched roof and low eaves which came almost to the ground-floor windows. There were two small dormer windows in the roof where the upper rooms must be. Various outbuildings extended from the back of the house and, as she approached, Julie heard the sounds of animals stamping and shuffling in a barn somewhere.

The house was silent and, though it was almost dark, there was no light showing in the window.

Julie knocked on the door. There was no reply. She knocked again, louder. After a minute there was the flicker of a light as an inner door was opened. Finally the front door swung open and a large, rather fierce woman stood in the doorway.

Julie smiled and said in French, 'I'm Julie.'

Suddenly the woman smiled and nodded. She called something over her shoulder, then beckoned Julie in.

A small, squat man appeared from the back room and with a shy smile shook her hand. 'You are welcome, welcome. Please come in.'

She was shown to a chair by the kitchen range and offered coffee. Her uncle and aunt sat opposite, watching her and smiling politely. Julie realised they were nervous.

They were sitting upright in their seats, their hands clasped in their laps, looking strangely uncomfortable. For several moments no-one could think of anything to say.

'It's kind of you to have me to stay,' Julie said at last.

Her uncle smiled. 'Not at all, not at all.'

Her aunt took a decisive breath and said, 'Well, let's make sure you're comfortable. First, have you had something to eat?'

'I had a sandwich on the train.'

'Perhaps you would like some soup?'

'Oh, thank you.' Julie smiled gratefully.

Her aunt got up and put a pan on the stove. She turned and started to speak again, quicker this time. Julie concentrated on what was being said, but to her chagrin, missed several key words. Before she could ask her aunt to repeat them her uncle was speaking and Julie realised with bitter disappointment that she could not understand all he was saying either. It was the accent, perhaps, or maybe her French was rustier than she thought.

At one point her relatives started to speak in Breton until, remembering Julie was there, they returned apologetically to French.

Julie suddenly felt depressed. She'd assumed that because her father came from this village she would have some bond with these people, some feeling of belonging. Instead she felt a complete stranger, a foreigner who knew and understood nothing.

And it was clear that her uncle and aunt found her equally strange. They'd probably never met an English person before – nor, for that matter, any kind of foreigner. She was beginning to realise just how remote the village was.

It was clear too that the farmer and his wife were not used to having guests. Julie had the feeling that she was upsetting the routine of the small household, and that they didn't really know what to do with her. When finally she said she was tired and they showed her to a tiny upstairs room, she knew they were relieved.

The next day started well. Julie tried hard to make conversation and offered to help her aunt with the chores. But soon she was depressed again. Her aunt was obviously uneasy about something and refused to let Julie help her with even the simplest tasks, while her uncle treated her with rigid politeness and exaggerated respect. The effect was rather chilling.

That evening it came to a head. They had finished supper and Tante Marie started to clear away the dishes. Julie got quickly to her feet and carried the cheese and butter towards the larder.

'No, no!' Tante Marie made her put the plates down. 'We can't have you doing these things.'

'But I must help, otherwise . . .' Julie struggled to find the right word. 'I will be a burden.'

Tante Marie looked crosser than ever. 'But you are a guest. You must not work!'

'But please . . . I feel I am imposing on you.'

'It is no imposition.' Tante Marie looked quite shocked.

'You are kind. But you must let me pay you, for my food and my bed, just until I can find a room to rent. I will look for one tomorrow.'

'A room?'

'Yes, a room to rent.'

'But – why?'

Julie stared at the older woman. She began to wonder what they had understood from her letter.

'Well, I can't stay with you for ever.'

Her uncle and aunt exchanged glances. Her aunt sat down slowly. 'You mean, you're staying a long time?'

'Yes, I want to.' She laughed nervously.

Gently Tante Marie took her hand and patted it. Then Julie found it easy to explain everything they hadn't understood from the letter: how she wanted to stay in the village, how she was going to find a room, then a job . . .

It was more difficult to talk about the baby, of course, particularly when she had to explain about the husband who was meant to have deserted her. But she did it, because they'd have to know some time and it might as well be now.

After she'd told them, she felt much better. At least everything was out in the open.

It was different then. In some strange way, her aunt and uncle were pleased. They insisted she stay with them. Terms for board and lodging were soon agreed. Everything was settled.

They went out of their way to make her feel at home. Her uncle prepared a room for her at the back of the house in the lower of two rooms which had once been used for storage; her aunt allowed her to help with the chores; and the formality of the evenings was replaced by what Julie realised was a well-established routine of occasional conversation interspersed with long silences.

But it was a long time before she did feel at home, partly because the way of life *was* so different and partly because she was lonely. The villagers did not take easily to strangers, let alone foreigners. And she had the unpleasant feeling they had heard the story about the disappearing husband and not believed it. Doubtless one or two of them were aware that she was entered on the Aliens Registration at Morlaix as Juliette Lescaux, not Juliette Howard, the name she had called herself when she arrived in France. She had chosen it after her favourite film actor, Leslie Howard, and then laughed at her stupidity: 'H' was the one letter the French could not pronounce.

Finding a job was the hardest part. There weren't many jobs around, even for those who spoke good French and weren't pregnant. But she persevered. At last, when her

money was beginning to run low, she was taken on as a
secretary to a vegetable wholesaler in Morlaix. She suspected that the manager was tickled by her English accent,
but whatever the reason, she wasn't going to turn the job
down.

She was still there, three years and a baby later.

Peter was like a lead weight on her shoulders. She said,
'You're breaking my back. I'm going to chase you home!'

Peter giggled. 'I'll win! I'll win!'

She lowered Peter to the ground and the two of them
ran down into the village and along the main street.
Tregasnou was a small village, no more than a scattering
of cottages built around a crossroads. There was one shop
and a café. The shop sold bread brought in daily from the
larger village of Plougat, as well as butter, cheese, simple
provisions, and a rough local wine. For everything else you
had to go into Plougat itself, or, for really special shopping
expeditions, to Morlaix.

Because Julie worked in Morlaix she often delivered or
collected items for her neighbours. She was pleased to do
it because it helped her to get to know them. Not an easy
thing by any means. At one stage she despaired of being
accepted by them. But then she realised it was a mistake to
be too interested in their customs or to be too curious
about their lives. They distrusted that. It was better to
show polite interest and then offer information about
England and how things were done there. They respected
national pride and liked to hear about foreign customs, if
only to reassure themselves that, all things considered,
their way of doing things was the best.

Julie thought some of their ways were quaint, others
just out-of-date – it wasn't done for women to go into the
café for instance – but she never commented on it. That

was the way things had always been done around here, and she wasn't about to change them.

Now, on Sunday afternoon, when almost everyone in the village took a stroll, it was impossible for her to get down the street without stopping for a chat. Most people made a pretence of talking to Peter and she realised it was mainly shyness which had held them back. Some were intractable – the old people mainly, who distrusted French-speaking people, let alone foreigners – but most treated her with kindness and warmth.

Peter was running ahead, his small legs flying in a funny wheeling motion which was peculiarly his own. Julie walked briskly after him, waving briefly at an old woman sitting in her doorway, and to a fisherman and his wife strolling towards her. Because it was a Sunday people were in their best clothes, black for the older women, simple printed cotton frocks for the younger. The men wore ill-fitting suits and shirts too tight at the neck so that they ran their fingers inside their collars. Julie smiled. The women loved dressing up, but how the men hated it!

Peter disappeared into the lane that formed one arm of the crossroads. When Julie turned the corner and looked up the hill she saw that the small figure had slowed down and was waiting for her. She caught up with him and bent to kiss him, then together they climbed slowly towards the small house which stood alone on the brow of the hill.

After a while Peter began to drag his feet and look unhappy. His breath came in short pants, like a small steam engine. Julie reached down and, taking his hand, squeezed it.

She said, 'Not far now.'

He gripped her hand tightly and looked up. 'Mummy, it *is* a tall hill, isn't it?'

She nodded and smiled. She thought: Why can't it always be like this? Why did Monday ever have to come?

Finally they reached the house. Julie pulled the latch
and they entered the darkness of the front parlour. The
room was simply furnished with a large darkwood table,
six straight-backed chairs, and a dresser. The walls were
covered with a traditional Breton wallpaper, a pattern of
flowers on trelliswork, and were bare of pictures except
for a cheap religious print framed in gilt. The ceiling was
low and supported by heavy beams.

As they took their coats off there was a call from the
kitchen and Tante Marie appeared. As soon as she saw
Peter her round face broke into a smile.

She leaned down to pinch Peter's cheek. 'And how did
you enjoy your walk, my hero?'

'Oh, we saw a boat, and I picked Mummy some
flowers . . .'

Peter chattered on in his broken French, and Tante
Marie listened studiously, exclaiming loudly at the amazing
things that had happened, and sighing deeply at the list of
creatures that had not, on this occasion, presented themselves for Peter's inspection. There had been no ants' nest
this time, nor a nesting plover.

Julie sank gratefully into a chair by the old stove and
watched Tante Marie's face as it went through all the
necessary reactions from astonishment to amazed delight.
Julie decided, not for the first time, that it had all turned
out pretty well. Not only did the old woman love Peter,
but she took trouble with him. During the day, while Julie
was away, she taught him things, about why plants and
flowers grew, and how things worked; and they drew
pictures and built paper castles together.

The old woman straightened up and, going to the larder
door, emerged with bread, cold meat and a dish of late
strawberries. 'Here, a surprise!' She put them on the table
and Peter wriggled up on to a chair, his little face glowing
with delight.

Tante Marie sat down on the other side of the kitchen

range and smiled as she watched Peter. 'I picked the strawberries this afternoon. We'll have a few more bowlfuls yet.'

When the old woman smiled her face was transformed. She was only about fifty, but she looked ten years older. Like many of the women in the village she made no effort with her appearance beyond neatness and cleanliness. Her grey-black hair was parted in the centre and scraped back into a bun at the nape of her neck. Her figure was full and round and it was a long time since she had made any attempt to lose weight. Now she thought it unimportant. Her clothes were simple to the point where she had two working dresses, which she wore alternate weeks, and one best dress. She hardly ever felt the cold and made no concession to the weather, except when there was snow on the ground, and then she wore a cardigan.

Her face was round and plain and red-cheeked. She thought life was too serious a business to smile about it. When her husband read from the newspaper she always tutted and shook her head: she thought the world mad and she viewed people's motives with distrust. The only important things, she believed, were the family, honest work and fear of God.

But with Peter she was different. With Peter she smiled a lot. She had never had children of her own.

Peter pushed the cold meat to one side and got down to the strawberries. Tante Marie turned to Julie and sighed. 'Your uncle is very worried. He thinks war will really come.'

Julie frowned. She really hadn't been following the news very carefully. Occasionally she glanced at her uncle's newspaper, or listened to a neighbour's wireless – there was none in her uncle's house – but her real passion was for books. In England she'd hardly read at all, it hadn't interested her. But in Brittany she'd started reading to fill the long evenings and improve her French. Now it was her greatest pleasure and she was rarely without a book in her hand.

People had talked about war, but she hadn't taken it seriously. Now she wished she'd read the papers more often.

'Do you think there'll be war?' Julie asked.

'I think people are selfish and cruel enough to do anything. Particularly the Germans.' Tante Marie had firm opinions about almost everything.

'But why? Why do the Germans want war?'

Tante Marie shrugged. 'You ask me? I wish I could tell you. The usual things, I suppose. Power and hate and jealousy.'

There was the sound of a door opening. Tante Marie inclined her head at the front parlour. 'Here's your uncle. Ask him. He's been down in the village talking about it most of the afternoon.'

The parlour door opened and Jean Cornou came in. He nodded a greeting.

Julie smiled up at her uncle. 'Hello. Did you have a good afternoon?'

He grunted and shook his head. He pulled up a chair and sat down, breathing heavily after his climb up the hill.

'The news is bad, bad.' He shook his head again.

Jean Cornou was short and square, with wide shoulders and muscular arms. He farmed the land around the house the only way he knew, and that was the old way, with little machinery and a lot of hard work and the help of a single farmhand. His face was uneven, open and kind. In his best clothes, which he wore now, his rough hands and face and muscular body looked oddly out of keeping with the dark three-piece suit and white shirt. The waistcoat was anyway too tight for him and his stomach bulged against the buttons.

He leant forward to take off his jacket, then unbuttoned his waistcoat and sighed deeply.

'The Germans look as though they are going to attack Poland. If they do there'll be a war. A war!' He snorted with disgust.

Julie frowned. 'But who . . . Which countries will fight?'

'Oh, Britain and France will fight Germany. Now that those filthy Russians have done the dirty and signed up with Germany, there'll be no stopping Hitler. Communists! They're not to be trusted. They've sold us down the river, just as I said they always would. Nothing but trouble, trouble. The great hope of France, they were meant to be. Yes, indeed. And what happens? They sell out at the first opportunity!'

Tante Marie shook her head and tutted quietly.

Peter had dropped a book on the floor and Julie automatically went to pick it up. Peter said, 'Mummy, read me a story!'

'Later, darling, I'm talking. Here, look at the pictures in this one. When you're finished I'll tell you a story. Promise.'

He nodded and started to turn the pages of the book. Julie stroked his head and returned to her chair.

She looked at Jean. 'So what'll happen? Will it last long? I mean, surely it'll be settled quickly?'

Her uncle shrugged. 'Who knows? With every country in Europe jostling for position, anything can happen. Who knows who will get involved and how far the fighting will spread? All I know is that, thanks to those spineless communists ganging up with Hitler, the cause of socialism has been set back fifty years. Everyone's anti-communist now – *and* anti-socialist. They put the two together, communist-socialist, socialist-communist! Everything that the working man has won in the last five years will be lost for ever, mark my words! We think of Hitler as a fascist – well, this Daladier government of ours is not far behind, not far at all! And speaking of communists, Michel was down at the café.'

Tante Marie glanced up from her knitting and they both

looked at Julie. She blushed, mainly because they were expecting her to. Michel Le Goff was Tante Marie's nephew. He came to the house quite often. Julie enjoyed his visits; he was clever, well informed and politically argumentative. He was probably quite attractive too, if you cared to think about him that way. But she did not, not at the moment anyway. She hadn't closed her mind to the possibility of liking him, but she wasn't ready to encourage him yet. Perhaps she never would be. But until her mind was made up, she did wish people wouldn't pair them off.

Peter was fidgeting at the table. 'Mummy, I've finished. Read me a story now. Please. You promised!'

'Yes, of course, darling. And it's almost bedtime, too.'

She picked him up and carried him through the back door of the kitchen into the extension. There were two rooms, one on the ground floor and, at the top of some steep, narrow stairs, a small attic bedroom. Julie used the main room as a bed-sitting room, though she nearly always sat in the kitchen during the evenings. The room was simply furnished with a bed, a chest of drawers, and a chair. Soon after her arrival she had whitewashed the walls and hung a couple of colourful pictures to brighten the room up. Though she didn't like needlework, she had even made some gay curtains for the window.

On the chest of drawers there were several framed photographs of Peter, and one of her mother. When Julie thought of her mother, she sighed. She wrote to her mother regularly, every month or so, but she rarely got a reply. The few letters she did get were bitter and full of reproach, begging her to come back to England and live in Plymouth again. Her mother never missed an opportunity to make it clear that she felt abandoned and betrayed. 'Disloyal' and 'ungrateful' were her favourite expressions.

It was clear to Julie that her mother could not have read any of her replies, otherwise she would have understood.

Julie had explained that she was happy here, that she enjoyed her work and she loved the people. But now, after so much time, Julie suspected that Mother did not want to understand. Mother hated the idea of Julie liking Father's people and living the kind of life Father had lived and which Mother had tried so hard to drag him away from. The suspicion made her sad but all the more determined not to go back. Life at the little house in Plymouth would suffocate her. Here at least she was free.

She undressed Peter and gave him a quick wash. As she dried him he wriggled away from her and dashed off round the room attempting as usual to evade capture, pyjamas and bed. Julie chased after him, roaring like a lion. At last she caught a flying arm and threw him giggling on to the bed.

Peter cried, 'Again!'

Julie put her head on one side and listened; there was the sound of a new voice from the kitchen. It was Michel's. She said firmly to Peter, 'No.'

Peter began to whine. 'If you don't, I'll cry.'

'And if you don't let me put these pyjamas on, there'll be big trouble.' She gave him a mock glare.

Peter's lower lip wobbled and he began to cry, though rather half-heartedly. He often cried when he was tired. She kissed him and felt the soft, cool arms encircle her neck. She put her arms round his small irate body and, taking him on her knee, began to rock him gently back and forth as she had when he was a baby.

After a while she felt a kiss on her ear and a small voice said, 'Story now?'

'Yes, we'll have *two* stories tonight.'

She read him three stories because he'd been a good boy and because she always read him one more than she said she would. Then she carried him up the narrow stairs to the attic bedroom. It was a small room, with one bed and a tiny window, but it was snug and Peter loved it because when he woke up in the night he could call down to her and, in the morning when he crawled into her bed, it wasn't far for him to come.

She gave him a last kiss and went down the stairs to the chest of drawers. She opened the top drawer and, taking out a small mirror, examined herself critically. She didn't like her face much. Its shape was all right – oval – and her skin was as clear as a bell, but the face seemed to her incredibly *ordinary*. Her best feature, she supposed, was her eyes, which were large and dark and fairly pretty – but she'd never dared pluck her eyebrows as the fashionable women did and so her eyes probably made little impression. Nose – all right but definitely nothing special. She sighed: really there was nothing very special about any of her.

Except her hair. That *was* something she was proud of. It was dark – dark *auburn*, they called it – and naturally curly where it met her shoulders. She never did much to it, usually parting it in the middle and holding it back with a comb at either side. She'd tried a fancy rolled style once or twice, but the hairdo seemed to detract from the hair itself and she'd let it down again.

She brushed it now until it shone, added a touch of lipstick, and stood back.

No, nothing special about her tonight. Anyway, it was only Michel.

But at least he was a man, and unmarried at that. And she didn't meet very many of those. She was beginning to think it would be a good idea for her to have a husband. She took a last look in the mirror and thought: I'm nearly twenty-four, I mustn't leave it too late. She smiled ruefully; some people would say she was already on the shelf.

She straightened her dress and walked into the kitchen.

Michel's voice was saying, 'But you have to understand, it's only political expediency – political *survival* – that's

all!' Julie's heart sank a little as it always did when Michel
and Jean started on politics.

Michel spotted her and, getting quickly to his feet,
stared into her face. His gaze was hard and penetrating.
Julie decided, not for the first time, that there was something altogether too earnest about Michel. After a moment
he smiled quickly and stooped to kiss her on both cheeks.

He said apologetically, 'I'm defending myself again.
Jean thinks my politics stink.' He shrugged slightly, and
half smiled. But Julie knew that, behind the casual manner,
he was deadly serious about his opinions. Michel nodded
slightly and sat down to face Jean again, saying, 'Look, it's
not something the Soviet Union wanted to do, but they
had no choice, don't you see? We and the British, we
offered them nothing, no guarantees, no treaties, just hot
air . . .'

Julie listened quietly, trying to follow the arguments.
There was something about the intensity of Michel's
opinions which was rather unnerving. He spoke with an
earnest fury that tolerated no opposition. It was a pity, she
decided, because in most other ways he had a lot to
recommend him.

He was dark, like many of the French: his hair was
almost black and his eyes deep brown. He was pleasant
looking, though he had a way of frowning which made
him look severe. He dressed well, and Julie guessed his
clothes cost a lot. She smiled to herself: only in France
could you find a communist who dressed like a capitalist.
But then half the population were communist when it
suited them. The rest of the time they were socialists, or
Republicans, depending on their mood.

Michel worked in Morlaix, in an insurance office. She
sometimes bumped into him when she was out shopping
in her lunch hour and occasionally he would buy her a
coffee. Then – when he was off the subject of politics – she

enjoyed his company much more. He had a dry wit and an interesting way of describing everyday things. But she'd avoided seeing him in the evenings; that would imply there was more to their relationship than family friendship, and she didn't want that.

She concentrated again on the conversation. Michel was speaking forcefully, his fists clenched.

'The Soviet Union does not want war. So what's wrong with her manoeuvring to avoid it? If we had any sense that's what we'd be doing too instead of pledging support to Poland, which is undefendable anyway!'

Jean Cornou leaned forward in his chair and, picking up a poker, flipped open the door of the stove. He stabbed thoughtfully at the fire. 'But someone has to protect countries that need protecting. Your precious Russia, she doesn't care about anyone else at all. She may be avoiding war for herself, but not for everyone else!'

'Nonsense, war should be avoided at all costs. Who wants to fight? You? Me? Of course not! The end justifies the means!'

Julie said suddenly, 'There's nothing wrong with avoiding war – so long as it achieves real peace. If it just gives the bullies time to move into a stronger position, then it's no good, is it? That's what it's all about, it seems to me – bullying.' She added almost to herself, 'They should let the women run things, then we might have a bit of sensible government and people would be left to live in peace.'

Everyone was looking at her in surprise. She'd never spoken during a political argument before. There was a long silence and Julie dropped her eyes. She'd gone too far.

She added nervously, 'Anyway, why don't we talk about something else for a change. This subject is very depressing.'

Tante Marie put down her knitting. 'A good idea. I'll put some supper on the table. Michel, will you stay for a bit?'

There was no reply and Julie looked up. Michel was staring at her.

'A fine speech!'

There was a mocking note in his voice and she wasn't sure if he was laughing at her or not. She got up and helped Tante Marie to lay the table. As she passed Michel's chair he said, 'Really, it was a fine speech.'

He looked as though he meant it and she thought that maybe she'd misjudged him. She put her hand on his arm and smiled.

They sat down at the table and talked about the harvest and the fishing industry, the weather and the fruit crop.

Eventually Michel said, 'And what about your job, Julie? Are you happy there?'

'Yes, happy enough. It's quite interesting really. I've become something of an expert on vegetable prices.' She didn't add that she was often bored. But it was a job and it brought the money in. That was all that mattered.

'I only wish—' She paused. 'I only wish I had more spare time.'

Michel leant forward. 'You should ask for shorter hours!' The subject of long hours was one of his favourite subjects. He considered anything over a forty-hour week to be slave labour. 'The other way is to give up work altogether.'

Julie gave a short laugh. 'And how would I live then?'

He shot her a glance. 'You could find someone to support you.'

She felt herself blushing and looked furiously at the table. I walked straight into that one, she thought.

Michel was looking at her with a rather smug, self-satisfied expression. Suddenly she wanted to wipe the smirk right off his face.

She said crossly, 'I'm not interested in marrying just to find someone to support me. Women who do that are fools and the men who marry them even more stupid. When I

find a man I want to marry, *then* I'll be happy to let him
pay the bills!'

Michel looked at his hands and said quietly, 'But
marriage is a practical arrangement. If you think it's made
in heaven, well – then you are not as clever as I thought
you were.'

He was warming up for an argument, Julie could see
that. He would call it a discussion, but it would really be a
sparring match. Michel always won those kinds of arguments. He had a way of twisting words and turning logic
until his opponent's opinions appeared ridiculous.

Suddenly Julie wanted to be on her own. She made an
elaborate pantomime of looking at the clock over the
mantelpiece. 'Goodness! Is that the time? I really must get
to bed.'

She stood up and made herself smile. 'It was nice to see
you Michel. Good night.' They kissed each other on both
cheeks, and she saw that he was looking pleased with
himself again. Damn him, she thought, why does he have
to be so *satisfied* with himself?

Later, when she lay in bed, she went over the conversation again in her mind. Until now she'd thought Michel
kind and thoughtful under his façade of cleverness and
indifference. But now she was having second thoughts. He
wasn't kind at all; he was conceited and intolerant. There
was no question of letting their friendship develop; it
would never work. She'd never be happy with a man who
had to score off everyone as if the whole of life were a
political debate. And she hated the way he was amused by
almost everything she said, like a patronising father listening to a child.

No, whatever happened, she could never love Michel.

She thought of the alternatives – none – and wondered
if she was being too fussy. A lot of women grabbed the
first man who came their way and lived happily ever after.
Or did they? One never knew.

All she wanted was someone kind, thoughtful and reasonable to look at. She smiled to herself. Not much! Just what everyone else was after too.

She turned over and tried to sleep. She remembered rather guiltily that she hadn't given another thought to this war. It was a very worrying thing. And yet it was difficult to be worried about an event which everyone must be working so hard to prevent. If it *did* happen it would, of course, be dreadful. But she couldn't help thinking how lucky it was that Peter and she lived so far from the German border, and that her uncle was too old to fight. The war, if it came, would hardly touch them at all. It was awful to think so selfishly, but one couldn't help it.

No: whatever happened, her little family would be safe.

It was a comforting thought and almost immediately she fell into a dreamless sleep.

Chapter 6

DAVID LOOKED AT the note on his desk. It read: Please report to the Director at your earliest convenience.

The message was innocent enough, but it gave David a twinge of uneasiness. In the past few days the laboratories had been rife with rumour. It was said that several projects were to be cancelled and that many more of the clerical and administrative staff would be liable for conscription. Already some seventy of the non-scientific personnel had been called up.

David took off his white coat and pulled on his jacket. Absent-mindedly he pushed his hair out of his eyes and looked at the note again. Best to get it over with, whatever it was. Automatically he checked his desk to make sure there were no confidential files lying around. He always did that; you could never be too careful.

The Director's office was on the third floor and David decided to walk up the stairs rather than use the lift: it would be good for him. He really wasn't as fit as he should be. He only wished he could find more time for exercise.

He arrived in the outer office breathing heavily and, when the secretary asked him to wait, he was glad of the chance to sit down for a moment. They'd never asked him to wait before. The Director usually made a point of not keeping the senior scientists waiting, and on minor matters he liked to come down to the laboratories rather than call them away from their work. Still, one shouldn't attach any undue importance to that. It probably meant nothing.

There had been other incidents, of course, and David was well aware that they *did* mean something. When a new steering committee had been set up within the Gema Company he and another scientist had been excluded from it. Both of them were Jewish. Shortly afterwards, for no apparent reason, he had been told that he would not be attending a demonstration of the new Wassermann early-warning radar system.

And then there were the small things: the way people avoided him, the way he seemed to be left off circulation lists of important documents. David knew that it all meant something and it left him apprehensive. But at the same time David trusted the Director. They had worked well together for a long time. The man had gone behind Schmidt's back and provided David with facilities and a decent budget for the Valve Development Project. The man knew the importance of science. And, David thought without vanity, he knows the value of a top-rate scientist.

Ten minutes later the secretary showed him into the Director's office. The Director was sitting behind his desk, busily reading some papers.

'Do be seated, please.'

David noticed that he didn't look up.

Eventually the Director shuffled the papers into an untidy pile and glanced quickly at David. 'Herr Freymann—' He looked out of the window, then down at the desk. 'I regret to tell you that due to a major policy decision all long-term research is to be cancelled. This has come from the highest level, you understand. It is out of my hands. In fact –' he met David's eyes '– the order came from the Fuehrer himself.'

'So the Valve Project is to go?'

'Yes.'

David wasn't entirely surprised. The project was, after all, a shot in the dark as far as Gema were concerned. Back in 1936 Schmidt had produced a document which 'proved' that short-wave radar was not only impossible to develop but not worth developing anyway. By supporting David for the last two years – albeit secretly – the Director had gone out on a limb. He couldn't be blamed for backing out now.

The Director cleared his throat. 'It's not as if you had achieved concrete results. I mean, the valve does not produce the required power, does it?'

David looked him straight in the eye and said, 'No, I'm afraid it appears not to.'

The other man nodded, relieved. 'Well, there we are then.' He picked up a paperweight and moved it nervously from hand to hand. 'There is also another problem and that is – this special scientific status. It appears that this special status is to go and . . . there is to be no widespread immunity from the draft.' He pursed his lips. 'Only those involved in work vital to our present needs are to be kept on.'

'You mean—' David frowned. He didn't understand.

The Director spoke rapidly. 'I mean that only those essential to the development of existing systems like the Freya and the Wassermann are to stay. All others are to go. Your work on the development of new systems is too futuristic and . . . and your contract is not to be renewed.'

'But it has two years to run. I can continue to work on *something*.'

The Director looked uncomfortable. 'No, it has been decided to let you go. Immediately.'

David stared at him and felt a tremor of fear. 'I am to go?'

'Yes, I am sorry, but these are my instructions. It is out of my hands. I have been *told*, you understand.'

David's throat was dry and he swallowed repeatedly. He was trying to understand, he wanted to understand . . . But all he could see was a great hole opening up in front of him. Without his scientific status, without protection, he would be completely vulnerable ... open to dispossession and God only knew what else. He felt as if his feet were being knocked from under him.

The Director was examining the paperweight and looking unhappy. David said, 'Herr Director, we have known each other for a long time. You realise what this means for me? You know that without special status I am – I have no *protection*.'

'I am sorry. There is nothing I can do. I myself am most upset about this treatment we are getting. Science is obviously not very highly rated by those in authority. It is most unfair! Most unfair! Really – there is nothing I can do. I am sorry.'

The man was avoiding his eyes and David stared disbelievingly. The decision itself was bad enough, but this – this cold impersonal expression of regret, it was terrible. This man had been his colleague, his workmate ...

'Herr Director, I realise that perhaps you cannot help me directly – work here – but you can help me in other ways—'

David thought rapidly. Without protection he and Ellen and Cecile would have to leave. There was no other choice, not if one wanted to work and live freely. What would he need? His passport was in order, thank God, complete with its red 'J'; Cecile was on Ellen's passport, so that was all right; but they would need emigration papers. Or what did they call them now? Deportation papers, that was it, deportation papers ... David asked, 'Could you help me to get deportation papers? If I can't continue with my work it would be best to leave. I hear that one needs help to get these papers. Would you? Help, I mean?'

'I'm sorry, I really don't think I can help. If I could, believe me, I would. Now, if you'll excuse me ...'

David sat frozen in the chair. He could hardly believe his ears. Perhaps the Director had not understood. It would only take a word from him, a telephone call, that was all.

'Please, all I ask is your backing. Just to leave. That's all I want to do. Really, it won't be much trouble.'

'Herr Freymann, I cannot help. It would not be *right* of me to interfere. It would not be appropriate, you understand. I try to keep out of politics – and such matters.' He stood up. 'I am sorry.'

David got unsteadily to his feet and opened the door.

'Oh, and—' There was a note of embarrassment in the Director's voice. 'I will need all your confidential papers. I will send my secretary to collect them shortly.'

David nodded and made his way back to his office. He walked again, but this time because he needed to be alone. He was stunned; he felt like a child who was being punished for something he hadn't done. Not only had he done nothing to be ashamed of, he had worked hard and with brilliant results. He couldn't believe that such achievements could be overlooked and ignored. It was incredible. He thought: How can they do this? How can they do this?

But even as he thought it, he knew they could – they *had*!

He felt tremendous anger, but not at them: at himself for being so ostrich-like. He had hidden behind his scientific status; he had believed he was important enough to escape this persecution. He shook his head. What a fool he had been, what a fool. He had made the mistake of thinking he was *different*. The sin of pride!

He closed the door of his office and sat heavily on his chair. Almost immediately there was a knock on the door and Hans came in.

'David, David. What can I say?'

'Nothing.'

'What will you do?'

'Oh, try to get out, I suppose. Except that it's probably too late for that.' He laughed bitterly.

'And your special research?'

David shook his head. 'Ended. I go, it goes. All for nothing.'

'But it was going well?'

There was a pause. David looked into Hans' eyes. 'Don't ask me, just don't ask me. It's better that way.'

There was a sound from the door and David jumped slightly. It was the Director's secretary. She was already in the room.

He thought: Now they're not even knocking before they come in. Without a word, he got up and unlocked his filing cabinet. He took out the batch of files marked with a red star and handed them to her. She nodded and left the room.

Hans asked, 'Your results?'

'Yes, everything.'

Hans sat down and put his head in his hands. 'Is there no end to their stupidity? Have you heard? Singers and entertainers are to escape conscription – apparently they are indispensable – but not scientists. Hitler has no idea, no idea!'

'No.'

Hans looked up. 'What will you do?'

'There's nothing I *can* do. I imagine they will confiscate my identity card and issue me with a new one – with the name Israel, just like everyone else. I mean,' he smiled ruefully, 'just like other *Jews*.'

And there'd be more, David knew: there'd be the star on his clothes, the declaration of his wealth and, shortly afterwards, the confiscation of all his belongings.

'Haven't you protected yourself?'

'Oh the house is in Ellen's name, and some of our savings. But I couldn't transfer everything. They stopped all that.'

'But Ellen. Your marriage is privileged, isn't it? I mean she's not Jewish, is she?'

'The special status of mixed marriages ended some time ago.'

'Oh, I didn't realise.'

'Nothing can save me, Hans. I have been a fool, a fool.' He felt himself near to tears, and turned his head away.

Hans said anxiously, 'I wish I could help.'

David shook his head. 'No, my friend, I don't think you can. My only hope is to buy some deportation papers. I hear they're very expensive, but . . . I might have enough money.'

'If there's anything I can do . . .'

For a moment David felt a glimmer of hope. 'Not unless you know an official? Someone with influence?'

Hans frowned. 'No, I'm sorry.'

Everyone seemed to be saying they were sorry today. Sorry but unable to help. At least Hans meant what he said; he was a good sort. But David made him leave: he couldn't bear to be pitied any more. Besides, he wanted to be alone. Hans said he would look in again before the end of the day. But he didn't: they both knew there wasn't any point.

David sat in the chair for a long time, staring out of the window. No-one came to see him and eventually he heard people leaving for home. Finally everything was quiet. At seven he heard the night watchman closing doors and checking windows. He put on his reading light and spread some papers on his desk. When the watchman put his head round the door David was engrossed in his work.

The watchman wanted to know how long David expected to stay in the building. David replied that he would be gone by ten, and the watchman nodded and left.

As soon as he had gone, David got up and went to the door. He listened and, satisfied that the building was empty, walked quietly down the corridor to the first laboratory. He went straight to a small cabinet and tried the door. It was locked. He crossed to a desk and feeling behind a drawer found the spare set of keys the technicians kept there.

The key which fitted the cabinet was smaller than the rest and David found it immediately. He opened the door of the cabinet and took out the camera and rolls of film which he knew he would find there.

David went back to his office and opened the filing cabinet. His mouth was dry with excitement. The file he wanted was marked 'Corporate Structure'. The papers it normally contained were unclassified and uninteresting; it was a file people hardly ever bothered to look at, which was why David had chosen it.

He took out the file and laid the papers on the desk. He loaded the camera, checked the exposure and, putting the first page under the light, pressed the shutter.

At first he couldn't keep the camera still and realised it was because his hands were shaking. He sat down for a moment and tried to calm down. It was vital to get good pictures; it was the only hope.

He stood up again and this time he could see the page clearly through the viewfinder. The job took over an hour, because he took two pictures of each of the ten pages and checked the exposure every time.

He wound the film on to the take-up spool and took it out of the camera. He replaced the camera in the laboratory cabinet and then returned to his office. He picked up all the papers that he had photographed and, putting them in the waste paper basket, set fire to them.

It gave him a curious feeling, to watch the beautiful drawings and the results of the last two years' work crinkle up and blacken in front of his eyes. So much work! So much love! He felt a stab of uncertainty. It was such a final act, this burning. It meant there was no going back. But then there had been no going back the moment he had lied to the Director about the Valve Project. The Director had asked him if the valve was producing the necessary power and David had said it wasn't. There had been no point in telling the truth. The decision to cancel long-term research had been taken at the highest level. The truth wouldn't have saved his project – or himself.

Why had he concealed the truth all this time? He still wasn't sure. It was partly caution – he wanted to announce his results only when they were fully proven so that Schmidt couldn't tear them to ribbons. And it was partly – what? Foreboding, an uneasy feeling that he might after all be vulnerable to the Nazi campaign? Yes, that too. But also – and he was ashamed to admit it – also pride. He wanted to keep the glory for himself, to show them that they were wrong and that he had been right all along, and show them in a dramatic way, by demonstrating a short-wave radar itself. That was still a good way off yet, and he would have needed more resources and at least ten assist-ants. It would have been difficult to keep it quiet much longer . . .

Over the last few months he'd been falsifying the test results, only a little – but just enough to make the Director think the valve was not going to be a success. Only his assistant had seen the results, but he was young and easily persuaded that there were still immense problems to be solved.

But there were no immense problems. Once he had discovered the best way of combining the two types of valve, he was there. Within a few months he'd produced a valve which generated 500 watts on the very high fre-quency of 3,000 megacycles. Despite its immense power the valve could be made very small, just as he had predicted. The radar that could be developed from the valve would be very small too. And he had predicted that too.

He felt a glow of pride. He had been *right* and Schmidt *wrong*.

It was a pity Schmidt would never know.

He tucked the spool into an inside pocket of his jacket and, wiping the sweat from his forehead, took a last look round the office.

This had been his second home, the place where he had come to do the work he loved, the place he associated with contentment and security and achievement. And he would never see it again.

Oh dear Lord. He wiped the tears from his cheeks and, closing the door behind him, walked down the passage.

As he approached the main entrance he felt a stab of pain in his stomach. Heartburn, probably. He always got it when he was late for a meal. Then, as he emerged into the darkness, it occurred to him that it was not heartburn at all, but fear.

He looked over his shoulder and, pulling his hat down over his face, walked rapidly into the night.

The room was hot and stuffy and David found it difficult to stay awake. At about four he nodded off. A loud voice announced 'Next!' and David woke with a start. He looked rapidly around him. There were three people ahead of him and about fifty behind – there would be many more, perhaps a hundred, in the street. With a bit of luck he might get in today. Otherwise he would have to wait outside in the street all night until they reopened the office in the morning. He'd already been waiting three days.

He looked at the man ahead of him. He was well dressed and prosperous-looking; he'd probably been a jeweller or a clothing manufacturer before the crack-down. They would have confiscated his business by now. Looking at him, David guessed he'd been clever and hidden plenty of money and valuables. Otherwise he wouldn't have bothered to come here. Yes, he looked the clever sort. Not like me, David thought, with no money and no influence.

It was stupid to come here really. But he was doing it

out of duty to Ellen and Cecile. He had to *try* to get the papers, he owed them that much at least.

It was five when he finally got into the *Gauleiter*'s office; David was the last before they closed for the day. A young man looked at his papers and asked, 'What are your means?'

David thought rapidly. Did they want to know what he was supposed to have or what he *actually* had? After confiscation you weren't meant to have much left.

He answered, 'Enough'.

'Are you sure?'

'Yes.'

The young man gave him a hard stare and waved him through to the next room. It was a long palatial office at the end of which was a large desk. Behind it sat a gross figure smoking a Bavarian pipe, and beside him a male assistant with a red ledger in front of him.

David stood in front of the desk. The large man was reading a newspaper. He took no notice of David.

Without looking up the assistant said, 'Deportation papers will cost you 250,000 marks. How do you intend to pay?'

David gulped. When he'd last heard they had been priced at 150,000 marks which he might have been able to borrow from Ellen's father. But this!

'Well?' The assistant was impatient. It had been a long day and he wanted to get home.

David thought: I must say something – anything – just in case. He said, 'I'll pay in cash – but it'll take a week.'

The assistant looked at the fat man. 'Herr Deputy Gauleiter, he wants a week to pay.'

'What?' The fat man looked irritated at being disturbed. 'No, no, no! Get him out! No money, no papers.'

It was all happening so fast. David tried to think. He said, 'Tomorrow then! Tomorrow!'

The assistant stared at him, then nodded briefly. He

scribbled on a card and handed it across the desk. 'This will get you straight in here tomorrow. But if you do not have the money you will be arrested for wasting the Deputy Gauleiter's time.'

David went out into the street and leant against the wall. He was tired, so tired. He looked at the long line of waiting people, each wearing a star, each with a look of resignation on his face. Probably one in fifty could raise 250,000 marks. For some people it amounted to a lifetime's pay. For David it was about ten year's salary.

There was only one source he could get the money from: Ellen's father. But it would represent a vast amount of money to him, more than his life savings. David shook his head and began to walk. How much was he worth to his father-in-law? Not that much, never that much.

Why then had he bothered to go through that play-acting back there? It was a waste of time: he'd known it was no use the moment he'd heard the amount they wanted.

There was no point in going back, tomorrow or ever.

Suddenly David made up his mind and walked briskly away. He'd given them their chance; he'd tried to do things their way. Now they left him no choice.

He took a tram to the Tiergarten. On the south side of the park were some of the principal embassies in Berlin. He hadn't thought which embassy he would try first: perhaps the British, then the French. If he had no luck there he would try the Americans or one of the Scandinavian countries.

He got off at the end of Tiergartenstrasse and walked. In the park he could see a group of *Jungvolk* training for their initiation into the Hitler Youth. Some were running the compulsory sixty metres, others jumping the 2.75 metre long jump. Another group were sitting in a circle chanting the *Schwertworte*, the short version of the Nazi dogma which had to be learnt by heart. The children looked so sweet, sitting there in the sun in their neat uniforms, that David stopped to watch them for a moment.

As he neared the embassies he pulled his raincoat on. It wasn't raining but he wanted to hide the star stitched onto his jacket. They might stop him otherwise; they might prevent him from going in.

The first embassy was just visible through a thick screen of trees, an imposing white mansion set back from the road behind metal railings. David was fairly sure it was the United States Embassy. Perhaps he should try there first: in the last ten years the country had taken a lot of Jews in. Yet at the same time it was neutral – perhaps they wouldn't be interested in trading his information.

David strode on, still undecided. Suddenly he stopped and frowned. There was a group of people on the pavement, standing quietly, waiting. Between them and the gates of the mansion were stormtroopers. The troopers were facing the people, weapons held ready across their chests.

David walked slowly up. It was definitely the United States Embassy. The waiting people were Jewish. No-one was being allowed in. He asked one of the waiting men: no-one had been allowed in for weeks.

It was the same outside the French Embassy, and the British. Except that there were fewer people waiting.

He thought: I'm so stupid; of course they're not going to let people in. Of course!

The telephone, he should have used the telephone. He walked rapidly throught the streets until he found a post office. He went up to the counter and asked for a booth. The girl behind the counter was young and quite pretty. She glanced up and then stared at him hard. David thought: There's going to be trouble; she's going to make trouble. The girl blinked then asked, loudly and deliberately, for his identity papers. The other counter staff fell silent; people looked. David felt in his jacket pocket and passed over his papers. Quickly, he pulled open his raincoat: it was a serious offence to hide the star on his jacket. The girl looked at him triumphantly and said, 'Non-Aryans are not permitted to use the telephones here.'

It was a new restriction David had never heard of. In fact he was certain that no such restriction existed. But there could be no argument: that was one thing he'd learnt during the last week.

They watched him as he turned and walked into the street. He heard the girl laughing as he closed the door, and the heat of humiliation burnt his cheeks. He shrank into the porch and leant against the cold stone. The tiredness hit him like a hammer. He hadn't slept properly for three days and now he felt sick with fatigue.

He looked at the time: it was nearly six. The embassy staff would have shut their offices by now anyway. It was too late to do anything more today. Another day gone and nothing achieved.

He thought: I'm tired, just tired.

He went to the station and took the train home. As he walked towards his house he passed the little shoe shop and looked in the window. The posters marked 'Jew!' had long since disappeared. Now there was one small notice discreetly placed among the shoes on display. It read: Under new management. David wondered what had happened to Finstein. No-one bothered to ask about their neighbours any more; it was better not to know.

When he came round the bend in the road the sight of the small cosy house no longer thrilled David. Instead it reminded him of his family and his responsibilities. He wanted to protect his family, to provide and care for them. If a man couldn't do that then he wasn't worth much.

As he opened the door he wondered if Ellen would be crying again. She had been crying almost continuously since he had lost his job. He couldn't blame her, of course; she had every reason to cry.

He called a hello and waited for Cecile to come bounding into the hall and give him a hug as she always did.

There was silence and he called again.

The kitchen door opened and Cecile came out. She was sobbing into a handkerchief. She didn't run up to him but hovered miserably by the door, shaking her head from side to side. 'Oh Daddy, Daddy!'

David stepped forward, his arms outstretched. 'My little rabbit, whatever is the matter?' Cecile had never cried before, not like this. She was usually so brave, so fearless.

Ellen appeared in the doorway behind her. 'It was no good, I suppose? You haven't got the papers?'

He shook his head. 'They wanted . . . too much.'

Ellen said firmly, 'Go upstairs, Cecile. I want to talk to your father.'

Cecile gave a sob and ran past him up the stairs. David looked at Ellen in bewilderment. She beckoned him into the living room.

'David, I have something to tell you.' She paused and started fiddling with a china dog on the mantelpiece. Eventually she said, 'Cecile and I are going away. I've been talking to my father and we've agreed that it's the only way.'

David looked at her blankly. 'What do you mean?'

Ellen took a breath and turned to face him. 'We want the best for Cecile, don't we? Well, there's only one way to be sure she doesn't suffer. And that's to get right away. I'm sorry, David, but I think it will be better if we . . .' She licked her lips nervously, '. . . if we live apart.'

'Live apart?'

'Yes, Cecile and I are going away, to a new place.'

'A new place? But . . . it'll be so difficult for Cecile . . . settling into a new school. And . . . at least everyone knows us here, accepts us . . .'

'Accepts us? Are you mad? Don't you realise what it's been like for me? And for *Cecile*? You have no idea what she's been through at school. They all *know* about you, they all know that Cecile is partly Jewish. They all taunt her, do you hear me, they *taunt her*!' Ellen was spitting at him, her eyes blazing.

David sank into a chair and murmured, 'Oh God, oh God.'

'I told you it was happening, but as usual you had your head in the clouds, where it always is. I told you last November when ... when ... those awful things happened, but you wouldn't listen!'

She was referring to Crystal Night, a major pogrom against the Jews; many synagogues, shops and flats had been destroyed.

David shook his head. 'But wherever you move to they'll still *know*. You'll still be my wife and you can't hide that.'

Ellen drew a deep breath. 'I am going to divorce you, David. I'm going to take a new name and make a fresh start. For Cecile, it's for Cecile. You must see ... how important it is, for her sake.'

David was dumbfounded.

She couldn't be doing this to him. The idea of losing his little rabbit was almost more than he could bear. They sat in silence for a while. Then a terrible thought came into his mind. He trembled as he asked, 'When? When are you going?'

'Tonight. My father's coming to collect us in the car.'

David felt as if a vice were tightening around his heart. He gasped, 'Oh no, oh no. Not yet, please not yet.' Then he remembered the telephone call and how he would sell his invention. He looked up and said brightly, 'You *mustn't* go, not yet. I forgot to tell you. I've got to make a telephone call in the morning. There's a really good chance we'll get papers. Really! The best chance yet! I'll go to the post office first thing in the morning.'

Ellen moved impatiently towards the door. 'David, these

schemes of yours . . .' She shook her head. 'Anyway, I don't want to live abroad. I want to stay here with my family.'

David cried bitterly, 'I'm your family too, remember!'

But she had gone.

Oh God! He tried to think, he tried to make himself think, but it was no good, he was just too tired. Hopelessness and despair overwhelmed him.

Dear Lord, what have I done? What have I done?

After a while he climbed the stairs to Cecile's room. He found her lying on the bed, crying silently. He went to her and touched her arm. She reached out to him and together they sat on the edge of the bed, their arms around each other, rocking gently.

David thought: Everything I want is here, my family, my daughter. Is it so very much to ask? What did I do that they should take it away from me?

Finally, after a long time, he said, 'My little rabbit, it's for the best, you know, your mother is right. You will be safer with a new name and a new place to live.' She started crying again and he said, 'I want you to be very brave. I want you to go away and to make a success of your life. And to forget about me.'

'I couldn't, Daddy, I couldn't.'

'But you must. I'm going to go abroad. I can't be a proper father to you when I'm away.'

'But you'll always be my Daddy.'

'Yes, yes, I'll always be your Daddy.' David hugged her tightly and wept quietly.

Then there were sounds from below and, without a word, Ellen came and took Cecile downstairs. David couldn't bring himself to watch them go. Instead he sat on Cecile's bed and put his head in his hands.

The silence pressed in on him and, when he couldn't bear it any longer, he lay down and put his arms over his head. Finally he fell asleep and dreamed that Cecile was dead.

When David woke it was dawn and he was very cold. For a while he lay on the bed watching the thin, grey light illuminate the toys and gay pictures that decorated the neat, feminine room. The room looked cold and unused, as if Cecile had been gone a long time.

He sat up. His head ached viciously. Lack of sleep and food.

Mechanically, he got up and went into the bathroom to wash. In the main bedroom he found a clean shirt and his best suit, and put them on.

He went downstairs. The house was deathly quiet. Normally Cecile would be chattering away in the kitchen while Ellen made the breakfast. He decided to turn the wireless on as soon as he got into the kitchen.

But first he went into the dining room and, reaching up to the top of the dresser, felt for the black canister. As his fingers closed over it he felt a thrill of excitement. So much in such a small container!

But small though it was, it was still too large. It would be impossible to hide on his body. Any good search would soon discover it under his arm, or strapped to his leg. He opened the canister and took out the roll of film. It was only half an inch high and an eighth of an inch in diameter.

He went into the kitchen and found a piece of grease-proof paper. He cut an oblong strip and rolled it round the film, then tied the ends with cotton.

David was pleased. It was small enough now to be hidden in his mouth. Or even in other places where people wouldn't look. Well, hopefully not.

Getting the film developed had been the most difficult part. The local photographic shop had been out of the question; they would have reported him straight away. There was a man at Gema whose hobby was developing and printing his own photographs, but it would have been far too dangerous to contact him. Then David remembered the processing laboratory which the Gema Company used for all its photographic work, and he went there. He went there straight away, before the laboratory knew he had been dismissed. He went there while he was still angry and had the nerve to ask them to process the film and transfer it onto the smallest possible negative. He said it was top secret, and they mustn't talk about it. His own daring had amazed him.

It was the strangeness of the request which made the laboratory carry out the work without question. The technicians were called in from the processing lab and everyone was so engrossed in deciding how the reduction could be done they didn't stop to query it. They didn't even notice the sweat on David's brow or the way his hands shook as he passed over the film.

Now David held the tiny packet in his hand and wondered where he should hide it for the moment. Best to be on the safe side. He took some surgical tape from the first aid box in the bathroom and stuck the roll on to the under side of his upper arm. It was not very satisfactory – if they were actually looking for a roll of film they would find it straight away – but it would have to do.

He found some bratwurst and black bread in the kitchen. There was a spoonful of coffee in a jar; he put it in a strainer and poured hot water over it. It tasted foul. He sat at the kitchen table and looked out at the small, neat garden. In the summer they always spent Sunday afternoons there, just the three of them. David turned on the wireless. The set was a new *Volksempfanger* People's Receiver; he had bought it as a present for Ellen's birthday.

David listened half-heartedly, thinking of Cecile. The announcements were always the same nowadays. People

were exhorted to greater service and sacrifice for the
Fatherland; they must unite against the enemies of
Germany; the young men must be ready to serve in the
cause of the Fatherland. Today the enemy seemed to be
Poland who were even at this moment threatening the very
security of the beloved Homeland. Poland? It had been
Czechoslovakia for so long that David couldn't get used to
all this talk about Poland. But perhaps Poland had been
the enemy for some time; he hadn't been listening to the
wireless very much recently.

The announcer turned to home news: today another
great step had been taken in the eradication of the common
enemy! The filthy Jews would no longer be permitted
wireless sets. No longer would they be permitted to enjoy
the fruits of their thieving and usury! Millions of honest,
working Germans would now be free to listen in peace, in
the knowledge that not a single conniving Jew was listening
to their beloved programmes!

David froze with a piece of bread halfway to his mouth,
and felt vaguely sick. He should have realised that this
campaign was much, much worse than the ones before.
And now it was almost too late. But not quite.

He washed up the breakfast things and went into the
hall. It was eight-thirty. He looked at the telephone which
stood on a small table beside the stairs. The embassy offices
would be staffed by now; he should call as soon as possible.
And yet – not from here. The operator might have instructions to report all calls made to embassies; she might listen
in; *they* might listen in. No, he would go to the post office;
that would be safer.

At the post office there was a queue for the telephones.
David waited quietly. He did not mind waiting. The
important thing was not to attract attention or get in
anyone's way. At one point a large woman came bustling
in and, seeing the line of people, sighed loudly. Without a
word David stood back and let her take his place. She

started to say something but, seeing the star on his jacket, tightened her lips and turned away.

Eventually there was only one person ahead of him and no-one behind. David eyed the girl at the desk nervously. She looked all right but you could never tell. When his turn came she glanced up quickly and, without comment, directed him to a booth.

So far, so good.

He gave the operator the number of the British Embassy and waited, swallowing nervously. He hadn't really thought of what he would say. It was so difficult to know when you didn't even know who you'd be speaking to.

There were several loud clicks on the line and a woman's voice said in German, 'British Embassy.'

'Hello. I wish to speak to . . .' He thought: *Who?* '. . . to the attaché who deals with scientific matters.'

There was another click. A man's voice said, 'Yes?'

'I am a scientist,' David began lamely. 'I wish to emigrate. I—'

The voice interrupted, 'The immigration section of this embassy has closed. We are not dealing with any new applications.'

'But you don't understand, I . . . I have special information.' David hated to say such a thing over the telephone but he had the feeling the man would soon ring off.

'Who are you?'

David paused unhappily. 'I'd rather not say . . . it's too risky. Can't I meet someone? Or come to the embassy?'

'One moment please.'

David waited uneasily. He hadn't thought about the problems of making contact. It was horribly dangerous . . .

The voice said, 'It is regretted, but we cannot be of assistance.'

David felt his heart lurch. 'What do you mean? I have vital information, of great value!'

'We regret but, in view of the gravity of the international situation, it is impossible for us to become involved.'

David stared at the wall of the booth, the receiver forgotten in his hand.

The voice spoke again. 'Hello?'

'Yes.'

There was a pause as if the owner of the voice was considering what to say. 'We are not alone. Do you understand what I mean?'

'Yes.' David understood. The conversation was being listened to.

He replaced the receiver, and tried to think. He was confused; the certain knowledge that they were listening had been a shock. He hadn't been ready for that. He must think again.

Perhaps the Swedes? Yes, the good neutral Swedes. He found the number in the directory and gave it to the operator.

After a few seconds there was a reply. David was about to speak when there were two loud clicks. David froze, then slowly replaced the receiver.

He paid for the calls and left the post office.

He had to think: *he had to think*.

He walked into the street, his head down, his mind working. One thing was clear, absolutely clear: to try to contact an embassy would be suicide. He would never get near them. If he arranged a meeting the Gestapo would be there first. If he tried to deliver a message they would intercept it.

It was awful to give up the idea – but there was no choice. What else could he do?

What did that leave? He thought desperately, but there wasn't much. Only escape. Escape without papers, without help . . . He shook his head and strode on, head down, carefully avoiding other pedestrians.

The black jackboots were right in front of him before
he saw them. He tried to step sideways but a second pair
of boots blocked his way. David looked up and felt a stab
of fear. Two young SS men were facing him; they were
both smiling. David stepped quickly against the wall and
tried to slide along it. The young men laughed and shouted.
He felt a sharp blow on his head. He knew he had to run.
They were coming for him again. He gathered his strength
and made for a new gap between a uniformed body and
the wall. He pushed through the gap, felt a blow on his
shoulder, pushed again, and was through.

He ran. He ran as he used to do at school; fast, his chest
out, his arms pumping. His lungs were bursting, they
wouldn't draw enough air. His legs felt heavy as lead. He
rounded a corner and staggered against a wall, his chest
heaving, his head pounding.

He looked behind. There was no-one.

Thank God. Thank God.

How stupid! How stupid! Must be more careful, must
be more careful.

He walked slowly on towards home, his heart still
hammering, his breath still rasping in his throat. So unfit!
So pathetically unfit!

Finally he neared the house and paused. The windows
were dark, the front door closed as he had left it.

The house was quiet. The front door yielded easily to
the key. He went in quickly and closed the door. The living
room looked untouched, as neat and ordered as usual. He
peered out of the window into the street. Nothing.

But there wasn't much time, he knew that now.

He sat for a moment so that his hands would stop
shaking and thought: I'm too old for all this, too old and
too tired.

Then he got up and looked through the bookcase until
he found Cecile's World Atlas. He knelt on the carpet and
studied the map of Europe. He would go west, that was

certain; the east was trouble. That meant Switzerland or France or Belgium or Holland. Switzerland was out; they were too uncharitable and, even if you got over the border, it was rumoured that they sent you back again. Belgium or Holland; he wasn't sure about them. But France . . . France had taken lots of Jews, he knew that. And even if he couldn't stay there they would send him on somewhere else, he was sure of that.

France . . . he turned to a map which showed the Franco-German border more clearly. He stared at the long winding line and wondered where it would be best to cross. It would all be heavily militarised, of course, but it shouldn't be too difficult to get through, not if he was patient.

A long section of the border ran along the Rhine, so that was no good; the bridges would be heavily guarded and he couldn't swim. Where the border turned west then, towards Luxembourg. He put his finger on the Saar region. What was wrong with the map there? Of course! He sighed; the atlas was pre-1935 and didn't show the new border. In 1935 the Saar region had become German again. He didn't dare cross there; it would be hopeless if he didn't even know where the border was. That left the stretch to the east of Saarbrucken.

He looked at the railway lines. How far could he get without risking being picked up? Mannheim perhaps. Then what? It was sixty kilometres from Mannheim to the border. He made up his mind: although he was unfit, he would walk. He would *make* himself walk. He'd been quite a walker in his day. When he was a student he used to go hiking in the Bavarian Alps; he had covered twenty kilometres a day sometimes.

He would need food, money and equipment. He tore the page out of the atlas and put the book away. He stood up and tried to remember what there was in the house. Money: he had enough to buy his train ticket and a few meals, no more; but it should be sufficient. Anyway he would be taking as much food as possible. He went into the kitchen and looked in the cupboards. There were cans of sauerkraut, beef, and fruit. He decided to take them all. But he would need something to carry them in. Not a briefcase; people associated them with wealth and money, and he might be robbed. A shopping bag? Even that wasn't very safe nowadays. He looked round the kitchen. There was nothing else: the shopping bag would have to do. It was made of woven straw and should be fairly strong. He would make straps for it, to carry it on his back. He thought of the lovely rucksack he had in his bedroom, but that was out of the question; it was far too obvious.

He took a sharp knife from the kitchen drawer and wedged it into the bottom of the bag. What else? A small torch, some string, a can opener . . . But he mustn't take too much. He had a long way to walk.

Shoes, he would need good shoes, and some warm clothing. But again he mustn't take too much. A raincoat, a warm sweater . . .

Finally it was done. He tried to think of what he might have forgotten, but everything else of use was too heavy and bulky to be carried.

When should he go? It was a long journey to Mannheim – at least a day, even by express. It would be best to start first thing in the morning so that he could complete the rail journey in a single day and avoid arriving at Mannheim in the middle of the night, when they would pick him up more easily. He should leave first thing the next morning then. In the meantime he would rest and go over all the details.

He went to his room and lay on the bed. Occasionally he took out the map and had another look at it. Towards evening he made himself a hot meal of eggs and sausage and then went upstairs for a bath. He removed the package from under his arm and put it in the pocket of his jacket.

He would fix it back on in the morning. After his bath he went straight to bed, his clothes for the morning ready folded beside him.

He didn't sleep immediately, but stared out of the window and watched the clouds darkening in the gathering dusk. He was really quite pleased with his preparations. Ellen had always accused him of never getting on with things. Well, she couldn't say that now. He had planned it all and he was going to go through with it. And when he got to France he would sell them his secret and buy himself a new life. One day he would send for them, Ellen and Cecile, and they would be proud of him. Yes, proud.

He fell asleep surprisingly easily and awoke only when a dog barked in the next door garden. He flicked on the light and looked at the time. It was five to twelve.

He went straight back to sleep and dreamed that Cecile was in the kitchen, laughing in the sunlight.

When the crash came he thought it was part of the dream, a plate dropped on the floor.

Then he was wide awake.

There was a moment of ear-splitting silence.

Then there was another crash and he heard a loud drumming noise. The noise got louder. It was the sound of people running up the stairs.

David sat up and started to get out of bed.

The door burst open and David knew it was too late. It was too late for everything. In that instant he knew that he would never see his little rabbit again.

There were two of them in the room. They grabbed him and dragged him on to the landing. He heard a dull thud and realised his head had crashed against the door frame. At the top of the stairs he was pushed. He fell forward, putting his arms out to break his fall. He came to a stop halfway down. He got slowly to his knees, holding onto the banisters while he caught his breath.

When the kick came it took him entirely by surprise. He

couldn't understand why the hall was rushing up towards him. He put his arms out in front of him, but he knew he was going too fast, too fast. There was a sickening crunch, he felt his head snap round and he thought: They've killed me!

Then he was being pulled to his feet and a terrible pain shot through his shoulder. He cried out. But they were dragging him again, pulling on his shoulder, and he nearly fainted with the pain. He could hear them talking, but it seemed a long, long way away.

They threw him down and, after a while, he opened his eyes. He was in the living room. All the lights in the house were blazing; they hurt his eyes. He could hear movements above and dull thuds and crashes; they were going from room to room. He thought: they're searching. He groaned: *Oh God*, they're searching for the *film*. It was sitting in his jacket pocket. They would find it straight away. *God, how could I have been so stupid?*

He sat up gently and leant against an armchair. The shoulder was agony, probably broken somewhere.

Boots drummed down the stairs and David felt his stomach turn. The footsteps went into the kitchen and there was a deafening sound of breaking china and glass. He waited, his heart hammering against his chest.

Finally they came in. David was surprised to see that they were quite young, only about twenty. There were three of them, not two. They had some of Ellen's jewellery and the nice piece of Meissen china she kept on the dressing table. David felt relief: perhaps that was all they'd been after.

'Up Jew! Now!'

David struggled to his feet. Although he had pyjamas on he felt naked and bare. Why hadn't he slept in his clothes? That would have been the sensible thing to do. *Oh God.*

Two of them came up to him and David felt his bowels turn to water. One said, 'Where's the gold, Jew?'

'I have no gold.' David saw this would not please them and added quickly, 'Only money. Upstairs in my wallet.'

'Where's the gold, Jew?'

'I have none.'

They punched him in the stomach first, then around the head. Then, when he was down, they kicked him.

Then they pulled him to his feet and told him they were going to break his fingers.

Through his swollen face David said, 'There's no gold, I promise.'

One of them grabbed his hand and David closed his eyes. He felt himself dirtying his trousers. Then he fainted.

They slapped his face until he came round.

One of them said, 'Put him in the truck.'

David knew he had to do or say something now, or it would be too late. 'Please, can I put my clothes on?'

There was no reply.

'Please, I've dirtied myself.'

The leader pulled a face of disgust and indicated he could go upstairs.

David clambered up the stairs to his room and went to his jacket.

The film was still there. *Thank God.*

He started to pull his pyjamas off. He fumbled with the buttons, then tore at them. He was taking too long: they would come for him. He tried to hurry but his hands wouldn't stop shaking and his shoulder was agony.

He pulled on his shirt, some underpants, and started to climb into his trousers.

He heard clattering on the stairs again and pulled desperately at the trousers. As he fumbled with the buttons a young corporal came in and started to pull at his arm.

David yelled, 'My jacket! My jacket!'

The corporal stopped while David picked it up. God, David thought, I nearly lost it again. God!

He ran quickly down the stairs. He was learning, learning: if you didn't run you got pushed.

They were taking a last look round. David waited by the door, leaning against the wall. When they weren't looking he took the packet out of his pocket and slipped it into his mouth.

When they had taken all they wanted they took him out of the house and pushed him into the back of a truck. It drove off so fast that David had only a moment to look back at the house. It seemed so strange, its lights still blazing, its front door open. David almost shouted for them to stop so that he could go back and lock up. It was wrong to leave it like that, so vulnerable, so open.

But then he realised it didn't matter. What hadn't been smashed or stolen tonight would be taken the next morning anyway.

Part Two

———◆———

1940–1941

Chapter 7

—·—

THE WAITING WAS the worst.

Vasson lay on his bed and listened to the approaching rumble of cannon and the occasional blast of a distant explosion. The cannon was German, he decided, and the explosions were French. The gallant French Army was presumably pausing long enough in its rapid retreat to destroy fuel dumps. About all they had managed to do, Vasson thought with contempt.

By afternoon he knew he was right about the fuel dumps. The sky over the city had turned black with the smoke of burning oil. It was as dark as night. Paris looked like a lost city: there were no lights, hardly any people and total blackness.

Then the rain came. It was a steady downpour and it fell in thick black droplets, streaking houses, pavements, and the odd passer-by with oily grime.

Vasson was annoyed. He had planned to go out for a pastis at about five – assuming somewhere would be open – but now he'd have to stay in or risk having his clothes ruined.

Several times during the afternoon he went downstairs to the front door and looked out. The streets were almost deserted, except for the occasional refugee making a last attempt at flight.

Vasson couldn't see any point in leaving the city. For days people had been packing up their belongings and setting out with nothing more than a few pathetic bundles tied on to bicycles or handcarts. They had no idea where they were going, nor where they would get food and shelter. It was madness. They would starve – or get shot. It was much better to stay in the city, Vasson decided. The Germans wouldn't eat everybody. Life would continue, one way or another.

The war had been going on for nine months now. In that time Vasson had been busy. As soon as war was declared he spent all his savings on stockings, petrol and car tyres. It was an enormous risk to spend every penny, yet it was hard to see how he could go wrong. He bought himself a cheap secondhand car and stored the stuff in a rented garage out in the suburbs at Clichy. As soon as things started to get short, he began to sell.

He sold slowly, carefully, realising only enough cash to buy new stock, when he could find it. He travelled to small towns, to the suburbs of northern cities and the outskirts of Paris. When the price was right he bought more stockings as well as perfume and lingerie. He also bought more food: coffee and sugar mainly. The prices were high, but not half so high as the selling prices in central Paris.

It took him five months to double his stock; now he looked forward to the real pay-off. It wouldn't come for a while of course. He knew he'd have to be patient. It would take time for the Occupation to take effect. But when rationing and severe shortages bit, he'd be ready to clean up.

The war was going to be a little gold mine, no doubt about it.

But the waiting was the worst.

It was a short night. The sounds of explosions and cannon fire continued until two in the morning. Then there was silence. For a long time Vasson did not sleep, but lay awake smoking and thinking about money. Finally, at about three, he dozed off. As the early summer dawn broke, the motorcycles came. They were far away, probably on one of the main boulevards, but the sound carried a long way on the still June air. Vasson was instantly awake. So they were here at last.

Later, at about six, he went to the front door and peered out, but the streets were deserted. The Germans wouldn't bother with Montmartre yet, he reasoned; they would tie up the city centre and the military posts first. He went back to bed and, at about seven, sank into a dreamless sleep.

He woke at midday. He got up straight away, washed thoroughly and dressed. He chose his best clothes, such as they were. It was silly to bother really, but he wanted to look good.

He left the rooming house and went towards the Etoile and the Champs Elysées, because if anything was happening it would be happening there. He walked because he wanted the exercise and because he wanted to see the Germans.

He saw his first German at Pigalle. There were six of them in an armoured car. They were looking relaxed and at ease. They know they've won, Vasson thought, they know there won't be any trouble. He watched them for five minutes. They laughed and joked and pointed at things which interested them. They watched the Parisians politely, but did not attempt to talk to them. It was just as Vasson had thought: they didn't want to stir up trouble, they just wanted life to go on as usual.

Most of the cafés were closed, some boarded up, but Vasson found one which was open and stopped for some breakfast. He had no trouble buying a coffee but there was no bread, so he ate biscuits instead. The proprietor and his wife were talking loudly as they served their customers. Death to the Germans! They would rather die, they said, than serve the filthy Boches. They would make the scum realise they weren't welcome here! Vasson thought: A month and they'll be serving the Germans happily at double their normal prices.

He walked on towards the Champs Elysées. When he
arrived he found a large crowd was already lining the long
boulevard. Everyone was waiting, but no-one knew what
for. There was no information, but then that was nothing
new: there had been no information for weeks. Vasson
leant against a tree and lit a cigarette. People should
welcome the Germans: they couldn't be any worse than
the French Government. Not only had the Government left
Paris without telling anyone, but they had left everything
totally disorganised. There had been no call for resistance,
no advice on what people should do, no organised evacuation. All they had done was put up posters telling people
to 'keep calm'. The newspapers had been censored for
weeks, so that no-one knew what was happening until they
heard the fighting and saw the troops retreating. It was
laughable!

The Germans could only be an improvement.

When they came, they came in style. In triumph. There
were tanks, armoured cars, mounted troops, and ranks of
field-grey infantry marching in precise formation. It was
an incredible sight. Most of the people stared in silence,
their faces angry or disbelieving; some shouted bitter
comments. Vasson watched, his face impassive, and wondered how long it would be before the Germans emptied
all the shops and set him up for life.

The first month was all brass bands, martial songs and
jackboots. The Germans seemed to be everywhere, their
music blaring out day and night in every part of the city.
Posters appeared saying: TRUST THE GERMAN SOLDIERS.
Strange new newspapers came on to the news-stands:
Aujourd'hui, La France du Travail, their pages full of
German propaganda. Even the long-established *Le Matin*
and *Paris-Soir* weren't slow to be forced into line and
before long they too came out with glowing pro-Nazi

headlines. The swastika appeared over hundreds of buildings.

The first week was good for the retail trade – or so people believed. The Germans made straight for the shops and swept up all the lingerie, perfumes and stockings they could find. And paid for them. Motor coaches brought hundreds of soldiers up into Montmartre to see the sights – ostensibly the Sacré-Cœur, but really the nightclubs and the girls. The Parisians were pleasantly surprised.

By the end of the month there was chaos. The Germans had paid for everything in Occupation money which was found to be worthless; the food disappeared from the markets to feed the German Army; petrol suddenly disappeared from the filling stations; and, overnight, prices shot up.

Vasson began trading. He started by selling coffee and petrol to the French. He dealt only in francs, in cash. As soon as he had money he spent it again, increasing his stock.

A few weeks later it was time to start dealing with the Germans. They had an almost insatiable desire for stockings, lingerie and perfume. Now that they'd emptied the shops they were happy to buy on the black market. But Vasson needed a contact: someone in supplies, who would buy his luxuries in exchange for food or tyres or petrol – he wasn't prepared to deal in worthless German money.

It didn't take long to find his man, a quartermaster sergeant called Seiger. Vasson would have preferred to deal with an officer, to make the operation more permanent and above board, but right from the start Seiger and he understood each other perfectly. It was too good an opportunity to miss. By September Vasson had doubled his stock, rented a decent apartment, and bought himself two new suits.

This time Vasson was determined not to fall into any traps. He would go carefully, always consolidating, always spreading the risks. The best way to spread the risks was, he realised, to branch out into other businesses. He started looking for opportunities. The girls racket was no good: everyone was on to that one and anyway half the girls had developed a bad case of patriotism and wouldn't go with Germans. The clubs were no good either; they were still wrapped up too tight.

For a while he settled for dealing in a wider range of goods – more foods, more imported goods – but he still wasn't happy: if for some reason he was closed down he would have nothing to fall back on.

Then he stumbled on the answer, accidentally.

He'd been tipped off about a large quantity of lingerie in a warehouse in the southern suburbs. He'd never been to the place before, he didn't know who ran it, but that didn't matter. He'd discovered that, when offered cash on the spot, people were quite happy to do business with him. This one would be no exception.

But he was wrong. The warehouse was run by an old Jew called Goldberg, and Goldberg did not want to do business with him. Not on any terms, not at any price. He would not say why; instead he was belligerent and rude. He called Vasson a leech and a verminous parasite. He shut the door in his face.

Vasson went to Seiger; Seiger arranged a meeting with a smart young man in the black uniform of the SS; the smart young man took him to see a man in civilian clothes, someone by the name of Kloffer. They met in an apartment in the Rue Lalo behind the elegant Avenue Foch.

Kloffer was different from the Germans Vasson had met before. He was quiet, cool and slim, like a snake. He hardly spoke while Vasson told him about the Jew with the warehouse full of lingerie. He merely nodded slightly and, when Vasson had finished, gave a small bow and left.

Kloffer left so quickly that there was no time to ask questions. Vasson was left in the air. He felt slightly cheated. Would they do anything? He wasn't sure. And, if they did, would they tell him?

After a few days Vasson could bear the uncertainty no longer. He drove to the Jew's warehouse to see if anything had happened. As he neared the place he felt a delicious sense of anticipation, as if he was about to be given a treat. He was not disappointed. The doors of the warehouse were open, the interior gaping and empty. The glass in the windows had exploded from the force of a fire which, from the scorch marks on the walls, must have raged for hours. Vasson was pleased; the Germans must have been impressed by what he told them. As for Goldberg, he'd deserved it. He hadn't listened.

Vasson expected to see Kloffer again, but he heard nothing. He was disappointed. He wanted to see Kloffer again, to talk about the raid, to go over the details and to remind Kloffer that it was he, Vasson, who had provided the information. He wanted his contribution to be recognised; yes, damn it, and properly acknowledged. But there was nothing.

During the rest of September and October the Germans dropped their softly-softly approach to the population: the honeymoon was over. There were arrests of communists, trade unionists and leftist-intellectuals; the bread ration was low, unemployment was high.

In November there was more trouble: a mass demonstration by students in the Champs Elysées on Armistice Day. The Germans arrested the ringleaders for left-wing activities.

Every week Vasson went to meet Seiger. They always met in a small bar near the Porte de Clichy. The place had two advantages for Vasson: no-one knew him there and it was near the rented garage where he kept his stock.

Early in December Vasson bought a batch of high-quality stockings off a little shopkeeper in the *vingtième*. He decided to offer them straight to Seiger. He would ask for cigarettes in return; cigarettes always sold well and at the moment they were fetching particularly high prices.

He walked into the bar feeling excited, as he always did. He enjoyed doing business. It was lovely and clean and *definite*. He liked thrashing out the terms with Seiger, playing the game they always played: hedging and evading, stating and overstating, until finally the bargain was struck. There was nothing like it.

But today there was no Seiger. He searched the small bar for the familiar uniform; but it was missing. How irritating! Vasson did not like arrangements to go wrong.

Vasson took another look round the bar. No, there was no Seiger. Instead – Vasson's heart gave a small thud – instead there was Kloffer. He was sitting alone at a table. He gave no sign that he had recognised Vasson. Vasson looked round again, wondering what to do. Should he go up to Kloffer and admit he knew him? Or should he ignore him? He decided it would be safer to ignore him. He went to the bar and sat down. The proprietor sniffed at him, 'Your friend not here today then?'

'No.'

The man sneered, 'Well, that's a loss, isn't it?'

Vasson ignored him. Another cheap patriot. He ordered a coffee, then changed his mind and asked for a pastis. He looked round at Kloffer. The German was sitting staring out of the window. Vasson downed his drink and, as he put the empty glass on the counter, he saw Kloffer get up and leave the bar. Vasson paid and followed the German out.

When Vasson reached the street he looked quickly up and down. Kloffer was disappearing round a corner to the left. Vasson walked quickly to the corner and rounded it. There was a black Citroën beside the kerb. Kloffer was waiting at the open rear door. There were two men in raincoats and fedora hats sitting in the front. They might as well have a sign on the side saying 'Gestapo'. Kloffer said, 'Get in.'

Vasson got in followed by Kloffer. The car sped south, towards the Etoile. Vasson asked nervously, 'May I ask where we're going?'

Kloffer stared straight ahead. For a moment Vasson thought he wouldn't answer, then he said, 'To my office.'

Vasson wondered where that would be. But he didn't ask. There was something about Kloffer's manner that discouraged questions.

The car rounded the Etoile and turned into the Avenue Foch. Vasson suddenly realised where they must be going and his mouth went dry. The Gestapo and the SS lived down here: the street was fast getting the pseudonym Avenue Boches. But why were they bringing him here? A nasty suspicion flashed through his mind and for a moment he thought: They're busting me, they're going to close me down. Then he decided not. If they were busting him they would have got him at the garage and taken his stock and ransacked his apartment.

The car drove under the archway of number 82 and stopped. This was the lion's mouth. It was well-known: Gestapo Headquarters. Its two neighbours, numbers 84 and 86, were occupied by the SS.

Vasson followed Kloffer up the stairs to the third floor. When they finally entered a large room with deep carpets and a large empire-style desk, he felt calmer. It was difficult to believe that anything terrible could happen in these surroundings. Vasson looked at the luxurious décor and realised that Kloffer was important.

Kloffer took off his hat and coat and told Vasson to sit down. When they were both seated Kloffer stared straight at Vasson and asked, 'What is your name?'

Vasson almost let the surprise show on his face, but he covered it quickly and said, 'You know my name: it's Jean-Marie Biolet.'

'No, your real name.'

'That *is* my real name.'

A flicker of impatience crossed Kloffer's face. 'Come now, I know it is not.'

Vasson thought quickly: How? How did he know? It *must* be a guess. Vasson had *never* been taken in by the police, not once; no-one had checked his identity since he arrived in Paris.

It had to be a bluff.

'It's my real name,' Vasson repeated.

'We could get the préfecture to check it. Somehow I don't think your thumb print would match that on your identity card.'

Vasson shrugged. 'So check them. You'd be wasting your time. I am Jean-Marie Biolet and I come from St Etienne.' He added, 'Anyway, what does it matter? Either I can help you or I can't.'

Kloffer's sharp rat-like eyes fell to the pad on the desk in front of him. Vasson realised he wasn't going to press the matter. *Thank God.*

'Very well,' Kloffer said, 'I want someone. I think you can find him for me.'

Vasson felt the relief flooding over him. So that was all they wanted – a person. It was to be a job like the one he'd done on Goldberg. Find and identify. Simple. But he was puzzled. Who could it be? He didn't know anyone these people might want.

Kloffer continued, 'The person we want is a communist agitator by the name of Cohen. He is a professor at the Sorbonne but has recently . . . gone to ground.'

'But I've never heard of Cohen, I don't know Cohen . . .'

'Exactly. You will be perfect for the job.'

Vasson began to understand. This was no Goldberg job. This wasn't a simple matter of pointing out an insignificant Jewish wholesaler, it was more, much more.

Vasson said stiffly, 'But why me?'

'Oh, come now. You will be excellent for the job. You have all the qualifications. You have already proved that.'

'But supposing I fail . . .?'

Kloffer looked impatient. 'Oh you won't do that. I have a feeling about you.' He stabbed a finger at Vasson. 'I have a feeling that you will be very good at the little tasks I ask you to do.'

'But . . . where would I start? How will I find him?'

Kloffer smiled thinly. 'We have some information. Cohen is a history professor at the Sorbonne. He is also the leader of a communist cell. We have detained most of them. Now I want Cohen himself. We picked up his girlfriend the other day, her name's Marie Boulevont. We released her but—' Kloffer cleared his throat and looked unhappy '– but we lost her. She was living at 56, Rue Brezin. Now she too has disappeared.'

In other words, Vasson thought, they've made a mess of it.

'We will give you a new name and student's papers and anything else that might be useful. Normally we would wait for someone to tell us where Cohen is, but in this case we want him in a hurry. As soon as possible. You understand?'

Vasson was trying to sort out his thoughts. He'd expected all kinds of things. But this . . . It would be difficult, and very dangerous. Political activists would not be kind if they caught him. Christ, they'd kill him without a second thought.

The money would have to be good, bloody good. Vasson looked up sharply: the German hadn't mentioned that.

Vasson said, 'I'd want good money for the job, in francs or gold, on delivery. What are you offering?'

Kloffer looked amused. 'Oh, a great deal. Freedom from arrest. Your little black market operation is, after all, totally illegal. It could get you into a lot of trouble. Also

freedom from investigation into your background and your
– what shall we say? – dubious identity.'

Vasson waited. Kloffer said, 'That is all.'

God! Kloffer was nothing but a cheap blackmailer. He
might have known. The humiliation burnt Vasson's cheeks.
He thought: No, you're bloody well not going to get away
with it.

Vasson looked calmly down at his hands and said
casually, 'No.'

'What do you mean?'

'I mean that I don't accept your terms. I have nothing
to hide. You can close me down if you like.'

Kloffer stared across the desk.

Vasson glanced out of the window. 'Now if we were to
come to a sensible arrangement I could do a first-class
job . . .'

'Go on.'

'I mean that you could get any rat to do a mediocre job
on those terms. But me? If I am paid a decent rate for the
job, I will do it well. And *quickly*. If not . . .' he shrugged.
'If not, well, it would take you a lot longer to find your
man, wouldn't it? Bust me if you wish – it really makes no
difference.' Vasson stared him straight in the eye and
thought how it would, of course, make a hell of a
difference: it would put him right back in shit street
without any money.

Kloffer put his fingertips together and touched his lips
thoughtfully. 'How much would you require, Monsieur
Biolet?'

'Fifty thousand francs.'

'Out of the question.'

'How much are you offering?'

'Ten.'

They settled on ten. Vasson didn't want to argue. He
didn't want Kloffer to lose too much face, otherwise he'd

bear a grudge. Anyway, Vasson thought, I'm bloody lucky to get anything at all. It would be silly to push his luck.

He could always ask for more next time.

He knew there *would* be a next time. The job was right up his street. He liked everything about it except the idea of getting caught: *that* terrified him. But the rest? Yes, very nice.

He liked the idea of a new identity, a new personality which, after the job, would disappear without trace. It was neat. A clean *out*, with no come-back. It was a challenge, too, something to get to grips with. It would give him a chance to show what he could do. He liked that.

And then there was the money, the lovely money.

The next day Vasson went back to the Avenue Foch, to an anonymous office on the ground floor, and collected a complete set of cards covering identity, student status, food ration, tobacco ration and military service, all of them in the name of Legrand. When Vasson saw the cards he went white with anger: the cards were hard, clean and unscuffed. They looked brand new, which was exactly what they were. He wondered if Kloffer was trying to nail him, or just being stupid. It was probably stupidity fuelled by the German passion for efficiency.

Another thing: there was no student enrolment card, which was necessary for the Sorbonne. Furthermore the card would be inspected frequently, so it would have to be genuine.

He went up to the third floor and told Kloffer what he wanted.

Kloffer was not pleased. 'What you ask is very difficult as well as unnecessary.'

'It's essential.'

Kloffer nodded curtly. It was agreed.

Vasson returned to the ground floor and settled down
to wait because he didn't want to be seen going in and out
of the building too often. Eventually, late in the afternoon,
a sergeant called him into the ground floor office and
passed him a new set of cards. The name was now Philippe
Roche, and the student enrolment card was obviously
genuine. Vasson guessed the other cards were genuine too:
they were soiled and scuffed. He was uneasy again: suppose
this Philippe Roche had been at the Sorbonne? Suppose
Vasson bumped into someone who knew him?

Vasson looked up. 'Is this person known at the
university?'

The sergeant smiled. 'No.'

'Did he ever go there?'

The sergeant eyed him lazily. 'No he never went there.
He never started his course.'

Vasson nodded. He didn't want to know any more.

On the way back to Montmartre Vasson bought some
slacks, two casual shirts, two sweaters and a donkey jacket
from a cheap shop. Back in his room he crumpled and
dirtied them a little, then changed, leaving all his own
clothes behind. He packed a small bag containing his
washing things and some pyjamas, then left. He went
straight to the Left Bank and wandered around the book-
stalls beside the river until he found some old textbooks
on French history. At a stationery shop nearby he bought
a couple of blank pads, some pencils and a pen. Finally he
wandered into Montparnasse and found a room to rent.

Then he was ready.

He would start with the girl, the girl who was meant to
be a special friend of Cohen's.

But first he spent a morning just walking round the
Sorbonne and the Left Bank cafés, watching the students,
listening to their conversation. It was fairly easy to gauge
their mood: most of them were angry, either about the
Armistice Parade arrests, or the disappearance of university

staff, or the curbs on student activities. Some even spoke of countermeasures, of demonstrations and open defiance.

They were incredibly naive, Vasson decided. They talked openly, in public places, without realising the need for discretion. Beyond lowering their voices they had no sense of secrecy, no idea that informers might be listening. Vasson thought: This could be easier than I imagined.

In the afternoon he went to 56, Rue Brezin, the last known address of the girlfriend, Marie Boulevont. Now that Kloffer's watchers had gone, she might have returned. But she hadn't. The *concierge* hadn't seen her for weeks and didn't know where she'd moved to. Vasson wasn't surprised. The girl would have been stupid to return.

He would have to start from scratch then. In a strange way he didn't mind. It was more of a challenge that way.

The next morning he examined the mass of notice boards in the history department at the Sorbonne and decided to go to the lecture on Enlightened Despotism in the Eighteenth Century. It was well attended and he had a job getting in. The lecture was long and tedious. Vasson spent his time looking at the hundreds of faces around the hall. They all looked the same: like communists. Finally, when the lecture was over and everyone was crowding through the exits, he chose a group of five students who were talking heatedly. They looked as if they might be political types. He followed them to a café on the Boulevard St Germain.

He sat at an adjoining table and listened. They were still talking heatedly – about lectures clashing because of the appalling new timetable. Vasson waited impatiently. This group was a dead end, he could sense it. Damn. He would have to think of a surer way.

Then Vasson realised that their voices had dropped and only the occasional word was reaching him. One of them was saying how terrible something was and the others were agreeing. Vasson strained to hear.

'. . . he was arrested . . . that is certain . . .'

The voices dropped again and Vasson lost the reply. Then a third voice said, 'But it's terrible to sit and do nothing!'

How right you are, Vasson thought.

Impulsively he got up and stepped over to the students' table. 'I . . .' He hovered nervously. 'I saw you in the lecture . . . I'm a new student. May I . . .?' He indicated his chair and looked suitably uncertain.

One of the students nodded. Vasson stuttered 'Thanks' and drew up his chair. They made room for him and he sat down.

They stared at him expectantly. Vasson laughed nervously and said, 'It's hard to find your way around!'

They nodded and one, a boy with thick pebble glasses, said, 'We've been here a year and we still can't find our way round!'

Vasson smiled anxiously and said, 'Is there—' he searched for the words '– is there a lot of trouble in the university? I mean, what should one *know* about?' He peered round the table earnestly.

'Oh, just don't get involved in – well, anything political.'

Vasson nodded violently.

There was a silence. Vasson looked pensive. 'And . . . have there been many arrests?'

The boy with the pebble glasses sighed. 'Yes, students and staff. Efforts are made to discover what has happened to them but . . .' He trailed off and shrugged.

Vasson looked grave. 'I was assigned to Professor Cohen, but now I am to be in another group. Did he—? Was he . . . taken?'

Pebble-glasses shrugged. 'Nobody's sure what happened to him. It's thought he's in hiding, but I wouldn't know.'

Vasson stared at him and realised with disappointment that he was telling the truth.

It was worth one more shot. He said, 'Also I was given

the name of a friend of his, by a friend of my family. But –
well, it's very upsetting, because she too has been taken
or –' He shook his head bitterly '– or disappeared. And I
don't know what to tell this friend. It's all very tragic, very
tragic.'

'Who's Cohen's friend?'

'Ah!' Vasson made a show of looking through his
pockets as if for a scrap of paper which he couldn't find.
By an effort of concentration he suddenly remembered the
name. 'Er. Oh yes, Yes, it was Marie, Marie Boulevont.
That was it!'

One asked, 'Marie Boulevont?'

Vasson stared vacantly into the distance and nodded
slowly.

They were shaking their heads. Vasson stood up, still
saying, 'Very sad, very sad.' He added brightly, 'Well,
thank you for telling me the form. See you again soon!'

Damn.

He would have to find a better way. There was only one
problem: he couldn't think of one.

Damn.

The next day he looked more carefully round the lecture
room and chose a serious-looking student of about twenty-
seven. He looked much more the type: thoughtful and
politically committed. But the student went back to his
rooms and stayed there all day. It was another dead end.

The following day was Friday. There was no major
history lecture that day but a series of smaller seminars on
specialist subjects. Vasson thought: What would a communist be studying? He decided on European History from
1860 to 1930, the period covering the Russian Revolution.

There were only thirty students in the seminar. Vasson
looked casually round the room a couple of times, taking
a careful look at each student. One, he noticed, was staring
at him. He was about twenty-two, with short curly hair
and glasses. His stare was intense and hard; he was

summing Vasson up. When their eyes met the student looked away and a few seconds later Vasson saw him exchange an almost imperceptible glance with another student across the room. Vasson felt a quickening of the pulse. This one was clever and sophisticated enough, that was certain.

The seminar was about the decline of nineteenth-century liberalism and was interminable. At one point the professor asked each student for a definition of liberalism. Vasson felt a moment of panic. He hadn't reckoned on that. But in the end it was easy, he just gave a garbled version of two earlier replies, defining it as freedom of the individual from excessive central control. As he spoke he was aware that Curly Head was watching him. When it came to Curly Head's turn his reply was clipped and informed; he was obviously a thinker. There was also a hint of intolerance and dogma in his speech. He even dared to differ with the professor on a point concerning 'old' liberalism versus 'new'.

Vasson stiffened: this one was a political animal.

At the end of the seminar, when they all got up, Vasson stood aside to let Curly Head pass. The student went by with his head averted. But Vasson thought: He knows I'm here, he knows it very well.

Vasson let Curly Head disappear down the corridor, then asked a student next to him, 'Who was the one going on about new liberalism?'

The student was in a hurry. He was irritated at being detained but answered, 'Eh? Oh, Laval.'

Vasson picked up Laval-Curly Head as he left the building. It was four, almost dusk. The student was heading south down the broad pavement of the Boulevard St Michel. He was walking fast, his thick woollen coat flapping out behind him, his head thrust forward. Vasson followed at a safe distance, his pace settling into a steady rhythm.

Quite suddenly Curly Head glanced over his shoulder and looked straight at Vasson. Vasson thought: He's on to me.

Curly Head hurried on. Vasson slowed his pace, walking more casually, and made a point of keeping his head down and his eyes on the pavement. At the next corner he turned down a side street, away from the main boulevard. When he guessed he was out of Curly Head's view he crossed the street and doubled back at a run. At the corner he stopped and looked carefully round until he could see up the length of the boulevard. Curly Head was some way away, still walking fast. Vasson pulled his coat up round his ears and followed. After a few moments Curly Head looked back again, but Vasson stepped quickly behind another pedestrian. This time he was not seen.

Curly Head walked across the south side of the Jardin du Luxembourg and into the streets of Montparnasse. He looked behind him only once more, just before he turned into a small rooming house. Again, Vasson was certain he hadn't been seen. He took up station near the house, but on the same side of the street so that he couldn't be spotted from the windows. It was bitterly cold and after an hour it began to rain.

Vasson sheltered in a doorway and thought of going back to his own room. But he decided not: the wait wouldn't do him any harm.

By seven the feeling had gone in his feet. All he could think about was drinking hot soup and red wine in a warm bistro.

At almost eight Curly Head came out. It was so dark Vasson almost missed him. Curly Head seemed more relaxed than before and strolled along quite casually. He didn't go far; just to a café in the next street. Vasson peered through the window. The black-out curtains were too effective and he couldn't see anything. He went to the door. Here there was a slight crack between the frame and the black cardboard stuck to the inside of the window. Vasson put his eye to the crack and saw that Curly Head had joined a group of people at a table. Vasson thought he recognised two of them; one was the student who had exchanged the glance with Curly Head at the seminar; and the other, a girl, had been there too, sitting at the back.

Vasson walked away and looked for another café where he might get something to eat and warm up. But there was nowhere. In disgust he settled down to wait in a doorway opposite Curly Head's café.

It was a quarter to ten and very cold when they drifted out. It was too risky to follow Curly Head again and anyway there wasn't much point: he was probably going straight back to his rooms. Vasson decided on the girl instead; she might be an easier nut to crack. She didn't live far away. She went straight to a cheap rooming house, rather like the one Curly Head lived in. Nothing was likely to happen that night, Vasson decided. He noted the address and went back to his room to sleep.

He returned to the girl's place early, at seven. The girl wouldn't have gone out yet. He was right: she didn't emerge until midday. He followed her to the Boulevard St Germain. She went shopping. Vasson began to wonder if this was going to be another dead end, but then she went into a glass-enclosed pavement café and sat at a table on her own. She started to read a book, looking up only to ask for a coffee. She did not look into the street. She obviously wasn't expecting anyone.

He went into the café and walked past her table, then doubled back and stooped down to look at her. 'Hello, aren't you—? Haven't we met—?'

She looked up at him curiously. She was plain, with thick black eyebrows, dark lanky hair and unattractive glasses. Definitely the intellectual type. Brainy but not clever, Vasson decided. She said, 'Sorry. I don't remember . . .'

Vasson shook his head and introduced himself. 'No, why should you remember? We only met briefly, ages ago. And then I saw you in the seminar yesterday. I've just switched courses, from geography.'

She squinted at him through her spectacles. 'Where did we meet first then?'

'Ah, well . . .' He looked carefully round the café. 'Perhaps it's best to stay at mutual friends, and leave it at that.'

She said nothing but licked her lips uncertainly.

Vasson dropped his voice. 'One can't be too careful.'

She nodded and frowned.

'I saw Laval in the seminar too, but I didn't contact him. Too dangerous. Anyway he may not remember me. Did he mention seeing me yesterday?'

She shook her head. 'No . . . He said nothing.'

Vasson nodded. 'Just as well.'

'Shall I mention seeing you? To Jean, I mean.'

Jean must be Laval. 'No, no. Best not to. I—' Vasson tried to look hunted. 'I have to be very careful . . .'

She said in a low voice, 'One cannot be too careful, that's for sure.'

'If only more precautions had been taken in the beginning.'

'Yes.'

A waiter came up and Vasson ordered coffee. He smiled brightly at the girl. 'I don't even know your name!'

For a moment she looked startled, then said quietly, 'Sophie.'

'What a beautiful name!' He thought: For such an ugly girl.

She was pleased. 'Oh. Thank you!'

Vasson looked down at the parcels beside her. 'Been shopping?'

'Yes. My allowance came through – I needed some clothes. There isn't much in the shops but . . .' She laughed and pushed some strands of greasy hair back from her forehead. 'I found a couple of things.'

God, she's plain, Vasson thought, plain and boring. But he felt he should let the conversation continue in the same vein. He bought her another coffee and they talked about her life, her family and the poor opportunities for women in publishing, where she hoped to get a job.

He listened attentively for twenty minutes, then decided the moment had come. He leant towards her and, looking deep into her eyes, said, 'I can't tell you how good it's been talking to you. I'd love to see you again. Can we meet later, for a bit of food? It would be fun.' He touched her hand.

'Oh. Yes. I – er – yes.' There was a blush on her cheeks.

Vasson hoped he wouldn't have to keep this up much longer.

The girl was flustered and confused. She was making a mess of gathering her belongings. Vasson picked a package off the floor and smiled at her. 'I can see I'm going to have to look after you!' Her face went scarlet and she looked down at the floor.

He suddenly looked serious. 'By the way, perhaps you can tell me—' He put his hand on her arm. 'I've been a bit out of touch. On purpose, of course. But—' he lowered his voice to a whisper '– I've been dying to know . . . Is Cohen all right, have you heard?'

Her eyes came straight up to his. She said immediately, 'He's all right. He's safe.'

Vasson made a show of beating his hand on his forehead. 'Thank God. Thank God for that!'

She started to pull on her coat while still in her seat and was soon struggling with a sleeve. Vasson jumped up to help her. When the coat was on he let his arm brush across her shoulders. Then he sat down again and put his face close to hers.

'We'll win in the end, you know. We *will* because we *must*!'

She nodded emphatically, her eyes shining up at him.

They stood up. Then he touched her arm and pulled her down into her chair again.

'One thing—' He frowned. 'I have reason to believe Marie may be in danger.'

She gasped. 'Marie . . .?'

He nodded.

The girl looked at him. 'Oh no! Why?'

'The word is that they're looking for her again. I don't know how to warn her.'

The girl said, 'Oh God. She was in a safe house, but now . . .' She trailed off unhappily.

'Now—?'

'I'm not sure . . .'

'I looked for her at the Rue Brezin, but of course she hasn't been back there.'

'Oh no, she wouldn't go back there. The Boches have been watching it. It isn't safe. She's – Well, I *think* she may be at Su's place.' She used the expression *chez Su*.

'Su's.'

The girl nodded. 'Yes, Su's.' Obviously this Su was well known. Suzanne perhaps?

'Ah . . . Where do I find Su nowadays?'

The girl looked at him sharply and stared. A shiver ran up Vasson's spine. Something was wrong: he'd made a mistake.

She said, 'Surely . . . You must know . . .'

He tried again. 'I just haven't seen Su for some time . . . You know how it is . . .'

She said slowly, 'But you are acquainted with her?'

Vasson smiled. 'Of course.'

The girl's face went sheet white. She got up from the table and, grabbing her possessions, stumbled out. Vasson followed, cursing softly.

Su? Who the hell was Su?

When he got out of the café he soon spotted the girl, half-running, half-walking down the street. From time to time she twisted round and looked back. She didn't see Vasson. He guessed she was short-sighted.

She crossed the boulevard and hurried towards the Sorbonne. She passed the main university building and turned down a narrow back street. Vasson got to the corner and paused. He edged slowly along the last few inches of wall and peered cautiously round.

The girl was two yards away, coming straight towards him.

He yanked his head back and sprinted away. He dived into a recessed doorway and pressed his body against it, panting hard.

The girl came into his field of vision. She looked anxiously up and down the street, then turned on her heel and disappeared.

He left it five seconds and looked out. No-one. He approached the corner again and peered round.

She was walking away from him. She began to turn her head. He pulled back.

He looked again. She had gone.

He walked towards the spot where she had disappeared.

There were three doorways in the vicinity. One belonged to a dingy restaurant. He glanced at the name over the door.

It was called Chez Le Maréchal Suchet.

Chez Su.

Vasson groaned inwardly. No wonder she was on to him. Every student must know this place. Su was no lady; Su was a bloody *maréchal*.

He wondered what to do next. The girlfriend, Marie Boulevont, might be here. If she was, she'd have to come out some time. But most likely she'd go straight to ground. Damn! He'd really blown it.

He decided to wait. There was nothing else to do.

Half an hour later the girl poked her nose out of the door. She looked carefully up and down the street. Even from several yards away Vasson could see that her face was bright red. She'd probably been crying. She took a last look up the street and disappeared into the doorway. When she came out again there was another girl with her, someone older, prettier, more self-assured. She was carrying a small case. Marie Boulevont?

Yes, Vasson decided, Marie Boulevont.

At the end of the street the women stopped, spoke excitedly for a moment and split up. Vasson followed Marie.

She was clever. He almost lost her twice. At the Boulevard St Germain she took the Métro to the Étoile, then hopped on a bus just as it was leaving. Vasson was lucky to jump on another bus going in the same direction. She got off at Montparnasse, almost back where they'd started. Then she walked again, constantly looking over her shoulder. At one point she dived into a shop. Vasson took a guess and sprinted round the block to the back of the building. There was a tradesman's entrance. Just as he got there, the door opened and Marie came out.

Got you! Vasson thought.

Then she walked again, quickly. She doubled back once more, looked over her shoulder one last time and disappeared into a doorway beside an *épicerie*.

Vasson waited uncertainly. He had no idea what this place was. It might be a safe house she was going to use. It might just be a friend's place. There was no certainty Cohen was there.

After an hour she came out again. She was nervous. She looked up and down the street, then walked quickly off. She was empty-handed. That meant she had left her case inside. That meant she was coming back.

Vasson came to a decision. He walked in the opposite direction until he found a telephone. He called Kloffer.

He said, 'Just two men – and not with Gestapo written all over them.'

'What do you mean?' Kloffer replied.

'I mean choose fellows without leather coats and felt hats – people with *French* clothes for Christ's sake.'

Then he went back and waited. God, Kloffer's men were taking for ever. The girl would be back soon. Shit!

After ten minutes Vasson swore again, louder.

Finally he saw Kloffer's men. They still looked like Krauts.

'Come on!'

Vasson led the way angrily along the street and into the door Marie had come out of. The house was on five floors. Off each of the two landings there were three doors.

Vasson guessed at a front room. They knocked on the first door. There was no reply and one of the Germans opened it with his shoulder. Nothing. A door at the back of the house flew open and an old woman thrust her head out. Nothing there either. The old woman said the third room wasn't occupied.

They went to the next floor.

Cohen was in the front room.

Vasson knew it was him the moment the pale, narrow face appeared round the door. He was small, dark and insignificant looking. He came out quietly, with resignation. Vasson felt vaguely disappointed. The man hadn't even tried to escape.

Kloffer's men searched Cohen, then the room.

Vasson was impatient to go. 'Come on!'

The Germans went first, Cohen between them. Vasson hung back and followed them at a distance. In the next street was the inevitable black Citroën. Vasson sat uneasily in the front. He didn't like being seen with Kloffer's heavies. On the other hand he wanted to be there when Cohen was brought in. He wanted to see Kloffer's face.

There was no sound from Cohen in the back. Vasson half turned his head. 'You should always choose a room with another way out, you know. That was silly of you. The girl was stupid as well – she led me straight to you.' He shook his head. 'It was all too easy.'

There was silence. Vasson craned his head round until he could see the man's face. 'You weren't very clever, professor.'

Cohen was looking out of the window, his face white and expressionless.

Vasson stared for a moment then turned back, uneasy and vaguely angry. The sight of the man was disturbing. His silence was accusing. Vasson decided it had been a mistake to travel in the same car. The next time he would take care not to.

The driver glanced across at Vasson and, smiling, said, 'Don't worry. He won't be so quiet when we've started talking to him.'

Vasson shuddered and looked out of the window, wishing the journey would end quickly.

When the car finally arrived at 82, Avenue Foch, Vasson got out hurriedly and ran into the building without looking back. He didn't feel comfortable until he was shown into Kloffer's office.

The German had a faint smile on his face. 'Very good. Very good.'

Vasson relaxed. Kloffer was obviously more than satisfied with him. Immediately he wondered if he could double his price next time – perhaps even treble it.

There was only one loose end. The plain girl with glasses. She could identify him. That had been a silly slip, about Su's. He would have to be more careful in future.

He gave Kloffer her name and the address of her room.

Then he pushed her out of his mind. He didn't want to know what Kloffer would do with her. It was none of his affair any more.

That night he returned to his apartment, burnt the student clothes, carefully hid the bundle of student identity papers, and assumed the name of Biolet again.

He went to bed content. All things considered it had gone pretty well really. Though it hadn't been as neat as it might have been – there had been a slip or two. He must be careful not to let that happen again, it might not be so easy to cover himself next time.

Chapter 8

JULIE TOOK A last look round the small whitewashed room, picked up her bag and went through the kitchen into the front parlour. She saw that Tante Marie and Peter were already outside, standing by the waiting fish truck. As she came out of the house and closed the front door behind her she thought: I might never see this place again. It seemed all wrong, to be going. This was her home, her life, and she was abandoning it like a rat leaving a sinking ship.

Peter was in Tante Marie's arms, a frown of bewilderment on his face, his eyes fixed intently on the tears running down the old woman's cheeks. Julie could see that he still didn't understand why they were going. But then why should he? He was four years old: Germans and conquerors meant nothing to him.

Nor, for that matter, did the problems of having a British passport in a country occupied by an enemy power.

During the last few days Julie had tried to imagine what that might mean. At best the two of them might be deported back to England. But Uncle Jean thought that unlikely; the Germans weren't that considerate, he said. So what *would* happen? Perhaps they would be interned or sent away; perhaps they'd be forced to work in camps; or worst of all, separated. Julie couldn't bear the idea of Peter being taken away from her and ill-treated or half-starved: it was unthinkable. It was her duty to get him away. That was what she was doing. Her duty.

Uncle Jean came round the front of the truck and, taking Julie's bag, threw it into the back. He turned to her and put his hands on her shoulders.

'Now Georges here will drive you to Morlaix. The boat you're going on is called *Fleur*. Make sure Georges takes you all the way to the boat and gets your bags on board for you. There's chaos everywhere, they say, so be sure to stick with him, eh?'

Julie nodded and Jean went on, 'It's a good boat, *Fleur*, it's one of the newest and biggest in Morlaix. It'll get you safely to England.' Then he embraced her with a ferocious loving hug which left Julie breathless and a little tearful.

Jean took Peter and handed him up into the cab. Julie and Tante Marie embraced and the old woman said, 'It's for the best, you know that. We'll be happy because we'll know you're safe.'

Julie nodded and got up into the cab. The engine coughed into life and they were off, bumping down the road, away from the little house. Peter jumped up and down, waving wildly, as if it were a day outing. Julie waved more slowly and, when the house and the two figures standing in front of it had disappeared from sight, she blew her nose and stared doggedly at the road ahead.

Peter craned his head to stare at her face. 'What's the matter, Mummy?'

'Oh, I'm just thinking.' She smiled briefly.

'When will we be coming home again?'

'Well, darling, as soon as the Germans have gone.'

Peter frowned and put his head on one side. 'When will that be, Mummy?'

Julie sighed, as much from the relentless questioning as the problem of finding an anwer. 'I honestly don't know, darling. It depends on lots of things . . . Perhaps it'll be a long time, a very long time.'

'They won't kill Uncle Jean and Tante Marie, will they?'

'No! Of course not! Only soldiers get killed.'

'They'll be all right, then?'

'Yes.' She gave him a reassuring hug, and wondered if the old couple *would* be all right. She knew she'd worry herself sick about them. There were bound to be shortages and severe hardships. Already meat was on sale only three days a week; the *patisseries* were closed two days a week; petrol was rationed. And that was *before* the defeat. Under the Germans . . . It would be worse, much worse.

Still, Julie remembered, this was an independent, self-sufficient community. They should be able to manage. Tante Marie had told her about terrible droughts and unusually cold winters in the past when people had almost starved. Those hardest hit were helped by the others with donations of food. Then later, when things were better, the debts were repaid in kind and with interest.

This time there was one major difference, though. The shortages might go on for years . . .

As the lorry bumped gently through the soft greens and bright yellows of the lovely June countryside, Julie tried to imagine the Germans here, with their trucks, their tanks, their hard grey efficiency. They would take over everything; they would be able to bully anyone they chose.

They'd be here in just two days, so it was said. That was the incredible part. Julie didn't understand how it could happen: how Paris could fall so easily, almost without a murmur; how the Germans could sweep across the country in so short a time. But then she knew nothing about fighting. She just hadn't understood what was happening.

At the same time it was strange that no-one else had guessed what was happening either. There had been no warnings until the Germans were already inside the country, almost at Paris. Why hadn't the Government said something? Why had they avoided telling anyone? It seemed extraordinary.

The driver, Georges, said, 'There might be a delay when

we get near the town. Evidently some of the roads are almost impassable in places.'

Julie looked at him questioningly.

'The people. Thousands of them. All on their way to Brest, to get on ships and get the hell out of here. Can't blame them either!'

They saw the first of them just before reaching the main Lannion–Morlaix road. There were people sitting in the hedgerows, resting and sleeping, while others foraged in the fields, pulling up vegetables and chewing on them, raw. Some waved to the fish truck and shouted, 'Any food?' Julie shook her head unhappily.

When they got to the junction itself there were many, many more people: women pushing prams piled high with bags and children; men striding along with heavy bundles on their backs; one family with a cage full of rabbits on the back of a bicycle. Again, there were cries of, 'Food? Some food? Anything to spare, friend?' Julie stared dismally out of the window. Every family, every child that she saw wrung her heart.

She murmured, 'I wish I could give them something.'

The driver shook his head. 'No. It's each man for himself. You have some food with you?'

She nodded.

'Well, my advice is, keep it! And guard it well. I think we'll all have to look after our possessions from now on!'

The truck slowed to a crawl as they came up behind a knot of people who stayed obstinately on the centre of the road. Julie guessed they were just too tired to step aside. Where had they come from? Paris? Even further? It must have taken them days to get this far. And where had they slept? Had they eaten?

It took half an hour to do the last three kilometres. The road leading to the quay was thronged with people. Most were standing in lines outside food shops, waiting silently, a look of resignation on their faces. At one corner there was an angry scene with groups of men pushing and shouting at each other. Two of them were trying to tear down a poster. Julie recognised the poster; it was one which had been pasted up all over the town. It read: WE WILL WIN BECAUSE WE'RE THE STRONGEST. As the fish truck passed, two men started to fight, their arms flailing in the air. Julie shuddered. 'Why are they fighting?'

Georges shrugged. 'Disgust at the Government, I should think. After all, we're not the strongest and we've lost, haven't we!'

At last the truck turned on to the quay and Georges said, 'This is it. The boat's just down there.' Julie gasped. The port was a mass of fishing boats. She had never seen so many in harbour, not even when a storm was blowing. Groups of refugees were standing on the quay, looking hopefully at one or two of the boats, but most were walking dispiritedly away.

Georges nodded at the boats. 'They can't take all this lot, so they're only taking servicemen and special cases.' He opened the door and added with contempt, 'That is, those boats which are going at all.'

Julie asked, 'Are you going?'

'Oh yes! I'll go and fight with the British, or anyone else for that matter. Well, I'm not going to stay here and say good day to the Germans, am I?'

Julie handed Peter down to Georges and said, 'No, I don't suppose you are.'

Georges shouted at a man on a nearby boat who nodded back, then Georges led the way on to the deck of the boat nearest to the quay. They had to cross the decks and climb the bulwarks of four boats before Georges finally said, 'Here we are.'

Julie passed Peter over the last bulwark then climbed aboard herself. Carefully she checked that the two cases were all right and that she hadn't forgotten the small basket of food that Tante Marie had given her. The luggage and the food made her feel secure, as if nothing could happen to her and Peter while she had them.

Georges was leaving and Julie thanked him. Then someone – Julie supposed it was one of the crew – took her cases and told her to sit on deck. She sat on a hatch-cover with Peter on her knee and waited, watching the people on the quay, some queuing for bread outside a *boulangerie*, others staring at the boats. They're wishing they were here in my place, she thought. It made her feel guilty, mainly because she was so glad it *was* her and not them.

She wondered how long it would be before the boat left. She knew that the fishermen always left on the tide. Morlaix was quite a distance from the sea, up a winding river. At low tide the upper reaches of the river were too shallow, but at Morlaix there was a lock which kept a good depth of water in the basin. The lock opened only for a few hours around high water.

Fleur was a large boat, about eighty feet long; she would need the full height of the tide to get down the river, Julie guessed. Jean had arranged for Julie to come on this boat because she was larger and safer for a Channel crossing, and because he knew the men who had built her.

A truck drew up on the quay. Some soldiers, apparently wounded, were helped out. A group of fishermen were mustered and the wounded were carried or helped across the boats. Julie suddenly realised they were coming towards *Fleur*.

The soldiers were taken below to where Julie guessed there must be a small cabin. Now there were more people arriving. Like her, they were civilians. Most were carrying heavy luggage and wearing thick coats and jackets. Julie began to feel a little nervous. There were more than twenty passengers on the deck now but, she guessed, nowhere for them to shelter. The soldiers had the cabin, and the small wheelhouse was clearly the crew's domain. Those on deck would have to stay on deck. If the weather turned bad, they would freeze . . .

She looked anxiously at Peter's coat. It was warm, but not waterproof. If it rained he would get soaked to the skin. And her own coat . . . She grimaced: such vanity! She had worn her best coat – a lightweight linen one – with a raincoat over it. She felt cold already.

One of the crew was passing. Julie touched his arm. 'Do I have time to get something from my luggage? Some warmer clothes?'

'Ah!' he shrugged. 'The bags are piled up in the hold. It'll be a job to get yours out now. Look, we're just leaving. If you're cold I'll find you something later. All right?'

Julie hesitated: she felt she should press the matter, but then it was too late, he was gone. The boat's engine throbbed into life and they were moving, first into the lock, and then down the long, narrow river through fields and tree-covered slopes towards the sea. A young man shouted, '*Vive la France Libre!*' And everyone laughed and cheered.

A man sitting next to Julie grinned. 'We live to fight another day. Eh?'

Julie smiled back. Suddenly she felt happy; the laughter and cheerfulness were infectious. And he was right; by going to England they could at least *do* something to fight back.

After a while the river widened into the flat expanse of the estuary. The sky was overcast but the sun was making a brave attempt to shine through a patch of thinner cloud. Suddenly it succeeded and the land turned from a dark sombre grey to a paler shade of green. Over to the right, beyond the low hills, was Tregasnou. Already it seemed distant and remote.

But I'll be back, Julie thought. She hugged Peter and said, 'Everything's going to be all right, darling. Wait and see!'

As the boat emerged into the open sea a stiff wind began to blow across the deck and Julie pulled her coat more tightly about her. She looked around for somewhere sheltered to sit. The deck was long and exposed. The only place that might offer some protection was the side, next to the deep bulwarks. Julie was just about to move Peter across when the boat rolled and water splashed up through some sort of drain holes. Soon the part of the deck where she had planned to sit was drenched with water.

It would have to be somewhere else. The bow was high and flared, with a tiny triangle of decking. It might just offer a bit of protection. Anyway it was better than nothing. Holding tightly to Peter's hand, Julie made her way unsteadily forward. The boat rolled again and she made a grab for the rail. Her hand missed and she staggered sideways, falling over someone's leg and almost sitting on a man's lap. A voice said, 'Hey! Watch where you're going!'

Peter cried, 'Mummy, Mummy! I've bumped my knee.'

Julie gasped, 'Sorry', and got to her feet. Holding Peter firmly in one hand, she held tightly to the rail with the other, and started forward again. Holding on made the trip much easier and they got to the bow without further trouble.

In the bow there was a large winch which, Julie guessed, was for pulling up the anchor. Around it there were several coils of wide oily rope. Julie sat on the largest and pulled Peter down beside her.

Almost immediately he said, 'I'm cold, Mummy.'

'Well, come on to my lap then.' She undid her coat and

raincoat and stretched them round Peter's body, hugging him to her.

It was definitely less windy up here, Julie decided. On the other hand the motion of the boat seemed worse – or maybe it was her imagination. The roll was the same, but now the deck was going up and down as well. She closed her eyes and tried not to think about it. Then the boat lurched and seemed to plunge into thin air. Julie felt her stomach take off and she reached down as if to hold it.

Peter said, 'Mummy, I feel funny.'

Oh God, Julie thought. She said calmly, 'Well, lie down darling, then you'll feel better.' She stretched him out across the coil of rope and laid his head on her lap. His face was sheet white and he burped slightly. He'll be sick in a second, Julie thought. She looked around for the nearest place to take him. The sides of the boat were too high here; she would have to take him several yards down the deck before they were low enough to hold his head over the water. Perhaps it wasn't so clever to have come up here after all.

She looked down at Peter again. His eyes were shut and his mouth slightly open: he was sound asleep. She relaxed and leant back against the rope. Thank goodness for that. It would be nice if she could sleep too . . .

The boat leapt again and Julie felt her stomach twist. She shivered and thought: Why didn't I get those clothes? She felt Peter's cheek and hands: he was cold too. What a fool she'd been! But it wasn't too late; she would go and fetch the extra clothes now.

It meant a trip to the wheelhouse to ask one of the crew. She looked down the deck: it suddenly seemed rather a long way, and the deck was treacherous with running water. It wouldn't be so bad if she didn't feel so tired . . .

The other passengers were lying across the top of the

hold or draped over the rail being sick. One woman raised her head and vomited on the deck. The sight of it made Julie retch and she knew she couldn't make it down the deck, at least not quite yet. If only she could get her head down . . .

She lifted Peter's head and shifted her body until she was more or less lying on her side, then moved him until he was lying in the curve of her body. It was wonderful to lie down; she felt much better. And the cold didn't seem to matter so much like this. She closed her eyes and thought: I'll definitely get the clothes in a minute.

A cry woke her and she looked up to see some of the passengers brushing spray off their clothes. The motion was worse than before and now and again the bow came down with a terrible shudder, as if the boat had hit something. The wind was reaching into the bow section now, whistling round, icy and chill against Julie's skin. She shivered again and wondered how much longer she dared leave it before she got the clothes. The longer she left it, the worse it would be. And yet she knew she would be sick if she got up, and she daren't leave Peter . . .

She thought: I'm just making excuses.

She made herself sit up. She tucked Peter into the coil of rope and, getting to her feet, started gingerly down the deck. The wind blew her hair into her eyes and then something cold and solid hit the back of her head. She gasped with the shock. Cold water seeped down her neck.

She got halfway to the wheelhouse and leant over the rail. A vague memory came to her, something someone had said about feeling seasick: first you want to die but then you're afraid you're not going to. Who'd said that? She couldn't remember. Whoever it was, he was right.

But afterwards, when her stomach was empty, she was surprised to find she felt much better, and she started down the deck with new determination. The crew member she had spoken to before was standing outside the wheelhouse.

As she reached him he held out a helping hand and she grasped it gratefully.

She gasped, 'Thank you so much. It's a bit rough for me, I'm afraid.' She looked up at him, a smile on her face. He began to smile back, then his face froze and he stared past her at a point over her head, his mouth open.

Suddenly he was shouting, so loudly that Julie stared at him in amazement. Suddenly everyone was yelling and pointing and Julie turned to see what they were looking at.

It was a plane.

It was coming straight for them, low over the sea.

The yelling stopped and there was silence. Everyone was watching the plane. It came closer and closer, its grey outline getting darker, more solid. Julie felt her heart beating against her chest. It couldn't be, surely . . .

The plane tipped its wings and went off at an angle, then tipped the other way: it was circling round them. A voice yelled, 'It's German! It's a German!'

There was a crash; it was the wheelhouse door opening. A large, red-faced man came roaring out, shaking his fist at the plane. 'Bloody swine! Bloody swine!' Julie guessed it was the skipper.

'What should we do? What should we do?' someone said.

The skipper shouted, 'Nothing, that's what. Absolutely nothing!'

The plane straightened up and flew in the direction of Morlaix, waggling its wings. Then it turned back towards them. But it didn't circle again. Instead it came straight for the boat, passing so low over the masts that Julie thought it would hit them.

A passenger cried, 'Turn back! He's trying to tell us to turn back. Quick, otherwise he'll shoot us all!'

People started arguing and shouting. One man – a fairly well-dressed man in his fifties – got to his feet, lurched up to the skipper and ordered him to turn around. The skipper told him to do something unpleasant to himself and, when he'd finished, to mind his own business. The passenger started to yell at him, his voice shrieking above the sound of the wind and the waves. A couple of women screamed as the plane made another pass close over the masts.

Julie thought: They've all gone mad. It's a nightmare.

She watched the plane turn and head towards the boat again. The noise, when it came, was staccato but very faint, as if it didn't come from the plane at all. At first Julie didn't understand what the noise meant and she was puzzled to see everyone throwing themselves on to the deck. For a second she stood there against the rail, frozen with surprise. Then at last she realised: bullets. She dropped like a stone and crawled against the raised side of the hold.

She thought: Peter! and looked up along the deck to the bow. There was someone in her way and she craned her head up further.

He was sitting up, looking bemused. He was swinging his feet over the rope coil and putting them on the deck.

He was going to stand up.

Julie screamed, 'Peter! *Get down! Get down!*'

He was looking around, searching for her.

Then he stood up.

The plane swooped over in a roar of noise.

Julie got up and started to run.

She started well, keeping her balance as she ran up the deck. The boat rolled and she swerved sideways. There was a sharp blow to her ankle, and then pain. She got a grip on the rail and ran on. The bow sank into a wave with a thunderous roar and a sheet of spray came swooping across the boat. She saw it coming and wondered for an instant whether to duck. But then it had slapped into her and she gasped at the coldness of the water: it had gone straight through her clothes.

Another two strides and she reached Peter. She rolled

into the coil of rope, pulling him down with her and sobbed with relief.

Peter pushed away from her and said crossly, 'Mummy, you're all wet! You're all wet!'

'Yes, darling.' She caught her breath then looked back along the deck, trying to gauge what was happening. She had a feeling they were turning: the wind was blowing differently, and the boat was not bumping so ferociously into the waves. Turning . . .

She listened for the plane, but there was nothing. She stood up quickly and looked around. Yes, they were definitely turning: the land was almost ahead of the boat now. They were going back towards Morlaix.

Julie knew she should be disappointed, but all she could feel was an overwhelming sense of relief; somehow nothing ashore could possibly be worse than staying out here on this awful boat, feeling like death and being fired at . . . All she wanted was to be warm, dry and safe again.

The sound of the plane's engine came softly over the water, a faint buzz gathering into a deep drone as it approached once more. Julie crouched down beside Peter. This time the plane did not fire, but swooped straight over the boat. Everyone froze where they lay, listening and watching, but it flew straight on, heading into the distance until, no more than a small black speck near the horizon, it was lost in the low grey cloud.

'And good riddance!' It was the skipper. He was smiling broadly and talking excitedly. As he spoke, a few people cheered and someone cried again, 'Vive la France Libre.' Some of the passengers still looked unhappy and a few were arguing. But then, Julie thought, there were bound to be some people who didn't like turning back. It was inevitable. Well, at least they weren't about to die out here, shot like rabbits or drowned. That was something to be grateful for.

The skipper strode into the wheelhouse and Julie sank

back on to the rope coil. Her teeth were chattering so loudly she had to clench her jaws to stop the noise. She remembered the clothes again. She really should make the effort to get them, but her mind was frozen and numb. It was rather nice, the numbness, like a dream. Nothing seemed very important any more, nothing except sleeping and lying here . . .

The bow hit a wave and water splattered and sloshed over the deck. People complained again. Then there was another wave and, as the bow fell fast, down into the void, Julie felt herself and Peter almost lifted off the deck.

Suddenly Julie was awake. Why were they hitting waves again? What had happened? She staggered to her feet and looked for the land. It was *behind* them. They had turned again. They were heading back towards England.

No, Julie thought, it's the wrong thing to do. Wrong.

Suddenly she was angry and frightened. She swayed down the deck again and opened the wheelhouse door. The skipper was at the wheel, a cigarette clamped between his teeth.

Julie asked, 'Why? Why have we turned back?'

The skipper glanced at her. 'Because, dear lady, we are going to England. And no stupid Boches are going to make me change my mind! That's why.'

'But what if they come back? They'll shoot us.'

'Don't worry your head about that.'

'But I do – we must. People could get hurt.'

The skipper drew hard on his cigarette and looked at her through narrowed eyes. 'Look, we go on. And that's final. Now go back on deck.'

'But what does everyone else want? Aren't they worried too?'

'Look, lady, we go on, all right? You wanted to go to England, didn't you? Well, it's a bit late to change your mind. I can see the problem – you're wet, you're sick, and it all seems a bad idea now. Well, you ladies are never happy at sea, but I'm afraid you're just going to have to put up with it. We go on!' He shook his head knowingly. 'That plane won't come back again, I know it!'

For a moment Julie didn't trust herself to speak. His attitude was exasperating. How did he know the plane wouldn't come back? It seemed highly likely to Julie that it would come back and soon.

She made an effort to pull herself together and said, 'But suppose the plane *does* come back . . . What then?'

The skipper turned and shouted down into the small cabin below, 'Someone! Show this lady back on to the deck!'

Julie found herself shaking with anger and tiredness. She tried to calm herself. 'Don't worry, I'm going. But please, my son and I, we're wet and cold . . . do you have anything warm . . .?' She trailed off.

'Here.' He passed her a jacket from a peg on the side of the wheelhouse. He looked at her pityingly and added, 'If it gets much worse we'll see if we can find your child a place in the cabin.'

Julie's anger melted away and she nodded with gratitude. 'Thank you.'

She wiped a hand over her face, put the jacket on and started the long awkward journey back to the bow. Halfway along the deck she waited a moment while spray flew across the boat, then, when the coast was clear, she set out on the last few yards. But before she reached the protection of the bow she felt the thud of the boat meeting a wave and a curtain of spray rose into the air in front of her. The water looked insubstantial but when it hit her it was like something solid, as if a powerful man had slapped her in the face. The force took her breath away and for a moment she almost lost her footing.

She gripped the rail more firmly and hurried into the shelter of the bow. The jacket had kept some of the water off her clothes but now an ice-cold river of seawater was streaming down her back. She said, 'Oh God!' and gritted her teeth as she lay down beside Peter and pulled him inside the jacket.

Despite the jacket she found herself shivering violently. Peter was still cold too; his skin was cool against her cheek. She found herself praying: Dear Lord, please let this end soon, please let it be over, please get us there *quickly*. But she knew it was hopeless; the journey had only just begun. They must be only ten or fifteen miles from the coast, and the English Channel was at least eighty – or was it a hundred miles wide? She couldn't remember. However far, it would take hours, all night and most of the next day at least. She couldn't even imagine that amount of time.

The plane came back half an hour later.

This time it did not bother to circle. It started firing straight away. The noise was much louder this time; the staccato rat-at-at of the bullets seemed to fill the boat. There were loud pings, too, and the sound of tearing wood. As the plane roared overhead someone screamed, a piercing and dreadful scream. It was a man; he was clutching his stomach, a look of horror on his face. Julie found herself staring: she had never heard a man screaming before.

Peter was sobbing, 'Mummy, Mummy! What's happening?'

Julie hugged him tight, then something caught the corner of her eye. It was the plane. She could see it banking behind the boat, then levelling up. It was coming in for another run. It was heading straight for her. Straight for Peter.

She looked around desperately. There was nowhere to hide, nothing . . . Just the winch.

It might just be big enough.

She pulled Peter to his feet and yanked him across the deck. He tripped and the deadweight of his body pulled at her shoulder. He was crying now. She gripped him under the arms and swung him in behind the winch. She crouched in front of him and put her arms round him. She tried to make herself as narrow as possible. The winch base was about two feet wide: she had the feeling her shoulders must be sticking out . . .

As she put her head down the din started. This time it was deafening: the clanging of metal, the whistle and thud of the bullets. There was another scream and several shouts.

The seconds stretched out endlessly. She heard each bullet as it hissed and thudded around her. She waited for the one that would tear into her body.

It never came.

In a roar of engines the plane was overhead and gone again. And they were both alive. Julie whispered into Peter's hair, 'Oh my darling, my little darling. It's all right, it's all right.'

She looked at him, at his big round frightened eyes, and said, 'Now, stay here. Right here, do you understand? I'll be back in a moment.'

Peter screamed, 'No! Mummy, don't go! Don't go!'

But Julie was already on her feet. '*Stay there!*'

She ran down the deck and straight into the wheelhouse. When she opened the door she was almost sick. Two men were lying on the floor: one had a terrible red oozing mass of brains and bloody flesh instead of a face. The other was the skipper. His eyes were staring straight at her, sightless and also quite dead.

She gulped and forced her eyes up to the man at the wheel. He was staring at her, his mouth gaping and his eyes dazed.

Julie said firmly, 'Turn round! Turn towards the land!'

He stared back, his mouth moving noiselessly.

Julie drew breath and said again, 'Turn now or we'll all be dead!'

The buzz of the plane was getting louder again. Julie

reached over and started to turn the wheel. The man's eyes suddenly focused and his hands fumbled at the wheel too.

The boat began to turn, but slowly, so slowly. The noise of the engines was getting much louder again.

Julie sobbed, 'Oh *please, please.*'

At last the boat was turning more quickly.

The plane roared over. There were no bullets this time.

They were going to be all right.

Julie waited to see that the helmsman was keeping the boat on course, then closed the wheelhouse door and walked quickly back to Peter.

They were going home.

Perhaps, Julie thought, we were never meant to go away at all.

The boat couldn't get up the river; it was low tide. Instead they picked up a mooring off a small fishing village at the top of the estuary, where it narrows into the Morlaix River. The dead were covered with canvas and left on board, the living were ferried ashore in a small rowing boat.

As they waited their turn for the boat Julie stood at the rail with Peter in her arms, looking at the quiet, golden land and thinking it was like a dream. There in the shelter of the river the air was warm and languid; a perfect summer day. The afternoon sun burned hot on her back, warming her slowly, deliciously. Like a dream. It was hard to imagine that the appalling boat trip belonged to the same day.

At last it was Julie and Peter's turn to go ashore. They squeezed in the back of the dinghy next to a young man. Julie recognised him: he was the one who had cried '*Vive la France Libre!*' when they set out. Now there was no laughter in his face; he was silent, staring blankly into the distance ahead.

They landed at a stone slipway. When Julie stepped ashore and felt the solid stone beneath her feet she sighed with relief. The young man passed Peter across and Julie hugged him tightly to her. 'It's all over, darling. It's all over.'

The young man carried their baggage as far as the main road, then left. Julie sat Peter down on a grassy bank and stretched out beside him. For a moment she closed her eyes and let the sun warm her face. The relief of being on dry land was almost as great as the comfort of knowing they were safe. She reached for Peter's hand and said, 'I love you, darling.'

Peter rubbed his eyes. 'Mummy, I'm hungry and I want to go home.'

'Of course, sweetheart. We'll start with some food!'

Julie unpacked the food basket and they ate. She was surprised to find she was ravenous. The two of them consumed a whole section of sausage, a large slice of hard cheese, four chunks of bread, and two apples. It was wonderful to eat in peace and quiet, the land steady beneath one's feet, the wind no more than a slight breeze rustling in the trees.

While they ate Julie began to think. This village was the wrong side of the river for Tregasnou. To get home they would have to go all the way inland to Morlaix and then double back on the other side of the river. It was a long way. The alternative was to find someone to ferry them across the river. But the river was still very wide at this point. And the country on the other side was pretty remote; she wasn't sure if they'd be able to find any transport once they got there.

The thought of home was wonderful. More than anything she wanted to return to the safety of the small grey house. Yet the problem of having a British passport remained. Peter would still be at risk. For his sake perhaps it was wrong to give up so easily. Perhaps she should make another attempt to get away. To Brest: that was where the ships were. Perhaps there'd be a place on one of them . . .

It was so difficult to decide. In her heart she wanted to stay, yet her main responsibility was to Peter.

She would think about what to do on the way to Morlaix, she suddenly decided. Morlaix was the way home *and* the way to Brest. Yes, she would make up her mind there.

One thing was soon clear: if they wanted to get into the town they would have to walk. While they had been eating only one car had come out of the village and, though Julie had stood up and waved, it hadn't stopped. There was a bus stop, but the next bus wasn't due for another two hours. If it came at all.

As soon as they finished eating Julie stood up. It was six in the evening; they must get to town before dark. The bags were a problem: she hadn't packed very much, but there was still too much to carry. She took the essential clothes and crammed them into one suitcase, leaving the other by the roadside. She wrapped the remaining food in some paper and put it in her raincoat pocket. Now she had one case, her handbag – and Peter.

She wondered how far a four-year-old could walk before he got tired. One thing was sure: it wouldn't be as far as Morlaix.

He was very good to begin with, marching well, his little arms swinging back and forth. Then, after twenty minutes, he began to flag. Their pace slowed. After another fifteen minutes Peter said, 'Mummy, please can we stop? I'm so tired.'

Julie smiled down at him. 'Of course, darling. We'll stop for a minute.' They sat at the roadside. When they started off again, Julie tried to make a game of it, pretending they were soldiers marching off to save Morlaix from ferocious bandits. It worked for a while, then Peter flagged again.

For a while Julie half carried, half pulled him along. Later she put him on her shoulders, though the extra weight made her arms and back shoot with pain, and she often had to stop and catch her breath. Her feet were agony and she cursed herself for wearing unsuitable shoes. But then hiking hadn't been part of the plan.

In the end it took three hours to do the twelve kilometres. The bus never came; Julie'd had a feeling it wouldn't.

When finally they arrived in Morlaix it was strangely quiet, the streets empty of people, the shops and restaurants shut and boarded. Only a few bars were open, their customers peering furtively out as if they were expecting the Germans at any second. Perhaps they are, thought Julie. She didn't honestly care. She sat on a bench near the port, her head back and her legs outstretched, and Peter cuddled against her side. She decided that whatever happened they would go no further tonight.

She thought of going to her employer's house. He lived on the edge of town, a ten minute walk away. Or there was a girl who worked in her office who had an apartment nearby. Or there was Michel.

Michel would know the best thing to do; she would go to Michel. She knew the building he lived in; it was five minutes away. She looked at Peter: he was asleep. She left him on the bench for a moment and looked for a place to leave the case. In the end she left it under a parked van. If anyone drove the van off, it was too bad.

She took Peter in her arms and walked. The rest on the bench had been a mistake: it had given her feet a chance to swell up and the blisters to weep. She stopped, kicked off her shoes and tucked them into the top of her handbag. It was a great improvement.

When she reached the apartment building the door was locked and a ring on the *concierge*'s bell produced no answer. There were individual bells for each apartment.

Beside each bell was a number but no name. She didn't
know which apartment was Michel's, so she pressed them
all. At last a man opened the door. It wasn't Michel, but
he let her in and told her which apartment she wanted.

When she reached the apartment door there was no
answer to her knock, so with Peter fast asleep in her arms,
she sat outside the door and waited.

He came back at eleven.

When he saw her, he stared.

She smiled stupidly at him and said, 'Thank you for
coming back.'

When she first woke up she couldn't remember where she
was. The room was dark and shuttered and she couldn't
make out its features. Then she remembered and, hugging
Peter's warm body closer to her, closed her eyes and slept
again.

Later she was woken by someone opening the shutters.
Brilliant sunshine streamed into the room and she screwed
up her eyes against the light. She was lying on the sofa
where she'd sat on her arrival the night before. She hadn't
had the energy to move, though Michel had offered to take
the sofa and give her his bed.

Now he was beside her, holding out a cup of coffee. He
was frowning. 'I found your case all right.'

Julie exclaimed, 'Oh! I'd forgotten about it!' Then said
hurriedly, 'Thank you.'

Michel nodded briefly. 'Now, there isn't much time, so
we've got to hurry.'

Julie stared at him. 'What do you mean?'

'I mean that the Germans are almost here. They'll arrive
some time today. At least that's my interpretation of the
complete black-out on news. There's nothing on the wireless except people telling us to keep calm. That *must* mean
we're for it!' He spoke with a bitter smile.

Peter was waking up, rubbing his eyes and looking round at the strange room.

Julie said, 'Then – should we go to Brest? Get on a ship?'

Michel laughed. 'Hah! There is nothing but good French chaos there.' He shook his head. 'A friend has just come back. He told me all about it. Evidently there are thousands of people at the port all trying to get on ships that do not exist. The military got away all right, then they started to let civilians on the few remaining ships. Some got away, but one large ship had a collision with a naval boat and sank. Right there, just outside Brest.' He lit a cigarette. 'Now? Well, there are no ships left, apparently. Just people trying to hide, running round in circles because there's nowhere to go. They also say that it's as black as night all day long. The fuel dumps at Maison Blanche were set on fire. It sounds like Dante's *Inferno*!'

Julie shivered. Thank God she hadn't gone there. She was frightened by crowds and disorder. That's what she'd hated most on the boat, the hysteria, the loss of control when the plane had fired on them.

She said calmly, 'Then I shall go home.'

'Yes. But first we have work to do—' He indicated that she should get to her feet. 'Comb your hair, change your dress. We're going out.'

He was so firm, so definite, that it never occurred to her to question him. Instead she looked at herself. She *did* look dreadful. Quickly she washed, tidied her hair and put on a clean dress. She changed Peter's shirt and trousers, gave him a *tartine* of bread and jam to chew on, and came back into the living room. 'We're ready.'

Michel stuffed his wallet into the back pocket of his trousers and led the way out. She followed, pulling Peter along with her. Michel walked fast and Julie had to pick Peter up and half-run to keep up with him. She was too breathless to ask where they were going.

They turned a corner, then another, until they came to
some double doors set in a high stone wall. Michel took
out a key and, unlocking the padlock, swung open one of
the doors. He brought out a *vélo*.

He locked the door again and said, 'Hop on.'

The little motor coughed into life and they were off,
Michel bicycling furiously to get up speed and Peter
giggling with delight on Julie's lap.

In contrast to the night before, the streets were busy this
morning, people hurrying everywhere with baskets and
bags in their hands. There were long queues outside the
boulangeries and the *charcuteries* again. After a few minutes they came into a square and stopped. Michel got off.
He jerked his head in the direction of a large building and
said briefly, 'We're going in there.' Julie recognised it
immediately: it was the *Sous-Préfecture*.

She followed Michel in. Inside there was chaos: people
were milling around, rushing from office to office, shouting, looking harassed. All the doors were open, showing
empty desks and stacks of papers. Two women were going
towards the main door carrying boxes. One said to Julie in
amazement, 'These are all to be burnt! I ask you – burnt!'
Michel lifted Peter into his arms and took Julie's hand. He
led her up the stairs and along a corridor with numerous
doors leading off it. He looked at the labels on the doors
and finally said, 'Ha, here we are!'

The office was empty. Michel gave Peter to Julie, went
straight in and started searching the drawers and filing
cabinets. Julie stared in astonishment. 'Michel!' she
exclaimed. 'Stop! Stop! What are you *doing*? Someone
might come!'

There was an old safe sitting on the floor in the corner.
Michel tried the handle. It was locked. He told Julie to
wait and left the room. Julie sat down and tried to work
out what was happening. Why had Michel brought her

here? What was all this to do with her? In a moment Michel was back. With him was a woman. The woman went to the safe and opened it with a key from a large ring hanging on her belt. She nodded at Michel, said, 'It's a pleasure,' and left. She didn't even look at Julie.

Whatever was going on, the woman was in on it too. Julie took Peter off her knee and stood up. 'Michel, please tell me what's going on!'

Michel grunted, 'Here we are!' He took two cards off the top of a pile and passed them to Julie. 'Start to fill one in, will you? The second's just a spare. I must go and make sure your name vanishes from the Aliens Registration and appears on all the voting lists.'

Julie stared at the cards. They were identity cards. They were blank.

Michel was disappearing down the passage. Julie ran and called after him, 'Michel, I may be down under the name of Howard as well as Lescaux!'

He waved an acknowledgement and vanished into another doorway.

Shaking her head, Julie went back and sat at the desk. Suddenly she smiled. Peter looked up at her and asked, 'Happy Mummy?'

She grinned down at him. 'Yes, very happy Mummy!'

She looked at the blank card and thought carefully. After a moment she began to write in some of the details. She kept her name, Lescaux, and entered her father's name correctly. But instead of her mother's name she put 'Jeannette Lescaux'. For her mother's maiden name she put 'Leforge' because it was the first name that came into her head. Under the heading 'Name Before Marriage' she put nothing. To pretend to be married would complicate matters. She slipped the second identity card into her handbag.

She sat back and smiled at Peter. Then her eye caught

the safe. It was still open, the pile of blank identity cards visible at the front of the shelf. On an impulse Julie reached in and took a batch off the top.

She stuffed them into her bag, her heart beating furiously. It was rather risky. But why *not* take them? They might be useful. She had never stolen anything in her life before.

Michel came back. He looked at her new card, nodded, and looked through the rubber stamps on the desk. He found the one he wanted, picked it up, inked it and stamped her new card. He then inked her thumb and pressed it on the space left for thumbprints. 'And again. Here.' He pressed her thumb on an official form. It was an application for an identity card.

Julie whispered. 'You're a magician!'

Michel shrugged, but Julie could see he was pleased.

'How on earth did you *do* it though? I mean, why did that woman open the safe for us?'

'Oh I told her the Germans would torture and kill you if we couldn't find you a proper identity.'

Julie shook her head. 'You're amazing!' And I mean that, she thought. She added, 'I owe you a debt of gratitude. I hope I can repay you one day.'

'It's nothing. Anyway—' he looked into her eyes '– it is an honour to do it for you.'

Julie blushed and stood up. Perhaps – perhaps she'd been wrong. Perhaps she had misjudged him and he was rather nice after all.

Her eye caught the rubber stamp. 'Are there two of those?'

'Why?'

'I want one, that's all.'

Michel looked at her in surprise. 'Good God, what for?'

'I don't know . . . just in case, I suppose.'

He handed her the stamp. 'Just don't get caught with it, that's all.'

They walked quickly down the passage and out of the building. By the *vélo* Michel asked, 'Can you drive one of these things?'

'I think so, but – what about you?'

'I have things to do. You drive back to Tregasnou. I'll deliver your suitcase and pick the machine up another time.' He glanced nervously round the square and Julie suddenly thought: He's going to stir up trouble somewhere. She said, 'Do be careful. You're not going to do anything silly are you?'

'My friends and I have got to make our plans, that's all.'

Julie looked at Michel with admiration: already he was making plans against the Germans, arranging meetings, doing something positive. She said, 'I won't ask what you're planning. But whatever you do, be careful. Don't risk your neck! And good luck!'

'What?' He looked at her in mild surprise.

'I mean, the Germans . . . they might catch you . . .' She trailed off, uncertain.

'Ha! I won't be going in for cheap heroics, if that's what you mean. I'm not going to risk my neck. Quite the opposite. I think the Germans and I might get on very well.'

Julie blinked. 'What do you mean?'

Michel leant over the bike until his face was close to hers. 'My dear, I'm with whoever rids us of the scum corrupting this country – the right-wing dictators who've robbed the working people of their rightful inheritance for more than a hundred years. I'm for whoever's against them!'

'But you're not going to work *with* the Germans?'

He shrugged. 'Who knows? It depends what there is to be gained.'

'But they're overrunning our country. They're – enemies!'

'Yes, but they won't stay for ever. And after the war – *after* – there'll be a chance to build a new state, a people's state. In fact, it's the best chance we've ever had to sweep the system clean!'

Julie got silently on to the *vélo*, lifting Peter up in front of her. Michel untied a piece of cord attached to the small luggage rack and gave it to Julie. 'Here, you'll need this to keep Peter on.' Julie took it and looped it round both her own and Peter's waists, then tied a knot.

Michel was saying, 'You shouldn't meet any Germans yet. But do watch out for planes. If you hear one, make for the ditch, and fast.' He took her face in his hands and without warning kissed her firmly on the lips.

Julie didn't move or respond. While he kissed her she stared at the side of his head and his closed eyes and thought: Why did I ever think I might like this man?

Michel stood back and said, 'Juliette, keep yourself safe for me, won't you?'

Julie stared at the ground then looked up at him. She said, 'No!' and saw a look of surprise on Michel's face. 'Look, I owe you a big favour which I will try to repay one day. But while you ... you play your dirty games, forget anything else. Especially friendship! How you can consider dealing with the Germans is ... beyond me!'

He was annoyed. 'You just don't understand.'

'That's right, I don't. Goodbye, Michel.'

She pedalled slowly away, wobbling slightly as she got her balance.

He was shouting. 'I'll send your suitcase over when I can.'

She didn't turn round but pedalled rapidly until the motor fired.

Peter squealed with excitement. 'Mummy, we're going so fast!'

Julie didn't answer. She was thinking about Michel. How could he? How *could* he? Whatever one believed it must be wrong to actually *help* the enemy. That would mean helping to prolong the war. It might even mean helping to kill one's fellow countrymen. As she rode along she shook her head and muttered in disbelief. God only knew what Tante Marie would say when she heard . . .

The thought of Tante Marie and the small grey-stone house cheered her up. She bent slightly and briefly kissed Peter's head.

Peter's small voice came floating up. 'Mummy, are we going home?'

Julie said firmly, 'Oh yes, darling! We're going home.'

Chapter 9

AT LAST A tender came into sight, nosing its way round the end of the distant pier and heading towards the warship anchored in the middle of the large natural harbour. Although the harbour was well protected from the rolling Channel seas and long Atlantic swells, a blustery west wind was funnelling between the hills, creating an unpleasant little chop which made the tender roll slightly as it progressed steadily across the water.

Richard Ashley watched it approach and thought longingly of sleep. He'd snatched only a couple of catnaps in the last thirty-six hours and now he was dog-tired. It would be sensible to go back to his bunk and turn in. But he couldn't bring himself to do it. An evening's run ashore was not something to be given up lightly, not when you'd gone without leave for three weeks. And particularly when the leave was here in Falmouth.

The place had happy memories for him – of sailing here in *Dancer*, first, in the early days, with his father, then later with friends from Dartmouth. Once, though, he had come here alone. He'd been on passage to the Scillies, and Falmouth, being the most westerly port on the English mainland, had been the last stopping place before setting out on the final sixty miles of open sea. He remembered that holiday among the beautiful, bleak Scillies with especial fondness.

A group of ratings clustered at the rail, waiting

impatiently for the tender. For them, Falmouth was just another port with another lot of pubs.

Not that pubs weren't a consideration for Ashley too. He enjoyed drinking. Just as he enjoyed the other opportunities ashore. In his wallet he had the telephone number of a girl he vaguely knew who lived not far away. He would take her out to dinner if she were free. It had been well over a month since he'd spent an evening with a girl.

A night out would cheer him up. Like everyone else in the ship he needed it. They'd had a rotten couple of months. After Dunkirk they'd started convoywork, escorting ships along the south coast and through the Dover Straits, fighting off increasingly heavy air attacks. By the end of July they were losing ships at an alarming rate and, when three destroyers were lost in the space of a few days, the Admiralty was forced to abandon day-time passages through the eastern half of the Channel. Now even the western Channel was difficult. On this last convoy, which had been westward bound, they had been attacked by Stukas south of the Isle of Wight and had lost a horrifying five ships before the attack had been driven off. It seemed to Ashley that, ever since Dunkirk, the Navy was being forced inexorably out of the Channel.

The tender was closer now, and turning in a long slow arc which would bring it neatly alongside the destroyer. Ashley put his face up to the blustery west wind and breathed deeply, willing himself to wake up.

'God, they're not letting you loose too, are they, Ashley?'

He turned and saw Blythe, the gunnery officer, also in best shore-going uniform.

Ashley smiled. 'Of course. Begged me to go actually.' He thought how trite and out of place the old jokes sounded now, yet one trotted them out as a matter of course, to maintain a feeling of normality.

Blythe said, 'Want to join forces? I thought of sampling the ale in a few of the local establishments.'

Ashley watched the tender bump alongside and considered. An evening with Blythe would be ruinous. The two of them had been out drinking together once before and ended up speechless and legless on the floor of a hotel ballroom in Weymouth. His hangover had lasted two days.

He chuckled at the memory. 'Just a quick one then. But I won't be able to stay long.'

'Aha!' Blythe gave him a steely glare. 'A woman, is it?'

Ashley grinned enigmatically and started down the gangway to where the tender was waiting, already crowded with the ratings who, anxious to start their precious leave, had swarmed aboard the moment it came alongside.

As the two men took their seats the boat drew away and Ashley turned to get a good view of the forward bulwarks, where a damage repair party was working on a series of dented, hole-peppered plates. A gunner had died up there during the last air attack. Although they'd been at war for a year, it was the first time Ashley had seen a man die at close quarters. The scene was still vivid in his mind.

He shook his head and muttered to Blythe in an undertone, 'You feel so damned ineffectual.' Blythe nodded; he knew exactly what Ashley meant. In company with another destroyer they had been trying to protect fourteen ships against a dozen or more enemy aircraft: an unpleasantly one-sided fight.

Ashley added, 'Let's hope the RAF have some more luck soon.' The Battle of Britain had been raging for a couple of months and still the bombers came, against convoys, against ports and military establishments and, increasingly now, against cities and civilian targets.

The tender buffeted its way up-wind towards the town nestling comfortably in the lee of a hill, its buildings rising haphazardly from the water's edge. Eventually they came to the small-boat moorings, where coastal patrol boats, oyster smacks and the occasional yacht lay swinging to the tide.

Suddenly Ashley peered ahead. An MFV – a motor fishing vessel – lay close under the town. She was painted dull grey and had obviously been requisitioned as an inshore patrol boat. Yet there was something unusual about her, something that didn't quite fit. For a moment he couldn't place what it was, but then, as the trawler came into full view, he had it.

The vessel was French. It was nothing definite, nothing you could tie down. But her lines and the long canoe stern definitely looked more Breton than Cornish. As the tender passed astern of her, Ashley saw someone come out of the deckhouse and saunter to the rail. He was wearing plain overalls and was bare-headed. A cigarette hung from his lower lip in the Gallic manner.

Ashley had seen French fishing boats in England before – everyone had. They had been appearing regularly since the fall of France in June, three months before. But this was the first time he had seen one under the white ensign. He wondered if the crewman on deck had been a French fisherman and, if so, how he liked Naval discipline. Not, he guessed, very much at all.

The tender came alongside a stone quay. Ashley was the first off, running up the steps two at a time and striding away across the cobblestones. Blythe was panting when he caught up with him. 'Gosh, what's the hurry, old man?'

'I spied a pub, Blythe, and I didn't want it to get away.' In truth he had been in a hurry to feel the land under his feet and he had run up the steps for the sheer pleasure of it. Like most people who loved the sea, he hated to spend too long on it and, after a few weeks, felt desperate for the land again.

Blythe laughed and followed Ashley up a narrow street and into the saloon bar of a pub with a low door and thick oak beams. Ashley knew immediately that it was the sort of pub he liked – old, rather dowdy and, most important of all, unpretentious. It would be very easy to stay here all evening and drink several pints too many. Instead, he had just one pint and went out to find the nearest telephone box.

He called his parents first, at their home in Hampshire. As always, his mother was light-hearted and gay. She considered it bad form to mention any anxieties she might have about her family, and always made a point of imparting only good or amusing news, usually about one of her many dogs. His father, now back in the Navy at a desk job after more than ten years' retirement, was more serious, and listened attentively to his son's news, limited though it was by the constraints of secrecy. When the conversation was over, Ashley put the telephone down with regret. He liked his parents very much.

Then he called the girl.

He'd met her twice, once at a party given by his sister and once when staying with an old schoolfriend. She was a good-looker in a cool English sort of way. She was the sort who liked riding and hunting and going to dances. She wasn't exactly a ball of fire, he remembered, and she certainly wouldn't offer him more than a kiss on the cheek – but she might be quite fun all the same.

She was at home when he called, and in her cool voice said that yes, she would like to come out to dinner very much. She would borrow her father's car and meet him in an hour.

He walked back to the pub to find that it had filled up considerably. He spotted Blythe at the bar, well into another drink, and made his way through the crowd towards him. Ashley felt far less tired now; he decided he was in the mood for a party. He slapped Blythe on the back and grinned. Blythe nodded briefly then returned to the discussion he was having with two men, one a balding, overweight civilian wearing the armband of the Auxiliary Fire Service, the other a silver-haired merchant navy officer. For a change, they were talking about the war.

With a sigh, Ashley settled down to listen. The AFS man was wagging his finger vehemently. 'They'll invade before the end of the month, mark my words. The bombing of London and the ports – that's just to soften us up, you know. As soon as they've knocked the RAF out of the sky, then they'll be on their way!'

Ashley interrupted brightly, 'Hello', and introduced himself to the two men. They shook hands.

Blythe resumed, 'But the Jerries won't be able to do that. Knock the RAF out of the sky, I mean.'

'But they will – they are!' the AFS man insisted. 'Oh, the BBC tell us it's all going all right, but you don't want to believe them, you know. They just tell us what they want us to believe.'

A professional pessimist, Ashley noted. He interrupted lightly, 'Now, old chap, that sort of talk isn't going to win the war, is it?'

'That's as may be, but we might as well face facts!'

Ashley smiled charmingly at him. 'Then what do you suggest we do to stop the Germans coming?'

'Ha! Not much we can do now. It's too damn late.' The AFS man tutted with contempt and took another sip from his drink.

The merchant seaman looked thoughtful and said, 'I still don't understand how France went under so quickly . . . I just don't understand even now.'

The AFS man dropped his glass to the bar with a bang. 'I'll tell you why – because the Frenchies aren't fighting men, that's why. In fact, they ran backwards the moment they saw the first German tank.'

Ashley felt the adrenalin pump into his blood. He said coolly, 'That's not true.'

'Well, they didn't put up much of a fight, did they?'

'Incorrect, old boy. They held Dunkirk while we got out. They fought all the way.'

The AFS man was determined to press on. 'But if they fought so hard, how did the Jerries get from Paris to Brest in five days, eh?' He turned to Blythe and laughed. 'Seems mighty strange, doesn't it?'

Blythe looked nervously towards Ashley and muttered, 'Er, how about another drink . . .?'

Ashley knew he should turn away and laugh it off, but he couldn't. After a moment's pause he said in a low voice, 'You're speaking about friends of mine.'

The AFS man shrugged a little. 'Well, facts are facts, and when the invasion comes it'll be no thanks to the French.'

'Nor, I'm sure, to you!'

'Now look here—!'

Blythe tugged at Ashley's sleeve. 'Er, how about another pub, Richard? Come on, it's just not worth it.'

Ashley looked into the AFS man's belligerent piglike eyes and knew Blythe was right. With an enormous effort he closed his mouth and, putting his drink on the bar, turned to leave.

At the last moment he couldn't resist a parting shot. He leant towards the man and whispered, 'When you're next fighting a fire, careful you don't get your hose up the wrong passage!' He turned and pushed his way quickly through the press of bodies to the cold freshness of the street.

He heard Blythe come up behind him and said half to himself, 'Slow strangulation for that one. I could cheerfully kill types like that.'

'I agree.'

'Murder by degrees.'

'Yes, but it's never worth it . . .'

Suddenly it all seemed rather ridiculous and Ashley

laughed out loud. 'No, it could be the ruination of my brilliantly promising career!'

Blythe smiled with relief. 'Not to mention your prospects.'

Ashley chuckled. He could laugh now, but his future in the Navy had been a touchy point until the war. He'd blotted his copy book by answering an admiral back in something less than respectful terms. He knew Blythe had heard about it – everyone had – and now he enjoyed making a feature of it. It gave him the reputation of being rather a devil in the wardroom.

Blythe said cheerfully, 'How about going to another boozer? There's the Admiral Something-or-another up the hill.'

'No.' Ashley suddenly felt tired again. More drinking wouldn't help. 'I've other plans. I'll see you tomorrow.'

Blythe winked. 'Aha! Tender loving care, is it? Good luck!' With a quick wave, he walked off up the hill.

Ashley looked at the time. He still had half an hour before meeting the girl. He decided to wander down to the water, to rid himself of the last taste of the unpleasantness in the pub.

The moment he stepped back onto the quay he was glad he had come. The early evening sunlight had ripened into a warm yellowy gold, illuminating the soft purple-green Cornish hills with a mantle of vibrant colour. Looking across to Flushing, its small cottages gleaming white above the water's edge, and watching the small-craft catch the golden light as they swung quietly and obediently to their moorings, it was difficult to imagine losing all this to the Germans. More than that, it was unthinkable. And if, like the AFS man, one ever started to believe it, then that was the beginning of the end.

He thought again: Nasty little man. And determined to forget about him.

He walked idly along the length of the quay and paused.

Jutting out from the maze of houses and workshops that lined the waterfront there were a number of quays and jetties, with harbour craft and fishing vessels tied alongside. Against one, he could just make out the masts and upper-works of what looked like a grey MFV.

Ashley stared for a moment, then, carefully gauging the distance, walked up to the main street and made his way along it until he guessed he was above the boat. Then, at the first alley, he cut down towards the water again.

It was the right quay. The MFV lay close against the wall beside a fuel pump.

He went closer. It was the French boat all right. He took a long look at her. She was in good condition, the grey paint bright and fresh on her sides and the sails clean and neatly furled. The original fishing gear had been left intact: on the main deck there were two large winches for hauling the nets and against the bulwarks on the afterdeck, two trawl boards.

There was no-one about. Ashley crouched on his heels and called down.

After a few moments a face appeared at the window of the deckhouse. The face watched Ashley to see if he would go away and, seeing that he wasn't going to, emerged reluctantly on to the deck. It was the man Ashley had spotted from the tender. He was still wearing overalls and smoking. He raised his eyebrows.

Ashley smiled. 'Hello. Just wondered where the boat came from originally.'

There was a frown of puzzlement.

Ashley took a guess and, switching to his inadequate French, tried again.

'Ah!' the man nodded. 'Concarneau!'

Ashley smiled to himself; he'd been right about the boat then. Concarneau was on the south coast of Brittany and a well-known fishing harbour. Ashley had been there once. He said so and the Frenchman nodded slowly and smiled.

Ashley wanted to say how hospitable the people had been and how much he'd enjoyed it, but his French wasn't up to it. Instead he said that the town was very nice.

He would have liked to know what the boat was doing nowadays but, since the beginning of the war, one didn't ask questions like that. Instead he asked, 'And where did you go to fish . . . er . . . before?'

'On the banks.'

'A long way?' Ashley gestured to show what he meant.

The man shrugged. 'Away four days or so.'

Someone else appeared from the deckhouse. An RNVR lieutenant, dressed in uniform jacket and battered cap. He smiled up at Ashley. 'Evening. What can we do for you?'

Ashley switched back to English with relief. 'Just interested to see a Concarneau boat after all this time.'

'Ah. You know Concarneau?' With surprise Ashley realised the lieutenant wasn't English; there was a slight accent that was almost but not quite American.

He replied, 'I've sailed around there.'

The lieutenant nodded politely. 'In a small boat?'

'A sloop. Smallish. Twenty-five feet overall.'

'Very nice. You cruised a lot?'

'Yes, most of Normandy and Brittany.'

There was a pause. The lieutenant asked, 'What ship now?'

'Destroyer. A bit more solid underfoot.'

The lieutenant smiled. Ashley stood up. 'Well, I must be going now.' He said to the fisherman, '*Au revoir! Bonne chance!*' And, waving to the lieutenant, turned to go.

'Hey, wait a moment.' The officer vanished behind the wall and, after a few seconds, appeared over the top of the ladder. 'Look, er, how about coming aboard for a drink this evening?'

Ashley looked at his watch. He was late already. 'Sorry, got to dash.'

'Perhaps later then?'

Ashley hesitated. 'Where do you come from?'

'I'm a French-Canadian, from Quebec. But then you speak French too, don't you?'

Ashley threw back his head and laughed. 'Exceptionally badly!'

The Canadian smiled but his eyes were serious. He asked for Ashley's name, then said, 'Try and drop by later. I'd like to show you the boat.'

'I'll do my best.' Ashley waved again and walked off, glancing briefly over the boat as he left.

When he was half way up the main street he stopped in his tracks. There was something wrong with that MFV.

He walked on, not quite certain what it was. It was only when he got to the hotel where he was due to meet the girl that it came to him. That boat was going to make a rotten patrol boat.

It had no guns.

The girl was beautiful, well-bred and boring. Ashley wouldn't have minded if she'd had a sense of humour, but if she had one, it was well hidden. Nor would he have minded if she'd been especially attractive. But she was too cool for that. Making love to her would be like embracing a cucumber – a distinctly one-sided experience.

He decided he must be getting more discerning in his old age. A few years ago he wouldn't have cared what a woman's conversation was like if she was as lovely as this one. But now he was more particular. He liked his women warm, attractive and – what? Funny, earthy, capable of laughter. And this one most definitely was not.

By nine the conversation was drifting aimlessly and Ashley found himself drinking too much. By ten he was bored and restless.

When she started talking about the problems of finding

young men to come to the austerity dance that her father was giving for her in London, Ashley knew he had to get away. He made a show of looking at his watch and said he had to be back at his ship at eleven, which was not quite true.

The moment he'd seen her off he felt a wonderful relief. There was still a good hour before the last boat left, still time to have some fun. He sauntered down the dark main street, wondering whether to go in search of Blythe. Almost immediately he decided against it. He could drink with Blythe any time.

Instead he made his way down to the water again, going carefully because of the blackout. After a while he heard the sound of lapping water and knew he must be nearing the edge of the quay. The dark outlines of a vessel showed black against the night. It was the MFV, riding high on the top of the tide.

He called across. After a moment there was a sound and a voice challenged him. He recognised it as the Canadian's and said, 'It's Ashley. I've come to claim that drink!'

The Canadian said, 'I thought you might.'

Ashley climbed on board and followed the other man down the companionway. Once below, the Canadian led the way forward into a wardroom which must originally have been the fish hold – and quite recently, Ashley guessed; the place still reeked of fish. Now there were two wooden bunks, a centre table, and an oil lamp hanging from the deckhead.

'Very nice!'

'Not bad considering this was a working boat just a few months ago.' the Canadian put out his hand and smiled. 'My name's Laperrine, by the way. Have a drink.'

Ashley chose gin and sat down. 'Your crew . . .' he began, 'are they all French?'

'Only the one. The man you met. He – well, he knows his way around and was willing to sign on, so we took him. The rest are British, ex-fishermen mainly.'

'And—' Ashley paused, wondering whether his question would be considered too probing. But what the hell. The drink had made him reckless. He asked, 'Will you be patrolling this part of the coast?'

Laperrine sat down on the opposite side of the table. 'Here ... and hereabouts. Tell me, have you been in destroyers long?'

Ashley wondered what lay behind the question. He replied, 'A couple of years. Before that I did a stint on torpedo boats.'

'You enjoyed that?'

Ashley nodded. 'Yes, very much. Fast, exciting stuff. But with war coming I thought I might not see a lot of action. So I transferred back to proper ships again. Not very popular with the brass!' He laughed.

Laperrine smiled. 'Well, the top speed of this thing is six knots. Not exactly fast and exciting.'

Ashley leant forward. 'But there are compensations?'

The Canadian smiled. 'I think so.'

An infinitesimal shudder of excitement went down Ashley's spine and the effects of the drink cleared from his brain. 'May I ask a leading question? Why don't you have any guns?'

'Ah ... Well, we do.'

'But nothing mounted on deck.'

'No. We keep our weapons out of sight.'

The man was going to tell him more, Ashley was certain of it. Smiling, he pressed, 'Because—?'

Laperrine paused, as if weighing him up. 'You must say nothing – And I only tell you because – well, I think you might be interested.' He took a breath. 'We're going to the other side, to mingle with the fishing fleets off the west coast, to ... exchange things.'

Ashley had guessed it would be something like that. He suppressed a smile of exhilaration. Then he remembered the grey paint. 'But – you can't go like this, surely.'

'Oh no. She'll look just like any other Concarneau trawler by the time we've finished with her.'

Ashley said quickly, 'Go on.'

'There's not much more to it really. We're only just setting up the operation. But we do need more people. To be exact, someone who would command another boat. You would be ... ideal. You know the coast, you know the people and you speak French—'

'Not very well!'

'But you understand it?'

Ashley nodded confidently, as if it were entirely true, which it wasn't. His French was really quite poor. He asked, 'But what about the fishing fleets – surely they're kept under guard?'

'Yes, guard boats go out with the fleets, but the Concarneau trawlers are allowed out for as much as two to three days at a time. It should be easy to slip in amongst them at night.'

Yes, of course it would. Ashley could imagine it. Pretending to fish, closing with the other trawlers, passing arms, receiving information. He could see it all and the idea thrilled him.

He looked up at the Canadian. 'I wouldn't mind knowing more.'

Laperrine smiled because he had been right about Ashley, and because he could see the glint of excitement in the other man's eyes. 'Good. I'll tell the Department.'

They had another drink then Ashley got up to leave. 'By the way, where on earth are you going to take her, to get her repainted?

'Somewhere quiet, away from curious eyes. Our base is to be at Helford. We'll probably do it there.'

The Helford River was just south of Falmouth, a quiet,

beautiful place, but overlooked by a couple of small villages and a number of large houses. Ashley thought: It won't be any good.

He shook his head. 'You should go somewhere more isolated. What about the Scillies? Somewhere like New Grimsby. No-one would ever see you there.'

Laperrine smiled and shook Ashley's hand. 'It sounds a good idea.'

It was late. Ashley had to hurry to catch the last boat back to the ship. As he walked briskly along the dark deserted streets he felt euphoric.

The whole thing was mad. Going over to the other side, masquerading as a working boat, mingling with the fleet under the noses of the Germans. It was the stuff that boys' adventure books were made of, the sort of thing he had loved to read about as a child.

That, he realised, must be why the idea appealed to him so much. He had always suspected that, in some ways, he had never grown up.

He laughed out loud. What the hell did it matter?

He adored the idea, he couldn't resist it. He couldn't wait to be frightened out of his wits and exhilarated at the same time. It was what he'd been waiting for all his life.

Chapter 10

DAVID CURLED HIS body up into the foetal position and thought about a field full of flowers. Flowers got him off to sleep faster than anything else. Some days he didn't need to think of anything, he just fell asleep the moment he lay down on the wooden boards. But when he was in pain it was different. It was usually his stomach which gave him trouble; sometimes the pain was awful. But today it was his knee; heavy rain had made the quarry treacherous and he had fallen heavily, twisting his knee and splitting open the skin. So today he needed to think of something, and it was best to think of flowers.

The sounds of the hut did not bother him. The continuous moaning and sighing, the sounds of suffering, the coughing and rasping of breath did not touch him at all. His ears heard the sounds but his mind cut them out, because his mind did not want to hear them.

He lay still, concentrating on the flowers, ignoring the pain, waiting for the escape into unconsciousness. Sleep was the one thing he looked forward to: it was God-given, miraculous, a gift from heaven. He waited for a long time, and then the sleep came at last, drifting in like fog out of a valley.

His mind was closed to sounds – yet he heard. He heard the sudden clatter of a stick being run along the side of the hut. Everyone heard it. Even before the door of the hut was opened men were getting off the wooden bunks and

standing up, their faces impassive, their eyes staring disin-
terestedly at a point on the opposite wall.

Automatically David climbed down from the flat
wooden shelf that was called a bunk – it was the top tier
of three – and stood in the passage that ran the length of
the hut. He felt nothing, showed nothing. He concentrated
on standing upright despite the pain in his knee.

Two of the *Prominente* marched in, beating their sticks
loudly against the door until all three hundred men were
standing silently. There was no moaning or sighing now;
the *Prominente* beat you if you made too much noise.

'You will wait!'

So they waited. David stared at the wall opposite and
thought of the flowers again. The field was very large and
quite overgrown with tall grass. But rising from the grass
were tall poppies, brilliant red and moving gently in the
breeze. A stronger wind came rippling across the grass,
turning the colour of the grass from green to yellow, and
bowing the poppies' heads over, as if in shame . . .

David liked to concentrate on a different picture each
day. From the moment he reached the quarry in the
morning until he lay down to sleep at night, his body
crying for rest, he liked to develop a picture, to find each
small detail and fit it in place, until the composition was
complete.

Otherwise he did not bother to think at all. Thinking
was a great mistake. Those who thought of their past, of
things they had lost, of families they were unlikely to see
again: those were the ones who suffered.

David had been in Dachau almost a year. Soon after his
arrival he learnt that you survived only by living each
moment as it came, second by second. It was important to
question nothing, challenge nothing, desire nothing. If you
desired such things as freedom, food, clean water, you
simply went mad.

He also learnt not to get angry. He wasn't angry now at

being disturbed from his sleep. Anger was pointless. You just lived each second, each minute as it came . . .

They had taken him first to Sachsenhausen. After two days they put him on a train and transferred him here, to Dachau. They had been the worst, those first few days; afterwards everything had seemed almost bearable. On the train each truck was crammed tightly with people. There was no food or water. When finally the door of the truck was opened and David, blinking in the strong light, saw that some had died and were being piled at the side of the track, he began to realise that you must live each minute, second by second, without thought, without question.

The most difficult thing was understanding the system and the rules – understanding how to survive. Oddly, the SS were the easiest to deal with. They liked order, numbers that tallied and obedience. One could cope with that. On arrival there had been prisoner registration. They had waited, the two thousand Jews off the train, in a long line. They had been allowed to sit until it was their turn to stand and advance to the desk of one of the four clerks sitting in the middle of the central compound. Their names, professions, and the details of their parentage were all carefully typed on forms; they were issued with a number; then they passed on to delousing and uniform issue.

Order and numbers: one could cope with that.

It was the *Prominente*'s rules that were impossible because they had none. They had been hand-picked by Himmler, these *Prominente*, from jails across Germany. They were all serving long sentences, for violent crimes mostly. It was said that the majority had been here since 1933 when Himmler personally created this, his show-piece, his first concentration camp.

The *Prominente* had no rules. They kicked, beat, hacked . . . sometimes they pushed men off the highest point of the quarry and watched them fall to their deaths. If you worked too slowly they might shoot you – or they might drop a heavy stone on your foot, or club you, or beat you round the head. They loved their work, these men. They picked people at random. You never knew who would be next. *That* was their secret: there was no order, no pattern, just uncertainty and fear. You never knew what might happen. But if you were clever you learnt not to care. It might be you, it might be your neighbour. Some weeks before, two men – David had not known them – had stood together at the top of the quarry, embraced briefly, and jumped to their deaths. It had been their own choice. It seemed to David that the gesture was noble, something fine and clean in the stinking cesspit of the camp. Those men, by choosing to die, had placed themselves high, high above the contemptible creatures who ran the camp and dared to call themselves human beings.

David envied the two men their courage. It was a courage he lacked. But then he'd probably die soon anyway. If you didn't die at the quarry, dysentery or disease got you. David's bunk-mate had died of typhoid the day before; that's why there'd been room on the bunk for David to curl up.

David had probably caught the disease already. The thought didn't bother him too much. When it came to living or dying, he didn't care much either way.

The *Prominente* shouted, 'Attention!'

David made the effort to bring his heels together and stand straight. He reckoned he could stand another five minutes at the most. That should be enough.

Two SS officers came in. They wore the insignia of the Death Head battalion. One referred to a list clipped on to a board and said, 'Stand forward the following: Abraham, Freymann . . .'

David stepped forward. His heart was hammering hard against his ribs. Perhaps . . .?

Perhaps, dear God, this is the end.

An overwhelming regret came over him: a regret for

everything that had been taken away from him – his beloved little rabbit, his home, his work. Everything he had ever cared about. *I loved it all so much.*

The other names had been read out – there were only five of them – and now the prisoners fell into line and followed the SS men out of the hut. The procession made its way quickly across the compound.

David tried to keep up, but the knee slowed him down. He began to lag behind. He suddenly thought: So what? If he was to die anyway, what difference did it make if it was now or five minutes later against a wall outside the compound?

The thought calmed him and he stopped trying to keep up.

He was getting used to the idea of dying. His first response had been emotional, the response of a man who had something to live for. But now, as he limped painfully along, he could see the rational side of it. There was nothing to live for. Death would, after all, be a merciful release – his stomach trouble was getting worse and sometimes he sicked up blood. A bleeding ulcer probably. The work at the quarry had been getting more difficult for him: he was breathless, weak and more prone to fall. Each day the effort of working, of pushing his body to do things it was no longer capable of doing, was more agonising.

One of the SS men had turned and was looking down the short line of walking men. He saw David, now ten yards behind. David thought: He'll probably club me.

But the SS man did not stride angrily towards him. Instead he waited.

David struggled on. When he came level with the soldier he braced his body for a blow. Three more steps and he was past. There was no blow. Through the corner of his eye David saw that the SS man was behind him, following slowly. He seemed quite happy. Good Lord, David thought, whatever next?

They passed through the main gates and approached a side compound surrounded by a single wire fence. There were three huts inside, all of them quite new and in good condition – raised off the ground and fitted with windows. They were like barracks, David realised. Why had they been brought here? For interrogation? Surely not after all this time. Perhaps for notification of a transfer. But one was never *told* of such things . . .

David thought: Whatever it is, they won't kill us here.

They waited outside one of the huts. David counted the prisoners in the group. Yes, seven in all. He recognised one: Meyer. Meyer had also been a scientist, a very important one and director of a large laboratory. Meyer looked terrible. The skin of his face and chin hung in folds, and he had the stoop of an old man. The striped uniform bagged out from his emaciated body. He was no more than fifty-five; he looked seventy.

I must look just as old, thought David. He too had lost weight so fast that the skin around his body was loose and wrinkled.

'In!' It was one of the SS men.

They filed into the hut and looked about them. The inside was clean and well fitted, the wood bright and new and sweet-smelling. Along the sides of the hut were wide benches with chairs in front of them. There were also three desks, a filing cabinet, and several typewriters. An interrogation centre? An office? It could be anything.

'Be seated!'

The prisoners looked around in surprise. You were not usually asked to sit down. One prisoner sat on the floor. The SS sergeant snapped, 'On the seats! The seats!'

When they were sitting down, an officer came in, and behind him, a soldier carrying a heavy object under a cover. The object was placed on a bench.

The officer faced them, his body erect, his manner efficient. 'Under the direct orders of Reichsfuehrer-SS

Himmler, this laboratory is to function forthwith! You, as prisoners of the Reich, are to serve in it to the fullest of your ability.'

David stared, dumbfounded. They were to *work* here! It was incredible. The significance of Meyer's presence suddenly dawned on him. Another top scientist . . . It must mean *scientific* work. Incredible!

The officer was saying, 'You will work on projects that will be assigned to you. Your first is here.' He indicated the object on the workbench. 'We have obtained a device from an enemy aircraft. You are to dismantle it, examine it and analyse your findings. We must know what it does, how it does it, and the way to produce it.'

David's heart lifted with hope. This was a genuine scientific project, requiring careful analysis . . . And by skilled scientists like him and Meyer. That meant they would be treated as special prisoners and not returned to the main camp.

Yet a part of him waited, listening carefully. Nobody who survived in this place ever believed what they were told. One must always wait and see. There could be a catch somewhere. There usually was.

The officer continued, 'Now, you are all qualified in this type of electronics, is that correct?'

Nobody was likely to admit they weren't, David thought wryly.

'Your leader will be—' he looked at his list '– Meyer. You will work under him. You will obey him. Is that understood?'

They stared blankly. No-one dared to speak.

'You will ask Sergeant Klammer for any equipment you may need. This project is of great importance. Herr Himmler himself is in personal control, you understand. You will work with all speed and concentration. You will produce results that will be of the highest excellence. Any questions?'

There was silence. Questions were not usually encouraged, they had got out of the habit of asking them. The officer nodded and was turning to leave, when a voice said, 'Yes, I have a question.'

David looked round nervously. It was Meyer. He was standing, looking straight at the officer. Silly old fool, David thought, why did he have to open his mouth! All eyes swivelled back to the officer. But there was no irritation on his face, no anger. Instead there was a slight pause and the officer said, 'Yes?'

Heads turned back to Meyer. The old man said, 'To work efficiently, we will need better quarters and better rations. I cannot have half my team down with disease and malnutrition.' His voice was steady and surprisingly clear.

David thought: My God! You amazing old man. What a nerve.

The eyes returned to the officer. He was nodding. 'Agreed.'

Just like that.

Then they were left alone to make a list of their technical requirements.

They sat in a group round Meyer and looked at each other, searching each other's faces for confirmation of what they couldn't yet believe. One man – his name was Richter – was sobbing violently, his head down on his knees, overcome by the improbability of it all.

David was still looking for the catch, and at last he had it. When they had analysed the device, when the work was done, suppose there were no more of these projects? What would happen then? They wouldn't be kept here. No, they would be taken back to the main camp, back to the quarry. It would be twice as bad, having to go back.

And yet . . . the work would take several weeks, maybe months . . . And a month in this place was a very long time indeed. Long enough to start hoping that it would last for ever . . .

It didn't occur to David that there was anything wrong in wanting to work until Meyer said, 'Whether or not we feel it is *right* to be involved in this project, we have no choice—'

The moral aspects hadn't entered David's mind. Here in this camp matters of principle were irrelevant, ridiculous even. You didn't consider whether things were right or wrong: if you did you would die of outrage. Wrong—? The idea had never occurred to him. Did it bother him, that he would be aiding the Nazis against their enemies? Did it matter when Jews were fighting for their very survival?

The answer was very simple. It came to David when his clean new uniform was issued to him, when he was able to take his first real shower in a year, when he had his first decent meal in as many months, and when he saw the sleeping quarters – clean, fresh, with individual bunks and a flushing lavatory. Then everything was very simple. You knew what you had to do: you had to survive. If you refused to work, someone else would take your place. A single gesture of defiance would change nothing.

That night, as he lay on his clean, sweet-smelling bunk in the sleeping quarters, he wept a little. Mainly from relief, but also from pity, both for himself and for his fragile pathetic hopes for the future, rekindled after so long. He thought of Cecile and Ellen and tried to imagine what their lives were like without him. It was more than a year since he'd seen them.

When finally he fell asleep he dreamed that he invented a magical device which would win the war for Germany. Suddenly he was a hero, he was freed from the camp and given the Iron Cross with Oak Leaves. But when he looked at himself he discovered, with horror, that they had given him an SS uniform. He told them it was a mistake and tried to tear it off, but the black cloth was stuck to his skin and as he tore at it, his flesh came away in his hands . . .

He woke with a start, his heart beating wildly. He thought: Is what I'm doing so bad? But no, it couldn't be, it really couldn't be. What would be bad would be to give his secret away; the small package of microfilm: *that* would be unforgivable.

The next morning, after roll call, David asked to collect something from his old hut. It was a request that would have been inconceivable two days before, but now they let him go.

When he got to the hut it was empty; the able-bodied had left for the quarry and the night's sick had been taken to the infirmary, euphemism for the hut which housed the rank stench and hopelessness of death and disease.

When he was sure he was quite alone he went behind the door and, using an old metal food bowl, scraped at the hard earth floor. He didn't get the right spot at first and had to search over a wider circle until, at last, his hand closed over the small package. He pushed the earth back into the hollow and stamped it down. Then, wedging the package under his arm, he walked back to the special compound. He hid the package behind the lavatory cistern in the sleeping quarters.

Then he went to work.

It was some sort of radar jamming device, that was obvious. But determining how it worked, and which type of German radar transmitter it was designed to jam, took longer. They split the device into twenty units and each took some pieces to analyse.

After two weeks they were getting somewhere. The device seemed to be aimed at the Freya early-warning system, which worked on a frequency of 125 megacycles and was capable of detecting enemy planes at a distance of seventy-five miles. David knew all about it. He should do – the Freya had been developed by the Gema Company.

As he worked on his section of the device David began to wonder how the British had discovered the existence of Freya and its frequency. Freya was a large unit fixed to the ground, it was not something that could be captured or examined by spies. They must have more sophisticated detection equipment than anyone had thought. But then, David realised, he was out of touch . . . *everyone* here was. It was a year since long-term research had stopped, a year since scientists had been called up or sent away to camps.

But David's thoughts went further: if the British could detect radar, then they themselves must be capable of developing it . . . The conclusion was inescapable. He discussed it with Meyer.

The older man said briefly, 'Yes, I expect they have radar by now.'

'To stay ahead Germany should have continued her research, then,' David said.

'Yes, in this business to stand still is to fall behind.'

'But there is still some development going on?'

Meyer exclaimed, 'No! As far as I can gather, we're all they have. Ironic, isn't it?'

David turned to him, amazed. 'Surely they've kept some laboratories going?'

'Oh, very few. And nothing of importance. I asked for detailed reports of any work that had been going on while I – in my absence. They were not able to give me anything. I tell you, we are Germany's principal electronics development laboratory now.' And Meyer laughed drily, 'We're cheaper this way, you see. No salaries to pay.'

David stared at the bench. For the first time he began to appreciate the importance of what they were doing. He asked, 'What are we going to tell them? I mean, when we give them our findings?'

Meyer said simply, 'We're going to tell them what we've found. But—' he lowered his voice '– we are not going to draw their conclusions for them. Let them discover the

hard way that the British have radar. I am not going to tell
them. Nor are you.'

David shook his head. 'No, I won't tell them.'

The knowledge made David feel better. It was only a
small act of omission, but at least it was something
positive, some small act of defiance.

David looked up from his work again. 'By the way, who
are we reporting to? Is it really Himmler?'

'I believe so. But copies also go to other departments,
including the Chief Scientist's.'

'Who is—?'

Meyer looked at him in surprise. 'Why Schmidt, of
course.'

Nothing changes, David thought. He wished it didn't
matter to him that it was Schmidt, but it did. It made his
stomach twist.

After a month they handed over their second stage
results. David began to wonder how much longer they
could spin out their work – another two weeks, four at the
most. The lab had the air of permanence about it, yet it
was impossible to believe that anything was permanent in
Dachau . . .

The thought of returning to the main compound
haunted him, as it haunted everyone. The seven of them
were relatively healthy now. They had warmth and security. They had hope. It was terrifying, to have so much.

There were several other laboratories, David discovered,
one was run by the SS Health Institute, another by the
Luftwaffe Research Bureau. You didn't know what was
done in them: you didn't ask such things in case the answer
sickened you. These labs also seemed permanent, but you
never knew about that either . . .

David remembered that Himmler had a passion for
specialised knowledge: that explained all the different labs.
Before the war Himmler had organised archaeological digs,
to prove some obscure theory, David couldn't remember

what exactly. Something about purely Germanic races being the forerunners of the Teutonic knights. The man was crazy. That he'd reached such high rank said a lot about the system.

A week later the workload was growing lighter and the scientists grew nervous. It would be difficult to spin things out much longer. Then, like manna from heaven, another object was delivered to the laboratory. This time they all exchanged smiles.

Like the first device this object was to be taken apart and analysed. With delight David and Meyer realised that it was something quite new, something they could only guess at. It would take weeks to understand properly.

They had been reprieved.

Sergeant Klammer shouted, 'Assemble!'

David looked up from the bench and felt a jump of alarm. Sergeant Klammer never interrupted them when they were working. It must be something out of the ordinary.

Sergeant Klammer waited impatiently while they got up and gathered in a group in front of him.

When he spoke, it was with such emphasis that spit flew from his mouth. 'You will cease work for the time-being, and tidy the laboratory. Within an hour it must look perfect. Then you will prepare answers to any questions that might be put to you concerning your work. Is that clear?'

Meyer nodded. They were dismissed. When Klammer had gone they turned questioningly to Meyer.

Meyer shrugged. 'Don't ask me.'

David thought: It must be Himmler. It was the only person it could be. He had been to the camp before. It was his creation: he liked to take a personal interest in it.

When the preparations were done they waited. They were denied permission to collect their midday meal, so they went without. Nor were they permitted to carry out any work which might make the lab untidy.

By three in the afternoon David felt faint. His stomach had got used to having food regularly, and it didn't like going without. His ulcer started to throb dully: soon the throb would grow into an angry pain.

At four they were still waiting.

Finally Klammer burst in. 'Attention!'

They stood up and stared fixedly at the opposite wall. One tries to look anonymous, David thought: faceless but servile; unimportant yet valuable. You look like they want you to look.

There were voices and the noise of feet on the steps. A group of men entered the hut. David stared at the wall, but from the corner of his eye he saw the black uniforms of high-ranking SS officers.

The group advanced into the hut. Someone laughed loudly. David thought: They've just had a good lunch.

As they came into his field of vision, David took a surreptitious look. Most were senior officers: he did not know their faces. Except – yes, Himmler. He recognised him from photographs. He was small, with close-cropped hair and a weak chin. His eyes were pale and cool behind rimless spectacles. He looked harmless, like a bank clerk.

There were others, some in civilian clothes. David glanced at them. He saw a face he knew.

It was Schmidt.

Schmidt was hanging back in a corner, looking uncomfortable. He took an occasional look at his surroundings, at the bare walls and simple equipment, with slight distaste. David thought: Well might you look uncomfortable, my friend. Schmidt hadn't spotted him yet. David watched him, waiting for the moment when he would, but Schmidt was keeping his eyes away from the prisoners' faces. David felt vaguely disappointed.

Himmler was strolling down the room, nodding as

pieces of the enemy devices were shown to him. Then he turned and searched for someone. His eyes fell on Schmidt and he smiled slightly. He beckoned the Chief Scientist towards him.

There was total silence.

'Herr Schmidt . . .' Himmler's voice was surprisingly soft, almost gentle. 'I trust you are pleased with what we have arranged here.'

Schmidt spoke in a near whisper. 'Yes, it seems most satisfactory.'

Himmler smiled benignly, like a kind schoolmaster. 'Well, I'm sure you will want to speak to some of the prisoners about their work. So please go ahead.'

Schmidt stared uncertainly.

Himmler made a small bow. 'Yes now, by all means. We are quite happy to wait.'

Schmidt looked unhappily around him, hoping for an escape. He focused on Meyer and stared hard. Then recognition sprang into his eyes and he relaxed visibly. David thought: Of course, he knows Meyer well. Schmidt went up to Meyer, and soon they were examining a cathode tube captured from a British bomber. A buzz of conversation sprang up around the room.

David wondered what had gone on there between Himmler and Schmidt. Perhaps Himmler was doing Schmidt a favour, and didn't want him to forget it. Perhaps Schmidt had been desperate for scientists and had been forced to ask the SS to provide them. You would think that the SS would be embarrassed to use Jews, the inferior race. But no: Himmler was obviously delighted with the laboratory. It was Schmidt who was uncomfortable here.

Schmidt was standing in front of him. 'Freymann . . .'

He was looking startled and David suddenly realised it was his physical appearance which Schmidt found so surprising.

Schmidt dragged his eyes down to the bench. 'And what have you been working on?'

David explained, as simply and briefly as possible. Schmidt seemed satisfied, and began to turn away. But then he paused and said, 'We looked into that shortwave radar idea again, that one you kept pressing. We established once and for all that it was not possible to develop it, nor indeed *wise*. It would be grossly inefficient.'

He was waiting for David to comment, but David stared past him and did not reply. He did not know what to say. Schmidt added irritably, 'It was a waste of time and money to research it. But of course, *you* knew best, didn't you?'

David said, 'Yes, it was a mistake. I see that now.'

The party began to leave, their boots shuffling across the wooden floor, their voices loud and raucous. Himmler was enjoying a joke with one of his junior officers, his lips pulled back in a pleasant smile. He had obviously enjoyed his day at Dachau.

As the door closed and silence fell, David sat down wearily on his chair. He felt terribly depressed.

To think he had worked willingly for these people. It made him feel ashamed. It had been vanity, really; wanting to show how brilliant he was, wanting to impress. Of course, he'd talked himself into believing he'd done it for the state and was working for a great common good which touched everyone equally. He'd separated the state – the people – from the Nazis. But he'd been quite wrong. The people, the state, the Nazis were all one. You only had to look at Schmidt to see that. How else could a scientist, a *thinking* man, visit this place and be untouched.

Vanity. It was leading him on even now. It was pricking him over the shortwave radar and that remark of Schmidt's. How he'd love to prove to Schmidt that he was wrong. How he'd love to show him!

Pure vanity.

Shaking his head, he got slowly to his feet and went back to work.

Chapter 11

THE STAFF CAR slowed to a crawl as it negotiated the wide streets of a town. The change of pace made Doenitz wake up and look out of the window.

His staff officer, a young man called Schneider, said from the front of the car, 'This is Morlaix, sir. We are approximately forty minutes from Brest.'

Doenitz nodded and stared at the monotonous procession of houses and shops. All French towns looked alike to him. He closed his eyes again. He often catnapped, particularly on long journeys. It helped to clarify his mind when he was working out difficult problems.

But, though he'd been over it time and time again, he could find no solution to his greatest problem: this early war with Britain.

When war was declared he'd had a meagre fifty-six U-boats of which only twenty or so were suitable for the Atlantic. Six months later he was down to a dangerously low total of thirty-two . . .

Only this miracle, the occupation of France, had saved the German war effort.

Doenitz stared out of the window at the Breton country-side and blessed the marvellous turn of fortune which had given him the long west coast of France and unlimited access to the Atlantic. It was everything he could have asked for. His boats no longer had to return to Germany round the north coast of Scotland and run the gauntlet of the shallow North Sea. Now they could reach their hunting grounds more safely and much, much quicker. Just three months after the Occupation, Doenitz had transferred two flotillas to Lorient and a third here to Brest.

The car turned a corner and Doenitz glimpsed the sparkle of water in the distance. He looked at his watch. They must be nearing Brest.

Doenitz said to Schneider, 'Please give me the details of the programme.'

There was a rustling of papers and Schneider said, 'Sir. At 1230 there will be lunch in a restaurant adjacent to the dockyard. At 1430 we meet Herr Dorsch, the architect from the Todt Organisation, and tour the dockyard. At 1600 we have a general review meeting with the Naval Commander, Brest. Also you will wish to meet U-319 when it returns. The last ETA we received was 1530.'

Doenitz nodded. 'Very well.'

U-319 was commanded by Kapitanleutnant Fischer. Fischer was a good man. He had done especially well on this patrol. Doenitz remembered the brief radio signal received at HQ in Paris yesterday. It had reported six ships sunk. Six! And by one boat during a five-day patrol. It was remarkable. Yet many of the other boats were achieving great successes too. The average sinkings per U-boat per day were way up. September should be a record month, with at least fifty ships sunk.

Fischer already wore the decoration of the Iron Cross of the Knight's Cross, First Class. Doenitz would present him with the Oak Leaves this afternoon. In the U-boat Arm they did not wait for boards of senior officers to approve awards; decorations were given immediately, on the dockside, when emotions were running at their highest and the men could share the recipient's moment of glory.

The car was travelling along the edge of a wide estuary. The occasional farmhouse had given way to a string of small villas: they were coming into Brest.

Doenitz considered the rest of the day's programme: the

planning session with the Todt Organisation man should be straightforward. It was a matter of discussing the construction of the necessary dockyard modifications. Work was already in progress. They were using Polish labour apparently, and Poles always worked hard.

The staff meeting would be the usual mixture of optimism and resignation. The staff did not bother – or maybe, Doenitz wondered, they did not dare – to ask for the one thing they knew he could not provide: more boats.

Only six new U-boats were being launched this month; in August it was a disastrous two. It had been the same in May, June, and July . . . Not enough even to replace losses!

The High Command always told him it was a matter of resources – what they really meant was that everything was going into Goering's precious Luftwaffe.

They were descending into the dockyard area. The car swept in through some large stone gates and approached an ugly grey stone building over which flew the flag of the Third Reich and the ensign of the Kriegsmarine. Waiting on the steps of the building were the commander of the 1st U-boat Flotilla and his staff. An ordinary seaman was keeping a tight rein on the flotilla's mascot, a goat draped with the flotilla's insignia. Doenitz was pleased. Back in 1935 this flotilla had been the one and only U-boat flotilla, and Doenitz himself had been its commander. Doenitz remembered with pride that the men themselves had thought them up, the insignia and the mascot.

Immediately the greetings were over they went to the restaurant. The lunch was indifferent. Doenitz considered French food to be very overrated. The wine, however, was excellent, though he drank very little.

He cut the lunch short and they started the tour of the dockyard early. Brest was a well-developed port, as one would expect of one of France's major naval bases, and considerable repair facilities already existed. It was a question of making modifications, Dorsch explained. The larger drydocks needed to be adapted to take two U-boats at a time; also more engineering shops and welding facilities would have to be created.

'How long will the work take?' Doenitz asked.

'Eight weeks at the most.'

'Good.' Once the work was done another flotilla could be moved to Brest from Kiel. Doenitz wanted as many boats as possible here, where they would be most effective.

As the party walked slowly back towards the cars the distant drone of a plane sounded high in the sky. Everyone looked up.

'One of ours.'

Doenitz nodded. So it should be. Goering had promised air supremacy: he'd better deliver it otherwise here in port the U-boats would be totally vulnerable to air attack. Rumour had it that the air battle with Britain was not going so well.

He turned to the architect. 'Herr Dorsch, how long would it take to create sail-in bunkers for my boats? Ones that would be invulnerable to air attack?'

Dorsch was taken by surprise. 'Oh? Er, I would think – allowing for the fact that the roof would have to be massively thick – my goodness, yes, very thick indeed . . . er, I would say, at least six months. All the concrete . . . all the labour. How many boats would need to be protected at once?'

'Ten, twelve, more if it was possible.'

'It would be . . . a massive project.'

'But possible?'

'Oh yes! Most certainly!'

Doenitz was pleased. If the air battle was lost then at least his boats would be safe in port.

That left one really vulnerable point: the run across the Bay of Biscay. It was here, in the approaches to his new French bases – Brest, Lorient, La Palice and St Nazaire –

that his boats were most exposed to enemy air patrols. Rather than search the open Atlantic, it was easier for the British to wait for departing or returning boats in the Bay.

He made a mental note to ask at the staff meeting about the current state of enemy air activity. What the U-boats really needed was proper air cover. But they never got it, Goering saw to that.

Back at headquarters the flotilla commander, Korvetten-kapitan Scheer, was waiting and the meeting began promptly.

The routine reports of successes, losses, and mechanical breakdowns were read out. The U-boat quotient – the average tonnage sunk per U-boat per day – was going up monthly. Everyone was pleased.

'But soon it will go up very much more,' Doenitz said. He explained that, as soon as another flotilla could be based on the French coast, they would have enough boats to reintroduce properly organised wolf pack tactics. The wolf pack would increase kills dramatically. Doenitz also promised first-class intelligence to help locate convoys.

Then they looked at the problems. Scheer, the flotilla commander, was most concerned about air attacks. The RAF had taken to carrying – and dropping – depth charges. And as Doenitz had foreseen, many of the attacks were being made in the Bay of Biscay.

'But the boats manage to dive in time?' Doenitz asked.

'Yes,' Scheer agreed, 'but sometimes it's closer than we'd like. In bad visibility the enemy never find us, of course. But in thin cloud they often see us first and, attacking from down-wind as they do, well ... Our men neither hear them nor see them until it's almost too late. And with these depth charges ...'

'But a good lookout solves the problem?'

'Well – yes,' admitted Scheer.

'That's the answer, then, isn't it?' Doenitz said a little

impatiently. 'And as many boats as possible should sail at dusk to benefit from the cover of darkness. Any other suggestions?'

There was a short silence, then someone said, 'Any chance of getting the magic eye?'

A few U-boats had been fitted with a large and cumbersome radar device just before the war, but the results had been so poor the idea of having radar in U-boats had been dropped and the sets removed. Since then all research into small sets had ceased.

Doenitz replied, 'No. There will be no radar. Tests prove that sets small enough to fit into our boats would be impossible to develop.' He remembered the Chief Scientist's report: it had been quite definite.

There was a knock at the door and a junior officer came in and saluted. 'Sir, U-319 has entered port. Estimated arrival time is 1610.' Doenitz looked at his watch. Fifteen minutes. He smiled. 'Good! Let's get down there.' He got to his feet and led the way out of the room. He always loved meeting the boats and he tried to do so as often as possible. In the old days, when his HQ was attached to the U-boat base at Kiel, he could meet every boat at the end of every patrol. Now – well, it was impossible. His HQ was in Paris and his bases scattered around the coast of the European continent.

As he walked briskly towards the dock Doenitz called to Schneider, 'You have everything?'

The staff officer replied, 'Yes, Admiral.'

The small party arrived at the dockside. They still had ten minutes to wait. Doenitz sat on a bollard and gazed in silence across the wide expanse of Brest Harbour. He looked round only once, when the braying of the mascot interrupted his thoughts. He saw that, in addition to the band and the official guard of honour, at least a hundred officers and men had gathered. It was always the same: everyone always made the effort to come out and welcome a boat home. It was part of the remarkable loyalty and camaraderie that united his men. He never felt less than immensely proud of them . . .

Though there were some he couldn't help feeling especially proud of: his two sons, one already in the service, the other in S-boats.

Someone shouted and everyone looked up. The nose of U-319 appeared from behind a jetty. There was loud cheering from the assembled crowd. The band struck up the Kretschmermarch. Doenitz felt a lump in his throat. This occasion, this moment of emotion and relief and pride, never failed to move him. His men were the best in Germany, the best in the world. They deserved to return like this, in triumph, for they were the bravest of them all . . .

The crew lining U-319's deck cheered back, waving and shouting to the crowd on the dock. They were in high spirits: obviously everything had gone well. As the submarine manoeuvred alongside there was some cheerful banter between the crew and the crowd. Doenitz smiled; he encouraged informality at moments like this. He reflected that, because of his presence, the comments were probably quite subdued. He could see Fischer in the conning tower, his face lit by a wide grin. The goat brayed loudly and everyone laughed.

When the boat was secure and the gangway rigged, the chatter of voices died away, the band stopped playing and there was a hushed silence. Everyone had guessed what was to happen. The crew stood in line along the decks. Fischer appeared through a hatchway still in his U-boat uniform of plain blue overalls and soft white cap, took a last look at his boat, and walked down the gangway. Doenitz stood waiting at the end and, as Fischer stepped on to the dock, the two men faced each other, saluted and shook hands.

The crowd waited expectantly as Doenitz said a few

words. Schneider then stepped forward, a small box in his hand, and opened it. Doenitz took out the simple iron cross with oak leaf on a long ribbon, and placed it round Fischer's neck. The two men saluted again, the band struck up a tune, and a great roar went up from the crowd. Scheer presented Fischer with a bouquet of flowers and the young U-boat commander, his face a picture of pride and joy, led Doenitz and Scheer aboard his boat to present his crew to their senior officers. To complete the formalities Fischer then inspected and saluted the guard of honour.

Scheer was at Doenitz's elbow. 'Sir, would you like to attend the debriefing? Or would a copy of Fischer's report be sufficient?'

'I will attend if I may.'

'Of course, Admiral!'

The formal question had been asked. The reply given. But, Doenitz thought, if they hadn't asked me I would have invited myself anyway.

Fischer sat near the window, his yellow hair lit gold by the late afternoon sun. From time to time he glanced at the written log on his knee to remind himself of precise times or sequences of events. But for the most part he spoke from memory, his pale blue eyes fixed at a point high on the opposite wall, his mind back in the North Atlantic. He told first how, on their way to their designated patrol area, they had come across a small convoy, probably from the Mediterranean. They had sunk two of the ships before being chased off by a destroyer. They then continued to their patrol area.

Fischer went on, 'In company with U-253 and U-90 we arrived at the grid reference point at 0700 on the fifteenth. We fanned out and zigzagged in twenty mile legs, covering a corridor fifty miles wide across the expected path of the convoy. U-90 spotted them at 1900 hours, dead ahead.

She reported the sighting to us by radio. I passed on the report to Command Headquarters. I then ordered U-253 to make her approach from the south and U-90 from the north. We ourselves would lie in wait dead ahead. At this stage it was impossible to gauge the speed of the convoy, or the pattern of its zigzag, but I ordered that there be no further communication between our boats until the action was completed, to lessen the risk of detection.'

Doenitz watched Fischer's abstracted face and was nostalgic for the time in 1915 when he himself had seen active service. Then he too had made reports like this: dispassionate, objective, but loaded with a multitude of things unsaid – fear, exhilaration, uncertainty. Would the convoy alter course at the last moment? Was it going faster than they had estimated? Which ship should they go for?

Fischer went on, 'We dived to periscope depth and manoeuvred to a position in front of the convoy and dead ahead of it. The convoy consisted of at least thirty ships, but it appeared to have a very small escort: we spotted only one frigate and three armed trawlers. Suddenly, as we waited, we saw the frigate detach herself from the convoy and steam away to the south. I thought she must have spotted U-253, but later I discovered that this was not in fact the case. We never found out why she dashed off in this way. We waited, keeping an eye on both the convoy and the frigate. At 2030 we spotted the frigate coming in to make a pass across the front of the convoy. Unfortunately, this pass would bring her very near to our position. I had a feeling the convoy was about to alter course and, though I had been planning to take us a bit further to the north, I had no choice but to dive. We stayed submerged for twelve minutes. We listened to the frigate pass then, using minimum speed, came to periscope depth again.'

Fischer paused, a look of exhilaration in his eyes. 'We could hardly believe it, but when we took a look around we discovered we had come up in the middle of the convoy!'

A ghost of a smile passed Doenitz's lips. It was indeed a remarkable stroke of luck! He could imagine the amazement and the excitement in the U-boat.

'There was a large tanker coming straight into the perfect target position. All we had to do was wait! However, since it was a very dark night and the convoy was well spread out, I decided to surface. There was a good chance of remaining unseen, and I wanted a more stable firing platform. We fired two torpedoes at the tanker. She went up straight away. We retreated so as not to be illuminated by the burning ship. Another ship came into target position. We got her with a single torpedo. Then we saw other ships on fire: U-253 and U-90 were obviously busy too. At this point the frigate came sniffing around so we went down to periscope depth, but she never found us. We continued to find targets in the centre of the convoy.'

Fischer looked down. 'We know to our certain knowledge that we sank four ships that night. We used only eight torpedoes.' There was a moment's silence. No-one liked the thought of ships being destroyed because men died, drowned or burnt alive.

'Finally, when the convoy had passed, we surfaced. Eventually we made radio contact with U-90 and U-253. They had scored four and six hits respectively. Thus we sunk approximately half the convoy.'

The senior officers exchanged glances of satisfaction. Doenitz nodded slowly. 'And so you were not detected by the enemy at any stage?' he asked.

'No, sir!' Fischer smiled. 'I don't think they had any *idea* of where we were. I believe that, when we're submerged, their Asdic can't distinguish the noise of our engines from those of the ships in the convoy. As long as we're sufficiently close to the ships, the Asdic won't pick us up.'

'I agree,' Doenitz said. 'Again, Kapitanleutnant Fischer,

my congratulations on your fine achievement. At this rate, our tiny band of boats will win the war!'

They think I am just saying that, thought Doenitz, but it is absolutely true.

The debriefing was over. Doenitz poised himself to get out of his chair.

'Sir, perhaps I did not answer quite accurately just now.' It was Fischer.

Doenitz looked up sharply. 'Yes?'

'We did have an engagement with the enemy, but it was much later. Just sixty miles from Brest, visibility one mile, the lookout thought he heard an aircraft engine. Fortunately he was a man with exceptionally sharp ears. I must admit I did not hear it, though I was in the conning tower. I took no chances and ordered a crash dive. We were just in time. The last man down saw a Sunderland appear to the south. It was banking sharply towards us. When we were down we heard one bomb explode, but it was some way off. After that, nothing.' Fischer shrugged, 'It was a fluke. But it was lucky we had such an excellent lookout.'

'Yes. It was lucky.' Doenitz stood up. 'And it banked only when it saw you, this plane?'

'Yes, sir.'

'A fluke then.' Doenitz put out his hand. 'Goodbye, Fischer. And I look forward to hearing about your future patrols. May all of them be equally successful!' He leant forward and said in an undertone that no-one else could hear. 'It is a long time since the early days at Kiel, isn't it?'

Fischer grinned. 'Yes, sir.'

'A long time . . .' Doenitz turned away and strode out of the room.

Chapter 12

THE APARTMENT WAS in a narrow street near the Porte d'Auteuil in the *seizième*. It was small, plainly furnished, and in every way unremarkable. It was just what Vasson wanted. It was high time to move. He'd been in the other place six months, ever since the previous December when he'd started working for Kloffer. It had been too long. He moved in at noon and carefully unpacked the contents of two of his three suitcases. In the bedroom there was a single narrow wardrobe with just enough room for his suits. His shirts, casual trousers, pullovers and best underwear he folded carefully and placed in the drawers of a large chest in the corner. He put two mothballs in each of the drawers and another four in the wardrobe. He didn't want to get back and find all his best clothes peppered with holes.

He opened the third suitcase and checked the contents. One inexpensive badly-cut suit, three cotton shirts, three pairs of cheap casual trousers, socks, shoes, underwear – his working clothes.

He took out his wallet. Papers in the name of Lebrun, a hundred francs, and the special travel permit which he would destroy once he was over the border in Belgium. He looked again at the money: would it be enough? He couldn't think of anything he could possibly spend it on between now and the border. He had already paid six months' rent in advance and given the *concierge* a float to cover the electricity and any other bills that might turn up.

No, he wouldn't need any more cash; anyway the less French money he had on him the better.

He looked at his watch. Three-thirty. Just time to go to Sèvres, then Clichy, and back by seven.

He shut the suitcase, placed it ready by the front door and left the apartment. He shouted a word to the *concierge* and went into the street. His car, a six-year-old Citroën, was three minutes' walk away. It was a habit, now, to leave his car at least two streets away from wherever he was living. Possessing a car was not so unusual, but having enough petrol to use it every day certainly was.

When he got to the car he went straight to the boot and unlocked it. The large leather grip was still there, as he knew it would be. It amused him to think of all the people who must have walked past the car in the last few hours without having the slightest inkling of what the vehicle contained.

He closed and locked the boot, and got into the car. Since the Occupation almost a year ago the traffic in Paris had thinned down considerably; the trip to Sèvres should take fifteen minutes at the most.

In fact he reached the Porte de Sèvres in five minutes and the Rue du Vieux Moulin in twelve.

Sèvres was a suburb on the south-west outskirts of the city. Vasson had chosen it because it was quiet, genteel, and, like everything else in his life nowadays, unremark-able. Rue du Vieux Moulin was a sleepy street of two-storey late nineteenth-century houses set back from the road in their own gardens. The villas, once impressive, now had the unmistakable air of decay, as if their once-affluent owners could no longer afford to keep them up.

Vasson drove the full length of the street to make sure that everything was quiet, parked in a nearby street, then, taking the leather grip from the boot, set off on foot for Number 22, Rue du Vieux Moulin.

A few moments later he wished that, for once, he had

parked outside the house; the bag was heavy. But it was too late now.

He wondered if Madame Roche would be in. It didn't really matter either way: the old woman was incapable of a suspicious thought. You could go in with a mask over your face and blood on your hands and she wouldn't notice.

He reached the house at last and opened the gate in the low wall surrounding the austere garden, which was laid to gravel and shrubs. In the balmy air of the warm summer day, the house was quiet and most of the shutters drawn. The old woman was probably having a nap.

Vasson walked round to the side of the house where some steps led down to the semi-basement level. At the bottom of the steps was a door which he opened with a key. Inside, there was a passage with four rooms leading off it. The first, which must once have been a servant's room, was now a bed-sitter; the second was a primitive washroom with a stone sink and lavatory; the other two were storage rooms.

Vasson went into the bed-sitting room, laid the leather bag on the bed, and listened for sounds from the upper floors. Still nothing. He crossed to the wardrobe and opened the door. He kept a spare set of clothes here, as well as two sets of papers which Kloffer didn't know about. The papers were strapped to the underside of a shelf at the bottom. They were still there.

He picked up the bag and, leaving the room, started down the passage towards the store rooms. It was dark and he had to feel his way along the wall. Finally he reached a door and, opening it, fumbled for the light switch.

The room was square and windowless except for four small ventilation grilles near the ceiling. Once it must have been stacked with wine but now only a few dusty bottles lay forgotten in an old rack. The room had an earthen floor which, because it kept the air cool, made it perfect for wine storage. The earthen floor also made the room perfect for storing articles like gold Louis and *demi-barres*.

Vasson locked the door and crossed the room. A wooden table straddled one corner. On it was some ancient photographic equipment: two developing trays, an enlarger, and five bottles of chemicals. Vasson had picked them up for a few francs in a pawnbroker's. Photography was what he was supposed to be doing when he locked himself in this room.

He moved the table and, taking a trowel from the leather bag, started to dig. He made a hole ten inches deep then, removing two small canvas sacks of coins and a solid bar from the bag, carefully buried them. He spent some time flattening the earth and beating it down with his feet before replacing the table.

That made two hundred thousand francs in gold. A tidy sum – but not enough, not enough by far.

It had taken months and months to wrest a decent wage out of Kloffer; even then it was in paper money and Vasson had been forced to go to the black market for gold. It had cost him dear. But gold it had to be; with inflation, paper money wouldn't be worth a *sou* in a couple of years. Then, in May, Vasson had finally persuaded Kloffer to pay him directly in gold. It didn't cost Kloffer anything – he and his friends were stealing vast quantities of the stuff – but it did save Vasson a lot of time and money.

He should have been paid in gold from the beginning, of course. It made him angry to remember how he'd had to beg, cajole and threaten to get what was, after all, only his due. He'd been shabbily treated, no doubt about that.

He replaced the trowel in the bag, closed the store room door and went back to the bed-sitting room. He left six months' rent money on the bed with a note saying that he wouldn't be back for some time, and left. The old woman thought he was a commercial traveller.

The house was still quiet, the old woman probably on the point of getting up. It was the perfect place for a cache. But then it was bound to be: he'd taken a lot of time and trouble to find it.

The drive to Clichy took thirty minutes. The lock-up garage still had quite a lot of stuff in it – stockings, perfume and petrol – but there was just enough room for the car. He parked it and locked up carefully. As he walked towards the nearest boulevard he thought about the remaining stock and wondered whether it would be a good time to sell. But he couldn't make up his mind; he hadn't been following the market recently and he didn't know how prices were. What he *did* know was that new stock was almost impossible to come by; most of his old sources had dried up. Also ... what? He'd lost interest, that was what. The market bored him: it was too restricted and the profit too hard to come by. Besides, the big boys had moved in and begun to squeeze everyone out, just like they always did. Diversifying was the wisest thing he'd ever done.

He reached the Rue Jean Jaurés and looked for a *vélo-taxi*, but it was almost five-thirty, the rush hour, and the few that he saw were already occupied. He cursed and walked towards the nearest Métro at Porte de Clichy.

He hated the idea of taking the Métro: it was too – well, public. Ever since the last operation he had kept away from crowds. He'd had a feeling, an indefinable but distinct feeling, that he was no longer safe. The project had been straightforward. He had bust a small escape line taking shot-down pilots from North-East France through Paris to Spain. The members of the line had been typically trusting and weak on security, but somewhere, somehow he'd disturbed something else. There was a loose end some-where. He didn't exactly know what ... But he was certain, absolutely sure, he was no longer safe. Someone

was on to him. The word was out; it was time for him to
go.

The Métro was even worse than he'd feared. He hated
confined spaces and, after changing at St Lazare, the train
was horribly crowded. The bodies pressed close against
him and he shuddered with the beginnings of panic. He
changed again at Miromesnil. The train was slightly less
crowded this time, but he still had to stand. After a few
moments he felt a tingling in his spine. It was a feeling he
never ignored. Without moving his head he looked at the
reflection of the other passengers in the window. A man
behind him seemed to be staring at him. Vasson studied
the face desperately. Did he know him? No. He was certain
he didn't. He relaxed again. It was his nerves. He was
imagining things. Christ, it really was time to get away.

He got back to the apartment in Auteuil at six-fifteen.
He stripped off and washed the whole of his body.
Washing always made him feel good. He lay on the bed,
smoking thoughtfully, until six-fifty, then dressed. When
the bell rang he picked up the suitcase, locked the apartment behind him, and slid the key under the *concierge*'s
door.

A car was waiting at the kerb. It looked like a taxi, though
Vasson knew it wasn't. Even the driver looked French.
Vasson thought: Kloffer's learning at last.

Kloffer was sitting in the back, looking like a fat cat.
Vasson sank on to the seat beside him. The car moved off
and the German asked 'Any problems?'

'No.'

Vasson waited. Kloffer was here for a reason; he wasn't
seeing Vasson off out of the kindness of his heart.

Eventually Kloffer said, 'This car will take you all the
way to Brussels.'

'I thought—'

'We decided against the train. We don't want anyone to see you leave.'

Vasson shrugged. 'Very well.'

'I think you'll agree that it's wise . . .' Kloffer turned and looked at Vasson. 'Your old apartment – we caught someone waiting outside. He had a weapon. It seems he wanted to kill you.'

I knew it, Vasson thought.

Kloffer smiled. 'We don't want you dead when I've promised you to Brussels. They would think me *most* inefficient!' He giggled slightly.

Vasson was wondering where he'd gone wrong. He hated loose ends, he hated not knowing. He asked, 'Who was the man? The one who was waiting for me?'

'Oh, the brother of one of the girls we arrested last week.'

'Was he working on his own?'

'We don't know. He says nothing.'

Vasson cursed. That meant it would be unsafe for him to return . . . Not until he knew for sure. Damn. He said suddenly, 'I must know – whether he was on his own. Also if he had a description of me, and how he knew where I was living. Everything!'

'We will do our best.'

'You'd better. Otherwise—' *Otherwise I'm as good as dead.* 'Otherwise I won't come back here. You understand?'

'Indeed.' Kloffer looked quite happy about it. Vasson had the feeling that there was more to this Brussels trip than Kloffer was admitting to. Perhaps there was a deal. If so, Kloffer would never tell him the terms.

'Have you any more information about the Brussels operation?'

Kloffer shrugged. 'Not really. But apparently there is just the one organisation. It seems that they collect the airmen not only in Belgium but some in France too and send them all the way down to Spain. A long way – there must be hundreds of people involved. Yet we haven't succeeded in stopping them. Amazing. You'd think someone would talk!' He sniffed with irritation. 'Your operation against the Paris couriers – that was excellent while it lasted. But we have evidence that all the people we removed have been replaced. No, there's only one way to get these pests, and that is from Brussels. Otherwise we'll just go on wasting our time.'

'What's been tried so far?'

'I'm not sure – you must ask them. But I gather that attempts at infiltration have failed.' Kloffer looked pleased.

Ah, thought Vasson, so that's it. The Brussels people had failed; Kloffer was coming to the rescue with his own man. No wonder Kloffer wasn't shedding any tears. All the more glory for him.

They were approaching the Avenue Foch. Kloffer said to the driver, 'Drop me on the next corner.'

Vasson said, 'And the money? Are they clear about the method of payment? I want that agreed before I get there.'

'Yes, yes,' Kloffer said impatiently.

Gold was to be deposited in the Banque de Paris and the receipt slips sent to Brussels, poste restante. It was quite simple, Vasson thought, but you'd think I was asking for the bloody moon.

The car came to a halt and Kloffer opened the door. 'Goodbye. All success. I know that if anyone can do it, you can.'

Praise indeed. Kloffer was getting quite pleasant in his old age.

Kloffer got out of the car and leant in through the door. He was smiling, though Vasson noticed that his eyes were sharp as a cat's. Kloffer said softly, 'Oh, by the way, are you happy with your papers?'

He never usually enquired. Vasson was instantly suspicious. 'Yes, why?'

'I thought you might not like the name we chose.'

Vasson waited.

'Well, it's Paul Lebrun, isn't it? I thought you might not care for the Paul.' Kloffer grinned briefly and was gone. The car drew rapidly away and Vasson was thrown against the seat. He stared blindly ahead, unable to breathe, a vice around his heart.

Kloffer knew his name.

God!

He felt angry, then sick with fear.

Kloffer knew his name.

Kloffer must know that Vasson was wanted in Marseilles ... Kloffer could blackmail him ... Kloffer *was* blackmailing him?

Vasson tried to assimilate the awful fact into his brain, but it hurt, *it hurt*. And it was being vulnerable, the dreadful realisation that he could be pressurised – humiliated – that hurt the most.

Where had he gone wrong? How had Kloffer found out?

He didn't know, and he would never know unless Kloffer chose to tell him. And he was sure Kloffer *wouldn't* choose to tell him; instead the German would let the question fester in his mind. Yes, that was Kloffer's way.

He was sure of another thing too: the timing of Kloffer's little bombshell was carefully planned. The German wanted to remind Vasson who was in control; he wanted Vasson to come back afterwards, like a good boy.

Vasson shuddered with humiliation. To hell with Kloffer!

But even as he thought it he knew he had lost. Kloffer had him, just *there*.

As the car sped into the gathering darkness Vasson pressed his head into the corner, his face contorted with rage and bitterness, and thought: It's all so *unfair*. Why does it always happen to me? *Why me?*

At midnight the car stopped outside a cheap hotel. Vasson had no idea where he was, except that it was somewhere in Brussels. The driver said he'd been told to take Vasson there. The hotel wasn't expecting him. At first the proprietor said he had no rooms, then he decided he had one after all, but, being his best room, it would cost a bit extra. When Vasson saw the room he realised he'd been had again – the room was dreadful: depressingly airless and none too clean. A single unshaded light hung from the ceiling. It was not his day.

For a few moments he sat on the bed and looked in despair at his surroundings. The room brought back memories of other squalid rooms: the ones in Montmartre, all shabby, all depressing; the ones in the Old Quarter, hot and claustrophobic; the bare cell at the Jesuit school, white and unspeakably barren; and – so long ago – that other room. *God . . .*

He undressed slowly and got into the bed. At least the sheets were clean.

Tomorrow he would spell it out to the Boches: no more cheap hotels, no more squalor. Lots of cash, lots of information, and no interference. In one way it was irritating to have to educate them, the way he'd educated Kloffer, but at the same time he was rather looking forward to it. It was a challenge, and he would win it, the way he'd won with Kloffer.

Except that Kloffer knew his name . . .

After a long time he fell asleep.

He was in the old lady's house in Sèvres, walking along the passage, when he saw that the door to the store room was open and the light on. There were voices inside. He tried to get to the door but he couldn't move. He looked down and saw he had weights on his feet. Then Kloffer came out. He was carrying the gold. Kloffer grinned and said, 'I knew it was here all the time! I knew! Goodbye! Goodbye!' Then Vasson's arms were grabbed from behind and he was dragged out. Kloffer called, 'They're going to cut off your head, isn't that interesting?'

They put him in a cell. It was like the one at the school: bare, soulless, destroying. Father Ignatius was leaning over him. 'Eternal Father, I confirm; Eternal Son, I confirm; Eternal Holy Spirit, I confirm. May the Lord forgive you, Paul, for you have sinned. Like your mother sinned.'

What had his mother done? What sin could be so terrible? He heard himself ask, 'What sin? What sin?' and Father Ignatius shook his head gently and said, 'It is better that you do not ask, my son.' 'But why doesn't she come?' 'She doesn't choose to, Paul, and it's better that she doesn't.' 'But Father Francis told me she was dead.' 'Well, she is in a way, Paul.' 'I don't understand, I don't understand!' 'It is not for us to understand, my son, we must accept God's will – and with love in our hearts.'

I don't understand. I never have. Why doesn't she come to me? What has she done that is so terrible? Why did she beat me? *Why does she hate me so?*

I don't understand.

German efficiency was enough to drive anyone mad, with its rigid structures, its unyielding demands and its inevitable duplications. But it did mean everything got written down.

It was all there in the files. Every operation against the escape line which operated from Brussels. There was tons of it, much of it irrelevant, but Vasson wasn't complaining, although it took hours to sort out what was useful and what wasn't.

Generally, reports to be seen by senior officers were far

too optimistic and evasive to be useful. Much better were the situation reports with limited circulation. Names, places, hypotheses, action to be taken . . . it was all there.

Gradually Vasson built up a picture. The airmen got themselves to a farm or whatever, presumably having buried their parachutes and any other evidence of where they had landed. The farmer harboured them, or quickly passed them on to someone who would. Then, as soon as could be arranged, they were picked up by the organisation proper. How were they transported? Impossible to say, but for the longer parts of the journey it was certainly by train. Several of the couriers arrested so far were young girls. Vasson could imagine them: innocent-looking, charming, pretty enough to distract if necessary. Yes, the system must work well.

The couriers were probably changed at Brussels and again at Paris and maybe a third time on the way down to the Spanish border. He wondered how careful they were: whether or not the couriers actually met and knew each other or whether they operated a cut-off system whereby the airmen were taken to a park bench by one courier and left there for ten minutes before the next came to pick them up.

He looked up the interrogation reports. Some of those arrested had talked, but they appeared to be small fry – collectors or minor couriers. None of them had known the names of the main couriers, those who must be in touch with the central organisers. Other hadn't talked even when they were about to die. Extraordinary how little value people put on their own lives.

The infiltration operations mounted so far had been amateurish – and that was putting it kindly. The SD had sent two of its men into the Belgian countryside dressed as Canadian airmen. They were found four days later, dead. It was no surprise to Vasson; the two men probably spoke English with a German accent and didn't know what maple syrup was. The line must have an interrogation centre somewhere, where airmen's credentials were checked. Well, even if they hadn't they certainly would now, after that little fiasco.

Another time a Belgian-born SD agent had infiltrated the line as a courier, had sprung his trap far too soon and managed to catch only two people. The agent had then run like hell out of Brussels and was never seen again. An amateur.

One operation had been quite successful, however. Twenty arrests were made. But Vasson couldn't find the details; the report was marked: Refer to Luftwaffe Intelligence. He must ask about that.

He looked at the current situation report: there appeared to be only two leads at present; a young girl, the sister of a girl in custody, plus an older woman whose address had been found in the apartment of a minor courier. Both women had gone to ground. Nothing about this surprised Vasson: the Gestapo had probably gone straight round to their homes in full view of all the neighbours and waited for them to return. Subtlety and patience were not the Germans' strong points.

He noted the names of all the suspects to date and took brief details of addresses, possible roles in the line, and probable leads. It didn't add up to much. In their usual blundering way the Germans had fouled up everything that might have been worth pursuing.

Vasson went back to Mueller's office. Mueller was his liaison man: quite senior, a colonel in the SD. For some reason Vasson didn't understand, here in Belgium escaping airmen came under the Nazi security service or Luftwaffe Intelligence, and not the secret police.

Mueller was pale and fat, rather like a large slug. He looked as though he had indigestion; from time to time he unhappily patted his obscene stomach which pressed relentlessly against the field grey cloth of his uniform.

'Well?' he asked impatiently. 'Have you seen everything you need to see?'

'I think so.' Vasson sat down, though he had not been invited to do so. Mueller would not object. Mueller, for all his arrogance and impatience, was not a problem: he was a realistic man. He wanted results and he'd made it clear he was prepared to pay for them. Vasson's anger at being put in the seedy hotel was forgotten when Mueller had agreed to all his requests.

Vasson said, 'But there is one thing. An operation involving Luftwaffe Intelligence. The report's not in the file.'

'Ah yes. That was a joint operation. Extremely successful. For a week or so we operated a loop in the escape line.'

'A loop?'

Mueller looked patronisingly at Vasson. 'Ah? You do not know? No, why should you. We invented the idea!' His fat face crinkled up in what Vasson realised was a smile. 'A loop is an extra link in the escape chain which the organisers do not realise is there and which we create to extract intelligence. We pretend we are Resistance interrogators who must check the bona fides of the airmen. We ask them to tell us everything about their units and operations so we can check the facts with London.' He shrugged. 'It works every time. During this last operation they told us everything ... Most useful for the Luftwaffe and most useful for us too; we got several good descriptions of the people harbouring airmen. We made a number of arrests.'

Twenty to be precise. But, Vasson thought, they can never use that one again, not with this line anyway.

'One more thing,' Vasson said. 'Is the line in direct communication with Britain? Can they actually check the airmen's identities by radio?'

'We believe not. At one time we picked up clandestine

radio transmissions from this area, but no longer ... We must have got the operator.'

'So they have no contact ...'

'But they have back-up from London; a department of the British Ministry of Defence, called MI9, sends them money regularly, and probably arms too. The British have a name for the line – they call it Meteor.'

'Meteor ...'

Mueller sat upright and looked impatient again. 'Now! We have provided you with cash, we have provided you with information; what else do you require, may I ask?'

'A work permit in the name of Paul Lebrun. My occupation should be given as Engineer and the place of employment as some engineering works in, say Lyons. Then in brackets it should say: On secondment duties to Wehrmacht.'

'You want to say you're working for the Wehrmacht?'

'That's right. I'll also need a special travel permit which allows me frequent journeys between my base in Lyons and the occupied territories.'

'That's all?'

'Yes.'

'Now!' Mueller said disparagingly, 'How exactly do you propose to bring off this amazing success that I am told you will achieve?'

'I don't know.'

Mueller's face showed uncertainty: he wasn't sure if Vasson was purposely misleading him or just being difficult. 'I suggest you inform me when you *do* have a plan.'

'Certainly. But for a few days I want to get to know the city and feel my way around.'

Mueller eyed him suspiciously. 'You will not start anything without informing me, will you, Lebrun?'

'No.'

As Vasson left, Mueller repeated, 'And you have no plan at all?'

Vasson shrugged. 'In good time. You didn't give me many leads . . .'

Mueller nodded abruptly. 'Please report back in two days.'

Vasson hurried out, thinking: Like hell! He would report only when he was ready, and even then he wouldn't tell Mueller a damn thing about what he was doing. The Germans would only foul it up. Anyway he loved to have it all to himself; he hated to share it until the last possible moment.

His plan was the same as always: he had it all worked out. But this time it would take longer, he realised that there were so many people involved, so many contacts to make. Yes, it would take time . . . But he didn't mind; it added to the challenge and the excitement.

This one would be the best one yet, he felt it in his bones. This would be his greatest triumph.

Chapter 13

FALMOUTH. AT LEAST it *should* be. Since the first invasion scare all the railway signs had been removed, so one had to use timetables and guesswork to decide your location. Smithe-Webb stepped off the train, sniffed the sharp, salty Cornish air and thought how wonderfully refreshing it was after the smoke and grime of London.

It *was* Falmouth: there was a naval staff car outside the station, waiting to take him to Helford. The Major settled back in his seat and admired the rolling green countryside. He only wished he could get away from London more often. But his department of MI9 was based at the War Office in Whitehall and he hardly got away at all.

In his year at MI9 he'd heard a few whispers about Helford and the naval unit there – but nothing very definite. It was a clandestine outfit, and, although he'd guessed that they went over to what was known as the Other Side, he'd heard little else. He'd had few dealings with the Navy: almost all the Allied servicemen stranded in Europe – his customers, as he called them – were airmen and soldiers.

But since MI9 had asked for the Navy's help, Smithe-Webb had been finding out a bit more. The DDOD(I), the head of the Navy's Irregular Operations Division, had told him a bit about the Helford operations and, what was more important, had promised to help. He had, however, suggested that the major go down to Helford and talk to someone who knew the Other Side well, someone who could advise him on the practical problems his people were likely to meet. The inference was clear: the Navy could manage their end of the operation all right, but could MI9 control *theirs*?

Smithe-Webb took the point; that was why he was here.

After half an hour the road descended steeply towards the dull glint of water visible in the distance. They passed through a picturesque village and came to the banks of a wide river. The car stopped and Smithe-Webb got out. A launch with two ratings was waiting at the jetty and, as soon as he had climbed in, it set off towards a cluster of vessels moored in the main stream of the river. There was a large three-masted yacht which had a number of dinghies tied to it – some kind of mother ship perhaps; then, moored around it, four or five largish fishing boats. Most of them were painted regulation grey, but one had a strange combination of colours. Her superstructure and most of her topsides were grey, but her aft end was bright scarlet with some kind of pattern on it. There were several men standing in a small boat, painting the scarlet with grey. The launch made a neat semi-circle and approached the many-coloured boat. As they drew near Smithe-Webb saw the shadow of a name on the stern. It read: *Marie-Claire. Brest.*

The launch came alongside and a rating threw a line to someone on deck. Smithe-Webb looked up and stared in amazement. The fellow was a sight: unshaven, dirty and dressed like a fisherman. If they were playing at pirates, Smithe-Webb thought, they certainly looked the part.

Smithe-Webb put a foot up on the rubbing strake and hoisted himself over the gunwale onto the deck. He looked expectantly at the piratical figure, but after making fast the launch's painter the fellow sauntered off down the deck.

Suddenly there was a voice from behind. 'Good morning!'

Smithe-Webb turned and was met by a pair of penetrating blue eyes and an outstretched hand. Like the other fellow, this chap looked a mess: his clothing was shabby and oil-stained, he had two days' growth of beard, and, if the major wasn't mistaken, his breath reeked of alcohol. Smithe-Webb asked uncertainly, 'Er – Lieutenant Ashley?'

'Yes, I'm Ashley. But, if it doesn't seem impolite, who on earth are you?'

Richard Ashley smiled ruefully. 'Sorry, didn't mean to be rude, but we've just got back and . . . we're not at our best. Come and have a cup of something. I'm not sure what we can offer you . . .'

'Not to worry,' said Smithe-Webb hastily. 'Don't want to put you out or anything.'

'No, no. Must find you something, This is after all a ship of His Majesty's Navy and traditions must be upheld . . .' He laughed and Smithe-Webb saw that, despite the smiling mouth, the face was strained and drawn.

Smithe-Webb followed Ashley down the deck. He noticed that two men were grafting a plank of wood into a gap in the gunwale and that the deckhouse was riddled with bullet holes. Ashley turned and caught his gaze. 'We were badly straffed. One dead and two wounded. We've never been caught like that before.' He led the way into the deckhouse and indicated that Smithe-Webb should take a seat. 'That's the problem with going down to the Bay: it's fine once you're there, looking like any other old fishing boat, but it's an awful long way there and back. We get some air cover on the way out, but . . .' He smiled thinly. '. . . well, it's awfully lonely on the way home.' He reached down into a locker and pulled out a bottle of cognac. 'Don't suppose you'd like a glass of this delicious brew?'

Smithe-Webb shook his head. 'A bit early for me.'

Ashley nodded. 'I'll order you a tea then – I think that's all we've got.' He opened the door and shouted down the deck. He came back in and smiled. 'For myself, I'm going to have a large one of these. One of the few perks of the job. The fishermen with whom we, shall we say, *trade*, they give us this stuff. And magic it is too!'

A minute later one of the crew brought the tea, which was dark brown and very sweet and had obviously been brewing for some time. Smithe-Webb gritted his teeth and took a sip. The tea was ghastly and he grimaced. Ashley was talking to the sailor about the repair work and didn't see.

Smithe-Webb took the opportunity to take a look at the lieutenant. He reckoned the chap was somewhere in his late twenties, though he looked older, probably because of the tiredness. He was average-looking: of medium height, unremarkable features and, Smithe-Webb guessed, with a tendency to put on weight. But the blue eyes were extraordinary; you noticed them straight away. Another unusual thing was the way the man talked. His face was immensely alive and – what was the word? – magnetic. You couldn't take your eyes off him.

The sailor was asking a couple of questions. Like the rest of the crew he was fairly unkempt and Smithe-Webb noticed he had a strong foreign accent.

When the sailor had gone the major asked, 'Your crew, are they – RN?'

Ashley laughed. 'Most of them! The rest could be loosely described as on loan. Free French, ex-fishermen and very fine lads they are too.'

Ashley sat down, the brandy glass at his elbow, and lit a cigarette. 'I must apologise again for my rudeness. Quite honestly, I forgot you were coming. They did tell me, but you know how it is . . .!'

'Yes, I can imagine.'

'In this kind of operation, you ignore half the rules – and the other half don't apply. Orders never get written down . . . Besides which my memory is—' he laughed, '– not of the best!' Smithe-Webb felt sure it was perfectly adequate, but smiled nonetheless.

Ashley asked, 'So how can I be of help?'

Smithe-Webb said, 'Right. Perhaps I'd better tell you a bit about my department first. Basically, our job is to help our chaps to get out of Occupied Europe. Immediately after Dunkirk most of our customers were soldiers who got left behind after the evacuation. Quite a few made it back by getting help from the locals and making their way to neutral territory. Since then it's been mainly airmen, though we still get quite a few soldiers and even the odd sailor. Obviously it's pretty difficult for chaps to escape once the Germans have got them, but some do manage to get over the wire and our job is to try to make it easy for them once they're out. Having said that, by far the greatest number of our customers are evaders – men who've been shot down or whatever and have managed to keep *out* of German hands. We encourage the locals to look after them and get them back to us safely. Obviously I can't give you the details of how this is done . . .'

Ashley nodded. 'No, of course.'

'Our problem is that our present . . . er, methods . . . are under a lot of pressure, both from the Germans and from the sheer scale of the operations. The number of evading airmen is increasing and quite apart from not wanting to let our men fall into enemy hands, we *need* them. Those pilots are absolutely invaluable to the war effort. We have to get them back.' Without thinking Smithe-Webb sipped at the mug of tea and immediately choked.

'Bloody awful, isn't it?' Ashley smiled. 'But try and persuade Leading Seaman Evans to make it any other way and there'd be a mutiny. Change your mind and have a brandy?'

Smithe-Webb raised his eyebrows. 'No, really.' Ashley

poured himself another drink and Smithe-Webb wondered if the fellow always drank like this. He brought his mind back to the matter in hand. 'So . . . we're trying to open up more routes. There's an idea under consideration which would involve your outfit. At this point we're having a good look at the plan to see if it's really on or not. And that's where you come in . . .'

'Yes, I'd heard something about it. Glad to help, of course. I've already picked up quite a few airmen. I never know when they're coming, mind, they just get bundled aboard. But there's never any problem.'

'Yes, indeed. But this would be more organised, and the numbers much greater. Also . . . we weren't thinking of the Bay . . . Rather, we were thinking of going straight across. To North Brittany.'

Ashley sat up. 'Ah! I see!'

'I was hoping you might be able to tell me what would be involved.'

Ashley frowned, but he was obviously excited by the idea. 'Well of course the whole thing would have to be organised differently. It'd be no good using these boats, for a start. MGBs would be much better.'

'Yes, that's what your department suggested.'

'We're getting two, did you know that?'

The major nodded.

'They'll make a lot of difference to your sort of operation. We can go in at night, really fast, do the job and then be out again before anyone knows we were there. In fact, it has already been tried once or twice.'

'Oh?'

'Dropping off the odd person with their luggage, that kind of thing. Not your department, of course?'

Smithe-Webb shook his head. 'No, one of the others. SOE, in all probability, sending in agents.'

'The only real problem has been to get the passengers from the boat to the shore in one piece and not half-drowned. Even in a fairly sheltered spot the surf can be pretty rough. But that's being looked at . . . Our chaps are trying to come up with a special surfboat.' He paused. 'But having said that, MGBs are definitely the answer. We could pick up ten, twenty, maybe even thirty men in a night.'

The major smiled. 'That would be excellent. But what about the North Brittany coast? Your CO thought it might be difficult . . .?'

'Oh, did he? Well, let's have a look, shall we?' He called out of the door. 'Evans! Get over to *Spray* and fetch me some charts, would you? North Brittany and English Channel.' He said to Smithe-Webb. 'We only carry three charts on this boat and they're French. Wouldn't do to be caught with a set of best Admiralty charts, would it?'

Ashley was enjoying himself, Smithe-Webb could see. The signs of strain had gone from his face. The major found himself liking the chap. He was a straightforward sort of person, which Smithe-Webb always admired, and he had a sort of easy charm that made you warm to him. Just as long as he knew what he was doing. Smithe-Webb had the feeling he did.

'Good Lord!' exclaimed Smithe-Webb softly. There were rocks everywhere. Unless he was reading it wrong the chart showed the coast to be completely impenetrable. Even the estuaries seemed littered with dangers. 'Good Lord!' he repeated.

'It's not as bad as it looks,' Ashley said slowly. 'Many of these rocks are covered except at dead low water. If one studies it carefully one can usually find a way through. Now, where roughly were you thinking of mounting your operation?'

Smithe-Webb put his finger on the coast north-east of Morlaix. 'Somewhere around here if possible.'

'Right, let's look at the large-scale chart.' He pulled out

another chart and stared at it intently. 'Yes, there are several spots that are possible from my point of view. But we have to find a place that's good for your people too. Have they come up with any suggestions?'

'Not yet. Communications are a bit difficult at the moment.' Which meant he had no wireless operator there. Oh, that he had! It had taken long enough to persuade DDMI(P/W) that wireless operators were essential, then there'd been delays in finding volunteers and training them. After all, not everyone wanted to be a sitting duck for the Gestapo's wireless detectors.

'But you will be getting some local intelligence? On the siting of gun emplacements, and patrols and so on . . .?'

'Oh yes, in due course.'

'Right. Until then, let's assume that the main headlands are to be avoided. That would give us this cove here, and this bay . . .' He traced the coastline thoughtfully. 'No, not this one. The cliff's absolutely sheer at this point and there's no path . . .'

Smithe-Webb looked up, astonished. 'How on earth do you know that?'

'I tried to climb it once!'

'Good God!' Smithe-Webb was impressed.

'Here . . . this cove here . . .' Ashley stabbed a finger at the chart. 'This would be ideal. The approach is reasonably straightforward, there'd be no problem anchoring, and I can't see the Germans having guns and sentries in the bay itself . . . Also there's decent access to the beach from the cliff, or so it would appear. I've never been there myself so I couldn't be sure.'

Smithe-Webb was staring in disbelief. It was too good to be true. The place was only a mile or two from Tregasnou. What a stroke of luck! But perhaps there were disadvantages he hadn't spotted. He asked, 'What do my people need to look for when they recce the place? What are the problems going to be?'

'Well, we'll only be able to operate on moonless nights so some sort of signalling arrangement will be essential – by shaded torch or whatever – so there really mustn't be any Germans anywhere near by. It would be useful to know exactly how bad the surf gets too . . . You can never tell whether one spot's going to be worse than another.' He paused and thought for a moment. 'Also your people will have to be prepared for some long waits on the beach; we could never give a definite time of arrival. Some nights we might not be able to turn up at all. You know – weather or engine failure or whatever. They'd have to be prepared for that . . . have contingency plans to hide all the passengers again, and so on. Oh, and we couldn't operate in high summer . . .'

'What?' Smithe-Webb frowned.

'No, I'm afraid not. The nights in mid-summer just wouldn't be long enough to get us over and back in time. From Dartmouth, where the MGBs will be based, it's a hundred miles. That's well over four hours even in a fast boat. Allowing one to two hours for approach and pick-up and four hours back, that's ten hours – call it twelve. We could probably operate as late as April with a bit of luck. In winter there's more bad weather, of course, but at least you can slow down and take it easy and know you have plenty of darkness to hide under.'

Ashley looked up at Smithe-Webb and smiled cheerfully. 'It's August now. By the time the thing is set up we'll be into autumn. So we'll have at least six months. We could get an awful lot of airmen out in that time! All it needs is reasonably good communications and some efficient organisation at your end.'

Smithe-Webb stared back at the chart and wished he could smile as cheerfully. Organisation was the one thing he couldn't guarantee. He hadn't mentioned that, and didn't intend to. No point in getting a sour note into the proceedings.

Richard Ashley said, 'The pick-up must be fast and well thought out – on both sides – otherwise . . .'

Smithe-Webb nodded. He had the message loud and clear. If there was a muck-up then everyone would get caught.

'. . . But I'm sure your people will be first class. The Bretons usually are.'

'They're good people,' Smithe-Webb agreed. He wasn't sure he could say the same for the Free French officer who was meant to be organising the line. Smithe-Webb hadn't liked the chap at all. But no point in fretting about it; they'd been forced to use him. The Free French had to be humoured and that was all there was to it. But, Smithe-Webb thought sadly, it was not the same as choosing your own man, not the same at all.

But on this side of the operation he might be able to get the man he wanted. He asked Ashley, 'Do you think you might be able to do the job yourself? You used to be on MGBs, didn't you? It would be tremendous from our point of view.'

Ashley stroked his chin. 'I was on torpedo boats actually, not gun boats. But . . . well, I *am* rather tempted. They say the new boats can do 30 knots. Very useful for getting out of trouble!' He smiled. 'Yes, I'd love to give it a go.'

He shot a glance at Smithe-Webb, and said mischievously, 'We could fix it between us. If you tell the Admiralty that you need me and then I volunteer, they can't refuse, can they?' Suddenly he laughed, his eyes sparkling with amusement, and Smithe-Webb had the feeling that few people refused Richard Ashley anything.

Smithe-Webb found himself smiling too. His feeling of optimism returned. If these MGBs could get there and back, then they were halfway there.

*

Ashley watched the launch heading back towards the jetty and wondered if he should have gone into the problems in more detail.

He walked slowly along the deck. God, he felt tired. He sat on the hatch coaming, and lighting a cigarette, inhaled deeply.

He tried to think, but the tiredness was clouding his brain. Or perhaps his mind was addled by the cigarettes and the brandy. Just as likely.

Problems . . . There'd certainly be a few. He'd made it sound easy and it wasn't. He should have told the major about the navigation problems: the tricky tides and the lack of navigation aids. He should have admitted that it would be bloody difficult to find the right place at all.

Then there was the weather: he should have spelt out the problems in more detail. Even in fairly rough conditions they might have to cancel operations; in gales they most certainly would.

Damn. He should have made the whole thing plainer.

Still . . . they should be able to get across pretty often. A lot depended on the efficiency of the organisation on the other side, of course. The major had been a little evasive about that . . .

Perhaps the escape line was brand new, or badly run or perhaps it was a complete shambles. Yes, there was always that possibility, though he'd be surprised. The Bretons were a cool, determined, closely-knit people. He'd be surprised if they mucked things up.

Well, whatever the situation, he'd give it a go. It was a marvellous challenge.

Besides, he had been on the Bay run for over nine months now and it was getting to him. Pretending to be a fishing boat was too much like sitting waiting to be a target at the Germans' convenience. The boat had an engine, to be sure – but it produced only six knots. As much good as a wound-up elastic band. And then there was the small problem about being captured when disguised as a French fisherman. According to the powers-that-be all you had to do was to pop a Royal Navy Issue cap on your head, show your papers, and you'd be treated as a prisoner of war. Ashley wasn't so sure: he had the feeling the Germans would politely ignore the caps and line you up against a wall for target practice.

He thought back to the last trip . . . It had gone wrong from the start. They'd gone to the Scillies as usual, to their secret anchorage, and turned the boat from a grey MFV into a Concarnean trawler, complete with bright orange paint and a few fancy patterns on the transom. But as soon as they'd left, the weather had turned bad and they'd had an uncomfortable trip. When they eventually got to the Bay it had taken far too long to make contact with the fleet, and a *Raumboot* had got suspicious and almost put a landing party aboard. Finally, on the way back, they'd been caught. Good and proper. In his mind's eye he saw it all again: everyone reaching for weapons, the low-flying plane, the bullets tearing into Jean-Pierre's body . . . He shuddered.

Perhaps he was losing his nerve. He took out another cigarette and lit it. He looked at the hand holding the cigarette: its fingers were bright yellow with nicotine and shook slightly. Too many cigarettes. Too much booze. Definitely time for a change.

A tern called overhead and he looked up. He followed it as it soared towards the river mouth and the open sea. Any time now it would be flying south to its winter quarters on some Atlantic island. This summer there had been thousands of terns on Scilly.

The islands: that was the one thing he would miss.

Whenever they'd sailed to the secret anchorage in the north of the islands, to paint the fishing boat, he'd been happy.

The secret anchorage lay between two islands – Tresco

and Bryher – in the small inlet known as New Grimsby
Harbour. He had remembered coming there before the war
– when was it? – '35? Some time then. The narrow inlet
had been empty then, not a fishing boat or islanders' gig to
be seen. He had anchored *Dancer* in the centre of the
basin, and rowed across to Bryher and made a camp on
the shore, and walked round the island and watched the
incredible surf in Hell Bay and wondered what it would be,
like to be shipwrecked. In the evening he had made a fire
and cooked a couple of mackerel and slept under a
tarpaulin in the shelter of a rock. The dawn had been still
and yellow and he had watched a cormorant diving into
the cool depths of the secret harbour. Later an oyster-
catcher had appeared, its long yellow beak probing the
stones uncovered by the falling tide. He had sat for a long
time, quite motionless, not wanting anything to change,
hoping it would be like that for ever.

He'd been twenty-one then, fresh out of Dartmouth,
and greedy for everything, preferably all at once. Strange
how everyone told you there was no going back, that the
simplicity of your youth could never be recaptured; strange
how right they were. But one day, when the world was
sane again, he'd go back. One day, when there were no
grey ships of war to ruin the quiet of that marvellous place,
only *Dancer* tugging gently at her chain . . .

In the meantime he would miss the place.

He rubbed his eyes. His head ached terribly. He got
wearily to his feet. He found himself reaching automatically for a cigarette and stopped in mid air. He must get fit.
Soon he'd be running a proper ship again, crewed by the
lads in blue. He was rather looking forward to it.

Chapter 14

---·---

JULIE DREW THE curtains over the tiny window and took a last look at the child in the bed. Peter was already fast asleep, his mouth slightly open, his breathing slow and steady. She pulled the covers up round his neck and kissed him softly on the cheek. He was such a big boy now, five and a half, and tall, oh so tall. She could hardly believe it – the time had gone so quickly. It seemed only yesterday that he was a baby.

She took a last look at him, then, picking up the flickering oil lamp, went down the steep staircase to her room. She paused and listened carefully. There was quite a wind; it was blowing round the house in long sighs. Outside, one of the cattle moved noisily against the side of the barn. Somewhere down in the village a dog was barking. Then, from almost overhead, a creaking noise. Julie stiffened, then relaxed as she recognised the sound of Peter settling more comfortably in his bed.

It was a habit now, listening. And not just for Peter – that was instinctive – but for other human sounds. The sounds of people arriving with messages or sometimes even 'parcels': foreign airmen with pale, frightened faces who were taken off into the night to some other more welcoming farmhouse. The comings and goings went on all the time now that autumn had come. She dreaded them; they made her horribly nervous. Yet – she had an awful urge to *know*. It was like being punished: the sooner you knew what was in store the easier it was to cope with.

And now she heard something. The sound of the back door opening. Someone had come then. Her heart sank. She opened the bedroom door and went quietly through into the kitchen. The figure of her uncle was leaning against the open doorway talking quietly and urgently to someone outside in the darkness.

Julie looked at the clock on the mantelpiece. It was eight o'clock.

They must have forgotten the time. They must have! She hovered uncertainly, wondering whether she should interrupt.

Now the person outside was speaking. The voice was louder, less secretive. Julie recognised it: the voice of the stranger, the *leader*, as he was meant to be. He was making no attempt to be discreet; he never did. But at this time of the evening Julie could hardly believe it. The man was mad ... or stupid! Worse, from the way he was talking, Julie had a feeling he wasn't going to stop.

The voice was saying, '... No, no, there is no problem there. I have Gaston from Plouga in charge. I have given him orders to bring the ten parcels from Madame Lelouche's place. It is all organised, I assure you ...'

Julie sighed with frustration. Surely Jean must realise the time and how dangerous it was ... She looked at the clock again. It was two minutes past eight. She could bear it no longer. She came up beside her uncle and looked worriedly at the leader, waiting for a break in the conversation. But he continued to speak and Julie suddenly realised that he was doing it to impress her, to show her how important he was. She bit her lip with the effort of staying silent. Eventually the man said, 'Ah, Madame! Good evening. I am sorry to disturb the household ...'

'Monsieur, ... please, the soldiers will be back soon. You ... your visits here put us in danger! Wouldn't it be possible to come back later? Please!'

The stranger smiled thinly. 'Madame, our business has

to be properly planned! You obviously don't understand what is involved ... And I assure you that there is no danger.'

Julie thought: This man is impossible, like a brick wall. 'Monsieur, surely the planning could be less – public!'

Jean shuffled uneasily and the stranger began to look annoyed. Julie couldn't help feeling glad; at least she was getting through to them. The stranger said coldly, 'Madame, you would do better to keep out of matters that do not concern you!'

Julie felt a surge of anger. 'Monsieur, they concern me directly – which you seem to forget at your convenience!'

Jean put a hand on Julie's shoulder and said gently, 'It's all right, he's just going. Really.'

'Not a moment too soon!' She turned and strode over to the stove. She began to stir the soup too quickly and immediately slopped some of the liquid over the side of the pan. There was a spitting and hissing as the soup hit the hotplate. Julie reached impatiently for a cloth and dabbed the remaining liquid off the stove. She was shaking with anger. She hated losing her temper. She knew she should try to calm down but while this dreadful man was still at the door she just couldn't. A pity Tante Marie was looking after Madame Gillet for the evening: she would have given him short shrift.

The burning soup was hissing loudly; Julie missed the sound of the front door opening and the steps crossing the front parlour. The rap on the parlour door made her jump so much that she jerked at the spoon and hot liquid spattered over her apron. She stared in horror as the door opened and the two familiar uniforms appeared. The two soldiers smiled politely at her as they always did, then looked curiously past her to where her uncle and the leader stood at the open back door.

For a moment they were all frozen, like a tableau: Julie at the stove, the soldiers in the doorway and the two men at the open back door. Then Jean gave the Germans a slight nod, turned his back on them and said to the man, 'Well, I'll deliver that grain in the morning, then. But I've only four kilos to spare – and I'll have to charge you a good price for it!'

The man smiled. 'Fair enough. I know how it is – we must be commercial about this! Oh, and you won't forget the other matter?'

Julie realised with dismay that the leader was enjoying the scene. He was going to play it out! He thought he was being so clever. Julie thought: What conceit! And she had the feeling he was fooling no-one: the two soldiers looked distinctly suspicious. Julie clattered some plates and said rather too loudly, 'The soup is ready. Please go and sit down.'

The soldiers looked surprised: normally Julie never spoke to them. They shuffled back into the parlour and as soon as she heard them drawing up their chairs, she took in a tray with two bowls of soup and some bread on it. As she put the bowls on the table she heard the distant sound of the back door closing. The horrid man had gone. At last!

One of the soldiers started to speak to her, something about what a cold day it was. She ignored him as she usually did and he fell silent. Good. One might have to provide accommodation and two meals a day for them, but there was no law that said one had to speak to them. Julie left the room, closing the door firmly behind her.

Her uncle was standing by the stove. He made a wide expansive gesture with his hands, as if to say, What could I do?

Julie slumped into a chair and her uncle drew up another close beside her. They sat in silence until, finally, they heard the sound of chairs being scraped back in the parlour and the front door opening and closing again. The

Germans had gone out for their customary drink. After a few minutes Julie spoke.

'That man . . .' She shook her head. 'He is a *danger*. I know it – everyone knows it.'

'Yes, but . . . Julie, please realise, we have to put up with him. He's the only contact we have, the only hope of getting all the parcels away.'

'Yes, but at what cost?'

The old man sighed. 'I know, I know. But you must understand that there are no fewer than thirty parcels waiting to be sent away. If we can't make contact with the British and have boats sent over, we'll be stuck with them. The longer these parcels are here, the greater the risk for those hiding them. And there are more arriving every day! We must, we *must*, keep that contact, otherwise what are we to do? Give them over to the Germans, eh? Wait until our houses are bulging with British airmen and pretend they're really French. Eh?'

Julie nodded wearily. She had to acknowledge the difficulty of passing the British off as local people. Quite apart from the language difference, they *looked* so alien. She said with a sigh, 'I do see the problem. But I can't understand why you should have to put up with that – that person. Surely the line could be run just with local people and perhaps one outside wireless operator. Surely!'

'Ah, but that's the problem. The only wireless operator is far away – in Paris, I think. And this fellow, he is the only person with contact. The British sent him over. What can we do?'

'Make him be quiet for a start!' Julie found herself getting angry again. 'Even I, a person who tries *not* to hear anything, even I know exactly who's in the organisation. I could give you a list right now! And if I know, then the whole village knows, not to mention the whole of the Côtes du Nord!'

'But who would talk? No Breton! Never!'

Julie laughed bitterly. 'I wish I had your faith in human nature!'

Then she sighed and patted her uncle's hand. He looked so old and worried that she hated to depress him.

The old man said softly, 'But we have to do something, don't we? We can't stand aside and just watch, can we?'

'I don't know. Sometimes I wonder if all these terrible risks are worthwhile.' She looked at her uncle and said simply, 'Anyway, look at me. I do nothing and *my* conscience is clear.' She looked away and patted his hand again. 'But I can see that you must do what you must. I don't blame you for that. Just . . . *do* try to keep it away from us, Jean, please. I worry so much about Peter . . .'

Jean nodded, and said thoughtfully, 'But Juliette, we don't hide parcels here. We agreed that. For *your* sake, and Peter's. So there is really very little risk for you. For me – ah, well, that doesn't matter. I'm an old man.'

Julie said heavily, 'Even then, they take hostages, don't they? And shoot them? Innocent women and children. Oh, the children!' She could hardly bear to think of it. There had been an incident in Morlaix, after a German had been shot. They had taken twenty women and children, lined them up and mown them down. Julie had heard the shots from her office. She had cried out and wept with rage and uselessness.

Jean said impatiently, 'That was the communists! Stupid fools. They just kill Germans and never think of the consequences. *They*'re the real dangers! I'll never help that lot of anarchists, never! And—' he wagged a finger '– I will never have another one of them in my house again. And that includes Michel—'

'I agree that their methods are – wrong. But they *are* on our side, uncle.'

'When it suits them! Ha!' Jean stood up, went to the

mantelpiece and picked up his pipe which he tapped angrily against the chimney. 'They were on the German side at first, remember! Remember? Then, when the Germans did the dirty on Russia – which anyone of any brain could have seen coming – then they changed sides. Very convenient! Ha!'

He filled his pipe with a plug of tobacco and lit it in a cloud of smoke. Julie hoped he wouldn't regret it: the tobacco was his last until the beginning of the month.

The old man puffed more calmly at his pipe and said quietly, 'I'm sorry about Michel – but I feel rather strongly about the matter. I told him to his face. I told him he wasn't welcome here!'

Julie frowned. 'When?'

The old man stared at her. 'But ... didn't you know? He's back.'

'What!'

'Yes, he's here, God rot his soul. I saw him in the village today. I thought your aunt had told you? Anyway, I told him that, with regret, he was not to set foot in this house again. I told him—'

Julie got to her feet. 'Where is he?'

The old man looked at her sharply and shrugged.

She went to the table and picked up her purse. 'I'm going down to the village – to see if I can find him.'

The old man said, 'God in heaven, why?'

'Because ... Well...' It was difficult to think of a reason. Finally she said, 'He *is* one of the family ... Maybe he needs help.'

And, she thought, because I want to see him anyway, I want to see him very much indeed. She said, 'I don't mean any disrespect, uncle, and I understand about not having him in the house, but—'

Jean raised his hand. 'Stop! Don't say any more. Talk to him if you must, but if you take my advice you won't be seen with him. And don't tell me what he's up to. I don't want to know!' He added automatically, 'And be careful down the lane. I never trust those soldiers.'

'I'll be careful.' She blew him a kiss and, pulling on her warmest coat, hurried out into the night.

It was very dark. The wind was howling in from the sea, tearing at the hedgerows and whistling through the occasional solitary pine, bent into a tortured shape by a hundred storms.

Julie shivered slightly and walked more quickly, her head bent low, her eyes on the dark road ahead.

Yes, she wanted to see Michel, she wanted to see him very much. She had been thinking about him increasingly in the last few months, hoping he'd come back . . .

The last two years had been lonely. When Peter was small and needed her so much she hadn't minded being on her own. But since he'd been at school and often went out to play with his friends the loneliness was awful, like a terrible weight pressing down on her.

Sometimes she felt guilty at being lonely. She'd been so happy here, she'd adored the peace and tranquillity, she'd been so grateful for finding a home: in those early days she'd loved everything about it. She still did! And yet . . . the thought of staying here for ever, with only Peter and Jean and Tante Marie and her books for company, filled her with dread. She was twenty-five and the years were beginning to slip away. Twenty-five! Her chances of – why couldn't she say it? – *of finding a husband* were getting slimmer all the time. And she *did* want a husband, she knew that. Often she lay awake at night imagining what it would be like . . . Having someone to talk to and laugh with, having someone *there*. What she wanted more than anything was to *share* – her life, Peter, everything. When she imagined being married, the lovely feeling of warmth and tenderness, she wanted it very badly.

There was no mistaking the café in the darkness: light was leaking from its blacked-out windows in a dozen places and the sound of voices and laughter floated on the air. Julie approached slowly. If Michel wasn't here, then someone would probably know where he was.

She waited: there was no question of going in on her own. At last someone came out. It was an old man called Pierre, a cowherd from a nearby farm. He'd had several glasses too many. She gave him her message and directed him gently back into the café.

A few moments later the old man reappeared, nodded to her and went off into the night.

Then the door opened again and Michel was standing there.

Julie started to smile. 'Michel, how lovely to . . .' But he was looking behind him. Then, taking her arm, he pulled her quickly away from the café.

They walked briskly, in silence. Presently they came to a barn at the edge of the village. His voice whispered, 'In here!' Inside it was pitch dark. Julie could hear Michel tramping across a bed of straw to the far side. She put out her hands and felt her way forward. She tripped over a bale of straw, recovered, and bumped her shoulder against the side of what was probably a cart.

'All right?' His voice was close by.

'I think so.' She sat down carefully and heard him sit beside her.

She asked gently, 'Are you in trouble? What's the matter?'

'Mmmm?' He laughed softly. 'No, I'm not in trouble. Well – no more than usual.'

'Then, why all this?'

'I just thought it would be better if you weren't seen with me, that's all.'

'Better for who?' But she knew what he meant.

'Why, better for you, of course! Your uncle doesn't

want me in his house, half the village think my politics stink, the other half are prepared to argue with me over a glass of wine – but none of them would let his daughter be seen with me. Better for *you*!'

She asked, 'Where have you been all this time?'

'Oh, away.'

She could tell that he didn't want to say any more. But she ventured, 'You've been all right though? Safe, I mean?'

'Oh, yes. Don't worry your head about me. I always look after myself.'

'Michel, I must ask . . . You haven't been working with the Germans, have you? I couldn't bear that.'

'Good God, no!'

He sounded outraged and Julie said quickly, 'I mean, you did talk about it . . . In Morlaix. Don't you remember?'

'Ha! That was a long time ago. And I never worked with the Germans then anyway. Now? I can assure you that I kill them, blow them up and destroy them whenever I can. But the less said about that the better.'

'Yes, yes. I'm sorry. I didn't mean to . . .'

'Forget it.'

Julie peered through the darkness and said wistfully, 'I wish I could see your face.'

He laughed. 'It hasn't changed. Just older. Here, I'll have a cigarette. That'll shed some light. I've been longing for a smoke for hours, but I'm too mean to share any of my hard-earned cigarettes with the old fools back there. They think anyone from the town has plenty to spare.'

She heard him fumbling in his pockets, then there was a sudden blaze of light and he was drawing on a cigarette. She looked at his face and was slightly shocked. She'd forgotten how deep his frown was and how narrow his mouth. She'd forgotten, too, how bitter was his expression. She realised she'd forgotten a lot about him . . .

He was asking, 'And how have you been?'

'Oh. All right really. We have just about enough to eat.

There's no help on the farm any more, so Jean has to keep it going by himself. Tante Marie and I help when we can . . . And Peter does too, of course.'

'Peter, he must be quite a young man by now.'

'Yes. Five and a half.'

'And he's well too?'

'Yes.' She didn't elaborate. His question had been polite but automatic. She had the feeling he wasn't really interested.

'Are you still working in that place at Morlaix?'

She nodded in the darkness. 'Yes, the same old place. Sometimes I think I'll be there when I'm sixty.'

'But your papers. They've stood up all right?'

'Oh yes!' She reached out and found his wrist. 'I can't tell you what a difference it's made. Knowing they're all right – genuine. It's given me peace of mind. I can't thank you enough!'

She fumbled for his hand, but there was no answering squeeze and his hand felt limp in hers. Blushing in the darkness, she withdrew. He asked, 'Did you ever use that stamp and those papers you pinched?'

She frowned. 'No. I still don't really know why I took them. It seemed a sort of safeguard at the time.'

'Well, hang on to them. You never know when they might come in useful. But for God's sake don't tell anyone about them and don't leave them lying around. Have you got them hidden?'

'Of course.' Julie felt a little hurt: did he really think she would leave them lying around? 'I've got them well hidden where no-one can find them. We've got two soldiers billeted on us, you know.'

'What!'

His voice was very sharp and she wondered why he was so surprised. She said quickly, 'Yes, lots of people have. It's nothing unusual.'

'But your uncle – he's involved with this escape line.'

Julie gulped and stared at the glow of Michel's cigarette, wondering what on earth she should say. Jean certainly wouldn't have told Michel about his involvement. How, then, did Michel know?

'Well?'

'I . . . I can't say. We don't talk about those sorts of things.'

He sighed impatiently. 'Come on, Julie, don't be silly! I know all about it. I heard within five minutes of coming back to the area. My people in Morlaix not only know who works the line, but they know all the operational details.'

'Oh no—'

'It's common knowledge. Among my comrades, anyway.'

Julie felt her heart turn to ice. 'The Germans . . .' she whispered. 'Do they know?'

'I wouldn't be surprised. And what bothers me is that, when the trouble breaks as it surely will, the finger of blame will probably be pointed at me and my friends when in fact it's that lunatic who's running your line who should be shot. He's obviously never heard of the word "security". Where did they find him, eh?'

'London.'

'Ah, a Free French hero then?'

'Yes.'

Michel exclaimed, 'The sooner you're rid of him the better.'

'I know, I know. I hate the horrid little man. He's so conceited, you have no idea. Everyone – well, they go along with him because he's the only link with London.' She sighed deeply. 'I wish they could see what madness it is.'

'My only advice is to keep well out of it. Don't get involved! The work is best left to men and old ones at that, then it doesn't matter so much when they get shot.'

So practical – or callous, depending on how you looked at it. Julie stared into the darkness, trying to understand how one came to think like that.

She heard Michel stand up and saw the glow of the cigarette disappear as he stubbed it against the side of the cart. A couple of sparks floated down and Julie automatically reached out to catch them before they touched the straw.

He said, 'Come on! It's time we got back. We don't want Jean to think that I'm filling your head with revolution, do we?'

Julie thought: But we haven't even begun to talk ... Then she remembered what she'd wanted to talk about. Suddenly it didn't seem very important any more.

She heard him move off towards the crack of grey light which marked the door. Julie got hurriedly to her feet and followed him, stumbling across the bundles of straw. When she reached the door he had opened it and was waiting. In the faint grey illumination of the night she could just make out his features. They were severe and hard. Julie looked at him curiously, wondering how she could have forgotten how very serious he was and how very – unyielding.

He said, 'By the way, do they tell you when a boat's coming?'

'No. I never ask – and they never tell me. Why?'

'Well, just keep out of the way tomorrow night. According to my information, there's going to be an operation then. I'm sure the information's good. No moon, you see, and the country crawling with hidden airmen longing to get home. If it isn't tomorrow night then it must be soon after. But my friends say it'll be tomorrow – and they don't usually get these things wrong.'

Julie closed her eyes. Was there anything he didn't know? She said slowly, 'I'll ... take Peter away for the night ... Thanks for telling me.'

He took her arm and guided her out into the road. They

walked in silence until they reached the crossroads at the centre of the village. People were coming out of the café. Instinctively they drew into the darkness at the side of the road and followed the wall round until they were in the lane and heading up the hill towards the house.

Julie didn't want him to come any further. She turned and whispered, 'Goodbye, Michel.' On an impulse she added passionately, 'Don't kill Germans if you can avoid it. They'll only take hostages again. Children . . . They take children, Michel.'

'Same soft-hearted Julie.' There was a trace of scorn in his voice and she felt hurt. How could he be so hard? And why did he have to make her feel foolish? He went on, 'Of course we do try to avoid killing Germans. But when it comes to blowing up something important, we have to do it, and that's all there is to it. Children suffer anyway, from bombing raids, starvation, lots of things. The destruction of a factory is more important than – many things. But it's nothing to how the Russian peasants are suffering . . . They're dying in their thousands!'

Julie could think of nothing to say. He added, 'Anyway, you'd do best not to think about such things. They'll happen whether you worry about them or not.'

Julie suddenly felt sad and tired. She said softly, 'Good-bye, Michel,' and walked away. He hurried after her and took her arm. 'Julie, remember one thing – don't get involved!'

'Yes, you told me.'

'But you might get into trouble without realising it. You . . . don't know how they can drag you into these things.'

Anyone would think she was a seventeen-year-old straight out of school. She pulled in her breath and said tightly, 'I'll remember that.'

She walked away and this time he did not follow her. Despite the steepness of the hill she walked rapidly, hitting the road with her feet, pumping her legs in steady rhythm, climbing faster and faster until she realised she was almost home. But she didn't want to go into the house yet and she walked on towards the open cliffs and the low roar of the distant surf.

For a moment she almost continued past the end of the made-up road and onto the track which led through the fields to the open heathland. Then she remembered that there were patrols along the clifftop and they shot on sight. She stopped and leaned against a low wall and wrapped her arms tightly about her and sighed deeply.

She tried to separate her thoughts, to look at them coolly so that her anger would go away.

For one thing, it was obvious that he didn't care for her. He pretended to be concerned for her safety, but she couldn't help wondering why. There must be a reason. Because in every other way he was as cold as ice. No, he didn't care for her. The strange thing was, she didn't mind a bit now. In fact, she was rather glad because she realised she didn't care for *him* either. It was impossible to care for someone as hard and callous as that. She had forgotten just how cold he was . . .

There was something else, too. She hated to admit it, but her pride had been hurt. She had gone to meet him, imagining he would be glad to see her – and he had treated her like a child. He had humiliated her – very subtly but very definitely – and it made her shudder.

She was angry – but not with Michel, with herself. What a fool she'd been! She'd built up a picture of Michel that bore no resemblance to the person he really was. She'd imagined him as a husband, as a lover; she'd made him into what she wanted him to be. It was self-delusion. Puppy love!

It began to rain, the drops driven by the wind into a horizontal curtain of penetrating wetness. Julie pulled her coat more tightly about her and began to walk slowly back down the lane. She wasn't angry any more, just rather cross and sad.

One thing: she wouldn't be so stupid again.

The most important thing in her life was Peter. He was the only one who really mattered. Tomorrow night she would take him to stay in the village, in a safe house, away from everything. Then if anything went wrong . . . *neither* of them would get caught.

A floorboard creaked and Julie woke with a start. It had taken her an hour to get to sleep and now she was wide awake again. It was hopeless: she was as jumpy as a cat and she knew it would take just as long to get back to sleep again. Being in a strange bed was half the problem; Madame Boulet's house was only a short distance down the lane, in the centre of the village, but it might as well be a hundred miles away. Apart from anything else, the bed was lumpy.

She put out an arm and touched the sleeping figure beside her. That was another thing: though it was lovely to share a bed with Peter, she found it difficult to relax in case she should move in her sleep and disturb him. It was disconcerting, too, to hear the steady breathing and occasional sighs of someone sleeping beside you, even when that someone was your own child.

But what really made it impossible to sleep was knowing what was happening – out *there*, in the fields and down on the beach. Julie began to wonder how they got the airmen to the beach. Did they creep across the fields like shadows? Or did they walk brazenly along the roads? Whichever way, the risk was tremendous. Sometimes the Germans sent out extra patrols . . . And then how did the boat find the right beach? Did they signal? No, surely not . . .

She couldn't see how it could be done safely. There were too many things to go wrong.

Best to try to sleep. She closed her eyes and made a conscious effort to relax her body.

Suddenly there was a faint moan. Instantly she was tense and alert again. It had sounded like someone in terrible anguish, sighing . . . She listened, straining to pick up the slightest noise, but all she could hear was the roar of silence.

Then it came again. A slight moaning which began as a low murmur and grew into a whine.

Julie suddenly relaxed with a groan. What a nervous idiot she was becoming! It was the wind. Only the wind!

She closed her eyes again and tried to calm herself. The wind . . . It sounded so different here. At home it whistled or, sometimes, when it was really blowing, it howled like an animal in pain. But this moaning . . . it made her feel uneasy. She tried to guess how strong the wind was now. A gale at least. The sea would be rough then, and there would be large breakers on the beach. She tried to imagine what it must be like for the British boat, trying to get in towards the land. Perhaps enormous waves were breaking right over it . . .

There was a faint tapping on the door. Julie almost jumped out of her skin. She lay rigid.

The tapping came again, soft but insistent.

Julie got quickly out of bed, pulled the covers up over Peter, and dragged on her dressing gown. She tiptoed to the door and opened it.

Madame Boulet was standing there, her anxious face illuminated by the candle in her hand. Immediately Julie knew something was wrong. 'What is it?'

The older woman whispered, 'Come down. Please. Now.'

Julie tied her dressing-gown cord and, closing the door

behind her, followed Madame Boulet down the stairs. The hall was in darkness, but light was coming from the kitchen door which was slightly open. As they approached Julie could hear the low murmur of a man's voice.

The two women went in. Monsieur Boulet was sitting by the stove, fully dressed, his face solemn. Another man who Julie knew only vaguely was sitting opposite, talking urgently. When they saw the women they rose to their feet, anxiety on their faces. Julie thought: God, the Germans have found out. Everyone's been captured. Everyone's been killed!

Julie said, 'What is it? Please tell me!'

The second man said quickly, 'Nothing's happened! Not yet anyway. But we need your help, Madame.'

Julie let out a sigh of relief and sat down weakly on a chair. 'Thank God ... I thought for a moment ...' Then she remembered what the man had said. 'Help? How can I help?'

'Madame, believe me I would not ask ... except that you are the only person ... Madame, we need someone who speaks English. There is a young pilot. He is injured. We have done what we can for him but ... Please come and talk to him. Otherwise – Otherwise we are all in trouble. Please, Madame.'

'I don't understand ... What do I have to do?'

'Madame, please, I beg of you. It isn't far. Just at Roget's farm, up near the point. You will understand when we arrive. Please, we have no time ...' He glanced at the clock on the mantelpiece. Julie saw that it was almost midnight. She looked back at the man. She remembered that he was a farmer from the next village, a nice man who usually smiled. Now, as he waited for her reply, his face was deathly serious.

They were all watching her, waiting for her to speak. Julie felt the beginnings of panic. How could she possibly decide at a moment's notice? It really wasn't fair!

Then she realised they must be desperate. For them to ask her something like this – and in the middle of the night – something must be very wrong. Perhaps this pilot had terrible injuries . . . Perhaps he needed help . . . And he was young, the man had said . . .

Julie said abruptly, 'I'll go and get dressed,' because it was easier to say that than to refuse. She hurried from the room before she changed her mind.

In the darkness of the bedroom she found some clothes and started to pull them on, wondering what she was getting herself into.

She dropped a shoe which clattered to the floor. Peter turned over and moaned quietly. Julie found the shoe and put it on. She went over to the bed and, leaning down, put her face against the soft, gentle cheek.

She took a last look at him, murmured, 'I love you,' and left the room.

The staircase was in total darkness and she had to feel her way down. When she reached the kitchen the lights were out and the back door already open. A blast of cold air came from the door, making her shiver. Someone helped her on with her coat and then she was outside, following the man as he led the way down the side of the house.

They turned a corner of the house and met the full force of the wind. It tore at Julie's coat and blew her hair across her eyes until she could hardly see. She pulled the coat back round her and held her hair back from her face and saw that they had reached the road.

In the blackness Julie could just make out the figure of the farmer as he strode off in the direction of Roget's farm. She followed quickly before she lost him in the murk. So they did use the roads on these night jaunts. Julie glanced nervously behind her. Sometimes she'd heard German trucks driving through the village in the middle of the night. If one came along now what would they do?

Jump over the wall into a field, presumably. If there was time.

The farmer's pace was relentless and when they came to the steep hill which led up to the point Julie had to make an effort to keep up. She thought of asking him to slow down, but then she remembered what he'd said about there being no time and she pushed herself on, concentrating on each step, closing her mind to everything except the rhythm of her stride.

At one point she looked up and he was gone, melted into the pitch darkness ahead. But then he reappeared again, standing, waiting for her to catch up. He whispered, 'Nearly there,' and set off again briskly. Julie made a final effort, pumping her legs, swinging her arms, and then at last they arrived. The black bulk of a building loomed up ahead and a low voice came out of the darkness. The farmer answered with a single word and then they entered the farmhouse.

Someone took her arm and led her along a passage. Another door was opened and there was a sudden blaze of light. Julie blinked.

She found herself in what was obviously the front parlour. It was full of people. At least twenty. At first it was difficult to make out the faces, but then her eyes became accustomed to the light and she saw several people she knew, villagers and men from outlying farms. The rest – perhaps ten or twelve of them – were strangers, all young men, all slightly out of place despite their rough working clothes.

Everyone was staring at Julie, some with a kind of horror on their faces, some with hope and relief. No-one spoke. Julie cast around, looking for some kind of clue. She expected to see a figure on a stretcher, but there was none. Perhaps he was upstairs . . .

A villager glanced nervously towards the far end of the

room, someone else did the same ... Julie followed their eyes. And then she saw.

One of the young men was standing by the fireplace. He had a bandage round his head and a frightened look in his eyes.

In his hand was a gun. It was pointing at the other people in the room.

Suddenly Julie understood.

She had been brought here to get the gun out of his hand.

For a long time she stood quite still, looking at the young man, and wondering where to start. Finally she took a step forward and smiled at him. 'Hello, my name's Julie. Who are you?'

The young man stared at her, his face taut and uncertain. The gun waved slightly in his hand.

Julie thought: I must try something else. She took a breath and said brightly, 'There's obviously something the matter. Would you like to tell me about it?'

The young man blinked rapidly and tried to focus his eyes.

Suddenly he spoke, so loudly it made Julie jump. 'I know who you are! You're a spy too!' The voice was high-pitched and tense, the accent Welsh.

'A spy?' Julie laughed gently. 'Goodness gracious me no. I'm English!' In the pause that followed she realised that this may not appear very logical and added, 'No, you see I just happen to live here ... among these good people and ... They're trying to help you, you know, to get you home. You do realise that, don't you?'

'No! No! They're not to be trusted, they're not! They're spies! I saw one with a German!'

'But ... if they were spies they would have handed you over to the Germans long ago, wouldn't they? They wouldn't have bothered to hide you for so long, would they? Not if they were going to give you up.' She smiled gently. 'Haven't they cared for you? Haven't they bandaged your head?'

'But I saw one talking to a Kraut!'

'Maybe the German asked him something. It would have looked odd if he hadn't replied, wouldn't it? We have to reply to the Germans, however much we hate it. I give you my solemn word that no-one here is on the Germans' side. I am telling you the truth, believe me.'

The young man frowned and clamped his lips together.

'Why don't I tell you all about myself and then you can tell me all about your family and your home. Eh? Wouldn't that be nice? Why don't we get rid of everyone else and talk, just the two of us?' She walked slowly across the room towards him. As she started to move, his eyes leapt with fear. But then they relaxed a little and followed her, searching her face, half hopeful, half uncertain. Julie felt a surge of confidence. She could see that he wanted to believe in her; he was only frightened.

Finally she stood in front of him. He did not move. She said, 'We'll tell the others to go away, shall we? And then we can talk.' She turned and signalled to one of the villagers for them to go. People started standing up and shuffling towards the door. He shouted, 'No, no! They must stay.'

Everyone stopped. Julie smiled and, reaching out, touched his hand, the one holding the gun. 'They only want to go down to the boat and get you people home. You want to get home too, don't you?'

He shook his head. 'Yes, yes . . . But . . .' He closed his eyes and said wearily, 'It's all so crazy.'

'I know, I know. You've had a tough time, I can see that. Poor old thing, poor old thing. I bet it's been terrible.'

'Yes, yes! Jesus Christ, Oh God . . .!' His voice cracked and Julie felt a moment of fear.

She said quickly, 'Remember your duty!'

'My duty?' The young man looked at her, puzzled, trying to understand.

'Yes. Your duty. It's quite clear, you know. You must get back to England. That is what they want you to do. And you know why? So that they can get you back home to your family. That's what they want you to do. They're not going to ask you to fight again, you know . . . not after all you've done. You can go home, back to where you belong. Back to your family. Really.' The young man's face cleared a little and Julie thought: I'm on the right track. She prompted gently, 'You have a family?'

He nodded slightly and for a moment she thought he would cry. He whispered, 'Mum . . . and Dad . . . And my sister, Susan.'

'And a girl? You have a girl?'

He looked at her as if his heart would break. 'Yes, yes . . .' His eyes filled with tears and he bowed his head and began to sob quietly. Slowly, Julie reached forward and removed the gun from his hand. She passed it to one of the men and then, reaching out, took the young pilot and cradled him in her arms. He clutched at her, his head on her shoulder, his tears warm on her neck.

She thought: But he's no more than a boy; just a boy. And they send children like this to war . . . what madness it all is. She patted his back and said, 'It's all right now. Everything's all right now.'

There was activity behind her: people were moving about and whispering. Someone touched her arm and breathed, 'We must go now or it will be too late. Will you bring him? Down to the beach?'

Julie hesitated. The beach . . . No-one ever went to the beach. It had barbed wire and patrols.

The young pilot clutched at her, still sobbing. She held his head to her shoulder and patted his back again. She

looked at the man waiting beside her and nodded slowly.
'Yes, I'll bring him. Just tell me what to do.'

Julie felt the pilot stumble behind her. She held tightly to
his hand and turned her head. She saw that he had regained
his balance and was tentatively stepping forward again.
She whispered, 'Are you all right?' but the wind tore her
words away and he didn't hear. She asked again, louder.

He nodded, 'Yes, I'm okay.'

Julie squeezed his hand and said, 'Well done. Not far
now!'

She peered down the path to where the man ahead of
her had been. But there was no-one now, not even a
shadow against the greys and blacks of the night mosaic.
Julie drew in her breath and started forward again. The
path was uneven and narrow, carved uncertainly into the
side of the cliff and descending rapidly to the beach below.
Sometimes, when a rock protruded, it disappeared
altogether and Julie had to reach down with her foot until
she found it again some distance below. She went forward
carefully, leaning slightly inwards towards the cliff face,
her leading hand feeling along the safe hardness of the
solid rock. She tried not to think of what lay below.

At one point she stepped on a loose stone and almost
lost her footing. She was wearing the wrong kind of shoes,
of course: leather with a slight heel – horribly slippery. She
should have brought canvas shoes. She also wished for the
hundredth time that she'd worn a scarf: when the wind
tore down the cliff it blew her hair across her face until she
could hardly see.

The path seemed interminable. Behind, the pilot stumbled again; she gripped his hand again and turned to make
sure that he had regained his balance.

Above the dull roar of the wind it was just possible to
hear a low rumbling, like muffled thunder. As they went

down it grew steadily louder. The sound of the surf. Julie's spirits rose: they must be very near the beach now.

Without warning the path suddenly fell sharply away beneath her feet. Julie felt down the slope with her foot, but there was nothing: no ledge, no rock, no sign of the path. She sat down, pulled the pilot down beside her and, letting go of his hand, levered herself over the edge. She felt a jolt of fear as she began to slide downwards, faster and faster. Then, just as she grabbed for a handhold, she saw the beach rushing up towards her. With a soft crunch, she landed on the pebbles.

She got to her feet and dusted her coat down. The young pilot hadn't appeared yet. She called up, 'It's all right. The beach is just here! Just slide down like I did!'

There was no reply. For a moment she thought she was going to have to climb back up again. Then she heard his voice, almost carried away by the wind. 'You sure?'

'Yes, yes. Just slide!'

There was a moment's pause, then a figure shot down and fell on to the pebbles beside her. Julie said, 'Well done.' She helped him up and, holding hands again, they started slowly down the beach.

Julie could just make out a line of pale grey that revealed the breaking surf and, to the left, a blackness, much inkier than the sky, which marked the high cliffs around the cove. But where were they meant to go? Where were the others? She stopped uncertainly and looked around, peering into the darkness.

'What's happening?' The pilot's voice sounded frightened again.

'It's all right. I'm just waiting for them to find us.'

She only wished they would.

As if in answer, a shadow, darker than the rest, emerged in front of them. A voice said, 'Here! Follow me!' Julie sighed with relief and, pulling the pilot behind her, followed the dark figure along the beach. They came to a finger of rock which protruded from the cliff. The rest of the group were waiting on one side of it, some of them sitting against the rock, their faces pale and indistinguishable in the gloom, others standing in groups of two or three. As Julie walked up she was surprised to hear the sounds of raised voices. With dismay she realised that there was a row going on.

The pilot pulled at her hand. 'What the hell's going on?'

It was a good question. But she said, 'Don't worry. It doesn't mean anything. They're just having a friendly argument.'

'Jesus . . . Can't they shut up, for Chrissake?'

Julie found a place against the rock and sat down with the pilot next to her. She listened anxiously as the angry voices continued. The pilot was right: it would be a good idea if they shut up. She wondered what on earth they could be arguing about. What could possibly be so important at a time like this? She peered at a man who sat down wearily on the other side of her. She thought she recognised him. She asked softly in French, 'Who's that?'

The reply came back, 'One of us.'

Julie whispered, 'Can you tell me what's happening?'

'Well, we're waiting for the boat but . . . it may be badly delayed by the weather.' He bent over towards her. 'In truth, it's doubtful it'll come at all . . .'

Julie's heart sank. The thought of having to look after her pilot for much longer filled her with despair. She imagined having to lead him up the cliff again. That was bad enough. But then what? Would they expect her to keep the young man with her? To hide him at the house? No, it was impossible! She said to the villager, 'What happens, then, if the boat doesn't come?'

'We all go home – with our guests, I suppose.'

'Do they go back to – where they were before?'

'I have no idea. You'll have to ask our leader.' There was contempt in his voice as he spoke the word 'leader', and Julie realised he disliked the man too. She asked, 'But why's everyone arguing?'

'Because the whole thing's a mess. No-one knows who's meant to be doing what. Virtually all our helpers are down here on the beach when some should still be up on the cliff. Half say the boat won't come, the other half want to wait. Our leader is telling all those who want to stay to go and all those who want to go to stay. Marvellous, isn't it?' The man spat with contempt.

Julie looked around. The mention of the dreadful man reminded her of Michel's warning. It had been quite clear. He'd said that the Germans probably knew all about this . . . If he was right and they did . . .

God.

She closed her eyes. She was terribly frightened, that was all. Just frightened. And yet . . . she couldn't shake off a terrible sense of foreboding. She was certain it was all going to go wrong. It was partly instinct and partly a feeling that nothing could go right while this leader was in charge . . .

Something had changed. Julie opened her eyes. It was the arguing – it had stopped. Instead everyone was staring out to sea. Involuntarily Julie squeezed the pilot's hand.

There was a sudden burst of activity. Orders were passed. Three men ran down the beach. Others came along the line and told the waiting passengers to be ready to move. Julie and her pilot stood up. A tall, lanky figure detached himself from Julie's group and started moving down the beach. A dark figure ran after him and pushed him back against the rock, saying in ragged English, 'Wait! When I say!'

Julie stared at the line of surf, straining her eyes to distinguish the shadows in the darkness. At first she thought she was mistaken, but then she saw it: the dark shape of a small boat coming through the surf, and then there were men jumping out, two or three of them, pulling the boat up the beach and blending with the men who had run down to meet them. Incredible. The boat had come in spite of the weather. It had not forgotten them after all.

Now four people were being led down the beach. Julie's pilot said plaintively, 'Why not me? What the hell's happening?'

He sounded tearful again and Julie said soothingly, 'It's all right. You'll be next. I expect the boat can't take everyone at once.'

The shape of the boat showed black against the whiteness of the surf and Julie realised it had been launched again. Dark figures climbed in, a curtain of water rose up as the boat met a wave, and then they were gone, vanished into the night.

Julie wondered how on earth the small boat found the large one in the darkness. She hadn't seen a single light.

It was twenty minutes before they returned. The pilot kept saying, 'Christ, they're not coming back! They're not coming back!' And Julie replied, 'Of course they are. Honestly, I promise they are, I promise.'

And then at last the boat was back and it was time for Julie's pilot to go. She started to say goodbye but one of the villagers hissed at her, 'No, you must come too. Now! Come!'

'What?' But he didn't reply and Julie found herself hand in hand with the pilot again, stumbling uneasily down the pebbles towards the water. As they approached the boat two men detached themselves from the waiting group and came towards them.

A man next to Julie said, 'She's here, over here.'

The two figures came up and a voice said, 'Hello, do you speak English?'

Julie laughed nervously. 'Yes.'

'Look, there's this walkie-talkie we'd like to give you. I was trying to explain how it worked. Do you think you could remember a few instructions?' His voice was very English and upper class: an officer.

'I'll try.' Julie made the effort to concentrate as he handed her the walkie-talkie, a small oblong object which was surprisingly light. The British officer spoke slowly and carefully, repeating everything twice. He spoke about frequencies, range, aerials, batteries, and procedures. Eventually he said, 'Do you think you've got all that?'

'Yes, I think so.'

'It's always best to explain it verbally, but it is all written down as well, on the plate on the side. Look, why don't you give it a go? Turn it on now and then you can listen to me talking to the MGB and get the idea. Okay?'

'Yes.'

The officer looked nervously round. 'Must go now! Bye!'

Julie had a ridiculous urge to ask him to stay for a while, but he was gone, striding towards the boat which was already being pushed down into the water. Julie looked for her pilot, but couldn't distinguish him among the group of people waiting round the boat. In case he could see her she raised her hand and waved goodbye before walking back up the beach.

When she reached the finger of rock she sat down and turned on the radio. There was a slight hissing and crackling. Then suddenly there was a voice which made her jump.

'Safely launched and on the way.'

'Roger.' The acknowledgement was so clear it sounded as though it had come from a few feet away. Julie listened, waiting for more. But there was nothing, just the hiss of the receiver.

A figure came up beside her and said, 'Come on! Time to go! Hurry!'

She got to her feet and reached for the button to switch the radio off.

Suddenly a voice crackled, 'Have run my distance but no visual yet.'

'Try further west.'

'Roger.'

Julie waited, mesmerised.

'Found a rock. Any ideas?'

There was a short silence. A new voice came on, stronger than the one before. 'Go north, Jimmy, you forgot the tide. And look out for more rocks on the way.'

'Roger.'

The man at Julie's elbow hissed, 'We *must* go. Come! Come!'

The radio had a strap. Julie hooked it over her shoulder and began to follow the man along the beach, back to the path. She left the radio on. It couldn't do any harm while they were down on the beach blanketed by the sound of the rumbling surf.

They were almost at the path when the radio crackled again.

The strong voice said, 'Got you, Jimmy. Turn east, fifty yards.'

'Roger. Yes, visual now.'

There was a pause, then, 'Where the hell are you going, Number One?'

'Avoiding a rock, sir.'

The radio hissed, then, 'Well, try and avoid the scenic route, will you?'

Reluctantly Julie turned the radio off and handed it to the man who was waiting to push her up the slide, the steep slope immediately above the beach. Another villager was waiting on the path above, ready to pull her up.

Halfway up the slope Julie almost slipped and slid back on to the beach again, but then she managed to find a foothold and push herself up until she could reach the hand of the man above. Once on the path the climb was much easier than the descent had been. It felt safer, going up, and her shoes seemed to grip the stony surface better.

As she climbed she felt ridiculously happy. The mixture of fear and elation made her want to laugh. Then she remembered the awful row on the beach and the risks they had all taken and realised it was relief that had made her lightheaded.

As they reached the clifftop, she remembered too that there was still a long way to go. She didn't think about laughing again until they had crossed the heathland and reached the fields, and her uncle had emerged from the shadows and taken her arm and led her firmly back to the farmhouse: only then did she smile. She suddenly understood why men enjoyed danger so much. She'd never felt so alive in her life!

It took her until dawn to sleep. She heard the clank of the milking pails and the sound of Tante Marie leaving to fetch Peter from Madame Boulet's before she finally began to doze off.

She kept remembering the scene on the beach and the dark silhouette of the boat against the surf. There was something warm and comforting in the memory, in the sight of the boat and the sound of the voices on the radio. The voices made her feel nostalgic, almost homesick. It had been a long time since she'd heard an English voice.

She remembered her childhood: the school outings to the beach, the occasional walks along the Hoe, the lovely view over the Sound, the chatter of her school friends . . . Yes: carefree days. She rather missed them.

Then she remembered what had come after. Peter's father had had a crisp upper-class accent just like the voices of those officers on the radio. Suddenly the memories weren't warm and comforting any more.

It was stupid to think about home.

There was no going back. There never would be.

But, even as she fell asleep, the nostalgia remained.

Part Three

—•—

1942–February 1943

Chapter 15

FISCHER FELT HIS eyes begin to close and, blinking rapidly, pulled himself quickly upright. He moved to the other side of the conning tower and stared out into the murk.

Not far now. They were well into the Bay – or as it was called by the lads, the Black Pit. Fortunately it was living up to its name this morning: it was a filthy day. A south-westerly gale was blowing, it was overcast and visibility was down to no more than a mile. Perfect cover for a submarine.

The weather was also bitterly cold, but Fischer didn't mind that either: nothing could be as cold as the place they'd come from.

It had been one of the longest patrols they'd ever been on. They'd gone up almost as far as Greenland – a hundred miles short of it, to be precise. And then they'd waited. It was so cold that the boat had iced up every few hours. They'd had to half-submerge then, to get the guns under-water and melt the ice off them. Not that the seawater was exactly warm, but it was just above freezing and that was all that mattered.

The wind hadn't been kind either: it had blown a gale or more almost the whole time. Conditions below had been worse than normal, and that was saying something in a Type VIIC. The accommodation had been running with water, both from the terrible condensation and from the waves that inevitably slopped down the conning tower hatch. The men had put up with the damp and the discomfort with their usual good humour. The only time Fischer had heard rumblings of discontent was during a storm when, instead of diving to escape the pounding and rolling, he'd been forced to keep U-319 on the surface to watch for a convoy. A lot of the crew had got sick and after six hours few except Fischer cared whether they ever found any targets or not.

They didn't find the convoy that day. Somehow Fischer had known they wouldn't. But he'd been ordered to watch for it, so watch he did.

It was four days later when they eventually found a target. It was a small convoy – only ten ships and one tanker – and well escorted by two destroyers. Fischer made contact with the other U-boats in his pack and they closed in. It was a disappointing fight: Fischer had just lined U-319 up for the tanker when the destroyer suddenly came straight for them and they were forced to dive. The ship dropped a few depth charges and by the time Fischer had got U-319 away and surfaced the convoy had got well ahead. It took him two hours to manoeuvre back into position; even then he managed to fire only two torpedoes before the destroyer was on to him again. And what was worse, the torpedoes had missed – at least there had been no *sound* of an explosion. It was all very unsatisfactory.

They did manage to find another convoy and sink two small ships before they ran out of torpedoes. But two ships was a poor tally and Fischer couldn't decide whether he'd suffered from bad luck, poor intelligence, or a simple lack of convoys. How did one ever know?

One thing was certain though: targets were not as easy to come by nowadays. He remembered the autumn of 1940, The Happy Time, it was called, when it was easy to sink eight, maybe even ten ships on a single patrol. Now, in this January of 1942, nothing was easy.

There was always something that conspired against

such achievements: the weather, the convoy escorts, Allied air cover, something . . .

Maybe the debriefing would shed some light. It wouldn't be long now . . .

Fischer glanced at his watch and saw that it was almost 0800. Time to get some sleep. He nodded to the second watch officer and climbed down to the attack room below.

The *Leitender* – the Chief – and two of the technicians were crouched round the periscope which was in the raised position despite the fact they were on the surface.

'Still having trouble, Chief?'

'Yes, Herr Kaleu. Hydraulics leaking somewhere. Haven't much chance of locating the fault before we get in, I'm afraid.'

Fischer nodded. There was always something. He asked, 'Can we raise it manually?'

'Oh, I can still give you hydraulic power, but a bit slower, that's all. I'll just have to keep topping up the oil. Don't worry, Herr Kaleu, you'll have your *Spargel*.'

Fischer smiled. *Spargel* meant asparagus; it was their nickname for the periscope. They had an abbreviation or nickname for most things – even himself. They called him Herr Kaleu, short for Kapitanleutnant. Emblems of authority were favourite targets: they had nicknamed the swastika *Wollhandkrabbe*, after a particularly unpleasant freshwater crab.

Fischer removed his wet weather gear and climbed down into the control room, wondering if the periscope would ever get fixed properly. Half the repairs carried out in the dockyards never held up for very long and broke down at the worst possible moments. They were still having problems with one of the hydroplanes and that had been going on for three patrols now.

Fischer automatically glanced round the control room before making his way forward to what was politely called the commander's cabin. It was in fact nothing more than a tiny recess with a curtain across the front of it. Still, it was an awful lot better than his men got. Fischer had heard that the British submarines were quite luxurious, with one bunk to each man. Here on the Type VIIC most of the lower ranks slept where they could, in hammocks or on the floor or between the torpedoes. They were allowed hardly any possessions, just a clean set of underwear and a few odds and ends.

Fischer supposed the whole boat must stink by now, but they were all so used to the intertwined smells of lavatories, diesel and sweat that nobody noticed.

When Fischer reached his cabin he paused only to hang up his cap before lying down and closing his eyes.

He never had trouble getting to sleep and when he was dog-tired as he was now it was that much easier. And the sleep when it came was the sleep of the just: deep, untroubled and dreamless.

It seemed to Fischer he was awake a fraction of a second before the klaxon blared. By the time it was in full cry he was running. Three seconds after it sounded he was in the control room, just in time to see the first man tumbling down from the conning tower.

The diving procedure was well under way: the men were running forward to get their weight into the nose, the hydroplanes were fully angled; the boat was starting to tilt downwards as she began to submerge at full speed. He looked quickly round to see if any problems were developing in the control room. None. He looked up to see if all the men were down from the tower and the hatch closed. Not yet. He watched, trying to judge from the angle of dive exactly how long the men had before the hatch had to be closed, whether or not any remained on the wrong side.

The last man fell down, the hatch clanged shut.

Now they had to wait. Diving took between forty and sixty seconds. Even on a good day it was an awfully long time.

Even now it was only eight seconds since the klaxon had sounded.

There was an instant of silence. The men stared across the cramped control room, their eyes locked on each other's faces.

Then for the second time that night Fischer had the strange sensation that he knew what was coming a moment before it actually happened. It seemed to him that he grabbed at a rail and tensed his body a fraction of a second before the bomb actually exploded.

The roar blasted his ears and jarred his senses. He felt the boat thresh violently, like a rat shaken by an angry dog.

Then darkness. A faint glow of light. Smoke. And the acrid smell of white-hot electrics.

Fischer yelled, 'Damage control reports!'

Voices started screaming at him, 'No rudder control!'

'Fire in the afterends!'

Fischer shouted, 'Pressure tanks?'

'Pressure normal!'

'Pressure hull?'

'No leaks!'

There was a pause, then, 'Fire in afterends extinguished, Herr Kaleu!'

'Any further damage?'

An engineer appeared from aft. 'Herr Kaleu! Starboard shaft buckled. Port shaft bent.'

'How bent?'

He was a young sailor, no more than nineteen. He didn't have an answer. Then his face brightened and he said, 'Well it's still turning!'

'I want a full report from the Chief at his convenience!'

'Yes, Herr Kaleu!'

Fischer absorbed the information. No rudder, no shafts.

Christ, the bomb had blown the whole of the bloody back end off!

But the pressure hull was intact: that was the important thing. They were still diving. There was no loss of diving control. He looked at the depth indicator. 'Level off at twenty metres.'

'Yes, Herr Kaleu!'

What they lacked was steering. He looked at the compass bearing. It was veering round. They were turning slowly to port.

'Trim?'

'Stable.'

The turn wasn't too sharp then. Hope yet.

The Chief hurried into the control room. 'Starboard shaft unserviceable, Herr Kaleu. Port shaft just about serviceable. But I can't give you more than – say, a knot submerged and two surfaced. Even then the engine might not like it.'

Fischer nodded.

It was decision time. He knew immediately that there was only one decision he could make.

He turned to the First Watch Officer. 'We'll give it fifteen minutes, then we'll go to periscope depth and send a signal to Brest, asking for assistance. I'll dictate the message in just a moment. In the meantime . . .' He looked round until he saw the figure of the man who'd been on watch, the Second Watch Officer, standing in his dripping oilskins, his face sheet-white. 'I want an incident report. Now!'

'There was no warning, Herr Kaleu. It even came from the north-east, downwind, so we didn't hear it until it was almost on top of us. All of a sudden there it was, coming straight for us . . .'

'This is very important,' Fischer interrupted. 'Are you sure it was coming straight for us?'

'Yes! No doubt about that.'

Fischer nodded. 'Continue.'

The Second Watch Officer gulped. 'I could see that it was a big plane, a bomber, and that it was close, awfully close. I knew that by the time we got to the guns it would be on top of us, so I ordered diving stations straight away . . .' He looked up anxiously.

If Fischer had been there he would have ordered the men to the guns, to get in at least one burst. On the other hand there had been so little time . . . He said quietly, 'I think there was nothing we could have done either way. At least the dive has protected us from a second attack.'

The young man looked relieved and continued, 'As I closed the hatch I reckon the plane was no more than, say, twenty metres away.'

'Tell me, was it still overcast and the visibility low?'

'Yes, Herr Kaleu. You were there, you saw what it was like . . .'

'Yes, yes,' Fischer said impatiently. 'I just wanted to know if it had changed suddenly . . .'

'Oh no. Just the same.'

'Thank you. That's all.'

The young officer left. For a while Fischer sat motionless on the seat, then he walked slowly back into the control room. A chart of the Bay of Biscay lay open on the tiny chart table. Fischer stared at it blankly.

Bad weather, overcast conditions, poor visibility . . . Perfect cover for a submarine.

Like hell!

The plane must have known they were there; it must have!

He stared at the chart as if it might explain it all. But there was no simple answer, he knew that. Nothing that fitted any of the known facts.

The plane had *known*! And U-319 had been just like a sitting duck. Intensely vulnerable. Unable to defend herself. It – changed everything.

Fischer murmured wearily, 'God in heaven!' Then, reaching for a pad and pencil, he started to draft a wireless signal.

Doenitz picked up the signal and read the last few lines again. '. . . ENEMY CAME STRAIGHT IN TO ATTACK IN POOR VISIBILITY. IMPOSSIBLE THAT ENEMY HAD ADVANCE VISUAL SIGHTING. REPEAT IMPOSSIBLE. CONCLUDE ENEMY PINPOINTED US BY NON-VISUAL MEANS . . .'

Non-visual means . . .

Doenitz laid down the signal. This was the third time in a month. On three occasions boats had reported sudden unexpected attacks, on three occasions they had been caught unawares on the surface. He could believe that the first two boats might have had sleepy lookouts, he could believe that their commanders might have underestimated the visibility . . .

But U-319? Fischer? Impossible. Fischer would never conceal the facts. If Fischer said the visibility was poor, then it was.

Doenitz called through to his staff officer, 'Get me Herr Schmidt at the Reich Research Directorate in Berlin.'

While he waited for the call to go through, Doenitz reflected on his previous conversations with Herr Schmidt. There had been several in the last six months. On each occasion Doenitz had asked if there was any information about new British antisubmarine devices. Three times he had come right out and asked the vital question itself: Was it possible that the British planes had search radar? Schmidt had hedged round the answer. His favourite expressions were 'very unlikely', 'improbable', and 'our information suggests not'. The man always promised to look into the matter again, but Doenitz had the suspicion that nobody was looking into it at all.

Well, this time there could be no doubt. This time Herr Schmidt would be forced to admit that the British not only possessed a search device, but that it was extremely effective. He wondered how Herr Schmidt would try to explain the phenomenon.

And however he did explain it, he had better be able to suggest a countermeasure. Otherwise ... Doenitz sighed grimly. Otherwise the effectiveness of the fleet would be severely curtailed. He would have to order the boats to submerge as they crossed the Bay. And if the British extended their air patrols further out into the Atlantic, then the boats would have to stay dived for even longer.

That meant it would take them twice as long to reach their patrol area: most U-boats could travel at a top speed of only seven knots submerged, compared to seventeen on the surface. Worse, at some time during their submerged run across the Bay, the boats would have to surface – for air and to recharge their batteries. Then ... then they would be desperately vulnerable.

If too many boats were caught on the surface and lost, it would be disastrous. The U-boat Arm was still desperately short of operational craft: instead of the three hundred or so he'd hoped for, Doenitz still had only ninety, and that was after more than two years of war. As before, the building programme was disastrously short of target and now, as if to forestall any chance of improving the situation, the winter was so severe that the Baltic ports were iced up and trials of new boats and training of new personnel had come to a complete standstill.

For Doenitz the shortage was doubly frustrating because, against his and Raeder's advice, Hitler had personally ordered much of the fleet to be redeployed. There were twenty-three boats – far too many – in the Mediterranean, where the waters were shallow and dangerous. Now, in the latest madness, twenty-six boats had been ordered to defend Norway against a supposed Allied invasion which, from what Doenitz heard, was very far from certain. Using U-boats as sentries was a waste of time; they could achieve much more spectacular results by squeezing the supply lines dry. But OKW – the High Command – was unconvinced. Doenitz could only advise. What more could he do?

And now this! A new threat, a new problem.

The telephone rang. The staff officer announced Herr Schmidt and put him through. Doenitz kept the formalities to a minimum, then told Schmidt the facts. He continued, 'I am having a meeting here in Paris with the Navy Technical Branch tomorrow. It is essential that you or your representative be here, Herr Schmidt. This matter is of the gravest consequence.'

The voice at the other end of the line was conciliatory. 'Of course I will come myself, Herr Admiral. If I set off now I can be with you first thing in the morning. I will have one of my people with me. He will have all the available data . . .'

Doenitz replaced the receiver, puzzled. Schmidt hadn't sounded at all surprised. Far from it. It was as if he'd been expecting the call. And his tone had been odd, too: evasive yet positive, almost as if he had a solution ready to pull out of his hat . . .

Doenitz rubbed his forehead. The politics of dealing with section chiefs in Berlin always gave him a headache. Doubtless he would find out what Schmidt had up his sleeve when the man chose to tell him. Hopefully tomorrow.

In the meantime he must take the painful decision to protect his boats. Even though it would slow them down considerably, he must order his boats to cross the Bay submerged.

He called for his staff officer. 'Werner, take a directive to all flotillas, Operational Area West.'

*

'As it happens, we think we can tell you exactly what it is,' Schmidt said calmly. 'Although we will have to make further checks, of course.'

Doenitz said sharply, 'Yes?'

'Well, it appears that the British bombers are being fitted with a type of radar . . .'

Doenitz blinked. There was a deathly silence round the table. The technical staff stared at the Chief Scientist in horror.

Schmidt licked his lips nervously. '. . . a compact search radar.'

'Are you sure of this?' Doenitz asked.

'A detection station in Normandy picked up a signal from an airborne source. It was quite definitely an intermittent signal. That means it was rotating . . . A search radar.'

Doenitz frowned and said slowly, 'I always understood that radar could not be made small enough to fit into an aircraft.'

There was an awkward silence. Schmidt looked cross.

Doenitz sighed and asked quietly, 'What about the wavelength? Is it one we understand?'

'Oh yes!' Schmidt replied immediately. 'They are using a 1.5 metre wavelength similar to our own systems. It's nothing new.'

'So?'

'We can manufacture a radar detector. This would pick up signals from approaching aircraft and give your vessels good warning.'

'How good?'

Schmidt shrugged. 'Ten, maybe fifteen miles . . .'

Ten miles . . . It was adequate – *if* Schmidt was right.

Doenitz asked, 'But how soon could these be manufactured?'

'It would take a lot of development. The receiver itself wouldn't be too complex . . . But the aerial—' He shook his head. 'That would have to survive submergence ... It would take time to develop ...'

Doenitz leant forward in his chair. 'But we don't *have* time!'

Schmidt looked uncomfortable. At length he said, 'Well, perhaps a mobile aerial might be possible ... But it would have to be assembled every time the U-boat surfaced and taken down again every time it dived. It wouldn't be ideal—'

'I don't care!' Doenitz interrupted. 'If it works we must have it! We have absolutely no choice.'

He gave the Chief Scientist a harsh look. 'I don't care what the thing looks like, Herr Schmidt, I don't care if it's made out of plywood – but I want that detector in sufficient quantity, and I want it *now*!'

Chapter 16

THEY CAME FOR David one cold February morning.

There was no warning. Sergeant Klammer and a soldier just marched in and told David to pack his belongings and be ready in five minutes. Just David, no-one else.

David stared, shocked. 'Where am I going?'

Klammer shrugged; he didn't know.

When the two guards had gone David looked at Meyer in horror. The old man patted his arm and said, 'Remember, they're allowing you some belongings. That's a good sign!' The faces of the other scientists were apologetic, guilty even, because they were being allowed to stay. David didn't blame them; he would have felt the same himself.

Meyer helped him pack his belongings. It didn't take long – they fitted into a small bundle. Then the two men sat down to wait.

When the soldiers came back David turned to Meyer, wanting to say many things. But he muttered only 'Goodbye', and, unable to say any more, followed Klammer quickly out of the hut into the bitter morning cold.

There was thick snow on the ground and more was falling. The path was slippery underfoot and David had to walk carefully. Suddenly he stopped in utter panic. He'd forgotten the most important thing of all! He shouted at Klammer's back, 'Please! One moment!' Then, before Klammer could say anything, he hurried back to the hut.

Inside, Meyer looked round in surprise. David cried, 'My medicine! I forgot my medicine!' Meyer took his arm and together they searched for it. They found it on the windowsill above David's bunk. David grasped the bottle and praised God. Shaking slightly, he placed it in his bundle, carefully wrapped in some overalls.

'Nothing else you've forgotten?' Meyer asked kindly.

David tried to think, but his mind was in a jumble. Klammer arrived and barked, 'Hurry!' David whispered desperately to Meyer, 'I don't think so.' Then, wringing Meyer's hand once more, he stumbled out into the snow.

Klammer led the way to the main gates, where a soldier was waiting to take over. The soldier marched David up the road towards the railway station. David approached it with foreboding. He hadn't seen the place since his arrival all those months before and he'd forgotten how bleak it was. The solitary station building loomed dark against the stark whiteness of the snow, and the wind was howling across the desolate expanse of sidings.

There was only one train, a train made up of cattle trucks.

David's mouth went dry. He remembered the horror of the journey from Sachsenhausen, the stench, the cries, the dying people. He couldn't believe that he must go through it all over again.

He stumbled and fell in the snow. As he picked himself up, his stomach stabbed with pain. He started off again but staggered, unsteady on his feet. The attacks often affected him that way. He thought: I'll never survive another journey.

The soldier led the way down the train. The trucks stank of excrement and, it seemed to David, of human suffering too. He struggled on, his head bowed against the driving snow.

They approached the end of the train. Here there was a single carriage, painted dark grey with windows. The soldier indicated that David should get in. David's heart lifted slightly.

Inside the carriage there were compartments with plain wooden seats and overhead luggage racks. The soldier pushed him into one and closed and locked the door. It was very dark inside, but after a while David's eyes became accustomed to the faint glimmers of light that seeped in through the drawn blinds.

He couldn't believe his luck. There must be a catch somewhere.

After a couple of hours the train started. Almost immediately the door was flung open and the compartment flooded with light. David jumped slightly. It was the guard, coming to tell him that he had two minutes to go to the lavatory. Later they brought him a blanket, some food – sausage and dry bread – and a cup of water.

David relaxed. He was going to be all right after all.

Slowly he stretched out on the long wooden seat and pulled the blanket over him. He tried to think, to work out where they might be taking him. He remembered, too, everything he was leaving behind – his work, half-completed; the safe, comforting routine of his day; the warmth of companionship. He had got very fond of his colleagues; he would miss them dreadfully.

Finally the steady rhythm of the clicking wheels lulled him into an almost dreamless sleep. Only when the train suddenly stopped did he wake. It stopped many times through the afternoon and early night, sometimes for hours at a time.

Once David woke in the night and tried to guess what time it was. Probably about three or four. He rubbed his eyes and realised he was mistaken. It must be much later: a crack of thin grey light had appeared at the edge of the blind. It was dawn. He must have slept much longer than he'd thought.

The train was going very slowly now; the sound of the wheels had fallen to a lazy rhythmic click. There was a loud squeal of brakes. Perhaps they were approaching a station. If they were going north, then they might be at Nuremberg by now, or Leipzig.

He sat up from where he had been lying on the seat and put his eye to the crack in the blind. The blind was permanently drawn, the section of heavy black canvas fastened to the window frame with nails at three-inch intervals. But between two of the nails the fabric bagged slightly. By pulling at it with one's finger and pressing one's eye close to the gap, it was just possible to see out.

He saw several railway lines, sheds, some sidings: a largish town then, maybe even a city. The brakes squealed again and the train juddered as it slowed still further. There was a loud clattering and the carriage suddenly jerked to one side: they were crossing onto another line. More sheds; a marshalling area. They came up alongside a stationary line of cattle trucks.

Then they stopped.

Suddenly there was a loud clanging and shouting. Soldiers were pulling back the doors of the cattle trucks. Men came pouring out, jumping on to the ground, standing blinking in the sudden light. The men were poorly dressed and foreign-looking, thin but not starving.

The men were moving now, walking obediently across the tracks towards David's train. There was more clanging and the sound of large metal doors sliding; they were getting into David's train.

After an hour there was more shouting and from far away at the head of the train David could hear the locomotive panting in long deep gasps as it pulled on its heavy load. The clank of couplings sounded down the train and the carriage jerked forward. From beneath there was the low rumble of the wheels on metal tracks.

David sat up and returned to his vantage point. They were slipping through the sidings and crossing junctions again until he guessed they were back on the main line. A stationary goods train appeared on the next track. David peered at the words chalked on each truck, trying to read the destinations. He saw Mannheim, Frankfurt, Mannheim again . . . Cities in the west.

Then the train was on the main line, going straighter and faster. With excitement David saw that they were approaching a station. There were platforms, station buildings, and a name . . .

Mannheim.

Something stirred in his memory.

Of course, David remembered and smiled to himself. This was the place he had planned to make for in his great escape from Berlin. This was the place he was going to reach without any trouble, by getting on a train and sitting quietly in a corner.

David shook his head slowly. What a child.

The train passed through several small stations, but the names flashed by too fast to read them.

After a while David dozed again, rocked by the motion of the train, and it was not until much later when the brakes squealed that he woke again.

It was Saarbrucken.

They were at the French border.

He sat for a long time, quite immobile, waiting. At last the train started moving again.

A small village. Name: Wendel. German name, German architecture.

Then a small town with a long name. He missed seeing it on his side of the train because they were going so fast. He had to stand up quickly to catch it from the corridor window.

Faulquemont.

French name. French architecture. French vehicles . . .!

Then he laughed. What a joke!

The Germans were taking him to France! They were taking him where he had wanted to go all those months ago.

He smiled for a long time. France . . .! What a joke! What a joke!

Suddenly he wasn't smiling any more. Pain came suddenly, without warning. It came in a great stab that took the breath out of him. He bent over and, clutching his stomach, reached for the precious bottle of medicine. He swigged a mouthful and waited for the soothing liquid to quench the burning in his belly.

Trembling, he lay down and, all euphoria gone, thought disconsolately: When all is said and done, France, Germany, it makes no difference, not if I'm dying.

And I started dying a long time ago.

After that David lost track of the hours. The pain dulled his brain and the darkness confused him, and he slept most of the time. Life became a dream, a nightmare of dim awareness.

Only when the guard slid the door open with a bang did David wake up, blinking at the sudden light. Usually the guard placed the food hastily on the floor and left, or waited impassively while David went to the lavatory. But one day he shouted, 'Out! Out! Come on!'

David tried to gather his wits. How long had he been in the train? Three days? Longer? He stumbled towards the door. It was a moment before he remembered his bundle; he'd left it on the seat. He reached down, picked it up and followed the guard out of the door, bumping into the wall as he tried to find his balance.

He stepped down off the train. Sidings again. Warehouses and sheds. A large city. But very French, still very French.

The labourers were pouring out of the train too. David saw that many of them were staggering and falling. Those who didn't get up were kicked or beaten with rifle butts, then thrown against the side of the track to where the dead and dying already lay in a pathetic pile of ragged limbs.

He tore his eyes away and followed the guard across the tracks. Suddenly there was a *crack!* Then another: the sharp whine of bullets. David winced but made himself keep walking. Why look back? He knew what he would see. They were killing the weak, finishing off the dying. Why look back? It only broke your heart.

They came to a lorry. The guard indicated that David should get in the back. It was a high lorry and David had difficulty climbing up. The guard, a boy of about twenty, helped him up.

David scrambled in and the guard came in behind him. For a while David sat quietly, then asked, 'Where are we?'

The guard looked surprised at David's German. Then he snapped, 'No questions!'

David nodded. 'Just asking.'

There was short silence, then the guard murmured, 'Brest.'

'Ah!' David exclaimed. He nodded as if he'd known all the time.

Brest: where was it? David had never been very good at geography. Brest . . . A port, surely, right on the west coast. So he'd reached the sea after all! The idea gave him pleasure.

The truck moved off. The sidings and marshalling yards gave way to warehouses and sheds, and then they were climbing a hill. David's eye was caught by the sparkle of light on water. He watched fascinated as a great natural harbour opened out before him, a wide expanse of water that seemed to be bounded by gently sloping woodland on every side.

Then the water was obscured by houses and they were skirting round the edge of the city, which appeared to be built on a small plateau overlooking the harbour. The houses disappeared again and, as the truck turned inland, David saw that there was a man-made harbour immediately below, with several warships at its quays. There were dry docks too. And a submarine, which was moving across the harbour, its wake a line of darker grey against the brilliant whites of the sparkling water.

The road dropped away and turned, and then they were down almost at water level. They crossed over a small canal and rumbled through another commercial area before coming to a sudden halt.

Almost immediately the truck started off again and David realised they had passed through the gates of a defence establishment: there were several guards on the gate, as well as barracks and military vehicles. Most of the personnel were wearing naval uniform.

David relaxed a little: he liked the Navy. Though formal and correct, they always seemed straightforward and trustworthy. The officers were of the old school: proper gentlemen, many from the old families, and few real Nazis among them. It would be good to work here . . .

The truck stopped outside a squat brick building. The guard jumped out and indicated that David should follow.

Inside the building a girl showed him up to an office and ushered him in. When David looked back he saw that the guard had gone.

There was a German naval officer sitting behind a desk. He stood up, a thin, nervous-looking young man. 'I am Kapitanleutnant Geissler. Please be seated.'

David waited for the officer to sit down then lowered himself gingerly on to a chair and waited.

'Herr Freymann, we understand you are highly qualified in radioelectrics and that you have been working for some time on the design of radio ranging devices.'

David nodded, a little taken back by the 'Herr'. It was a long time since anyone had called him that.

The officer went on. 'There is a company here in Brest

which we have appropriated to produce electronic and radio components for us. They are making one particular piece of equipment which has the highest priority. It is essential that this device is produced with all speed and in some quantity ...' The officer looked a little unhappy. 'However there have been problems ... Problems of a technical nature. We wish you, Herr Freymann, to supervise the technical side of the operation.'

David nodded and waited for the rest.

'The device is needed to protect our U-boats from enemy attack.' The officer stood up and picked up a thin file from the top of a filing cabinet. 'I have the technical specifications here. If you could study them immediately – then I will take you over to the manufacturing unit and you can see the organisation for yourself.'

David frowned. Protecting U-boats, but from what exactly? He still felt woolly-headed from the journey. As he took the file and opened it, he tried desperately to clear his brain.

There were a few pages of written specifications and a fold-out plan. Both were headed: *Project Metox. Most Secret*. David started to read the first page of the specifications.

He blinked.

It was an anti-*radar* device.

His pulse quickened and his mind cleared. This meant that the British had radar, just as Meyer and he had guessed.

He looked again at the specification. It stated the necessity for the Metox device to pick up signals at maximum possible range, up to thirty nautical miles. The absolute minimum tolerable range was six miles. That seemed very precise ...

David looked up and asked, 'Why this six miles? What is so special about six miles?'

The officer replied, 'Ah. You see, our U-boats must have

plenty of warning. They need at least one minute to dive, and another thirty seconds to get below bombing depth!'

Bombing . . .? David stared with incomprehension. Bombing. 'You mean *aircraft* attack . . .?'

'Yes, indeed!' The young man exclaimed. 'These aircraft approach at over 200 knots, you must realise. We need warning of over five miles to give enough time . . .'

But David wasn't listening. The British had succeeded in putting radar in aircraft. That meant they had made it small enough. But *how?* How had they done it?

Rapidly he searched down the first page of the specifications and then flipped impatiently over to the second. Where on earth was it? There! At last!

The detection device was to cover the wavelengths 1.4 to 1.8 metres.

David stared, trying to understand.

The British radar wasn't shortwave after all. It was within a range of wavelengths Germany had been using for some time.

Nothing new at all.

David felt a mixture of relief and anxiety – relief that no-one had got to the shortwave idea before him and anxiety that perhaps he had got it wrong and it wasn't possible after all.

He dragged himself back to the rest of the specification and read through it, glancing at the large-scale drawing. It was all quite simple. Whoever had designed this detecting device had got the basic idea right. There was a simple aerial, which led to a radio receiver. When the receiver picked up a radar signal from an approaching plane it emitted a high-pitched warning signal. The main problem, David saw immediately, was to get the emitter to give off a strong signal whatever the range and frequency of the incoming radar waves. The receiver itself was relatively straightforward.

'What problems have you been having, then?' he asked.

The Kapitanleutnant breathed in with obvious annoyance. 'It is difficult to be precise. Most of the devices produced so far have had small but serious defects. We don't know why. We need you to tell us and to prevent it happening in the future.'

'I see. And the technicians at this factory, are they competent?'

'Apparently so.'

'And the components, where have they been manufactured?'

'Mainly in Germany, a few in France. They all appear to be up to standard, but . . .! There always seems to be something wrong with the finished sets. We need someone to make sure these faults are stamped out!'

David closed the file and stood up. 'I am ready then. At your convenience.'

It took two days at Goulvent, Pescard et Cie for David to realise that the Metox project was a shambles. Some of the components weren't up to standard, the assembly line was disorganised and the French personnel were less skilled than he'd been led to expect.

The problems could be solved, no doubt about that. As always, it was a question of identifying the trouble spots and eliminating them. But it would take time – rather a long time by present standards. From the moment he arrived David had run into an unexpected difficulty: he was virtually unable to communicate.

He was more than a little surprised when the factory personnel failed to understand more than a few words of his French. He spoke the language badly, admittedly, but not *that* badly. Of course, it would have helped if some of the French personnel had spoken German, but they didn't and that was that. To make matters worse, the anxious young Kapitanleutnant kept hanging over David's shoulder, listening to his hesitant questions and staring angrily at the French technicians when they shrugged or gave the briefest of replies.

Secretly, David was glad most of the replies were short because then at least he could understand them. When one of the French started a monologue delivered at high speed and great length his heart sank. There was absolutely no hope of following it, and he could almost believe they were doing it on purpose, just to confuse him.

For a man who loved to communicate precisely and economically the frustration was terrible. David felt as if he were foundering in cotton wool.

The evenings only served to make him more depressed. He was escorted back to a cold bare room in some barracks within the dockyard compound. The food, sent over from a naval canteen, was good, but otherwise David found the accommodation almost unbearable. He was not used to being on his own. The silence and the smallness of the room pressed in on him: for the first time in his life he could guess at the terror of solitary confinement. Before, he had always been with people, whether working, living, or suffering, and he missed them. He even missed Fengal, the most irascible of the team back at the laboratory! Even him, the old shark.

The situation was ironic, he had to admit. Never had he been safer – never had he felt so discontented. It was, of course, because they had given him back so much . . . He had got to expect things.

The answer was work. Work always made him happy.

He paced his room and decided on some priorities.

The first was easy: he would make a success of the project even if it killed him.

The second was not so easy: Kapitanleutnant Geissler had to go.

And while he was about it he might as well have a third: to ask for another billet, one nearer other prisoners, somewhere with a bit of company. The request would probably be refused, but it never did any harm to ask.

He took a scrap of paper from the table and rummaged for the pencil stub which he always kept in his small bundle along with his other treasures: an eraser, a small slide rule and a picture postcard of Berlin – all possessions he'd been allowed to acquire while in the camp laboratory.

Taking up the pencil he wrote a work list for the next day, itemising each action in his neat handwriting made necessarily larger by the bluntness of the pencil.

When he had finished he regarded the list critically. It was not much, but it did at least make him feel that he had started.

He went to sleep immediately and woke early, his mind already busy. He jumped out of bed, examined his job list, then waited impatiently to be picked up for work. When the van finally deposited him at the factory door, he went straight to his office. He got out two blueprints of the Metox device, one in German, the other in French and, by comparing them, made a careful crib of all the technical words he would need for his conversations with the French technicians.

Next came the more difficult part: the Kapitanleutnant.

Geissler arrived sharp at eight, as he always did. David forced a warm smile, offered him a chair, and then, his heart in his mouth, dived straight in. 'Herr Kapitanleutnant, may I ask you a great favour?'

Geissler looked a little suspicious. He murmured uncertainly, 'Ask.'

David smiled briefly, then put on a suitably serious expression. 'I need to get deeply into the operation here. I need to talk to the men – at length. I also . . . have a need to do everything at my own pace . . . In short, Herr Kapitanleutnant, I need to work on my own. Of course,' he added hastily, 'I will report to you regularly. Every day, if you wish! Every few hours, if you wish! But . . .'

Geissler had got to his feet and was holding up his hand, as if stopping some imaginary traffic. David stood up uncertainly. The officer shook his head and David's heart sank. Then Geissler said, 'Say no more. I understand perfectly. If you feel you will get better results on your own, then your request is automatically granted!'

The officer clicked his heels and left. David sat down in surprise. It had been so easy! He rubbed his hands. He felt a surge of excitement similar to those he had felt when starting new projects in the old days.

Next, to battle with the French language. David picked up his files and left his office. He was careful to avoid the director, an effusive, overbearing man, and went in search of the chief technician, a man called Gallois. He found him in a corner of the main workshop, staring disconsolately at some components on the bench.

David mustered his best French and said, 'Good morning. May I have a word with you?'

Gallois looked up and then past David's shoulder. 'Ah! No lieutenant today!'

'No.'

The Frenchman raised his eyebrows. 'You are in charge, then?'

David wanted to say: Hardly. But he didn't know the word and settled for, 'No, *they* are always in charge.'

'Ah! So what can I do for you?'

'Could we talk, please, about the problems on the Metox?' David spoke slowly and distinctly.

'Certainly. I am at your service.'

David was rather pleased: the fellow seemed to have understood him. They began to walk towards the drawing office.

Suddenly the Frenchman asked, 'You are German?'

'Yes.'

There was short silence, then, 'And you work for the German Navy?'

'Work?' David laughed. 'I "work" for the people I must!'

'But – you are employed by them?'

David frowned. He didn't understand the verb. 'Employed?'

'Yes. You earn money?'

David smiled grimly. 'Ha! No! No, my friend. I am a prisoner.' A look of confusion came over Gallois's face. David added, 'A prisoner, just like . . .' He searched for the word for labourers '. . . the workers I saw on the train.'

Understanding came over the Frenchman's face. 'Ahhh,' he murmured.

The mention of the labourers reminded David. He stopped and faced Gallois. 'Why are they brought here? What work do they do, all those people?'

'They are Poles. They are building the U-boat pens. Great shelters of concrete to stop bombs . . .' He threw out his hands to demonstrate a massive explosion.

They walked on.

The Frenchman asked, 'Why are you a prisoner?'

'I'm Jewish.'

The Frenchman nodded. 'I see.' And walked on in silence.

When they were sitting with the plans spread out in front of them, the Frenchman asked, 'What happens if you cannot solve the problems? What if this Metox does not work very well?'

'Ah!' David snorted. He indicated with his head. 'Back there, I suppose, to where I came from. But don't worry. It won't happen. We will make the thing work . . .'

They began with the problem of the aerial connection, then went on to the placing of the valves, and the suitability of the proposed amplifier.

To David's surprise they managed to cover the three main problems within an hour, in each case arriving at agreement as to the necessary action to be taken. Strangely,

David's French seemed to have improved dramatically. He was elated.

David folded the large-scale drawing and beamed at the Frenchman. 'A simple device, with simple problems. I knew we could sort it out!'

Gallois nodded slowly. 'Yes, one can always sort these things out . . .' He smiled ruefully.

David regarded him for a moment, then said impulsively, 'Tell me, was my French so awful – when I arrived?'

The Frenchman looked down. 'Awful?'

'Yes, you know . . . No-one seemed to understand me.'

'Oh, we never understand Germans very well.'

'Ah.' David frowned. Some confusing, unsettling thoughts drifted through his mind. 'The matters we've been discussing . . .' He paused and looked sideways at the Frenchman. 'The problems with the Metox . . . why was it you were unable to solve them before . . .?'

Gallois made a face. 'Ah! The Germans, they never provide the information and equipment we need . . . We've asked and asked . . .' He trailed off and shrugged.

David nodded slowly. 'Yes . . . quite . . .' He thought of asking why the Germans had not responded to these demands, but something about Gallois's manner did not invite any more questions.

'Well,' said David brightly. 'I am sure the project will be a great success!'

'Without doubt,' the Frenchman replied coolly.

David walked quickly back to his office, his mind already going through the letters he would have to write and telephone calls he would have to make, and realised with mild surprise that his stomach hadn't been hurting at all today. In fact he hadn't felt so well in months.

It was the challenge of the work. As he thought, it was just what he needed.

Chapter 17

MOTOR GUNBOAT 309 had two outstanding character-istics: she was wet and she was as explosive as a bomb.

The south-westerly Force 6 was revealing the first of her attributes: her speed was reduced to thirteen knots and she was twisting and bucking like a wild horse. Every few seconds she dug her nose deep into a wave and chucked a wall of cold, very solid, water back along her 110-foot length, up and over the open bridge, drenching the four men who stood there peering into the impenetrable darkness.

There was a loud thud and a particularly large wave flew up over the bows. Ashley ducked instinctively behind the reinforced glass screen. The water hit the bridge with a dull slap, showering spray in all directions. Ashley felt a rivulet of freezing water running down his back and reflected that things might be worse: an E-boat could at this minute be firing at them and igniting the perfect mixture of air and high-octane petrol in their fuel tanks. And what a lovely bang they would make, he thought. A nice big orange whooomph! And the Jerries wouldn't have to worry about looking for survivors: there wouldn't be any. Instant cremation.

All things considered, he'd rather be wet.

As if reading his mind, Jones, the coxswain, shouted, 'When are we getting these new boats then, sir?'

'Ah, cox, when indeed? According to the Master Plan we already have them!'

'Yes, sir.'

'But according to the grapevine, it'll be some time at the end of the year.'

Jones blew the saltwater off his lips and exclaimed, 'About bleedin' time too, sir. This old girl's as wet as Glasgow on a Saturday night! If I'd wanted to be a submariner, I would have bleedin' well volunteered.'

Ashley smiled. 'On the other hand, Jones, a diesel-powered boat could be a real bore! A dry bridge, reliable engines, non-explosive fuel – there'd be no feeling of adventure. That first pint back in Dartmouth wouldn't taste the same at all!'

'Ha!' the coxswain retorted. 'After a ride on the Hamoaze ferry, lemonade tastes like bloody champagne to me, sir! But, you know, sir, I wouldn't mind about the weather, 'cept we've been having it all bleedin' winter. Not a break 'ave we 'ad, not a single one.'

'No, cox,' Ashley admitted. 'We can't have been saying our prayers right.'

In fact, there had been breaks in the weather, but they had come during the full moon, or when 309's engines were out of action, or when there was no operation planned. Whenever an operation *had* been set up it had blown Force 5 or more. Nothing unusual for winter in the English Channel, but uncomfortable, wet and – for this kind of job – dangerously slow. A delay on the outward journey meant a late arrival, a nervous wait at the pick-up point, and a mad dash to get back across no-man's-land to British coastal waters before dawn.

Ashley peered at the luminous hands of his watch: it was already 2330 and, he guessed, another two to two-and-a-half-hours to the pinpoint. An 0200 arrival would give them only forty-five minutes – or an hour at the most – to make the pick-up. It would be horribly tight. In this wind it would take the beach party at least twenty minutes to reach the shore. Five minutes to sort out the passengers and get them loaded. On the way back they would have the wind behind them but it would still take, say, fifteen minutes. Horribly tight.

Worse, he had the unpleasant feeling the wind was freshening.

They'd had miserable luck all winter, one way and another. First they'd had an inexperienced navigator and, on one occasion, had waited at the wrong beach for over three hours. Then, a week or so later, the engines had started to play up. As the Chief, an inevitable Scot by the name of McFee, was always saying, 'Seawater and petrol don't mix.' He did his best with the three supercharged Hall Scott engines but even he couldn't make the damn things work when they weren't in the mood. Bad weather made them especially temperamental; 'Like a woman caught in the rain,' the Chief said contemptuously. A week before, they'd packed up two miles off the Brittany coast, just as they were being opened up for the journey home. The Chief had managed to coax a couple of knots out of the starboard engine, just enough to get them out of sight of land before dawn. Eventually, water was found in the fuel system, was cleared, and they managed to get under way again, but not before getting a nasty fright from a patrolling E-boat.

Ever since, the engines had been giving trouble of some kind or another and they needed constant nursing to keep them going.

But at least they had got rid of the dodgy navigator: that was something. All they needed now was a break in the weather.

Ashley poked his head outside the screen: yes, he could swear the wind was increasing. The barometer was probably dropping through the floor. He reached for the voice pipe and called down, 'Macleod! How's the barometer?'

A voice came floating up, 'The *Jimmy*'s in sick bay, sir! Elliott here.'

'Sick bay!' Ashley sighed and said 'Bugger!' under his breath. He put his mouth to the pipe again. 'On my way!'

As Ashley climbed down the exposed bridge ladder he felt the MGB's bows dive into a wave and instinctively flattened himself against the side of the boat. The action avoided the worst of the water: instead of pouring down his neck the sheet of water slapped into his back. As he made his way aft he felt the wetness seeping through his oilskins into his clothes. So much for oilskins.

He reached the door, yanked it open, and climbed down into the relative peace of the accommodation. The sick bay was not as grand as it sounded: it was an ordinary bunk which happened to be situated next to the locker housing the medical stores. The First Lieutenant was lying on the bunk, his face white and his breathing irregular. Two seamen were taking off his boots and covering him with a blanket. There was an ominous black bucket on the floor beside him.

Ashley looked at one of the seamen. 'What's up?'

'Sick, sir. Chucking up and – the other, sir.'

Ashley went to the side of the bunk. 'Christ, Number One, couldn't you have thought of something more original? Been overdoing the champagne and smoked salmon, eh?'

'Sorry, must have been something I ate.' The voice was soft with a gentle Canadian accent. 'I'll be all right in a moment, I'm sure. Once I've . . .' A look of disbelief came over the man's face and he suddenly threw himself over the bucket. Ashley looked away; the sight of vomit always made him retch.

When Macleod had sunk back onto the bunk Ashley turned back and said, 'I don't think you'll be fit for anything, Macleod. You'd best stay here.'

'No! I'll be okay. Really!'

'Stay here! That's an order. We'll manage without you. Very well, in fact. You'd be surprised!' He grinned.

Macleod smiled faintly and closed his eyes. The smile vanished from Ashley's face and he said quietly to one of the seamen, 'Keep an eye on him – temperature, pulse, everything. He looks bloody awful to me.'

He turned and made his way back to the deck, thinking: Damn!

The Canadian was his best man; very keen and very able. He must be really ill to have agreed to lie down; if he was capable of getting to his feet, he would. Ashley gritted his teeth. He'd have to find a replacement – Macleod was leader of the beach party. Macleod was the only one who spoke decent French.

Apart from himself there was only one other officer on the boat: the navigator, a man called Tusker. He was RN (Retired) and had bamboozled his way back into active service by nagging the Admiralty to death. Unlike the first navigator, Tusker was brilliant at his job. He'd got *309* through rocks and narrow channels into countless pick-up points, in filthy weather and without a decent navigation aid in sight.

There was only one problem: he was forty-five and had a gammy leg.

Ashley made his way forward again, gripping tightly on to the available handholds. The boat pitched sharply forwards and then, trembling and shivering, heaved herself up once more, ready for the next wave.

Ashley climbed into the small space optimistically called the chart room. It was a wooden structure built on to the deck just in front of the bridge. Tusker was crouching over the collapsible chart table – a simple device which, when the boat pounded heavily, often lived up to its name. As usual, Tusker was making careful calculations. He never stopped, from the moment they left until the moment they got back, reworking the tides, the course, the speed, and the ETA.

'How we doing, Tusker?'

'Ah, should reach Les Vaches at 0135, and drop anchor at 0200.' He always used Les Vaches, a large pair of odd-shaped rocks three miles off the beach, as a navigation point. He aimed the MGB straight for them and then, as he liked to point out, when they almost hit them they knew exactly where they were. He'd never failed to find them yet, despite a shortage of navigation aids. All there was to confirm the dead reckoning position was an echo sounder ticking away in the corner of the chart room.

Tusker wiped some drips off the transparent plastic chart cover and pointed at the chart. 'We crossed the Hurd Deep forty-five minutes ago. I hope to pick up the edge of the Plateau de Triagoz in just over an hour. That'll give us a good lead in. Unless of course we have to reduce speed still further . . .?'

'No, we must bash on, whatever the weather. Otherwise we'll be too late. We're cutting it a bit fine as it is.'

The two men braced themselves as *309*'s bows rose into the air and began to descend rapidly towards an approaching wave. There was a loud crash and the boat shuddered. Cascades of water thundered over the chart room, pouring down the windows and penetrating the cracks in the wood. Tusker methodically wiped the drips away and gazed down at the chart again. 'Whatever the revs say, I'd be surprised if we were doing thirteen knots in this sea.'

Ashley nodded. 'I've allowed a bit for the sea conditions, but I dare say you're right. I still want to press on, though. Once we reach the plateau we'll start to get in the lee of the land. Things should improve then.' He blew out his cheeks. 'By the way, Macleod's sick, so I'll be leading the beach party. That means you'll be in charge until I get back.'

Tusker's eyebrows shot up. 'I say, that's a bit irregular, isn't it? I mean, why not send Talbot or Eddington to the beach? They'd do the job all right.'

'No, I'd rather go myself,' Ashley said crisply. He didn't

want a discussion. He was perfectly well aware that a commander shouldn't leave his ship, but this was a very small ship and the circumstances rather unusual. 'No, I'd prefer Talbot and Eddington to stay here. You'll want them if there's a fight. It's more important to leave the ship properly manned. Anyway . . .' He smiled breezily at Tusker, '. . . after all this time I want to have a look at this beach and meet some of our Breton friends.'

Tusker nodded reluctantly. 'As you say.'

'Now, this is the form. You are to wait until 0315, at the very latest, and then you are to leave, even if we haven't returned. Is that understood?'

The other man nodded.

'And if there's any sign of trouble, the usual rules apply – get out and as quickly as possible. Just because I'm ashore, don't try to be clever and wait around. Understood?'

'Understood.'

'Good!'

It was raining now, drumming against the window, mingling with the salt spray in a steady deluge of running water.

Ashley murmured, 'Christ! We're not going to see very much at this rate.'

'No, but it may not last. We've still got an hour before we need to start worrying about visibility.

Ashley sighed. 'I just wish that, for once, we'd have a bit of luck. It would make a pleasant bloody change!'

It was 0140. There was no sign of Les Vaches. Although the seas were much lower here in the shadow of the land and the boat was riding the waves more easily, the weather was still foul. Every few minutes heavy showers came through, obliterating the few precious yards of visibility, turning the already dark night into a wall of black.

Ashley stood at the side of the bridge, his teeth set, his eyes straining to penetrate the inky darkness. He tried to resist the temptation to call down to Tusker again, but failed. He reached for the voice pipe. 'Tusker! Any ideas?'

'Give it five minutes, then we can try turning east.'

'Five minutes is a hell of a long time!' Ashley knew he was sounding testy but, damn it, he was.

'Yes, five minutes should get us right up to Les Vaches,' came the calm response.

'I thought we were meant to be there already!'

'Well, allowing for losing some time in those seas . . .'

'Okay! Five minutes!'

He threw the pipe back into its socket and stared back into the darkness. He had four men on the bridge now, all of them looking – for anything: any sign, any indication of rocks, land, E-boats, anything. A hundred miles, they'd travelled, and now they were looking for two rocks in the middle of the sea. Ridiculous!

Nothing. Not even the customary smell of the land. Ashley thought: Tusker's finally blown it.

The rain stopped. Strange new shadows flickered across the pattern of the night. Ashley screwed up his eyes. It was almost impossible to know what you were seeing . . . But the visibility had definitely improved, no doubt about that.

'Sir! Port bow! I think I see something, sir!'

They all turned and stared, no-one speaking, an electric silence filling the bridge.

'Yes, sir.' It was the coxswain's voice, steady and firm. 'Just fine on the port bow, sir. A rock, I would say.'

Ashley looked again, and saw it this time. It was a large rock. One of two. Les Vaches.

Ashley breathed out slowly, his body sagging as the tension eased away. He called down the pipe, 'Well done, Tusker. Your rock's popped up on the port bow.'

Thank goodness it had. He always had a vision of getting the boat lost and steaming on to a barely submerged rock and the boat tearing her guts out . . . He tried not to think of such things, but on bad nights one couldn't help it . . .

Tusker took some bearings and they pressed on towards the land. Because the wind was offshore and would carry the sound of their engines away from the ears of German sentries, Richard decided to risk a fast approach. Time was ticking away. It was 0150.

At two miles they reduced speed to five knots, searching for the familiar landmarks, feeling their way in towards the anchorage. Finally they were on station, one mile offshore in the open arms of a wide, rocky bay, lying to their grass-rope anchor. It was 0215. Only one hour at the most.

The beach lay in a cove in the western arc of the bay, its sides guarded by a myriad of small rocks. The surfboat was already in the water, the two crew waiting at their oars which were muffled with heavy sacking.

Ashley jumped down and sat in the stern, a compass in his hand and the wireless on the seat beside him. At his feet was their new gadget, a hydrophone, which, when its sensor was dropped in the water, would pick up the sound of 309's echo sounder and guide them back to her. They would need it tonight.

The surfboat buffeted her way through the waves, the water hissing and slapping at her sides. Already the MGB was a shadow in the deeper darkness behind them.

Ashley looked at his watch. It was 0222.

He couldn't help thinking that for once they really were cutting it a bit fine.

The clock ticked loudly on the mantelpiece, syncopating with the gentle snores of Tante Marie, asleep in the chair on the opposite side of the hearth.

Julie stared at the book which lay open but unread on

her lap and listened intently to the other sounds, the sounds of the night. A wind was blowing, quite a strong one, vibrating the windows and moaning softly around the buildings; and there was rain, coming in sudden squalls, drumming loudly on the outhouse roof, pit-patting against the glass.

She listened and almost imagined she heard the rumbling of the surf down in the cove and the scrunch of boats as they grounded on the pebbles. Almost imagined, too, that she heard the sound of footsteps as the guides led the passengers past the farmhouse down to the beach . . .

With a sigh, Julie returned to her book. Always imagining things!

But she stared at the pages, unseeing, and thought of the waiting men and the steep path to the beach and the dark cover again. She hadn't been back to the beach since that night, four months ago now. In one way she was sorry – she'd rather enjoyed it – but she was determined not to get involved too deeply. Her instincts still told her that it would all go wrong, that, sooner or later, it would end in disaster. And she couldn't bear the thought of being caught. Nothing could be worth that.

At the same time she couldn't help worrying. Especially tonight.

The night had a bad aura about it, an indefinable atmosphere of depression and doom. She couldn't say why, or in what way. At ten she had gone to bed and tried to sleep, but her feeling of despair had been so strong that she had come down to sit with Tante Marie and wait. Of course a man would laugh at the whole idea of *feeling* these things, but for her it was almost tangible.

Except that now, two hours later, she wasn't quite so certain as before. Perhaps nothing was going to happen after all. She rubbed her eyes. She was beginning to feel tired. It might be worth trying to go back to sleep again.

It was comfortable there by the stove. She rested her head against the chair-back and closed her eyes. She'd make the effort to go to bed in a moment.

Suddenly she stiffened.

There was a slight unidentifiable sound, something that hadn't been there before . . .

She stood up and, dousing the small oil lamp, went to the door and opened it.

The wind was sighing and rustling round the farmyard, a cow shuffled restlessly in the barn, then . . . Yes, it was there! *Something* . . . Julie felt her blood run cold.

But what was it! *What?*

Machines? Men?

Whatever – it was something that shouldn't be there.

Quickly she closed the door, lit a candle and took it to her room. She found warm clothes: vest, woollen blouse, thick sweater, trousers, socks, sturdy shoes. Back in the kitchen she took a waterproof cowman's jacket from the back of the door and Jean's beret, pulling it low over her head and tucking her hair up inside the crown.

She touched Tante Marie's arm. The old woman woke with a start and looked at Julie in horror. She exclaimed, 'Where are you going? What's the matter?'

'Don't worry! I just have to get out, that's all. Just to listen . . . and watch for them.'

'Julie, don't go!' Tante Marie hissed. 'You don't know where the patrols are! You might stumble into one of them. Don't go, I tell you!'

Julie shook her head. 'I'll be careful . . . I just want to see that everything's all right. That's all. Don't worry.'

She turned quickly and went to the door. Waving briefly to the old woman, she stepped out into the night. She waited a moment to get her eyes accustomed to the darkness, then walked quietly round the side of the house to the road.

She paused and listened. Whatever that sound had been, it had gone. There was nothing now, only the rustling of the trees and the sigh of the wind.

But still, she had to go. She set off along the road, walking rapidly, her shoes making no sound on the hard surface. After five minutes she had made good progress: almost halfway up the hill that led to the open heathland. She walked steadily, her hands deep in her pockets, her mind locked on the necessity of reaching the clifftop. Once there she would wait and listen until she knew everyone was all right.

She stopped dead. There was that sound again.

It was a low whining, far off, back towards the village.

It was like the whining she'd heard in her imagination once: the whining of trucks. Trucks climbing.

Up the hill towards her.

She froze, still listening, unbelieving . . .

. . . the sound of trucks climbing. Oh God!

Then she ran, she ran fast and straight; she ran along the dark narrow lane, up and up, on and on, until the air rasped in her throat and the heavy shoes were like lead on her feet.

She ran with grim determination, absolutely certain that she must reach the clifftop: absolutely sure that she must get there before *them*.

She ran until her lungs were bursting and her heart was hammering in her ears.

And she didn't look back – she didn't dare. She just ran. Push, push . . . On, on . . . Think of nothing . . . Just trucks! Climbing! *Oh God, let me get there first!*

She was slowing. She panted, 'Come on! Come on!'

The heathland, at last. Now gorse reared up and pulled at her clothing; and the uneven ground rose and fell unexpectedly before her, jarring her legs, unbalancing her body. She stumbled and picked herself up again, still running.

It was dark, very dark. She tried to get her bearings. It was a long cliff and there were several paths, all leading down. Only one path was the right one. She looked ahead, trying to read the contours of the land. It all looked the same!

Now the effort was terrible. At every breath her lungs shot with pain and at every stride her legs flailed, less and less controllable, until she was half-running, half-staggering.

She sobbed, 'Come on! Come on!'

She tripped and fell. She put out her hands, too late. Her head hit the ground with a dull thud. For a moment she was dazed then she thought: *Get up!* She pulled herself up and staggered forward again.

Now at last there was something paler ahead. The wide expanse of the sea. Bordering it was the dark rim of the clifftop. Sobbing with relief she looked wildly to right and left. Which way?

Right. Yes: right.

She ran, looking desperately for familiar landmarks.

Then she saw a hillock, and a hollow . . . She was there. At the path.

She stopped, panting wildly. There was nobody. She called softly. Nobody. Perhaps the lookout was further along the cliff.

She hesitated for a moment, then set off, down the steep path towards the rumble of the surf. This time she took the path much faster, half-falling, half-running, stumbling against the larger rocks and scrabbling at the loose stone hill for handholds. A rock came up and knocked her chin and she heard her teeth close with a sharp snap. The warm, unfamiliar taste of blood filled her mouth.

The ground fell away: she had reached the slide at the bottom. She thought of jumping, but it was at least six feet and she was too tired. Wearily, she sat down and slid. The beach rushed up, she braced her legs. They gave way under her and she landed heavily on her side.

Slowly she got to her feet and staggered across the pebbles. She was so tired she'd almost forgotten why she had come. She called softly. Nothing. She called louder. Where were they? She thought: Oh God! Please let them be here. *Please!*

The finger of rock was deserted: no-one was waiting there. Down to the water then.

Suddenly, close by, there was a voice. Julie jumped and gave an involuntary cry. The voice repeated, 'St Brieuc!' It must be a password and she didn't know the response.

She was shaking violently. She cried, 'It's me, Julie Lescaux. I don't know the password. Please – I've come to warn you . . .'

'We can't go now! The surfboat's already on its way!'

There was a short silence, the men huddled in a nervous group, their faces hidden in the darkness. Then everyone spoke at once. One voice emerged high above the rest. Julie recognised it immediately: it was the leader. 'We must go now! Now! We must abandon the mission!' His voice was shrill, anguished. 'Come on! Let's go!'

Again, there were many voices. Julie realised with a shock that one of them was Jean's. Then there was a lone voice, a strong voice, someone who commanded, 'Stop!' And there was silence again. The strong voice went on, 'Those who want to go, go now! The rest of us stay and get our passengers away.' There were mutterings of agreement, then the leader was speaking again, louder, shriller, 'It's madness to stay! We must go now! Now!' The strong voice said, 'Go then!' Julie realised it was the voice of the man who'd sat next to her by the rock, that first time, a man she'd later realised to be a fisherman from a small cove in the next bay: a man called Gérard.

Now Gérard came close to her, saying, 'Here, Julie, the wireless! Try to make contact with them! Warn them!'

The hard oblong box was thrust into her hand. Julie grasped it. She walked unsteadily away and sat on a rock, trying to remember how it worked. Her body was still shaking with exhaustion and she fumbled clumsily with the knobs. She tried the on/off button. It was difficult to know if it was working: the surf was roaring and the wind whistling so loudly that she couldn't hear. She put the receiver part to her ear: there was a faint crackling. Now the aerial. She pulled it up, found the transmitting button, and pressed it. She called, 'Hello.' There was nothing. She tried again: still nothing.

She thought: I'm doing something wrong.

She peered at the various buttons and remembered something about two different frequencies. She found a sliding switch and pushed it the other way. She called again, 'Hello.'

The wireless crackled and, above the rumble of the surf, she heard a tinny voice, 'Bertie here, Please identify. Over.' Julie shivered with surprise.

Then she remembered that she was meant to say something: a password. But it was no good, she couldn't remember it. She pressed the transmitter and said, 'Beach here.' Now what? Information. She said hastily, 'You may be in danger. The Germans are searching the cliffs.'

The wireless crackled, 'Understood. But our party's arrived, hasn't it? Over.'

Julie was confused until she realised she was talking to the ship, not the boat. She looked quickly along the beach. Yes – he was right – something was happening. The men had gathered at the water's edge and a shape was showing dark against the whiteness of the breaking waves: the surfboat.

She pressed the transmitter. 'They're here. We'll get them off again as soon as possible.' She left her finger on

the button but couldn't think of anything else to say. She
released it, then pressed it again hurriedly and said, 'Over.'
When she let go again the man on the ship was already
speaking, '. . . short message when they leave. Out.'

Julie blinked and wondered whether to reply, but 'Out'
probably meant that the man had signed off. She'd understood what he meant: they wanted to know when the
surfboat left. Best not to talk again and confuse the matter.
She switched off the wireless and, getting up, walked along
the edge of the water towards the surfboat.

It was terribly windy: she had to lean her body forward
in order to walk. The surf was very loud, too, and it was
impossible to hear anything above the thunderous roar.
Julie hoped someone was keeping a good lookout up on
the clifftop . . .

As she approached the boat, she saw frantic activity:
the men were dragging things out of it and removing the
oars from the rowlocks. She saw with horror that one of
the oars was broken. Most of the men went to one side
of the boat and, with a heave, tipped it right over.
Water poured out and Julie realised it must have been half
full.

Suddenly the firm voice of Gérard was at her elbow
again. 'Julie! Come!' His tone was urgent, authoritative.
He led her past the men working on the boat to a figure
who stood slightly apart from the rest.

Gérard pulled her in front of the figure and said, 'Please
explain that the Germans are near!'

Julie realised it was one of the British crew. She said in
English, 'We think the Germans are about! Searching the
clifftop. They may know you're here. You must get away
quickly, straight away!'

The figure stepped closer and she felt a strong hand grip
her arm. 'Tell your friend, it's not just the oar that's broken
– there's a hole in the boat too! We've got to find something
to stuff in it, and quick!'

She translated quickly and turned back, saying, 'Yes, he understands that.'

The hand was still on her arm. 'And tell him we can only take six passengers. It's just too rough out there to risk any more.'

Again, Julie translated. Gérard nodded. The British officer said, 'Right! Let's get going!' The men were already at work: tearing a wool jacket in half to make a bung, sorting out passengers, cutting cord to whip together the two pieces of broken oar.

So little time! Julie stood, frozen with worry, willing them to finish.

But a moment later there was an exclamation. It came from someone standing a little way up the beach. There was something about the shout which made everyone stop and look up. The man was running frantically towards them, hissing, 'A light . . . A signal!'

Julie looked up at the cliff and felt a thud of fear.

There was a dim red light, blinking through the darkness.

A warning. Blood-red.

For a second there was silence, then Gérard's voice floated over the thundering surf. 'The boat! We must hide the boat! In the rocks on the point. Quick!' Everyone jerked into action, hauling on the boat, dragging it along the beach.

The British officer ran up to her and grabbed her arm. 'What in hell . . .?'

'The Germans! They're coming!'

'Christ!' He turned and shouted, 'Jenkins! Turner! Pick up your weapons! Get this boat hidden, then follow these men!'

The boat was halfway up the beach now. Her heart in her mouth, Julie ran as fast as she could over the slippery pebbles, following the rapidly moving shadows of the men as they fled across the beach to the rocks.

By the time she reached the point, the men had hidden the boat behind a large rock and were covering it with seaweed. As soon as the boat was camouflaged people moved quickly away towards the jumble of rocks and boulders that tumbled down from the headland above, and slid quietly into the shadows of the crevices.

Julie looked blindly around, panic rising in her throat. Where was Jean? And Gérard? She stumbled closer to the rocks, searching desperately. Then Jean was beside her, taking her arm, guiding her in towards the rocks. She cried, 'Oh Jean!'

'Julie, it'll be all right. All we have to do is keep quiet! Now, go in here. In here!' He pushed her into a crevice between two tall rocks. She settled herself on the stones and then realised Jean hadn't followed her. Where was he? Why hadn't he followed?

All around her there were clicking noises: Julie realised the men were checking their weapons. She felt sick. *Where was Jean?*

Suddenly he was back, pushing another figure towards her. With surprise she realised it was the British officer. She hissed, 'Jean! Jean! Where are you going?'

'I'll just be next door! Next rock!'

The officer had crawled in beside her and was tugging gently at the strap on her shoulder. She'd forgotten about the wireless.

'Sorry,' he whispered. 'But I must contact my boat. Our own set got wet.'

'Of course.' She felt a fool, for having panicked. She passed over the wireless and listened as he clicked the switches. There was a hum and he said, 'Bertie, Bertie, this is Alfie calling. Over.'

There was a silence, then he tried again. Still nothing. Julie felt for him. Suddenly she felt guilty. She should have thought of calling the ship herself as she came along the beach. The wireless probably would have worked then, out in the open. Stupid of her!

She started to say, 'I'm sorry, I . . .' But he said 'Shush!' and she bit her lip.

After another two minutes he called into the wireless again. Still there was nothing. She heard the click of switches again and realised he was putting the wireless down onto the ground. He sighed and said very quietly, 'I think that perhaps it just isn't my day.'

Then he leant closer to her and whispered, 'Sorry, I didn't mean to shut you up just then, but I thought I heard something . . .'

'That's all right.'

'You've been a great help. Thank you.'

Julie nodded briefly in the darkness, then turned her head to listen for sounds from the beach. She strained her ears but it was impossible to hear anything over the rumbling of the surf. Suddenly there was a scraping noise; the officer was moving forward. His figure became a silhouette against the paler black of the sky, a weapon just visible in his hand.

Tentatively Julie followed until she too could see down to the impenetrable darkness of the beach.

After a while, she realised quite a lot of time had passed. Half an hour, maybe more. And still there was nothing.

Perhaps they were going to be safe after all.

Suddenly she sensed the officer stiffen. He got up on one knee, then rose and walked forward until he was standing just clear of the rocks.

Then she heard a sound: the sound of an engine. Not a truck, not from the cliff. It was something more familiar. She tried to place it. It was the sound of an engine over water, like a fishing boat's but deeper, throatier . . .

She heard the Englishman say, 'Christ All Bloody Mighty!' Then he turned and crawled slowly back in beside her. She thought she heard him laugh; she must have misheard. But no, there it was again.

She whispered, 'What is it?'

He said bitterly, 'I think I've just missed my bloody boat!'

Ashley opened his eyes and frowned slightly. Hanging from the ceiling above him there was a model aeroplane made of cardboard and paper. He turned his head. On the walls there were a couple of bright paintings – one of a tractor, the other of a car – and two posters of Paris. A child's room. A rather small child at that: he looked down and saw that his feet were protruding from the end of the totally inadequate bed. It was the coldness of his toes which had woken him.

He looked at his watch: nine-thirty. GMT, that was: an hour later in France. He must have been asleep for three hours then.

They had waited in the rocks until five when a lookout had come to tell them that the Germans had gone. Then the Bretons had had a short conference to decide who was going to take charge of the airmen, and who Ashley and his crew. Ashley tried to understand what arrangements were being decided, but the men whispered in Breton or, once or twice, in heavily accented French, and he couldn't catch it. Then he'd searched for the girl and asked her and she had told him that his men were to be hidden in a safe house – she wouldn't tell him where – and he in another. He'd asked if he couldn't be hidden in the same house, and she'd said no, there wasn't room. She was quite abrupt.

'Well,' he said, 'just tell me who to follow.'

'Me. You're to be hidden in my house.'

He tried to see her face in the darkness. 'How very kind . . .'

'Hardly! There's nowhere else, that's all.'

She was cross, he could tell, though he couldn't guess why. Best not to say any more then. He'd followed her without a word, up a steep path to the top of the cliff and then across some heathland to a road. She'd started off at a cracking pace, up the cliff, but then slowed and at one point she staggered and almost fell. He'd reached for her arm, but, politely but firmly, she'd pulled away.

When they reached the back door of the house she'd told him to wait outside. Within a minute she was back, leading him into a warm room, very dark: a kitchen he guessed. Again he'd waited while she disappeared into a back room. This time it was several minutes before she returned. She guided him through a door and up some narrow steep stairs to an attic – this attic.

All she'd said before going was, 'Don't make a sound and don't put your face to the window! Oh, and your clothes, they're wet, I suppose? Leave them at the top of the stairs, just here!' And then she was gone.

Two thoughts had entered his mind before he fell asleep: the first, that someone had just been asleep in this bed, it was so warm, and the second, that the cross English-speaking lady was not very pleased to have him here, not very pleased at all.

Now, in the morning light that filtered through the one small window, he took another look round the child's room, pulled his feet in out of the cold and closed his eyes. He might as well go back to sleep again: he wasn't going anywhere – and certainly not without any clothes on.

Suddenly he was wide awake again. A door had closed in the room immediately beneath. Someone was climbing the stairs. He reached down to the floor and, picking up his gun, pointed it towards the top of the stairwell.

A head appeared, with dark, longish hair. The girl.

He relaxed and put the gun back on the floor.

She was carrying some bread and a mug of hot liquid, her head bent down, intent on preventing the liquid from spilling. She came up to the bed and, crouching down, placed the mug on the floor. The bread was more difficult: she thought of balancing it on top of the mug, but put it on the bed instead. Then she looked up at him.

He stared at her in astonishment.

He realised with a shock that he knew her.

But where on earth from? He couldn't think. He examined her face for clues: dark eyes – tired today, with grey shadows under them – neat features, a lovely mouth, and fabulous clear pale skin. Very attractive – lovely even. But *where* had he met her?

He realised he was staring: she had looked away, embarrassed, and had started to speak. '. . . we've found some clothes for you. I'll bring them up directly. It's best not to wear your other ones – they look far too Navy if you're seen. And you *must* take care not to be seen – we have soldiers billeted here.'

Ashley blinked in amazement. 'What?'

'Yes, two of them. They sleep in the main part of the house, at the front. They're up at six-thirty, out by seven and back at about eight in the evening. For a meal. Then they usually go out for a drink – until about ten.'

Ashley raised his eyebrows. 'It's a bit close for comfort, I must say . . .'

'On the other hand,' the girl said, 'they wouldn't think of looking for anyone in the same house, would they? I mean, you're probably safer here than somewhere more isolated.'

He smiled. 'Yes, I hadn't thought of that.' He looked at her with new admiration.

'Just as long as you're *not* seen.' She was looking at him sternly. 'I'm afraid that means not going out. And no noise, either. It's vital. You do understand that, don't you?'

He sat up in bed and looked down at her. 'I understand that very well – I understand the risk you're running. And I'm very grateful, believe me.'

'Fine, well as long as you obey the rules there'll be no problems.' She was so schoolmarmish that Ashley couldn't help hiding a smile. She glanced up, saw his amusement, and flushed.

'Right,' she said tightly, getting to her feet. 'I'll get those clothes then.' She brushed at her skirt with agitation.

He could see he had annoyed her. He said hurriedly, 'Thank you. I'm really most grateful. And I'm really most sorry for the trouble I've caused.'

She hesitated, searching his face. Then she nodded slightly. 'Don't mind me. It's just been a long night and – they arrested some people.'

Ashley said, 'I'm so sorry.'

She went on, 'Three people, two local and one from – elsewhere. It could have been worse, of course. We're grateful there weren't more.'

Ashley thought for a moment. He said, 'Did these people know about the beach, about our visits . . .?'

'Oh yes.'

'So—' He didn't know how to put it '– so the Germans might extract the information from them.'

She hesitated. 'It's possible.'

'Then . . . that beach might be risky. Well,' he said brightly, 'there must be other beaches near here! We'll arrange a pick-up as soon as possible and get ourselves off your hands!'

She nodded briefly, then frowned. 'There's only one problem. One of the men arrested was the leader – he was the one with access to the wireless operator, somewhere near Paris. It'll take time to set up another link, particularly if the wireless operator has to go into hiding, or gets caught . . .'

Ashley sighed heavily. He didn't like the idea of being cooped up here for any length of time. All he wanted was to get back to his boat; he hated to think of the old tub being commanded by anyone else, even if it was Jimmy

Macleod. He hated, too, the prospect of not being able to move around, of being a virtual prisoner. He looked around the room with dismay: it was tiny. What the hell was he going to do all day?

The girl had come closer. She said softly, 'I'm sorry. It's going to be rotten for you, stuck up here all day long. But I'll bring you some books – some English books. And I've got a cribbage board—' She shrugged. 'If you play, of course.'

He looked at her and grinned. 'Under the circumstances, I'll be glad of anything, anything at all!'

She smiled back and he thought how lovely she looked when she was happy.

Then, suddenly, he had it. Where he'd seen her before. Plymouth! He'd met her in Plymouth – the girl who'd come sailing with him that day! How extraordinary!

His stare had flustered her; she was turning to walk away.

'Wait a minute!' he exclaimed. 'D'you realise we've met before?'

Julie's heart sank. She'd known, from the moment she'd looked into his eyes, that she had met him before. It had taken her some minutes to fix the exact time and place. But then she'd remembered it all: the sunny afternoon, the boat, the sail round the harbour.

And now her heart sank because she wanted it forgotten and he had remembered.

She turned and said lightly, 'Oh yes?'

He smiled. 'Absolutely! You came sailing with me. Around Plymouth Sound.'

She inclined her head. 'Oh really?'

'Yes.' He looked rather surprised that she hadn't remembered. 'In *Dancer* – my 25-footer ... Don't you remember?' He put on a half-hurt half-amused expression.

She nodded, as if it had just come back to her. 'Oh yes. I think I remember now. It was such a long time ago . . .'

'Yes, I suppose it was,' he laughed. His expression changed and he said, 'But what are you doing, living here?'

'My family – they live here. My uncle and aunt.'

'And the child, is that yours?'

Julie hesitated. She didn't want him to know anything about Peter, nothing at all. She said abruptly, 'Yes.'

'How old is he – or is it a she?'

Julie went cold. Now the questions – next the mathematics. It wouldn't take him long to work it out. She thought quickly and decided it might be all right if she took a few months off. 'Five. His name is Pierre. He's at school.' She wasn't lying about his name: ever since the Occupation she'd made sure he was known by the French version of his name.

'Well, I look forward to meeting him, if only to tell him I'm very sorry for pinching his bed. He wasn't too put out, I hope?'

'No.'

'Still, it must have been rotten going into a cold bed.' He smiled warmly. 'I look forward to meeting him.' She saw that he was about to ask another question and, indicating the mug on the floor, she said quickly, 'Your coffee's getting cold.'

He exclaimed, 'Oh!' And beat his hand against his head in an exaggerated gesture of stupidity. He looked at her, his eyes twinkling, and said, 'I promise to be a better guest in future!'

She smiled faintly and turned to go down the stairs.

He called softly, 'And your husband? Is he here?'

She paused at the first stair and, not looking at him, said, 'No, there's no husband.'

'Oh! I'm sorry. I—'

Julie immediately wished she hadn't said it. He would think she had a husband who was killed in the fighting.

But it would be a mistake to explain further; it would mean telling less than the truth, and she hated lying. Instead she murmured, 'I'll go and get those clothes then.'

'Thanks. And one more thing!'

'Yes.'

'I'm sorry,' he said apologetically, 'but I've forgotten your name.'

'Julie.' Immediately she realised that this too had been a mistake. The less he knew about her the better, in case he was caught. She decided she was hopeless at all this intrigue.

He was smiling. 'Of course. Julie. What a lovely name. I remember it now. You've probably forgotten my name too. After all, why *should* you remember it! Anyway it's Richard. Richard Ashley.'

She nodded. 'Yes, I remember now.' She started down the stairs.

'Oh, and Julie.' His voice was very soft now.

She stopped, a strange feeling in her throat. It was the way he had spoken her name: so familiar, even intimate. She swallowed, 'Yes?'

'I *will* try to be good.' He sighed. 'But I'm not used to being cooped up. It's going to drive me quietly bonkers, I'm afraid. And not knowing what's happened to my ship doesn't help, either. For all I know they might have met an E-boat on the way out . . . Look – if I get bloody impossible or moan and gripe too much, just tell me I'm being tiresome, will you? Just be firm with me, and I'll behave. Honestly!'

She couldn't help smiling. 'Yes,' she laughed. 'I'll tell you.'

'Thanks! And,' he added solemnly, 'for my part, I promise to obey the rules. To the letter, ma'am!' He touched his forehead in a mock salute and then smiled, just a little sheepishly, an apologetic expression on his face.

He was making fun of her, she knew. But it was

impossible to take offence: he had done it so amiably. And his eyes – they were so nice and friendly. She couldn't be angry with him.

Instead she smiled at him and, blushing slightly, went quickly down the stairs.

Chapter 18

———•———

YOU COULD TELL Americans anywhere, Vasson decided. They looked different in every way. There was the colouring – often blue-eyed and fair-haired, rather like the Germans themselves; the height – many of them were well over six feet tall; and, most telling of all, the well-fed look. Somehow people who ate lots of meat looked different from those who ate bread and starch: in fact, they looked rather like the fat cattle they ate. They sat differently, too, lounging on the train seats instead of sitting upright as the Europeans did. Some even had bright yellow nicotine stains on their fingers: something you never got from French and Belgian cigarettes. It was only because the Germans were so blind to anything but pieces of paper that these obviously alien creatures could travel on trains at all.

There were six of them, sitting in different places around the open carriage. All were airmen who'd ditched over Belgium and been found by 'friends'.

They were travelling to Paris, where they would be transferred to a south-bound train. Vasson was their courier. Eventually they would be led over the Pyrénées into Spain.

Or so they thought. Vasson viewed them with contempt: they were so naive, these people. They had no idea at all.

There was also a seventh man. The Americans thought he was Czech and a pilot in the RAF. They were almost right about the first bit – in fact, he came from the Czech–German border. But they were quite wrong about the second bit. The man did not work for the RAF, he worked for Vasson. And he was going to tell Vasson every detail about the escape line, every courier and safe house all the way down to Spain.

It was a lot to ask of one man, but Vasson had spent four weeks briefing him. He had also arranged for his wife and child to be placed under arrest, just in case.

Vasson glanced round the carriage again. One of the flyers – a young, fresh-faced boy with an awful American haircut – winked at Vasson. Vasson stared back coldly. The boy had been a problem ever since Brussels, when Vasson had taken the group over. The boy had started chewing gum, quite oblivious to the stares of the other passengers. Then he'd started to whisper in English to his friend. Vasson had had to separate them.

Now, under Vasson's cold stare, the boy dropped his eyes and looked out of the window. There were no more winks.

They were approaching the Gare du Nord. Almost home. Vasson missed Paris very much; Brussels was dull by comparison. This was his fifth run to Paris, but he never got to stay for any length of time, and this visit would be the shortest yet. After seeing Kloffer he would catch the next train back. But for once he didn't mind too much: Brussels promised a great deal of excitement over the next two days.

The train ground to a halt. Vasson stood up. The airmen got to their feet, their eyes on Vasson.

Vasson joined the throng of people leaving the train and strolled down the platform towards the barrier. He could feel the others following him. At the barrier there were two French policemen checking papers and two *Feldgendarmen* examining people's faces. Vasson knew they would get through all right: he'd arranged it with Kloffer.

The gendarme looked at Vasson's papers and pushed

them quickly back into his hand. Yes: he'd been briefed all right.

Vasson wandered slowly into the main concourse and glanced around, as if looking for someone. He glanced casually behind him and saw that all the airmen were through the barrier.

He waited until they had all found him again, then walked out of the station into the Rue de Dunkerque.

There were only two people at the bus stop. Vasson strolled up and stood behind them. The airmen followed suit. Vasson moved closer to the Americans' leader and muttered, 'I'm off now. Wait for a girl wearing a purple hat. Bye.'

Vasson went through his pantomime of looking at his watch, glancing up the street for a bus and then, after shaking his head, moving away. The other Americans looked around uncertainly, wondering whether they should follow Vasson, but, seeing that their leader did not, settled down to wait.

Vasson walked back to the station, went into the booking hall and, very casually, turned back until he could watch the bus stop from the darkness of the doorway.

The next courier was meant to pick up the passengers – or parcels, as they insisted on calling them – in five minutes. In fact she arrived in eight.

It was the same girl as before: a dark, rather plain girl with a permanent frown. She was wearing the purple hat. She stood patiently behind the group until a bus destination 'République–Bastille' came along. Then she moved forward to the front of the line and got into the bus. The airmen got in behind her.

It was the classic cut-out rendezvous. The two couriers never met, never saw each other and were incapable of identifying each other. Vasson smiled: doubtless the organisers were very proud of the method. After all, it worked very well – so long as everyone was on the same side.

As the bus drew away Vasson saw the Czech sitting in the back of the bus, staring calmly out of the window. He was going to be all right, that man. He'd deliver the goods.

But there was a back-up, just in case. It was only good for the first part of the journey, but if the Czech failed it would be better than nothing. He'd asked Kloffer to provide a tail.

He looked around for signs of one. There hadn't been anyone in the bus queue, he was sure of that. A car then. But there were no black Citroëns in sight. The only possibility was a battered old Peugeot which pulled out from the kerb and went off in the same direction as the bus. Yes, perhaps that was it. If so, Kloffer was definitely improving.

The concourse was crowded when Vasson got back into the station and it took him some time to get across to the other side. The plain unmarked door was behind the men's lavatories, next to the railway security office. But he didn't go straight there. Instead he went into the lavatories, glancing behind him as he went. No-one. He used the urinal and went out into the concourse again. This time he paused and took a good look round. Still no-one. He'd known there wouldn't be, but it was always best to make sure.

He strolled towards the unmarked door, took one last look, and slipped inside.

Kloffer was there, waiting.

They nodded at each other. Vasson sat down and said, 'You've done as I suggested?'

'Yes, we have several tails on them. They'll be followed as far as possible.'

'And the tails, they're not your usual gorillas, I trust?'

Kloffer looked annoyed. His men's appearance was an old bone of contention. He said testily, 'They will do their job well, don't worry.'

Vasson said, 'Good.'

'And your man, will he do *his* job? It's a lot to ask of one man – and not one of *my* men at that.'

'He's been properly briefed. As long as he can make contact all right, then nothing will go wrong.'

'Yes. As long as he *can* . . .'

'He will.'

'So!' Kloffer put his fingertips together. 'That takes care of that then . . .'

'Yes.' Vasson's only regret was that he wouldn't be in on all the arrests. He would have liked that.

Kloffer examined Vasson with his cold, hard eyes. 'Now, the Brussels end. Are you sure you have it under control?'

'Oh yes. I'll give you the lot within three days.'

'But the leader – have you identified him?'

'Yes. Finally.'

'And—?'

'Tomorrow. You'll have him by tomorrow.'

Kloffer nodded and stood up. 'After – when you've finished there – you'd better come back to Paris.'

'That was what I intended.'

Kloffer said deliberately, 'But not for too long. And you must stay away from your old haunts. You're no use to me if you're dead.' He smiled faintly. 'And you would be dead – very quickly.'

Vasson sighed, 'You're just saying that, Kloffer. Just to keep me in order. I'm beginning not to believe you any more.'

'Ah . . . but there's only one way to find out if I'm lying. And that might be fatal for you, might it not? Besides . . .,' Kloffer went on carefully, 'if you were dead you wouldn't be able to spend any of that money you're so carefully accumulating. That would be a pity, wouldn't it?'

Vasson suppressed his irritation. Kloffer thought he did it just for the money. He was a stupid man.

He decided that he couldn't be bothered to argue the

point. Anyway perhaps Kloffer was right – better to be out of Paris and alive than shot in the back.

'Okay. So I don't stay in Paris. So where do I go?'

Kloffer said, 'Ah! Where? Who knows? We'll see.' He smiled, enjoying what he imagined to be his little moment of power. Vasson thought: Screw you.

Kloffer stood up and put on his hat. 'But I promise you the job will be equally interesting and rewarding.'

First the stick, then the carrot. Kloffer was so predictable.

Kloffer paused at the door. 'Goodbye, and we look forward to some excellent results in Brussels.'

'And I look forward to some excellent results in the money department, Kloffer.'

'Don't be greedy. You earn enough.'

'But am I paid what I'm worth? That's the question.'

'You could be worth nothing. Remember that, *Marseillais!*'

Kloffer opened the door and chuckled to himself. 'Goodbye. That's what I always call you, you know – The *Marseillais!*' He watched Vasson's face, then, smiling still, went out.

The door closed and Vasson clenched his fists. He took a long, deep breath to calm himself.

The bastard must have taken his thumb print and had it sent round to every police station in the country. It was the only way he could have found out.

It all came back to that filthy foreign woman . . . If it hadn't been for her, he'd never have been on file . . .

It was her fault, the bitch.

Vasson shivered and stood up.

He hated Kloffer for knowing.

One day he'd get Kloffer. One day.

He looked at his watch. There was a train for Brussels in ten minutes.

As he walked angrily across the station he thought

about the Brussels job. He saw the faces of the smug
intellectuals running the operation, and imagined their
expressions when they realised they'd been betrayed. It
was the only thing that consoled him.

The train was late arriving. Vasson decided to go straight
to the Café Mirabeau for dinner. The journey had made
him hungry. Also Anne-Marie might be there and she
would tell him the news. Or rather the lack of news. Even
if there had been some early arrests south of Paris, no-one
in Brussels could possibly have heard anything yet.

Anne-Marie. He'd be glad to be rid of her. She'd become
a bore. When he'd first met her, she'd been rather sweet
and it had been quite enjoyable to win her over. It had
taken time, of course, because she had been very cautious.
She'd only just been released by Mueller and she was
suspicious of everything. But he'd been patient. He'd led
her on, slowly but surely. In the end she had come to trust
him completely, just as he knew she would. When she'd
introduced him to her friends they'd given him simple jobs
at first: running messages and errands and that kind of
thing. Then at last had come the courier's job: the real test.
After that he was home and dry.

Anne-Marie. The trouble had started when she'd tricked
him, that terrible evening. He'd quite liked her until then.
He'd even imagined what it would be like to touch her,
naked, and to hold her down, tight . . .

Then she spoilt it all. She tricked him by saying she
loved him and that she just wanted to put her arms round
him. *It was all her fault.* She'd flaunted herself, showing
her knees, having those large breasts, smelling of sex . . .
He'd found himself feeling her body and then she was
naked and instead of staying still she *kept moving* – putting
her arms round him, trying to kiss him on the lips. It had

revolted him. In the end he'd put his arm across her neck and stopped her moving until he'd finished.

After that she disgusted him. He could hardly bear to look at her, particularly when she stared at him with those large reproachful eyes. Why couldn't she have left him alone? Why did she have to do *dirty* things?

But he still had to make the effort to see her, otherwise all his work would be for nothing. It almost killed him. Whenever she moved he could see those large breasts . . .

But it was just for one more day. That was all. He must remember that. He gritted his teeth and went into the café.

The bitch was there, sitting in a corner. He could tell she'd been waiting for him. She looked worried: she was probably going to be difficult.

As soon as he sat down she said, 'Everything all right?'

Vasson nodded. 'I think so.'

'Not sure?'

'I don't know. I always think I see shadows . . . You know.' It was important to sow a slight seed of doubt, just in case news of the Paris arrests reached Brussels before he'd finished the job.

She nodded. 'Probably nothing to worry about. But you—?' She looked at him with concern and touched his hand. It was all he could do not to snatch it away. 'Are *you* all right?'

'Sure. Why shouldn't I be?'

'It was just . . . you've been so . . . withdrawn . . . well, cold,' she finished painfully.

'Oh? Well, it doesn't mean anything.'

She brightened a little and he realised crossly that she had misinterpreted his words.

She said, 'Oh, I'm so pleased. I thought – Well, quite honestly I didn't know what to think. After . . . you know. I've been very confused.'

'I've just been feeling the strain, that's all.'

'But – you seemed so angry! It's been torturing me. What did I do wrong? Why were you so cross? And – why, oh *why*, Paul, did you hurt me?'

He sighed impatiently. 'Did I?'

'Yes. *Yes*.' She spoke angrily, reproachfully.

'Well, it was just the strain, as I say. Let's just forget it, eh? You're really getting things out of proportion.'

She gave him an agonised look. 'Oh dear, I really don't know what to think . . .'

Vasson thought: Christ, she's going to go on and on unless I shut her up. He breathed deeply and said, 'Look, dear, I'm truly sorry for what happened. I was upset, you see. I had a girl once – I've never told you this before – but . . .' He made a face as if the memory gave him terrible pain. '. . . she died you see. And whenever . . . Well, whenever . . . I remember her I want to die too!' He looked away as if it was too much to bear. He couldn't help thinking what a good performance he was giving.

She said, 'Oh! Oh, I see. I had no idea . . .'

She was buying it. Good. Time to ease off the subject. 'Look, I'd rather not talk about it. D'you understand?' She still looked unhappy, but nodded gently.

He said quickly, 'How are things here, then? Quiet?'

She nodded.

He looked pleased – he *was* pleased. Then he put on a frown. 'Look, there are a couple of things I'm a bit worried about – to do with security and, well, other things. I'd like to discuss them with Guy. Can you arrange a meeting, here or somewhere near?'

'But – does it have to be Guy himself?'

'Yes, it does.' Of course it had to be Guy: he was the most important one of all. 'And Patrice, too. Any chance of arranging something for tomorrow morning at about eleven?'

'I don't know . . . It's a bit unusual. They don't like too

many of us to meet at once. And, well, they'll want to know *why*.'

What a stupid woman, looking for problems. He was so irritated with her he could shake her by the throat. He said calmly, 'Look, I'm really worried and I do think it's important to talk the thing over with them. Really! Can't you just take my word for it? It's important. I have to have that meeting.'

She blinked. 'All right. I'll try.'

'Good.' He got up to leave. She frowned anxiously and said, 'Where are you going?'

'Mmm? Oh, home, I expect.'

'Don't you want to eat?'

The answer was yes but he didn't want to eat with her. It would spoil his appetite. He answered, 'No, I'm going straight to bed. I'll see you in the morning. You will arrange that meeting, won't you? It's important.'

She nodded, her face drawn and pale.

He realised she still wasn't convinced. Better make sure. He put his hands on the table. 'Look, after tomorrow, perhaps we'll go out for the day. Into the country. Would you like that? It would be nice to – well, relax a little. I have been feeling the strain, I can see that . . . Shall we do that? After the meeting?'

Her face was a mixture of relief and uncertainty. 'Yes. That would be nice.'

He forced himself to smile at her and then turned hurriedly away. Anything to keep the bitch happy. Anything to keep her quiet until after tomorrow. God! The things he had to do. But it would be worth it, he was sure of that.

It was a spectacular morning, the light as bright and clear as glass. Though it was still winter it was just warm enough to sit at a pavement table without feeling the cold. Vasson turned his face to the sun and thought that he'd never felt as good as he did today.

He ordered a second pastis and looked at his watch. Five minutes to go. His pulse quickened and he felt a delicious sense of anticipation.

It was almost the best part, the anticipation.

Anne-Marie was the first. She walked along the pavement towards him, her head down, her expression serious. She always looked serious. Well, today she really had something to worry about! The thought amused him and he had to lower his head to hide a smile.

She saw him and, giving a slight wave, weaved her way through the tables towards him.

As she sat down he asked, 'Everything fixed?'

She nodded.

He smiled brilliantly. 'Excellent! Now what would you like to drink? Pernod? Coffee? Yes? Then coffee it shall be!'

She was watching him, trying to gauge his mood. He smiled at her, elated. She said, 'You're very happy today.'

'Yes! Well, something's happened!'

'What?'

He held up his hand. 'All in good time! All in good time!'

She smiled thinly, but her eyes were serious, questioning. She was a bit wary, he decided. Nothing to worry about though, he could deal with her all right.

Stupid bitch. He smiled at her again. 'It's such a beautiful day, isn't it?'

'Yes.' She looked around nervously.

'What's the matter?'

She said quickly, 'Oh nothing. I'm just a bit jumpy today, I don't know why.'

Vasson eyed her sharply and wondered if she'd guessed something after all. She couldn't see Mueller and his men, of course: they were well hidden in a florist's shop across the street. And Vasson himself had given nothing away. He decided, finally, that she was just the nervous type.

Patrice, the number two in the organisation, was next. He was a doctor, one of the types who worked with the poor and the needy. His halo was so bright it was almost dazzling. Vasson watched him approach with satisfaction. Two down and one to go.

The doctor drew up a chair. Vasson said smoothly, 'My dear fellow, a glass of something? A Pernod?'

The doctor smiled kindly and said, 'No, thank you so much. Just a coffee.'

'Oh, but I did so want us to have a drink together!'

The doctor and Anne-Marie exchanged glances. Vasson realised he was pushing it. He said quickly, 'It's just that we hardly ever see each other and it's good to drink with one's friends.'

The doctor smiled. 'Another time, really.'

At last the leader, Guy, came. Vasson spotted him while he was still some distance away on the other side of the street. The man walked casually but with infinite caution, missing nothing. A wily man – a worthy opponent.

The leader arrived at the table and, taking a last look round, sat down.

Vasson beamed at him. 'Now I hope I have a customer for a drink! How about it? A pastis? A cognac?'

Guy eyed him and said quietly, 'No, let's have a drink after we have discussed our business. What, exactly, have you to tell us?'

A cool one, Vasson thought, a cool one. 'Ah!' He raised a finger and smiled. 'Good news, very good news.'

'But I thought there was something worrying you?'

'*Yes*, there is that too.' Vasson tried to look suitably serious. 'But to be precise it's something that should be worrying *you*.'

A nice little joke, that.

Out of the corner of his eye Vasson saw Mueller and his men coming out of the florist's shop. Only a minute left, then.

A look of concern had come into Guy's eyes and he said, 'What exactly is the problem? Spit it out!'

'The problem is that the Boches are on to you!'

The three of them froze, their eyes fastened on Vasson, waiting for him to go on. Vasson raised his eyebrows and shrugged mysteriously.

They exchanged glances, then stared back at Vasson, a mixture of uncertainty and cold horror growing on their faces.

Vasson looked past them to where Mueller and the men in black leather raincoats were making their way through the outer ring of tables. Then, just before the Germans arrived, Vasson smiled.

The two men realised almost simultaneously. They jumped to their feet and looked desperately around them. Anne-Marie was still staring stupidly across the table.

The men saw the black leather raincoats and froze like animals gauging the wind. Vasson wondered if they would try to run for it. He hoped not: it would draw attention.

The men turned and looked at each other, fear and terrible understanding written all over their faces. Vasson realised with satisfaction they were not going to run for it. Slowly, they sat down again and first one then the other stared at Vasson. The girl was still looking dully across the table, her mouth open.

Vasson said to the two men, 'Right. Now if you just tell me where to find the courier Francine, then we can be going.'

There was silence.

'If you don't tell me your wives and children will be arrested within the hour.'

'You bastard?' It was the girl. The dull look had gone and her eyes were blazing. 'You bastard! You filthy swine!

You—!' Suddenly she screamed and, picking up an ashtray, raised it above her head. Before she could throw it one of Mueller's men swung at her. There was a *crack!* as his leather-gloved hand hit her cheekbone. The ashtray fell to the ground.

Shaking with anger, Vasson leant forward in his chair. 'That'll teach you, you bitch. Next time we'll make your face into pulp!'

Vasson leaned back in his chair and took a deep breath. 'Where do I find the courier Francine?'

The men were looking away now, their expressions grim. Only the girl was staring at him again.

They weren't going to talk. It didn't matter; he could send a false message to the courier and lure her out that way. Vasson said stiffly, 'Very well. If you wish to sacrifice your families . . .'

The girl had been quiet but now she let out a cry of agony and for a moment Vasson thought she'd reach across the table and try to scratch him. But she sank back in her seat, her face a picture of hate and self-loathing, and shouted, 'Oh God! Oh God!'

Vasson indicated to Mueller and one of his men yanked the girl out of her seat and took her away. She screamed as she was dragged across the pavement. Vasson wished she wouldn't make so much noise; people were staring.

Vasson said to Mueller, 'And the others!'

As the doctor was pulled to his feet he turned towards Vasson and said quietly, 'I feel very sorry for you. May God forgive you.'

Vasson forced a smile and said, 'Sod you too!'

He finished his drink and nodded to one of Mueller's men, who made a show of arresting Vasson. Vasson pretended to struggle a little, then walked quietly across the street to the waiting car.

*

In Room 900 of the War Office, Smithe-Webb of the
French Section of M19 was waiting for news.

There had been no news from Meteor for three days.
Meteor, the largest of the evasion lines, had two wireless
operators. Neither of them had made contact.

The major had to remind himself that this in itself
meant nothing; wireless operators often had trouble getting
through.

But then there was the silence from the Spanish end of
the line. No airmen had come over the border for four
days.

And then there were the rumours. They'd started
coming in the previous day, from other evasion lines and
from agents of the Special Operations Executive.

The rumours hinted at a disaster in the Meteor line.

All Smithe-Webb could do was to hope it wasn't true –
and wait for news.

The news came at four that afternoon. From the Coding
and Signals Section of MI9 headquarters at Beaconsfield,
just outside London. The section had received a message.
It was from Xavier, one of the Meteor wireless operators.
The message was perfectly routine, asking for arms and
money to be dropped in three days' time; the code used
was correct; and the 'touch', the operator's unique and
personally identifiable Morse style, was definitely Xavier's.

But something was missing, something which made
Smithe-Webb's heart sink. One of the security checks had
been left out. One of the two intentional mistakes that
operators were trained to put into their messages had been
omitted.

That meant only one thing. It meant that Xavier was
operating under German control.

Over the next three days more and more information
filtered through and Smithe-Webb's worst fears were
realised.

Meteor had been devastated. It was as if the line had

never existed. Over a hundred and fifty arrests had been made: men and women, some in their seventies, others no more than eighteen.

It was a disaster.

When the news broke, the Head of MI9 shielded Room 900 from the worst of the flak which rained down on them from the Department's enemies in high places.

But Smithe-Webb didn't care either way. There was only one thing he cared about – finding out how it had happened so that it could never, ever happen again.

The next day his prayers were answered. A long signal arrived from the British Consulate in Lisbon. A man claiming to be a member of the Meteor line had reached Portugal by means of the Pyrénées and a Spanish jail. His code name was Gaston and he had operated in Brussels. Before escaping from the city, he had heard a whisper, passed from someone who had called up to the leader, Guy, in his prison cell. The whisper was that it was a traitor who had caused the disaster, a man who called himself Lebrun.

A traitor from within.

Smithe-Webb sighed. It was the one thing that was so very difficult to guard against.

All he could do was to help them prevent it happening again.

He would press for money to train agents, agents who could be sent over to start new evasion lines, people who, above all, would be skilled in *security* . . .

He started planning straight away. It would be a mistake to set up another large-scale Belgium–Spain line too soon; the aftermath of the Meteor disaster would rumble on for a long time.

Instead he would reinforce the existing, smaller *réseaux*, particularly those well away from the Meteor route.

He looked at the north coast of Brittany. The recent upset there had been no more than a temporary hiccup.

Most of the line was still intact. So too were the MGBs, though minus Ashley and his crew.

Yes, Brittany it must be. A new organiser, a new security system, and a much larger operation.

The line would need a new name.

He thought for a moment, then came up with the name which had been his mother's before she married. He would call the new *réseau* the Sheldon line.

Chapter 19

TANTE MARIE TOOK a last look into the front parlour, closed the door, and nodded to Julie. Julie picked up a plate of fish stew from the stove, a knife and fork from the table, and carried them quickly into her bedroom. Tante Marie closed the door behind her.

Julie walked through the room and started to climb the narrow stairs. Whispers and a small chuckle floated down from the room above. Her eyes reached floor level and she saw the two heads bent over some fascinating object on the floor.

They heard her and looked up. Richard grinned. For a moment she met his gaze and smiled back. Then she directed her eyes towards her son. Peter acknowledged her arrival with a matter-of-fact glance and said in his high-pitched monotone, 'Maman, look at this. It's nearly finished!'

Julie obediently inspected the rough model ship lying on the floor and said, 'It's lovely, darling. Really super!'

Richard got to his feet and reached out for the plate. 'Shall I relieve you of this? It looks too good to go cold.'

'Oh yes! Sorry!' Julie laughed and looked up into his face. He was still smiling, but there was something else, too: an enquiring, watchful look, as if he were trying to catch her out at some game they were playing.

She looked away and said to Peter, rather too quickly, 'Come on! Bedtime, young man.'

'But I'm not tired!'

'That's as may be, but it's still bedtime.'

'Oh, no! We were just going to stick the funnel on, weren't we, Richard?' He pronounced 'Richard' in the French way, softly and with no 'd', just as Julie had taught him. She was terrified that he would blurt the name out at school.

Richard put on a stern face. 'It can wait until tomorrow. Go on, *jeune homme*. Do as your mother says!'

Peter made a face, then nodded obediently and got up. Julie reached down to take his hand, but he said crossly, 'No, I want to walk by myself!' Julie sighed. Such an independent little beast, her son, and hardly six. She shrugged, rolled her eyes at Richard, and followed Peter's stamping feet down the stairs.

She knew the bed-time stories so well that she could read them automatically while she thought of other things. Up until three weeks ago, she had thought about the shopping and the mending and Peter's clothes. But now . . . Now she thought about the evening ahead.

She was fascinated by Richard's view of the world.

Certain things – like politics – he found amusing; something the French would never do. He said that anything so serious which was so badly managed had to be funny. She wasn't sure she agreed with him, but the way he talked made her laugh – most things he said made her laugh. But then at other times he could be very serious, and those laughing eyes became as hard as stone, and she guessed he could be very determined when he chose to be. Particularly about things he cared about, like loyalty and integrity and duty. When he talked about things like that he reminded her of an earnest schoolboy – or perhaps a knight of old: chivalrous, honest and true.

And yet – whenever he was talking seriously he would add almost in the same breath something so irreverent that it made her gasp. At first his wickeder remarks had taken her aback and – well, shocked her. Then she'd started to find them rather funny and it dawned on her that he said them for that very reason: to make her laugh.

He made her talk too, about herself and what she believed in and what she cared about. She wasn't used to having long discussions. The conversations in the farmhouse kitchen were inclined to be short, almost monosyllabic. At first she found it difficult to express herself, but then, gradually, the words had come more easily.

'*Maman*, a kiss!'

She leant down and kissed the small round cheek. 'Good night, darling. I'll try not to wake you when I come to bed.'

'Night-night.' He was already half asleep.

Julie hurried to the mirror and peered into it. She brushed her hair a couple of times then examined herself critically. She really didn't look bad at all, she decided. She was doing her hair a new way – with a side parting – and it rather suited her.

She made her way to the stairs and went up, happy and confident.

He was sitting on the bed, finishing his meal. When he saw her he put the plate down and said, 'I'm putting on weight, you know. You'll have to stop feeding me like this!'

She sat down on the floor and smiled. 'Well, it's not exactly Cordon Bleu – and I wouldn't enquire about the vegetables you had in that stew. But we do our best!'

'It's wonderful!' And Julie had the feeling he wasn't referring to the food. She said quickly, 'Do you want to play crib tonight? It's about time you played an honest game and beat me!'

'Are you suggesting I cheat?' he asked.

'Yes!' Julie laughed.

He looked horrified. 'How did you guess?'

'Because I win so much.'

'Ah! I can't argue with that logic! I promise never to

cheat again. Guide's honour.' Julie smiled because he didn't mean a word of it.

He looked at her more seriously and exclaimed, 'No, *don't* let's play cribbage. Let's talk instead! Come on . . .' He settled himself more comfortably. 'I want to hear the story of your life.'

She felt a stab of fear. She said quickly, 'No. There's nothing to tell.' There was an awkward pause. She looked for something else to say. 'I heard about your crew, by the way. Did I tell you? They're fine, apparently, but still very restless. D'you want another message sent over to them?'

Ashley shook his head absently. 'No. It'll wait a couple of days.'

He was watching her carefully. She went on quickly, 'But still no news from outside, I'm afraid. There's been a big clamp-down round Paris and the wireless operators have gone to ground. We still haven't managed to get a message through . . .'

He frowned. 'This Paris thing – is it connected with what happened here?'

'No . . . they don't think so. Our – incident – happened before the troubles up there. No, our problem was that leader of ours. We think he just talked too much and the wrong people heard . . .'

'But – will he have talked? To the Gestapo?'

Julie stared at him for a moment. 'No . . . Thank goodness, there's no possibility of that.'

'Why?'

'Ah. Well, he died, you see. On the way to St Brieuc, to Gestapo headquarters.'

'Oh . . . He—' Richard searched her face. 'He died immediately, did he?'

Julie thought: He's quick, he understands completely. She said quietly, 'Yes . . . The Germans found him dead on arrival. But then he would have died anyway—'

Richard nodded. 'Quite.'

Julie had been relieved to hear of the leader's death. It was amazing how hard and realistic you could be when it was your child and your family who were at stake.

Julie shook her head. 'But none of it need have happened. If we'd had our own people running it *their* way . . .'

Richard nodded sympathetically. 'Well, for what it's worth I'll put in a word with the powers-that-be when I get back.' He laughed. '*If* I get back!'

Julie said gently, 'I'm sorry there's no news.'

He leaned forward and touched her arm. 'Don't worry on my behalf. Actually, to be honest, I'm rather enjoying it in some ways. I've done a lot of thinking – much more than in the whole of the last few years. And I'm getting a lot of satisfaction out of making this model with your young man. Then, of course . . .' He paused and stared at her meaningfully. '. . . it's really rather nice to be locked up with you.'

Julie gave him a look of amused disbelief and said, 'You're just saying that!' But secretly she was pleased.

There was a pause. He said quietly, 'You very cleverly put me off just now, when I asked you about your life. But come on, Julie, don't be such a mystery woman. Tell me . . .'

Julie said softly, 'No, I'm really not ready to talk about it yet. I'm sorry.'

He gave her a questioning look. She was tempted to explain but instead she got up and fetched the upturned packing case they used for playing cards.

He gave a small laugh. 'All right. Cribbage then.'

He won the first game easily and Julie said, 'There, you see! When you concentrate you can beat me every time!'

He let her win the next game and the next, then she accused him of not trying.

He replied half-heartedly, 'Of course I'm trying.' But she knew he wasn't.

Julie looked at her watch and got to her feet. 'Well, work tomorrow as usual. About time I turned in.' She smoothed down her skirt and looked up with a smile. 'Good night, then!'

She turned to go but he stood up and touched her arm. 'Julie . . .' His voice was very soft. 'I wish you'd tell me . . .' He sighed. 'You know what I mean.' He held her by the arms and, moving closer, kissed her on the forehead, very gently, his lips barely brushing her skin. Then, for a single moment, he leant down and put his cheek against hers and Julie thought: I'm not going to survive this. He turned and whispered into her hair, 'Julie, I want you so much . . .'

Julie pulled away and looked unhappily at the floor. Then without a word she turned and made quickly for the stairs.

'Julie — ?'

But she was hurrying down. As soon as she reached the bedroom she pulled off her skirt and top and quickly got into bed next to Peter. She closed her eyes tightly and thought: God, please help me to live through the next few minutes. She listened to the sounds upstairs. For several minutes he didn't move, then she heard him walk slowly across the room to the bed.

She stared into the darkness for a long time, full of longings, wretched with misery.

She wanted him too, of course she did. She wanted him with all her heart.

But there could be no question of that. He wouldn't care for her if he knew the truth. He wouldn't respect her. The humiliation would be terrible.

She closed her eyes tightly, thinking that sometimes life could be very unfair.

Richard eyed her critically. 'You look terrible!'

'Thanks!' Julie managed the ghost of a smile. She was

feeling an awful lot better than she had first thing that morning. She'd woken with a thundering headache and it hadn't faded until the afternoon. Now, she was just feeling tired.

She put the plate down on the packing case and looked at him a little nervously. She hadn't seen him since the night before. She breathed deeply and said, 'If you don't mind, I think I'll go straight to bed tonight. I'm rather tired.'

He got up slowly, a frown on his face, and took her hand. 'Julie, if it's anything I said last night . . . If I offended you in any way . . . I'm terribly sorry . . .'

'No! Really.' She smiled and gripped his hand. 'No, I'm just tired, that's all.'

'Well . . . if you're sure.' He looked uncertain. 'You promise that I didn't upset you . . .?'

Julie said, 'Honestly,' and wished he would let go of her hand. It was embarrassing her.

He said softly, 'If I did upset you, Julie, I assure you it was the last thing I intended . . . You know that, don't you?'

She nodded. 'I know that.'

Very gently he released her hand and said breezily, 'Well how about a nightcap?'

'A nightcap?' she repeated dully.

'Yes, I did a little bit of bartering with your uncle. He ended up with three cigarettes and I got a bottle of wine. Rather a good deal, don't you think? Though who for, I couldn't say!' He laughed and leant down to pick up the bottle. 'Look, why don't you have a quick glass. It'll do you good! And make you sleep! Come on, keep me company! Just for a minute.'

Julie knew that if she didn't go to bed now she might stay all evening. She began, 'I really would, except . . .' Then she closed her eyes, and smiled faintly and said, 'All right.'

He grinned at her: he was pleased.

She sat on the floor and accepted a glass. He was right about the wine: it did make her feel better. After a while she felt beautifully calm and almost content again. Richard told some stupid stories about a pet goat his family had once owned and suddenly she found herself laughing again. It was as if nothing had changed . . .

Except that it had.

They talked about all the usual things and he looked at her with the same eyes, alive and sparkling with fun, but . . . it was all subtly different. The words from the previous night hung in the air.

She began to feel deliciously drowsy; she hardly ever drank wine. She said, 'I really must get some sleep now . . .'

'Of course.' He leaned forward and helped her up. 'But wait! Just for a second . . .'

He went to the candle and blew it out. She heard him move across the room and the next moment a square of light appeared where he had pulled the curtain back from the window. 'Come and see!'

She came up beside him and stared out. It was a brilliantly clear night. A myriad stars carpeted the sky, like silver on black velvet.

He said, 'I used to sit on *Dancer* and watch the night sky for hours on end . . .'

She said, 'It *is* lovely.'

'It's even better when you're sitting on deck. Then you can see everything, all the constellations.'

They stared in silence.

He said pensively, 'After the war I'll take *Dancer* cruising again, to all the old places.'

'To the Scillies?'

He turned. 'How did you know that?'

'Well – you must have told me.'

'Not since I've been here. I wouldn't have.' He was very definite. 'You know, you must have remembered that from *before*. In Plymouth.' He laughed softly. 'And there you were, pretending you didn't even remember *me*! You quite hurt my feelings, you know!'

'Rubbish!' Julie said firmly. 'It did you good, not to be remembered. Otherwise you'd have got a big head.'

'But you *did* remember me, didn't you?'

Eventually she said, 'Yes, but I couldn't remember exactly where it was that I'd met you.'

'Well, I knew! I enjoyed that day we spent together, and I was rather disappointed when you announced – right at the last moment – that you were just about to go away!'

He touched her shoulder and, sitting on the bed, waited for her to sit down beside him in the darkness. He said, 'Tell me. About you.'

She murmured, 'I'd rather not.'

'But why? Do you think I won't try to understand? Whatever it is you don't want to talk about – well, it can't be that bad, Julie. It can't be so bad that I wouldn't—' There was a pause. '– that I wouldn't care for you any more. You know I care, don't you?'

Julie couldn't speak.

He moved closer and took her hand. 'Tell me at least . . . What happened to your husband?'

Julie stared into the darkness and thought: Whatever I say will be wrong. The past was like a terrible monster that kept rearing up in front of her, breathing shame and guilt and eternal damnation. However much he believed he would understand, he wouldn't. He would pity and despise her.

She sighed and looked up at the window. The sky seemed even darker now, the glittering stars like lights on a tree. Taking a deep breath, she said slowly, 'Peter never knew his father. And I – I haven't seen him since Peter was born.'

Richard gently squeezed her hand. 'More fool him. He must be mad. So then . . . he's not likely to show up again.'

'Hardly!' She couldn't keep the bitterness out of her voice. 'You see ...' She bit her lip. 'We ...' She spoke so softly that he leant closer to hear her. 'We were never married.'

For a moment he didn't speak and Julie thought that she had been right and that he wouldn't understand.

But then he put his arm round her shoulder and said, 'Bad luck!'

'For me, yes!'

He said quickly, 'But you mustn't think it matters any more.' He was stroking her hair, slowly, softly. 'You have a lovely boy. You have nothing to be ashamed of.'

'... Oh yes I do!' She pulled herself away from him and blew noisily into her hanky. 'I feel ashamed that it ever happened ... Except for Peter, that is. If only ...' She sighed angrily.

'But Julie, lots of people have affairs, and ... well, indiscretions, without being married. Society's incredibly hypocritical about all that kind of thing. They say it's forbidden – but they're doing it all the time. The secret is not to worry about it ... about the past, I mean. It's not that important.'

'It's important to *me*. I mind! And Peter will mind when he grows up and finds out. No ... I made a terrible mistake and, one way and another, I'm going to pay for it for the rest of my life!'

He said, 'But how are you going to pay for it? Nobody's going to make you pay, Julie! You'll only suffer for it if *you* let it bother you. Why should you ever *pay* for it?'

'You know what I mean,' she said miserably. 'People talk, people don't forgive.'

'Do they know round here?'

'Oh, they've guessed.'

'But they still accept you?'

'Well ... yes.'

'There you are then! What's the problem? Julie, I can

assure you of one thing – it doesn't matter a damn to me!'
He squeezed her hand again.

She breathed in deeply. 'Well, thank you for saying
so.'

'It was meant.' He leant down and she heard him
pouring another glass of wine. He handed her the glass. 'Is
that why you came to Brittany? To have Peter?'

'Yes, but please – don't ask any more!'

'All right.' He stroked her hair. 'But all I meant was,
have you been here all this time? With your uncle and
aunt?'

'Yes.'

'Not much fun.'

'At least I was welcome – which was more than I was at
home.'

'Ah. Your parents didn't understand?'

'Just my mother. My father's dead. We're still not
speaking, my mother and me.'

'After the war, though, you'll want to come back, won't
you?'

'I don't know. The war . . .'

'It won't last for ever.'

'I suppose not.'

'And then—' he paused. 'You might come on *Dancer*
again perhaps. For a cruise. Would you like that?'

'I'm a rotten sailor.'

'I'll teach you.'

'No, I meant—'

He laughed. 'I know what you meant.'

He put his arm round her shoulder and they sat for a
long while, watching the night sky and talking quietly.

Eventually he stood up. 'Time you went to sleep. You
still look terrible!'

She smiled faintly. 'Thanks!'

He took her face in his hands and kissed her on the
mouth, warmly and for a long time.

As she went down the stairs he called softly, 'Julie, I'm glad you told me.'

A little later, when she lay in bed beside Peter, she thought: Perhaps, given time, everything might be all right after all.

'Be careful. The door's creaky.' The boy's whisper was loud in his ear.

'Right-o.'

Ashley turned the handle and felt the door open. He pulled at it gently, trying to lessen the squeak of the hinges. Finally the gap was large enough for him to squeeze through. He stepped out into the darkness of the farmyard.

He began to close the door behind him, but there was something in the way. He realised it was the boy. He whispered, 'Hey! What are you doing?'

'Coming with you!'

'Oh no you're not. Get back inside!' Ashley tried to push the boy back through the door, but the small body wriggled past him and shot off into the night. Ashley could hear the pad of his feet receding into the distance.

He swore under his breath and, closing the door, followed after him, stumbling slightly as his foot met an obstruction.

The boy was waiting at the gate which led into the pasture behind the house. He was jumping up and down with glee. 'Beat you!'

'Look, young man, your mother will kill you if she finds out!' He thought: She'll kill me too.

Peter sighed with the exasperation of dealing with an adult. 'But I often sneak out here on my own.' He clambered on to the top of the gate. 'Anyway she's not back from work yet. She won't know!'

'That's not the point,' said Ashley reasonably. 'We might get caught.'

'Oh no. The soldiers never come here. Come on! Let's go up the hill. Sometimes you can see the lighthouse from there.' He jumped to the ground and hopped impatiently up and down while Ashley climbed over the gate.

Then he was off again, running across the grass, a small black blur fading into the grey of the early winter evening. Ashley gave up the idea of chasing after him, and strode forward, stretching the muscles of his legs, breathing the cool fresh air, drinking in the delicious moments of freedom.

How he had needed this. He hated being cooped up. It drove him mad. He knew how animals felt now, doomed to stay in cages for ever. Slow death.

He pressed on, pushing harder, wanting to feel the sweat on his body and the ache of tiredness in his limbs.

He hated the thought of being locked up for much longer. The only compensation was Julie, of course. He had been intrigued by her from the beginning. She had an other-worldliness, a gentle serenity that appealed to him. At the same time she was quick to laugh, and he liked that too. Damn it, he liked a lot about her.

But the revelations of the previous evening had subtly changed things. It had cost her a lot to tell him the truth, he had seen that, and he admired her for it. But it made him feel – what? – a sort of responsibility towards her, and that rather frightened him.

Yet he knew he cared for her. Nothing had changed that.

And nothing had changed the fact that he wanted to make love to her. Quite apart from being lovely she had an earthiness, a suggestion of passion, that made her extremely attractive. What was more, he was sure that she wanted him too.

He tramped on, thinking that perhaps responsibility wasn't a bad thing. After all, it had to come at some point in one's life.

'Woo-hoo.' The soft cry came from a short way ahead. Ashley climbed the last few yards to a wall at the top of the hill and peered around. There was no sign of the boy. 'Come out, you rascal.'

There was a giggle. Ashley followed it and, reaching over the wall, lifted the boy up and into the air. 'Got you!'

Peter wriggled and tried to get free. Ashley held him high for a moment longer then let him fall into his arms. The boy dropped his head against Ashley's chest and lay there, panting slightly. Ashley hugged him and thought how much fun it would be to have a child of his own one day.

The giggling started again. Peter squirmed out of his arms and dropped to the ground. 'Come on. I'll show you the rabbit warren.'

They investigated the warren, although there wasn't much to see in the darkness. Then they looked for the beam of the lighthouse, but saw nothing and decided there were no convoys passing that night. Ashley stared into the darkness, trying to make out the deeper shadows of the sea, and thought longingly of the MGB. Later they walked again, along the wall and round the other side of the hill.

It wasn't until Ashley saw the hooded headlights of a vehicle on the road that he realised they'd been gone a long time. He ran back to the top of the hill and looked down. The headlamps had stopped outside the farmhouse.

The boy came panting up behind him and saw the lights too. As they watched, the headlights went out.

The boy grasped Ashley's sleeve and cried, 'It's the Germans! The Germans!'

'Yes. I'm afraid you're right.' Ashley took the boy's hand and led him back to the darkness of the wall. 'I think we'd better wait here, don't you?'

*

Julie felt sick.

She looked at the clock again. Half past eight. And still no sign.

She sat absolutely still, her eyes on the wall, her hands tightly clasped in her lap. Tante Marie sat opposite, her face tortured with worry. Neither spoke: neither could begin to imagine what they would do if something dreadful had happened.

The familiar sound of scraping chairs came from the parlour. The two soldiers had finished their meal. The front door banged as they went out. Julie sprang to her feet and, going to the back door, opened it a crack. The soldiers had brought an armoured car with them tonight, she had no idea why. They had parked it in the yard. Now they were getting into it and slamming the doors. She prayed that, if Richard and Peter were out there, they wouldn't choose this moment to return.

The car started with a roar and two dull beams of light sprang out and illuminated a corner of the farm yard. Then the lights were swinging away and the sound of the engine faded into the distance.

Julie took a jacket off the back of the door and hurried out into the night. When her eyes were accustomed to the darkness she started up the yard, towards the back pasture. She couldn't be sure they had gone this way, but it seemed likely. They certainly wouldn't have gone on the road.

She opened the gate and went into the pasture. She let out a small gasp.

Two figures, one small, one tall, were running towards her.

She stood waiting for them, shuddering with relief, then stepped forward and scooped Peter up into her arms. Without a word she carried the child back through the yard, into the kitchen and straight to bed.

As she undressed him, Peter glanced nervously at her face. 'Sorry, Mummy.'

Julie narrowed her lips and said at last, 'I'm going to say this once and only once. Don't ever, ever do that again. If you do, I'll hit you so hard you won't know what time of day it is. D'you understand?'

'Yes, Mummy.'

She tucked him up and, without another word, turned out the light.

She went into the kitchen and, ignoring Ashley, crossed to the mantelpiece and shook a cigarette out of a packet. Her hand was trembling as she lit it.

'Julie, I'm very sorry ... I meant to go out just for a second or two, but ...'

Julie inhaled deeply on the cigarette and, gritting her teeth, stared dumbly at the mantelpiece. She didn't trust herself to speak yet.

'Peter followed me. Of his own accord. That's not to say I shouldn't have dragged him back ...' He put his hand on her shoulder. 'It won't happen again.'

Eventually she said stiffly, 'We've done out best, you know. To make it bearable for you. I know that going outside for a few minutes at midnight isn't as much fun as walking round the entire countryside ...' She made a wheeling gesture with her hand. 'But it was safest. For you – and for us!' She spat out the last words, then exhaling, shook her head. 'If you knew what I'd been through in the last hour you'd ... understand!' The unaccustomed cigarette was making her dizzy and she stubbed it out.

He sighed heavily. 'I'll go back to my room.' The way he said it, it might have been prison.

She realised it *was* a prison to him. She turned to say something softer, more understanding, but he was already gone.

After a moment she lit a candle and followed him. She climbed the narrow staircase and, through the banisters, saw him lying on the bed staring at the ceiling. She paused at the top and said matter-of-factly, 'I know it's awful for you, I do realise that. But it shouldn't be long now. Before you can get away.'

He stood up and came over to her. 'I *will* go mad if I have to stay much longer. You see that, don't you?'

She nodded and said briskly, 'And you must understand that I'll go mad if you take any more risks.'

He smiled ruefully. 'It's a bargain. Anything to avoid your wrath again.'

She said firmly, 'I was only angry because I was so worried.'

'Thank you.'

'Not at all.' She turned quickly and went down the stairs.

Most of the potatoes were half rotten. Methodically, Julie cut out the bad sections, peeled the remainder, however small, and chucked them into the pot. Nowadays you wasted nothing.

Tante Marie was tenderising a piece of beef, beating it with a large wooden mallet, until the meat was almost flat. They always had meat on Saturday evenings and, because they had their own chickens and cattle, often twice during the week as well. Most people were not so lucky.

Tante Marie put the meat into a pan on the stove, added dripping, garlic and herbs, and left it to cook.

Julie smelled the aroma of garlic and herbs and remembered that it was Sunday the next day and she could spend all day with him.

She smiled and realised she was staring into the pot, the potatoes forgotten. Tante Marie was watching her, a frown on her forehead. 'Juliette . . . Your uncle will be a little late tonight. I think—' She lowered her voice. 'I think there's some news.'

Julie looked up sharply. 'Some news?'

'From – away. But I'm only guessing. I'm not sure. I just thought . . . I might warn you.'

Julie tried to hold on to her thoughts, but they were shooting off at tangents. News. A boat? Coming soon, probably, then he would go away, she would be alone, he would be safe, she would be miserable . . .

After she had put Peter to bed she went up to see him and they talked and she thought: It will never be better than this. I'll never feel closer or warmer towards anyone than I do now.

It was not until nine that Jean returned. Richard was just telling her about his sister who was married and lived in Sussex when Julie suddenly tensed. Somewhere in the house there was the sound of a door opening.

Richard looked at her. 'What is it?'

'Nothing. Just my uncle. I'll be back in a moment.' She left him and hurried down the stairs and found Jean already at the bedroom door, waiting for her.

She followed him into the kitchen. He whispered, 'We've heard! They're sending a boat on Wednesday. Unless the weather's bad. We'll know for sure on the night – the BBC will broadcast a message.'

'And the boat will take everyone – the sailors and the airmen?'

He nodded.

Julie blinked. 'Wednesday night, then.' She touched her uncle's arm in thanks and went back into her room. She closed the door and leant against it for a moment. It was only four days away.

She climbed the narrow stairs, slowly, and didn't turn her head until she reached the top. The moment Richard saw her face he stood up and frowned. He said, 'What is it?'

She made herself smile and said brightly, 'It looks as though you're going home!'

He came towards her and grasped her arms. 'When?'

'Wednesday night – unless the weather's bad.'

'Good Lord above!' he laughed. 'Marvellous! Marvellous!' He closed his eyes and clenched his fists and threw back his head and grinned with delight. 'Oh, marvellous!'

Julie smiled gently and tried to look glad, for his sake.

He took hold of her arms again. 'Julie, I'll miss you . . .'

She nodded silently.

'Wednesday . . . that's four days. Let's make it the best four days we've ever had! What do you say? Let's have a wonderful time! I'll take you out to the Ritz for dinner tomorrow night.' He smiled wrily. 'That means I'll buy another bottle of wine off your uncle and we'll eat off the packing case *together*, properly . . . Then the next night—!'

As he talked she watched him and thought: Only four days.

She reached out and touched his face. He stopped talking and smiled at her. Then, when he saw the expression in her eyes, he leaned towards her and kissed her on the mouth, gently at first, then, when he felt her mouth moving under his, much harder.

He said, 'I want you, Julie.'

She put her lips to his ear and whispered, 'I want you too!'

She cried. Afterwards.

He touched her cheek and felt the tears and said, 'Julie, Julie! What is it?'

She pressed her head against his shoulder and said, 'Nothing, nothing. I'm so happy, that's all.'

He turned towards her and stroked her back, following her spine with his fingers until he reached the curve of her bottom. Then he pulled her against him and kissed her again, very softly, murmuring, 'Julie, Julie . . . silly old thing, don't cry!'

'But it's only because . . . it was so lovely!'

'Yes!' He squeezed her against him. 'It was, wasn't it?'

And then she cried again, very softly, not only because it had been so lovely but because she could see the past six years for what they really were: barren and lonely. All the routines, Peter, meals, work, going through the motions of life . . . And all that time she had only dimly imagined what it would be like to have all this.

'No more tears?'

'No,' she laughed, 'I promise!'

'Julie, four days is a long, long time!'

'Yes, yes!' She kissed his mouth and his cheek, then his ear and his forehead . . .

'Julie, if you go on like that—'

She paused and pulled back, uncertain.

'No!' he laughed. 'What I meant was – go on! Please don't stop!'

But she did because she didn't know the rules and she still felt a little awkward about the order of things. She wanted him to tell her, to whisper to her . . .

And then it was starting all over again and he was touching her in a special way, and she felt the beginnings of that extraordinary warmth, that quite incredible pleasure.

Later, much later, she lay in the darkness and thought that, whatever happened – even after he'd gone – she'd never feel completely alone again.

Chapter 20

————•————

IT WAS A triumph.

Output had risen to fifty units a week – and fifty working units at that. David walked slowly round the despatch room and peered at the packing cases. Each was labelled 'Tested and passed', and each label had been stamped and countersigned with the initials of the Technician-in-Charge. It was a new idea, to have one person testing and sealing each unit before despatch. David had introduced the system because it was one which had worked well before. He had asked for – and got – a German naval technician for the job because he'd wanted someone he could communicate with. He hadn't wanted a German for any other reason – and certainly not because he didn't trust the two Frenchmen who'd done the job before. It hadn't occurred to him not to trust them.

Another new idea had been introduced, too. It was Kapitanleutnant Geissler's idea this time, though David had endorsed it and put it into operation. Each device was now the responsibility of an individual on the assembly line. If a Metox was faulty it was returned to the man concerned. If the fault was not rectified within a day, then the man was summoned for an explanation. If the fault was still not cured, the man was fired and the special exemptions on his military papers removed. Everyone knew what that meant: you could be called up for forced labour.

In the six months that David had been with the company

no-one had been fired. At the same time output and quality had shot up. Yes, it was a triumph. Kapitanleutnant Geissler was pleased. Presumably the Navy were also pleased. And doubtless the submarine commanders were grateful now that they had their Metox receivers to warn them of enemy planes.

A triumph. And, thought David, the worst thing I've ever done.

He paused in the doorway of the main workshop and stared at the line of men working at the bench. There was a gap in the line. David closed his eyes. Only yesterday a man had stood there, brave and alive. Today he was dead.

And it was David's fault. *David's*.

He had been too taken up by the challenge of the problem-solving, too intoxicated by the freedom of action to see what had been happening.

The workers had been sabotaging the Metox, from the very beginning.

There had been nothing obvious – no extra wires or smashed valves. Instead, for no apparent reason, small components had failed to function or valves had burnt out. David could see now that too much current must have been forced through them or reverse polarity applied.

He should have realised of course. It should have been obvious. But he hadn't *wanted* to see. When small suspicions had begun to enter his mind he'd dismissed them. No-one would dare to do such things, he had decided. The penalty, after all, was death.

Then David's new measures had come into operation. The subtle forms of sabotage which had been so successful were no longer effective. The men had been forced to use more open and dangerous methods. Yesterday one of them had been caught.

The penalty was death, and the man had died.

And, whichever way David looked at the event, he couldn't help feeling that it was his fault.

He stared blankly at the gap in the line of working men. One of the technicians glanced up and David looked quickly away. He couldn't meet the man's eyes; he couldn't look at any of them. They thought him as bad as the rest: just another Nazi. Him! A Nazi!

David turned away, full of shame.

In the passage he almost bumped into someone. It was Gallois, the French chief technician. Gallois nodded and, stepping aside, waited for David to pass. David almost spoke but changed his mind. It would be no use. Gallois must despise him. He must think David worse than a mere German – he must think him a traitor!

David walked quickly towards the front of the building, muttering angrily to himself. He went down the front steps and out into the road in full view of the guard. He had permission to do that, to walk the short distance to his quarters under the eye of the guard. Why? Because they trusted him. And why did they trust him? Because he had shown himself to be such a good German, that was why! He laughed bitterly. What an irony.

He should have died back there in the camp. It would have been better for everyone.

He walked rapidly along the road until he came to a compound surrounded by barbed wire. He walked in past the guard and along the side of a large warehouse. The warehouse served as a barracks for the East European labourers who worked on the U-boat pens. At one end of it was a long wooden hut where the guards lived. David had a cubicle to himself there. Geissler had arranged it. David had been very pleased with the cubicle. It was infinitely better than the solitary room in the naval barracks. Here, at least, he had company. He often chatted with the guards; he enjoyed talking German again. They baited him, of course, but for much of the time they overlooked his race because it was convenient to them – they sometimes needed a fourth at cards. He, in his turn, ignored the fact that they were soldiers and beat up Poles every day.

David went into the box-like cubicle and closed the door.

He lay down on the bed and, drawing himself into a ball, covered his eyes with his hands. He was a disgrace. A disgusting disgrace. A deeply selfish and despicable man without principles or integrity. All those scruples he had pretended to have back in the camp laboratory. All the concern for whether he was doing the right thing. And what had he done? He had done as he was told. As time had gone on he had even been happy to obey. He had worked with all his heart and soul. What had happened to him, that he could have forgotten? Where had he lost his way?

He could see now that it had happened slowly, so slowly. His greed for security had pushed all other thoughts out of his mind. He had thought only of himself, his health, his next meal, and of the vital need to survive and preserve his life at all costs.

I have betrayed everything and everyone. My race. My Cecile. Most of all I have betrayed myself. I am not a proud man.

After a while, when the self-pity had passed, he lay and thought about the future.

Then he had the idea. It came to him quite suddenly, but the moment it appeared he knew it was the answer.

He sat up and, dropping on to his knees, put his hand underneath the metal frame of the bed. He touched the familiar flat shape of the small package and, pulling it out, held it tightly in his hand.

They had travelled so far together, he and this package, that he had almost forgotten the real meaning of it. He'd tucked it away in the back of his mind as something for the future: his passport to Britain or America when the war was over, a sort of insurance policy for his old age.

But now . . .

He held it in his hand and remembered the pages of plans and specifications for the secret device.

Shortwave radar. Germany would never be able to develop it, not while her laboratories were closed and her research programmes at a standstill. And if she didn't have shortwave radar she couldn't defend herself against it.

Certainly the Metox would be useless against it. He smiled a little.

It would only be a question of getting the plans to the British. They should be able to develop it fairly quickly.

It would be the perfect act of sabotage. The U-boats would be defenceless against it and, in a single blow, David's work here would be undone.

He hugged the small package to him. Then he looked up and said gently, 'Dear God, you are looking now at a miserable worthless old man. But one who is going to try to do his best. Give me the strength to succeed. And, if You should also deign to give me positive assistance, I thank You. If not – then, dear God, I will have done my best!'

He lay down and thought to himself: What better thing can a man do than be brave just once in his life?

David often came into work early, at about six so that he could enjoy two hours of peace and quiet before everyone else arrived. In the calm of the early morning he could think more clearly than later in the day. This morning he had arrived well before six – and yet he still couldn't make up his mind what to do.

Gallois. He should try Gallois.

It was the obvious choice. David couldn't be sure that he was involved in the sabotage, of course, but he must *know*. Even if he himself was not involved, he must have *guessed*.

Yes, he would try Gallois.

He rose unsteadily from his chair and went next door to the drawing office where a young trainee was standing at a high desk. 'Go and ask Monsieur Gallois to come to my office, would you?' The young man nodded and went off in the direction of the main assembly shop.

David went back to his desk and sat down unhappily.

There were footsteps in the corridor. A bead of sweat trickled down David's forehead and he reached into his trouser pocket for a handkerchief. He mopped his brow and looked up. Gallois was already in the room, watching him. David started with surprise and, half rising, smiled a little and indicated a seat. 'Do sit down, please.'

The door was still open and David got up to close it. 'Well, well. Lovely weather we're having, aren't we?'

'Yes.'

David sat down again. 'It always makes life pleasanter, doesn't it, if the sun is shining?'

The Frenchman nodded, but David could see he wasn't in the least interested in the weather.

David drew breath and began again. 'I – wanted to talk to you about a rather delicate matter . . .'

The Frenchman stared back across the desk, his face blank and uninterested. He was not going to give David any help, that was obvious.

'It's . . . Well, it must seem to you that I have had every sympathy . . . every desire to make a success of this project . . . Indeed, I did at the beginning. I saw it as a wonderful opportunity to use my skills and to – give meaning to my life again. Do you understand that?'

Gallois made a gesture which seemed to indicate: If you say so.

David leant forward. 'Please – do you see that?'

'Yes—' He shrugged. 'I know you had no choice.'

'But I worked hard, didn't I? For success.' David frowned and looked down at his hands. 'I forgot, you see.

I put my own satisfaction above . . . other considerations.'
He looked up again. 'But now – I can see I was mistaken.
I should not have done what I did – so wholeheartedly. I
was wrong.'

Gallois was watching carefully now, studying David's
face.

'The point is . . .' David went on, '. . . I want to help.'

There was silence. He was suspicious, and who could
blame him? David leant forward urgently. 'Look, I am well
aware of what was going on in this place when I arrived.
Most of the devices were being deliberately sabotaged. I
know that now. But I have said nothing. So you see –
despite what you may think – I *am* in sympathy with your
cause.'

Gallois had not moved a muscle. He sat as still as stone.

David wished the Frenchman would give him a sign,
some indication of encouragement. The sphinx-like silence
was – difficult. 'Look, I realise it's hard for you to say
anything . . . After all, why *should* you? I can only tell you
that I do wish to help . . . and that I am in a position to do
so in a very definite, a very concrete, way.'

Suddenly Gallois moved. He sat forward in his chair
and cleared his throat. 'Monsieur Freymann, I cannot
imagine where you have obtained these strange ideas. For
one thing, there has never been any sabotage at this
company. It is, if I may say so, an absurd idea! And second,
I really cannot be involved with any activity against – the
interests of this company. I don't know why you have
approached me, monsieur, but I assure you I cannot help.'

He was getting to his feet. David sprang up and hurried
round the desk. Gallois said, 'I think it is best if we do not
continue this conversation. Really, monsieur, I cannot help
you. Nor can anyone here. We are straightforward working men. We keep out of trouble.' He turned and reached
for the door handle.

For a moment David was frozen with indecision. Then,

just as Gallois was opening the door, he lunged forward and grabbed the Frenchman's sleeve. 'Please, you don't understand!' David looked nervously into the open passageway to see if anyone had heard, then stared imploringly at Gallois.

Very slowly, Gallois closed the door again. 'What exactly don't I understand?'

David thought miserably: I am going to have to tell him! In all this time he had never told a living soul.

As he stared up at Gallois, searching for the words, acid bit into his stomach and suddenly a piercing pain hit his abdomen. The room seemed to move in on him and he gasped for breath. He felt as if he was falling and reached out. A firm hand took hold of his arm and suddenly there was a chair under him and he was leaning forward with his head between his knees. 'My tablets . . . They're on the desk there . . .'

The bottle was thrust, open, into his hand. He took out three tablets and chewed them hard because they worked quicker that way.

Gallois' voice said from close by, 'Are you all right?'

David nodded. 'I'll be better in a minute. In just a minute . . . Don't go, please.' He reached out and gripped the other man's arm for a moment. After a while the pain eased a little and David leant his head on his hands and whispered, 'Don't judge me too harshly. I just ask you now, please, to listen to what I have to say . . .' He sat up slowly and leant back against the chair with his eyes closed. He felt very faint and his heart was thudding like a drum. 'I need *your* help . . .' He smiled gently. 'Not the other way round.'

He paused to take a few deep breaths. It often helped the pain. 'The thing is . . . before they made me leave my job in Germany – before the war – I stole something. A secret. A secret that could be very, very important – in the

war. I am the only one who knows about it – it was my
idea, you see.' He stopped to look at Gallois, to see that he
had understood. He thought: Now is the moment of belief
or disbelief. He pulled himself upright and grasped the
Frenchman's arm again. 'I have always wanted to get the
secret to the British, so they can use it. But . . . there was
never the opportunity. And then, I came here and it seemed
easier to carry on and do my job . . . You see, I was so
happy just to be alive. This place, it seemed like heaven
after . . . the camp.'

He sighed deeply. 'But now . . . Now I must do something about it, do you understand?' He shook his head. 'I
just cannot do nothing – like before. If you knew what the
camps were like! I must do something for *them*, do you
see? I must in some way help *them*. And this is the one
thing I can do.' He looked anxiously into Gallois' face.
'Tell me – do you understand what I am saying?'

Gallois looked down, as if making up his mind what to
do. When he looked up again his expression was guarded,
worried. He sighed and whispered firmly, 'Dear Monsieur
Freymann, I am so sorry that you are unwell. I know you
have been through a lot. I only wish there was something I
could do to help but, really, there is nothing.'

'But I just want to take my secret to England . . .'

'I'm sorry.' The Frenchman's tone was cooler now.
'There is really nothing I can do.'

A terrible tiredness came over David and he slumped in
his chair. It had all been for nothing.

Gallois looked over his shoulder and lowered his voice.
'Really, I think it is very dangerous to talk about this . . .
Forgive me, but it really is unwise.' He moved towards the
door. 'You're all right, are you? Do you want me to send
someone along?'

David covered his face with his hands and shook his
head. He heard the door close and got off his chair and lay

on the floor. It often helped his stomach. But nothing, he knew, would remove the dull ache in his heart.

One week later a new project was announced. Goulvent, Pescart et Cie was to build larger radar detection devices suitable for ships. The pioneering work had been done elsewhere; all that was required was to assemble components which would be sent from Germany.

For David, however, there was still a lot of work to be done, developing test programmes and equipment. He worked long hours but only because he couldn't bear to go back to his room any more. He had stopped playing cards with the guards. He had stopped talking to them – or indeed to anyone. He just wanted to be left alone. Whenever there was a discussion, he cut it short. He even barked at Geissler.

He didn't bother with meals; he hated having to go to the canteen to collect them. He knew it wasn't doing him any good – he felt awful – but he didn't care.

He hated his work. He hated his life. He hated himself.

Then Geissler summoned him to his office. 'It seems that they want you elsewhere, Herr Freymann.' The Kapitanleutnant picked up a letter from his desk and examined it. 'They don't say when ... However,' he smiled coolly, 'we need you more, so we are protesting at this proposed transfer. We have put in a request through the appropriate channels and expect to hear shortly.'

David was looking past Geissler to the window. Between a gap in the buildings it was just possible to glimpse the sea, misty today, but still beautiful. David said quietly, 'Where?'

'Excuse me?'

'Where do they want to send me?'

'Ah! Let me see ... It's not a naval project, that I do know.' He examined the letter again. 'All I have here is a

code number and prefix. Perhaps . . . Wait one minute . . .'
Geissler picked up the telephone and asked for HQ. He
spoke for a few seconds then replaced the receiver. He
coughed nervously. 'I cannot unfortunately tell you where
exactly – we do not have details – but apparently the prefix
denotes an SS establishment . . .' He added unhappily,
'That is perhaps another reason why it would be best for
you to stay here.'

Germany. Perhaps even a camp. Back into the pit.

'Herr Freymann, I will let you know the minute I myself
hear the decision. In the meantime we must proceed with
the preparation for the new project. Yes?'

'Yes.'

'I will do my best, Herr Freymann. I will try to persuade
them to let you stay . . .'

'Yes, thank you.' He was sincere, Geissler, but there
would be nothing he could do. David stood up and,
nodding briefly, walked out. The escort was waiting. David
led the way down to the entrance and into the van. They
began the short drive back to Goulvent, Pescart et Cie.

The van deposited him at the door. He went up to his
office and finished his day's work. New component specifications, details of new testing equipment: work that could
easily be done by someone less qualified. He would begin
the business of handing over in the morning.

That night he slept badly for the first time in months.
He dreamed he was back on a bare wooden bunk, crushed
between two dying men. The *Prominente* came and made
them get up and go to the quarry. It was still the middle of
the night. The *Prominente* thought it was very funny, to
make them get up in the night. Then they started beating
people. David woke up.

For a while he couldn't get back to sleep and then, when
he was tired again, there was pain in his stomach. In the
end he hardly slept at all.

The next morning he went to the office early and began

working out how best to delegate his work load. Feverishly, he started making lists of jobs and responsibilities, grouping them under different names and departments.

There was a knock at the door. David glanced at the clock on the desk. It was still only seven. 'Come in.'

It was Gallois. He took a seat. 'Good morning.'

David said, 'I'm glad you called in. I need to discuss this with you. It's a list of jobs that will need to be taken over by you and others when I go.'

Gallois said, 'You're going?'

'In all probability. Now, when this is typed, perhaps—'

'Where will they send you?'

David put down his pencil and said shortly, 'I don't know. Probably back to where I came from.'

'But you have done well . . . Surely they are pleased?'

David rubbed his eyes. He felt dreadfully tired. With effort he replied, 'Ah, but you don't understand the way they work. There are no rules, you see. You do badly, they send you back to a camp. You do well – the same thing happens. There are no rules.'

Gallois hesitated. 'You'll work on electronics, though. You'll have a skilled job?'

David shrugged. 'Perhaps. It's not really important.'

'Surely you want to work?'

'What I want isn't relevant. Anyway, I don't care. Not any more.'

Later there was a meeting about the new project. The atmosphere in the room was claustrophobic, hot and smoky. David felt enormously irritated with everyone. They were so slow to grasp the basics and he had to explain the simplest things to them. He couldn't believe how stupid they were. Someone – a junior technician – asked yet another idiotic question. David closed his eyes for a moment to stop himself from shouting, then he said between clenched teeth, 'Can't you understand *anything*? Why do you have to be so stupid? Are you *trying* to make

things difficult? Really! It's impossible to deal with you
people . . .'

They were all staring at him and he realised he had been
shouting after all.

A second later his stomach ulcer ruptured. The pain hit
him like a sledgehammer. It was incredibly sharp, like a
fire burning inside. As soon as it started he knew it was
different from anything he'd felt before. He also knew that
in a few more seconds it would be so bad that he would
have to scream. But then the room started to blur and he
felt very cold and everything began to slip away. He was
grateful. It was nice to slip away.

Peace and beauty always. A hundred years at least.
Whenever the fire came back they pressed the black thing
on his face and he was floating again . . .

He wanted to sleep for ever. The sleep was gentle, like
clouds, floating . . . Flowers, there were flowers. Then
whiteness again, soft and gentle . . . He wanted to sleep for
ever.

They wouldn't let him. The *Prominente* were beating
him, slapping his face. Someone was shouting at him. He
moaned and tried to close his eyes again. But the voice was
shouting again. It was a woman. She was speaking in
French. 'Come on! Wake up now! Come on!'

He felt the pain again and moaned, 'No. No!'

Then they let him sleep again. He had won.

Someone slapped his face again. Why couldn't they
leave him alone? The pain was more persistent now. It
wouldn't let him sleep. He murmured, 'The pain. Please,
can I have something?'

A woman's voice said, 'Not yet. When you're awake.'

He woke up only because the pain wouldn't let him
sleep. Then at last they gave him something. It didn't help
much. He discovered that nothing helped very much. The
days blended into one another, he slept only when he was
exhausted with the pain.

Then he woke up one day and realised that for once he had slept well. The pain was much less. He sat up and let them feed him with watery milk. He felt better. His only regret was having to face the world again.

Another day he woke up and found Gallois sitting beside the bed. The Frenchman smiled and said, 'How are you?'

David said what was expected of him. 'I'm all right.'

They exchanged more platitudes, then David was tired and the Frenchman left. As David fell asleep something nagged at his memory. He should have said something to the Frenchman, something important, but he couldn't remember what . . .

The next day he remembered and groaned because it was too late and the Frenchman was no longer there.

But it wasn't too late. Gallois returned. When he came into the room David stared at him in disbelief and, reaching out, grasped the Frenchman's hands.

Gallois smiled and asked again, 'How are you?'

David said, 'Never mind. Please listen. I have something to ask you. Something important.' He pulled himself up in the bed. 'Monsieur Gallois, when we had our conversation some weeks ago, you said you could not help me. That's as may be. But I'm sure you know of a way to get a small package to England. The information I told you about, it's all in a small package. I wanted to go with it, before. But since it's impossible now, then the information must go on its own.'

Gallois started to speak but David held up his hand. 'No, please don't bother with denials and so on. Whether or not you personally can find a way of getting this to its destination is irrelevant. Just come back, please, and tell me that you can get it to the right people! Please!' He leant back against the pillows, exhausted.

Gallois said firmly, 'I'll find out.'

David patted his hands; he felt sure that the Frenchman would find a way. He fell asleep happy.

Kapitanleutnant Geissler came to see him next. 'Well, are they taking care of you here? I am proud to say that we managed to bend the rules and get you put in here. It's rather a good hospital. I trust you like it here?'

'Oh yes. It's very good. Very good.'

Geissler looked awkward. David guessed he did not like sickness. Eventually he said, 'What I thought you might like to know is that you are to stay with us here in Brest. It's all been decided. Of course, that's as long as you manage to regain your fitness ... You will, won't you, Herr Freymann?'

David nodded, dumbfounded.

'Good! Well, we look forward to seeing you back at your desk as soon as convenient then. In the meantime, I wish you good health!'

David stared at the door for a long time after Geissler had gone. He was to stay ... after all. He frowned; he had been so sure, so certain that they would send him away. It was most confusing. Another reprieve. Life was nothing but a series of reprieves. He didn't know what was worse: living in hope of life or in certainty of death.

He didn't feel glad, he didn't feel angry. If anything he felt a little annoyed. It was the constant chopping and changing that got him down ...

The next day a nurse came in, a nurse he hadn't seen before. As she made a show of tucking in the bed clothes she started whispering to him. At first David didn't understand what she was saying. Then, suddenly, he realised. The nurse was saying, 'I have a message for you. Your friends will deliver both packages. They repeat: *Both* packages.'

He clasped his hands together and let the understanding slowly dawn on him. His prayers had been answered. He was to be allowed his small act of sabotage after all.

Chapter 21

THE BOOKSHOP WINDOWS looked blank and cold. Julie lowered her eyes and kept walking until she reached the shop door. She went straight in. A bell jangled loudly.

The proprietor was sitting behind the counter. He peered at her over his spectacles.

Julie said, 'I'd like a copy of *La Grande Chance*, please.'

'Is that by Maurik?'

'No, Lefarge.'

The shopkeeper looked quickly around. 'Follow me, I'll see if I have it in the back.' He led the way through some heavy curtains into the darkness of the store room behind. For a moment Julie couldn't see anything, then she realised there was a figure standing before her. A voice said, 'Thank you for coming.'

'That's all right.'

The figure came closer and Julie made out the features. It was the new man, Maurice. He had come from England with a wireless operator called Jacques.

Maurice led her towards the back of the storeroom. There was more light here. Maurice said, 'The same as before, if you don't mind. There are two of them.' His voice was quiet, calm and authoritative. It was like his face: trustworthy. The moment he'd started reorganising the line Julie had known he'd be all right. He'd discarded many of the helpers and reduced their numbers to a small tight group. Most important, he was very very careful.

He indicated a door which led to a small box room. 'The first's waiting in here.' He smiled. 'All right?'

'Oh yes!' It was easy now, not like the first time.

Julie walked in, sat down and faced the young man who sat at the small table. He certainly looked American, with his round face and his extraordinary haircut.

She smiled briefly. 'Where do you come from?'

'I'm from Milwaukee, ma'am.'

Julie regarded the airman as if she knew precisely where Milwaukee was. 'And which State is that in?'

'Wisconsin, ma'am.'

Julie tried to remember where Wisconsin was. Somewhere on the Great Lakes, she thought. Mid-West, anyway. She said, 'That's near New York, isn't it?'

The airman laughed drily. 'Goodness me, no, ma'am! Don't let nobody from Wisconsin hear you say that! Chicago – that's the nearest big city. New York! Why that's a thousand miles away.' He laughed again.

This one was genuine, no doubt about that. But best to make sure. 'You should be back in four weeks or so. Are you looking forward to that?'

The young man grinned. 'You bet. Haven't seen my family for over a year now.'

'Yes, let me see, it's late November now. You should be back in time for Thanksgiving then, shouldn't you?'

The airman frowned. 'Why, no, ma'am. We've just had Thanksgiving. Just four days ago!' He shook his head. 'No, no way I'll get Thanksgiving with my family till next year, ma'am.'

Julie smiled. 'No, of course not.' She stood up. 'You wait here. They'll come and collect you in a moment.'

The airman nodded and sank back in his seat. Julie went back into the storeroom. Maurice came forward. She nodded and said, 'That one's all right, I'm certain.'

Maurice looked pleased. 'Good.' He said over his shoulder, 'Get that one back into the cellar, Henri, and bring up the other one. Don't let them talk to each other.'

Julie leant against a bookshelf to wait. This was the third time they'd asked her to come to the bookshop. The first time had been difficult: she hadn't known what to ask and she'd found herself going through two generations of the Americans' family histories before she struck on the idea of asking questions about Thanksgiving. Now she could do an interview in as little as five minutes.

Stool-pigeons. *Mouchards.* She was pretty sure she hadn't let any through yet. *God forbid.*

She watched Maurice as he leant back against a bookshelf and lit a cigarette. He was about forty, stocky, and she was pretty sure he was a Belgian – but one didn't ask. After the fiasco of the previous winter no-one asked anything any more.

He ran the line with a firm hand. No unnecessary contact, no unnecessary knowledge. That's why everyone trusted him.

Maurice came up to her. 'The other one's in there now. He's the one we're concerned about. He turned up near Rennes, saying he'd walked all the way from the north somewhere. That's a hell of a long walk without any help . . . Also he looks very nervous. We checked him out with London, of course. Everything all right there, but . . .!' He shrugged.

Julie nodded and went back into the box room.

The airman jumped when she came into the room: he was nervous all right. Julie took a good look at him. He was blond, blue-eyed and pale-skinned. He looked miserable. Julie began with the usual questions: name, rank, serial number, aircraft, squadron, where stationed. These facts had already been checked, but she asked the questions again so that she could watch him and listen to his voice.

There was a strange inflection in his voice: not quite an accent, more a hint of one.

She asked, 'Where are you from?'

'Omaha.'

'Have your family always lived there?'

'No.'

He was not very forthcoming. Julie tried again. 'Where did they come from originally?'

'Europe.'

'Where exactly?'

There was a silence. The boy narrowed his lips. Julie thought: Oh dear, this one's going to be difficult. On a hunch she asked, 'Was it from Germany?'

The young man was looking upset. 'Back to that again! You're going to be like the rest.'

'What do you mean?' Julie asked softly.

'They—' He was unable to speak and shook his head. Finally he said, 'They – hate me! They call me a Hun! And now I suppose you're going to accuse me of being a German spy!'

'Your family *were* German?'

He nodded slowly. 'But I'm an American! I'm as American as any of them! I suppose they've been telling you different?'

'No. No, they haven't. Really. But your name – Smith?'

'My family's name was Schmidt. They went to America a long, long time ago! We changed our name – oh, fifteen years ago.'

'That must have been about the time you went to school.' He didn't look much more than twenty.

He nodded.

'Where did you go to school?'

She took him through everything she could think of. School, summer camps, baseball, football, the movies he had seen, the girls he had known – not many, she guessed correctly – even the house his family lived in. She had no idea if his answers were right. She only knew that his eyes were honest and he never stopped to search for an answer and, when he spoke of home, his face lit up.

She asked him about his journey from Northern France. He had walked, he said, because he felt safer that way. He thought the local people might not be friendly so he'd avoided them and stolen food as he went along. He described the places he'd been to, how he'd narrowly escaped a patrol and had to hide in a tree. It all sounded plausible, Julie decided. She couldn't imagine anyone making up such a long and involved story.

Finally she said, 'Well, if everything goes smoothly you should be home soon – in about a month. That'll get you home at the end of December, won't it?'

He smiled and it transformed his face. 'Yes! Will it really be that soon?'

That makes a change, Julie thought. Most of them complained because they weren't being airlifted back in the morning. She said, 'If all goes well.' Then she smiled. 'But you might just miss Thanksgiving, I'm afraid.'

He shrugged. 'I don't care – just so long as I can see my folks.'

Julie thought: Blast, he hasn't risen to it. I'll have to keep going.

Suddenly the young man said, 'Hey! But we've just had Thanksgiving!'

'Of course!' Julie laughed. 'How silly of me.'

When she came out Maurice and the others were standing among the dusty book shelves, waiting for her expectantly. She said, 'I think he's genuine. But I can't guarantee it.' She hated giving them a woolly answer, but there was one awful possibility she could not rule out: his background might be everything he said it was, but he might have chosen to move back to Germany just before the war. He might be a superb liar. She said, 'He certainly lived in America as a child but whether or not he chose to stay there I cannot say. His family were German.'

Maurice touched her shoulder. 'Good enough. He stays with the others, then. But we keep an eye on him.' He turned to Julie. 'Thank you for your help. It's just what we need.'

Julie flushed with pleasure. 'I'm just sorry I couldn't be more certain—'

'No, no! Better to have doubts than pretend to be sure. Thank you again. We've kept you long enough. You should go now. Take care.'

Julie put her hand on his arm. 'One thing – you will call on me, won't you, for beach duty, when the boat comes?'

Maurice looked at her thoughtfully. 'If you wish. It would certainly be useful to have you there. But – it means more risk, you know that?'

'Yes, I know that.'

He nodded.

Julie waved briefly, then went to the thick curtain and waited behind it, listening. There was no sound and, tentatively, she pulled the curtain aside until she could see through into the shop. There were no customers: only the proprietor, standing behind the counter.

She stepped out briskly and went round the end of the counter. Near the shop door she paused, as if looking at one of the books on the shelf, then nodding to the proprietor, went casually out into the street.

She resisted the temptation to look over her shoulder. That would never do. Instead she looked at her watch. Her lunch hour was nearly over. She'd have to go straight back to the office. It wasn't far, only five minutes away.

She walked calmly, not too fast, not too slow. She kept her manner casual, glancing at the occasional shop window, or into the faces of passers-by. She had never realised it was so difficult to look natural. She wondered if she was fooling anyone. Her heart was beating wildly and she felt horribly conspicuous. She decided she'd never get used to this kind of thing.

When she arrived at the office it was quiet: her boss was away for the afternoon. She finished some accounts and typed three letters, then looked at the pile of copy invoices waiting to be filed. She hated filing: it could wait.

Instead she flicked through her diary, trying to work out when the next moonless night would be . . . That was when he would come . . .

It was seven months since she had seen him. She'd thought about him constantly, so much so that sometimes she couldn't remember what his voice sounded like or the exact shape of his nose. Not that those things mattered . . . But it did make him seem unreal and that frightened her. Sometimes she could even persuade herself that she'd never see him again.

He, his crew, and the stranded airmen had finally been collected in March. The boat had come back four times after that, on routine missions. It was then that she'd expected to see him. But he hadn't been on board. Instead there had been messages, usually relayed by the leader of the beach party.

Hoping to come soon. Please be careful.

Take care. Don't know when I'll be able to come.

In April the nights had got too short and the boats had not come any more. The summer seemed to last for ever – and not just for her but for the people hiding the growing number of airmen. Now it was autumn again and he still hadn't come. There were messages like the ones before, but no Richard.

Maybe he would never come again. But she'd go to the beach anyway, just in case.

That was why she was helping Maurice – to make sure she got to the beach. She was ashamed of her motives. Either one was committed or one wasn't. She had to make up her mind.

Immediately, she knew it was impossible. She couldn't

choose between the safety of her son and seeing Richard again. She was greedy; she wanted *both*.

After. She'd make up her mind after she'd seen Richard. Yes: that was the answer.

She shivered slightly and got up to do the filing.

She left the office early. There was no more work to do and, by getting the five o'clock bus, she could have an extra hour with Peter before bedtime.

It was only a five-minute walk to the bus stop, but she'd still have to hurry. She walked rapidly, head down and arms swinging. She looked at her watch again. There should be enough time ... But she hated cutting things fine. She ran a little way until she was out of breath, then walked again. She arrived at the bus stop with four minutes to spare.

She flopped into a seat, breathless and rather hot. Why had she hurried? Because I'm a worrier, she thought with a sigh, and I'll never change now. She took the morning edition of *Ouest-France* out of her bag and, unfolding it, started to read. There wasn't very much of it – only two pages – and it was, she guessed, heavily censored, but some news was better than none at all and, like everyone else, she read what she could.

She was aware of someone sitting down in the seat beside her, then, with a lurch, the bus set off. After so many years Julie knew the route like the back of her hand. She didn't have to look up to know exactly where they were on the forty-minute journey.

The person next to her shifted in his seat. Suddenly there was a voice in her ear. 'You left work early!'

Julie started and looked round.

She sighed with relief and laid her hands over her heart. 'Michel! You gave me a terrible fright!'

He smiled briskly. 'My apologies.'

The bus drew to a halt at the checkpoint which marked the beginning of the Zone Interdite, the coastal zone restricted to all but those with the necessary permit. Julie got out her papers and glanced at the permit which had appeared in Michel's hand. She noticed that it was in a false name.

When the *Feldgendarmen* had glanced at the papers and the bus was on its way again, Julie stole a glance at Michel. 'Where have you been all this time?' How long had it been? Months.

'Morlaix. Mainly.'

'But I haven't seen you around. I thought you must have gone away!'

'No.' It was a statement.

'Anyway—' She took another look at him. 'What are you doing on this bus?'

'Going your way.'

'Ah.' She didn't ask why. With Michel, she never liked to enquire too closely. He was probably planning to blow up more Germans.

He read her mind and said quietly, 'I'll be behaving myself, don't worry.'

Julie glanced surreptitiously over her shoulder. Behind, there were two large country women sitting with baskets of vegetables on their laps. In front, there was a girl reading a book. No-one was listening.

Michel whispered, 'I hear that things have got a bit more organised around Tregasnou.'

Julie stiffened. How dare he! She said calmly, 'What do you mean, Michel?'

'There's a new set-up, isn't there? A new organisation to get people out?'

'If there is, I know nothing about it.'

Michel smiled. 'Of course. I must say your security's much better. Nobody's talking. That's very good.'

Julie said coldly, 'So how did you hear this story? If security is so good.'

'Ah. Small things ... Guesswork mainly. And the silence.'

'The silence?'

'Yes. No-one's talking. That always means there's something going on!' He smiled at her.

Self-satisfied as ever, Julie thought. But he doesn't know as much as he pretends. That's the important thing. She said, 'If there *is* something going on, I really don't know. I keep well out of these things nowadays.'

'I hope so. Whatever they may think, they're still a bunch of amateurs.'

'I think not.'

Michel looked at her quizzically. 'You seem very definite.'

'I've just formed an opinion, that's all.'

He regarded her for a moment. 'You've changed, Julie—'

She frowned. 'Why do you say that?'

'You're more – self-confident. You never used to be.'

'You're making judgements again.'

'Yes. I think I'm quite good at them.'

Julie sighed with exasperation. 'But – you're so sure of yourself. And so intolerant of everyone else, Michel! It's really very trying.'

'You mean, like everyone else in your quiet neck of the woods, you think my politics stink! Well, I tell you – after the war you'll be sorry. You'll find you're living in a France run by fascists, just like it was before the Germans came!'

Julie shook her head. 'There, you see – you immediately turn everything into a political argument. All I meant was you're very difficult to talk to!'

'Ah! But how very sure of yourself *you* have become, Julie. You're quite a different lady from the one I used to know. What *have* you been up to? I think you're busier than you'll admit to. Yes, a very busy lady!'

How she hated his games. She said impatiently, 'I am just the same person, Michel. Nothing's changed.'

He gave her a mocking glance. 'If you say so.'

The bus had stopped at a village. More people got on. With a loud roar the bus started again, juddering slowly up through the gears. Like most buses in Brittany, it had seen better days.

Michel leant closer. 'All right – no more discussions. I'll tell you. I caught this bus purposely – so that I could see you.'

Julie peered sideways at him. Again, she wasn't sure what he meant. She smiled and said archly, 'Oh really? I didn't know you cared so much, Michel. After all, you've managed to keep away from me for at least six months!'

He looked irritated. 'No . . . Well, of course it's nice to see you – but actually it's about something else.'

'Yes?'

He said, 'Whether or not you know who's involved in . . . local activities . . . you must know someone who knows *someone*. Anyway, I have an important message for them.' He turned and looked at her. 'If I give it to you, will it get to its destination?'

'But why me? Why not send it more . . . directly?'

'Directly? You're joking. There's undeclared war between your lot and mine. Or didn't you know? If your lot had their way we'd never touch so much as a hair of a German's head. Well, that's not our idea of how to fight.'

'But when you kill it means reprisals.'

'I thought we weren't going to argue . . . Look, you're the best contact I have. Are you going to pass this message or not?'

Julie looked him straight in the eye. 'Well . . . I can't promise anything, but . . .' She shrugged and pretended to consider. '. . . if it's that important I'll do my best.'

said heavily, 'Who can tell? Michel has always had extreme views. To him, anything is justified if it furthers his cause.'

Julie could bear it no longer. She said to Maurice, 'But he would not betray us, I'm sure of that. After all, we *are* his family. He wouldn't betray us to the Germans, I'm sure . . .'

'Family—?'

'Yes!' Julie exclaimed. 'Cousins. He used to come here often . . .'

There was silence again. Finally Maurice said, 'It's what happens *before* we take delivery of this fellow that's the problem. There is no way we can be sure he's authentic. We're going to have to take *their* word for that. If they've been fooled . . . well, we'll have no defence . . . We'll get nabbed at the hand-over. When you think about it, it could be the perfect set-up.'

The others nodded slightly. Julie shook her head.

'But . . . Why would they make up this story about him being ill, if he's really a Gestapo agent? It sounds unlikely . . . Doesn't it?' Suddenly she was as uncertain as the other three. It was impossible to be sure.

Maurice grunted and passed a hand over his face. 'Looking on the black side, the Gestapo might need the extra time to train up their agent. Who knows?'

The fisherman, Gérard, said, 'But what if this scientist *is* genuine and he *does* have this secret, what then?'

Maurice suddenly slapped his hands on his knees and said, 'Well, I suggest we do this – we ask for as many details about this man as possible. We try to check him out with London. You never know, they might have some information on him – if he really is a top brain. Then . . . We take as many precautions as possible. We risk only one person at the pick-up, we blindfold this fellow, we guard him twenty-four hours a day . . .'

'So we go ahead?'

'Yes, I think we have to.' Maurice looked at Julie. 'Can

you ask for more details about this man? And also ask if they guarantee his authenticity.'

Julie nodded. 'I'll ask.'

'Okay. That's it for the moment then.'

They all got up. Gérard said a quick good night and left immediately. Maurice paused and came up to Julie. He put a hand on her shoulder. 'May I speak with you one moment?'

'Of course.'

He led her to the other side of the table and they sat down. He said softly, 'Look, I'm concerned that you've become involved in all this when perhaps you didn't mean to. If – well, if you should decide to change your mind, that is understood. You only have to tell me. And there'll be no recriminations.'

He was asking her to choose. She thought of Peter asleep upstairs and instinctively looked upwards. There was no simple answer . . .

She said, 'I'll do what I can for the moment . . . I'll deliver the message and bring back the reply and all that. Perhaps when this scientist is delivered, perhaps then I might . . . want to be not quite so involved . . .' She trailed off, thinking what a half-baked person she was.

But Maurice was nodding. 'That's fine, then. We'll do that. But I do think we shouldn't be using your real name. I think we must find another for you. Would Marie-Claire suit you?'

The question took Julie by surprise. 'Er – yes.'

'Right, Marie-Claire you are then.'

A false name. Julie shivered slightly.

Maurice was getting up. 'Oh, and the boat. Sunday. It's coming on Sunday. You'll help bring parcels to the beach?'

Julie breathed, 'Oh yes! That'll be no problem!'

Sunday. It was three days away.

*

The darkness was made up of a million small dots which jumped and danced before your eyes. One moment you could see the outline of a rock against the sea, the next it had gone and there was nothing except the shimmering blackness. If you stared too long you began to see strange indistinct shapes that moved and faded and darted away. Then you had to look away and rest your eyes.

One thing at least, thought Julie, it was a perfect night for the gunboat. The sentries up on the headland wouldn't be able to see further than the cliff edge. Also, there was hardly any wind. That meant the boat would have a fast passage. They would come, she knew it. The BBC message had said so. It had come at eight. *Benedictine is a sweet liqueur.*

Whatever happened, it would be a great relief when all the parcels were gone. There were thirty-nine of them, there on the beach at that very moment. It was a terrifying number, but they had been accumulating fast in the last few weeks. Many had been diverted away, to Spain via Bordeaux, but those who had been sent down the line to Brittany – by train from Paris to St Brieuc – had all been hidden, some for as long as a month.

Now, miraculously, they were all on the beach. And restless. Julie could hear them muttering between themselves. She got up and, walking over to the voices, whispered, 'Please don't talk. The sound may carry.'

'But how long do we have to wait?'

'It's impossible to say. Just be patient. Please.'

They were quiet and Julie returned to her place. She felt very calm. She was sure everything would be all right. She had a feeling about it.

There was silence apart from the faint lapping of waves on sand.

She saw someone move, probably Gérard. Then another man. Then there was a sound, an infinitesimal, soft swishing . . .

They were here.

Her heart thudded. She made herself concentrate on what had to be done. She moved along the groups of airmen and said to each, 'You will see two small boats arriving soon. You must not move until you are told. Do you understand?' Then she crouched beside them and waited.

The surfboats seemed to take a long time. Then at last they were there, first one then the other gliding in to the beach, two solid dark shapes against the paler sea. Julie waited half a minute, then stood up and called softly, 'Groups One and Two?' The men – it should be fourteen in all – rose and followed her down towards the waiting boats. The surfboat crews came forward and Julie directed the two groups to different boats. The surfboat crews were in a hurry. They were already pushing their boats out and bundling their passengers in. Julie tried to get a look at their faces. But he wasn't there, she already knew it. Then they were gone.

Twenty minutes later the boats were back. Julie called two more groups of airmen forward. This time some of them didn't listen to her instructions and too many men peeled off in the direction of the first boat. Julie sorted them out and took the three extra men across to the second boat, which was already loaded and waiting. The three men waded into the water, rolled into the boat, and then it was gone.

Julie stared after it for a moment before turning away. One more journey, and they would be finished.

Someone was hurrying along the sand towards her. Gérard? No, too tall.

Then suddenly she knew exactly who it was.

She moved tentatively forward, laughing a little. Then he was hugging her, so tight she could hardly breathe. He put his cheek against hers and with a sudden shock she remembered the feel of his skin and the lovely animal scent of him. And she remembered his body, and how lovely it had felt against hers, and she murmured, 'Oh, how I've missed you.'

'Julie—'

He pulled away, trying to see her face in the darkness. He whispered, 'There's not much time and I must know – First, are you all right?'

'Yes, yes! *I'm* all right!'

'But is it safe? I bet it isn't!'

'It's fine, now. Really! Everyone's very careful. Really!' She laughed and pushed herself up on tiptoe and put her arms round his neck and kissed him. He kissed her back, hard. Then, after a while, he pulled away again. 'Julie, listen – I've had an idea. It's all been okayed. I've cleared it with everyone . . . Julie, you and Peter must come back to England. On the gunboat.'

Julie frowned in the darkness. 'What—? I—'

'Look, we can fix it for the next trip. You can just disappear. No-one will ever guess where you've gone. And then you'll be safe, *both* of you. Julie, say you will!'

'But . . . I don't know. I . . . I'll have to think about it.'

'But Julie, it *must* be the right thing to do! You're running terrible risks, don't you realise that? If you got caught, well – what *then*?'

'Yes, I . . . I suppose you're right.' She'd never thought about going herself. It had never occurred to her. But it wasn't that simple – and she couldn't explain.

He said urgently, 'Please, say you'll come!'

'I don't know – I don't know! I need time!'

'There may not *be* any time . . .'

She could hear the disappointment in his voice, and understood. He must have been planning this for ages, and now she was being reluctant and ungrateful. She said, 'Please – I love you with all my heart. But I must *think*. My family are here, and the others, and . . . It's all so sudden, Richard. Please, let me think and plan . . . And, next time you come, I'll tell you for sure, I promise. You *will* be coming again, won't you?'

'Yes. Yes . . .'

He was still disappointed, she could tell. She pulled at his arm and sat down on the sand. He sat beside her and put his arm round her. 'Julie – I thought you'd *want* to . . .'

'But I do! I do!'

'Then?'

Julie thought: He's right. I should go. I should get Peter to safety. I should be with him – I *want* to be with him. She said, 'Yes . . . perhaps you're right! I'll try. I promise!'

He squeezed her arm. 'Good! Good!' Then he chuckled. 'I thought for a moment your affections had been stolen by a tall, dark Frenchman!'

She laughed quietly. 'No, I ran after him, but he wouldn't have me!'

'He must have been mad!'

They grinned at each other in the darkness.

After a while there was the gentle sound of muffled oars and she stiffened. He pulled her to her feet. She suddenly realised she hadn't mustered the airmen. She said, 'I'd better get the passengers,' and, before he could reply, ran quickly up the beach. When she got back the boats were ready and waiting and there was no more time.

She found him by the second boat. He said, 'We'll be back in a week or so. Come then, Julie! Please!'

'I'll try!'

He kissed her and ran quickly into the water to where the boat was waiting.

Then he was gone, vanished into the darkness that was the sea.

Chapter 22

THERE WAS CLOUD at two thousand feet. The moon shed a soft silvery sheen over it as it appeared in a rapidly growing mantle beneath the cruising Wellington.

The pilot leant his head against the side cockpit window and looked down. The cloud was thickening all the time. He regarded it with satisfaction. The U-boats would think they were safely hidden under that lot.

The pilot peered at his watch and said into his mike, 'How long to turnaround, Wally?'

There was a crackle and the navigator's voice came through the earphones, 'Fifteen minutes, sir.'

'Right-ho.'

They were flying to the limit tonight, like they always did. Eight hundred miles west-south-west into the Atlantic, then a zigzag course east-south-east, across the Bay of Biscay to the French coast, then home. The pattern might yield up a U-boat or two. The only problem was, the U-boats usually knew they were coming.

It had all been so simple when they'd first got the ASV radar more than a year before. If the conditions were right you just turned the thing on and waited for the magic words, 'Radar to Skipper. Target thirteen miles to port. Angle twenty degrees.' Then you turned into the darkest part of the sky and approached up-moon, so that the U-boat was beautifully silhouetted against the moon-path. By the time the U-boat spotted you it was too late for them to dive – or even fight. The pilot had got a good tally in those days: two definite hits and a probable.

Of course, it hadn't been *that* easy. The radar was a bit temperamental and it was no good in rain, snow, sleet or heavy seas. But when the conditions *were* good, it could work quite well.

Then it all changed and the devilish U-boats kept disappearing before one's very eyes. You'd pick them up all right, but by the time you homed in on them they'd bloody disappeared. Of course, there was only one way they could do it so consistently – by counter-measure. A radar detector.

Bound to happen, of course, but still frustrating. Eventually Coastal Command worked out a counter-strategy. As soon as a target was picked up you ordered the radar scanner to be stopped and the radar aimed aft, where its waves couldn't be picked up. Then you manoeuvred slowly into position, asking for the radar to be turned through a full circle only once every minute or so, just to make sure you hadn't lost the U-boat. Only on the final run in did you leave the radar on continuously. At between one and two miles you turned on the two-million-candle-power Leigh light and, even if you didn't pick the U-boat up immediately, with a bit of luck the U-boat gunners wouldn't be able to resist the temptation of firing at it, thus, most obligingly, guiding you straight in to your target.

The strategy worked fairly well, but as often as not the U-boat sussed you out before you ever got near. Real cat and mouse stuff. Trouble was, the mouse got away with it far too often.

It would be nice to gain the upper hand again.

And, with a bit of luck, they might. There was a new box of tricks on board. An experimental device. He was rather proud of the fact that his old girl was the first in Coastal Command to be fitted with one.

H_2S, the boffins called it. Which, if he remembered his school chemistry correctly, was the chemical formula that stunk of rotten eggs. Some boffin somewhere had a sense of humour.

It was a new radar. They'd explained it to him. A completely new type, they said, which would give wonderful definition in *every* direction. Read the sea and the land like a map.

Certainly the radar operators were mad keen on it. The navigator, too – finding his way back to the coast was a piece of cake.

The new-fangled device had been fitted only three days before, so they were continuing to use the old ASV radar as well, to be on the safe side.

The pilot looked at his watch. Two minutes to the final turn and the start of the journey home. They were deep into the Bay now, only twenty miles from the French coast. They'd run parallel to the coast as far as Brest, then turn for home.

They turned. The engines droned on. An hour passed.

'Captain to Navigator. Position, Wally?'

'Fifty miles south-west of Lorient, Skipper.'

Good hunting country, this. Close to both Lorient and St Nazaire. 'Captain to crew. Extra sharp lookout now – above *and* below.' Fighters weren't much of a problem in the Bay, but you never knew.

The acknowledgements from the nine-man crew came back through the ear-phones, one by one. The pilot leant his face against the side-screen and looked down at the thick cloud below. No chance of a visual. But somewhere down there was a U-boat, perhaps *several*.

Damn it, all he wanted was a stab at one. *Just a stab*.

The young officer watched the long nose of the submarine carve swathes of white foam through the dark sea and could hardly believe this great monster was really his.

Even now it seemed incredible that they had given him command. He was just twenty-six and had been an Ober-leutnant zur See for only a year.

He wished he felt completely confident – but it was impossible. Not when he'd looked up to the great U-boat commanders for so long: men like Gunther Prien who took U47 into Scapa Flow and sank the *Royal Oak*; or Karl Fischer, the commander with the greatest single tally of ships sunk. How could he think of himself on the same level? It was impossible.

He looked up. A thin veil of cloud was covering the moon. That would give them some cover at least. They needed it: the air patrols were heavy nowadays. He remem-bered the beginning of the war when he was a Leutnant zur See fresh from training. Then enemy aircraft had been rare and usually came in daylight.

It was five hours since they'd left St Nazaire. They'd left late, because of engine problems, and they'd left dis-organised, because of last-minute crew changes. Half the men on board had been transferred from another, crippled, boat and at least ten were fresh recruits who'd completed only half their proper training. It was unsatisfactory, to say the least. As soon as they were clear of the Bay he would put the men through their paces and do some intensive training sessions. It wouldn't make up for the lack of an experienced, well-trained crew, but it would have to do.

He looked at his watch. Seven hours of darkness left. Not enough to clear the Bay. He stamped his feet. The winter had come early this year and it was very cold.

The junior watch officer was at his shoulder. 'Radar bleep, Herr Oberleu.'

The young commander nodded. It was nothing to get excited about. The radar detector bleeped and whined and whistled all the time. Often the thing drove commanders so mad that they ordered it to be turned off. The device seemed to hear planes everywhere.

Still, better check it. After all, he was responsible now.

He stepped across to the other side of the bridge and looked at the aerial. It had been introduced as a temporary measure when the British first started using radar, and had quickly been dubbed the Biscay Cross. Now, a year later, they were still using it. This one had certainly seen better days. It looked as though it had been thrown hastily down the hatch and patched together dozens of times. Nevertheless the fragile wooden structure was correctly positioned and the wires properly connected. Nothing wrong there then.

He nodded to the second watch officer and went down the hatch to the control room. The Metox technician was bent over the set, fiddling with a knob. The set emitted a piercing shriek. The technician saw the young commander and said, 'Sorry, Herr Oberleu, it seems to be playing up. Shall I open it up and have a look? It would mean turning it off for a while . . .'

By habit the young officer almost referred the matter to the commander until he remembered with a slight shock that he *was* the commander. The eyes of several of the men were on him. Decision time.

He hesitated. The men's eyes hardened. He *must* decide. Suddenly he said, 'No! Don't dismantle it until we're clear of the Bay. Leave it on!'

The technician nodded. The young commander turned away and went to the chart table, to give himself time to recover. He'd almost made a fool of himself.

He turned on his heel and climbed purposefully back up the conning tower.

On the bridge the men moved aside in deference. The young commander stepped forward and stared purposefully ahead. It was darker now. He looked up. The cloud cover was much thicker: both the moon and the stars had disappeared. Good! This darkness was safer and more cocoon-like.

Suddenly he began to feel more optimistic.

'Radar bleep, Herr Oberleu.'

The young commander nodded.

'Another radar bleep.'

Automatically he searched the sky, but there was nothing.

There was tension on the bridge now, as everyone waited for another bleep. If they came at regular intervals, then it might be an aircraft . . .

'Interference on Metox . . . Permanent signal.'

The young officer gripped the coaming. The cursed thing was really playing up. Useless. It was quite useless. It was said in the Officers' Mess that the device worked well only when the enemy were making their final run-in. That gave just enough time to alert the gunners and fire a few bursts on the 20 mm's. Not enough – but better than nothing at all.

'Metox functioning. No signal.'

He relaxed a little and looked out into the night.

Five minutes passed. There were no further reports from the control room.

There was no aircraft then.

The pilot was just beginning to think it wasn't going to be his night.

Then it came. 'Radar to Skipper. Target twenty miles to starboard. Angle ten degrees.'

The familiar excitement clutched at him. He gulped involuntarily and said, 'Stop scanner. Radar aft.' He switched the controls to manual and banked the aircraft to port, automatically beginning the manoeuvres that would bring them into position down-moon.

'Radar to Skipper. You don't want the H₂S scanner off too, do you, sir?'

'Is it picking up the target?'

'Loud and clear, sir. Only one that is. I had nothing on the old set at all.'

Of course. The range had been twenty miles: the old set had rarely managed that. He said, 'Leave it on then.'

They flew north-west until Radar gave the target bearing due east. Then they flew north-east until the target was bearing due south. Now the target would be in the path of any moonlight that might be filtering through the cloud. They turned for the final run-in.

So far so good. The U-boat, if it was one, hadn't dived.

'Captain to Radar. Keep it dead on the nose now.'

'Roger.'

'Still a good target, is it?'

'Oh, loud and clear, sir!'

It was too good to be true. Despite the cold, the pilot's hands were sweating as they gripped the stick.

'Radar to Captain. Range four miles. Dead on the nose.'

A minute and a half to go then. The pilot took her down to four hundred feet and they broke through the cloud base.

'Radar to Captain. Target three degrees to starboard.'

The pilot made the necessary course alteration. The target was moving west then: outward bound. The Wellington was down to three hundred feet.

'Radar to Captain. Target dead ahead. Range three miles.'

'Roger. Captain to Navigator. Bomb doors open.'

Normally they switched on the Leigh light at two miles. But with this much certainty the pilot decided to wait.

Hell, but it had better be a U-boat and not a bloody fisherman out after hours!

'Radar to Captain. Target dead ahead. Range two miles.'

'Roger. Call distances at every half mile now.'

'Will do.'

'Captain to Navigator. I want the Leigh light on at *one* mile, and, Co-pilot, keep shouting my height, will you? Yell if it gets too near a hundred feet.'

'Right-ho, sir.'

'Radar to Captain. One and a half miles, dead on the nose.'

The pilot peered into the murk ahead, but there was no moonpath. No sea, nothing. He was at a hundred and twenty feet now. He could feel the sweat running down his body and his heart hammering against his chest. God, but it had better be a U-boat!

'Radar to Captain. One mile and dead on the nose!'

Navigator to Captain. Leigh light *on*!'

The powerful beam sprang out from the starboard wing, carving a path of light far into the night ahead.

For a moment the pilot could see nothing.

Bloody hell! Where the devil—!

Suddenly there was a yell. 'There!'

And there she was.

Black. Sleek. Long.

A great big beautiful fat U-boat, a perfect target – just for them.

The pilot grunted with excitement. He knew, even before he released the depth charges, that nothing could save her. They had the beautiful black beast absolutely cold.

The young officer felt drained. He hadn't realised how tense he had been. Presumably it was something one got used to.

He rubbed his eyes.

When he opened them again he thought for a moment his sight had gone. He was almost blinded by light . . .

There was a scream from his right. 'Enemy starboard ninety!'

He spun round.

A massive light was blazing out of the sky, a great ball of white fire which dazzled the eyes. The entire submarine was covered in a bath of vicious cold light. The young officer wanted to order the light away so that they could slip back into the darkness and hide . . .

Simultaneously he heard the whine of approaching engines.

He began to scream, 'Fire! Fire! Fire all guns!' Even as he screamed the guns opened up, their staccato *rat-tat-tat* tearing into the eerie silence. The tracers wove their way up towards the blinding light.

But still the light came.

He yelled, 'Get the light! The light!' And then realised it was far too late for all that.

The light was so close, so dazzling, it filled the sky. The ominous drone of the engines grew to a higher pitch.

Behind the circle of light the dark shape of the plane was visible. Large. Like a bird of prey.

And still it came inexorably nearer. The young man was filled with blind rage.

He screamed, 'Fire! Fire! Fire!' as if his words would travel through the air and extinguish the terrible light.

Then the noise was a great roar, and the plane seemed to lift up and up, and suddenly its black belly was swooping over them and he raised his fists and cried, 'No-o-oooo!'

The plane was gone. There was an instant when the engine noise was receding and the darkness was descending round the U-boat like a protective blanket – an instant when he felt a flicker of hope.

Then, a brief moment later, he knew with awful certainty that there was to be no escape after all.

The boat gave a great shudder and the deck lurched under his feet.

There was a slow rumble which grew into a thunderous boom. The shock hit his ears and buffeted his body.

The young commander realised with astonishment that the deck was continuing to fall away under his feet. He looked up and saw the boat rolling slowly, almost leisurely, to port.

The deck lurched again, violently, and there was another roar, much closer. The blast threw him against the side of the bridge and he heard his head meet the metal with a dull thud. Then water was in his eyes, in his mouth, pouring down his face. He spluttered fiercely and gasped for breath.

He suddenly thought: I must tell them.

He got to his feet and, pulling himself up the slanting deck, gripped the coaming and shouted, 'Abandon ship!' But his voice was weak and there was too much noise. Men were running and screaming. Even if they heard, it would make no difference.

He almost shouted again, but his eye was caught by the astonishing sight of the bow, just visible in the darkness. It was out of the water.

As he watched he realised with amazement that it was rising slowly but remorselessly up into the sky.

There was another explosion, this time from deep within the boat. Then another. The boat staggered, then continued her terrible climb into the sky.

It was only when he saw the sea rising up towards the conning tower that he realised she wasn't climbing at all, but sliding ... backwards, deeper and deeper, backwards ...

There was frantic activity on the forward deck. Some men were trying to release the rafts. They were tearing at the hatch covers with their hands. The hatches would not open. A man began to scream ...

The young commander felt water round his legs. He noticed in vague surprise that the sea was pouring into the conning tower. The sight made him desperately sad.

When the water reached his neck he swam for a while, thinking of his home and his parents and how much he loved and respected them, and crying because he had failed them so completely, and because he was so terribly afraid to die.

Then the waves were breaking over his head and he was swallowing water and it was incredibly cold and he knew it wouldn't be much longer.

It was twenty minutes, in fact. But he lost consciousness before he drowned and there are worse ways to die.

The streets of Berlin were dark and almost deserted. Rain and sleet were falling in a cold flurry, whipped sideways by the icy northerly wind. The roads were slippery from the long winter freeze and the staff car went slowly, the driver peering nervously through the windscreen at the unlit road ahead.

The weather had been bad for weeks. One storm after another, snow, Arctic temperatures. Doenitz reflected that even the elements seemed to be against them. Stalingrad was under siege, the Army was in retreat; at sea the U-boat crews were achieving remarkable results under terrible conditions. It seemed that the winter would go on for ever.

He could do nothing about the weather.

But he could and would fight against the other problems besetting the Navy. Like complete lack of air cover and reconnaissance for his U-boats. Like lack of steel for the building programme. Like the usual continental-minded attitudes of the leadership, Hitler still had not grasped the fact that he had to win the war at sea to win the war on land. Always the same problems.

Tomorrow Doenitz would get Hitler to approve the

steel allocation. And he was slowly winning on the matter of air cover, too. Goering had actually been pleasant to him the last time they met at Fuehrer Headquarters, and Hitler had pressed Doenitz rather than Goering to stay to breakfast. Promising signs.

Doenitz fingered the gold bands on his arm. How much difference power made!

He had been Commander-in-Chief of the Navy for three weeks, ever since Raeder's sudden resignation. Raeder had resigned over Hitler's decision to lay up the battleships, which the leader dubbed 'useless'. Doenitz, on taking up his new post, had also fought the decision – and won. Since then Hitler had treated him with the greatest consideration and respect. Strange justice!

The trouble was, it might all be too late. The worst mistakes had been made and were difficult to put right.

Like the business of this radar.

Schmidt had requested an urgent meeting to discuss 'a radar problem'. Even Goering was going to be there. It must be something serious.

The car drew up outside the Chancellery. Doenitz got out and climbed briskly up the steps into the first of the vast halls, his two staff officers on his heels. The meeting was in one of the smaller conference rooms. Originally the meeting was to have been held in Goering's ostentatious Air Ministry building, but early the day before a bomb had fallen nearby and shattered all the windows. And it was Goering who'd promised that Allied bombers would never reach Berlin!

The others were already there. As Doenitz entered everyone except Goering got to his feet. Goering was sitting at the head of the table, his massive weight wedged into a large ornate gilt chair. He smiled benignly at Doenitz. Doenitz carefully sat at the opposite end of the table, in an equally grand chair. He nodded at Goering and noticed that the man's eyes looked rather odd. It was said that Goering took drugs: that would account for it.

The meeting began. Schmidt was sitting on Goering's right, looking unhappy, his eyes firmly on the papers on the table in front of him. Hesitantly he started to read from what Doenitz realised was a carefully prepared statement.

After a few seconds Doenitz felt his hackles begin to rise. Schmidt was saying, '. . . the enemy aircraft was shot down near Rotterdam on the night of February 12th 1943. Routine examination of the wreckage by Luftwaffe personnel revealed a box which was badly damaged and covered with blood. However the box was sufficiently intact for it to be confirmed that nothing similar had ever been seen before. Superior technicians were called in but were unable to guess at the function of the box. The only clue was the words "Experimental 6" written in pencil on the side.' Schmidt turned a page and went on, 'Luftwaffe Headquarters ordered the box to be dismantled and brought to Berlin for closer examination . . . The Rotterdam Apparatus, as we decided to call it, was then examined by my staff in our laboratory. However . . .' Schmidt paused and looked even more unhappy '. . . two days ago, the RAF scored a direct hit on the laboratory, killing some of my staff and destroying parts of the apparatus. My staff climbed into the ruins of the laboratory and retrieved what they could. We are now trying to reconstruct the apparatus, using the parts which are left to us.'

'Herr Schmidt now has the use of the best possible laboratory,' Goering interrupted. 'It is properly fortified so that this cannot happen again.' The Luftwaffe staff officers nodded. Doenitz waited. He wanted to hear the rest.

Schmidt looked to see if Goering had finished then returned to his notes. 'With the components now in our possession it is impossible for us to reconstruct this apparatus to the point where we can make it function. We

cannot therefore report on the performance, range or
characteristics of the device – not unless we obtain another
apparatus, more or less intact, from a crashed enemy
bomber. However, it *is* possible to draw two basic conclusions: one, that it is a form of radar – a form that we
have never seen before . . .' Schmidt's voice was down
almost to a whisper. He had his elbows on the table and
his head in his hands, so that his face was hidden. 'And
two, that it works on very short wave, possibly as little as
ten centimetres.'

There was a long silence. Doenitz's staff eyed their
commander nervously. Goering frowned and, staring out
of the window, thoughtfully patted his large belly.

Doenitz stared at Schmidt, but didn't see him. His mind
was in the Bay of Biscay, seeing the enemy bombers
hunting, tracking, killing his U-boats with their magic new
eyes; and on the convoy routes, in the wastes of the North
Atlantic, seeing British destroyers lying in wait, ready to
pounce, without warning . . .

'May we understand this more completely?' Doenitz
spoke softly. Everyone looked at him. 'Are you saying that
this radar is completely unknown to us?'

Schmidt licked his lips. 'Yes.'

'And – you believe it might be very effective?'

'We have no way of knowing, not yet . . .'

'And are you saying that, in the event of it becoming
widely used by the British, we have no defensive measures
against it?'

The Chief Scientist shifted uneasily in his chair. 'We do
not have any way of detecting it at present . . .'

Doenitz leant forward. 'But *will* we?'

'It . . . would take time. We would have to understand
exactly how this new apparatus worked. It is based on
entirely different principles, you understand; *entirely
different*!'

'Entirely different . . .' Doenitz echoed. 'I see. I will not enquire as to why we ourselves have never investigated these entirely different principles!'

Goering gave Doenitz a hard stare. 'May I remind you, Herr Admiral, that our radar has proved to be extremely effective in everything except this, er, field! We have led Britain, led the world, in early warning systems. Not a British bomber nears Germany without our knowing about it!'

Doenitz nodded and said testily, 'Yes, Herr Reichsmarschall, most effective when defending a land mass, but not very effective for protecting U-boats, wouldn't you agree?'

There was an awkward pause. Suddenly Goering slapped the table. 'Quite so! I assure you, my dear Admiral, that everything possible is being done! I have taken every possible measure to ensure that we crack this Rotterdam problem as soon as possible. First—' For emphasis the Reichsmarschall pushed his right fist into the open palm of his left hand. '— *First*, all firms in this field have been ordered to start research! Second, we are releasing all the necessary personnel from active service, *however* many people are needed!' He turned abruptly to Schmidt. 'How many, Schmidt, five thousand? Ten thousand?'

'Impossible to say yet, Herr Reichsmarschall. But maybe as many as ten thousand. Yes.'

Doenitz asked, 'Why so many?'

Schmidt frowned. 'We have to follow several avenues of research . . . We have to try lots of different approaches to make sure we find the right one.'

My God, thought Doenitz, they haven't a clue, not a clue. He said, 'But how long will it take to develop a warning device?'

'Ah, not too long, hopefully.'

'In the meantime . . .' Doenitz stared at Goering. 'In the meantime, we are defenceless.'

'Not entirely!' exclaimed Goering with a smile. 'Telefunken tell me they have not entirely stopped research into other wavelengths. They might be able to produce a detector quite quickly.'

'Might?'

'You will be kept fully in the picture, Herr Admiral, I assure you!'

'Yes,' Doenitz said tightly. Doubtless the picture would be the same as ever – the bare minimum imparted with the maximum reluctance. 'And shortwave radar itself. What would be its advantages?'

Schmidt said, 'It is small . . . compact. For the rest, as I say, we cannot be sure, not until we can actually get a Rotterdam Apparatus working.'

'And when could we have this radar ourselves?'

Schmidt breathed deeply. 'Eighteen months . . . Or two years.'

For ever. Doenitz looked at Schmidt with contempt. The man had sworn that shortwave radar was impossible. The man was incompetent. Doenitz said shortly, 'There is no more to be discussed, then, is there?'

Except, he thought, with the Fuehrer, in private. Then he would make quite sure Hitler knew who was to blame for this appalling catastrophe.

Everyone began shuffling papers. Suddenly a thought stirred in the back of Doenitz's mind. 'Schmidt!' he called sharply.

'Yes, Herr Grossadmiral.'

'A long time ago, on the *Welle*, when you first demonstrated radar to us . . .'

'Yes, Herr Grossadmiral.'

'. . . there was a scientist of yours, someone who'd worked on radar from the beginning. He talked to me about shortwave radar. He said it was possible.'

Schmidt looked pale. 'I – I don't remember exactly . . .'

'But I do! He was a round, jolly little man. One of *your* men, Herr Schmidt. I can have him looked up if you like.

I'm sure I'll recognise the name when I see it. I remember speaking to him: he was quite definite about shortwave radar. He said it could be done.' Doenitz shook his head. 'I'm surprised you don't remember. You seemed quite agitated about the matter at the time.'

There was an indefinable electricity around the table. There might be a fight, the staff sensed it.

'Ah . . .' Schmidt said, as if remembering for the first time. 'I think I know who you must mean. A fellow called Freymann.'

'Yes, that was the man. That was him.'

Schmidt said quickly, 'Herr Grossadmiral, we have already asked for this man! Of course we have! He was an obvious first choice! Yes indeed, he has been earmarked for the main team . . .'

'But his ideas were not worth investigating before?'

Schmidt looked injured. 'Why indeed they were! But they were unworkable, quite mad! Whatever this new device may be, I'm sure it can't be anything like Freymann's ideas!'

Doenitz was unconvinced. He said, 'I see. But he *is* about to join your staff?'

'Yes, indeed! We have made a request!'

'A request?'

'Yes. Of the SS.'

'Ah! He was detained?'

'He is a Jew.'

'Where is he detained?'

'Ah.' Schmidt smiled slightly. 'We have just been informed that he is working at a Naval establishment – at Brest in France!'

There was a short embarrassed silence. 'And a request has been made?'

'Through the appropriate channels.

Doenitz barked, 'I find it surprising, Herr Schmidt, that

this request was not made immediately, direct to myself. I
am sure that, addressed through the highest possible channels, Freymann would be with you by now!'

Schmidt looked as if he had indigestion. 'But until we
realised the nature of the device we were not to know . . .'

'That this man was vital?'

Schmidt coughed. 'Indeed.'

'What about documents – research papers and so on.
Surely something of his work remains?'

'Nothing. Apparently it was all mislaid.'

'Then I hope to hear that he is with you very shortly!'
Doenitz stood up. 'And I look forward to hearing that the
research programme is progressing with all speed. Until
then, good day!'

There was a shuffling as people got to their feet. No-
one bothered with Heil Hitlers nowadays.

Schmidt watched Doenitz stride angrily from the room
and sighed. It was a nightmare, the whole thing. But not as
bad as it would be if Freymann didn't come up with the
answer. When Doenitz had called Freymann 'vital' he'd hit
the nail on the head.

Without Freymann it would take months, years.

It pained Schmidt to admit it, but that conceited little
Jew was their only hope.

Chapter 23

'You look wonderful today, madame!'

'Thank you, madame.' Julie smiled broadly at the shopkeeper and, picking up her basket from the counter, went out into the road. She walked briskly, waving and nodding to the people she met. Some of the villagers looked at her rather strangely. No woman had ever worn trousers in Tregasnou before. But then few women had ever been cowhands before. She grinned to herself. They would soon get used to it.

She'd given up her job before Christmas and it was the best thing she'd ever done. She now worked for Jean – which meant she worked from dawn until well after dusk for her keep and no money. But it was the best salary she'd ever had; she'd never been happier. The outdoor life suited her, the physical work made her feel better than she had in years, and, best of all, she saw much more of Peter. A pity she hadn't done it years ago.

It was the second big decision she'd taken.

The first had been even more important: she'd decided to escape to England.

At the right time. To disappear overnight would be to put her family at risk. She'd decided to do the thing properly. First, she'd left her job. Then she'd told people she was thinking of moving away – to Rennes, or another large city. Now all that remained was to leave, quite publicly, with farewells and luggage.

She'd even set her departure date: she'd told everyone
she was going in two weeks.

Julie walked over the crossroads and down the road
that led to the west of the village. Ahead, a front door
opened and an old lady in Breton dress emerged from one
of the smaller cottages. The old lady nodded at Julie, her
tall white lace coiffe bobbing forward, and mumbled,
'You're away, I hear. Thought you'd be off sooner or
later!'

Julie smiled and passed on. She thought: Silly old
woman. But nothing could annoy her today: she was too
happy. It wasn't just the thought of the actual journey and
of being with Richard, it was the way everything had
changed. For the first time she felt as if she was really in
control of her own life. The decision to go had been hard
– but once made, it was as if an enormous weight had been
taken off her shoulders.

She'd seen Richard only three times the whole winter.
The weather had been atrocious. Sometimes the boat didn't
come at all; sometimes it was so late there was barely time
to load any passengers; at other times she guessed he had
had to stay on board because of the terrible conditions out
at the anchorage. The last time she'd seen him he had
urged her to leave straight away. But there were always so
many passengers waiting to go, always more than there
were places for, that she couldn't.

Also there was Maurice and the group. They still needed
her and that was important to her. She'd never felt really
useful before and, well, she liked it. She couldn't let them
down. It would be disloyal and she wanted to be honour-
able and to do what was right. By staying this extra time,
until the scientist was well enough to go, she would have
done enough. After that she could leave with an easy mind.

She swung round a corner into a tiny lane that led
between a number of small cottages. She knocked firmly

on the front door of a cottage and, without waiting for a reply, walked straight in.

There was an old man beside the hearth.

'Good morning, Monsieur!'

The old man nodded and Julie went past him, through a door into a back room.

Maurice was already there.

'All right?' he asked.

She nodded happily. 'Yes. And you?'

'Fine.'

She sat down and, delving into the pocket of her trousers, handed him an envelope. He opened it and pulled out an identity card and a small box.

She said, pointing to the small box, 'I brought the ink pad. All it needs is the thumb print and the photograph, then give it back to me and I'll stamp it.' She had inserted the name – a totally fictitious one – and the details of birth and parentage. Maurice had already given her the age and colouring of the new owner.

She had only two cards left after this. But Maurice knew they were precious: he wouldn't have asked her for one unless it was important.

Maurice nodded. 'Right. We'll do the card in just a moment.'

Julie glanced up in surprise. That must mean that the new owner of the card was here, or nearby. She wondered who it could be. But she didn't ask: one had learnt not to.

Maurice began, 'First, the scientist. What's the news?'

Julie remembered the brief talk she'd had with Michel the day before. 'Everything's set for this week, but I don't know any more. They wouldn't give me any more details.'

'They wouldn't say exactly when?'

'No.'

'But the scientist's out of the hospital?'

'Yes.'

'And fit enough to travel?'

'So they say.'

Maurice made a wry face. 'I hope they're right.' He thought for a moment. 'We'd better aim to get him away in about ten days, then. I don't want him hanging about, but at the same time I do want to be sure he's everything he says he is ... There's still something about the whole set-up that makes me uneasy ...'

He looked hard at Julie. 'Will you help me to interrogate him? You have an instinct for it, you know.'

Julie smiled self-consciously. 'Thank you. Yes, of course I'll help if I can.'

'There'll be someone else, too. Helping us, I mean.'

'Oh?'

'Yes, a friend. From Paris. He's been with us for some time now, but further up the line.'

Julie frowned. A stranger. She had a dread of strangers. 'But – why's he come here?'

'He needs to lie low for a bit. He was spotted at Gare Montparnasse the other day and now the Boches are on the lookout for him. It was too dangerous.'

Julie looked down unhappily. Whatever the reasons, she wished the man hadn't come here.

Maurice watched her questioningly. 'This fellow will be useful to us, Marie-Claire. He was with Meteor. He's seen the sort of bogus airmen the Boches tried to pass down the line there. And he knew the traitor, Lebrun. He always suspected him, apparently. He's going to be very good on security.'

She asked. 'But how did he find us?'

'A mutual contact.'

'And he's ...' She wondered how to put it. 'He's – definitely all right?'

Maurice nodded. 'I had him checked out very carefully. I had the mutual friend verify him personally. Face to face in the presence of one of our couriers. Then I had him checked with London. They know him well. He'd been with Meteor for some time.'

Julie nodded. 'Ah.'

'And since he's been with us, he's been doing very good work, I assure you.'

She smiled briefly. It must be all right. She was just worrying too much as usual.

Maurice stood up. 'You might as well meet him now. I'll call him in, shall I?'

She looked up in surprise. 'He's here?'

'Yes. In the next room.' Maurice went to a back door, opened it, and spoke quietly. He returned and sat down.

Julie waited expectantly. Slowly, almost imperceptibly, a shadow fell on the open door then, without a sound, a man appeared, silhouetted against the light. Julie had the strangest feeling he'd been there all the time, just behind the door, listening.

For a moment the man paused, his face in darkness. Then he came forward, and Julie saw that he was looking at her carefully, his eyes hard and searching.

Then he smiled, his lips curving into a friendly grin, the eyes warming a little. Julie automatically smiled back and put out her hand to shake his.

Maurice said, 'This is Roger. Roger, this is Marie-Claire.' Roger wouldn't be his real name, of course.

They sat down. 'Now,' Maurice began immediately, 'let's look at security procedures. As a first defence I think we should aim for a new series of security checks further up the line . . .' As Julie listened she stole the occasional glance at the stranger. He had a thin face with rather sallow skin and straight black hair which flopped over his forehead in untidy straggles. He was dressed in rough clothes, but she noticed that on one hand he wore a thick gold ring. His eyes were so dark they were almost black and you had the feeling they didn't miss a thing. At one point they flicked up and looked straight into Julie's eyes. She glanced hurriedly away.

'. . . So Marie-Claire, you take the Americans and the British,' Maurice was saying, 'and Roger, you the other nationalities. All right so far?'

Julie nodded.

Roger said, his voice low and soft, 'Those already in hiding? Have they been checked?'

Maurice nodded. 'Pretty well.'

'No so-called Czechs or Poles?'

'No, none. But – there is one odd passenger we've been asked to take. A German by nationality, no less.'

Julie glanced at Roger. He remained impassive. 'A German?'

'Yes, but a reluctant one, apparently. A Jew who's doing forced labour for the Navy in Brest. He wants out with some vital documents.'

Roger said gently, 'What vital documents?'

'Ah, some scientific marvel that would be very valuable. We don't know the details.'

'And he's in a Navy establishment?'

'Yes.'

Roger asked softly, 'Which one?'

He was asking a lot of questions. Perhaps that was his way, Julie thought, perhaps that was how things were done in Paris.

Maurice shrugged. 'We don't know.'

Roger's eyes fell. 'And how is he to be removed?'

'Ah,' sighed Maurice, 'that's to be arranged by some – er, friends.'

Roger nodded very slowly. 'It does sound rather risky. I'd certainly like to interrogate him.'

'Of course. We all want to be certain about him!' Maurice sat forward in his chair. 'Right, let's call it a day. Unless you have any questions . . .?'

Julie looked at Roger. He was shaking his head. She looked back at Maurice and almost spoke – she wanted to confirm the arrangements for her and Peter. But she changed her mind; it didn't seem to be the right moment any more.

Maurice took the identity card from the table. 'Right, Roger. Here's your new identity. If we can bother you for a thumb print . . .?'

Julie watched as Roger rolled his right thumb on the ink pad and placed his print carefully on the card.

Maurice looked at Roger. 'And the photograph?'

'Of course!' He felt in his jacket pocket and brought out a small photograph.

Maurice handed the card and photograph to Julie. She pushed them into her trouser pocket and stood up. Roger sprang to his feet and bowed slightly.

On a whim she said, 'The Meteor thing . . . How did you escape?'

'A friend warned me, just before I walked into the trap.'

'But the others—?'

He looked down, sighed deeply and shook his head. 'Most of them gone . . .' He looked genuinely upset and Julie felt a little guilty for having asked. She said, 'Sorry – I . . .'

His eyes came up suddenly. 'No – please don't worry. That's the price we have to pay sometimes, isn't it? They knew that. They knew the risks. All one can do is learn the lessons.'

She nodded. 'Yes, of course . . .'

The distress had disappeared and now he was smiling slightly. She noticed, though, that his eyes were cold.

She muttered goodbye to Maurice and, turning back to Roger, said, 'I'll have your card ready in an hour.'

He bowed again. 'Thank you, madame.'

Julie went quietly through the house and out into the lane. Her happiness had evaporated. The presence of Roger troubled her, not just because he was a stranger, but because he was something new, and new elements made her nervous.

And there was something else. What? Yes – he frightened her. It was those cold watchful eyes.

A shiver went down her spine and, shoving her hands in her pockets, she walked quickly in the direction of home.

Vasson watched her go and wondered why she had been wary.

It was probably just native suspicion. She was like the rest of them: distrustful of anything from outside. There was nothing more to it than that. After all, she had no reason to be suspicious. No, she was an earnest, well-meaning type, but definitely not too bright.

He turned back to Maurice. 'A good girl, that.'

Maurice nodded. 'Yes, the best.'

Vasson sat down again. He waited for Maurice to speak: it would show the proper subservience.

Maurice said, 'Right. Now, I'll try to get the rest of your new papers by Thursday, but no promises. In the meantime, lie low—'

'But I've still got my own papers – I could use them.'

'No! You've been using them in Paris, haven't you? And you're known there.'

'Well – yes.' He had to admit it: the owner of the papers, a man called Fougères, had indeed used them in Paris before he found his way into Kloffer's dungeon. Kloffer's office had then replaced the identity photographs with Vasson's – and a very professional job they'd made of it, too.

Maurice looked stern. 'Then it would be much too dangerous to use them! No, you stay here until your new papers are ready. If you *were* spotted at the Gare Montparnasse as you suspect, then they might be on to you! No! You must wait!'

Vasson nodded thoughtfully. 'Of course! Whatever you say!' It didn't make any difference: he had three other identities to choose from, any one of which would do perfectly well if he needed to slip away from the village. And the Gare Montparnasse thing was a nonsense, of course: he'd made it up.

'When your papers are fixed, then we'll send you to Morlaix or St Brieuc to interview parcels as soon as they come off the train.'

Morlaix was very convenient: it housed his local contact.

Vasson thought: Now for a little touch of finesse. He said softly, 'What about people *within* the *réseau*? Have they been checked recently?'

'No, but then there's hardly anyone who hasn't been with me from the beginning. Those who do join . . . Well, I check them very carefully.'

That was true enough. At the beginning Maurice had kept Vasson under close watch until his identity had been checked, first with London, who had okayed him straight away – they would, of course: Fougères was a long-standing member of the Meteor line – and then with the contact in Paris, the one who had got him the introduction to the Brittany *réseau*. The contact had, in fact, been under Kloffer's supervision for some two weeks. If Vasson remembered correctly, Kloffer had the man's wife in the basement at the Avenue Foch. Anyway, the man had done what was required and, in front of a witness, sworn to Vasson's identity as Paul Fougères. Vasson rather liked the name: it had an aristocratic ring to it.

Vasson stood up and walked to the window. 'So what can I do until Thursday?'

'Nothing.'

That suited Vasson very well. It would give him the time he needed.

But not if he was cooped up. He said with feeling, 'I'll go mad if I have to stay inside all the time. All right if I stretch my legs in the evenings?'

There was a pause. Maurice said reluctantly, 'If you have to. But stay in the village and keep out of sight of Germans.'

'Certainly. I'll be very careful.' Which was true: he would do his reconnaissance of the village very carefully indeed.

Maurice stood up. 'Right. I'm off now. Any problems, just leave a message at the café.'

They nodded to each other and Maurice left.

For a while Vasson sat quite still, thinking that it was all going quite well. There were, of course, a few minor problems; but then there always were.

He lit a cigarette and drew on it deeply. First, there was the security of the line. Unfortunately it was very good. Maurice had done an excellent job. It would be impossible to slip a bogus American or Britisher through, not with that girl interviewing them. And a Czech or Pole – well, everyone knew that was how Meteor had fallen. It would be tempting fate to try the same trick again. No, a plant really wouldn't do.

So – what could he get on his own? The Bretons were close people, very suspicious of strangers. It would take ten years to get trusted around here. No hope of confidences then. No way of locating the safe houses easily. Nor of identifying more than two of the couriers: Maurice had made sure of that. So what did that leave him with?

Quite a lot, in fact.

He could get the organisers, no trouble there. Maurice, the girl and the people who actually went on beach operations, he could get them all right. And they, after all, were the real plums.

Then the Gestapo would have to do some of their own work for a change. They would have to extract the names of the small fry. It wouldn't do them any harm – he'd been handing them things on a plate for long enough.

It wouldn't be as clean and satisfying as Meteor had been. But what the hell? After this job he would be a very rich man. As long as he delivered most of the goods, what did it matter?

Anyway, he'd go mad if he stayed in this place too long. The silence was deafening, except for the racket of bleating sheep and the bloody wind howling the place down. And the cold! He'd never been so cold in his life. They'd never heard of heating in bedrooms, or bedwarmers. And the food – solid and inedible. It was the end of the bloody earth.

No: he'd just hit them hard and quick and then he'd be off, back to Paris. And Kloffer could threaten him all he wanted: Vasson would *stay* in Paris. This time he was going home.

He got up and went through into the messy, smelly back room he'd been given. It was like a rat-hole: disgusting.

There was a bottle of wine beside the bed. He picked it up and swigged at it. There was no point in going out until dark, but Christ! it seemed a long time away.

He lay and looked at the ceiling. He suddenly realised he'd forgotten something. Ah! Of course. There was the other matter: the scientist. What the hell was he going to do about that?

He could always do nothing, of course. But if the Jew really was important, then it might just be worth his while to organise something . . .

The main problem was to find out exactly who this

fellow might be. It would be no good asking Baum, his Gestapo contact at Morlaix. The fool would probably blow it straight away by going to Brest and asking questions.

No, better to keep Baum out of it. That meant he'd have to handle it himself.

In the meantime there was nothing to do but wait.

He swigged at the wine again, gulping the liquid down in long draughts. It was the only way to drink the stuff: it was rough as hell. Then he lay back on the bed and slept fitfully through the afternoon.

At dusk he got up. He put an old cap on his head, a canvas working man's bag over his shoulder, and some identity papers in his pocket. Then, looking carefully out of the door, he slipped quietly into the night.

The dawn was pale and misty and very cold. Julie stepped into the yard, gulped the fresh, cold air and watched her breath floating away in long clouds, up into the white opalescent sky.

'Maman, are we *really* going in the van?' Peter ran up to her, skipping with excitement.

Julie smiled. 'Yes – well, I hope so! Uncle Jean got it going yesterday and it seems to be working. But we'll see.'

She opened the barn door and climbed into the ancient Peugeot van. Peter hovered next to the passenger door while she turned on the ignition, took out the starting handle and, coming round to the front of the vehicle, swung energetically on the handle. After four attempts, the engine fired a couple of times; at the fifth it started.

Peter squealed with excitement and, flinging open the door, jumped in.

'Got your school things?'

Peter nodded violently. Julie wiped her hands on her overalls, climbed in and slowly eased in the clutch. The van lurched out into the yard. Soon they were off, bumping down the lane and through the village. Julie tried to change into second gear. There was a loud grinding noise. She double de-clutched and tried again. Another rasping and clattering and then the engine settled on to a lower note: they were in second gear.

Julie sighed with relief then looked across at Peter. He was laughing uncontrollably, his little face creased with delight. She exclaimed, 'Well I never promised to be the world's best driver!' And then she was laughing too.

She concentrated on the road. It was a cross-country route to Kernibon, through narrow one-track lanes. Fortunately there was no traffic – few people had petrol nowadays – and it wasn't necessary to stop to let anyone pass. After ten minutes a stretch of misty water came into view: the Morlaix estuary. Julie looked into the distance, across the wide river to the village opposite, the one where she and Peter had landed after that terrible fishing boat journey. It all seemed a long time ago now.

Julie found the right farmhouse and drove into the yard. Eventually the farmer came out and grunted at her. She could see by his expression that he, too, had never seen a woman in trousers before. He waved her up to a shed, then opened the van doors and slid a plank of wood up into the back. He disappeared into the shed and emerged a moment later pulling an angry squealing sow on a length of rope. He pushed and shoved the pig into the van, then closed the doors. He grunted again. Julie smiled because he sounded just like his pig. Or rather, *their* pig, as it was now. Julie politely refused the customary invitation to coffee and, waving goodbye, restarted the van.

Peter said, 'Maman, couldn't we go down to the village for a minute?'

'Goodness, why?'

'I've never been there before!'

Julie stared at him, a little taken aback. Overcome with

remorse, she said, 'Of course, darling! Though we can't be very long, otherwise we'll be late for school.'

Peter nodded happily and they set off down a slight hill, the pig snorting and squealing in the back. The village was nothing much, a few cottages built around a haven formed by a small peninsula which protruded into the estuary. There were half a dozen fishing boats moored in the centre of the inlet. It looked as if some had just come in: men were offloading baskets into small boats floating alongside.

Julie turned the van round and they got out. She said, 'There! Even smaller than Tregasnou!'

'Yes!' Peter exclaimed. He obviously thought smallness a great recommendation. 'Look at the boats! Do they go a long, long way?'

'No, darling. They're not allowed to go far.' She saw that all the boats had sails furled to their masts. With the lack of fuel fishing boats had to rely on the wind again, just as they had done a few years back, before the advent of engines.

Something caught Julie's eye. A figure had emerged from behind a stone barn on the far side of the inlet. She glanced away, then, curious, looked at the figure again. She stiffened: there was something about him that was familiar . . .

The man came nearer, then turned down between two cottages and disappeared. Julie frowned with disappointment.

A moment later he was back again, pushing a *vélo* which he must have collected from the alleyway. Julie frowned. It looked just like Michel.

The man got on the *vélo* and started pedalling towards her. Julie stared, trying to catch a proper sight of his face. After a moment the man looked up into her face, and wobbled.

He had recognised her too.

It *was* him!

But what was he doing here? Julie couldn't understand
it.

He pedalled up to her and dismounted. His face was
serious and unsmiling. He said sharply, 'What are you
doing here?'

'I might ask the same of you.'

He sighed impatiently. 'Come on – what *are* you doing
here?'

'Collecting a pig. I'm a farmhand now, you know!'

He glared at her. 'So I see!'

Peter was looking uneasy. Julie reached down and
pulled him to her. 'We were just going anyway . . .'

She turned and, opening the door of the van, pushed
Peter up into the seat.

'Julie—' He came up and held the door open for her. 'As
a favour to me – don't tell anyone you've seen me here.'

Julie got into the van and turned to look at him. His
face was even more severe than usual and she noticed that
there were deep shadows under his eyes. He looked as
though he hadn't slept for days.

She said, 'All right. If that's what you want. Though—'
She looked away.

'Yes?'

She sighed. 'You're not creating trouble, are you,
Michel?'

He dismissed the idea with a shake of the head. 'I
promise.'

'In that case . . .' She picked up the starting handle and
opened the door to get out again, but he took the handle
from her and, going round to the front of the van, cranked
the engine into life.

When he brought the handle back, she suddenly remembered the scientist. She said, 'By the way, no more news
about the – delivery?'

He shook his head. 'No, nothing new. He'll be with you
shortly, safe and sound.'

She put the van into gear. 'Goodbye then.'

He nodded, his face tight and angry, and turned quickly away.

Peter said, 'Mummy, why was he so cross?'

'What? Oh darling, I don't know. Really.' She smiled brightly. 'Come on, let's get you off to school!'

But all the way there, Julie kept thinking: He's up to something, I know he is! Oh Michel, what on earth is it now?

Chapter 24

IT WAS QUITE a farewell. Most of the senior staff had assembled. Geissler was there, of course, and Gallois.

Geissler held out his hand. 'So, Herr Freymann, I'm sorry we are to lose you after all, but I am sure that you will enjoy your new position. A great honour, a great honour!' On this occasion Geissler had not thought of questioning the order: it had come from the High Command itself, marked 'Most Urgent', and he was impressed. He smiled at David. 'I expect you will be most happy to see Berlin again.'

'Yes. Yes.'

Geissler inclined his head slightly in the German style. 'Are you sure, Herr Freymann, that you prefer to walk to your quarters?'

'Yes, thank you.' David nodded, then smiled in the general direction of the factory personnel. But he couldn't bring himself to look at Gallois in case guilt and conspiracy should show all over his face. He felt sick.

He turned and, grasping his briefcase tightly under his arm, walked slowly down the steps. The guard acknowledged him with a slight blink then glanced away.

David stepped on to the pavement and, his heart hammering in his ears, began the short walk down the road to the compound.

It would be any minute now. A car, probably; sweeping round the corner, opening its door, pulling him in, roaring off ... David imagined the guard watching curiously, trying to work out what the car was doing, slowly realising, pulling the rifle up to his shoulder, firing at David while he was still inches from the safety of the car . . .

He felt his back itching and shivered. The urge to look round was almost compulsive. He resisted and kept walking, slowly, to give them time.

He came to the access road that led down the side of the factory. He paused at the kerb, looked to left and right, stepped down and crossed the road.

Now, surely! He reached the opposite pavement and went even slower. But it was difficult walking slowly. He swayed and almost lost his balance. His legs were still weak.

The compound gates were getting closer now, the guards almost visible. David began to worry: it would be very risky to leave it any longer.

He paused and leant against the wire fence, as if he were resting. He listened carefully, but the road behind him was silent: no engine noises, no cars. Nothing stirred.

They weren't coming.

He moved away from the fence and began walking again. Almost immediately the guard post came into sight. The uniformed figures stared at him, their faces uninterested and bored. He turned in through the gates and walked past them, as he had a hundred times.

They hadn't come.

David went automatically towards the hut, opened the door and walked up the corridor to his cubicle at the end. He sat on the bed and stared at the wall, the briefcase still tucked under his arm.

The message had said they would come for him. He tried very hard to think how they would do it. Perhaps they'd come later. But *how*? Getting him out of here would be impossible.

Perhaps never, then. In which case he'd been deceived.

He thought: I'm no good at this sort of thing. I don't understand.

He wasn't due to leave for Berlin until early morning, at seven. He'd wait until then, ready dressed, just in case. In the meantime he was tired; the walk, like any physical exertion nowadays, had tired him out. He lay down.

After a while he sat up and, opening his briefcase, took out a sandwich of bread and cheese which he'd kept specially for the journey. He ate it slowly, chewing each mouthful several times. He closed the briefcase carefully, lay down again, and dozed.

Much later he woke suddenly and pulled himself up. He guessed it was late, probably about one or two in the morning. Something had woken him. A sound. He got unsteadily to his feet and went to the window. There was a moon and the outlines of the buildings were just visible in the pale light. Nothing moved.

He was turning to go back to bed when he felt the floor shudder. He put his hand up to the wall to steady himself. A flash of light flickered against the walls of the cubicle. He turned back to the window, confused.

A low rumble sounded from far away, the window shook, another flash of light illuminated the night sky.

An air raid. They were common enough. Only this time the Germans hadn't had time to sound the siren.

There was another flash, much closer this time. Then orange and yellow lights flickered against the buildings: an incendiary. David frowned: there was something strange about all this. What was it? Yes – he'd heard no planes. Usually you could hear the drone of the bombers as they passed overhead. There were no searchlights either.

A siren sounded. It was from close by. Inside the hut there was a deafening noise of banging doors and running feet and shouting men. A moment later the guards streamed out of the hut, running in the direction of the flickering lights.

David opened the window and stuck his head out. There was another sound now, a drumming, as if people were beating sticks against a wall. Angry people. And there were voices, too, a thousand voices shouting and yelling while they beat the sticks against the walls.

It was the workers, the Poles. They were trying to break out.

David shook his head and cried, 'Oh no! Oh no!' and beat his fist against the wall. What *were* they trying to achieve? What did they hope to gain? It would mean death for many of them; death. In despair he murmured again, 'No! No!'

He froze. Something caught his eye: a movement away to the right, in the shadow of one of the buildings. A figure, running stealthily in a crouched position.

David pulled his head back inside the window and watched, motionless. The figure paused in the darkness of the nearest building, then ran again. He was coming straight for David. David felt a stab of fear and pulled himself back into the room.

The figure disappeared beneath his line of sight. Then, after a few seconds, a hand suddenly appeared over the sill. A head followed. David pressed himself against the wall.

A voice. 'Freymann?'

David stared at the silhouette of the head and whispered, 'Yes.'

'Quick! Climb out and follow me! *Quick!*'

David fumbled for his briefcase and, tucking it under his arm, approached the window. He said breathlessly, 'Are you – from . . .?'

'Shut up. No time for that. Come *now!*'

David looked at the height of the sill and said, 'I can't.'

The figure hissed, 'You *must!*'

David nodded and pushed the briefcase through the window. It disappeared rapidly. He got his left foot up onto the sill and pushed his leg out. It was impossible to get a second leg up: the frame was too narrow. He pulled his body up onto the sill and felt the window-catch dig into his thigh. He levered himself safely to one side of it and, sitting astride the sill, rested for a moment, breathing heavily.

'Come on!' The dark figure was pulling at his sleeve.

'All right! All right! I'm doing my best!' David looked down: it was a long drop, a man's height at least, and he only had one leg to land on. 'You'll have to catch me, otherwise I'll fall.' The figure seemed to nod and David levered himself out until he was hanging from the window, his right leg still over the sill. He tried to pull the leg out, but some of his weight was on it and it wouldn't come.

'Have you got me?'

'*Yes! Yes!*'

Only one thing to do, then. Let go.

He felt himself falling, body first, his left foot nowhere near the ground. A hand clutched at his arm and twisted him round. His right foot met the ground, followed shortly by his shoulder and his hip. He felt his head shoot back to hit the concrete.

He staggered to his feet, shaking slightly, and brushed himself down.

The man had hold of his arm and David found himself being pulled along behind. The man stopped at the end of the building and David bumped into him. Then the man was off again, running faster, his hand still grasping David's sleeve.

David ran as best he could, but he was already breathing hard. His legs felt like rubber and wouldn't do what was required of them. For some reason he couldn't swing his right arm either.

They approached the perimeter fence at the eastern side of the compound. With alarm David wondered why they were going that way. There was no way out here.

Normally the fence was brilliantly lit, but now it was in darkness. They stopped at the side of a small shed and waited. The man was listening, as tense as a cat. David put his head against the wall and tried to regain his breath.

Suddenly they were off again. The fence loomed up in front of them. The man looked up and down the length of the fence, pulled David a short way to the right, then dropped to his hands and knees. David saw that there was a gaping hole in the wire. The man hissed 'Down!' and David got on to his knees.

The man threw the briefcase through then put a hand behind David and pushed. David crawled through. The man came quickly after, picked up David's case and pulled him to his feet. He grabbed David's sleeve again and then they were running across open ground to the dark wall of a warehouse. They stopped, David gasped for breath.

Another pull. David said, 'Please! Please! Not so fast. I can't go so fast!' The man slowed down a little. They skirted three more buildings and came to another fence. This time there was no hole. David eyed it apprehensively. But then they reached a gate and the gate was open and they were through into a road.

A lorry was parked in the road. The man took David round to the tailgate. It was closed. David breathed, 'I can't . . . I can't . . .'

The man reached down and, grasping David's foot, heaved. David sprawled over the tailgate, unable to pull himself up. The man pushed again and David landed head first in the lorry's load, which smelt strongly of cabbage.

'Hide yourself!'

David panted, 'What?'

'Hide yourself under the vegetables!'

'. . . under?'

There was a thud as something landed beside David in the cabbages. 'Your case. Goodbye.'

There was silence. David took hold of the briefcase and

crawled slowly over the vegetables to the far end of the lorry. How did one bury oneself in a load of cabbages? Painstakingly he began to remove the cabbages one by one until he had made a hollow in them, then he lay down, his case at his side, and pulled the vegetables back over himself.

It wasn't difficult to lie still – at that moment it was all he'd ever wanted.

Five minutes passed and the lorry hadn't moved. He wished they would hurry. He could hear the sounds of activity in the compound and the docks: trucks roaring back and forth, the distant sound of shouting and the occasional report of a rifle shot. It must be the Poles they were shooting at.

But why wasn't the lorry moving? Come on! Come on! If they didn't get going soon, they'd never get away!

But the lorry didn't move. After half an hour David realised it wasn't going to. Not for a long time. Perhaps not until daylight. He wished they'd told him.

Eventually he fell into an uneasy sleep, waking frequently. Finally he saw a tinge of grey light through the gaps in the cabbages above his head. He drifted off again.

Suddenly there was a loud crash from immediately behind David's head. He jumped, his heart racing. Someone started whistling and the next moment there was a loud whirring and the lorry's engine burst into life.

The whistler broke into song. 'I'm dreaming of you, my love, wherever you may be . . .'

The lorry stopped and started a few times. Once David heard the driver talking to someone, but then they were on their way again. The singer began to whistle once more, but softly, and the drone of the wheels fell to a steady hum.

*

There was silence. David realised that the lorry had stopped and the engine had been turned off. He waited, tense.

The driver was whistling loudly. The cab door slammed and footsteps came round to the back of the vehicle. The tailgate was lowered with a loud bang.

There was a moment's silence, then a voice called, 'Hello, friend. We've arrived.'

David wasn't sure what to do. He stayed still.

But the voice came again. 'You're safe, friend. Time to get out.'

David pushed the cabbages away from his face and tried to move, but he was very stiff. He reached up and, gripping the metal side of the lorry, hauled himself up into a sitting position. He blinked and, looking out, saw that the lorry was backed up against the doors of a wooden building. A man of about forty dressed in an old cap and working jacket was standing by the tailgate.

On seeing David, the man climbed up into the lorry and walked over the vegetables towards him. 'Here. I'll give you a hand.'

'Thank you. That's most kind.'

The man pulled David to his feet, picked up the briefcase, and helped him across the uneven surface of the cabbages to the open tailgate and down on to the ground.

David now saw that the building was a barn. The man led him quickly inside and into a corner behind a pile of sacks. 'Here! You're to wait here.'

'Thank you.' David looked around. The floor at this point was thick with straw and, gratefully, he sank down on to it.

The man had turned to leave.

David called, 'Wait! Please – tell me, what was the fire last night?'

The man paused and looked uncertain. Eventually he said, 'One of the fuel dumps.'

'But the Poles. Why did they try to break out?'

'They didn't.'

David looked blank. 'But the noise?'

'Noise. That's all it was.'

'But – why?'

'Because they were asked to. It was a favour.' The man turned again. 'Best not to know any more, friend.'

The barn door closed, the lorry's engine started up and slowly faded away. Then there was silence. David lay down on the straw. He tried to sleep, but it was impossible, so he lay still and rested instead.

Much later there was a sound. David opened his eyes. It was a creaking. A door opening. Someone was coming into the barn. He pushed himself up on one arm, but he couldn't see: his view of the door was obscured by the pile of sacks.

The person was advancing slowly up the barn: David could feel the movement rather than hear it. Finally, very slowly, the person came into view.

David's heart went to his mouth. It was a man. He was wearing a scarf over the lower part of his face. The man said gruffly, 'Turn around.' David turned and, almost immediately, something was placed round his eyes and tied behind his head.

The voice said, 'Don't move unless I tell you.' There was a rustling of straw as the man moved away, then silence.

The darkness was awful, like being in a pit. David tried to relax. They meant him no harm.

A long time passed. David's stomach began to ache with hunger.

Then there were low voices and footsteps. Someone walked up to him. The straw rustled as the person sat or knelt beside him.

'Hello.' It was the voice of a woman, rather breathless.

David cleared his throat. 'Good morning.'

'Are you all right?' The voice was warm, concerned.

He nodded. 'Oh yes! Yes! Very well, thank you. Yes, very well!'

'Good. We – er – heard you had been ill.'

'Ah. Yes, I was. But better now, thank you.'

There was a pause. 'Some others will be coming soon. To meet you. We have to ask you some questions.'

'Questions?'

'Yes . . . It's necessary. I'm sorry.'

David was disappointed. Questions? It sounded as if they were going to interrogate him. It had never occurred to him that they wouldn't trust him. He said half-heartedly, 'Yes. Of course.'

There was the sound of paper crackling. 'Here, I thought you might be hungry.'

'I am, thank you.' Something was placed in his hand. 'Thank you.' It was a roll. He bit into it. Cheese. He took another bite.

Julie watched him eat and felt sorry for him. He seemed so lost and bewildered. She'd be very surprised indeed if he were a German spy – he looked far too harmless for that. Certainly he was too frail to take anyone on; he wouldn't be able to hurt a fly. The hands were thin and veined and she noticed that when he brought the bread to his mouth they shook slightly. The face beneath the blindfold was lined and pouchy, rather like a dog's. She could see that he had been ill. Also, he was much older than she'd expected.

It was a pity to have to put him through an interrogation but there was no way round it. Maurice would allow no exceptions.

She peered at her wristwatch. The others were late. But she must wait. It would be wrong to start the questions without them.

Finally, there was a creaking. The barn door opened

and two people slipped in. One was the unmistakable squat figure of Maurice, the other the taller, slimmer frame of Roger.

Maurice came up and looked questioningly at Julie. She nodded slightly to show all was well and, satisfied, Maurice turned to look at the old man sitting on the bed of straw. Julie glanced at Roger. He was approaching slowly, his eyes fixed on the corner of the sack pile. Suddenly he stopped in mid-step and Julie guessed he had caught his first sight of the old man. For a moment he stared, then he relaxed and leant casually against a wooden pillar.

His eyes darted up to Julie's. She looked hurriedly away. He was always catching her out that way.

Maurice was sitting on the straw, talking to the old man in a low voice. Julie went closer and sat down beside him. '. . . interrogation is necessary for our self-protection, do you understand?' The old man nodded briefly.

Maurice continued, 'Right, please tell us everything. First, your name and background.'

'Freymann, David Freymann. I lived most of my life just outside Berlin, in a suburb called Hennigsdorf . . .' Out of the corner of her eye Julie saw Roger come closer and crouch silently on the straw just behind Maurice.

'. . . mainly I worked on radio-wave development. Then just before the war started, it all got difficult. Because I was Jewish, you see. I was put in a camp . . .'

'Where?' Maurice interrupted.

'Near Munich. Called Dachau. I was there some time – two, maybe three years, I don't know. Time – is difficult to judge.' He spoke matter-of-factly.

'Then?'

'Then they sent me to Brest.'

'Why?'

'They needed me. There are very few scientists who are experienced in radar. They had to swallow their pride.'

Roger said, 'Explain, please. What is radar?'

The old man sighed deeply. 'I'll try to explain simply. It's ... a way of using radio waves so that you can see with them. At night, in bad weather ... it doesn't matter. You can see the echo of any large metallic object – a ship, an aeroplane, whatever ... You can discover its range, and in the case of a plane its height. Nothing can hide from you ...'

Maurice asked, 'And this is the information you're bringing with you?'

Freymann quickly shook his head. 'No, radar is already known. No ...' He paused, as if debating something. His hands moved nervously. Finally he said, 'No ... what I'm bringing is a refinement of it. A type which can see like a map, draw pictures almost. It will – create a great advantage.'

Maurice frowned. 'In what way?'

'For one thing, the Germans could not detect it as they do the existing radar. So they would have no warning of the enemy's approach. For another, well – it will, I believe, provide enormous detail so that for the bombers it will be like having a map of the country underneath.' He cocked his head slightly. 'Do you understand what I say?'

'Yes, I think so.'

Suddenly Freymann sat forward and felt for Maurice's arm. Maurice looked surprised. The old man said, 'Look, you cannot possibly know that what I'm telling you is the truth, can you?'

Julie looked quickly at Maurice. He dropped his eyes and smiled slightly. 'No, you're quite right. I can't.'

'Right. But you believe I am Jewish?'

'Well – yes.'

'Right. So I'm Jewish. Now what do you suppose would make a Jew want to help the Nazis?'

'Force? Coercion?'

'Yes. But I'm a free man now. That leaves coercion. But

I have no family for them to threaten me with. My family disowned me a long time ago!'

'I can't be sure of that.'

Freymann started in surprise. 'Ah...!' He paused, taken aback, then nodded gently. 'Of course.' He seemed so downcast that Julie had the urge to lean forward and pat his shoulder.

'So – then, it is a simple question of whether you believe me or not.' He spoke quietly and with resignation. Julie wanted to say, I believe you.

Maurice looked at Julie then Roger. 'Any questions?'

Julie said, 'When you talk of your family, who do you mean?'

'My wife. My daughter.'

'And they've disowned you?'

'Yes. My wife was not Jewish, you see.'

'But your daughter?'

'She'll have forgotten me by now – and the best thing too!' His voice almost broke. 'She was pretty, you see. And clever. She had everything before her. It was *better*, you understand. *Better*.'

Roger leant forward and said sharply, 'What company did you work for in Brest?'

'Goulvent, Pescart et Cie.'

'Under what authority – what German authority?'

'The Navy. But I was on loan, so to speak, from the SS.'

'And when you were working in Germany, what company then?'

'Gema. The Gema Company.'

There was a short silence, then Maurice got to his feet. Julie and Roger followed him across the barn until they were out of earshot.

Maurice looked at Julie. 'Well?'

Julie said, 'I believe him. Everything about him seems – right.'

They both looked at Roger. He was glancing down, his eyes hooded and unreadable. Slowly, the eyes came up to Maurice's. 'Yes, he's genuine.'

Maurice nodded. 'I agree.'

Roger said, 'So he goes, does he?'

'Yes.'

'When?'

Maurice looked hard at Roger. 'Soon. The fewer who know the exact date the better. You'll be told in good time.'

Roger smiled. 'Of course.' But he was put out, Julie could tell.

Julie touched Maurice's arm. 'Can't we take the blind-fold off? At least until we have to move him again.'

Maurice rubbed his lip thoughtfully.

Roger interrupted, 'No! It'll be much safer to leave him as he is!'

Julie gave Roger a hard look and said quickly to Maurice, 'Please. He's absolutely harmless. I'd stake my life on it. *Please.*'

Maurice smiled slightly. 'All right.'

Julie ran back. The old man shrank away at the sound of her steps. 'It's all right,' she said soothingly. 'I've come to take your blindfold off.'

'Thank you. How kind.' She leant over and untied the handkerchief from round his head. The old man blinked and put his hand up to his eyes. Then he smiled up at her. He had large, dark, sad eyes; again Julie was reminded of a rather mournful dog.

She smiled back at him. 'I'll bring you more food later. The guard has water when you want it.'

'Thank you. You really are very kind.'

Julie touched his hand quickly then went back to the others waiting by the door. Maurice exchanged smiles with her. Roger avoided her stare and put his face to the gap in the door.

'All clear?' Maurice asked.

Roger nodded and, opening the door, led the way out. As Julie stepped out into the daylight she looked up and found Roger staring at her. She almost gasped: there was rage and hatred in his eyes. For a moment she was bewildered. Why? The blindfold? Such a small incident – but what else could it be? She looked desperately at Maurice, but he had seen nothing.

God, Julie thought, the man's terrifying – and no-one knows it but me.

Vasson made himself smile to conceal his irritation.

The girl had outdone him, and he didn't like it.

It was time to get away. He said, 'I'll go now. Across the fields.'

Maurice looked up sharply. 'But do you know the way?'

'Oh, I'll find it, don't worry. Anyway, it's about time I found my way around. In case of trouble.'

'Careful not to speak to anyone.'

Vasson almost sighed with annoyance: Maurice must have told him a dozen times. 'Don't worry! I won't.'

'It's the accent. They'd know you were an outsider straight away.'

'But then they wouldn't tell, would they? Being good Bretons . . .' Before Maurice could answer, Vasson turned and walked briskly away.

He went round the barn, over a wall and into a field. He spotted a gate on the far side and began to make his way across the field towards it. Almost immediately he regretted it: the field had just been ploughed. He pressed on, cursing under his breath as his feet slipped and stumbled over the hard, bumpy ground.

Finally he reached the gate, went through, and paused. He looked over his shoulder: nothing. The others were going back by the road. He looked ahead: nothing either.

Away to the right he could hear the faint sound of surf and calling gulls: the sea.

He went on, across four smaller fields until the village came into view over a slight hill. There was a farmhouse immediately ahead and, he realised, a road beside it. He would have to cross the road then, to skirt the farmhouse and the village and reach the main Morlaix road.

He approached the wall which hid the road, peered over it and, climbing carefully up the rough stonework, jumped down. He crossed the road and prepared to climb the opposite wall. He stopped: there was someone walking down the road towards the village.

It was the girl.

She had seen him. He leant against the wall and waited. She approached, walking fast, her eyes down. When she was almost level with him she moved to the opposite side of the road. Then she was past, swinging on down the hill. He watched her for a moment. The trousers were ridiculous, he decided. They revealed and accentuated the movement of her bottom. She probably wore them on purpose. Bitch.

He shinned up the wall and dropped neatly over on to the other side. It was a pasture this time, with a few sheep pulling at the scant grass. The solitary farmhouse was nearby. He decided to skirt the buildings close, rather than risk being seen wandering across the fields.

He came up behind the barn and moved along until he could peer round the corner. There was a yard and, on the opposite side, the farmhouse itself. There were some iron railings with a gate which separated the yard from the pasture. He would have to walk along the railings in view of the farmhouse. He waited a moment, just to make sure that everything was quiet. Then, just as he was about to set off, he stopped.

Someone had entered the yard from the other end. It

was the girl again. She was walking slowly towards the farmhouse. She was looking around cautiously.

He ducked back behind the wall and wondered if she was looking for him.

He peered out again. She was at the back door of the farmhouse, pushing up the latch. She paused again and looked around.

He pulled back before she saw him.

There was the sound of voices. Hers, and a high-pitched voice: a child's. He put his eye back to the corner.

A small boy was jumping up and down beside the girl. She reached down and took his hand and, with one last look over her shoulder, pulled the child inside.

At last Vasson understood. The girl lived here!

She hadn't wanted him to know. He smiled to himself. It could be rather useful.

He looked at his watch: only fifteen minutes to go. There wasn't time to make the enormous detour which would keep him out of sight of the farmhouse.

He sauntered out from behind the wall and walked casually along the railings. He was being watched, he felt sure.

He walked past the house and then straight down the next field to a stile in the corner. He climbed over it and glanced back. He was out of sight of the farmhouse.

He went diagonally across the next field and the next so that he was skirting the village. Finally he reached the main Morlaix road and, after checking that it was empty, walked along it until he came to a small crossroads. Then he settled down to wait.

After half an hour he was still waiting. He wasn't surprised: everything in this bloody godforsaken place was always late.

Finally, the small battered bus came into view, its engine roaring. Vasson waved it down and jumped on board.

He settled himself in a seat and decided that the day might not turn out so badly after all: there was still time to get a decent lunch off Baum. There was only one thing still bothering him: the girl. She was suspicious of him. And he didn't like that, he didn't like it at all.

'Mummy, what are you staring at?'

Julie reached down and stroked Peter's head. 'Nothing, darling.' She moved away from the window and, going to the sink, started to peel some potatoes for the midday meal.

Jean came in through the parlour door and looked at Julie. 'I thought I just saw someone in the back pasture.'

Julie kept her eyes down. 'Oh?'

Jean reached onto the mantelpiece for his tobacco, then remembered he didn't have any. 'Yes, I'm sure I did. But . . . Probably just one of the lads. Eh?'

'Probably.'

It had been Roger; she had seen him.

He had been prowling around; he reminded her of a cat. She shuddered and thought: I don't like it any more. The sooner Peter and I are away the better. It wouldn't be long now. The moon was on the wane: the boat would come soon.

There was a rapping on the back door. Julie jumped and looked at her uncle. Jean shrugged and went to open it.

There was a short exclamation, then Michel strode into the room. His face was like thunder.

Julie gasped, 'What's the matter?'

Michel said bitterly, '*You* should be able to tell *me*!'

Julie pulled Peter up from the table. 'Go to your room.' The boy left, closing the door quietly behind him. Julie sat down. 'Now! Explain, please!'

Michel breathed in, then, pulling up a chair, began talking slowly, as if speaking to a disobedient child. 'Last

night, in Brest . . . The Germans were expecting us. At the
fuel dumps. Three of my comrades died. Three! We were
only able to fire one of the main tanks. The whole thing
was a fiasco—'

'Wait!' Julie said sharply. 'These fuel dumps, what have
they to do with us?'

'It was a diversion, of course!'

Julie was amazed. 'For the scientist? You did it
especially for *him*?'

Michel dismissed the question with an arm movement.
'Yes . . . No. Well, we were planning it anyway. But the
point is, they were waiting for us! *They were waiting for
us!* How did they know, Julie, *how*? My friends are asking
questions! They—'

Julie stood up. 'I think it would be better if you didn't
go on. To start with, nobody here ever knew *when* the
operation was to be—'

'But I told you!'

'You said only that it would be the end of the week.
Also we had no idea you were planning a diversion of that
kind. And, Michel, the old scientist *did* get away. If they'd
been warned, then they would hardly have let him escape!'

Michel stood up, his face hard and cruel, and hissed,
'But my comrades are *saying* this! They are saying, why is
it that the first time we work with your lot, we get sold
down the river! They are saying, we knew we should never
trust that lot and look what happens! They are saying ugly
things. They are talking of revenge. What am I to say to
them?'

Julie felt the anger rising in her throat. She walked up
to Michel until her face was close to his. 'You will tell
them this! That they should look for a shark in their own
ranks. Or bad planning! Or – something! Just don't look
to us for a scapegoat! Because it was not one of *us*!'

Jean tapped Michel firmly on the arm with his pipe.
'Perhaps some of your own people used the opportunity,

eh! Perhaps they wanted to get rid of some of their precious comrades, heh? And they wanted you to blame us!'

There was a silence. Michel looked unhappily from one to the other. Eventually he exclaimed, 'All right! I'll do my best to convince them! I just hope that—' He shook his head in frustration. '– that what you say is true! But, for God's sake, don't blame me if—'

Julie said coolly, 'If what?'

'If – emotions run high!'

She said, 'I think they already have!' She went to the back door and opened it wide. 'Goodbye, Michel. Please don't ever come here again.'

When he had gone she sat stunned, and thought: It's all falling apart again, just like before.

The pâté was very good but the steak was not as tender as it might have been. Vasson decided to leave the rest and, pushing the plate to one side, leant back in his chair.

Baum smiled across the desk. 'Better?'

'Much.'

'I'll send across for some of their *tarte maison*, if you like. It is really delicious.'

'Yes. And some decent cheese.'

'Of course!' Baum pressed the buzzer on his desk. Vasson noticed that he crooked his little finger as he did it. The man was probably a queer. Vasson wondered how he got his thrills.

Baum smiled again, his thick lips drawing back to reveal rather yellowing teeth. Vasson decided he would prefer to deal with Kloffer any day. Baum tapped the telephone and sighed. 'The Navy – not very efficient, you know. You would think they would have come back to us by now. When did we call? Yes, half an hour ago at least!' He picked up the piece of paper he'd written his notes on and peered at it. 'This – er – Freymann, he's a Jew, I suppose?'

Vasson nodded.

'Then I doubt he'll be of much consequence. Nevertheless—' He placed his fingers together in a neat arch. 'Nevertheless, it will be rather satisfying to sweep him up into our little net, won't it? Then we can deliver him back from whence he came. Yes?' He smiled sweetly across the table. A raving poof, Vasson decided.

Baum tapped his fingertips together impatiently. 'Now, now! Where *is* Schultz? You must have your dessert! *And* your cheese!' He leaned forward and pressed the button again. Vasson heard a buzzer sound in the office next door.

The door burst open. A young man, presumably Schultz, stood at the door. He looked as if he'd just seen a ghost. 'Herr Oberst! The telephone, it's Paris! General Oberg!'

For a moment Baum froze, then, swallowing hard, he reached for the telephone as if it were glass. He lifted the receiver carefully to his ear and said precisely, 'Ja? Ah, Herr General!'

In the next few moments Baum seemed to say 'Ja' rather a lot. Then the German jerked his head and looked hard at Vasson, a look of amazement on his face.

Vasson tensed. It was something big. Concerning him. And Freymann. It must be Freymann!

There was a torrent of German from Baum and then he was replacing the receiver carefully in its holder.

Baum stared at Vasson for a moment, his lips quivering nervously. Finally he said, 'That was General Oberg. The head of the *entire* Gestapo in France.' He paused, as if to assimilate the information, then continued, 'It appears that this man – Freymann – is important to us. In fact, more than that! Vital!'

Vasson smiled slightly.

Baum leant forward, his pale eyes round with anxiety. 'We *must* get him back, do you understand? We must not fail! It is absolutely essential!'

Vasson looked away, already calculating how he could take all the credit.

He regarded Baum for a moment and said casually, 'Nothing is ever guaranteed.'

Baum nearly went purple. 'What do you mean by that! I thought you *had* the man!'

'Oh, I do! I do! But, when I am relying on your men to close the trap, then nothing can ever be guaranteed.' Vasson stood up. 'Now, it's about time we made a plan, isn't it?'

Baum nodded violently. 'Yes! Yes! Whatever you say!'

Part Four

———◆———

March 1943

Chapter 25

JULIE EMBRACED TANTE Marie very hard and said, 'Thank you again. For everything.'

Tante Marie sniffed and, flapping her hand with irritation, said harshly, 'Go on! Be off with you! Go on!'

Julie kissed the old woman quickly on the cheek, then, taking Peter's hand, followed Jean's dark figure out of the kitchen and across the yard. She leant down and whispered to Peter, 'All right, darling?'

'Yes, Mummy, I'm fine.'

Julie squeezed his hand and felt very proud of him. For the past few weeks she had been telling him the same story she told everyone else: that they were moving to Rennes. It was only the previous night, when she'd heard the boat was coming, that she had told Peter the truth. Bless him, he'd taken it like a lamb. He even pretended to be looking forward to it, though she could see he was very nervous.

She hitched the strap of the haversack further up her shoulder. It was light enough: she'd taken almost nothing. Peter had his own bag, too, with spare clothes, a food parcel from Tante Marie and some of his favourite things: a toy lorry, his coloured pencils and, of course, the carved ship.

They started briskly up the road. A faint drizzle was drifting down and a film of dampness formed on Julie's face. She pulled her beret further over her forehead and put a hand down to Peter's head. He had already raised the hood of his jacket. Julie had chosen practical clothes for both of them: warm trousers and windcheater jacket for him, and trousers and a cowjacket for herself.

As they climbed the long hill the dampness turned to a steady drizzle. The faint patter of the falling rain sounded a gentle rhythm in the stillness of the night. Julie had sudden doubts about Peter's jacket; perhaps it wouldn't be up to all this rain. She would check it later. She touched him again and almost smiled. He was doing well, her son, striding along as fast as his legs would carry him.

They reached the heathland and turned right, up a slight hill. After a while the outlines of a small building came into view. It was a shepherd's hut, made of stone with a slate roof, caved in at the far end. Jean crouched and entered. Tightly clutching Peter's hand, Julie followed.

It was dark inside, but Julie could hear the sounds of the waiting people: slight rustlings and the occasional muffled cough. She felt her way to the side of the hut and sat down in a space, pulling Peter down beside her. She put her arm round the small shoulders and hugged him. 'Won't be long now.' His hand felt for hers and grasped it tightly.

Julie moved her leg and bumped it against someone else's. 'Sorry.'

'No, no. My fault. So sorry.'

The voice was familiar. Julie leant across and whispered, 'Herr Freymann?'

'Yes.'

'It's me, from the barn. Are you all right? Have you been looked after?'

'Oh yes, yes. Thank you, thank you. *Most* kind.'

Julie smiled and thought what a nice man he was. She wondered vaguely how he'd manage the path to the beach.

Peter coughed slightly. She turned back and, squeezing him against her, settled down to wait. Her stomach was fluttering uneasily, but she forced herself to be calm.

Whatever happened, she wasn't going to let herself think about all the things that could go wrong tonight.

She pressed her lips against Peter's hair and closed her eyes tightly and tried to imagine what life would be like in England after such a long time.

There was nowhere to shelter on the clifftop. Vasson was getting wet and he didn't like it. He pulled up the collar of his jacket and crouched down on his haunches.

The night was quiet: the only sound was the murmur of the sea far below and the steady splatter of the falling rain. It wasn't ideal for stalking – the air was too still – but it was good enough.

He took a look round. No sign of Baum. Thank God for that. The fool might not muck it up after all. Vasson worked out how long it would be before he could slip away and get to Baum's position. Half an hour maybe. After the passengers had gone down to the beach. Then he could sit on Baum – physically if necessary – until the right moment.

As always, it was a matter of timing.

He shivered and took another look round. What a good lookout he had become! Maurice *would* be impressed.

Clifftop lookout was his important new job. A promotion, no less. This was the first time Maurice had trusted him with beach duty. It was most ironic.

But the rain was a sod. Vasson cursed: the water was soaking right through his clothes to his skin. And bloody cold it was too.

Another look: still no sign of Baum. The man might stick to the plan yet.

He tried to guess what time it was. Eleven maybe. Not long before the first party would arrive.

Peering down into the darkness of the cove below, he

thought what a very neat trap it made, and allowed himself a smile.

Someone came into the hut and said in accented English, 'First group now.'

A voice said, 'Hooray!' Someone laughed nervously.

There was the sound of people moving and then the silhouette of figures against the doorway.

The old man grasped Julie's arm. 'Is that us?'

'No. We go last, on our own.'

A few minutes later the second group moved out. Then the voice of Gérard, the fisherman, was saying, 'Ready?' Julie stood up and helped Peter to his feet. She leant down and said in Peter's ear, 'Do you want to do a wee, darling, before we go?'

'No. I'm all right, thank you.' The small, high-pitched voice sounded so faint and uncertain that Julie reached down to give him one last hug. Then it was time to go.

Gérard led the old man out and Julie followed, grasping Peter's hand tightly. It was raining more heavily now, coming in a steady downpour that seeped down one's neck and through one's clothes.

Jean was waiting. It was time to say goodbye. Julie said nothing, but flung her arms round his neck and hugged him. Jean patted her back, then pushing her gently away, reached down and took Peter up in his arms. 'Take care, young man,' he whispered. Then, putting Peter down, he turned abruptly away and disappeared in the direction of the village.

Julie wiped her eyes and, taking Peter's hand, hurried off in the direction of the path. When they reached the clifftop Gérard was stepping on to the path, turning with an outstretched hand to help the old man down. As Julie waited, a dark shape caught her eye. It was a man. He was crouching a few feet away. The clifftop lookout.

As she watched him he uncurled and came towards her. He towered over her, his face a featureless blur. 'Is that the last?'

She recognised the voice: the man Roger. 'Yes.'

He turned and seemed to see Peter for the first time. Julie began to move towards the path, but Roger stepped in front of her and said, 'Why's he here?'

'He's coming with me.'

'But why?'

'We're going, both of us.'

'On the boat?'

'Yes. Now – please – let us pass.'

There was a pause, then a slight chuckle. 'Of course.' Roger put out his hand and touched Peter's cheek.

Julie pulled Peter close in behind her, stepped round Roger and began to negotiate the path.

The rain had turned the path to mud. Julie went slowly because she didn't want Peter to slip and frighten himself, and because it was impossible to overtake Gérard and the scientist anyway. She could hear Gérard coaxing the old man past rocks and down the steeper slopes. The old man must be wondering what he'd let himself in for.

Julie slipped, grabbed for a handhold and missed. She landed on her hip. She breathed, 'Damn!' Peter's voice said anxiously, 'You all right, Mummy?'

She pulled herself up and, trembling a little, laughed nervously. 'Yes, darling. I'm fine. Are you all right?'

'Yes.'

Julie felt her way forward again, even more slowly, until at long last she realised they were near the beach. She heard Gérard saying, 'Just let go' and saw the old man poised on the top of the slide. Suddenly he was off and she saw him disappear towards the paleness of the beach.

She sat down and waited for Peter to sit down beside

her. She whispered, 'It's the slide I told you about. We'll
go together, shall we?' He nodded violently and, holding
his hand, Julie pushed off. They shot down and landed
safely on the shingle. With relief Julie realised it was the
last time she would ever have to negotiate that path.

The other two were waiting for them. Julie picked
herself up and wiped the worst of the mud off the back
of Peter's jacket and trousers. Gérard moved off, with
Freymann following. Julie looked at the thin, stooped
figure of the scientist in his inadequate clothes, and then at
Peter, his small figure huddled against the relentless rain,
and thought: This is ridiculous. She moved forward to
catch Gérard's arm. 'What's the earliest the boat will
come?'

Gérard thought for a moment. 'Half an hour, I suppose.'

'Look, it's so wet and miserable, I'll take these two into
the rocks over there.' She indicated the far side of the cove.
'It might be a bit dryer.'

Gérard hesitated. 'All right. I'll come and collect you
when the time comes.'

Julie turned back to the two forlorn figures and said,
'Look, if we go further along we might find some shelter.
We mightn't get quite so wet. All right? Just follow me.'

They moved to follow her. Julie grasped Peter's hand
and led the way down to the water and along the sand.
She tried to remember the layout of the rocks from the last
time, all those months ago, but her memory wasn't very
clear.

They came to the lower rocks and began to scramble
over. Julie turned to Freymann. 'All right?'

'Oh yes. I can manage. Don't you worry about me!'

There were larger boulders now. It was somewhere near
here, Julie felt sure. Suddenly she recognised the dim
outlines of some larger rocks and, coming round the side
of one, saw the neat crevice where she had hidden before.
With Richard.

'In here!' she said triumphantly. Gently she pushed Peter forward. 'You first!'

When the old man and the boy had disappeared into the darkness of the crevice, she followed. It had been worth coming: the rocks curved in above their heads and formed a roof with only a slight gap in between. As long as one kept away from the drips that fell steadily from the bumps and lips of the overhangs, it was relatively dry. Julie said cheerfully, 'All right?'

Peter said plaintively, 'I am a bit wet, Mummy.' Julie felt his trousers and top, and said, 'Just a bit damp, that's all, darling. Really. You'll soon dry out. Think – sailors get wet all the time.'

'Yes,' Peter said thoughtfully. 'Mummy?'

'Mmmm?'

'Does Richard get wet all the time?'

'Oh, I think so. Yes! I'm sure he does.'

'Oh, that's all right then!' His voice sounded more cheerful now.

Julie was glad. She guessed he was beginning to enjoy his adventure.

Julie tried to see Freymann's face. 'And you, Monsieur Freymann? Are you all right?'

Freymann's voice said, 'Thank you. Thank you. Much better. How kind.'

David sat back against the rock and closed his eyes. Already he felt tired and the night had hardly started. The worst – the boat trip – was yet to come. Still, he'd come a long way, a long way.

He patted the bag tied round his waist. Everything in it must be wet by now. He himself was soaked through. Never mind. It could be worse, much worse. And he mustn't complain. Not when these people were being so kind and brave.

Anyway what was discomfort when one was a free man? Ha! He was amused by the idea. A free man. It sounded so grand. Although he wasn't sure he knew what real freedom was. Was it being able to do as one wished? Or was it having the opportunity for fulfilment within a rigidly structured society? He'd been thinking about it a lot recently, while he'd been hidden in the barn. He still wasn't sure what the answer was. Perhaps he was about to find out. Perhaps freedom would be a tangible state, a conscious understanding. How nice that would be.

Something caught his eye. The small boy was fidgeting. Such was the way of small boys. Slowly he leant across and said deliberately, 'Waiting's not much fun, is it?'

Silence. He could feel the boy's eyes staring at him. David thought: The boy thinks I am about to eat him.

'When I was your age I used to play a little word game to pass the time.'

Still nothing.

'Would you perhaps like to give it a try?'

A pause then a cautious, 'Yes, please.'

'Excellent. Shall I begin then?'

Vasson lowered himself on to his belly and, holding the torch in his hand, pressed the button once, twice, three times. He waited, dropping his head behind a tussock of grass. There was a knot of fear in his stomach: this was where Baum and his friends might just do something stupid, like blast him out of the ground.

Come on, where the hell were they?

He wiped the rain off his face, lifted the torch up and flashed the signal again.

Suddenly a small pinprick of blue light appeared through the downpour: once, twice, three times.

Vasson got cautiously to his feet and, moving away to his left, approached in a slight semicircle. The hunched silhouettes of helmeted men appeared black in the greyness. One of them moved. Then another. They were putting rifles to their shoulders. Vasson thought: Christ! And dropped to the ground. Then someone was striding out towards him and a foot kicked him hard in the ribs. Baum's voice said furiously, 'What the hell are you doing?'

'Get those bloody rifles off me!'

Baum snorted, 'Even if they had thought of shooting you, my stupid friend, they are not going to shoot me too, are they!'

Vasson got angrily to his feet and hissed, 'Just keep them away from me, do you understand!'

'Don't be a fool. People can hear you.'

Vasson swallowed hard. 'Just keep your *animals* under control, d'you hear me!'

Baum ignored him and said, 'They're all on the beach, are they – the lot of them? We'll move in, then.'

'No! We wait!'

'What!'

'Because you want the lot, don't you?'

'Yes, but—'

Vasson put his face close to the German's and spat, '*We wait.*'

The MGB stole quietly in towards the coast on one muffled engine. Ashley peered through the darkness and thought: Some luck at last. The weather had been foul all winter but now, finally, they'd been blessed with a calm night. The rain was a nuisance, of course, because it reduced visibility, but it was clearing away now and, with a bit more luck, should be gone by the time they reached the beach. Anyway, rain was better than a crystal clear night. Once, Ashley had seen the glow of a German sentry's cigarette up on the point.

The voice of Tusker, the navigator, came floating up. 'Course 165 degrees.'

'Course 165 degrees,' the coxswain repeated and turned the wheel.

In a moment Tusker would start calling out the depth until, finally, at five fathoms, they would anchor.

Already Ashley could smell the strong scent of the land, an aromatic mixture of vegetable matter and earth.

His mouth was dry and he swallowed several times. The adrenalin was working overtime tonight. It was the thought of Julie and Peter waiting on the beach. After so long.

When she'd first told him that it would be at least a month, probably two, before she could get away it had exasperated him. He'd made all the necessary plans and he was surprised and a little hurt that she hadn't wanted to come straight away. But then he'd looked at it from her point of view and begun to admire her for it. After all, he would have done the same. Waited and seen the job through.

The waiting had been terrible. That was because no-one that he'd met in the last few months had been a patch on Julie. It had taken a long time for him to realise how much he loved her. And Peter. He loved them both, and now, at last, he would take them home.

Tusker's voice called softly, 'Seven . . . seven . . . six . . .'

Ashley said, 'Stop engine.'

'All stopped, sir.'

There was a rock close by, Ashley could hear the water lapping against it. 'Port twenty.'

'Port twenty,' the coxswain whispered.

Ashley saw the dark shape of the rock slip past some five yards to starboard and recognised it. The best anchorage was a few yards further to the east. 'Steer 080 degrees.'

'. . . six . . . five fathoms . . . five . . . five . . .'

Ashley left it another minute then gave the order to lower the anchor. There was a slight plop then a swishing as the grass anchor rope unwound and raced out through the stemhead fairlead.

As he waited for the boat to settle to the anchor, Ashley stood listening to the night. Now that the rain had stopped, every sound was magnified by the stillness of the air. He could hear the gentle hissing of the surf in the cove, and the echo of the swell rumbling round partly submerged rocks.

They would have to be particularly quiet tonight; the slightest sound would carry for miles.

He waited impatiently for the men to launch the surf-boats and stow the gear, then he dropped into the first boat and they were off, rowing softly towards the beach.

With each stroke of the muffled oars, Ashley thought of the woman and the boy waiting in the darkness, and realised with no surprise at all that he had been looking forward to this night for a long, long time.

It had to be well past midnight. The rain had eased off and Julie could see some way along the beach. She strained her eyes for sight of a boat. But there was nothing. She looked back into the darkness of the rock cave. The word game had finished some time ago. Peter was asleep, his head on his bag. The old man was silent, probably sleeping too.

She closed her eyes for a while to rest them, then looked out through the gap in the rocks again. If you stared too hard the blackness seemed to dance before your eyes.

And yet . . .

She stiffened: there *was* something. A black blur on the water. It was moving. And up on the shingle there were other movements: dark figures running down towards the water's edge.

The boat. It must be the surfboat.

She cried out and raised her fist to the sky in a gesture of delight.

Peter woke up. 'Mummy?'

'Darling, it's come! The boat's here!'

'It's really Richard? He's really here?'

She laughed with excitement. 'Yes, darling!' She remembered the scientist. 'Monsieur? The boat. It's come!'

'Yes . . . yes . . .! I – I – It's wonderful. Yes!'

'Wait here, you two!' Julie went onto all fours and crawled out on to a flat rock. She stood up and peered into the night. The surfboat was there all right, just riding in towards the beach. A dark mass had appeared under the cliff – the first group of passengers being gathered together. It would take five minutes to load them and twenty minutes before the boat returned. Not long. *For ever.* She desperately wanted to run along the beach that very second – but there was Peter and she couldn't leave him.

She laughed with excitement. Richard. He was there, she knew he was. He would have come himself, just to make certain. She wanted to say, I'm here, darling, of course I'm here!

The boat flew on to the beach and figures jumped out. The dark mass of the passengers started down the beach.

They seemed to be going very slowly. She willed them to speed up.

At the water's edge there was some more movement – she guessed the crew were floating the surfboat off again, ready for the passengers.

Behind, another black shape slowly emerged from the darkness of the sea. That would be the second surfboat, coming in to the beach.

Julie watched with satisfaction. For once it was a perfect night. Everything was going smoothly. A marvellous piece of luck. She couldn't help thinking that it was *fate*; that, after all the storms of the winter, this calm night had been arranged, just for *her*.

The passengers had reached the water's edge at last. In a moment they would be in the surfboat and on their way.

She clenched her fists. *Hurry. Hurry up. This waiting is killing me.* And she laughed a little, because the anticipation was so sharp and warm.

Suddenly she gasped and froze, the last of the smile still on her lips.

Light.

There was light—!

The picture in front of her jumped from negative to positive, the blacks to whites.

She blinked and focused, disbelieving.

The surfboat and the figures around it were sharply illuminated, encircled with brilliant white.

Dear God—!

The brilliant whiteness was coming in a long shaft from the left – from the sea. She jerked her head towards it. The beam was radiating from a single point out in the bay.

She let out a small cry.

The British boat must be mad. What were they doing? *What were they doing?* She hissed, 'Turn it off! *Turn it off!*'

Suddenly she jumped.

There was more light. This time from the clifftop. A great cone of dazzling brilliance which swung from side to side across the cove, searching, trying to trap the running figures.

Crack! Crack! Gunfire from the clifftop. Then, almost immediately, a deep low *Bang!* from the bay, where fingers of yellow-tongued light flashed across the darkness.

Suddenly she understood. It was a *German* boat out in the bay, shining the light. Just as there were *Germans* up on the clifftop.

A shot rang out, closer, much closer. Then more shots. Shouting. Men running or pausing to shoot back. Men falling.

Julie shrieked, 'No!' and cried with rage. 'Please, dear God, No!'

A second great cone of light shone down from the clifftop, sweeping back and forth like the first, trapping running figures in its glare, figures which ran then fell, figures which froze, sometimes, and raised their hands. The guns were rat-tat-tatting in a continuous stream of noise, from the beach, from the clifftop, enveloping the cove. In one sweep of the light she saw a group of figures crouched behind the surfboat, guns aimed upwards, towards the clifftop.

'Mummy! Mummy!' Peter was pulling at her jacket. 'Mummy! Come back! Come back! Come back in – please!'

For a moment Julie was frozen, unable to comprehend, then, slowly, she realised it was Peter calling her. She shuffled backwards until she felt the rock against her back. Then, her eyes on the beach, she pushed herself into the rock cave. 'Dear God ... Dear God ...' She buried her face in her hands and, rocking back and forth, cried with rage and despair, loudly, to shut out the terrible noise. Peter hugged her back, patting her ineffectually, crying too.

On the beach the rat-tat-tatting of machine-gun fire became more spasmodic.

Out to sea the low boom of the big guns had ceased and the faint roar of deep-throated engines was fading into the distance.

Suddenly, there was a deathly silence.

Julie looked up. Light was still reflecting from the beach. Sick with fear, she crawled forward on her stomach and looked down.

There were soldiers everywhere, encircling the beach,

rifles at their shoulders. In the centre stood a ragged forlorn group, their hands above their heads.

Gérard . . . Maurice . . . Pierre . . . Many of the airmen, too.

But no oilskinned figure with a cap on his head—

Scattered around the beach were bodies lying inert on the pebbles. She stared at them in horror, terrified that she would spot some clue – a fleece-lined seaboot, a duffle coat . . .

Suddenly she realised she couldn't see the surfboat. She grabbed at the ray of hope. He must have got away. Yes, of course – he'd got away!

Then she remembered that the British boat had been chased away and that there was nowhere for him to escape to . . .

And she saw that some of the soldiers were down at the water's edge, raising their rifles to their shoulders, pointing out to sea, shouting . . . A light was shining from the sea again, but much closer.

Her heart sank. There were heads in the water, heads swimming around a waterlogged boat – the surfboat. For a moment the swimmers seemed undecided, then one tried to dive out of sight, surfacing some distance from the boat. But it was too calm. They spotted him the moment he came up. The sharp cracks of shots rang out.

Julie bit her knuckle and shook her head rapidly from side to side.

The lone swimmer held up a hand, as if in surrender, and began moving towards the shore. The others followed. There were four of them. They emerged slowly from the water and held up their hands.

She recognised him immediately. He walked through the other men and stood at the front. A soldier stepped forward and searched him roughly, then pushed him forward with his rifle butt.

Richard walked quickly to the group of prisoners and

pushed his way through them. Julie realised he was looking for somebody – *her*.

She cried very softly, 'I'm here, *I'm here*.'

Shouts again, and some of the prisoners were pushed towards the dead and wounded. With difficulty they picked them up and rejoined the group. More shouts and the prisoners formed a ragged line and moved off towards the cliff path, the dead and wounded carried like sacks between them.

The last she saw of him was when he paused at the bottom of the path and took a quick glance over his shoulder.

Then the lights went out.

Only the weak beams of torches remained. She watched them weave their way slowly up the path to the clifftop. Then they, too, were gone and there was nothing but darkness.

Julie whispered, 'Dear God. I'm so sorry. I'm so sorry. Please forgive me. Please!'

Then she beat her hands against the hard rock until they hurt, because she couldn't *do* anything and because, *somehow*, she had the terrible feeling that it was all her fault.

David opened his eyes. A long time had passed. Through the opening in the rocks he could see a cold grey light. Dawn. How he hated it. He'd never understood how people could rapture over it. Dusk was more beautiful every time.

He peered along the rock cave. The young woman was finally asleep, poor thing. How he had felt for her – she had suffered so terribly. The people on the beach, they had been her friends, perhaps even her family.

And the child: so young to understand such terrible things. What a world for a child, what a world.

But what now? The woman had been almost hysterical

with grief. What if she was still in a state? Who was to decide what they were to do? One thing was certain: David had no idea of how to get out of this place on his own.

He looked towards the patch of sky at the end of the crevice. At least it wasn't raining any more.

There was a sound. He turned. The woman was awake, her eyes open and staring. There was a hopeless look on her face. David recognised it: he'd seen it many times before. He whispered so as not to wake the boy, 'Good morning. How about some breakfast?'

She stared at him dully, her face blank. David smiled at her. 'I have – let me see—' He opened his bag and rummaged inside. 'Yes, cheese, *always* cheese. I think, one day I'll turn into a cheese! Then some bread. Yes, and an apple! I'm sure our young friend will like that won't he? We'll keep it for him. Just for him.'

She wasn't listening. She was looking into the distance. David could see that terrible thoughts were going through her head. She was remembering the night.

'Dear lady!' he said more firmly. 'I think we should begin our breakfast. *Then* we think! *No* thinking until then!' He wagged a finger at her.

She nodded vaguely and slowly sat up, trying not to disturb the boy on her lap. David broke off some cheese and handed it to her with a slice of bread. She stared at the remaining food lying in the paper on his knees. He realised she was checking to see how much was left. David said, 'It's all right. Plenty for me and the boy.'

She nodded and ate, slowly at first then hungrily. When she had finished she started to caress the boy's hair and he saw that she was crying again.

David pursed his lips. 'Well, now, let's make a plan! Let's be very practical!'

Her eyes focused and she blinked away the tears. 'Yes.'

'We need to decide what options are open to us. First . . .' He thought for a moment. 'First, can we just walk back up the beach?' Without waiting for her to reply he said, 'No. They'll have guards, won't they?'

'Up on the point. They have a post there. And ... they've probably got extra guards at the top of the path.'

'Yes.' There was silence while they both thought. David ventured, 'Perhaps at night ... Perhaps we can climb the cliff somewhere else?'

She shook her head. 'There's no other way that I know of. The cliff here is sheer. It's impossible to reach the next cove ... This place is cut off.'

The silence was longer this time. David thought: I wish I could think of something else, for *her* sake. For myself I don't care any more. Enough is enough.

She gave a bitter laugh. 'Not much choice, is there?'

He waved his hand from side to side. 'Nonsense! We will think of something. Defeat is in the mind!'

The woman sighed. 'I suppose so, but ...' She shook her head.

'What's your name?'

'Eh? Oh, Julie, it's Julie. Short for Juliette.'

'Well, Julie, there must be a way out of here. Mustn't there? Yes?'

She shrugged hopelessly. 'Maybe ...'

'For your boy's sake.'

She stared at him hard, her eyes round with anger and surprise. Then she softened and nodded gently. 'Yes. For his sake ...'

David smiled. 'We'll think of something.'

'Yes, you're right.' She rubbed her forehead. 'We'll *have* to.' She looked at him again and David noticed that her eyes had lost their lifelessness and were alert again. She said softly, 'But *what*?'

Then her face took on a preoccupied look and he guessed she was going through the possibilities again.

He said, 'There's always *diversion*.'

'Diversion?'

'You know, make a noise somewhere to attract their attention. Then slip past.' He made a snaking movement with his hand. 'It can work very well. I *know*!'

'Really? Yes . . . Perhaps you're right. I—'

She paused and stiffened, her face suddenly sheet white. Then, moving the boy's head quickly off her lap, she scrambled towards the entrance. A moment later she was back, her eyes round with fear.

'Soldiers! Coming down the path!'

David looked at their rock cave: it was no good. Far too easy to find. He grasped her arm. 'Quick! We must hide!'

'Where!'

'Try to hide the boy . . . Right under a rock, in the sand . . .'

'Yes!' The boy was already awake, dazed and frightened.

David crawled through the crevice to the far side, away from the beach. The woman followed and overtook him. She looked wildly to right and left, grabbed the boy and, scrabbling feverishly, pulled him up over a rock and out of sight.

David knew he couldn't go climbing after them. He was too slow. He might give them away. Better to stay.

He looked back into the crevice and decided against it: they'd find him straight away. He crawled round a corner and almost immediately found a much smaller gap, under the overhang of a large rock. This would do. He thought wrily: It will have to.

There was nowhere!

Julie wanted to scream. Smooth rocks. Gaps in between. Nowhere to hide! God!

And she was losing the cover of the massive boulders behind. The back of her head felt as if it were ten feet square: the Germans were probably watching her even now.

Nowhere! She looked down towards the water.

Perhaps the water . . .

Pulling Peter behind her, she crouched low and ran down a gully towards the sea.

In the water? Yes! She hissed, 'Peter, we might have to get wet!'

He nodded. She climbed on to a rock and looked down. There was a gap in the rocks beneath, where the water sucked gently back and forth with a gentle lapping noise. It didn't seem too deep and it looked as though there was an overhang—

She removed her rucksack and Peter's shoulder bag and squeezed them into a narrow fissure in the rock above, where they couldn't be seen. Then she jumped down. She caught her breath. The water came up to her thighs: it was icy. She stumbled, found firm sand, and turned for Peter.

She reached up for him and he jumped into her arms. She tried to hold him above the water but he was so heavy that he slipped through and he was up to his waist before she got a grip on him and hauled him back into her arms. She heard him gasp as he met the water.

Julie looked quickly around and immediately saw an overhang where they'd be invisible from everywhere but the sea. Moving Peter round on to her hip, she pushed herself under the rock and pressed her back against it. She kissed him on the cheek. 'I love you, darling.'

'I love you too, Mummy.' He turned his face to her and kissed her on the lips. He was shivering already.

She thought: How long could they last in this water? And the tide! She'd completely forgotten about that! God! Perhaps it was coming up . . .

Time. It passed in fractions of moments that lasted for ever. The icy water got colder. The blood too. Peter shivered.

She held him closer.

She tried to guess how the time was passing. Five minutes? No, seven. Maybe eight.

A stone fell some way away. Julie gripped Peter tighter.

Another sound: someone walking over the rocks. Heavy boots. Nearer. *Much* nearer.

God!

Crunch! From just above. Just overhead.

Close your eyes. Believe.

Another crunch. Feet shuffling.

Moving away. *Away!*

Heavy boots stepping from rock to rock. Moving away!

But wait . . . *Wait.* Until you're sure they've gone. It might be a trap!

She felt a great shudder go through Peter's body. She put her lips to his ear and whispered, 'It's all right, darling!' He nodded, but she could hear his teeth chattering. His skin was deathly cold.

But wait . . . Wait.

So she waited. Twenty minutes – it felt longer. Perhaps it was thirty minutes. Peter was weighing her down, heavier and heavier. A brisk wind was blowing in from the water, scything through her clothes, making Peter's cold skin the temperature of ice. She whispered, 'A little longer, just a little longer . . .'

She looked down and realised with a shock that the water was higher than before – quite a bit higher. It had reached her waist. The tide was coming up.

They would have to go, like it or not.

She smiled into Peter's taut pale face. 'We're going now, darling.'

He nodded, his jaws clamped together to stop the chattering.

She moved out and looked up. Empty sky. No Germans.

There was only one way out: up a smooth rock face. She couldn't do it with Peter in her arms. She said, 'I'll have to put you in the water. Just until I'm up. I'm sorry, darling . . .'

He nodded and, without a word, slid out of her arms into the water. It came up to his chest. He closed his eyes for a moment as the coldness hit him, then looked up to her.

'Right. I've got to get back up on to the rock. Give me a heave, will you?' She waited until he had moved out from under the rock then put her foot into a notch in the rock and pulled herself up. She felt Peter valiantly pushing from below. She paused, spreadeagled halfway up the smooth face, and took a long look round.

There was no-one in sight.

She looked for another handhold. She found one away to the right and hoisted herself up the last few feet. She looked again. No-one. She turned and lay down on the rock. Reaching down, she took Peter's hands and pulled. She raised him a few inches but could get him no further: she didn't have enough leverage. She lowered him back into the water. His lips quivered and silently he began to cry.

'Don't worry, darling, please!' She put her foot across on to another rock so that she was making a bridge across the gap and, reaching down, pulled. This time he came, desperately slowly, until he was halfway up the rock. 'Try and wedge yourself, darling!' He put out a foot to the rock opposite and locked himself against the rock face. Julie moved quickly across and, lying down on the rock again, pulled. Slowly Peter came up until he lay on the top, panting, in a pool of water.

Julie got to her feet and, taking the bags from the crack, pulled Peter to his feet. 'Come on, we'll get some dry clothes on!'

She led the way cautiously up the gully. No-one. Then they were on a plateau of rocks, hidden from the beach by the giant boulders. No-one.

Back to the crevice then. She crept forward, came round a large rock and they were facing the entrance.

Her heart was thudding in her ears. Perhaps they had got the dear old man . . . She stooped and looked inside.

'Hello, my dear!' Freymann's creased, smiling face peered out of the darkness at her. 'They've gone. I watched them go back up the cliff. There's no-one left.' He smiled again. 'How very delighted I am to see that you are safe!'

Julie smiled weakly. 'They've gone?'

'They've gone. They've given up! They think we have vanished into thin air! We're safe!'

Julie thought: But we're not, are we? It's only a reprieve.

Darkness again. Julie chewed on the bread and knew that she had to decide.

They had shared out the last of Peter's food parcel; most for Peter himself and the rest split between herself and the scientist. At first the old man had refused to take any, but she'd insisted. For drink they'd taken brackish rainwater from pools in the rocks.

Now there was no more food and the pools were drying out. Peter had put his one change of clothes on, but they weren't very warm and he'd been cold and shivery all day. He was probably catching a cold. Something would have to be done. But *what*? What could one do with a small boy and a sick old man?

The thought of having to take a decision made her feel slightly hysterical. She wanted to put it off. The longer they waited the better the chances might be . . . After a while the guards on the clifftop might go away. *Might* . . .

The decision was impossible. Perhaps if they waited another day . . .? Julie closed her eyes and started from the beginning again.

Freymann and she had been through it a dozen times since morning. The only thing they'd decided was to do nothing while it was light. Darkness offered the only hope. The old man favoured the diversionary tactic. He'd suggested that he should walk up the path and run, to lure the guard away while Julie and Peter escaped. Julie had pointed out that David would be shot instantly and bring the other guards from the headland within seconds.

After that, Freymann was silent for a long time. Julie asked him about his life and he told her about his childhood and the happy days in Berlin. He didn't tell her very much about what happened after that and she didn't press it.

She said, 'And what will you do in England?'

'Ah. Who knows? I've learnt not to think ahead.'

Then he'd been silent again, except to ask her to call him David.

'I'll try, monsieur.' Then she laughed. 'It's difficult not to call you monsieur . . . The only person of your age that I've ever called by his name is my uncle.'

'How old do you think I am then!'

'Well . . . Not *that* old. I – Oh dear, I've offended you.'

'No . . . No.'

'How old *are* you?'

'Fifty-two. Or fifty-three. I'm not sure.'

'Oh.' She was shocked. He looked well over sixty. 'Yes, of course. That's what I thought . . .'

He smiled at her because she'd lied to be kind. Then he settled down to sleep again and she was left to her own thoughts.

Now it was dark and the thinking still hadn't produced a solution.

It was Peter who gripped her arm and whispered, 'Mummy! There's something. A noise!'

Julie tensed and listened. The night was very still.

There was silence. Then, suddenly, a sound: a low whistle, long and low. A pause, then it came again. It was a man's whistle.

Silence. Then it came again, closer. Thoughts raced through Julie's mind: Friends? Germans! A clever trick? Oh yes: what a clever trick!

Now the sound was close. Panic began to grip her.

A voice called soft and low, '. . . Juliette . . . Are you there? . . . Julie . . .'

Julie froze. It could be a trick, an elaborate trick . . .

'. . . Julie, it's me . . . Michel.'

Julie sighed audibly and squeezed Peter's arm. She got up and climbed out onto the rocks. 'Michel . . .! Michel . . .! Here! We're here!' A moment later a dark figure emerged out of the night. Julie grasped his arms and sobbed with gratitude and relief. 'Oh, bless you! Bless you!'

'Quick!' His voice was harsh and businesslike. 'How many are you?'

'Just me and Peter and the old man.'

'The old man?'

'Freymann. The scientist.'

'Oh.' He sounded cross.

'Why?'

'He'll be slow, that's all.'

'He'll do his best. I know he will.'

'Right. Come on then. We've got to be quick.'

'Yes. Yes. I'll get the others.' Julie scrambled back into the crevice. 'Come on, darlings. We're going! Don't forget anything, will you? Have you got your bag, Peter?'

'Yes, Mummy.'

Julie pulled on her haversack. 'Ready?' she called.

She led the way up on to the rocks again and waited while first Peter then Freymann climbed out and started down the fall of rocks to the beach. She heard someone grunt: Freymann. She found him lying against a rock trying to regain his feet. 'Here, let me give you a hand.' She pulled him up and, holding his hand, helped him down to the sand where Michel and Peter were waiting.

Michel said brusquely, 'Right, no talking. No noise at all. And stick in line. Freymann, behind me. Then Peter. Julie, you come last.' Julie saw for the first time that Michel had a machine gun slung over his shoulder.

Julie whispered, 'What about guards? On the cliff?'

'There's no guard. Not if we're quick!'

They set off at a cracking pace. Julie immediately worried that Peter and the old man wouldn't be able to keep up. But they strode out, the two of them, and in no time they had reached the bottom of the path.

But the path was a different matter. Even before they were a short way up she could hear Freymann panting. He'd never make the top without a rest. Nor would Peter.

Freymann slowed up then stopped altogether. She heard him apologising breathlessly to Michel. Julie leant forward and caressed Peter's cheek. There was a pause, then they were off again, but much more slowly. After that they stopped regularly. It took twenty minutes to reach the rim of the cliff. She could almost feel Michel's impatience.

Just below the clifftop Michel signalled them to wait and crawled on ahead. Julie found herself praying. Then Michel was back, waving them forward.

Julie came up onto the clifftop just behind Peter and, seeing Michel move rapidly off, grabbed Peter's hand and started to run. Almost immediately she tripped over something and, glancing down, almost screamed. It was a body. Wearing a helmet. Lying inert. The guard.

She ran on, pulling Peter behind her. Ahead Freymann was in trouble again. As soon as she drew level with him she slowed down and stayed with him.

David thought: I can't go on! It's not physically possible. I'll ask them to leave me behind. Then I'll make my own way.

He staggered and fell to his knees, gasping for breath.

The girl stooped down beside him. 'Come on! You can do it. Not far now! Not far!'

There was fire in his lungs. He tried to speak but there was no breath to spare. Instead he shook his head.

Now the young man was back. 'Get up! Quick! We've got to get to the road! Come on!'

David rasped, 'Go . . . on . . . Don't . . . wait!'

The young man sighed impatiently. 'No! We can't leave you here. You'd be a bloody danger! Come on! You'd ruin it for *us*!'

David blinked. He hadn't thought of it like that. Right then. He got unsteadily to his feet and prepared to set off. Roughly, the young man thrust his shoulder under David's arm and half-carried, half-dragged him across the uneven ground.

It was downhill now. David tried to take more of his own weight: he could hear the young man panting with the effort of supporting him. But his legs were weak and, however hard he tried, he never seemed to be able to regain his breath.

Finally they came to a low wall. David disengaged himself and, determined to make an effort, climbed resolutely over. The others were over ahead of him and the young man led the way across what David realised to be a field. David followed unsteadily, wondering if he could ever keep up. The pace was slower now, the young man moving cautiously, like a cat. But even so, David knew he couldn't go on much longer.

Suddenly he realised that no one was paying any attention to him. He could hide here and no one would know. He wouldn't be a danger to them here.

Gradually he dropped back until the others vanished into the darkness ahead. Then, gently, gratefully, he dropped to his knees and lay down, one hand on the ground, one hand against his aching chest.

*

They were skirting the village, to the north. Where was Michel taking them? To Morlaix maybe ... But where could they hide there? At his apartment? Terribly risky. It would be risky wherever they went.

She turned to look for David. No sign. She waited for him to loom up out of the darkness. He didn't. Michel came up. 'What the hell's the matter?'

'It's David – I can't see him. I'll have to go back.'

'We haven't time!'

'Well, I'm certainly not going to leave him there! Here – look after Peter while I go to look.' She turned and strode away into the darkness.

Almost back at the wall ... He had to be somewhere near here.

Then she saw him. Lying on the ground. She ran up. 'David! David! Are you all right?'

For a moment she thought he was dead then he groaned slightly. 'Sorry ... sorry ... leave me here ... Leave me.'

'Absolutely not! Come on! You're too important. Anyway, I need you! Where you go, I go.'

'Leave me. It's no good ... Please ...'

'But the Germans will find you!'

'So?' he rasped. 'All they can do is kill me.'

'No. No! They'll take you back to Germany and make you work. They'll get hold of your family and force you to work. Don't you see? Come on. *Come on.* David, make an effort, *please.*'

He didn't move and for a moment Julie thought he had given up completely. Then at last he groaned and, leaning on her, got unsteadily to his feet. Slowly, his arm over her shoulder, they set off down the hill.

Michel and Peter were waiting. Michel said impatiently, 'Hurry! We've really got to hurry!'

They left the village behind and struck out across the fields towards the south-west. After a while Julie realised they must be approaching the small road that led from

Tregasnou to the estuary and Kernibon. Once they'd crossed the road, there was nothing but fields for miles. How far did Michel expect them to go? David was in a bad way, his breath coming in long shallow rasps. Peter was tired too, poor chap, dragging his feet, shoulders drooping.

A hedgerow loomed up. Then a gate leading onto the road. Michel disappeared into the darkness of the hedge. Perhaps they were to wait here for a while.

She followed Michel in towards the hedge, then stopped in alarm. Someone else was there, waiting in the shadows. She froze, but then recognised something familiar about the figure. Slowly she went forward. 'Jean!'

He took her arm. 'Quick! Into the van!'

'The van?'

Jean led her into the darkness of the tall hedge and there, parked close beside it, was the old Peugeot van.

Michel was opening the back door. He took Freymann's arm. 'In here. And you.' He helped Peter up into the back. 'Julie, you drive.'

'Me?'

'Yes, unless you want to take the Sten.'

For a moment she didn't understand what he meant, then she realised he meant the gun. It was an ugly great thing: she wouldn't have the first idea how to use it.

She grasped her uncle's arm. 'Jean, thank you! Thank you!'

'Don't thank me! It was Michel.'

'Take care of Tante Marie. And *please*, don't get caught! *Please!*'

He said gruffly, 'Off you go! Quick! There's no time to spare.'

She hugged him and, climbing in through the passenger door, eased herself across into the driver's seat.

Jean was opening the gate. He disappeared for a moment, then came back into view and waved them forward. Michel swung on the starting handle and the old engine burst into life with an ear-splitting roar. Michel jumped into the passenger seat. 'Out of the gate, turn right. Go!'

Her heart in her mouth, Julie threw the gear lever into first and the van jumped forward. She pulled the wheel hard over and they shot out of the gate into the lane. There was no chance to wave to Jean.

It was pitch black. 'I can't see anything!' she cried.

Michel reached down and flicked a switch. The lights came on but they had been well hooded: they cast only the faintest glow over the walls and hedgerows lining the road.

Julie peered forward, trying to keep the speed up. A sharp bend reared up and she almost missed it. She pulled the wheel over and the bumper crunched into the wall with a loud bang. 'Sorry.'

'Keep going!'

They shot through a tiny village and then down a hill towards some crossroads. Julie almost asked, 'Which way?' when Michel said, 'Straight over!'

She kept her foot down and the van shot across the crossroads. Michel looked rapidly right and left, then stuck his head out of the window to look behind. He pulled his head back in and said, 'Nothing!'

Another hill, leading down to the estuary. Julie realised they were on the road to Kernibon. It was a dead end.

As they neared the village Michel leant over and turned off the ignition. The engine petered out and they coasted down the hill in eerie silence. 'Right at the harbour!'

As they approached the bottom of the hill Julie resisted the temptation to brake too much and the van was still travelling fast as she yanked the wheel across. They shot round the corner and along the road encircling the land-ward side of the cove.

Finally the van slowed right down and Julie pulled in towards the side. Michel jumped out, opened the rear

doors and bundled the others out. Julie climbed out, trying
to stop herself shaking.

Peter ran up and took her hand, then they were following Michel along the side of the tiny harbour. Suddenly he
lowered himself over the sea wall and, climbing down,
disappeared.

There was a slight clatter, some muffled movements,
then Michel's voice floated up. 'The old man first!' Freymann lowered himself gingerly over the edge and hovered
for a moment, searching for a foothold, then he moved on
down the wall.

Julie peered over and saw that there was a metal ladder
and, below, a small dinghy floating on the water. She sat
Peter down and, turning him face to the wall, put his hands
on the rungs of the ladder. 'Careful. Take it slowly.'

When he was safely in the boat beside Freymann and
Michel, Julie lowered herself over. She hated heights almost
as much as she hated boats. Finally her foot was in the
boat and, wobbling violently, she threw herself into it. She
fell awkwardly into the bottom, bruising her shin. She
clenched her teeth and stayed silent.

The boat was moving away from the wall. Michel was
weaving an oar from side to side over the back. Julie
watched him, amazed: she'd never realised he could do this
kind of thing.

Then she remembered when she and Peter had come to
collect the sow, how they'd surprised him here at the
harbour and how secretive he'd been.

They were approaching the fishing boats moored in the
centre of the cove. Perhaps Michel was going to hide them
here, on one of the boats.

The dinghy bumped alongside one of the smaller boats.
Michel pushed the old man to his feet and helped him up
the side. Julie went next and, reaching down, pulled Peter
up beside her. Michel came last and tied the dinghy's rope
to the fishing boat.

Julie looked around. It was a small boat, completely open and without so much as a wheelhouse. There was nowhere to hide.

Michel was beside her. She pulled his sleeve and said, 'Michel, we can't hide here!'

'No. But it'll take you across.

'Across?'

'To England. That's where you want to go, isn't it?'

Julie gasped and stared at him in amazement. 'Yes but – in *this*?' It was much smaller than the fishing boat she and Peter had taken from Morlaix three years before. She saw that there was a small bit of decking at the front which came halfway back to the mast. But otherwise it was entirely open. She could imagine the waves coming straight in.

Michel said, 'Right. Here are some waterproofs. Fresh water and so on are up in the bow. Not much, but it's all I could get hold of.'

He moved along the boat to the far end and Julie followed, a feeling of hopelessness creeping over her. 'Right.' Michel was saying, 'Here's the tiller, for steering, and here, the compass. Now, I'll light the little oil lamp here, beside the compass, but keep it well masked until you're clear of the land. Now there *is* an engine but there's almost no fuel for it and anyway it's too noisy to use near the land so I think you'll be better off without it . . .'

'Michel! What do you mean?'

'The sails are quite straightforward. One large and one small. If the wind comes from ahead you'll need both, otherwise you could manage with just the large one . . .'

'*Michel! What are you saying!*'

He turned to her and said harshly, 'I'm sorry, I wish I could come with you, but I can't.' He shrugged. 'I *have* to stay. This is the best I can do for you, Julie—'

'*No! No!*' She grabbed his arms and tried to read his

face in the darkness. 'I *can't*, Michel! I don't know what to do!'

'But I'll get the boat ready and rigged and I'll sail out with you into the bay. Then all you have to do is point north—'

'*Michel, I can't!*'

He took her by the shoulders and shook her slightly. 'You *must*! It's not ideal, I'll admit, but it's a damn sight better than getting caught by the Gestapo. And *that's* the only alternative!'

Julie stared at him in disbelief. She repeated desperately, 'But I don't know how to sail!'

'I told you, I'll get you going in the right direction. But we must go *now*! We're losing the tide!' He ran forward to the mast and started heaving on lines. Julie grasped the side of the boat and watched him, horrified.

Peter was at her elbow. 'Mummy, I can help . . . I think. Richard told me all about sailing . . . Mummy?'

Julie looked down at the small pale face and automatically touched his hair. 'Oh darling! I – wish I . . .' Then she remembered what the Gestapo did to children and, holding the small face in her hands, she made an effort to smile. 'We'll do our best then, shall we? We'll sail to England, shall we?' But even as she said it she was filled with despair.

Peter nodded and clutched at her hand. Up by the mast Michel was pulling on a rope. There was a great flapping and beating as a black sail rose slowly into the sky. Then Michel was leaning over the front of the boat, pulling hard on something. Suddenly he ran back, pulled another rope and dived for the tiller. Julie realised the land was moving sideways: the boat was free of its mooring. The beating noise diminished then stopped. She looked up at the sail. Its black curved shape soared up into the darkness, huge against the sky.

The mouth of the tiny harbour reared up ahead. Julie winced and drew back involuntarily. The high brick mole rushed past, an arm's length away, then they were through, slipping rapidly out into the vast blackness of the night.

Julie felt the boat move under her and grabbed at the side. She felt sick. It was a nightmare. She didn't understand the first thing about any of it – not the first!

Michel was calling, 'Come here!'

Lurching unsteadily across the deck she reached his side. 'Now, listen very carefully. We've only got a few minutes. So *listen*! There's a torch here just behind me in the bo'sun's box. There are the waterproofs I told you about. Here—' He placed her hand on the tiller, '– here is the tiller. You push it the opposite way to the one you want to go in. You'll get used to it . . .'

Julie stared into the darkness, her throat constricted and dry.

'And now listen *very* carefully. The course . . .'

After a while Julie realised he had stopped speaking and was moving away from the tiller, leaving it in her hand.

'Best of luck, Julie!'

'*But*—'

Then he was untying something – the rope holding the dinghy – and climbing over the side.

She almost screamed.

The next moment he was gone.

Chapter 26

VASSON REACHED OUT and touched the painting. A tractor, bright red and crudely painted. Not bad, considering. Then it occurred to him – the mother probably gave the child some help with it. He imagined them sitting on the floor together, engrossed and happy in their task. The picture irritated him. He turned away.

There was a model plane hanging from the ceiling, a second picture and some posters of Paris. Angrily he yanked the cover off the bed; it was unmade, the blankets neatly folded, the calico bolster without a pillow case.

There was a wooden chest under the eaves. He pulled it out and, raising the lid, emptied the contents over the floor. Toys, clothes, old fabrics.

Rubbish.

As he moved towards the stairs his head brushed against the model plane. He pushed it impatiently aside. The fine thread holding it to the ceiling broke and it fell to the floor, one wing bent and broken. Vasson kicked it out of his way.

He went down the narrow stairs to the room below. The woman's room. It was clean and tidy, the bed neatly covered like the boy's.

She was expecting to be gone a long time, the bitch.

He pulled open the drawers of the dresser. The top one contained underwear, carefully folded. Scattered between the clothes were sachets which smelled of herbs. He pulled everything out on to the floor.

He leant down. In the next drawer were blouses, woollens – more rubbish. He threw them onto the floor as well. Impatiently he jerked open the bottom drawer. Papers. A ration card. Some letters. An old photograph.

He leafed through the letters. They were in English. They were signed 'Your Mother'. He stared at them, frowning. He didn't understand English. He threw them back in the drawer. The photograph showed two people sitting on a beach. One was the girl, much younger, maybe fourteen or fifteen. She was very slim, her angular body clad in an unbecoming, old-fashioned swimming costume. She was looking straight into the camera, her eyes screwed up against the sun. Beside her was a woman, much older, rather fat, dressed in a tight frock with a floral print on it. The mother.

Vasson flipped the photograph over and stared. There was some writing: English again. It said: Mummy and me. Cawsand. 1929.

Cawsand. It must be a place in England. The girl was not Breton at all then, but English. A worse thought – she was probably an agent, planted in France to spy. The thought made Vasson angry and uneasy. He had the unpleasant feeling that he'd been cleverly and ruthlessly deceived.

If Baum found out it would mean more stick and Vasson had had enough over the scientist. Vasson decided it would be best if Baum never found out.

He slid the photograph inside his jacket. It offered no clues as to where the bitch was now. And *that* was what he needed to know.

She had to be the key. She'd been with the scientist at the cliff. Now they were both missing. The girl must be hiding him.

Suddenly, he jumped.

A terrible cry came from the next room. Vasson shuddered and, bracing himself, stood up and went towards the door. He hesitated, half-revolted, half-fascinated by what he might see, then, his heart thudding, opened the door and walked through into the kitchen.

Baum was leaning against the mantelpiece, examining his nails. To the left, three of his men were huddled round a chair. Vasson moved across the room, his eyes on the backs of the men, until he could see between them into the chair. He swallowed hard and stared, fascinated. The figure lay inert. The face was a mess, the nose a pulp of blood and bones, and the eyes reduced to slits between the purple-red swellings of cheeks and eyelids. Apart from the hair, the old woman was unrecognisable.

Vasson glanced at Baum and raised his eyebrows. Baum made a face of disgust which indicated: Nothing.

Turning his eyes back to the monstrous sight in the chair, Vasson lowered himself on to a seat in the corner. One of Baum's men put his face down to the old woman's and chanted, 'Where is the girl?'

The old woman's mouth moved, as if to say something, then dropped open. With distaste Vasson saw that the gums were bare and devoid of teeth. She started to moan loudly.

The man standing directly in front of the chair turned to his companion and said something in German. The other nodded and, reaching into his pocket, pulled out some cord. It was in two sections. They took one piece each and tied the old woman's hands down to the arms of the chair. Vasson saw that they hadn't tied her by the wrists but across the width of the hands. Vasson moved his tongue around his mouth to remove the dryness.

The chant again. 'Where is the girl?'

The moan again.

They leant forward and each took a forefinger. Slowly they bent the forefingers backwards. The old woman's bloody eyes stared in disbelief, then she cried out, a loud shriek that filled the room. Suddenly she convulsed, her body arching upwards, straining against the cords, and she screamed, a long long, shrill, piercing scream. Vasson put his hands over his ears. The scream ceased. For a split second there was silence. Then there was an audible snap, quickly followed by another, and Vasson stared curiously at the two fingers. Though the men had moved away the fingers were still upright, at a strange angle to the hands.

The old woman's head had fallen back against the chair and she groaned, a long, low moan of despair.

'*Where's the girl?*'

The mouth dropped open again and tried to speak. Nothing happened. The old woman began to shake her head from side to side, first slowly then more rapidly until the movement became frenetic, like a mad animal's. Vasson felt uncomfortable and looked away. Suddenly the old woman's head dropped forward and he realised she was unconscious.

Baum shifted his weight and leant the other elbow on the mantelpiece. He said something in rapid German then turned to Vasson. 'We're getting nowhere.' The muscles in his jaw fluttered under the unnaturally pink skin. He said with irritation, 'What's so sickening is to think that this whole business need never have happened!'

Vasson snapped, 'But if your men had covered the beach properly, they would never have got away! *And*—' He stood up '– if the scientist had been properly guarded by the Navy, then he would never have escaped in the first place!'

Baum glared at Vasson and whispered, 'Don't get clever with me, you little pimp!' He raised a forefinger. 'And don't go spreading dirt behind my back. Just try, *just try* – and I'll carve you into little pieces, little pimp!'

Vasson smiled briefly. 'Don't get yourself in a state, my friend. We'll just have to find a way. What about the old man? The woman's husband?'

Baum rolled his eyes with exasperation. 'Yes! Yes! But

where is he now? Eh? I do not see him here, do I?' He put a hand over his eyes and rubbed his forehead.

Baum was right. They had nothing. Personally Vasson didn't care a damn – he was fed up with the whole job – but there was bound to be a scapegoat and he had the unpleasant feeling that Baum would try to nail the whole mess on him.

Wearily, Vasson sat down and lit a cigarette, thinking: It's all that bitch's fault; it's she who's fouled the whole thing up.

The old woman groaned. Baum nibbled at one of his nails, roused himself, and nodded to his men. They moved in towards the chair.

Simultaneously, there was the sound of boots crossing the front room. The door opened and a soldier appeared. He saluted and spoke to Baum in rapid German. The men looked quickly at Baum, their faces worried. Baum turned pink and looked apoplectic. There was a long silence, then Baum said very slowly in French, 'I thought you had *caught* these people!'

Vasson shifted on his seat and said carefully, 'Most of them, yes.'

Baum almost choked. 'Why, then, are my men being murdered?'

Vasson said sharply, 'Where? Where were your men killed?'

'One man. On the clifftop. Those filthy murdering swine . . . !'

Vasson sat up and thought: Good God, why would they want to get down to the beach again . . .? What on earth? Then he closed his eyes and swore quietly. There could only be one reason. Oh hell. He said out loud, '*Merde!*'

Baum looked at him quickly. 'What is it?'

'They were there all the time. On the beach.'

'Impossible—'

'They were there!'

Baum looked at him sourly. 'I don't see how—'

'Shut up!' Vasson thought quickly. He tried to imagine where the girl's friends would have taken her. He said, 'If they've escaped from the beach that means they must have gone into hiding again, somewhere nearby . . .'

'Ha!' Baum exclaimed contemptuously. 'But *where*!' He shook his head. 'I tell you, there's only one way to find out. We take hostages and we shoot them tomorrow. Twenty. No! Thirty. The families of these murderers. That's the only way!'

As Baum began to give orders, Vasson knew it would take too *long! Too long!* If only he'd got the old woman's husband. It was much more likely that *he* would know. Damn, damn. So *nearly* there. He clenched his first and swore under his breath.

There was a shout outside and the back door opened. A soldier came in, pulling the figure of a short, stocky man behind him. The man was sixty-ish and dressed in peasant's clothes.

As soon as the man saw the bent, bloody figure in the chair he threw himself at it, crying, 'Marie! Marie!' The old woman moaned and the man cried out, 'No! No!'

Suddenly, Vasson realised who the man was and laughed out loud. His prayers had been answered. That's what came of being lucky.

The old man was sobbing violently. Vasson wished Baum would put a stop to it.

Baum jerked his head at his men and they hauled the old man to his feet. 'Please, please!' The old man was still sobbing. 'Please, leave my wife alone! Please! She knows nothing! Nothing!'

Baum leant against the mantelpiece and waited.

'Please – I am giving myself up because she knows nothing, nothing . . . Please leave her alone!' The old man was panting, shaking his head from side to side.

Baum said calmly, 'And you know something?'

The old man nodded slowly, his eyes tightly closed. Then he stopped moving, his body sagging between the two men. 'Yes – I will tell you what you want to know.'

'Excellent.' Baum looked at his fingernails again, smiling slightly. 'Is the girl with the scientist?'

'Yes.'

'Where are they?'

'On a fishing boat.'

There was a pause. The smile had vanished from Baum's face. 'Where is this fishing boat?'

'At sea. But I don't know where it's going.'

'You don't know where it's going.'

'No, they didn't tell me.'

'I see,' Baum said stiffly. 'You realise we will extract the information from you one way or the other.'

The old man nodded furiously. 'Yes, yes. Please, it's the truth, they didn't tell me. I suppose England, but I don't know where exactly . . .'

Vasson said, 'Of course England! Where else would they go!'

The old man looked at Vasson for the first time, trying to understand who he was.

Vasson said, 'The girl, she used to live there, didn't she?'

The old man nodded again.

'Of course England!' Vasson snorted. 'Who else was on the boat?'

'I'm not sure . . .'

'The scientist, Freymann?'

There was a pause. 'Yes.'

'And the boy?'

The old man whispered, 'Yes', and began to weep.

'No-one else?'

'I don't know. I only heard about those three. That's all I know. Please believe me. And please, leave my wife alone. Please!' He looked at Tante Marie and, sobbing bitterly, tried to reach her again, but they held him back.

Baum came up to Vasson. 'If it's not the truth I'll get it out of him.'

'But suppose it is.'

Baum clenched his teeth and said unhappily, 'I will have to notify High Command and alert the coastal units. They can't have got far!'

Vasson thought: I hope you're right.

Baum turned away but Vasson caught his sleeve. 'The old man. He'll be shot, won't he?'

Baum blinked. 'In the end.'

Vasson nodded. 'Make it soon. He's seen my face.'

The telephone jangled loudly. Doenitz woke up and blinked. The room was in darkness. He guessed it was about one. So much for catching up on some sleep. He sat up and reached for the receiver.

The voice of his staff man said, 'Berlin, Herr Grossadmiral. Reichsmarschall Goering calling.'

Doenitz turned on the light. There were voices on the line, then clicks. Absent-mindedly Doenitz smoothed down the blanket. Finally Goering's voice said, 'Ah! Admiral Doenitz?'

'Good evening, Herr Reichsmarschall.'

'Herr Admiral. And how is Paris? How I envy you your little trips there. So much beauty! And so quiet, so quiet!' Quiet, Doenitz supposed, must mean there was no bombing, which was true enough.

Goering went on, 'Yes, how I wish we could all take our command posts to Paris . . .' The words were slurred. Doenitz sighed under his breath: the Reichsmarschall was heavily drugged again.

'. . . Very soon, of course, life will be quieter in Berlin,' Goering continued, 'but we must get this radar business under way.' Doenitz wondered where the conversation was leading to. He murmured a noncommittal, 'Indeed.'

'...A scientist we need has been *lost* by Himmler's idiots. We must get him back. He's at sea—'

'At sea?' Doenitz asked incredulously. Goering began a long, rambling explanation. As it proceeded, Doenitz felt his blood run cold. He could see what was coming.

Goering said finally, 'So we must get this person back. A search will have to be mounted. How soon can you arrange it, dear fellow?'

'I cannot!' Doenitz retorted. 'It's out of the question! It would be like looking for a needle in a haystack! Even if I had any units available, it would be a complete waste of time—'

'But I don't think you understand, Herr Admiral – the Fuehrer himself has ordered the search. The matter is absolutely vital! You have S-boats, don't you? And your enormous fleet of U-boats. Something can be spared, surely, for what is after all a vital matter?'

Doenitz squeezed the receiver hard. He said tightly, 'I will consider what is appropriate when I receive the order direct from Fuehrer Headquarters.'

'Of course, dear fellow. The order will be sent directly, I'm sure.'

Goering had never called him dear fellow before. Doenitz realised that this must be really important to him. If that was the case ... Doenitz said levelly, 'When – if – I receive this order, I will insist on air support. Several patrols will be needed to locate the fishing vessel. Then, and only then, might it be possible ...'

The thick voice interrupted, 'My dear fellow, you know that this cannot be done. The Luftwaffe's resources are fully stretched. We have to defend Germany, first and foremost. And the English Channel ... well, I cannot spare *anything* ...'

Oh no, Doenitz thought, I'm not going to let you get away with it this time. He said briskly, 'Without air support I cannot hope to find this vessel. In fact, I would almost certainly fail! I *must* have air support!'

There was a short silence. 'A reconnaissance aircraft then . . .' The voice was grudging. 'I'll see what's available. After all, I wish to help as much as possible. The Fuehrer is most anxious, you see . . . most anxious . . .' The voice became brighter. 'You'll find this scientist for us, won't you, Doenitz?'

It was an impossible question. Doenitz said tightly, 'I'll see what can be done.'

'Good. Remember, we *need* him. Got to sort out this radar business, haven't we? Essential to get it right, essential. You do appreciate that, don't you?'

'Yes,' Doenitz sighed. Of course he appreciated it – how could he fail to? Two more U-boats had disappeared the day before. He added, 'This scientist – why is he so vital?'

Goering laughed. 'Ah! He worked on this new kind of radar, a long time ago. He understands it. He'll save us a lot of time!'

A suspicion flashed into Doenitz's mind. 'And his name? What's his name?'

'Ah . . . One moment.' There was a pause, then, 'Um, Freymann. Yes, Freymann. A Jew – but there we are!'

Doenitz closed the conversation and replaced the receiver. Freymann! So . . . He had escaped and Goering wanted him back. Or rather, it must be *Schmidt* who wanted him back. If the Chief Scientist was so anxious to have Freymann that he was prepared to put the matter to Hitler himself, then Freymann must be really vital. Schmidt must have realised that Freymann had been on the right track all along, from the beginning . . . Memories of a day long ago came into Doenitz's mind: the trials ship, the strange, tubby little man and the wild ideas tossed about like sparks from a firework.

Sighing, he got up and pulled his uniform jacket on over the shirt and trousers he already wore. He remembered that Freymann had been based at a naval establishment. God forbid that the Navy were responsible for letting him escape! He finished buttoning the jacket and went into the adjacent room. His staff officer jumped to his feet. Doenitz said, 'I am expecting an order from Fuehrer Headquarters. Bring it to me the moment it arrives. In the meantime please tell Admiral Kohl that I wish to meet him in the plotting room in two minutes.' Protocol had to be observed. Admiral Kohl was C-in-C Gruppe West and this was his command post. Doenitz was a visitor here.

Doenitz waited one minute, then descended to the plotting room. He should wait for the Fuehrer-Command, but there was no harm in discussing the strategy. Anyway, he knew very well that the command would come. Goering had sounded very certain.

When he entered the plotting room there was a slight hush, then Admiral Kohl and his staff detached themselves from their work and followed him to the vast plotting tables. Doenitz stared at the array of wooden shapes that marked the positions of convoys and of each German vessel presently in the Atlantic. The black shapes representing U-boats were spread out far across the ocean, from the Mediterranean to the Caribbean, from the Cape Verde Islands to Iceland. Never before had there been so many U-boats at sea: a hundred and ten out of a total fleet of almost four hundred. The fleet was at last approaching the sort of size that Doenitz had always pressed for.

However there was not a single U-boat in the English Channel. The only vessels anywhere near were the *Schnellboote*, the fast torpedo boats with bases at Cherbourg and Guernsey.

The S-boats first then.

Admiral Kohl was waiting patiently. Doenitz said quietly, 'We are mounting a special operation. We are looking for a fishing boat which left this region, somewhere around the Morlaix River.' He took a pointer and placed it on the North Brittany coast. 'It left at some time this evening. We do not know the exact time. The craft is making for the English coast. Again, we do not know where exactly. But we must make every effort to find this vessel.'

There was silence. Doenitz could feel the officers exchanging glances behind his back. Eventually Kohl said, 'There are the S-boats. They would be our best bet.' He said over his shoulder, 'Werner, find out how many S-boats are operational at Cherbourg and Guernsey.'

Doenitz stared at the massive chart. 'I wish I could tell you course and speed, but apparently this is not available either . . .'

Kohl took the hint straight away. 'Well, I'm sure we can make an estimate. Is the fishing boat motor-powered, Herr Grossadmiral?'

'Unlikely . . . Unless they have managed to steal considerable amounts of fuel. And I believe the fishing fleet is searched regularly for excess supplies . . .' Doenitz looked questioningly at an intelligence officer, who nodded in confirmation. 'So,' Doenitz continued, 'I would imagine it's using sail.'

Kohl looked to one side. 'Braun! What's the weather situation?'

There was a rustle of paper. 'Channel area . . . Yes, north-easterly, Herr Admiral. Ten knots, increasing later, possibly veering to the north.'

Doenitz frowned. 'North-easterly . . .'

'Common in March, Herr Grossadmiral. The equinox.'

'Mmm. So – what speed?'

'Four knots?'

Doenitz nodded. 'Yes, I agree.'

Kohl went on, 'Course . . . it would have to be west of north. The best port to make for would be Falmouth. Otherwise . . . Well, there's nothing else west of there. No other major harbours. It would have to be Falmouth.'

Doenitz stared at the chart. The boat certainly couldn't hope to lay due north and reach Plymouth. So Kohl was right. The only major port on a north-westerly course was Falmouth. To the west of that was the Lizard, Land's End, then ... He glanced further west to the Scillies, then brought his eyes back to Falmouth. He said, 'Yes, Falmouth. So – if the boat set out say at eleven, it should be somewhere around here by now.' He pointed at a point some six miles off the coast. He turned to Kohl. 'How long before it gets out of S-boat patrol range, would you think?'

Kohl frowned. 'Well, we don't usually operate S-boats beyond forty miles from the coast at this point ... Enemy air patrols have been very heavy ...'

'Forty miles ... We have only until dawn, then. The escaper will be thirty to forty miles off by then ...'

Kohl nodded slowly.

Doenitz said abruptly, 'So the S-boats won't be much use to us!'

Kohl blew out his cheeks. 'The Luftwaffe ... I suppose there is no hope of an air patrol?'

Doenitz kept his eyes on the table. 'We have been promised air reconnaissance, yes.'

No-one spoke. They had been promised air support countless times before. It rarely turned up. And when it did the planes usually had very limited range.

'But even if we do receive air support, that will not be enough,' Doenitz said grimly. 'So we will have to deploy additional units ...'

Doenitz waited for Kohl to suggest the only solution, but he did not. Eventually Doenitz said, 'We'll have to send a U-boat.'

Kohl sighed deeply and asked quietly, 'Is it really that vital, Herr Grossadmiral?'

Doenitz nodded. 'Yes, I'm afraid it is.'

*

There were no brass bands any more, no garlands either. Nowadays the boats arrived and left as quietly as possible, sliding in and out of their dark, dank pens like snakes from a hole. Nor did the men smile any more: many of the old guard had gone now, long buried in their tomb-ships. The fresh recruits had never learnt to smile: they were too frightened.

Except for Fischer's men. Fischer's men thought their commander was as close to God as anyone could get because he had kept them alive so long and because they believed that, after all this time, he would keep them alive for ever. Quite simply, they believed in him.

It was one of the reasons Fischer couldn't sleep any more, even when he was desperately tired. No-one could sleep with that kind of responsibility.

He felt tired now, and the patrol had only just begun.

They were heading south-west from Brest, beginning a long loop out towards the North Atlantic. U-319 was travelling on the surface in company with two other submarines. The idea was that, in a group of three, the boats had a reasonable chance of fighting their way out of an air attack. In the event Fischer doubted that all three boats would actually escape a concerted attack – more like two. If that. The air patrols were efficient, heavy, and, if anything, getting worse.

He looked at the chart in front of him. Only sixty miles out. It should have been more but they'd left late: U-64 had been delayed with engine trouble. That meant they wouldn't be clear of the Bay by dawn . . .

The Bay. The Black Pit. Ever wider, ever deeper. Like everything else it got more difficult to face, more difficult to cross. The Happy Time was long gone.

Not that the kills weren't high – far from it. But Fischer sensed a desperation about the whole business that hadn't been there before: the satisfaction, the excitement, had gone.

'Herr Kaleu, Flotilla HQ are signalling.'

Fischer hurried over to the wireless area. The operator was typing a long signal into the Enigma cipher machine, his assistant copying down the deciphered letters as they appeared on the machine. Fischer peered over their shoulders, and his heart quickened. It was a personal signal from Doenitz. Fischer smiled. Just like the old days!

He began to read the body of the message and a small frown appeared on his face. When the staccato sound of the Morse ceased and the operator had typed in the last of the signal Fischer reached forward and picked up the sheet carrying the completed message. He read it again slowly, from the top.

It began in Doenitz's usual informal way: DOENITZ HERE. GOOD TO SPEAK TO YOU AGAIN, FISCHER. IT'S BEEN A LONG TIME.

Then came details of a special operation. *Imperative*, Doenitz called it. U-319 to abandon her patrol and proceed with all speed to search the following area – map references were given – to intercept a fishing boat believed to be at H17 P15 – another map reference – at 0100 hours, and now believed proceeding at 4 knots under sail on approximate course 330. Possible destination H24 P23. Occupants of boat to be captured but not harmed.

It was repeated that the orders were urgent and immediate. After acknowledgement U-319 was to maintain radio silence except in emergency. Doenitz signed off: IF ANYONE CAN DO IT, YOU CAN.

Fischer tried to absorb the information, to work out what it all meant. But however he looked at it, the whole thing was incredible.

He went to the chart table to check the map references, but he'd already worked out the rough position. The middle of the bloody English Channel.

If anyone but Doenitz had asked him he would have queried it, asked for confirmation, more information. But

Doenitz had guessed all that – which was why he'd asked
Fischer personally. *If anyone can do it, you can.* Fischer
thought: I hope you're right.

Fischer went back to the wireless operator and dictated
a reply: U-319 WILL PROCEED IMMEDIATELY. I WILL TRY
MY BEST.

Back at the chart table he pulled out the large-scale
chart of the English Channel and checked the map references again. The references were used by the Kriegsmarine
for security reasons. Triton, the U-boat cypher, was, of
course, secure and the Enigma machine itself invulnerable,
but, where vital information on the positions of German
vessels was concerned, the references were an additional
safeguard.

Fischer thought again: Incredible. What a hell of a job!

The search area lay between thirty and forty miles
south-south-east of the southernmost point of the English
mainland – the headland known as the Lizard.

Fischer drew a line between the last estimated position
of the – he almost called it 'target' then corrected himself –
of the *prey*, and the given destination, the port of Falmouth, which lay to the north-east of the Lizard. Where
the line intersected the search area he drew a cross.

He turned to the navigating officer, hovering at his
shoulder, and said, 'A course, please, to *there*.'

The navigator bent over the chart. Fischer said to his
first officer, 'A signal please to U-64 and U-402. Tell them
we have new orders and are leaving them directly.'

He returned to the chart. 'How far to the search
point?'

'One hundred and ten miles exactly.'

Fischer calculated how long it would take to do the
distance. On the surface, flat out at seventeen knots, seven
hours. He looked at his watch: 0130. Dawn was at 0700
roughly. Not enough time. At dawn he'd have to submerge

and he'd still be sixteen odd miles short of the search point. Still, he'd be in the right area and it wouldn't take long to complete the distance, even at the paltry seven knots they did under the surface. So, on target at about 0930.

Not bad. If this fishing craft was really doing four knots then they should be there well ahead of it. Even if it was doing six knots, they'd still be all right.

'Drop clear astern of U-64 and then turn to starboard on the course —?'

'008 degrees, Herr Kaleu, until abeam of Ushant.'

'Course 008.' The order was repeated by the first officer and the coxswain.

Fischer looked round for the Chief. He was standing in the after section of the control room. 'Chief, I'm going to need everything. Seventeen knots if you can manage it.'

The chief tried to frown, but Fischer could see that he was pleased. He liked a challenge. 'Right, Herr Kaleu. I'll see what I can do.' He disappeared in the direction of the engine room.

'Tell me when we're on course.'

After a few minutes the confirmation came. Fischer gave the order for full speed ahead.

The order was repeated through the control room. The whine of the diesels rose to a steady din and Fischer felt the vibration run through the boat. He ordered extra vigilance from the lookouts, then, with nothing further to be done, returned to the chart table to stare at the wide expanse of white paper that marked the English Channel.

It was a long time since he'd taken a U-boat into the Channel – it was a long time since anyone had. The British controlled it too effectively. He wondered what he'd find there – the lot probably: air patrols, motor torpedo boats, minesweepers . . .

Too much, far too much. There was only one point in U-319's favour: the British wouldn't be expecting anyone to take a U-boat into the waters where submarines had been proved so vulnerable. They wouldn't believe anyone could be so stupid.

It wasn't much of an advantage. But it was all he had.

From the outside the building looks solid and impenetrable – but not enormous. Certainly not large enough to house the operational headquarters of the British Admiralty. That is because most of the building is underground, a warren of subterranean rooms protected from bombing by concrete walls and roofs several feet thick. Not surprisingly, the building is called the Citadel. It lies in the heart of London, next to the main Admiralty buildings, to which it is connected by underground passages. Deep within it are two largish adjoining chambers which resemble billiard rooms. Both contain tables about nine feet square on which are enormous charts overhung by brilliant lights which shine day and night. In the first room is the Main Plot where Allied surface movements – both Allied and enemy – are plotted, as well as relevant air activity. Next door is the Submarine Tracking Room. Its sole purpose is to track enemy submarine movements in the Atlantic.

And, despite German beliefs to the contrary, it does it remarkably well.

On this occasion the night watchkeeper was busy. Although the main interpretation of the data was carried out by the day staff, a lot of information came in during the night and it was his job to decide if there was anything requiring immediate attention, and to generally sort things out ready for analysis in the morning.

He had a staff of three. They were sifting information into groups according to the known facts. They had five sources of information: sightings, aircraft radar fixes, radio direction finding, Special Intelligence, and tracking using a combination of all available information. Radio direction finding was very efficient as long as the U-boat transmitted for long enough. Then the various stations around the country could take cross-bearings on the signal and obtain a fix.

But it was the euphemistically named Special Intelligence which really nailed the U-boats. Also known as Ultra, the information came from Bletchley Park, the Government Code and Cipher School. No-one outside Bletchley Park really knew how the boffins had cracked the German codes, but cracked them they had, though it usually took them a day – sometimes more – to decipher the signals. Once, some months before, the Germans had changed their codes and there had been a hiatus while the ciphers were broken, but then, after a while, the information had come filtering through again.

Sometimes the deciphered signals arrived in a matter of hours. Then the ex-lawyer who headed the department acted quickly, passing information to the naval and air commands and diverting convoys from the path of the waiting wolf packs – when the politicians allowed. Sometimes they did *not* allow, fearful that the Germans would awake to the fact that their codes had been broken.

More often than not it was twenty-four hours before information came through, a time when the Head of Department had to take decisions and make calculated guesses as to what the U-boats might be doing. When the information finally appeared it was amazing how often the Head's hunches proved correct. He was an astonishing man.

For the third time in an hour the watchkeeper leafed through the decoded Ultra signals that had come in at 0200. Nothing out of the ordinary. Routine signals from headquarters. Brief acknowledgements from the U-boats. He had checked the U-boats' call-signs against those known to be at sea. They all tallied.

A teleprincess – one of the girls from the telex and communications room – came in and put a telex in front of him. It was from Bletchley Park: a decoded message sent to U-boat headquarters by an escort vessel. At 2300 the escort had reported dropping three U-boats at T3, the buoy which marked the end of the swept channel leading out of Brest. The U-boats concerned were U-64, U-402 and U-319.

The watchkeeper got up and, taking three tokens, marked them with the U-boats' numbers. He calculated the approximate distance the U-boats would have travelled since 2300 and placed the tokens on the plot, some fifty miles west of Brest.

U-319. He knew that number. Even before he looked it up on the list he remembered that it was Fischer's boat. Yes, there she was: U-319, Commander: Karl Fischer, Flotilla: Ninth, Base: Brest.

Fischer was well known. A very successful skipper, a German hero. He'd been around a long time.

The watchkeeper only wished he knew where the blighter was heading for. Sometimes one didn't find out until too late. Sometimes one never found out at all.

He returned to his desk. Almost immediately the telephone rang. It was Bletchley Park. He listened carefully, asked a couple of questions, and replaced the receiver. He stood up and stared thoughtfully at the plot.

U-boat headquarters had sent an unusually long message on the Atlantic U-boat frequency. The message had only just been intercepted and wouldn't be decoded for some hours yet, but it had had an urgent priority prefix. That was sufficiently unusual for Bletchley to call him.

Something was up then. The watchkeeper wondered what it could be. Perhaps German Intelligence had discovered the position of a convoy, perhaps a new strategy was being implemented . . .

He stared at the plot as if it could tell him the answer. But there was only one thing that could do that – the decode.

And that, as always, took time.

Chapter 27

NxW. NORTH BY WEST ... Where on earth was it? It had *disappeared* again.

Julie peered at the dimly-lit compass card and tried to read the letters. The boat lurched and she put up a hand to brace herself against the post that held the compass.

Come on! Which way? Which way?

Think. It was showing W – West. North was to the right. Therefore she wanted the card to swing – which way? She almost shouted with frustration: it was impossible to work out.

Frantically, she pulled the tiller towards her and watched the card.

It hesitated then swung slowly towards North.

She breathed a sigh of relief, then made herself concentrate again. NxW. North by West.

NxW for one hour. Don't forget. NxW – North by West.

The problem was the compass. It wouldn't stay still. It kept swaying from side to side. And it moved in the opposite direction to the one you expected. The tiller did too!

NxW for one hour then you'll be safe.

Then you'll be safe ... So there must be dangers either side, rocks, shoals, islands ... She remembered on placid summer days seeing the rocks in the estuary and, further out, black towers marking hidden plateaus.

She gulped and gritted her teeth and concentrated again

on the swinging card. However hard she tried it was absolutely impossible to keep it straight on NxW. The best she could do was to keep NxW in the centre of the swing. Even then, if she took her eyes away for a moment, it seemed to dive away.

She jerked the tiller towards her and realised the card was swinging the wrong way. 'Dear God!' She shoved the tiller away and the 'N' shot round towards the front of the compass. Too far! She yanked at the tiller again until NxW hovered for a moment on the marker before swinging inexorably away. She shouted out loud, 'Damn you!'

She closed her eyes tightly for a moment and made an effort to clear her mind.

She opened her eyes, breathed deeply and concentrated again. At last the compass evened out somewhere around NxW. She remembered something Richard had said, about boats having a feel to them, a balance . . . There was none that she could sense, none at all!

A sound floated back, a whimper . . . She peered towards the middle of the boat. 'Peter? Peter! Are you all right, darling?'

'Mummy!' The voice was tearful. 'Mummy, I'm awfully cold!'

'Yes, darling, I know. But—' Could she leave the tiller and get to him? No – it was too risky, even for a moment. She shouted, 'Darling, try to get under the deck at the front. And – look in your bag—'

'What?' His voice was faint, plaintive.

The course had veered again; Julie jerked at the tiller. 'Your bag, darling. Look inside it. There's another sweater somewhere!'

'What?'

Julie gripped the tiller and tried not to scream. She shouted angrily, 'Just do as I say and don't argue!'

There was a silence, then, 'I've got it.'

Julie calmed herself down. She said steadily, 'Take off your jacket and put on the sweater, then crawl up – No! Put the jacket back on *first, then* crawl up to the front. It'll be warmer there. Tell me when you get there.'

'All right.'

For an instant Julie wondered what had happened to the old man: he was very quiet. She thought of calling to him, then decided against it. Later. She had too much to think about now.

The boat moved suddenly and Julie reached for the post again, her heart lurching with fear. The waves – they were a little larger, she was sure of it. She shivered violently and looked quickly down at the compass. The boat was miles off course. She jerked at the tiller and thought: This is hopeless, *hopeless*! I can't *possibly* manage this on my own! God, why did Michel think I could!

If only there was someone else!

Richard . . . Best of all, *Richard* – why couldn't *he* be here? He would know exactly what to do. He must have been through lots of experiences like this. The thought encouraged her a little. She tried to remember other things he had told her about sailing, things that might help . . . But she could remember nothing very useful: he'd talked about compasses and courses – but he'd never explained how you actually held a course, far less how you managed the sails . . .

Peter's small voice floated back on the wind. 'Mummy, I'm here!' In the front, presumably.

Julie shouted, 'Try to go to sleep now, darling.'

'All right.'

She looked down at the compass. Good Lord: it actually read NxW. She giggled a little hysterically.

The night was so dark it was impossible to see anything clearly. The sky was slightly less dark than the sea – but that was all. Julie stared ahead, trying to make out shapes – something, anything. But there was no distance, no perspective and after a while the blackness seemed to rear up in front of her like a wall.

Quickly, she looked back at the compass. NW. She pulled the tiller towards her. NNW. Then, a sudden swing to N. She pushed the tiller away again. NxW – at last. *Stay there!*

She glanced up again, and shivered. It was eerie, the darkness. Unnerving. It made her feel utterly remote, like being on a hilltop, quite alone. And then there was the silence. Though it was broken by the whisper of the wind and the swishing of the water and the occasional slap of a wave on the boat's side, it was eerie too.

She shivered again, and couldn't stop. With faint surprise she realised she was terribly cold. No time to get more clothes on. Later. Later.

NxW for an hour – then you'll be safe.

How much time had passed? She had no idea. It felt like hours. She looked at her watch, but it was far too dark to read it. She put her wrist down to the compass and, leaning forward, tried to see the hands by the reflection of the compass light. The thing was a stupid woman's watch: it had a tiny face without numbers. Useless! She put her face closer. At last she thought she saw the hands. Midnight—?

An hour gone!

The compass had sheered violently off. She pulled on the tiller. Damn! Wrong way! Why did the blasted thing have to work *backwards*!

There: NxW. She put her wrist to the compass again and, steadying the boat, thrust her face down to the flickering light. It took half a minute to be sure, but yes: it was almost midnight. Nearly an hour gone! She'd wait another ten minutes to be on the safe side. Perhaps even more, to be absolutely sure. Then—! She felt the beginnings of relief. Over the first hurdle. Something anyway, to have got this far.

Half-smiling, half-miserable, she thought: Richard would be proud of me!

Then she remembered where he was and the despair settled on her like a lead weight.

Don't . . . Don't think . . .

Mechanically she glanced at the compass.

It wasn't there.

Her heart went to her mouth. She gulped. It had gone – the *light*! The light had gone!

There wasn't a flicker. She said out loud, 'No! Dear God!' And, clamping her hand over her mouth, thought: What on earth do I do *now*?

Relight the oil? But she had no match.

Think. What had Michel said? He'd mentioned something . . . A torch. Yes! Where? In a box. That was it, he'd said it was in a box. She knelt down, one hand still on the tiller, and felt around. Nothing. The other side, then. Floorboards . . . a rope . . . Further behind . . .

Her hand came to an upright wooden surface. She felt up to a top lip and a lid. It was a box, full of things: rough ropes, a square metal box, then – a round metal object. She almost cried out in triumph. Standing up again, she found the switch and a narrow beam of yellow light shot forward into the darkness. She was half-blinded. Fumbling she switched it off again. Far too bright.

She reached down into the box again and scrabbled around. At last she found a piece of cloth and, putting it over the torch, turned it on again, being careful to keep the beam pointing downwards. That was much better: the beam was reduced to a dull pool of light. She shone it at the compass. Not bad! Only NNW! She pulled the tiller towards her and the card swung back towards NxW. At last.

She switched off the torch. Mustn't waste the batteries.

She let her body sag. The boat leaned slightly and she stepped backwards to regain her balance. The back of her

knees came up against something hard and, feeling with
her hand, she realised it was a seat. Of course: a seat for
the helmsman. She sank back on to it and wedged her foot
up against the compass post. It was much more
comfortable.

She almost laughed.

She wondered if the full hour and a quarter had passed.
Probably not: best to wait.

She tried to concentrate on the steering, to keep on
course without having to shine the light too much. Sometimes it worked, sometimes not. Most of the time she just
stared forward, trying not to see the darkness rearing up in
front of her.

Finally she shone the torch on her watch. It was twenty
past twelve. She clenched her fists and, looking up, said,
'Thank you, God!' She almost shouted the news to Peter,
but decided not to: he was probably asleep by now.

What now? *Then anything between north-north-west
and north-east . . .* Or was it north-west and north-east?

She couldn't remember.

. . . No, he'd definitely said between NNW and NE.

Julie felt into the box for some rope and, resting the
tiller against her knee, unwound a coil. Her fingers were
dreadfully stiff from the cold and from gripping the tiller
so tight. Eventually she managed to tie a loop on to the
tiller. She went to the side of the boat and felt along it for
an anchor point. She found one on the top of the rail: a
wooden thing with a point sticking out either end. She'd
seen them used for tying up ropes before. She took the
rope and wound it several times round the wooden thing,
which had a name she couldn't remember.

Next she took the other end of the rope to the other
side of the boat and tied it to another wooden anchor
point. She shone the torch on the compass and watched.
NNW moving towards NW. She let off one side of the
rope and tightened the other, to move the tiller slightly

across. The course held steady on NW. She loosened the right-hand rope a little more. The course came up to NNW and she tightened it again. The course was holding. More or less.

Taking the torch she quickly made her way along the left side of the boat towards the front. She knelt down under the small expanse of decking and shone the shaded torch on to the floor. In the reflected light she saw Peter, curled in a ball, sleeping peacefully. She felt his cheek: warm enough, but not as warm as she'd like.

She shone the torch around and saw, right in the point at the front, some dark material folded under a lobster pot. She crawled forward and pulled the material out. It was a sack. Under it was another. She went on pulling until she had four. She crawled back and put two over Peter.

Now the old man. He must be on the right-hand side somewhere. She was still blinded from using the torch and waited until her eyes readjusted to the darkness. Then she saw him: a dark shape huddled under the steep side of the boat. She went over and knelt down beside him.

He was very still. She asked tentatively, 'Are you all right?'

Silence. Julie reached out and touched his arm.

There was a slight moan. She thought: Thank goodness, at least he's alive! 'Are you all right?' she repeated.

'Eh? Oh . . .' The old man's voice was low, rough. 'Oh . . . Yes, yes . . . I'm all right.' He tried to laugh. 'I'm just not as young as I used to be, that's all!'

'I'm so sorry, I didn't mean to wake you. I'm so sorry!'

'No, no, dear girl. Please . . . please don't apologise. I only wish I could help you. I'm of no use at all, I'm afraid. Perhaps later . . .' His voice was weak now, and breathless.

'No, you just stay there and rest. Don't worry about me. Honestly, I can manage! Here—' She put the two sacks over him. 'Are you comfortable here, or would you like to go up to the front? It's a bit more sheltered there.'

'No, thank you so much. I'm all right . . . Thank you.'

There was a loud slap: a wave against the side. Julie said sharply, 'I must go now – back to the steering . . . Just shout if you need me.'

And then she was gone. David pulled the sacks more tightly round his legs and wished he didn't feel so ill. He closed his eyes and leant his head back against the side. Immediately, he felt disorientated and his head began to swim. He opened his eyes again. The boat was rocking gently from side to side. If it went on rocking, he thought grimly, he would be sick.

He burped slightly and felt a pang of acid in his stomach. So he was to suffer that too! His stomach chose its moments very well.

He closed his eyes and tentatively let his head fall to one side. He decided he would be more comfortable lying down. Taking the bag from round his waist, he felt in it and found his tablets. He took one and, putting the bag on the deck, lay down with his head on it. Yes: that was better. He didn't feel so sick, lying down. He might even be able to sleep.

He would feel better later. Then he would give Julie a hand.

Julie untied the tiller and brought the boat back on course. Almost immediately she sighed with annoyance: she'd forgotten to get a sweater. But perhaps it wasn't necessary; it didn't seem quite so cold as before . . . Then she remembered that awful time on the fishing boat, and something Richard had said, about cold being the greatest danger of all, much more dangerous than the waves themselves, and she retied the tiller and set off towards the front.

Her bag was beside Peter, right up under the deck. She supposed Michel had put it there in case it rained. She undid the strap and felt around until she found the thick wool sweater. She took off the cowjacket, pulled the sweater on, and put the cowjacket back over the top. She felt warmer already. There was a scarf in the bag too; she rummaged around, found it, and tied it round her head.

Peter was sleeping peacefully. She went straight back to the tiller. When she shone the torch on the compass she almost laughed: the course had settled on NxW. She decided to leave the boat sailing by itself; the course was a good one and much steadier than anything she could achieve.

She sat on the helmsman's seat and tried to think. How far was it across the Channel? She had no idea. How long would it take to get across? She had no idea of that either.

Brilliant!

Try again. It must be at least a hundred miles across the Channel – perhaps even two hundred. Say a hundred and fifty. How fast were they going? Goodness only knew! It felt as if the boat was going quite fast – perhaps fifteen miles an hour. No: on second thoughts, that was quite a rate. What was walking speed? Five miles an hour, four? A bit faster than that, say six then.

Six miles an hour. A hundred and fifty miles. Mental arithmetic: always one of her worst subjects at school. Sixes into one hundred and fifty . . .

Eventually she got there: twenty-five. Of course. Six twenty-fives made a hundred and fifty.

Twenty-five hours then, call it twenty-four.

Immediately she felt depressed.

It was a dreadfully long time. A whole day out in the middle of the sea, a day when they would be exposed like a goldfish in a bowl. There were bound to be German patrols . . . aircraft . . .

If they survived the day, then there'd be most of the

next night, a night when the land would be getting closer and closer, rushing towards them. How on earth would she know where it was, the land? And how would she know when the boat was about to crash into it?

I can't do this, she thought, I just can't do it!

Silently she began to cry, the tears hot on her cheeks. It was all such a mess, the whole dreadful thing. Everyone at the village caught and dead or more probably tortured. Richard a prisoner. And here – Peter and the old man relying on *her*, probably the most incompetent person in the world!

Angrily, she wiped the tears away. Whatever happened, crying wouldn't do any good.

Later, she realised a long time must have passed – several hours at least. Apart from shining the torch on the compass from time to time she stared ahead into the darkness, her mind half on what had happened at the beach, half on the nightmare she was living through now. One event seemed to lead on from the other, in a horrible dreamlike way.

For a while she dozed, perched uneasily on the seat, terrible pictures drifting in and out of her mind, the beach and the boat blending into a terrible fantasy of water and blazing lights and anger and suffering. The Germans were taking everyone away ... Jean, Tante Marie, and Peter, *even Peter—*

Suddenly she was awake.

She looked blindly around, wondering what had woken her. The boat was still sailing along, the water hissing and gurgling past the hull. But the sky was different. It was clearer now: there were stars, thousands of them, carpeting the sky so that the sail stood out black against them. But there was something else and she couldn't place it. She shone the light at the compass. NW – North-west. The course had changed a little. But was that it? No.

Then she had it. The wind, it was much fresher. She felt it cold against her face, pulling at her scarf. A muted fluttering sound came from above, like a thousand birds beating their wings. Now and then there was the creaking of wood against wood.

Yes, there was more wind. She could feel it now, in the motion of the boat. The movements were much quicker than before and, instead of rocking gently from side to side, the craft was tilted stiffly over at a slight angle, its nose going down and up, down and up, like a rocking horse.

The bow hit a wave with a *crump!* and Julie realised that it was the sound which had woken her. A fine spray floated back on the air and drifted onto her face. Shaking slightly, she shone the light at the compass again. Still north-west, but tending to veer off towards the west. Not good enough. She untied the tiller and moved it until the compass read nearer to North.

Immediately the fluttering sound changed to a flapping and there was a fierce rattling as something close to Julie's head started to shake angrily.

She yanked the tiller back the other way. The flapping stopped, but when she looked at the compass the course was back west of North-West. Michel had specifically said she must steer between north-north-west and north-east. She was definitely *outside* that.

What should she do? She gripped the tiller, undecided. She could leave the boat on this course – but that *must* be wrong. The sails, then, she should stop them flapping. But how?

She tried bringing the boat back onto a northerly course once more, but the flapping started again, louder than ever. 'Damn!' She quickly pulled the tiller the other way. The flapping stopped. She breathed out sharply.

She stayed at the tiller steering north-west for a long

time, frozen with indecision. She should do something to the sails – she knew *that* much – but what? And if she didn't – God, she'd probably miss England altogether.

Impossible.

Because there was nothing else to do, she held the north-westerly course, thinking all the time: I'm failing! Miserably failing!

Perhaps if she held on, perhaps the wind would change . . .

A long time passed. Dimly she realised that she could see the side of the boat stretching away from her. When she looked again the bow itself was there, a faint black smudge against grey. Then the sea itself – waves; she could see waves like the ripples on an iced cake, but grey and murky. To the right, a thin line of pale white light appeared, stretching across the horizon from side to side; with a slight shock, Julie realised it *was* the horizon. The white light filtered gradually up into the sky, turning a delicate crystal yellow, the colour of pale primrose. One by one the stars disappeared until the sky became a clear unbroken dome over her head.

Dawn. It had come too soon.

Instinctively, Julie looked behind, but she could see nothing – it was still too dark. She looked again a few minutes later. It was difficult to tell: the grey area between the sea and the sky was too indistinct.

Half an hour later the southern horizon was visible, a grey line behind the boat. She looked carefully: there was no land in sight. They were clear of the coast, then. That was something at least.

Then, as she looked at the vast expanse of water appearing around her, stretching out barren and cold in every direction, she didn't feel so glad. It looked enormous.

Up in the front Peter's figure was clearly visible, curled up under the sacks. He was sleeping soundly. So was the old man, over on the right-hand side, against the side of the boat. Good. There was no point in everyone being tired.

Wearily, Julie looked at the compass, visible now in the grey light. Still North-west. Still the *wrong* course.

She should do something about it . . .

She stayed frozen at the tiller a moment longer then made herself stand up. *Time to get going.*

She said out loud, 'Right!' Gritting her teeth, she tied up the tiller and eyed the ropes that were coiled or fastened at various points round the boat. There were two sails. The first, a big sail, almost square, was fastened to the mast on its front edge, to a long wooden pole on its lower edge and to another, shorter, pole high up on its top edge. The fourth – back – edge wasn't fastened to anything. Up in front of the mast, there was another, smaller sail, triangular and attached to a sharp piece of wood that stuck out in front of the boat. She remembered: the piece of wood was called a bowsprit.

The big sail first. There was one rope which seemed to make the sail go in or out. The rope wound back and forth between wooden pulleys. She wasn't sure why – to make things easier perhaps.

The rope was tied off round a wooden anchor thing – was it called a *fastener*? Tentatively she reached forward and began to untie the rope. She paused, her heart hammering against her chest, then, very slowly, began to take off the last turn.

Suddenly there was an almighty jerk and the rope almost flew out of her hands. She cried out and, holding on grimly, tried to get a second turn of rope back onto the anchor-fastener. As she moved her hands the rope jerked out, pulling her knuckle sharply against the hard wood of the fastener. She gasped out in pain.

God, the pain!

She let go.

The rope whistled out from the coil, snaking up angrily

towards the sail. The next moment there was a thunderous noise: the racket of beating canvas and rattling pulleys. Julie looked up. The sail had gone mad; it was beating itself about in a frenzy, girating back and forth until the whole boat vibrated.

Julie stared, aghast.

What now?

She put her hands over her ears, to cut out the dreadful noise, and looked round in desperation.

There was still some rope left in the coil; it hadn't all run out. Shaking like a leaf, she reached down and picked up the rope and, cautiously, began to pull in on it.

'Mummy!'

Julie spun round. Peter was standing beside her, rubbing his eyes, and looking curiously up at the sail. 'Mummy, shouldn't we pull it in?'

Julie stared at him and shook her head. Then, trying to smile, said wearily, 'Yes, Peter, we should.'

'I'll help you, then!' He was shouting to make himself heard over the thrashing of the sail.

'Don't you dare touch it!' Julie screamed. 'Just – leave it!'

There was no reply and, looking down, she saw that he was looking hurt and shame-faced. She sighed, 'Sorry, I'm just tired, sweetheart, that's all. I'll be all right in a moment.' She wiped her eyes on her sleeve and said ruefully, 'The trouble is, I don't know *how* to get the sail in.'

'You put the rope under the cleat.'

'The cleat?'

'Yes.' Peter pointed at the wooden anchor-fastener thing. 'That's what it's called – a cleat. Richard told me. And I know you put the ropes round it to take the strain. That's what he said . . .' He trailed off.

'Thank you, darling!' She almost kissed him. 'Let's have a go then!' She picked up the rope and, with Peter tugging rather ineffectually behind, began to pull. Soon the rope was jerking in her hands. She leant down and slid the rope under the lower arm of the cleat. Alternately she pulled and rested, letting the cleat take the strain of the rope. The clattering of the sail lessened slightly.

Then she had the idea of standing on the other side of the deck, so that the rope was doubled back from the cleat. It was a great improvement: the rope seemed less inclined to jerk out of her hands.

The pull on the rope became much stronger and, though she put her full weight against it, she couldn't get it in any further. She rested for a moment, panting.

Suddenly the noise got much worse again. Julie looked up, bewildered, then realised the rope had gone almost limp in her hand. She pulled wildly, gathering in great lengths of it, until she could pull no more. Quickly, she tied the rope off round the cleat.

The noise stopped; the sail was full again. She waited. After a few moments the flapping started again. Quickly she pulled in on the rope.

She looked up at the sail: it was almost tight in!

Elated, she tied off the rope securely and looked at the compass. North by West – or thereabouts! And the sail full: a miracle.

How it had happened she had no idea. Then the flapping started again and she saw that the tiller had become untied. Perhaps that was something to do with it.

She took hold of the tiller, put the boat back on course, and grinned at Peter. What did it matter how it had happened? She'd got the sail in *and* the boat on course.

She went forward and hunted for the rope that controlled the other, smaller, sail at the front. She found it and, eyeing the sail with trepidation, undid the rope. It didn't have nearly so much pull on it and she was able to haul it in quite easily.

Returning to the tiller she undid the lines that tied it
and said gaily to Peter, 'I'll make a sailor yet!'

The child smiled back and, coming to her side, put his
hand in hers. 'Mummy, I'm hungry. Is there any breakfast?'

Julie's heart sank. Breakfast. She'd never thought of
breakfast. Her smile vanished. Had Michel said anything
about food? Water, yes, he'd definitely mentioned that.
But food? No.

She sighed. How did one tell a six-year-old that there
was nothing to eat? She said softly, 'There isn't any
breakfast, darling. Sorry.' She took a deep breath. 'We're
going to have to go without until we get to England.
Sorry.' She squeezed his hand.

'Without – anything?' The voice was small and subdued.

Julie looked away and tried to sound brisk and matter-
of-fact. 'Without anything. We finished all the food when
we were on the beach, remember?'

'Perhaps there's some on the boat somewhere . . .'

She sighed. It was very unlikely. 'Perhaps. Why don't
you go and have a look, eh?'

He nodded brightly and, dropping to his knees, started
rooting around in the large box where Julie had found the
torch.

It would, at least, keep him busy for a while.

A movement caught her eye: the old man was leaning
over the side of the boat, his head down, as if staring at
the water. For a moment Julie couldn't think what he was
doing then she heard a faint retching sound and looked
quickly away.

She'd quite forgotten about being sick. Extraordinary.
She couldn't understand why it hadn't happened to *her*.

There was a *crump!* from the bow and a thin veil of
spray came flying back into her face. More wind: definitely
more wind. The tiller felt different in her hand: it was
moving of its own accord and she had to push harder to
get the boat back on course. The boat was going faster,

too, haring along like the wind. Perhaps her calculations had been wrong; perhaps they'd get to England before nightfall. The idea of more wind made her very nervous but it might be a blessing after all.

There was a whoop from the front. Julie tensed. Peter's face appeared round the mast, waving madly. She frowned. What on earth was he so excited about?

He emerged, holding a bag, and weaved his way back down the boat. He dumped the bag at her feet in triumph. 'Food!' he yelped.

Julie blinked. 'Food?'

'Yes, tins, Mummy! Cans of fish and beef and potatoes and *petit pois* and . . .'

'Goodness gracious me!' She stared in astonishment as Peter opened the bag to reveal the cans, about ten of them, a little rusty but obviously quite usable. The whole thing was odd enough – Michel having this boat – but the food . . . A thought came to Julie and suddenly she understood everything.

This boat was for *Michel*'s escape. He'd planned it all – bought the boat, prepared it, put the food on board, even worked out the course for England. He'd planned it all – and then given the boat to her.

Crump! Spray flew into Julie's eyes and pattered against her jacket. 'Take the bag back to the bow, Peter, so it doesn't get wet. And you stay there too and have something to eat.'

'But it's awfully bumpy up there. Can't I stay here?' He was whining. Tiredness.

'Well – perhaps . . . All right! We'll eat here together then. See if you can find an opener or a knife or something.'

He disappeared into the box behind her and rummaged around, then looked up at her dispiritedly. 'Nothing here, Mummy, only this.' He held up a metal spike.

'Try the front, then.'

'The bow, you mean. That's its *proper* name.'

Julie made the effort not to clip his ear. 'Don't argue with me!' she shouted. 'Just go and look.'

He wandered off down the deck. Instantly Julie regretted her anger: she was tired and hungry too.

The bow rose then dipped suddenly. There was more spray, heavier this time and icy cold: she could feel it seeping through her trousers. The wind seemed colder too; she shivered despite the extra sweater.

Peter came back along the deck, his hair dripping with water.

'Oh darling, you're all wet!'

'There was a big wave!' His lower lip trembled and he started to cry.

'Come on, let's get some food inside you!'

'There's no opener!' He was crying in earnest now, his face creased up in despair.

One thing after another. Julie took a deep breath and said calmly, 'Let's use the spike then. That'll have to do.'

Pushing her back against the tiller to hold it steady, she reached into the bag for a can and, holding it against her leg, tried to puncture it with the spike. On the third attempt the spike slid off and dug into her thigh. Hopeless.

God, she felt tired.

She put her hand into the bag to see if there was an easier can, perhaps a flat sardine-type with its own opener. She felt around and came out with a long metallic object – a can opener. She clapped her hand to her forehead and shook her head. It was, of course, where any intelligent person would have put it.

She opened a can of meat and one of pilchards. 'When you've eaten, go and see if Monsieur Freymann wants anything, will you, Peter?' He nodded, his mouth full of meat. Julie looked to the rail, but David wasn't there any more and she saw that he was lying on the deck again. His face was sheet white; he wouldn't want anything to eat. A drink, maybe . . .

Where was that water Michel had talked about? Heaven only knew.

She stuffed a pilchard into her mouth and was surprised to find how hungry she was. She ate ravenously, then opened a can of potatoes and ate most of that, too, before passing it to Peter.

Crump! The water was flying over the bow more frequently now. Did it matter, all this water? She remembered how wet it had been on that large fishing boat when she and Peter had tried to escape before, yet the crew hadn't been worried.

Peter got a face full of water and she made him move to the uphill side of the deck where there seemed to be less spray. She moved across to the same side and took the tiller in her other hand.

As soon as she moved across she realised just how much the boat was tilting over on to one side. The deck was at a considerable slant and the mast was leaning over at a distinct angle. Each gust of wind made the tilt worse. What was there to stop the boat going right over?

She had a sudden memory of another time ... With Richard all those years ago. The boat had tipped over then, quite far. She remembered clinging to the side, terrified. But *he* hadn't been worried, not in the slightest. She whispered, 'Oh Richard, why the hell aren't you here!'

There was a whoosh and a swishing sound. Water was racing along the downhill side of the deck. Julie felt a rush of fear. *Where had it come from?* Immediately she thought: We're sinking!

She clutched at Peter. 'Oh God, darling!'

'It's all right, Mummy, it'll go out through the scuppers.'

Julie stared at him in amazement. 'The scuppers?'

'Yes. Richard told me when we were carving the model. They're the holes in the sides, down there. For letting water out.'

'... for letting water out ...'

She watched, fascinated, as the water gurgled away through the small slits. A moment later the boat tipped again and the water came back, only to gurgle harmlessly away as before. She turned to Peter. 'What else did Richard tell you?'

The little face went blank. Julie realised it was the wrong way to ask. She tried again. 'Did he talk about what to do in strong winds?'

Peter made a face of concentration. 'Ummm, well I know what you do in *gales*.'

Julie gripped his shoulder. 'Yes, darling!'

'You shorten sail!'

'Yes . . . and?'

'You reef! That's what you do!'

'Reef . . . That's what he told you?'

'Yes.'

Julie thought desperately but she had no idea what that meant. She looked down at Peter. He was still thinking, she could tell by his face. Eventually he said slowly, 'You let the sail down a bit, then you tie up the loose bit with all those ropes hanging from the sail there. Richard drew me a picture.'

'I see.'

She couldn't imagine how it was actually done, but at least she might have a vague idea if the worst came to the worst. But when did a strong wind become a gale? How did you *know* when to reef?

Her head was aching violently: she couldn't think. Damn it. One thing at a time. Gales might never happen!

She settled back on the helmsman's seat and forced herself to stop worrying. After all, things could be a lot worse.

At that moment David Freymann cried out in agony and, from far away in the eastern sky, there came the low hum of an approaching plane.

Chapter 28

————•————

THE WIND. IT was coming from the north-east and
freshening.

Fischer left the periscope and went to the chart table.
The prey certainly wouldn't be trying for Plymouth – the
course would put them hard on the wind. Too uncomfortable and too slow.

No: Falmouth it had to be.

But the speed estimate would have to be revised. Even a
small boat would be doing more than four knots in this
wind. Five, maybe more.

Fischer marked off two points along the prey's course
line. The first point marked the prey's position if he were
doing a steady six knots; the second, his position at four
knots. These, then, marked the limits of speed probability.
The gap between the two positions was twenty nautical
miles.

Now, course. If this fellow strayed from his course,
which way would he go? To the west almost certainly,
because of this freshening wind. Fischer marked off a
second course line ten degrees to the west of the first. He
now had a long thin box of approximately a hundred
square miles.

A hundred square miles . . . One hell of a lot of sea . . .

It would be impossible to search it all. No, the best
thing would be to patrol back and forth across the
probable track of the prey and wait for him to come to
them. A waiting game.

The soonest that the prey could possibly be here was
. . . right now. Unlikely, though, because he wouldn't have
been doing six knots the whole time. At the other extreme,
the latest he'd arrive was in five hours' time, at 1500 hours.

A waiting game.

In the meantime . . .

Fischer looked at the chart as a whole. Little danger of
meeting enemy surface units here: U-319 was in the
unofficial no-man's-land between Britain and France. But
nearer Britain there would be a lot of shipping – minesweepers, coastal convoys – and guarding the shipping
lane, maybe even some minefields. His chart showed one
mined area just to the north of him. But Fischer was
sceptical: in all likelihood the intelligence was out of date
and probably not too accurate in the first place.

But overhead there was no such thing as a no-man's-
land. The air was anybody's. Except that, around here, it
was mainly British. That was one of the reasons U-boats
didn't bother to operate in the Channel nowadays.

Fischer strolled thoughtfully back to the search periscope. A young seaman was manning it, circling slowly.
Fischer watched him for a moment, his mind on what
would happen if they did manage to find this fishing boat.
To capture the occupants they'd have to surface. The
operation would take a good fifteen to twenty minutes – if
they were lucky. It was an awful long time to be on the
surface in broad daylight.

Hell! What an operation!

The periscope stopped circling. The young seaman
yelled, 'Aircraft bearing 045! Range – four to five miles!'

Fischer pushed the young man aside and took a look. A
Catalina or something like it. Definitely one of the opposition's. Closing.

'Down periscope! Alter course forty-five degrees to
starboard!'

Fifteen minutes: he'd give it fifteen minutes before he took another look.

After five minutes he said again, 'Alter course forty-five degrees to starboard.' The order was echoed twice.

They waited, as they'd waited so many times before, the crew automatically falling into Silent Routine, though no ship was tracking them. Everyone was still and the only sound was the quiet hum of the electric motors.

After a long while Fischer looked at his watch. Time to have a look. 'Up periscope.'

The periscope hissed up and, quickly lowering the folding handles, Fischer looked through the eyepiece. He made a quick circle: nothing. Then a slower one: nothing. The plane had gone.

It had been on a routine reconnaissance patrol, Fischer decided. It was unlikely it had seen them.

Another two circles to search the horizon. No fishing boat in sight.

'Resume course. Resume Patrol Routine.'

The men relaxed and started to move around again. Fischer made another circle of the horizon. The sea was definitely rougher. From one point of view that was a good thing: it meant there was less chance of the periscope being seen. On the other hand it would be more difficult to spot the prey.

If they ever got anywhere near it, that was . . .

'Wireless signal, Herr Kaleu.'

With the resumption of Patrol Routine the rod aerial – also periscopic – had gone up. Fischer went over to the wireless operator and watched him tap the signal into the Enigma machine. Fischer tore off the decoded message, said, 'Strictly *no* acknowledgement!' and strode over to the chart table.

He was jubilant: the target had been spotted! By one of their own reconnaissance planes – which meant the position wouldn't be terribly accurate, aerial fixes never were – but it was a darn sight better than nothing.

He measured the co-ordinates off the side and top of the chart and pencilled in a cross. There! Seen *there* at 0930 hours!

Slow. Going much slower than he'd thought. Almost at the lower edge of the box he'd drawn – and to the west, *well* to the west! He frowned. Where could they be making for?

And the slow speed, that was a surprise, too. They had averaged only four knots. Perhaps the fishing boat had set out later than first thought, perhaps that first position was wrong . . . All supposition.

The point was, he must get U-319 further over to the west, into the prey's path . . .

And then?

Then he'd wait. Nothing had changed. It was still a waiting game.

In the Submarine Tracking Room the Head went over the information that had come in during the night. He sifted through it slowly, measuring it against the probable speed and track of the various boats, and tried to calculate where wolf packs might be forming.

The job was getting increasingly difficult. The problem was one of scale. Never had there been so many U-boats – four hundred in existence, two hundred and fifty operational and probably well over a hundred actually at sea. It was almost impossible to keep track of them all, though he and his staff did their very best. Especially *now*.

He remembered the morning meeting and the appalling statistics – twenty-one ships lost from just two convoys. He remembered the words of the Vice-Chief of Staff. *We have reached a crisis in the battle of the Atlantic.* The crisis was simple – if the U-boats weren't driven off, then the convoys couldn't get through.

No-one needed to be told the consequences of that.

To fight the menace there was to be a new strategy: Ultra information was to be used to the full and convoys always diverted out of the path of waiting wolf packs; all convoys were to get full support group protection; and, finally, production of the new H_2S radar, which trials had proved to be successful, was to be rapidly accelerated and units fitted to all bombers of Coastal Command.

It was make or break. The last ditch stand.

Doenitz knew that too.

Over the years the Head had learnt to understand the way Doenitz's mind worked. The U-boats' tactics reflected Doenitz's thinking, his favourite strategies, his master plan. A year before, when air patrols and radar had made things too difficult for the U-boats in the North Atlantic, the Grand Admiral had transferred the larger ones to the South Atlantic. And the Head had foreseen it. When that in turn got too hot for his boats Doenitz had sent them to the American coast. Again, the Head had guessed. Because he would have done the same himself.

Now Doenitz had put everything back into the North Atlantic.

This was Doenitz's last ditch stand too.

But for the Head it was hard work keeping the Plot up to date. The Head had a day staff of eleven track plotters and six DF plotters – not a lot to cover so many U-boats.

He re-examined the log entries made by the night watch, and the decodes.

Mainly routine. No specific evidence of a new wolf pack forming. The only unusual thing was the long message sent at 0115 hours and prefixed urgent.

A signal on the U-boat frequency – possibly an acknowledgement – had been sent ten minutes later. The signal was too short for the DF people to get a good fix on it, but a rough estimate had put the U-boat in the Bay of Biscay.

Just one acknowledgement . . . A single U-boat involved then. Curious. A change of orders perhaps? A new destination?

What he needed were the Ultra decodes.

An hour later he had them in an enormous pile.

Short messages, lots of them: acknowledgements, damage reports, notification of successful attacks (too many of them, always too many of them) . . . He passed them to his staff for routine processing.

He picked up the long signal and read the message with growing astonishment. Good Lord, what on earth did it all mean? A fishing boat, occupants to be captured but not harmed . . . Extraordinary.

He went to a side table. On it was a large chart marked with grid references. At the beginning of the war the Germans had made no attempt to disguise their grid references and, once a German chart had been obtained for the Tracking Room, it was a simple matter to read the references off. But now the references were disguised by a code which was changed every month and sometimes it took quite a while to crack it. At the moment they were still guessing. The code had only just been changed.

Grid references. The signal had dozens of the blasted things . . .

Some were familiar and did, he knew, lie somewhere in the Bay. Others were unfamiliar . . . H17 P15, for example. He knew the prefix 'H' and 'P', but he'd never seen them with those numbers and in that combination. Deduction – this boat was being sent somewhere different. Not into the Atlantic, nor to Greenland or Iceland.

Chasing a fishing boat . . . Biscay coast? Possibly. But there again the grid references didn't look right, certainly nothing like those used by U-boats close to the Biscay coast from where, after Allied air attacks, they sometimes had to call for assistance.

The North French coast then?

No U-boats had been into the Channel for a long time. Too dangerous and too few convoys to make it worthwhile.

He frowned, studying the signal again. The fishing boat was believed to be heading for another place with fairly similar co-ordinates – same prefixes, not too dissimilar numbers. So, somewhere fairly close to the first place? It would be easy to assume that the second place was a port or refuge – but it could just as easily be a point miles out to sea, a rendezvous . . .

The Head called across to one of his assistants and asked her to check with the various clandestine organisations, just in case they knew anything about a meeting with a fishing boat.

Back to the co-ordinates. Assuming the first of each pair of co-ordinates was the latitude, then the second position was at a higher latitude, assuming again that the code followed the normal practice and the numbers got higher the further from the equator you went . . .

An awful lot of assumptions.

But if the assumptions *were* right, then the second place was to the north of the first.

The fishing boat could conceivably be going north from somewhere like Bordeaux . . . But no, the co-ordinates would have been familiar. Also he felt that, instinctively, it didn't quite fit. They'd never send a U-boat if the fisherman was making a run for another part of Occupied France, or for neutral Spain, they'd send a coastal patrol boat or, even better, an E-boat.

That was it! Of course!

They had sent a U-boat.

Not anything else . . .

Why?

The mission was important, of course, as Doenitz had stressed. But there must be more to it than that. This fishing boat had to be going somewhere where *other* craft couldn't go. Like towards enemy territory. Or *past* enemy territory, where Allied air patrols were likely to be heavy. Yes, *yes*.

The English Channel.

It had to be.

But where *exactly*? East Channel? No. However vital the operation was, Doenitz would never send one of his boats on a suicide mission. It was so shallow in the East Channel the U-boat wouldn't stand a chance.

So West Channel. Why not?

The Head looked at the clock on the wall. He must decide quickly – he still had an awful lot of work to do.

He went to the plot and, picking up U-319's token which the night staff had placed outside Brest, placed it in the middle of the English Channel, to the south of Plymouth.

Then, pulling his ear thoughtfully, he lifted the telephone and asked for Coastal Command.

He might be wildly wrong, of course, and be sending the lads of Coastal Command off on a wild goose chase. But he had one of his feelings about this one.

It was Doenitz's postscript. *If anyone can do it you can.*

There could be only one reason Doenitz had said that. Because he was asking his man to do the impossible. He was asking him to go into the jaws of the lion.

Chapter 29

———•———

JULIE SLAPPED HIS face.

Awful, but it had to be done. 'Wake up! Please, wake up!'

He stirred slightly. 'Monsieur Freymann! David! David! Wake up!'

He was almost unconscious. In desperation she put her mouth to his ear and shouted, 'You've got to move!'

There was a *crump!* from the bow and, after a moment's pause, heavy spray came flying over the deck. Julie ducked her head but it was too late and the water trickled down her neck. The old man was getting soaked too: that's why he had to be moved.

His eyes had flickered open. The cold water must have woken him.

Julie shook him slightly. 'You've got to move. To the front, over *there*.' She indicated the bow. 'Otherwise you'll get soaked!'

He looked at her blankly then, closing his eyes with pain, nodded slightly. Taking his arm, Julie pushed him into a sitting position and began to pull him along the deck. At first she could feel him helping, shuffling sideways on his behind, but then he sagged and his weight fell against her leg. She saw that his face was white and contorted with pain.

She crouched down and, her arm round his shoulder, waited a while. The boat hit another wave and the inevitable deluge of heavy, cold spray rained down over them.

Julie blew the water off her lips, and, standing up again, tried to drag the old man along, but he was terribly heavy and she couldn't keep her balance on the unsteady deck. Panting heavily, she knelt down and shouted desperately. 'Please *try*, David. Please *try*.'

There was the faintest nod. Julie started pulling and felt him helping again. This time they reached the shelter of the small decked area under the bow. The motion of the boat was much more violent up here – Julie felt her stomach take off a couple of times – but at least it was dry.

'Just a bit further, then you'll be comfortable!'

The old man made a final effort and, at last, Julie managed to pull him up against some coils of rope. He lay back and closed his eyes. Julie covered him with sacking and placed a rolled-up section of tarpaulin under his head.

She looked at him fondly and, very gently, stroked his head. 'Sorry I had to slap you.' But he didn't hear: he was unconscious again. She examined his face anxiously. It was deathly white, with an almost green tinge to it, and his breath was coming in short, shallow pants through a gaping mouth.

The pills: the old man had mentioned pills. She should try to get some more down him. He'd thrown the last lot up.

She looked in his bag and found a small bottle half full of white tablets. It had to be them: there were no others. The bottle had no label and no instructions. She guessed at two tablets and shook them into her hand.

Water. She'd need water.

She found a large, rope-clad bottle full of clear liquid, up by the lobster pot in the bow. She opened it and dipped a finger in. Water. But no mug or cup.

She placed the tablets on the old man's tongue then, raising his head slightly, put the bottle to his lips and tried to tip it up. It was too heavy. She wedged her body against the side of the boat and, resting the old man's head against her chest, used both hands to tip the bottle. Water poured everywhere. Some went into the old man's mouth. He moaned loudly, then spluttered and coughed.

Julie patted his shoulder and watched him carefully. The pills seemed to have disappeared. It was something at least.

A moment later the old man groaned and, clutching his stomach, turned his head to one side, and threw up over Julie's leg.

Julie stared in slight revulsion then realised with unhappy certainty that unless she moved away the same thing would happen to her. There was an uncomfortable feeling in her stomach and it was rising fast towards her throat. She got up and, lurching towards the rail, swallowed hard and gulped at the fresh salt air. She turned her face to the wind and looked out at the wide expanse of sea.

After a while she felt better. She looked back at David. He seemed peaceful enough. She couldn't face going back, not just yet. The smell . . .

She turned away and, holding tight to the rail, made her way cautiously along the tilting deck to the tiller. Peter was curled up against the side of the boat on the uphill side, right at the back, where it was dry. He was asleep, a slight frown on his pale face.

Julie looked at the compass. The course had changed a little – slightly more westerly than before. She altered the tiller lines and the course improved slightly, but she could already hear a slight fluttering from the sails. They'd start flapping if she moved the tiller any further. The sails would need adjusting again. It would have to wait: with a bit of luck it might not be necessary and, anyway, she couldn't face it at the moment.

She searched the sky. No sign of that plane. It was quite

extraordinary: it had seen them, she was certain. It *must* have. It had changed its course slightly and flown almost directly overhead. Yet it hadn't come down to shoot at them, or even to look more closely.

Julie had taken Peter and dived under the bow and waited for the rat-tat-tat of bullets. But the sound had never come. Instead the plane had stayed high, the hum faint, and then the sound had faded slowly away into the distance.

She couldn't work it out at all.

But there was no sense in worrying about it. The point was, the plane hadn't come back, and that was all that mattered.

Time: almost noon. She felt dreadful. Her eyes were aching in their sockets and her head felt as if it were banded with iron. Sleep; she would have to sleep some time. But at the moment she felt oddly light-headed and awake and in need of *doing* something – as if by keeping busy everything would turn out all right.

Chores: she would get the chores done. Just like at home.

The compass light. It had to be repaired. She thought: But I don't have the first idea *how*.

She drew a deep breath. No harm in looking anyway.

To the side of the compass, mounted on the brass base, was a small flap fastened by a finger bolt. It undid quite easily. She looked. There was a wick. She touched it: quite dry. No fuel, then. Her heart lifted. It might be quite simple after all.

A filler cap: there had to be one. She peered into the small opening, then drew away sharply because it made her stomach feel queasy again. A moment for fresh air, then she took another look. Nothing.

Frowning, she looked all the way round the brass compass mount, and suddenly, there it was, on the forward side of the mount: a small brass cap which, when unscrewed, smelt of kerosene. She put a finger in. It came out dry.

All it needed was fuel. *All!*

She went to the box where she had found the torch. It was bound to be in there.

It wasn't.

She made her way up to the bow, choosing her moment between waves and flying spray. David seemed to be sleeping peacefully. She put a hand on his brow. He was warmer than before but his colour was still terrible. She wished there was something she could do for him.

Crouching, she went up into the point of the bow. Another rope-clad container. She opened it excitedly. More water.

She searched carefully under the lobster pots, ropes and the single tarpaulin. Nothing.

Where else?

She made her way back towards the tiller. Halfway along the deck, in the centre, was a raised section built up from the deck in a large square. It had a sort of lid on it. The way into the hold, presumably, where the fish were usually stored.

Would the kerosene be in there? She'd have a look anyway.

There were fastenings around the lid: clips. They were stiff. She tried to prise one open and tore a finger nail. She bit off the nail and tried again. It needed leverage. The spike. The one Peter had found in the box.

It was still there. She brought it back to the hatch cover and, putting it under the clip, levered outwards. The clip sprang open. Triumph!

The other clips opened more easily. Now, the cover itself. It was heavy, but, standing on the uphill side, she managed to lift it slightly, then, using the slant of the boat, to slide it downhill.

She looked over the edge of the opening into the hold.

Much of it was dark, but immediately below her there was a large square brilliantly illuminated by the open hatch.

Julie stared in disbelief, but there was no mistake.

The hold was full of running water.

Spray pattered onto Julie's back, but she didn't notice; she was mesmerised by the water flowing in a great torrent through the boat. After a moment she realised the water was streaming first one way then the other, as the boat seesawed its way across the waves. At its fastest the water made a great rushing noise then, as the boat reached the crest of a wave, the entrapped water slowed down and paused before beginning its frantic return journey.

There was tons of it.

Julie wondered how long it had been there – and how fast it was coming in.

'Mummy!'

Peter was standing by the rail, well aft, out of the spray. 'Mummy!' he called again. He was looking unhappy. Julie got to her feet. The bow hit a wave and spray flew back over the deck and into the hold. She should cover the hold again – but then there was so much water in it anyway, a bit more wouldn't make any difference.

When she got to Peter he held out his arms and she hugged him. 'Mummy, I need to go to . . . I want to do a poo, Mummy.'

Julie sighed. 'Of course, sweetheart.'

'But where, Mummy?'

'Oh.' She hadn't thought of that. Up till now it had just been a question of standing him near the scuppers. A bucket: that would have to do. She looked around desperately. Knowing Peter, there wasn't much time.

'Wait here.'

She looked in the large wooden box beside the tiller, then up in the bow. There *had* to be a bucket somewhere.

No bucket. But there was a square tin box full of fishing

tackle. She threw out the tackle and, grasping the tin box, ducked out from under the decking.

'Please . . . Please . . .' It was David. He was looking at her with pleading eyes.

Without waiting for an answer, she hurried down the deck. Just in time by the look on Peter's face. Without ceremony, she pulled down his trousers and sat him on the tin box.

'Ouch!'

'I can't help it! It's the best I could find!' She supported the child's weight, so he wouldn't have to sit on the sharp edges.

'Mummy, what about paper?'

Paper. Paper.

'Wait here.' The boy grabbed for the helmsman's seat as she let go of him.

Her brain was seizing up, she could feel it. She made an effort to think. Paper. On a boat? Never. Never! It'd be soaked in a moment. What then? A rag – yes, a rag.

The big wooden box let her down again: it was always letting her down. Back to the bow again. Only an oily black rag. It would have to do.

David was grasping her arm. 'Please, must talk . . . It's very important . . . *Please.*'

'Yes! Yes! In a minute. I promise!' She was begining to whine. She lowered her voice. 'Sorry . . . I really *will* be back – but I've got to take this to my son. All right?'

As she made her way aft for what felt like the twentieth time, Julie thought: It's just a matter of keeping going, that's all.

David watched her go. She looked worried. Perhaps things weren't going so well.

He made an effort to keep his eyes open. Musn't let go. *Not yet.*

He had to tell her, had to get it to her . . .

Before he couldn't any more.

He felt so weak. The pain was eating into him, gnawing away at his body, and it was impossible to fight it any more. He wanted to escape, to drift away so that there'd never be any pain again.

But first he *must* talk to the girl. After . . . *then* he'd close his eyes and slip away. And there'd be no more pain, just peace.

But not yet. Mustn't let go . . . Not yet.

When Julie got back David was asleep. Whatever he'd wanted to say would have to wait. She'd talk to him as soon as he woke up again.

In the meantime . . .

She searched the deck carefully. There had to be a way of getting the water out. 'Manning the pumps', that's what they used to do in the stories she'd read. But was this boat big enough to have a pump? And if so what would it look like?

There was nothing on the deck that looked remotely like anything that might be a pump.

Nothing for it then . . .

She stared for a while at the gaping hold then, taking the torch, lowered herself over the edge and down into the darkness. She found a foothold and stepped down into the swirling water up to her calves. Immediately, she wished she's taken her shoes off and left them on deck. Too late now.

The torchlight revealed an empty shell. Julie stooped down and shone the light right into the bow. Nothing: just the timber frame and, halfway down, the mast coming through the deck above. Behind, nothing either.

Crouching, she climbed forward and shone the torch

into the bow again. The water was surging round something heaped on the floor – the anchor chain.

No sign of any kerosene. No sign of a pump.

The boat lurched and she grabbed for the mast. The
nasty feeling began to rise in her throat again. She knew
she must get out, and fast!

As she let go of the mast something cold touched her
hand. *Must get up on deck . . .* Swallowing fast, she shone
the torch back on the mast, to where her hand had been.
A pipe. It ran parallel to the mast, down into the bottom
of the boat where it was lost in the murky water.

She gulped hard and pointed the torch upwards. The
pipe followed the mast until the spar disappeared through
the deck, then it ran horizontally for a short distance until
it stopped at a large metal object suspended from the
deckhead.

I'm going to be sick.

She rushed for the open hatch and hoisted herself
quickly over the edge of the coaming onto the deck.

She fell against the downhill rail and knew that nothing
would stop it now. She heaved miserably for several
minutes then began to feel better. She staggered back to
the helmsman's seat and, resting her head against the
compass, waited for the faintness to pass. It would be so
easy to sleep now, to let go.

After a few minutes she stood up and, still shaky, made
herself go forward to the mast. She looked to one side of
it, to where the metal thing must be just under the deck,
and there, set into the planking, was a short thick metal
post. She'd thought it was some kind of bollard, but now
she could see it was mechanical: it had a socket thing, and
bits that obviously moved.

Spray shot through the air and struck her coldly on the
cheek. She dropped on to her hands and knees and looked
more closely at the mechanical post. The socket was clearly

designed to take some sort of handle. Then it could be moved back and forth.

A handle. She was getting tired of looking for things . . .

She glanced around half-heartedly and saw, right beside her, attached by a clip to the mast, a long straight piece of pipe iron. A handle.

It fitted the socket.

She pulled the cover across the open hatch so that no more water should get in from above, and, sitting on the edge of the hatch, started to pump. At first the handle went back and forth quite easily then, suddenly, it became stiffer and she realised it was only now beginning to draw up water. She settled down into a rhythm and wondered how long it would take to empty the hold.

The pump was situated in what was probably the wettest part of the deck, where the spray was at its thickest. Water dribbled down her neck and into her clothing, which clung damp and sticky to her skin. But the action of the pumping was, at least, getting her nice and warm. She gave a small snort of amusement – you could make anything sound good if you tried.

After half an hour or so, she lifted the hatch cover and shone the torch down. Still tons of water. She'd half expected it. She settled back into the pumping, trying to clear her brain of everything but the necessity to pump. But her mind kept wandering; thoughts of home, and Jean, and Tante Marie, and *him* . . .

She made herself sing, and quite enjoyed it for a while, until she ran out of songs.

Her back began to ache. She took a rest, but it was a mistake: her back ached twice as much when she started pumping again.

After a while her hands blistered and she had to stop because of the pain. Wearily she lifted the corner of the hatch cover and shone the torch down. The water had almost gone. She nodded with satisfaction. Wrapping her hands in rags she pumped again, more quickly, desperately, until at long last there was a sucking noise and the pump was dry.

She put the handle back in its clip on the mast and slowly, shakily, made her way back to the tiller seat.

The course read North-west. *Too far west.* She rested her head against the glass bowl and closed her eyes.

'Mummy . . .' A small hand was placed on her arm. 'Mummy, are you all right?'

'Yes, darling, I feel fine.' It was about the last thing she felt.

'I opened another tin. I thought you might be hungry after all your pumping.'

She put her arms round his small waist and her head against his chest and said in a tight voice, 'Thank you, darling.'

A faint cry sounded from the bow. Julie looked round. It was David. His hand was raised as if to wave. She'd quite forgotten about him. He must want water.

Wearily, she got to her feet and began the long wet journey down the deck.

She was coming back at last!

David watched her fervently, willing her to complete her uncertain passage along the heaving deck. She paused halfway and for a moment he feared she'd changed her mind, but after waiting for a break between waves and ensuing spray, she came on, staggering slightly as the boat gave a sudden lurch forward.

As soon as she'd dropped on to her knees beside him, he grasped her hand. It was very hot. He was rather surprised because she looked so cold: her hair clung damply to her forehead and dropped in long wet strands around her shoulders. She looked worn out. Her face was very pale, apart from two bright patches of colour which burned on her cheeks, and her eyes were red and swollen, with dark smudges underneath.

David patted her hand. 'My dear, you must rest ... Some time.'

She squeezed his hand and smiled. It quite transformed her face. 'Don't you worry about me. I'm fit and healthy. It's you who must take care. Would you like some water? You must be desperate for some by now.'

She reached over for the large glass bottle and, removing the stopper, held it to his lips. He drank greedily. It tasted good.

As she replaced the stopper he opened the bag he wore round his waist and, reaching in, took out the small package.

He took hold of her hand and, concentrating hard on the words, said, 'You remember ... in the field. When you came back for me. I want to thank you.'

She smiled. 'Don't be silly. Of course I came back for you. I couldn't leave you, could I?'

'At the time ... Well ...' He coughed and breathed deeply to regain his breath. '... I wanted to give up. But I'm glad I didn't. You see—' He waited for a spasm of pain to pass.

She was patting his hand. 'Are you all right?'

'Yes, yes ...' As soon as he could, he went on. 'You were right ... about them making me work. They would've got hold of my Cecile ... they would have threatened things. This way I'm *protecting* her. Just like I promised. Thank you for that, thank you.'

She almost spoke, but he interrupted quickly. 'Look ... this package. It's got everything ... about my ideas. The drawings. The specifications. Please, you must take care of it. In case anything happens to me—'

'It won't!'

He shook his head irritably. 'You will promise,' he went

on slowly, 'that you'll take care of it . . . and hand it to the right people. It must be the right people . . . Do you understand?'

She still seemed unhappy about it, but nodded gently and, looking down at the small flat package, weighed it thoughtfully in her hand. She appeared to come to a decision and, turning slightly away, pushed the package down inside her jersey and buried it somewhere in her underwear.

David relaxed. He was free at last. It was like a weight off his shoulders. Now he could *really* sleep. He squeezed her hand. 'You're a good girl.'

She leaned forward and kissed him gently on the cheek. Then she stroked his forehead and asked, 'What about taking some of your pills?'

'Pain's not so bad now . . . Anyway . . . Make me sick. Better not.' It was a lie about the pain, it was as bad as ever, but he didn't want to bother her with it.

She was regarding him thoughtfully. 'You know, I should thank you too. For snapping me out of it when we were hiding on the beach. If you hadn't – well, I would probably have stayed in a daze . . . I only wish I hadn't got you into *this* mess.' She sighed and looked away.

She didn't understand at all. She thought she was failing.

David said desperately, 'No . . . No, we're *trying*. And that's worth *everything*! *Everything*! You must realise that *trying* is the most important thing of all . . .!'

She nodded uncertainly. 'If you say so. Now rest. Please. Try to sleep.' She leaned forward once again and kissed him softly on the cheek.

'Remember,' he murmured. 'Trying is the most important thing.'

'Yes!' She gave a small laugh and, touching his hand, got to her feet and set off towards the stern.

David lay back and closed his eyes. His mind was at

rest, he had done what had to be done; now, at last, he could sleep in peace.

Her body was seizing up like her mind. As she moved back along the deck she felt her whole body complaining. Her neck was almost unmovable and every time she turned her head a sharp pain shot through her temples.

Peter's face lit up at the sight of her. 'Mummy, here! You still haven't had any lunch. I've kept some for you!'

She sat down beside him, under the bulwark, and tried to eat. She didn't feel very hungry.

'Mummy, are you going to be better now?'

'I expect so. I'm . . . just tired, that's all.'

'Why don't you sleep and then I can keep watch?'

Sighing, she began, 'No, Peter, it—' Then she thought: Why not? The boat was sailing itself. Peter would probably keep a better lookout than she would. Yes: why not?

She finished her mouthful and looked at him. It was an awful responsibility for a six-year-old. But it would be night in a few hours. She'd have to be awake then and, without sleep – well, she'd never do it.

She said carefully, 'Darling . . . Would you promise to tell me the *moment* you saw anything?'

The small head nodded.

'Or the moment the weather changed . . . black clouds or more spray . . . or rain . . .?'

'Yes, Mummy.'

'If you saw a ship or . . . anything floating, or a plane . . . You'd wake me then too, wouldn't you?'

'I promise, Mummy.'

'Anything at all . . .'

He nodded again. 'Don't worry, Mummy. I'll keep a really sharp lookout!' He smiled excitedly and pulled himself up onto the helmsman's seat.

Julie stood up and took a long look round. The sky was

still clear, but now there was a slight haze around the horizon. The sea appeared as vast as ever – and as impossible to cross.

A sharp lookout . . . She lay down on the deck with her head on her arm and wondered if Peter had learnt that one from Richard too.

Richard. He must have been through this sort of thing countless times – the wet, the cold and the tiredness. The thought gave her comfort. Then she saw him in another setting – in a prison cell, hungry, cold, raging to be free, and hastily tried to shut the picture out of her mind before worse things appeared.

She closed her eyes and tried to sleep, but for a long time her body refused to relax. When she finally drifted into an uneasy doze a series of disconnected thoughts rampaged around her brain and several times made her wake with a terrible start. After a while her brain began to slow down. Only one thought remained. Something she should have done. What was it? As she drifted off into a deep sleep, she remembered at last. The course. It was still wrong. She hadn't reset the course.

Chapter 30

A NEEDLE IN a haystack.

And yet, and yet . . .

With his finger Fischer traced the fishing boat's course from Morlaix to the position the plane had reported, then followed the pencilled line on, in a straight projection. His finger arrived at a point midway between the Scillies and Land's End. It was the fifth time he'd checked the projection, but the result was always the same.

He still couldn't understand it. Where was the boat making for? Why go all the way round Land's End and then be faced with a long trek up the north coast of Cornwall, against the wind? The alternatives were – what? Wales or Ireland. Wales – again why bother? Ireland then. Now that *was* a possibility, particularly if the occupants of the fishing boat were seeking the safety of a neutral country. When one thought about it, the whole affair did smack of politics . . . Fischer decided that it was the most likely destination.

However there was still one thing that didn't make sense.

If the fishing boat was holding her course, why the devil hadn't they seen her yet?

U-319 was zigzagging four miles either side of the prey's projected track. The visibility was still good. Using the search periscope they should be able to spot even a small boat at four miles. She must have masts and sails which should be clearly visible against the skyline.

Even allowing for the worst: for U-319 speeding away from the approaching prey on the wrong leg of the zig-zag, and for the fishing boat being as much as four miles off course, they should still see her on the return leg because of their superior speed and because each leg of the zigzag took them very slightly forward along the fishing boat's track.

They should have seen her, but they hadn't.

Fischer sighed deeply and chucked the pencil down on to the chart.

The control room was quiet except for the gentle hum of the electric motors. The men were at their positions, silent except for the occasional whisper, engrossed in their jobs. The man at the periscope was swivelling slowly, his eyes fixed to the lens.

Fischer wondered how long it had been since he'd slept. He thought for a moment and decided that his last proper sleep must have been over thirty hours ago. He'd tried to sleep early that morning, but had managed only a short doze.

He should try to snatch some rest now but he knew he wouldn't be able to. Not yet. Not while the hunt was on.

Once darkness fell – once they'd missed the boat for certain – then he'd sleep. During the night there was nothing they could do; they had no way of hunting a small boat under cover of darkness. All he could do would be to manoeuvre U-319 into a position ahead of the fishing boat and lie in wait for it at dawn. By then the margin for error would be enormous – the prey might have changed course a dozen times. The chances would be slim.

A needle in a haystack . . .

Men were moving around the control room, changing places, whispering in muted voices. The watch change. 1600 hours.

He was tempted to go to the periscope and take a look,

but decided against it. A man from the new watch was just settling in. When the fellow finished his first trick at the periscope in about fifteen minutes, perhaps then he'd take a look. It was partly superstition: Fischer had the feeling that, by restraining himself from looking, the fishing boat was more likely to turn up. Ridiculous, of course . . .

Fischer wandered aft, towards the engine room. The Chief spotted him and, wiping his hands on an oily rag, made his way between the massive diesels to meet his commander.

Suddenly there was a muffled exclamation, the sound of voices from the direction of the control room. Fischer froze for a moment then, turning quickly, retraced his steps. Even as he turned he was thinking: No klaxon – not an aircraft. What then?

The first officer was at the periscope. '. . . bearing 280!'

Fischer strode up and tapped him on the shoulder. The first officer stood aside. 'A small craft, Herr Kaleu!' Fischer put his eye to the lens.

For a moment he could see nothing, just seas, larger than before. He checked the bearing – 280 degrees – and waited. A wave rose in front of the horizon then fell again.

There!

Fischer felt the adrenalin leap into his veins.

'Raise attack periscope!'

There was a hiss of hydraulics as the much larger attack periscope rose from the bowels of the boat. The search periscope had a wide field of vision, covering large areas of the sky as well as the sea, but had limited powers of magnification; the attack periscope, on the other hand, had a small field of vision but much greater magnification. Fischer pulled down the handles and, swinging the periscope round, put his eye to it.

Greatly magnified waves obscured the horizon. He waited. They fell away.

There she was!

A small boat. Under sail.

The silhouette was unmistakable, even from this distance. He guessed the range to be over four miles. He could see almost nothing of the hull – it was hidden among the waves – but the mainsail showed black and distinct, a tiny curved shape against the brilliant yellow of the western sky.

The boat was sailing north.

He allowed himself a moment of satisfaction, then let his natural caution take charge. It might be a British fishing boat . . . But unlikely in mid-Channel. It might be another escaped French fishing boat – equally unlikely. The coincidences of time and position were too great.

It *had* to be the prey.

Next – how to capture them. He'd have to approach submerged, then surface at the last minute. That way the occupants wouldn't have time to think about fighting. He wanted to avoid fighting, not only because he'd been told to bring back the occupants unharmed, but because the operation had to be completed in the shortest possible time, to avoid being caught on the surface.

He hated the idea of surfacing in broad daylight, particularly here. But it would have to be done.

Automatically he began to swing the periscope round, walking with it in a circle, sweeping the narrow band either side of the horizon. No ships. He couldn't see much of the sky, not with this periscope.

He stood back and let the first officer take a look.

It was time to close in. 'Alter course to —'

He broke off. Something was wrong: he identified it. The bloody stupid man on the search periscope wasn't swivelling it round, wasn't searching! Fischer felt a surge of anger.

'*Sweep!* Sweep the sky! Come on!'

The man glanced up, looked shaken, and rapidly spun the periscope.

Fischer clenched his fists. Bloody fool. That was the way
to get caught. An aircraft could spot the wake of the two
periscopes at a hell of a distance. But Fischer knew the
sailor at the periscope: normally he was a good man. He
decided to let the matter pass.

Now, the order to alter course.

A sharp cry, half-shout, half-scream, rent the air.

'*Enemy aircraft!*'

In reflex Fischer shouted, '*Down periscopes!*'

The two shafts began to hiss downwards.

'*Take her down! Alter course forty-five degrees to
starboard!*'

The order was repeated.

Fischer had no idea whether the plane had been close,
whether it was even making a bombing run, but he wasn't
going to take any chances. He strode to the chart and
looked at the depth of the water here. He barked, 'Take
her down to thirty metres!'

After what seemed a long, long time but which was only
a couple of seconds the submarine began to react to the re-
angled hydroplanes and her nose tilted downwards.
Slowly, peacefully, the boat slipped further and further
down into the depths.

Everyone tensed and reached out for a handhold, waiting for the shock of the depth charges.

The silence lasted a long, long time.

The voice of the coxswain sounded calmly through the
stillness. 'Depth fifteen metres ... eighteen metres ...
twenty metres ...'

'Alter course another forty-five degrees to starboard.'

'Altering course forty-five degrees starboard, Herr Kaleu.'

At last it came. 'Depth thirty metres.'

Fischer exhaled. The men shifted their weight and
exchanged glances. No depth charges. They were safe.

'You!' Fischer barked at the sailor who'd been manning
the search periscope.

The man approached, ashen white.

'Bearing and range of enemy plane?'

The man gulped. Fischer noticed that he was shaking like a leaf.

'*Bearing and range of enemy plane?*'

The man's mouth was gaping slightly and he glanced around like a frightened rabbit. Fischer raised his hand and quite deliberately slapped the sailor's face. The man fell back in surprise. For a moment Fischer thought he was going to cry.

Fischer repeated more quietly, 'Bearing and range of enemy plane.'

The man's eyes cleared. 'Behind us, Herr Kaleu,' he began breathlessly. 'No – slightly to starboard. Bearing about . . . I . . . I'm not sure.' He was shaking again.

Fischer said sharply, 'But a British plane?'

'Oh yes . . . A Catalina, I think.'

'Was he closing on us?'

The man nodded. 'Yes! Oh yes! Straight for us, it was coming straight for us.'

'Diving on us?'

'Yes – yes! Head on! About half a mile away. No – less. Less!'

Fischer nodded and said briskly, 'Stand down and pull yourself together!'

Fischer went to the chart table and leant over it, a wave of depression pressing in on him.

They might have been seen. It changed everything.

The enemy might send more aircraft, perhaps patrol boats . . .

They'd be hunted down.

Unless . . . unless they stayed submerged and slipped away. But the orders had been clear: he had no alternative but to close in and try to accomplish the task.

Damn! So near and yet so far.

He thought of the fishing boat sailing on, oblivious to

everything, a victim ready for the taking, yet maddeningly beyond his reach.

He daren't surface now. He wasn't even sure if he dared go to periscope depth and have a look.

Not yet anyway.

He'd take a look in half an hour, he decided. The plane might have given up by then. Even if it hadn't – well, he'd have to risk it, otherwise he'd lose the prey.

He passed the time bent over the chart, calculating and recalculating the course and speed necessary to stay on the fishing boat's tail. As before, the fishing boat had been slightly to the west of its projected track. Maybe the wind was backing. He redrew its course line and calculated the manoeuvres necessary to get the U-boat on to the new track.

At the end of an hour he checked with Sonar: there were no propeller noises. He gave the order to go to periscope depth. There was the muted hiss of blowing tanks.

'. . . Twenty-five metres . . . Twenty . . . Fifteen . . .' Then they were levelling off. Finally came the words, 'Periscope depth!'

Fischer pulled up the search periscope and, his heart in his mouth, put his eye to the lens. As he did so he thought: Please, dear God, let it still be there.

She was a long way away, in the country somewhere, lying in a barn, which accounted for the hard floor. Nearby was some soft straw which would be much better to lie on, but she couldn't get her limbs to move and carry her across to it. Her body was like stone, heavy and lifeless. For some unaccountable reason the barn was very noisy: there was a whistling and swishing and roaring which reverberated around the bare wooden walls. It was moving too, the barn, the floor tilting strangely . . . It was confusing, this place. Now something was shaking her. An animal – large, like a cow – was butting its head against her arm. The creature was getting more agitated . . .

'Mummy! Mummy! Wake up! Wake up!'

Julie opened her eyes. Instantly she closed them again: the light was blinding. Reality began to seep through into her consciousness: the awful awareness that a real night-mare was lying in wait for her, inescapable, ready to pounce on her if she awoke. She grasped at the image of the barn and tried to push her mind back towards it, back to the soft straw . . .

'Mummy, Mummy! *Please* wake up! There's a plane!'

Julie opened her eyes again and screwed them up against the light. A plane . . . She groaned slightly, and, rubbing her face with her hand, sat up. As she moved a sharp stabbing pain shot into her temples. Grasping the rail she pulled herself to her feet and the headache settled into a rhythm of dull throbbing blows that made her feel slightly sick.

'Plane . . .? Where . . .?' She looked around, her eyes refusing to focus properly.

'There! There!' Peter pointed away to the right. *'There!'*

Julie stared for several seconds before she saw it, a tiny black speck flying low just above the horizon. It looked a long way off. It was moving towards the north, rising now, gaining height. It seemed to hover for a moment, and Julie realised it was turning. She rubbed her eyes and looked again. It took a long curve away until it was hardly visible, then it was heading towards them, getting larger again. For a moment she thought it must have seen them, and was coming straight for them, but then she saw that the dot was banking and dropping down again, retracing its path along the far horizon, towards the south. It repeated the manoeuvre once more, and then again, going back and forth along its path several times.

The boat lurched and Julie clung to the rail to stop herself falling. Peter grasped at her jacket.

'Mummy, I'm hungry . . . and I want to go to sleep . . .'

The small face was pale and tired and a little frightened. He had done very well, considering. Julie tried to sound, if not cheerful, then reassuring. 'Of course, sweetheart. Let's open a can or two. Then you curl up down here.'

She bent down to search in the food bag and felt sick again. The boat was moving more jerkily now, its seesaws more violent. She fed Peter quickly and settled him down at the back of the boat under the high wooden side, out of the wind and spray.

She rubbed her aching temples and wished the headache would go away.

She looked for the plane again. It had gone.

She stared for a long time, but there was no sign. Maybe the plane had been German anyway.

She noticed that it had clouded over. High up, there was a solid ceiling of white; lower, there were angry black clouds scudding across the sky. The sea was grey and forbidding, the waves marching relentlessly towards the boat, their crests breaking with an audible hiss. Their onward procession was mesmerising, almost hypnotic.

She dragged her eyes away. *Must think* . . . David . . . She made her way slowly along the deck, trying unsuccessfully to dodge the spray and bumping sharply against the mast instead. The old man seemed all right. He was fairly warm and breathing normally. She lifted his head and put the water bottle to his lips. The motion of the boat was much worse up in the bows and it was a job to get any water into his mouth, but finally David nodded that he'd had enough and, falling back against the rope, closed his eyes.

The sickness was rising again. She hurried back to the tiller, shivering as water slopped over the side of the boat, splattered against her legs and seeped through her trousers.

Ignore the sickness. Wake up!

Course? WNW: West North-west. Still off-course – too far to the west. She frowned then grasped at an idea – perhaps it was a *good* thing. By heading too far west she'd probably miss the land altogether. Then she wouldn't have to worry about hitting it during the night. Once it was light again, *then* she could head the boat back towards the land.

It would solve a lot of problems.

Yes. She'd let the boat go where it wanted. Then – no land, no fighting with the sails, no worries. She felt a little more cheerful.

She looked at her watch. Five-thirty. God, was that all? She'd only slept for a couple of hours. No wonder she felt so terrible. Still, without any sleep at all she might have felt even worse.

She shivered again. So cold ... And the headache, still hammering away ...

She sat on the helmsman's seat and looked ahead into the greyness, watching the bow rise and fall against the pattern of the waves. It stopped her feeling sick. After a while she dozed, waking only when the boat lurched and threatened to slide her off her seat. Then she came to with a jerk and, getting back onto the seat, stared forward again, concentrating on the grey smudge of the horizon, which seemed increasingly distant.

She should take a good look round and search for ships, but she couldn't be bothered.

She thought: I don't care any more, I really don't. I just want this to *end* ... To get somewhere, *anywhere* ... I just want it to *end*. That's all.

I don't care any more, I really don't.

Later she dozed again and woke with a jump when spray pattered against her face. The spray had never come this far back before.

Disorientated, she looked around. The boat was tilting further over, the downhill side of the deck awash with running water. The bow was digging deeper into the waves, pushing up solid sheets of water which, caught by the wind, flew diagonally back over the boat and fell down the deck in heavy cascades to the scuppers on the lower side. As the boat met each wave it gave a great shudder, pausing in its tracks for a second to throw off the weight of the water before picking itself up and leaping forward to meet the next wave rushing towards it. The mast was leaning over at a sharp angle, and the big sail bellied out, taut and strained, except for the back edge which vibrated violently. Suddenly, the boat rolled and almost dipped her rail in the rushing water. Julie gasped. The boat came back a little and the water receded.

The boat rolled again, then again. Julie watched with terrible fascination as the rail came ever closer to the rushing water. She thought: What's to stop us rolling right over? Perhaps she needed to do this reefing business, perhaps that would slow the boat down . . .

Miserably, she regarded the enormous bulging sail and knew that it was hopeless: she wouldn't know where to start. It was impossible to do anything while the boat was like this, careering along like a mad thing.

The scene frightened her. After a while she realised what made it so terrifying.

The world was getting greyer, the outlines less distinct, the dark colours blacker.

The horizon was a blur, a featureless grey blending into the grey of the sea and the sky. The shape of the bows was beginning to fade . . .

Julie thought: I *might* have done something, I really *might*.

But not in the dark, not *ever* in the dark . . .

As night fell, and the greys faded into blackness, the fear gripped her even tighter, until it held her firmly, mindlessly, on her seat by the tiller.

*

Two hundred miles out in the Atlantic the Liberator swept high over the darkening sea, searching.

The patrol had been going on for four hours now, with another three to go. The plane was flying one leg of a gentle zigzag designed to take it over the likely path of U-boats heading north to their hunting grounds.

Then, suddenly, the wireless operator received a signal.

A few minutes later the plane abandoned her search pattern and, banking steeply, headed east.

At first the plane headed for the position given in the signal – the last known position of the U-boat – which was thirty miles south-south-east of Land's End.

Then, later, when the pilot had done some thinking and the navigator some calculations, the course was changed to take the plane towards the English coast.

The U-boat must have been submerged all day, the pilot reckoned, which meant her speed would have been no more than seven knots. If, as he'd been told, she was heading north, then he would intercept her near the coast.

Where on the coast was another matter. The U-boat was shadowing a small fishing boat, apparently, but its destination was unknown. Falmouth? Ireland? Could be anywhere.

He would have to make a single sweep along the coast at a distance of five miles off. The channel between the Scillies and Land's End must be covered, also the Lizard, and the approaches to Falmouth.

He wouldn't have time for much more, not with the freshening headwind.

Only one thing was certain. At some point during the night the U-boat would have to surface, to get air and to recharge her batteries. And for quite a long time, at that.

There was just a chance they might catch her . . .

But where should they start from? How far west might the U-boat have gone?

He decided, and said to the navigator, 'Course to the

Scillies, please. We're going to start from there and work
our way eastwards.'

They lie at the end of the world, the isles of Scilly: far
beyond the land; a nest of rocks and islets cut off from the
mainstream of British life. On a chart they are mere
pinpricks situated twenty-one nautical miles west-south-
west of Land's End: a cluster of small dots on the wide
immensity of the sea – the last fragment of land for three
thousand miles. Being so remote and isolated, they remain,
for the most part, unnoticed.

But sailors know and mark them well.

Sailing inward, towards the major European ports, ships
must find their way into the beckoning but treacherous
arms of the English Channel, between the rugged north
coast of Brittany on the one hand, and the Scillies, harbin-
ger of the English mainland, on the other. For many vessels
this will be their first landfall for thousands of miles. Even
in good conditions navigation can be the most uncertain of
sciences, but after long periods of bad weather, or in fog
or storm, the chances of error increase dramatically. When
the weather is thick the navigator can do little but make
his calculations, check the distance run – and then resort
to hope, optimism and prayer.

He has reason to pray. The Scillies lie in wait for the
unwary, eager to ensnare and reluctant to release.

The islands are unusually low – barely a hundred and
sixty feet at their highest point – and therefore difficult to
see from any real distance. In bad weather you can find
yourself very close, even hear the surf on the rocks, before
you realise you are on top of them.

Ships are led to their doom by the wind, which, for a
greater part of the time, blows from the west, pushing
ships speedily homeward, hastening the ship on her way,
so that sailors have reason to be grateful to it. That is,

unless the navigator is mistaken in his calculations. Then the wind blows the ship towards the crouching islands and the low teeth of the hidden reefs. A jagged grey mass of rocks is suddenly spotted close ahead, someone hears the thunder of surf on the ledges and the ship tries to turn, too late. All too late. Escape is impossible. The wind drives the vessel further and further onto the rocks, until she pounds heavily, and the teeth bite through, and the guts are torn out of her, and she is gone . . .

There are so many wrecks around the islands that even the inhabitants cannot count them. Hardly a year goes by without one, two – or in a bad year maybe a dozen – vessels meeting a lonely end on one of the outlying rocks.

The men who live here have a realistic, practical attitude towards shipwrecks. The Lord taketh away, the Lord giveth . . . There is money in salvage, there are sometimes rich pickings to be found on the long white beaches . . . Who would not take advantage of that which is given?

But they save the people first. Bravely, sometimes in gale-force winds, they set out in their open gigs and row to the dying ship to save whosoever they can . . .

Five islands are inhabited, four of them forming a circle round a shallow sound which was itself part of the land more than two thousand years ago. Most of the people live on St Mary's, the largest of the islands, which is just three miles wide. Across the sound to the north lie Bryher and Tresco, separated by an inlet which is the secret harbour of New Grimsby, where boats may hide . . .

Each of these islands has two distinct sides to it, like a coin. There is the windward side, bare and treeless, raked by the remorseless wind and salt spray, where only heather, hardy gorse, and a few stalwart flowers grow in the peaty soil. However, over the slight hills, in the lee of the land, it is possible to find shelter, and here, screened from the wind by tall hedges, of Pittosporum, Veronica and Tamarisk, there is a surprising fertility, with an abundance of early spring flowers, grain crops and grazing for domestic animals.

The fifth and smallest inhabited island, St Agnes, which lies to the south-west of St Mary's, is similar to the others – and yet somehow different. Lying outside the circle formed by the other four, it is surrounded by deep water, and has a feeling of isolation about it. Its western shore, craggy and strewn with massive red and silver granite boulders, marks what ancient men believed to be the end of the world.

Or very nearly . . . Because the land has not ended – not quite. Though few would call it land . . .

Strewn over the sea to the south-west for a distance of four nautical miles are numerous islets, rocks and half-hidden ledges. Some say that there are fifty islets around the main islands, some say a hundred. Many of them are here, to the south-west. No-one has tried to count the rocks.

Some of the larger rocks and islets support colonies of sea birds – puffins, shearwaters, petrels and gulls. Other rocks are coloured grey-green with lichen and coarse vegetation.

But many are quite bare. Washed by a hundred thousand Atlantic storms, the silver granite is unvisited, save for the seals who lie resting in the clefts before diving back into the restless rolling waves.

The most westerly of the rocks are so low that only the leaping, cascading surf reveals their position. In storms the angry white curtains of spray shoot high, high into the air – a terrible warning if you should be lucky enough to see it. The local people call these rocks ledges, though reefs might be a better name. They have ripped many a hull apart. Some vessels sank immediately; others pounded slowly and painfully to death, spilling cargo and people into the water for several days.

Once, a long time ago, the Royal Navy lost fifteen ships-of-the-line on the Western Rocks – the pride of the British fleet. Two thousand men drowned. Just over a hundred years ago during the height of the steamship era, a crack passenger ship died an agonised death on the Retarrier Ledges with the loss of three hundred lives.

The carnage had to be stopped. They decided to build a lighthouse. They chose the Bishop Rock, the last rock before the Atlantic, the final jagged point before the safe depths of the open sea. It is, unfortunately, a small rock, being only a few yards square. But they had no choice: there was nothing bigger.

They made three attempts. The first time the sea swept the structure away before the light was even lit. The second time the structure stayed up, but, pounded by winter storms, started to shake itself to death. Finally they built a third one around the second because it was easier that way – though nothing achieved in that wild, windswept desolation could ever be called easy. It took years of superhuman effort to build the third mighty tower – but it stayed up.

Now it stands proud and tall above the sea, unmoved even by the waves that sweep up and over its one hundred and sixty foot height – the tallest lighthouse in Britain. And the loneliest.

To navigators the light is a veritable godsend; in good conditions its powerful beam is visible eighteen nautical miles away. Even in poor conditions you are likely to see it before you are too close. In fog the loud blare of its foghorn will warn you away from the rocks. Sailors love the light: they have taken to asking how far out from the Bishop they have sailed, or how far back to the Bishop it might be, or how long it will take to reach the Bishop. To the sailor the Bishop means home.

The light is a veritable godsend.

. . . When it's lit, of course.

Tonight, like most nights during this war, it is not.

Only when a convoy is passing does the light flash twice every fifteen seconds, and then only dimly.

Tonight, like most nights, there is no convoy. The light is unlit, the revolving lens still.

The Western Rocks lie in total darkness, just as they always used to, before men dared to build the light.

Chapter 31

———·———

DAMN! DAMN!

He'd missed her.

He still couldn't understand it. Had he misjudged the distance? Or, while U-319 was down deep, hiding from the plane, had the little boat changed course?

Whatever had gone wrong, when they'd returned to periscope depth there'd been no fishing boat in sight. Fischer had ordered All Ahead – full speed – towards the north-west, thinking the prey had got ahead.

But nothing. *Nothing.*

He had stayed at the periscope himself, sweeping the horizon until the waves seemed to dance in front of his eyes.

But nothing.

Then darkness had fallen.

It was infuriating. Fischer had gone back to the chart and recalculated the fishing boat's course. This time he allowed for a slightly more westerly drift, laid off the effects of the tide – also running to the west for the next few hours – and projected the line forward.

It led straight to the Isles of Scilly.

He sighed. He should have considered that possibility before. It seemed a curious destination – but on second thoughts, a very clever one. No-one would ever think of it.

Whoever was in this little boat had brains and nerve, he had to give them that.

But it wouldn't make any difference: he'd still chase them, up to the very rocks if necessary.

There was one problem though, one major chance of failure. The little boat would reach the islands before dawn and if the skipper knew the islands well he might try to enter during darkness and slip out of Fischer's reach. If, on the other hand, he didn't know the islands well enough, he would *have* to hold off till dawn or run a high risk of wrecking his boat . . .

Fischer was willing to gamble that the skipper was a stranger to the islands.

He'd catch him at dawn, then, trying to creep in. But he'd have to get in close, to be sure.

He looked up to where the young navigator hovered attentively nearby and asked him to find the largest possible chart of the islands.

Even before he saw it he knew it wouldn't be very detailed, but it would have to do.

In the meantime . . . He had another problem. Recharging the batteries. He would have to surface to charge his batteries and compress some air for diving purposes. He had no choice. The power to the electric motors was already running low.

He called the Chief and together they calculated the minimum charging time they could get away with.

Six hours.

Full daylight at 0700. They'd have to get onto the surface by 0030 at the latest then.

Six hours. An awful long time. He shuddered involuntarily.

Then he had an idea.

It wouldn't eradicate the danger entirely, but it would reduce it considerably. It was risky: very.

But it was the only way.

The navigator brought the chart, the best he had. It covered the area from the Scillies to Falmouth. The islands were not shown as clearly as Fischer would have liked, but it would suffice.

The navigator said, 'There's also the pilot book, Herr Kaleu. I could make a larger sketch chart from that.'

'Very well.'

'Any particular features that you want me to study?'

Fischer stood back from the chart, 'Yes – rocks . . . Or rather a lack of them. We need an area near the islands which is safe from rocks, yet close enough to make us *look* like a rock . . . You see, we have to find somewhere to hide.'

The water came out of the darkness, flying across the deck in great sheets, drenching everything. Despite the water-proofs, Julie was soaked through. She could feel the icy water trickling down her neck, spreading slowly down, even into her crutch. Her eyes were sore, the eyelids sticky as if covered with glue, and her lips were swollen and tender from the salt. She didn't bother to duck when she felt the bow hit a wave. She didn't care any more.

She was hand-steering now, the tiller jerking and buck-ing in her hand. Since the wind had come up, the boat wouldn't sail by itself any more . . . Not that she knew which way the boat was heading half the time. The compass was unreadable. She'd completely forgotten about the oil for the compass light. It was too late now. From time to time, when she remembered, she shone the torch on the compass, but its beam was getting dimmer all the time and the course more difficult to read.

The course, when she did manage to read it, was all over the place. God only knew where they were heading.

But it didn't seem very important any more.

She stared forward into the darkness, her body braced against the violent bucking motion of the boat. It was so tempting to just let your mind slip away into nothingness.

The movements of the boat were hypnotic; so too the loud hissing and roaring of the wind and the waves. They rocked her into a state of mindless inertia. She saw the darkness as a friend now, a cocoon which encircled and protected . . .

Her eyes drooped, her head fell forward. She awoke with a jerk. God, her head ached . . .

She wondered if Peter was all right. And David. She hadn't heard from either of them for hours. She should go and see them, but she didn't. It was so much easier to stay here . . . and not to move, to let her mind drift . . .

She vaguely realised that the tiredness and the cold had paralysed her brain and frozen her will-power. It was weak and shameful to give in to it, she knew, but she was incapable of moving, of acting, of *doing* . . . She was in a sort of trance, half-believing that by staying still and ignoring things, the nightmare might somehow go away. She thought: I *would* pump the water out, I *would* go and see David and Peter . . . I *would* . . . But it's *safer* to stay here – and, oh God, *easier* too – And I've got to steer, haven't I? And, if the others had needed me, they would have shouted for me, wouldn't they? And I'm so tired, I can't do any more . . .

Her brain was so fuddled she couldn't sort the arguments out. They'd been scrambling in her mind for hours – though exactly how long she had no idea. Time seemed to spread out before her like a fan, wider and wider . . . until suddenly the fan closed and there was no time any more. She was confused . . . Sometimes she couldn't even remember how long she'd been at sea. One night? Four?

Once she saw grass growing out of the water . . . Another time she saw lights, sparkling . . .

Now, once again, she dozed.

Suddenly she was wide awake.

A noise. She could hear it, loud and distinct, above the persistent wail of the wind.

A *tearing* noise . . .

A second later there was a loud flogging.

The sails? – Or the mast . . .!

She murmured, 'God!' and stood up, feeling the first touches of panic. What to do? Christ, what to do?

'Mummy! Mummy!' Peter was almost screaming.

'It's all right! Just sit tight!' Julie shouted.

What to do?

The piece of rope was still fastened round the tiller. She took a loose end and tied it to the cleat on the uphill side of the boat. Then she made her way carefully across the deck and tied the other end to the lower cleat.

The flogging and rattling were deafening. Julie pocketed the torch and made her way forward along the uphill side of the deck. She lunged for the mast and found it. It was vibrating and shaking violently – but it was upright. Something at least.

An avalanche of spray poured down on her. She blew the water off her lips and wiped her eyes with her sleeve. She reached for the torch and shone it upwards at the sail.

Or what remained of it. She groaned. There was a tear right across the middle, from one side to the other. The tattered remnants of canvas were beating themselves to death, shaking the wooden spars like a dog shaking a rabbit.

They would have to come down . . . the lot: the sail, the long wooden pole at the bottom of the sail, the shorter pole at the top. She looked at the ends of the two poles: they were both held by ropes – ropes that must end here, at the bottom of the mast.

But which ones? There were a dozen ropes tied to cleats on a wooden frame at the base of the mast.

Trial and error. It was the only way. She undid one rope and, shining the torch upward, gently let the last turn slip off the cleat. Nothing: there was no tension on the rope. She tried the next. Ah! A lot of tension here. She

searched the sail for signs of something coming down . . .
Nothing. Without knowing why, she shone the torch
forward. The little sail – it was half down! Blast!

She hoisted it up again as best she could and tried
another rope. At last: the outer end of the lower pole was
moving downwards. Right: mark that one and look for the
ropes controlling the shorter, higher pole.

She found one finally and let it down until the outer end
was almost in the water. Now the other inner end, the one
joined to the mast. Triumphantly, she found that one too
and lowered it.

Now, the two poles were lying almost parallel to each
other, just a few feet above the water, but swung well out
from the boat. She would have to get them in somehow . . .

She went back and hauled in on the rope near the tiller,
the one she'd used to adjust the sail. There was much less
pressure on it now and, to her surprise, the lower pole
came in quite easily. She lowered it carefully on to the
deck. Panting hard, she regarded the upper pole. She
couldn't see any way of getting it in: in the dim yellow
light of the torch she could see no rope leading from its
end towards the boat.

The boat lurched and the pole suddenly swung inwards,
lunging over the deck. Aha! Julie thought. Nearly got you!

She waited for it to happen again. It swung in once, but
not so far and she couldn't reach it. Then at last it swung
right over, almost knocking her off her feet. She threw an
arm round it and held on for dear life. The boat rolled
back; she was jerked against the boat's side. She held on
grimly and looked for something to tie round the pole. She
felt around with her hand and touched a rope which was
fastened to the pole. She took hold of it and held tight.
The boat lurched and the pole tried to swing out again,
dragging her towards the rail. She gripped the rope tighter
until it ground into her flesh. Then the boat rolled back
and the pole swung in again. She stepped quickly back-

wards and, fumbling around the base of the mast, felt for a cleat. The pole started to pull outwards again but she got one turn of the rope onto the cleat; waited, then got two more turns.

She went to the other side of the mast and, finding the right rope again, lowered the pole onto the deck.

Triumph! As she leant panting against the mast, she smiled to herself in the darkness. She'd actually tackled something! – And *succeeded.*

She said aloud, 'Well done!'

She unfastened the rope which held up the little sail in front and tightened it a bit more, then rubbed her hands. What next? Yes: the other jobs! She had the ridiculous feeling she could do anything now. Getting the big sail down had been only half as difficult as it had looked. Now everything else would be easy!

First – David . . . She went forward and shone the dim yellow light of the torch into the area under the deck. It was still fairly dry here, thank God. David was awake and bewildered, his eyes large and staring. He tried to smile but it was an effort. He seemed to be in constant pain. 'Sorry . . . not helping . . .' he whispered.

'Don't be silly. No need to worry!' She patted his arm. 'Just you rest!' She put the water bottle to his lips. As she put it down she noticed a dark stain on his sleeve. Vomit . . . And – she stared, horrified – something dark, blood. 'Are you all right, David? Oh, David!'

'I'm . . . all right.'

But he wasn't, she could see that. She shook her head miserably. 'Oh dear, I shouldn't have let you come!'

'No! No!' He gripped her arm. 'I'm glad, very glad . . . I always wanted to get to England. Are we almost there?'

Julie blinked. 'I don't know.'

He nodded slightly and closed his eyes. Julie watched him anxiously for a moment, then pulled the sacking up round his chin and made her way back to the stern.

Peter next. He was crouching in the corner of the deck, sobbing quietly. She hugged him and whispered to him until, at last, she managed to calm him. She adjusted his jacket so that it protected his head better from the spray, then went to the tiller and shone the torch on the compass.

North-west – or thereabouts. Not bad! Not bad at all!

Gradually she realised something had changed ... It took her a moment to identify it. The boat was riding the waves much better now. There was less water coming over and the deck was not tipping so far. The tiller wasn't jerking about so much either, and the lines seemed to be holding the boat on course again. Yet the wind hadn't diminished. She realised dimly that it must be the loss of the sail that had made things easier. A blessing in disguise! She felt almost euphoric.

But the jobs now, the jobs! Pumping: that was essential. But before that, something she had been meaning to do for hours. She had noticed two life-rings on either side of the tiller, attached to the back of the boat. She found one and unhitched it and, leaning down, slipped it over Peter's head. She took the other one forward, to David and, waking him gently, made him put it on. There wasn't a third.

Then she went to the pump and, after inserting the handle in the socket, began to pump methodically, singing loudly as she rocked back and forward. Now and then she almost laughed. In the strangest way, she was ridiculously happy.

It took well over an hour this time. The sweat poured off her, and she felt hot and clammy inside her wet clothing. Her back ached terribly, but she ignored it, working herself harder and harder.

Once she paused in the eternal pumping and thought: I've discovered the secret of all this – perhaps it's the secret of everything. Never give in! Never give up! Richard wouldn't have. He would have enjoyed the challenge . . . Maurice too . . . Yes, the secret: Never give up!

Finally, when she could hardly pump any more, the handle went easy in her hand, the pipe sucking on empty air.

She staggered back to the stern and flopped down on to the helmsman's seat.

She made an effort to concentrate. There was one more thing . . . Yes, what David had said . . . About arriving . . . *When*, he had asked.

She had no idea. What had she worked out before? Twenty-four hours . . . That meant they should arrive *now*! God . . .!

But wait. They were going much slower now that the big sail was down. That would make a difference.

Also, they'd been west of their course for most of the time. She corrected herself: No, *all* the time . . . That meant they would miss the land altogether. It *must* do, otherwise —

She had a nasty thought. It had been in the back of her mind for some time. Perhaps Michel had given her a course to a *safe* part of the coast. Perhaps, by steering outside it, she was even now leading them straight for a dangerous, rocky part of the land . . .

Perhaps this north-westerly course *wasn't* safe after all . . .

She could think of only one thing to do. Steer even further west. To be absolutely sure.

Yes! *West* North-west. That would be the safe thing to do!

Until dawn at least. Then she would turn the boat towards the east again . . .

She decided to hand steer. But before she settled down, she reached into the oddments box and found another length of thin rope. She went to Peter and, kissing him, tied it round his waist. She tied the other round her own.

It was probably the wrong thing to do. If anything happened she would drag him down . . . She couldn't ever bear to think about it.

But whatever happened she wanted to be with him. She couldn't bear to think of him floating away from her . . . She murmured, 'Where you go, I go.' Then she untied the tiller and put the boat on to its new course.

'What you got, Radar?'

'The Scillies, bright and shining like a lot of little stars, Skipper!'

'Range?'

'Bishop Rock ten miles, bearing 030.'

'And how's the picture?'

'Good. There's a strong breeze blowing, about twenty-five knots, but I'm not getting too much clutter. The waves can't be that big, probably because the wind's offshore now.'

'Right-ho. Taff?'

'Yes, Skipper?'

'When we get within five miles of Bishop Rock give me a course to a point five miles south of the Lizard, then we'll take another leg in towards Falmouth.'

'Roger, Skipper.'

'And Radar, shout when you see anything, however small.'

'Always do, Skipper. Eyes skinned like hard-boiled eggs.'

The pilot grimaced at the expression.

He looked down into the blackness and thought about the submarine and wondered what she was doing at this very moment. Racing for home? Creeping between the Scillies and Land's End? Hiding near the shore?

There might just be time for more than one run. If so, he'd try another further south, then perhaps a sweep to the north of the islands. He'd decide nearer the time.

The intercom crackled.

'Radar to Skipper. Contact ten miles to starboard, angle twenty degrees.'

The pilot licked his lips. 'Where is it in relation to the islands?'

'Five miles south of St Mary's. But it's a really small target, Skipper. I mean, it doesn't *look* like a U-boat. Though I can't be sure . . .'

'Keep an eye on it. Taff?'

'Yes, Skipper.'

'Give us a course to the target.'

'Roger.'

'Wireless?'

'Yes, Skipper.'

'Have we been notified of any friends at sea in this area?'

'No, sir. No convoys. No MTBs or MGBs . . .'

'Radar, could it be a mine?'

'Don't think so, sir. And we don't usually pick up anything that low in the water . . .'

'But it's definitely a target?'

'Oh yes. No doubt about that.'

If it had been the old radar the pilot might have doubted him, but it wasn't, it was the H_2S and he believed him.

'Wireless to Skipper.'

'Go ahead.'

'We *were* notified that the U-boat was meant to be pursuing a small craft, sir. Maybe this is the small craft—?'

That was exactly what the pilot had been thinking. If so, then where was the U-boat?

The navigator's voice came over the earphones. 'Taff to Skipper, course for target 055 degrees, range ten miles.'

The pilot switched to manual and took the plane onto her new course, reducing height at the same time.

He exchanged glances with Reid, the co-pilot, and said into the mike, 'Might as well go and have a look.'

'Definitely!'

But the pilot had a feeling about this one – a bad feeling. Something told him it wasn't a U-boat.

'Range five miles, Skipper.'

'Right ho.' As the pilot took the plane down to seven hundred feet he felt the familiar exhilaration, the thrill of the chase.

'Radar to Skipper. Look . . . I may be nuts, but . . .'

'Out with it!'

'I've got a moving rock. Just to the south of St Agnes. Quite close in . . . But it's *moving*, sir.'

The pilot stared unseeing into the night, his mind racing.

It couldn't be! But even as he thought it, he knew it could . . . just possibly . . .

He said into the mike, 'Size of contact?'

There was a slight pause. 'Larger than the first, though still small. Not a ship at any rate. *Could* be a U-boat.'

Jesus Christ! *Yes!*

The bastard was hiding!

'Taff, guide me in to this second contact. Reid, keep me above the rocks. How high are they, Navigator?'

'Navigator to Skipper. If we make a run from the south-east to the north-west, there's nothing above seventy-five feet . . .'

'Right! Guide me in!'

He would go straight in. Straight in and light her up at one mile.

Then – *Bam!*

It was the U-boat, he *felt* it was the U-boat. And trying to hide, the bastard!

But there was no hiding place, not for U-boats. Not any more.

*

The sea was sluicing over the long, narrow bows, creating great swathes of phosphorescence which ran off in rivers of sparkling silver to the dark water beneath.

Normally Fischer would have worried about the phosphorescence, but U-319 was moving slowly so there was almost no wake to give them away. Besides, it was quite choppy and the luminescent path cut by the submarine would be indistinguishable from the multitude of breaking crests, flashing white and silver against the dark background of the night.

Fischer shivered: the north-east wind was cold. He pulled his scarf tighter round his neck and, moving over the hatch, shouted, 'Position?'

A voice came floating faintly up. 'Half a mile south of St Agnes Island.'

Fischer peered into the darkness. Nothing to be seen, but he couldn't help looking.

He hoped the navigator was right. After so long without a proper fix – visual or star – it was impossible to be positive about one's position. The navigator had got what he believed to be good bearings on radio beacons issuing from the French coast. Nevertheless Fischer had told the lookouts to keep a sharp watch for white water, just to be on the safe side . . .

These islands were the very devil. Lots of rocks and islets scattered around, especially here to the south-west. And the rocks rising steeply from the sea floor so that depth-soundings could give no warning.

The only warning they'd *ever* get would be white, breaking water . . .

U-319 was going at four knots, making tight circles in an area between a mile and half a mile to the south of St Agnes.

They'd been up on top for an hour now. Five to go. A hell of a time . . . Fischer hated being on the surface in a place like this, it made him nervous. But to enemy radar, U-319 would hopefully be just a tiny speck, another rock in the chaos of white blips that marked the Scillies.

He paced the small bridge then, on a whim, decided to go below to have another quick look at the chart. There was nothing to see up here anyway.

He half-slid, half-climbed down the ladder and, still in his wet-weather gear, went to the chart area. Just before dawn, at about six, he would take U-319 to the entrance to St Mary's Sound and wait for the prey. The little boat would have to go in that way: it seemed to be the only entrance into the islands – or at least the only *safe* entrance.

Then he'd grab the occupants – and quick. Once he was spotted all hell would break loose. He'd have five minutes – ten at the most. A slim chance. Was there any other way? He began to mull over the possibilities.

There was a muffled shout. Fischer tensed.

Then a cry. Fischer felt his blood run cold.

The klaxon shrieked through the silence, whooping obscenely. Twice.

'Dive! Dive! Dive!'

Fischer thought: *Oh God, no!*

There was a burst of noise.

Men were running forward to the bow to get the nose down; the watch were pouring down the tower from the bridge; the rest were busy in the control room, spinning stopcocks, handling levers, shouting as they completed each manoeuvre. There was a loud hissing noise as the main vents were opened, and Fischer stared at the depth-meter, waiting – *willing* – it to go down . . .

Christ! He remembered they were doing only four knots. At that speed it would take for ever. *Christ!*

Everything was happening with infinite slowness . . .

Fifteen seconds gone . . .

The last man fell down the tower and the hatch was clanged shut.

The depth-meter was just beginning to show something – *at last*. Come on. *Come on*. The water would barely be washing round the conning tower . . .

One metre! So slow . . .

Twenty seconds gone.

Fischer looked over the coxswain's shoulder. The stick was fully forward, the hydroplanes at maximum pitch, angling the nose down, down, down – but slowly, so slowly . . .

God, one could go mad in such a moment . . .

Thirty seconds gone.

They should have been down by now – safe!

Depth – four metres. Conning tower covered . . . Not deep enough!

She was going slightly faster now. Eight metres . . . Almost at periscope depth . . .

Forty seconds gone . . .

Perhaps they'd manage it after all.

Then time stood still. And U-319 took off.

Her port side shot up, up, up, twisting sideways and upwards by the bow. Fischer felt a momentary surprise as the floor rose up against his feet. Then the control room spun rapidly round and he realised he was falling.

Then came the noise, a vast long echoing boom which stunned the ears and reverberated in the brain.

There were shouts . . . Dull noises which dimly penetrated one's ringing ears . . . Men lying on the floor, reaching out . . .

Panting, Fischer pulled himself up. He tried to shout. But nothing came out. He tried again, 'Damage reports!'

The messages came back, slowly at first.

'Flooding in fore-ends. Watertight door closed!'

'Flooding in accommodation!'

The bow was settling down from its strange upward tilt, settling down – and falling.

He shouted, 'Blow forward tanks.' Christ, he had to

get more buoyancy into her, otherwise she'd sink like a stone.

The bow was already beginning to tilt more steeply downwards.

'Depth twenty metres!'

Fischer gulped: she was falling too fast!

'Forward tanks blown!'

'Blow aft tanks!' It was risky, but even if they came up stern first it was better than falling this fast.

Men were pouring aft now, out of the accommodation. As the last man came through, the watertight door was slammed and bolted shut.

'Accommodation flooding rapidly, Herr Kaleu. We couldn't stop it.'

Fischer's eyes fastened on the depth gauge. It was falling steadily.

'Aft tanks blown!'

Thirty metres . . . thirty three . . . still falling.

And they had blown all the main ballast tanks.

The nose was tilting further and further down . . .

Fischer raced for the chart. How deep—?

Sixty-eight metres.

Christ, they were going to hit the bottom *hard*.

Forty metres . . . Fischer tried to think: What else, what else!

He looked at the men who had crowded in from the forward sections and yelled, 'All you to the after-ends!'

The frightened faces were blank and stunned, but they obeyed, grabbing handholds to start the uphill climb to the after sections.

But the nose was tilting further and further down . . .

Depth: fifty metres and accelerating.

'Brace yourselves!'

Men flattened themselves against bulkheads or crouched against partitions. Then there was silence.

Those who could see the depth gauge watched it, their eyes round with horror.

Fifty five metres . . . Sixty . . .

She hit at sixty-one. The impact pushed in the first fifteen feet of her bow, opening up the already damaged forward compartment and completing the flooding process.

Fischer was aware of the breath being knocked out of his body, of his head meeting hard metal with a thud.

Then there was quiet, except for the hiss of leaking pressure pipes and the moans of men in pain.

U-319 was on the bottom.

Fischer pulled himself up against a partition. The floor was steeply tilted: the submarine was at an angle of about forty-five degrees, her stern high above the sea floor.

She was still moving though: twisting over, slowly and gently on to her port side.

Fischer brushed at the warm blood that was running into his eyes and looked round the control room. There was something wrong, something *else* . . .

He peered round the partition. Ahead was the bulkhead that separated the control room from the accommodation. The watertight door was still closed and locked tight. But to one side of it water was hissing out in a fan from the bulkhead itself. Fischer stumbled down the slope of the deck and fell against the bulkhead. He put his fingers to the metal. The water was spraying out from a wide fracture which ran from the deckhead almost to the floor.

He looked at it for a long time, then turned.

The men were watching him, their faces blank, patient, passive. Someone appeared from aft. 'Flooding in the engine room, Herr Kaleu. We're trying to patch it up now.'

They couldn't save her. They'd try of course, but Fischer knew it would be no good. Neither could they escape; no-one had ever made a free ascent from this depth and lived.

Fischer stared back at them. For the moment there was nothing he could say to them.

He would think of something later, something appropriate, something to prepare them for the end.

But all he could think of now was that they had put their faith in him and they had been wrong. Even now, they were waiting expectantly.

There is nothing I can do for you, my friends.

It might take them a day to die, maybe longer, depending on how long the air lasted.

Then he looked down at the gathering water and thought: No, it'll be quicker than that. We're going to drown first.

He shook his head and smiled at his brave uncomplaining men with affection.

He wanted to say: I never was a god. Why did you ever think I was?

But they already knew it. They could see it in his face and, one by one, they looked away.

Julie wished it wasn't so dark.

She wasn't so worried about the sailing now – the boat seemed to be dancing along quite happily – but she did wish she could see.

Still ... there was only this night to survive, and then, some time in the morning, land would come into sight – or a plane – help of some kind at any rate. Then – she could almost imagine it now – the massive overwhelming *relief*. And the peace.

A picture floated in front of her eyes, as real as if she had seen it herself: it was a picture of a small cottage, standing alone on a hilltop, with a wonderful view of the distant sea which was pale and sparkling in the sunshine. The cottage was whitewashed and surrounded by a small garden with borders of softly coloured flowers. Sitting in the garden were two people: she was one of them. The other was Richard. They had been there some time, living in the small cottage. They were very happy.

Extraordinary how clear it all was. She tried to hold on to it but other pictures flashed into her mind: a small terraced house – her mother's – a clifftop, her uncle and aunt walking on it, a dance at Plymouth . . . Then everything got jumbled up and people were laughing at her, and it was some kind of nightmare, and they were pointing at he . . . Then she was drifting away, out to sea, in a strange boat without a tiller . . .

She woke up. Reality.

She shone the dim torch at the compass and put the boat back on course. She looked around. Nothing had changed.

She peered down into the darkness by the stern. She could just make out the dark shape of Peter's body curled up in the corner.

Then she heard it.

A faint noise, so indistinct that at first she thought she was mistaken.

Wide awake now, she peered into the darkness ahead.

There it was again. A faint – something . . .

A whispering? No, more of a swishing . . .

She gulped and stood up.

Where was it coming from?

She looked around wildly. The sound seemed to be all around her. Or was it ahead, more?

It faded then died away. Perhaps she was imagining it . . .

No! There it was again, like muffled thunder, a soft boom which rolled, then fell away . . .

She stood still, frozen, gripped by fear.

Again, a low rumble. Closer. *Closer.*

She clamped her hand to her mouth.

Then she saw it and almost screamed. A flicker which grew into a long smudge of glimmering whiteness.

'God! God!'

It was water – white water, leaping, moving, rising, falling back, a great line that stretched across the sea in front of her.

She yanked the tiller towards her. Pulling, pulling until it would go no further.

'Turn! Turn! *Please* . . .' She pulled on the tiller until her hands hurt.

The boat turned on a wave and lurched over, throwing her sideways against the boat's side.

She grasped the rail and turned back to look.

White water . . . rising, thundering up against black walls, falling back . . .

She cried out, '*Oh God!*' And watched the terrible water, mesmerised, the fear gripping her like ice.

Then she remembered. The tiller: she had let it go. She reached out for it, found it, took hold of it, suddenly realised she had lost all sense of direction.

The white water was to her right now. Whimpering slightly she looked around her. Turn still more: she must turn still more.

Away, away, back to the open sea . . .

She pulled on the tiller, took another look at the white water . . . it was almost behind her . . . *behind* her . . . Yes, yes – behind her now . . . She shouted, 'Oh, go away! *Go away!*' For a moment it seemed that the white water was dragging her back, then she realised it was fading, turning grey again . . .

She collapsed, shaking and weak, on to the seat, murmuring, 'Oh, Oh . . .'

Something made her look up – a sound; a dull roar; falling water. Her blood froze.

Somebody screamed. She dimly realised it was herself.

Ahead of the boat was a wall of brilliant silver and white cascading downwards and backwards, rushing out towards the little boat. Then a wave rose, higher and higher, and Julie was aware of the little boat rushing forward, hurtling headlong towards a black mass rising into the sky, blacker than the night.

She grabbed for the tiller and pulled desperately, but the wild forward motion of the boat was inexorable. The black mass rose higher and larger, rushing forward to meet the boat.

She screamed again and turned to reach out for Peter. A second later the breath was pushed from her body and she was thrown forward, flying headlong. *Peter! Peter!* She was twisting in the air; turning; then landing on something brutal and hard which dug deep into her back.

She looked wildly about and screamed, 'Peter!'

Some way below her she saw the dim outline of the back of the boat, where Peter had been, but so dark that she couldn't see *inside*.

'Peter!'

Water came roaring towards her in a great deluge, flooding over the boat. She grabbed at something and, closing her eyes, held on tight. The water came thundering over her head, filling her eyes and ears and trying to drag her away. *Hold on, hold on.* She held on until her arms were breaking. Something jerked at her waist, pulling at her body.

The water subsided, sucking back in a great gasp, as if taking another breath.

She rasped for air and tried to move towards the stern, towards Peter, but the rope was tight around her waist, dragging her to the side.

'God, let me go! Let me go!'

She pulled on the rope, tried to yank it off, tried to tear it off, grappling wildly at the knot. *Get off!* Then she remembered – the rope! *The rope was Peter.* She screamed,

'*P-e-t-e-r!*' and slid down the deck in the direction of the rope. Nothing. She groped around. She touched something soft and reached for it just as the next wave came thundering over the deck, knocking her sideways, roaring into her mouth. She reached out through the water – grabbed – found – clung – pulled him into her body . . .

She clung to him. She clung to him as the water carried them forward, bumping, crashing them along, forward, forward . . .

Something hit her head with a great bang. She swallowed water. Then they were up against something hard, and now the other way, now they were being dragged back, back, back.

And she clung to him. And in that fraction of a moment she would have died for him, *wanted* to die for him, the child of her body. She would have held the water back with her bare hands and clawed at the rock with her fists and killed any man or anything that stood in her way . . .

But now the water was carrying them forward again, faster this time and angrier, a great crested wave that carried them up, up, racing forwards to hurl itself on the unyielding granite, forward on to the mighty rock which waited to break the back of the impudent wave, as it had broken a hundred thousand before it.

Julie was aware that the deck had disappeared from under her feet. Instead there was only the water, spinning her round, trying to drag her down. She swallowed water, tried to breathe, choked, gasped for breath, found some precious air, gulped water again, felt the sea close over her head . . . flung out an arm and tried to fight her way up . . .

Still the wave raced forward.

And still she clung to him.

Then they were falling, falling in the great cataract of water. Julie braced herself. In that instant of time she saw a great panorama before her: a split second which covered all the happiness and joy of her life.

Something hit the back of her body with a sickening impact, it hit her so hard that her chin met her chest and her breath was exploded from her lungs. Then the water was clawing at her, dragging her over rough, sharp, hurtful things . . .

Everything began to slip away . . . She was drifting gently . . . the world was purple . . . white . . . black. She was drifting . . .

In a moment of lucidity she was aware of a terrible pain in her side, as if a great weight were pressing hard against it. One last time she murmured the child's name.

Then she was slipping away again . . . into a cloud where a soft gentle wave enveloped her, soothing her aching head, removing all pain, making everything right again . . .

David thought: How strange that I should die here, in the sea.

The boat lurched again, slipping further down, wood scraping loudly and unhappily against granite.

The rushing waves came higher into the raised bow, grabbing at David's legs, trying to pull him away.

David thought: I'll be ready for you when you come.

He'd already said his last prayers and made his peace with God. Now he concentrated his mind on the small house in Germany, as it used to be, in the days when they had been so happy.

He started from the time when Cecile was very small. He remembered her podgy little arms reaching out to touch his nose, he remembered the three of them in the park . . .

A wave washed up to his chest and covered his head with spray. He was almost swept away, but managed to cling on.

Was that the one God had intended for him?

No. When he could hold on no more, *that* would be the one.

He had got to Cecile's school days when the wave finally came. It was larger than the rest. It washed right up into the bow with a thunderous roar and as it receded his hands were torn away from the boat and he was travelling with the water . . .

Free at last. In a way.

Then he made himself go limp and waited, suspended by the lifebuoy. Water filled his mouth and nose and he choked and spluttered and fought for breath. He was vaguely disappointed. He'd thought it would be easy, just a matter of closing your eyes and waiting.

But finally the fight for breath became more difficult. He had no strength left. He felt himself ebbing away.

For one brief moment the soft air touched his face, then a wave hissed over him and filled his mouth and he knew he wouldn't struggle any more.

The lifebuoy slipped up over his shoulders and he was floating downwards, drifting gently. In the last few moments panic gripped him, but he calmed himself by remembering that he was a lucky man: his troubles were finally over.

Chapter 32

JOE TRELEAVEN SNIFFED the air. Cold. Cold for March and cold for the islands. The low dormer window was opaque with condensation. Puffing a little, he pulled a heavy oiled sweater over his head and, leaning down, rubbed the wetness from the glass and peered through.

It was almost sunrise. The dawn light was clear and hard as a diamond, the sky a yellow dome above the blackness of the sea. It would stay cold all day, Joe decided.

Easterlies. He shook his head and stomped down the cottage stairs into the kitchen. Easterlies were the only winds which could bring this kind of cold to St Agnes. Perhaps there was something to be said for turning the fields over to vegetables after all. Before the war he'd grown nothing but flowers and flowers didn't like too much sharpness in the air.

Mind you, the bulbs kept coming up: you couldn't stop them. And now that the transportation of flowers was forbidden there were fancy prices to be had on the black market, so he'd heard. Four pounds for a box of daffodils. By jove, that was enough to keep a man for a month.

He riddled the stove, opened the vent and poured more coal into the top. He picked up the kettle and, opening the latch, went out into the yard. He paused, as he always did, and looked out towards the Western Rocks. The wind of the previous night had dropped away and the air was still. It might be a good fishing day. Perhaps he'd take the boat and go lining for scad. But then perhaps he wouldn't; perhaps he'd go weed-gathering for pigfeed instead.

He filled the kettle from the water barrel and, returning to the kitchen, put it on the stove. He made himself a breakfast of porridge and tea, then pulled on his jacket to go and feed the animals. As he approached, the pigs snorted in wild agitation. He gave them their usual mixture of vegetables and kelp, then threw the chickens a handful of grain.

The sun was up now, illuminating the tall Tamarisk hedges a vibrant green. Beyond the fields, over the rugged shoreline, the far-away lines of jagged rocks were lit a dull pink-gold in a sea of palest yellow.

There was a distant buzzing sound in the sky. Joe screwed up his eyes and spotted the glint of a plane far away above the needle-like Bishop, heading south.

After it had gone he gazed a little longer, but more casually, eyeing the weather and getting the feel of the day. He decided he should really go weed-gathering rather than fishing, though he wouldn't enjoy it half as much.

He began to turn away, but something made him pause and look back. He stared at the distant rocks for a long time, a slight frown on his face. Then, slowly, thoughtfully, he walked back into the cottage and closed the door behind him.

He cleared the breakfast things from the table and piled them in the washing-up bowl. Then he went into the front room to the mantelpiece. The telescope was an old one which his family had come by many years before – probably from a wreck, though no-one would own to it.

He took the telescope through the kitchen and up the stairs to the bedroom. The small window hadn't been opened all winter and was warped with damp, but it finally yielded. He extended the telescope, rested it on the still and peered through.

He stared for a long time before he was satisfied. He

closed the window, compressed the telescope and went down to the kitchen again. From the back of the door he took a long oilskin coat, a sou'wester and a towelling scarf, and placed them on the table. He removed his stout farmer's boots and pulled on a pair of long seaman's boots. Then, picking up the oilskins, he left the cottage and made his way up the lane towards Lower Town, one of the four settlements on St Agnes.

When he reached the handful of dwellings he went straight to a cottage near the beach and knocked on the door. A man appeared. 'Mornin', Jeremiah,' Joe said.

'Mornin', Joe.' The man eyed the oilskins.

'Ther's somethin' out on the rocks.'

The man nodded and without further comment disappeared inside. After a while he returned with oilskins and together the two men made their way to the beach. A heavy boat was sitting at the top of a long concrete slipway, two pairs of oars lying across the thwarts.

Without a word the two men threw their oilskins into the boat and began to drag her down the slipway. Once she was afloat they gave a last push, hopped effortlessly in, fitted the oars into the rowlocks, and started to pull away.

From the cove they crossed the expanse of Smith Sound and passed between the low rocks of the Hellweathers out into the open sea. From here it was two miles to the main group of the Western Rocks.

They rowed silently, each man intent on the slow, steady swing of his stroke. There was a swell running, the last remains of the waves whipped up by the gale the night before. But the surface itself was unruffled by wind and the sharp bow of the boat cut cleanly through the glass-like water.

Joe sat on the forward thwart, the better position for piloting. He had noted the thrust of the tide as they passed through Hellweathers Neck and every now and then he glanced over his shoulder to get his bearings on the rocks

ahead. They came abreast of Melledgan and the Muncoy
Ledges to the south then, after another fifteen minutes, Joe
saw the profile of Gorregan and the Rags out of the corner
of his eye. Not so far now.

He paused in his stroke and, turning his head, took a
good look at the rocks ahead. The other man paused also.
'Where d'ye reckon, Joe?'

Joe pursed his lips. 'I reckon Rosevean. Well, let's start
there at any rate.' They began to row again.

The two men had searched the rocks many times before.
Once, before the war, they had found the wreckage of a
small boat and, on one of the higher rocks, the body of a
man. He was on his knees, his hands clasped together as if
in prayer, his body crouched, his head pointing towards
the mighty Bishop Lighthouse as if in hope of rescue. When
they got to him he was cold and stiff as a board and it had
been the devil's own job to straighten him out.

Joe feathered his starboard oar to turn the boat to port
and head her between the Rags and Rosevear. As Rosevear
came up abeam he slowed the pace and examined the
rocky surface of the islet with a critical eye. Nothing there.
Only gulls, the occasional tuft of scurvy grass, and the
jagged patterns of the rocks themselves.

The boat passed on, going due south now. They came
to a scattering of small rocks, then, finally, the islet of
Rosevean, a little taller than its sister, Rosevear, but smaller
and utterly barren.

As they approached the islet they stopped rowing and
let the boat drift under her own momentum. The only
sound was the rumbling and swishing of the sea as the
swell rose up the sides of the rock and rushed and tumbled
in among the cracks and crevices, only to recede again, the
water falling away from the granite walls in tumbling
cascades.

The other man was pointing. Joe followed the direction

of his finger. There was something in the white froth at the base of the rock face. It looked like wood.

The boat drifted on. They came abreast of the islet. There were more fragments in the water here. Again, they looked like wood.

The two men scanned the uneven surface of the rock but Joe saw it first. It was the object he'd seen from the land. A great blob of darkness against the pallor of the rock.

They came closer and saw that it was a ragged triangle of reddish-black material, caught on a spur of rock some fifteen feet above the sea. It looked to Joe like canvas.

Joe began to row the boat round in a circle away from the islet. Still the men stared at the rock.

There was something else: a touch of bright scarlet. This, too, was quite high up, half hidden behind a knoll. Joe pointed to it and the other man nodded. As they rowed away, more of the object came into view. It was familiar, something both men had seen before: the brightly painted transom of a small boat.

'Better take a look.'

They rowed back towards the rock, to a ledge they knew well: a ledge a man could jump on to.

'I'll go,' Joe said.

'Right-ho'.

Joe shipped his oars and, as the other man brought the boat in towards the rock, he stood up. He waited while the swell took the boat down then, as the boat rose again, he placed a foot on the thwart and, in the moment that they hovered at the top of the wave, he stepped across on to the ledge.

From here there was a gully which led to the top. There was only one point which was difficult to climb, but Joe knew the handholds.

When he reached the top he clambered across the rock

to the side where he'd seen the blaze of scarlet. He peered down over the edge. It was wood all right, and, as he had thought, part of a boat. By the brightness of the paint, a fishing boat. By the gay designs, a French one.

He moved to where the triangle of reddish-black was spread across the rock. Yes: part of a sail. It was still attached to the gaff. The gaff was suspended by a halyard which had caught itself round the spur of rock.

But there was more.

Trapped by fingers of rock or marooned in rock pools and tiny plateaus there were all kinds of jetsam: rope, more pieces of tattered canvas, fragments of black-painted wood – even a lifebuoy.

The small boat had been smashed into a thousand pieces.

He climbed on, as close to the edge as he dared, peering down among the gullies and crevices.

He reached the northern side of the island and turned back. There was nothing worth risking his neck for.

Then he realised he'd missed something: a black sack-like object draped over a small outcrop. There was something else underneath it.

He went nearer until he could look directly down on the objects. He stared for a long moment then murmured, 'Poor devils.'

He clambered back to the other side of the islet until he could see the rowing boat. He whistled and indicated to the other man that he should row the boat round to the east side.

The other man nodded and Joe clambered back to the point directly above the sack-like object. With his face to the rock, he climbed carefully and slowly downwards. He paused to look down and get his bearings. Yes, at least one body and perhaps another.

The last few feet were difficult: almost vertical rock. He found a foothold and jumped the last few feet. He waited for the boat to appear round the corner and waved until he was sure that Jeremiah had seen him. Then he went over to the bodies.

He knelt down. One was a woman, her body arched backwards round a finger of rock, as if a wave had tried to pull her back into the sea and the rock had prevented it.

Beside her was a child of about seven or eight, his face white, his eyes closed.

The two were roped together.

Joe put his hand on the woman's forehead. Cold. He put his hand against her neck and felt for the artery. Nothing.

Then a flutter. A glimmer.

He moved quickly. He straightened the woman's body and laid her on her back. He saw that there was a nasty wound on her head.

He rubbed her hands vigorously then patted her cheeks. He felt her neck again. The fluttering was still very faint.

Something made him look up. He started with surprise.

The child's eyes were open, staring blankly.

Joe went to his side and took his hand. It was icy cold. The child was almost frozen to death. Joe rubbed his hands, roughly, almost angrily, then patted the sheet-white cheeks.

The child blinked.

'Now then, young fella, ye're goin' to be all right, you hear? I'm just goin' to get ye' something warm. Right?'

The child stared. Joe turned and shouted to Jeremiah, who threw a rope up. A few minutes later Joe had hoisted up the oilskins and an old piece of canvas they kept in the boat. He took off his own sweater and placed it over the child with an oilskin on top. Then he put the canvas and Jeremiah's oilskin over the woman.

He shouted down to Jeremiah. 'We'll need four more men, another boat, more warm clothes – oh, and a plank of wood to get them down on, Jeremiah.'

The other man called 'Right-ho', and rowed off in the direction of St Agnes.

Joe leant down beside the woman and went through his rubbing and patting treatment again. Warmth and blood-flow, that was what she needed. There was no response, but he kept going. It was probably the bump on the head that was doing the damage.

Then he returned to the child. This time the boy watched him as he approached.

'Hello, young lad.'

Fear came into the child's eyes and he looked desperately around, as if realising for the first time where he was. His lips moved but he couldn't speak, his teeth were chattering so much.

Joe smiled. 'Don't worry, we'll soon 'ave yer warm!'

Finally the child said, 'Mummy!' And tried to move nearer the woman.

Joe restrained him gently. 'She'll be all right, don' yer worry!'

'Mummy!' He was sobbing now.

Quickly Joe said, 'Look 'ere, who else was with yer? On the boat? Can yer tell me?'

The child was crying, rivers of tears falling from his cheeks, his face contorted with despair. 'M-M-ummy! P-p-lease let me g-go to M-M-Mummy!'

It was perplexing. Joe didn't know what to do. He'd never had dealings with children. He didn't know they could be so – strong-minded. 'Look 'ere, she's not too well. She's best left on 'er own, take my word for it!' He put a friendly but firm hand on the child. He didn't want the lad throwing himself around the place.

The child was sheet white now, his eyes staring. 'G-go away! Go away, you horrible man! L-leave us alone!'

Joe was taken aback. That was strong talk. He retreated a little and said uncertainly, 'Well . . . You won't touch 'er 'ead, will yer?'

'N-no!'

'Right, well . . .'

The child got to his knees and, crawling across to the woman, put his arms round her waist and pushed his head against her side. He murmured to her as if she were awake.

Joe shook his head. What a thing. He covered the boy with the clothing again and, when the child was calmer, asked him again, 'Was there no-one else with yer, lad?'

This time the child turned his head and nodded slightly.

'Yes? 'Ow many?'

The boy looked away and Joe thought he wasn't going to answer. Finally the child said, 'D-David. D-David.'

'David, was it?'

The child closed his eyes and pushed closer to his mother.

'Was it just 'im?'

The child said something. Joe put his head closer. 'What did you say?'

'Just him,' the child whispered.

Joe patted his arm reassuringly. He should say something but it was difficult to think of anything. Eventually he murmured, 'Well, don' yer worry. We'll find 'im. We'll find 'im. One way or the other.'

And they did. Four days later. When his body, bloated with gases, floated to the surface again.

Part Five

May 1943–June 1945

Chapter 33

THE CAR CAME to a halt. It wasn't difficult to see why. The road was blocked by fallen debris. A row of tall buildings had been almost totally destroyed. The ruins were smouldering in the dawn light, the heavy smoke in strange contrast to the pink blossom on the one surviving cherry tree.

Doenitz said suddenly, 'I'll walk from here.'

The driver leapt from his seat and opened the rear door. Doenitz stepped out and walked briskly away, picking his way round the piles of stone and mortar, his staff officer on his heels. The Hotel-am-Steinplatz was only just round the corner. Doenitz noted that the hotel was still standing: one of the few in central Berlin that still was.

He strode into the hotel and went down to the basement. But instead of going straight to the tracking room as usual, he turned into his office and closed the door behind him.

He needed time to think.

It was the day of decision.

The figures had been placed on his desk. He eyed them as he slowly and methodically pulled up the chair, sat down, and straightened his tunic. He picked up the sheet of statistics. It was now 23rd May. In the first twenty-one days of the month the U-boat arm had managed to sink 200,000 tons of Allied shipping – a lot less than in any of the previous three months but still a commendable total, considering—

He brought his eyes down to the paragraph marked 'U-boat Losses'.

Thirty-one boats lost in just twenty-one days.

It was an unprecedented rate.

It was a disaster.

Thirty-one . . .

Boats had been disappearing everywhere – while hunting in the open Atlantic, off Iceland and, as ever, on passage across the Bay of Biscay.

Nowhere was safe any more.

Thirty-one . . .

He gritted his teeth and tried not to imagine how it had been for the men . . . And, in particular, for one of them, the special one so close to his heart . . .

With effort he turned his thoughts back to the problem. What was the answer to it all? No-one could tell him exactly what system or secret the Allies had hit upon. No-one had offered a countermeasure. Maybe the British had spies in the Kriegsmarine itself, maybe they had broken the German ciphers, maybe . . .

Maybe that Rotterdam device which Schmidt and his scientists were still trying to rebuild held the key to it all . . .

Doenitz had the feeling it did.

But nobody could tell him one way or the other. Not with certainty.

Meanwhile his men died.

The men had a name for what was happening. They called it the Thunderbolt. This month of May was becoming known as the Month of the Thunderbolt.

The question was, what could he do to prevent it? He had been asking himself that question all night. And most of the previous day. And the answer was always the same.

Nothing, not directly anyhow.

He looked up at the safe neutral walls of his underground office. Head of the German Navy and powerless to protect his men. He had done his best – but it had not been enough.

He sighed. He was left with only one possible decision and he must make it now.

He must withdraw all his wolf packs from the North Atlantic.

He had been brooding on it all night; now he was certain. He couldn't go on sending his men to their deaths. Nothing could be worth that.

The consequences of the withdrawal would be grave. It would give the Allies the freedom to plan their invasion of Europe. It would also give them the means of achieving it. Once their convoys could get through from North America unimpeded, they would quickly stockpile weapons and supplies. Then there would be no stopping them.

He had told Hitler this, he had explained it all. Doenitz wasn't sure whether the Fuehrer had understood the implications fully, but Hitler had been sufficiently worried to summon Goering and ask for a progress report on the Rotterdam Device. Goering had brushed the matter aside, as he usually did, saying that radar probably wasn't at the root of the trouble anyway . . .

In the meantime the disaster gathered momentum. He must withdraw the wolf packs.

There was no choice. Not for the moment.

Later perhaps there might be a chance . . . There might be an opportunity to get the boats back into the North Atlantic when the scientists had discovered a counter-measure . . . Yes, one never knew. There was always a chance.

He sat forward in his chair and picked up the telephone. 'A meeting of senior staff in five minutes, Henker.' The Staff Officer acknowledged the order. Doenitz asked, 'What else must be attended to this morning?'

'Special meeting with Herr Scheer at eleven. That's to

discuss the shortfall in the U-boat programme, Herr Gross-admiral. Then some general correspondence. Oh, and some bereavement letters.'

'How many?'

'Five, Herr Grossadmiral.'

'Right.' He replaced the receiver.

Bereavement letters. Doenitz was in the habit of writing to the families of missing U-boat commanders personally, even though his present rank did not demand it. He'd always done it in the past, and he liked to continue the practice.

Five. He'd already done ten this week. He would do them directly after the staff meeting.

He must write another letter. To his wife. He'd written to her when the news of his son's loss had first come through. Somehow it hadn't been too bad then. But time was making it worse, not better, and it was becoming increasingly difficult to find the right words.

He covered his face with his hands. In the past he had always managed to avoid thinking about the boys. He had been careful to close them out of his mind so as to show no favour. One could not let emotion enter into one's judgement; one could not ask about a particular U-boat just because it carried one's own flesh.

Now – now he wished he'd thought about them more often. He wished he'd *seen* them more frequently.

Now one was lost.

He must write to his wife again. It would be impossible to find the right words.

He sat upright and breathed in sharply. In a sense, all the crews were his sons and now he must do his best to prevent any more of them from dying.

There was a knock at the door. Doenitz started slightly. He reached hastily into his pocket and, taking out a handkerchief, rubbed his eyes where some dust seemed to have got into them. The Staff Officer appeared in the doorway. 'The meeting is assembled, Herr Grossadmiral.'

Doenitz nodded, got to his feet and, straightening his tunic, marched from the room.

'It's here in Paris, the job.'

'I thought Paris was too dangerous for me.'

Kloffer shrugged. 'You worry too much. Time has passed. People forget.'

Vasson thought: They never forget.

They were sitting in the back of Kloffer's Citroën, parked in a side street near the Etoile. Vasson viewed the scene with annoyance. It seemed to him that there was an atmosphere to the city which hadn't been there before. The people were more optimistic, more defiant. The sullen desperation had gone.

'Yes,' Kloffer went on, 'it's the students again. Communists, agitators . . . Usual stuff—'

'Look, before we talk about this,' Vasson interrupted firmly, 'there's the matter of payment. I haven't had the second payment for the Brittany job.'

Kloffer turned his head and stared hard at him, his eyes gleaming angrily. He said, 'You never give up, do you? You never learn!' He tutted and sighed heavily. 'The job was a mess, remember? And you were the one who messed it up. I strongly advise you not to mention the money again. Otherwise – even I will lose patience!'

Vasson was so angry that he couldn't speak for a moment. Eventually he said deliberately, 'I've told you before, it was nothing to do with me. It was that disgusting queer, Baum. *He* made the mistakes!'

Kloffer shrugged. 'So you say, Vasson, but in Berlin it's *your* name that's got the mud all over it. Nothing will change that.'

Vasson clenched his teeth. He hated Kloffer using his name. He said with difficulty, 'So am I to understand that I will never be paid?'

'That's correct.' Kloffer spoke matter-of-factly, but there was an edge of impatience in his voice.

Vasson said stiffly, 'I see.' He stared straight ahead, his face impassive. It was the one thing he couldn't forgive. Not being paid.

Kloffer gave a small sigh of relief. 'Good. Now, where were we?'

'One more thing,' Vasson interrupted. 'Am I to be paid for *this* job?'

There was an infinitesimal pause. 'Of course.'

He was hiding something, Vasson could tell. 'What are the terms?'

'The best available, given the circumstances.'

Vasson's pulse quickened. The bastard was going to try and screw him. 'Tell me.'

'No more gold. There's none available.'

Vasson said nothing.

'Also this is going to be a simple job for you. It shouldn't take more than a week. The payment will be a single payment of five thousand. On completion.'

It was chicken-feed. Vasson let his rage rise and subside again. 'Tell me,' he said carefully, 'is it that I'm worth less than before . . . Or that you now regard me as expendable?'

Kloffer considered for a moment. 'Your price has gone down.' He shrugged. 'That's all there is to it.'

'I see.'

'You'd be blind *not* to see, Marseillais. You have to realise that things have changed. You're not as – Well, we don't need you so much as before . . . We've got other methods. And other people – people as good or better than you.'

It was a lie about the other people, Vasson knew it.

There wasn't anyone better. As for the other methods –
they were cruder, that was all. And less effective.

There was a silence.

Kloffer glanced at him. 'Shall we get on, then?' He
waited a moment, then began listing information and
instructions.

Vasson pretended to listen, but his mind was already
elsewhere, planning his moves, working out times and,
most important of all, calculating how best to cover himself
so that Kloffer would never find out the truth.

When Kloffer had finished, Vasson asked casually,
'Fougères. Is he dead?'

Kloffer said irritably, 'Fougères? Who's he?'

'The Meteor line. Based here. I used his identity in
Brittany.'

'Ah . . .' He thought for a moment and shrugged. 'Dead.
Yes, I'm almost certain.'

'And the other man? The one who swore to my
identity?'

'Yes, yes! Dead too! Why do you worry about such
things?'

Vasson managed the glimmer of a smile. 'I just like
things neat and tidy, that's all.'

'You mean, you're frightened!' Kloffer looked amused.

'Not at all.'

'But you should be.'

Vasson smiled grimly. 'I thought you said it wasn't
dangerous for me in Paris.'

'It's dangerous for you everywhere.' He removed a piece
of fluff from his sleeve. 'But don't worry, we'll protect
you.'

It was a lie. Vasson knew they would never protect him.

'All right? Are you clear about the job? Any questions?'

Vasson shook his head. 'No questions.'

'Oh? Well, well. Quite a change . . .' Suspicion flashed

into Kloffer's eyes. 'You're not planning anything stupid, are you?'

'What?'

'Running for it.'

Vasson snorted with amusement. 'No, Kloffer. As you always tell me, there's nowhere to hide.'

Kloffer nodded slowly. 'Yes, and don't you forget it, Paul Vasson.'

Vasson smiled at him, and thought: Goodbye, you bastard. May you rot in hell.

As soon as he reached the apartment near the Porte d'Auteuil he set feverishly to work.

He took the three suitcases down from the top of the wardrobe and left them open, two on the bed and the third, which was rather shabby, on the floor.

From the wardrobe and the chest of drawers he took his best clothes and packed them hurriedly in one of the better cases. The cheaper working clothes which he'd used in Paris he placed in the second. The oldest clothes and the ones he'd worn in Brittany he threw into the third, shabby case.

Then he pulled out a drawer and, turning it over, tore off a small flat package which was stuck to the underside. Inside there were two sets of identity papers. He took one set of papers, which he'd never used before, and slid them into his wallet. The second set, which were in the name of Fougères, he placed in an ashtray. With a shaking hand he put a match to them. When they were burning nicely he added another set of papers – those he'd been using since his return to Paris – and watched them as they curled in the flames. When both sets of papers were burnt he tipped the ash into an empty cigarette packet and threw it into the bin.

He closed all the suitcases and, picking up two of the

cases, carried them to the ground floor. He left them just inside the street door. He returned and, taking a last look round, picked up the third case and closed the apartment door behind him. When he reached the ground floor again he was slightly out of breath. He knocked on the *concierge*'s door.

When she appeared he said, 'I'm going. Urgent business. I won't be back. Are we up to date?'

The old woman shrugged. 'I suppose so!' Which meant they were up to date and he didn't owe her anything.

'Here. Take this.' He handed her the third suitcase. 'It's full of clothes I don't need. For a worthy cause.'

He picked up the two remaining cases and walked round the corner and across two streets until he came to the car.

He put the cases in the boot, got in and sat still for a moment until he felt calmer.

He started the car and took the familiar road to Sèvres and Number 22, Rue du Vieux Moulin.

He drove slowly past the house to take his customary look, then turned round and drove past again, just to be on the safe side. Then he parked two streets away and, leaving the cases in the boot, walked briskly back to the house.

The villa was deathly quiet, shrouded by its air of slow decay. Vasson hurried up the drive, his footsteps sounding horribly loud on the loose gravel. He ran the last few feet on tiptoe, then paused at the basement door and listened.

Nothing.

He let himself in and went to the bed-sitting room. From the underside of the shelf he took one of the two sets of papers that Kloffer didn't know about and slid them in his pocket. This particular set of papers was incomplete: no photographs, no thumb prints, only a name. The name belonged to a boy who'd been born and brought up in the French West Indies but had died just before the war, shortly after coming to France to work. The authorities didn't know he was dead. The identity was a marvellous one: it had taken a lot of research to find it.

He went along the passage to the storeroom and, moving the table, dug down until he found the waterproof bag he was looking for. It contained the only cash he had: sixty thousand francs. He put it in his inside pocket. The money would keep him for a year if necessary.

There was another bag lying at the bottom of the hole. He pulled it out and, opening it, looked at the contents thoughtfully. It was an Enfield No 2 revolver which he'd obtained from one of the Meteor line. With it were twelve bullets.

He'd never used the gun – nor *any* gun for that matter. But he knew he could if he had to. Should he take it now? A picture of Kloffer flashed into his mind and, without another thought, he loaded the revolver and thrust it into his pocket with the spare bullets.

He smoothed back the earth and, leaving some money and a note for the old lady, locked up and left.

Next, the car. He drove to the river and parked on the embankment. He waited a moment, thinking hard. How long would it take Kloffer to realise? A day? Two days? Maybe even longer.

Or was the German already suspicious?

He got out of the car, locked the door, removed the cases from the boot and threw the keys in the river.

He carried the cases to the side of the main boulevard and waited. It was soothing, standing anonymously by the road and he didn't mind having to wait. Finally, after half an hour, an empty taxi came along and he hailed it.

The *vélo* took him across the city to the Gare d'Orleans. He paid it off and, taking his cases, deposited them in the Left Luggage.

He looked at the station clock. Four. He might be lucky.

He found a public telephone and, after referring to a slip of paper in his wallet, lifted the receiver and asked for a number.

His heart was hammering against his chest. He gripped the receiver more tightly and held his breath.

Someone answered. It was the person he wanted. He spoke haltingly. A time and place were agreed.

Vasson replaced the receiver. His hand was damp with sweat.

He had a quick pastis at the station bar, then walked to the Métro and took a train east. After changing trains he got off at the Place Gambetta and started walking through some of the unfashionable areas of the *vingtième*.

He looked at several rooming houses before finding the right one. It was the right one because the *concierge* was drunk and didn't bother to take him up to the room herself. She didn't even look into his face.

At one point he thought he was wrong and she was going to be nosy after all. When he came downstairs again she asked him what he did for a living. He replied 'Doorman' and she was satisfied. 'Just don't want anyone who's going to be trouble, that's all!'

'No trouble.'

He paid for the room and left quickly.

Four hours until the meeting.

He went and had a meal. He ate very little but drank a great deal. He wanted to be very drunk by ten. He drank a bottle of wine and several glasses of rough cognac. The owner of the restaurant looked disapproving.

At half past nine he paid for the meal and went in search of a *vélo-taxi*. The driver dropped him near the Porte de Pantin and then Vasson walked.

The cool night air cleared his head a little. He swore quietly. He should have had more to drink. He wasn't drunk enough by far. 'Christ!' he said out loud.

He followed the directions he'd been given. Past the cattle market, down to the canal, turn left and the warehouse was a few yards along on the left.

The area round the canal was very dark but there was a moon and eventually he found the warehouse. He didn't know whether he was glad.

The other person hadn't arrived.

He paced back and forth. He felt very light-headed.

For a while he tried to think seriously, about what he might have forgotten and what he might have left undone. Was there anything that would lead Kloffer to him?

He shook his head. No. No. He'd forgotten nothing. Kloffer would never find him, not in a million years.

Kloffer thought he was being so clever. Kloffer had been going to feed him to the wolves.

But not any more.

Not after tonight and *this*. The thought of what was to come made Vasson's stomach turn and he closed his eyes.

There was a sound. Vasson jumped. A man stepped forward from the shadows. He was large, his head almost square on his massive shoulders. In the faint moonlight Vasson could just make out his features. His face was puffy and his nose broken: he looked like a former boxer, which was exactly what he was.

'*Salut.*'

Vasson stared, mesmerised. '*Salut.*'

'You're sure about this?'

Vasson gave a high-pitched laugh. 'Of course!'

'What exactly do you want?'

'What are you offering?' It was such a ludicrous question that Vasson giggled softly. It was nerves, but he couldn't stop himself.

'How different do you want to look?'

Vasson made an expansive gesture. 'Completely.'

'The money?'

'Here.' Vasson reached in his pocket and threw some notes on the ground. 'One thing—!'

'Yes.'

'I don't want to feel any pain. Please.'

'All right.' The man stepped forward. The fear leapt into Vasson's throat and he felt his knees begin to buckle.

He made a conscious effort to close his eyes, thinking: Dear God, please let it be quick and not too painful.

He needn't have worried on either count.

A fraction of a second later the boxer's right fist smashed into his face.

After the first shock Vasson never felt a thing.

The big man put everything into his first blow. Backed by sixteen stone of still solid muscle, his fist sank deep into Vasson's left cheek and shattered the bone. The force of the blow sent Vasson flying backwards against the side of the building. As he fell to the ground his head hit a stone and he lost consciousness.

The big man finished the job in his own time. He sat Vasson up and smashed the nose a couple of times, just to make sure it was broken properly. He smashed the right cheekbone to match the left, which had been flattened. Then he paused for a few minutes while he examined the results. He decided a smaller jaw might improve things, so he broke that too.

The eyes were difficult, of course. Not much one could do to make them look different. But he did his best, cutting the eyebrows deeply in a couple of places and, hopefully, thickening up the bones underneath.

Finally he was satisfied that he couldn't do any more without risking internal bleeding. He left Vasson lying on his side so that he shouldn't inhale his own blood, and walked away.

When he arrived at the nightclub where he worked he phoned a priest he knew and, disguising his voice, told him there was a seriously injured man down by the canal who couldn't, for political reasons, go to a hospital.

It wasn't kindness. He just didn't want the customer to bleed to death by mistake. He'd never killed anyone in his life.

He promptly forgot all about the incident. Which was a mistake.

Vasson never forgave him for calling the priest.

Three weeks later the big man was found dead in an alley, a neat nine-millimetre bullet hole in his back.

Chapter 34

————

ST MARY'S POST office was crowded, the people waiting patiently in a long line. The woman behind the counter seemed slower than ever. Finally it was Julie's turn. She stepped forward. 'Good afternoon. Do you have anything for me?'

'Name?'

The woman always asked her that. You'd think she'd know by now. Julie suppressed her irritation and said calmly, 'Lescaux. Madame Lescaux.' It was the way the major from MI9 had addressed her in the first letter.

The woman searched the rack but Julie knew, even before she turned round, that there would be no letter.

'Sorry, Mrs er – Lascoo.'

Julie managed a slight smile. 'Thank you.' She squeezed past the waiting people out into the main street, pausing to take a deep breath of the fresh May air. She crossed to the opposite pavement and began to walk, her eyes down, her face grim.

Every day it was the same: no letter. More doubts. Less hope. Every day it was more of an effort to be cheerful, to cope with life.

Some days it didn't seem worth bothering at all.

A voice said, 'Afternoon!'

Julie started slightly and looked up. It was a boatman, one of the men who ran ferries between St Mary's and the outlying islands.

She nodded and forced a smile.

The man shuffled his feet and asked kindly, 'Boy all right, is 'e then?'

'Yes, thank you. He's fine.'

'Amazin' 'ow they get over these things, these young people.'

'Yes.' Except, Julie thought, that he'll never get over it. He had seemed all right after the sinking, even when she'd told him about David. But later, when the letter had arrived, and she'd told him about Jean and the others, then he'd changed. He'd become quieter, more troubled. Not the Peter she used to know.

'You be stayin' with us awhile?'

She hesitated. 'Er – Yes, I think so.'

'Well, you always be welcome 'ere.' The boatman looked down, embarrassed.

'Thank you.'

'Bye for now, then!'

'Bye.' Julie smiled. 'And thank you again.'

She turned away with relief. They had all been very kind, the islanders, and they must think her ungrateful, the way she kept to herself and avoided their company. But she hated making conversation, particularly about the war. She just wanted to be left alone.

She walked briskly up the hill until she came to a place high above Hugh Town. She sat on the ground, her hands clasped round her knees, and looked out at the view. She often came here in the afternoons when she was waiting for Peter to come out of school. The scene was wonderful: you could see St Mary's Pool below and, away to the west, the glittering rock-strewn wastes that led to the open sea. To the north lay the Mediterranean-blue waters of St Mary's Road and the vivid green, yellow-fringed island of Tresco and, beyond, the starker, less brilliant Bryher.

There were rumours about these northern islands. It was said that fishing boats painted in French colours sometimes appeared from the open sea, crossed the sound, and disappeared between Tresco and Bryher towards New Grimsby Harbour. The craft were known locally as 'the mystery boats'.

Richard. He'd hinted at secret operations here in the islands. It would be just the sort of thing he'd have got involved with.

She thought of him all the time.

She thought of where he might be – in some hidden, secret place, perhaps. Or in a POW camp – it *was* just possible – or, when she was really depressed, she imagined him being cold and dead.

She thought of Jean, too. And Maurice. And the others.

She tried not to imagine what they had been through before they died.

That – *everything* – was a terrible torment.

But the thing that really hurt, now, was the suspicion that they – and she – had been forgotten.

Why, otherwise, had she had no more news?

She took the letter from her bag and looked at it for the hundredth time. She hated the very sight of it now: so efficient, so emotionless, so British: Dear Madame Lescaux . . . Thank you for letting me talk to you for so long . . . most useful . . . help prevent the loss of others . . . However I regret to inform you that news has now reached me from the other side . . . Your uncle, Jean Cornou, died in Rennes prison during the first week of April. So too did the agent known as Maurice, and at least ten others. Of your aunt I fear we have no news at present. If I receive any I will, of course, let you know . . . Deep regrets . . . You also enquired about Lieutenant Ashley. He has been posted missing. There is no record of him having entered a POW camp, nor of him being held by the German Security Forces. Indeed, there is no information about him at all. Enquiries have been instigated through the normal channels . . . Again, so sorry . . . If there is any news I will, of course, let you know. Some good news, however. The special parcel you delivered to me has been passed straight to the appropriate department and is receiving their immediate attention.

It was signed A. E. Smithe-Webb (Major).

She folded the letter and put it back in its envelope. She got up and paced along a narrow path that led to an old fort on the hill.

He'd said he would let her know ... That had been four weeks ago. Since then, nothing. It was driving her mad. She couldn't believe there was no news at all. *Something* must have filtered through from the other side. If not about Tante Marie, then about the survivors of the *réseau*.

And about the traitor.

It must have been a traitor. It *had* to be.

And she knew who that traitor was.

There was no proof, of course, but she *knew*.

The cool, calm Major hadn't believed her. He had listened patiently but he had been doubting, politely but firmly *doubting*. He had pointed out that 'Roger' – whose real name was Paul Fougères – had been vouched for and checked. Maurice had even had him personally identified. Perhaps, the major had suggested quietly, it had been someone else?

The hill steepened, but Julie kept her pace, pushing harder until the path levelled off again. She liked exerting herself: it made her tired and that helped her to sleep.

She sat on a rampart of the old fort and lifted her face to the warm sun. The islands were quite lovely now. Most of the heathland was covered in carpets of blooms – pink, yellow, white; flowers called sea pink, thrift, hottentot fig . . .

But no amount of loveliness could make things right again.

From the top of the hill it was possible to see some of the islands to the south-west. The tip of St Agnes and the beginnings of the Western Rocks. It was calm today. Hard to believe that they were the same rocks . . .

David was dead. They'd buried him in the quiet, shaded churchyard at Porth Hellick on the southern side of St Mary's, next to the dead from other shipwrecks of long ago. Every two days or so she walked there, picking a bunch of wild flowers from the hedgerows to place on his grave.

There was only one consolation for his death. His package had been delivered. It was something at least. It was the only thing that assuaged her guilt.

It was a quarter to four. Time to go and meet Peter. She made her way down the path towards the town and, reaching the school, waited outside the gate with the other mothers.

Sharp at four a door opened and the children poured out, skipping and running and making a lot of noise. After a while Julie spotted Peter, slightly apart from the crowd, walking quietly on his own. Her heart went out to him. He looked so lonely.

When he saw her he gave a small wave and quickened his pace. She leant down to kiss him. 'How was it, then?'

'All right.'

They began to walk slowly down towards the town. 'What did you do today?'

'Oh spelling. And arithmetic . . .'

'Do you hate it terribly?'

'No,' he said matter-of-factly. 'It's all right.'

They walked on in silence.

Julie glanced down at him. He was frowning slightly. 'What is it, Peter?'

'Nothing.'

But she could see he was disturbed about something. 'Come on. Much better to tell me.'

There was a long pause, then he murmured, 'I had a bad dream.'

'Why didn't you tell me about it before? What was it about?'

He bent his head and she knew he wasn't going to reply.

They were almost into the town, only a few yards from the lodgings. Julie paused; she didn't want to go into the boarding house while they were talking like this. Her eye caught the gleam of water down an alleyway between two houses.

'Let's go and watch the water.' She led him across the road and down the alleyway to the sea. They sat on the harbour wall and Julie asked again, 'What was the dream about, Peter?'

Eventually he whispered, 'Uncle Jean. And Tante Marie.'

'And it was a bad dream?'

'There was—' The high voice faltered. '– the Germans took them away.'

Julie stared out across the harbour. She often had dreams like that herself.

Peter asked suddenly, 'Is that where Tante Marie is, Mummy, with the Germans?'

She replied quietly, 'I don't know. I wish I did.'

He was silent again, picking at the stone wall with his fingers.

Julie said impulsively, 'Peter, suppose I went to London, do you think you could manage on your own for a few days? Mrs Eldon would look after you.'

He froze. 'Mummy, don't go away. Please!'

She took his hand. 'It would only be for a few days. Promise. I – I'm going to find out about Tante Marie.' She added, 'And maybe Richard too. If there's any news.'

He nodded slowly.

'I won't be long, promise. It's just that . . . I've got to find out. You do see, don't you?'

He looked crestfallen.

She added brightly, 'And I tell you what, since you've

finished *Swallows and Amazons*, I'll see if I can borrow another Arthur Ransome before I go in the morning. How about that?'

There was the faintest smile.

'But for now, how about helping me to send a telegram?'

He nodded again.

Julie jumped to her feet and, holding Peter's hand, made her way back to the post office. For the first time in a month, she almost felt cheerful.

Smithe-Webb looked at his watch and wondered when she'd arrive. The telegram hadn't been very specific.

She arrived, in fact, just ten minutes later.

As soon as she was announced, Smithe-Webb and his assistant, Forbes, went straight down to the main entrance.

She wasn't difficult to spot. She was waiting by the main door, a slim, nervous figure pacing back and forth over the stone floor. She was wearing a dress that was shabby and rather too large for her. Refugee issue, Smithe-Webb decided. It made her look particularly vulnerable.

'Mrs Lescaux?'

She spun round, as tense as a cat. Immediately Smithe-Webb noticed the wound on her head which, though almost healed, was still conspicuous.

He put out his hand. She shook it, her enormous dark eyes searching his face. He said straight away, 'No news, I'm afraid.'

She sagged visibly and looked down.

Smithe-Webb said quickly, 'Look, there's a flat we use not far from here. Shall we go and talk there?'

He led her by the elbow towards the door while Forbes went ahead and hailed a cab. During the ride she didn't speak but stared disconsolately out of the window. Smithe-Webb asked politely, 'How's the head? All healed up now?' She nodded vaguely and he didn't bother to speak again.

The flat was on the fourth floor of a mansion block in Victoria. Forbes unlocked the door and said cheerfully, 'What about some coffee, then?'

Smithe-Webb led the way into the sitting room and said, 'Do sit down. *Will* you have some coffee?'

She nodded. 'Thank you.'

She looked so thin and pale that he asked, 'How about something to eat?'

'Oh. Well, if you have anything . . .'

As he'd thought – she'd had no breakfast. He told Forbes to dig up a sandwich and said to her, 'Won't be a moment.'

She nodded. Smithe-Webb took out his pipe and tobacco pouch and began the solemn ritual of lighting up. Through the clouds of smoke he took a good look at her.

She was in a bad way, obviously very depressed. When she smiled she was probably rather a looker – she had lovely eyes, a clear skin and a wide, sensuous mouth. But at the moment she was frowning grimly.

Her eyes darted up to him. 'No news at all?'

'Sorry. We've put out a request about your aunt but . . . with no-one on the spot, well, it takes time.'

She was nodding. 'Yes, I understand.' She looked at him again. 'And Richard Ashley?'

Smithe-Webb frowned and examined his pipe. 'I have to admit that . . . the lack of news is worrying. He still hasn't been registered as a POW.'

'The Gestapo have him then.'

'It's by no means certain. All sorts of things could have happened—'

'Yes.'

She was very pale, sitting motionless on the edge of her chair. Forbes came bouncing in with a plate of food and a mug of steaming liquid and put them on a side table.

She didn't move.

'You must eat!' Smithe-Webb got up and put the plate on her lap.

Mechanically, she picked up the sandwich and took a bite. The taste seemed to revive her and she began to chew. She said, 'Major?'

'Yes, Mrs Lescaux?'

Her eyes were suddenly hard and bright. 'What about Roger – the man Paul Fougères? Have you had any more news of him?'

'Apparently he was executed in Paris quite recently.'

She looked startled. 'You're sure?'

'Not absolutely . . . It's hard to be definite.'

She was shaking her head slowly from side to side.

'You still think it was him?' asked the Major.

'Oh yes!'

Smithe-Webb raised his eyebrows and didn't reply.

'I *know* it was. As soon as you have contact with Brittany again, you'll hear it from there too, I'm sure! They'll know by now! They always find out . . .'

Smithe-Webb cleared his throat. 'I – er have heard from Rennes, through another organisation—'

She sat up.

'Apparently no-one has heard anything definite.'

'*Nothing?*'

'There's no certainty it was a traitor. Apparently.'

She stared at him, thunderstruck. 'But it *must* have been. Can't you find out more? Someone *must* know.'

The doorbell rang. As Forbes went to answer it, Smithe-Webb looked towards the door with relief. 'Look, there's a chap from the Scientific Intelligence Service who'd like to ask you a few more questions.'

'About the package?'

'I expect so.'

She nodded briefly. 'All right.'

The man from SIS was a round, balding man with pebble glasses – just what you'd expect.

He pumped the girl's hand warmly and sat down in a chair beside her. 'I'm a sort of intelligence officer – but on the scientific side,' he began. 'I just wanted to ask you a couple of things, Madame. I hope you don't mind—'

'Not at all. Please go ahead.'

The SIS man adjusted his glasses and began earnestly, 'When Freymann told you about the – er – device, what else did he tell you? Did he say *how* he got hold of the plans, for instance?'

She thought for a moment. 'Well, as I told the Major before, they were David's own plans. He'd been working on them. As I understood it, they were *his* alone.'

The SIS man nodded. 'But did he say if anyone *else* knew about them?'

'Well – he gave the *impression* that no-one else knew. But I couldn't be sure.'

'Did he mention destroying duplicate plans or anything like that?'

She shook her head, 'I don't remember. The Major – and the other people I talked to before – they asked me all these questions. And I'm afraid I still don't remember.'

The SIS man nodded. 'It was just that you'd had a big bump on the head then, and we thought that now you were fully recovered a few things might have come back to you.'

'No. Sorry. Is it really vital?'

'Yes. Very.'

She thought for a moment. 'I suppose you want to know if the Germans have got hold of the idea?'

'Yes, that's just what we'd like to know!'

'David's idea was a good one then?'

'Indeed.'

'Oh I'm so glad! I'm so glad!' She smiled a little, the first time Smithe-Webb had ever seen her smile. It transformed her face. She asked, 'It'll be really useful then – to Britain? To the war effort?'

The SIS man licked his lips nervously and looked at Smithe-Webb, as if for assistance. 'Well . . . er. In a way, yes. In a way.' He looked down awkwardly.

Smithe-Webb thought: My God, he's made a hash of it, bloody fool.

The girl was staring at the SIS man, confusion on her face. 'What do you mean – *in a way*?' She looked questioningly at Smithe-Webb, then back to the SIS man. 'Can't you use it after all? I thought you said — ?'

'No, please forgive me,' the SIS man said unhappily, 'Of *course* we can use it — '

'You're not telling me the truth!'

Smithe-Webb breathed in deeply and said, 'What he hasn't actually mentioned, Mrs Lescaux, is that – we already have this type of radar.' He hurried on, 'Now that doesn't mean that what you did was any the less important. You stopped the Germans getting hold of Freymann and the secret, and that *was really vital*.'

She stared at Smithe-Webb, a look of blank incomprehension on her face.

He added quickly, 'You see, it was vital that Freymann be brought out of France. Otherwise the Germans could have tortured the information out of him. They could have held his family prisoner and *made* him work for them. So you see — '

She murmured something. Smithe-Webb missed it and hesitated. She said again, 'So it was all for nothing. All for nothing.'

'No, Mrs Lescaux. Really — ' Rather exasperated, he turned to the scientist. 'You tell her, old chap.'

'Well . . .' The SIS man blinked nervously through his glasses. 'What Major Smithe-Webb says is absolutely right. The Germans don't have the radar and that gives us a tremendous edge . . . It means we can bomb their cities

really accurately and ... our planes can locate their
submarines on the surface ... But *they* don't have the
same advantage. Do you see—?'

'But there were other ways, weren't there?' she cried
bitterly. 'Like destroying his plans so they'd never be
found, like hiding him and stopping him from being
caught. Instead ... he died, trying so hard—!' She put a
hand over her face.

The SIS man was on his feet looking perplexed and
mildly alarmed. Smithe-Webb said, 'Better go, old chap.'

The man nodded and left. Smithe-Webb pulled up a
chair and patted the girl's arm. 'Now look, we wouldn't
make this thing up, you know. What Freymann did really
was important, you do believe that, don't you?'

She took a large breath and raised her head. Eventually
she said wearily, 'Yes, I believe you. Yes ... It was just
that ... I was so hoping that David's invention would be
useful. In a positive way. I wanted it for him – I—' She
sighed. 'I wanted him to have the *glory*.'

'Yes, I understand that. Yes, I do see. But what he did
was very brave, you know. And very positive. I mean, he
whisked the information away from under the German's
noses, didn't he? They'll kick themselves when they find
out.'

'Yes.'

Forbes brought in some fresh coffee and she sat drinking
quietly, staring blankly at the opposite wall. Smithe-Webb
could see that she was thinking hard.

Suddenly she put down her cup and looked hard at
Smithe-Webb. 'Send me back. I want to go back.'

Here it was, Smithe-Webb thought. She was bound to
ask. He sighed deeply. 'Mrs Lescaux, it would be most
unwise. Think about it. You'll be on the Gestapo's list of
most wanted people. They'll have your photograph, your
description. You couldn't go anywhere *near* North Brittany. They'd have you in a second!'

She frowned. 'But—'

'What could you achieve there? Think about it. What would you *do*?'

'What would I do!' she exclaimed. 'I'd find the others! And regroup the line! And I'd—'

'Find the traitor—?'

'I—' She hesitated, almost spoke, then shut her mouth again. Finally she said firmly, 'If I could. Yes.'

Smithe-Webb sighed. 'Well, with all due respect, I really don't think it would be wise for you to go looking for him on your own. As for regrouping the line ... Well, I'm afraid we wouldn't want that. We wouldn't want to inflict the risk on the same village again. In fact – well, I shouldn't tell you this – but we've already got plans to operate from another part of the coast. So you see, there really wouldn't have been a job for you to do. If there *had* been, well – you would have been the first person on our list ...'

'So you won't send me.'

'No.'

'I could do special training. Wireless, guns—'

'No.'

'But I could work in another district. Away from Tregasnou. Away from North Brittany altogether!'

Smithe-Webb shook his head firmly. 'No, Mrs Lescaux. You don't understand. Anyone who's been compromised – agents, members of the Resistance, it doesn't matter *who* – does *not* go back. It's an absolute rule. It's too dangerous for *others* ...'

She whispered tightly, 'I see.'

She stood up and walked over to the window and looked out for a long time.

Eventually she turned and said rather crossly, 'Don't think I've given up. I'll keep trying, you know. The Free French might send me.'

'Well, I can only tell you that no-one goes to France

without the approval of my superiors. And I'm afraid to say that they won't give it.'

Her shoulders sagged. Smithe-Webb felt rather sorry for her, but it was for the best. She had to accept the situation.

'All right,' she said quietly. 'All right.' She turned to face him. 'But will you promise me one thing? Will you promise to get me back the moment it's possible, the moment the Germans have gone?'

He stood up and shook his head. 'Well – it's jolly difficult to promise something like that.'

She came close to him. '*Please!* Promise me you'll try. *Please!*'

'Well . . . All I can say is that I'll do my best. But I can guess how it'll be after an invasion. They'll be ferrying tons of equipment across the Channel, there won't be any room for passengers . . .'

'I'll get across *somehow*. Just promise you'll get me some papers – or whatever I need – *permission. Please.*'

She was standing very close to him, looking up at him with those beautiful dark eyes. Suddenly she smiled a little. The effect was quite lovely and rather touching. Smithe-Webb softened. She *had* been very brave and MI9 *did* owe her a debt. He thought: What the hell. He nodded. 'All right. I'll do my best. But no promises!'

She gripped his hands. 'Thank you! Thank you!'

'You may have to wait a long time, you know,' he said gently.

She stopped and nodded slowly. 'Yes, I know that . . . A year? People are saying we'll invade in a year.'

'It may well be longer.'

She sat down. 'I'll wait, then. For as long as I have to.'

Chapter 35

———•———

IT WAS SEPTEMBER. The *next* year.

A whole year and four months later.

The Eighth Corps of Patton's Third Army had come and gone, sweeping the Germans before them, chasing them into the fortified west coast cities of Brest, St Nazaire, and Lorient where they rallied to fight again . . .

Behind them the Breton countryside seemed untouched. There was an occasional overturned jeep, a few cratered roads . . . But the fields themselves were gold with late crops and the rippling corn was largely undamaged by so much as a tyre track.

In the towns it was different; the towns didn't look the same at all. The marks of war were all too evident, in the ruins of the occasional house flattened by a shell; on the facades of the buildings riddled with bullet holes; in the empty shops, almost devoid of goods; and in the general air of decay. The townspeople were different too: thinner, harder and solemn with the knowledge that their troubles were far from over. It would be a long time before they'd have money in their pockets again.

And in the wake of the Germans' departure came the reopening of old wounds – public mourning for those who had been deported, tortured, killed . . . for the hostages, the innocents, the children . . . for the loss of pride and the deep humiliation of four years of occupation.

Among some of the people there was resentment, too, at the new occupation. At the small groups of cocky well-fed American troops who replaced the Germans at sentry duty and on street corners and in cafés. So brash, so *alien*, so lacking in understanding, these young men, none of them realising that all the French people wanted was to be left alone.

Left alone to their own lives and their own wars—

There were recriminations, often bitter. Against those who had done nothing ... Against those who had helped, supported, *collaborated* ... And not only against those who were *known* to have collaborated, but against those who *might* or *could* have collaborated ... It was a time of innuendo, suggestion, rumour ... It was a time to settle old scores. Men pointed fingers at their enemies and rivals, innocent or guilty. A few were ostracised: girls who'd been with Germans had their hair cut off; dead men appeared in alleys, summarily executed by their peers.

Of course, most rejoiced at the new freedom; most welcomed the new era with optimism. But for many the liberation brought fresh uncertainty, renewed bitterness, and in some, a hunger for revenge.

Amazingly the old bus was still running, though due to the shortage of fuel, it went only twice a day now.

As it progressed slowly through the country lanes, the shudderings and roarings were as bad as ever and, from the way the vehicle juddered and rabbit-hopped, it seemed that one of the gears had given up altogether.

Julie was rather glad. She didn't want anything to have changed, even the old bus. She sat by the window in a seat she'd occupied dozens of times before on the endless journeys to Morlaix and back. It made her feel at home.

As the bus ground up the slight hill towards Tregasnou she looked at the familiar countryside and felt a sense of unreality. Perhaps because she'd been dreaming about this moment for so long.

The bus stopped. Julie picked up her case and climbed out.

The bus roared off and Julie looked around. The village seemed untouched, the small grey cottages snuggling together as cosily and firmly as they had always done.

There was no-one about, not even nosy old Madame Gres who knew everyone's comings and goings. Julie strolled over to the café and paused at the door. She'd never been inside before. She walked straight in. The interior was dark and at first she couldn't see. Then, as she put down her case, she saw the *patron* standing behind the counter. He looked up and stared at her.

There was a moment's silence, then recognition spread over his face. 'Madame! Madame!' He said expansively. 'Welcome! Welcome!'

Julie nodded, smiled a little, and looked around. How extraordinary: this place wasn't frightening at all. There were two men drinking coffee at a table in the corner, otherwise the place was empty. She walked up to the bar and placed her hands on the counter.

'Madame – welcome, welcome!' the *patron* was repeating. 'Please! A little something – a glass of Pernod. Sadly we have no cognac . . .'

Julie said quietly, 'No, I won't. Thank you all the same.'

The *patron* nodded and waited expectantly.

Julie began, 'Monsieur, my aunt . . . Where is she, do you know?'

His face clouded and he dropped his eyes. He said carefully, 'Yes, madame. She's at Madame Boulet's . . .' He trailed off and looked away.

'How is she?'

The *patron* looked unhappy and shook his head. 'Not very well, madame. She – er . . . she's—' He dropped his voice and whispered confidentially. 'She's not of this world any more, if you understand me. But she's being well looked after, I assure you. Madame Boulet has nursed her like a saint, like a saint!'

It was just as the War Office had informed her. Over a year ago, in a letter. She asked, 'But does she know people? Does she recognise them?'

The *patron* pursed his lips. 'I believe ... I believe not *usually*, no. But I'm sure she'd recognise *you*, madame!' He was only saying it to please her, Julie could tell.

She said, 'What about – the old group?' She saw that he knew exactly what she meant and went on, 'Is there anyone left? I want to ... get in touch.'

'Ah.' He raised his eyebrows and said mournfully, 'Few left, madame. Most were taken, oh, more than a year ago now —'

'Yes, I know that,' she interrupted. 'But is there anyone left?'

He thought for a moment. 'There's old Rannou ... up the hill ... He ran a safe house ... Then there's Doctor Le Page in Plougat ... Lots of Americans stayed there ... But —' he shrugged, '– that's about it really.'

Julie couldn't remember meeting either of the people he mentioned. That was because Maurice's security had been so good. 'But what about the group *here* – in the village?'

'No.' He whispered. 'No, madame ... All gone. A sad day, that was ... A sad day ...'

'Did you ever hear what happened to the British crew, from the gun boat?'

'No ... We never heard. No. We thought they must have been taken to Rennes with the others. No-one ever saw them again.'

She nodded. Nothing new, then.

Only Rennes. Everything seemed to have happened in Rennes. The Gestapo had killed Jean and Maurice and the others there. They might have taken Richard there. It would be the best place to start.

'Thank you,' she murmured. 'I'd better go and see my

aunt now. Oh—' There was something else, '– the farm. My uncle's farm. What's happened to it?'

'The neighbours – they're looking after the animals and doing the harvesting. But the house ... That's empty, madame.'

'Yes.' She could imagine the house, damp, deserted and cold.

She moved away from the bar. 'Well, I'll go and visit my aunt now.'

The *patron* nodded, 'Of course.' He came out from behind the bar. 'It must be a long time since you last saw her. A long time since you went away.'

'Eighteen months.'

'A long time.'

Yes, Julie thought bitterly, far, far too long.

She said, 'Goodbye then. And thank you.'

She walked towards the door and picked up her case. Footsteps sounded on the bare wooden floor and she was aware of the *patron* at her elbow. At first she thought he'd hurried over to help her with the case, but then he took hold of her arm and gripped it tightly.

She looked up into his face with surprise.

He was wildly excited, his eyes dancing.

'Yes?' she asked.

'I quite forgot to tell you! Good news! Good news!'

She frowned. 'Yes!'

'The traitor! The traitor!'

Her heart leapt. 'Yes! *Yes*—!'

'They've got him!'

Her mouth dropped open. She stared, dumbfounded. 'Got him ...?'

'Yes, they charged him in Rennes a week ago. He was in Paris, about to make a run for it. Huh! But they were on his trail all right. No trouble! They brought him back to Rennes and now he'll pay the price!' He made a guillotine motion with his hand. 'Ha! He'll pay all right!'

Julie made the effort to speak. 'Who? *Who?*'

'Ah!' The *patron* was smiling and formed his lips to speak. Then quite suddenly his face froze and he put his hand to his mouth. 'Madame, I quite forgot . . . Oh dear God, I'm so sorry. I quite forgot! Oh madame, prepare yourself for a shock!'

She put her face up to his and shouted, '*Who?*'

'It's . . . it's Michel, madame. The communist. Michel Le Goff. Your cousin.'

Neither of the massive doors would budge. The top hinge of the right-hand door had broken, so that the door had fallen and wedged itself firmly against the other one.

The count gave a last ineffectual pull then stood back, panting hard and feeling his age, which was seventy-two. In the old days the coachmen and grooms would have sprung forward and opened the doors for him. In the old days a hinge would never have been allowed to fall into disrepair.

It was hopeless. These doors hadn't been opened since the beginning of the war: they obviously weren't going to open now. The count decided to give up and get into the coach house by means of the side door.

He made his way slowly round the wall of the coach house, which, with the stables and gardeners' cottages, was screened from the château by a long hedge, once carefully trimmed but now grown wild.

Through a gap in the hedge the count noticed that another section of drain pipe had broken loose from a wall of the main house. Too bad. Like everything else it would have to wait. Repairs took money, and money was the one thing he didn't have.

As he opened the side door to the coach house he wondered, not for the first time, where all the money had gone.

He peered into the darkness and, fumbling in his pocket, lit a match. He would need an oil lamp. He went back to the château and searched the dusty, empty rooms until he found one. It took him another twenty minutes to get the lamp clean and the wick trimmed.

Back at the coach house he lit the lamp, turned up the wick and peered into the darkness. The giant tarpaulin, once green but now grey with dust, sat humped over the massive object in the centre of the floor.

It was a long time since the count had been in here. He'd rather forgotten about the coach house and its contents. He eyed the tarpaulin thoughtfully. Better get it off and start dusting and polishing straight away. Before the war he'd never dusted or polished anything in his life but, since the staff had gone, he'd got used to all sorts of things, even cooking and washing-up.

He put down the lamp, then tugged at the tarpaulin. It was snagged somewhere. He went round the other side, freed a corner rope, and pulled again. The tarpaulin slid smoothly to the floor.

The count stood back. Not bad, not bad at all. It looked much better than he'd dared to hope.

The car gleamed magically in the flicker of the dim lamplight, its paint a deep, almost black ruby-red which glowed warmly in the drab darkness of the coach house. The great sweep of its body reached from the wall almost to the very doors.

It was a soft-top D8/120 Delage. His last great indulgence before the war. He'd bought it in '37, the same year he'd set up Elfie, the glorious Elfie, in an apartment in the Avenue Foch.

He sighed. Perhaps he *had* been just a little extravagant.

He found a piece of rag and began to dust the wings and bonnet. When he'd finished, he eyed the car critically. The chromework could do with a good clean. There was a shelf littered with jars and tins and he searched through them for some chrome polish. Once the chrome was brightened up, he decided, the car would really look very good indeed. He might even ask a bit more for it. The chap had sounded very keen: perhaps he might go as high as seventy thousand.

He wetted his lips. That kind of money would tide him over very nicely.

From outside there was a loud hissing noise, and the crunching of wheels on gravel.

The count hastily wiped his hands and went out of the side door into the drive.

It was the taxi from the village, wheezing and snorting like a wild animal. Like many vehicles, it had been converted to run off gas extracted from a charcoal furnace strapped to one side. A well-dressed young man had stepped out and was speaking to the driver.

At the sound of the count's footsteps the young man turned.

The count's gaze faltered for a moment. What an extraordinary face! It looked as if it had been horribly injured at some time: the nose had obviously been broken and the cheek and jaw bones were lopsided, giving the whole face a curiously crooked look. Thick white scars ran through the dark eyebrows and there was a longer, more livid scar down the length of one cheek.

The count stretched out a hand and smiled. 'How d'you do? Monsieur Lelouche, I presume?'

'Yes.' The young man hesitated, then shook the proffered hand briefly. He said immediately, 'Where is the car?'

'In here.' The count indicated the coach house. 'Unfortunately I have not been able to get the doors open. No help, you understand. Would you care to come round the side for the moment?'

The young man said coldly, 'No, let's open the doors.' He beckoned to the taxi driver and together they lifted the right-hand door and swung it open. The count pulled open the other door, which moved quite easily.

The car glinted brightly in the morning light, its colour now revealed as rich gleaming wine-red.

The sunlight also revealed that the count's rag had missed some patches of dust and that he had been right about wanting to clean the chromework, which looked decidedly dull. The count wished he'd started work on the car the day before.

'When was she built?'

'1937. That was when I bought her. Brand new. Hardly been used.'

'How long's she been sitting in here?'

'Since the war.' That didn't sound too good and the count added hastily, 'She's been looked after, though. Always checked regularly, polished and so on . . .' A lie, but then one had to embroider a little.

'And the body's by Letournier and Marchand?'

'Oh yes, only the best.'

The young man went in and walked round the car, his eyes gleaming thoughtfully, his fingers running gently over the sleek lines. 'Is it in running order?'

'It *should* be . . .'

The young man raised his eyebrows. The count had a feeling that the fellow hadn't believed a word of what he'd said. The old man's confidence began to wane: perhaps the young man wouldn't offer such a good price as he'd thought.

The young man opened the driver's door and leaned inside. The count realised he was letting off the handbrake. The young man closed the door, went round to the front of the car and the next moment the Delage was rolling out into the sunshine.

The young man paused for breath and remarked, 'The battery's flat, I suppose?'

'Well . . . er, I don't know.'

The young man got into the car, found the crank handle and passed it to the taxi driver who took it to the front and started winding. Nothing happened, not even a rumble. The engine sounded very dead indeed.

After fifteen minutes the young man put his head out of the window and said to the taxi driver, 'Can you fetch a mechanic from the town?'

The driver nodded and went off to restoke his charcoal burner.

Lelouche came over to the count. 'Shall we talk about price? Assuming the engine *does* work . . . Eventually.' He sounded very doubtful.

'Yes, yes. A good idea!' The count did some quick mental arithmetic and decided that, in view of the dead engine, he'd settle for sixty thousand. He'd paid a hundred and twenty for it seven years ago. Since then prices had doubled, more or less. So in real terms he'd be getting about a quarter of what he'd paid for it. Yes: that seemed fair enough.

The taxi went hissing and snorting away down the drive. The two men began to walk slowly along the drive, towards the front of the château. The young man was considering. He said suddenly, 'I'll give you twenty. Twenty thousand.'

The count felt the blood drain from his face. He could hardly believe his ears. He said weakly, 'Twenty? But it's worth at least – *at least* fifty!'

'I don't think so.' The eyes were very certain, very calm.

The count averted his gaze and said bravely, 'I won't accept a *sou* less than forty-five!'

The young man stopped. 'That's a pity. A great pity.' There was contempt in the hard black eyes. The count shuffled uneasily. 'I don't think you'll find many buyers around at the moment, even at a reasonable price,' the young man went on. 'And certainly none at that – unrealistic – price. There's no market for cars at the moment. None at all.'

He was right. The count knew he was right. It was infuriating.

Lelouche regarded the crumbling façade of the château with apparent indifference. 'If you want a sale you'll have to be a little more realistic.'

The count sighed. 'Very well. But twenty thousand is *ridiculous*, monsieur. Out of the question! What's your best offer?'

Lelouche shook his head. 'Twenty-five. And that's being very generous. It isn't worth any more. Twenty-five. And that's my final offer.'

The count swallowed hard. It was ludicrous, insulting! And yet without the money ... It didn't bear thinking about. He couldn't go on living here in penury and squalor. He wanted to get back to Paris, to his friends, to the comfort of a smart apartment ... He was too old to change now.

He'd advertised twice in *Auto* and this had been the only enquiry.

He shook his head. 'Forty. Forty, monsieur. Not a *sou* less.'

The young man's eyes were hard now, like bullets. 'I said my final offer was twenty-five. I meant it.' He turned on his heel and strode away.

The count watched in dismay as the young man walked to the coach house and leant against the wall. The old man's heart sank. He was beaten and he knew it.

He left it a few minutes then walked over with as much dignity as he could muster. 'Thirty-five.'

The young man sighed heavily. 'I said twenty-five.'

'All right! *All right!*' The count could have wept. What a waste! His lovely car, worth nothing. Nothing! Tears of humiliation and anger pricked his eyes and he sniffed loudly. He made the effort to pull himself together. Because he was an aristocrat and breeding was everything, he forced himself to smile and say, 'Well, monsieur, you drive a hard bargain, I must say!'

'Do I?' The young man shrugged slightly.

For some minutes the count found it difficult to speak. He kept thinking of what one used to be able to buy with a hundred thousand francs – and how little one could get for twenty-five nowadays.

Lelouche was walking round the car again. He stopped and, manipulating some clips, released the soft top and folded it back. He got into the car and sat at the wheel.

The count wandered over and leant unhappily against the door. After a while he found the silence embarrassing and, more out of politeness than interest, asked, 'You'll find enough petrol to run it, will you?'

The young man's lips narrowed. 'Yes, I've been saving my coupons.'

The count nodded. Out of a lifetime's habit of making conversation he eventually went on. 'There's so little of everything nowadays. Food. Necessities . . . It's been a long four years. Did you have a hard war, monsieur?'

The young man dropped his eyes. 'As hard as any.'

'You were in the fighting?'

A slight hesitation, as if not wanting to boast, then, 'Yes.'

'I thought so! By your face . . . If you'll excuse me saying so.'

There was a silence.

Despite the difficulty of the conversation, the count persevered. He wanted to show that he could rise above such petty considerations as resentment and hurt pride. 'Which service were you in?'

Again the slight pause. 'Airforce. I joined the British.'

'Ah.'

At that moment the taxi reappeared round the corner and the count was rather relieved.

It took an hour for the mechanic to clean the plugs and the points, change the oil and adjust the timing. Fortunately no actual parts were in need of replacement.

The mechanic closed the bonnet wiped his hands and, with some ceremony, cranked the handle. The Delage started first time, the engine purring smoothly like a large well-fed cat.

There hadn't been much wrong with her. The count began to feel rather sick.

The young man approached him and without a word counted twenty-five thousand francs off a roll that contained at least fifty.

The count took the money. 'We'll need a bill of sale . . .'

'I have one.' He went back towards the car and the count followed him. The young man took a document out of his pocket and, laying it on the car bonnet, wrote on it. Then he said, 'Sign here.'

The count looked at the document. It was a proper bill of sale. The young man's name, Lelouche, and an address in Paris were already entered, and the young man had apparently just added the car's details, the count's name and address, and the date. The young man was holding out a pen. The count took it and said, 'I'll need a copy of the details.'

The young man's eyes dropped. He looked cross. Eventually he said, 'All right.' And he tore a piece of paper out of a notebook, wrote down the details of the sale, and gave them to the count.

The count sighed. 'I'll get the car's papers,' he said. He went into the château, found the *Carnet de Route*, and handed it over.

The young man walked back to the car, got in and drove off.

It was only after the low throb of the exhaust had faded round the bend in the drive that the count realised that neither the taxi driver nor the mechanic had been paid.

Clenching his teeth, the old man took the roll of bills from his pocket and counted out some money.

As soon as he had turned the corner of the drive Vasson let out a great laugh of delight.

She was a beauty! Fantastic!

In need of some attention, of course. But it wasn't anything that a good mechanic, a little money and a bit of elbow grease couldn't cure.

He took the car carefully out on to the main road and concentrated on getting the feel of her. The steering was heavier than he was used to and the pedals stiffer. But it was only a question of familiarity. He pushed her gently up through the gears. Once in top he eased off the throttle and listened to the engine noise for signs of trouble. But she was going as sweetly as a bird. After a while he put his foot down a bit and heard the engine note change from a steady purr to a more urgent roar. The car surged forward.

The speedometer crept up. He felt the wind pulling at his hair and buffeting his cheeks. The tall poplars lining the road swished by, faster and faster. The long straight road stretched out ahead, empty of traffic, seductive, luring him onward.

He kept his foot down. The speedometer on the walnut dashboard read eighty . . . ninety . . . a hundred kilometres an hour.

He held his breath. His heart was almost bursting with joy and excitement . . .

Then he lost his nerve and slowed down for a while.

He found that he was shaking. He laughed to himself, and shook his head.

It had been worth all the effort. And all the waiting. He'd never been so happy in his life.

Then the slowness seemed rather tame. He wanted the intoxication – the exhilaration – of the speed again. He pressed gently on the accelerator and felt a wave of delicious physical pleasure . . .

Yes! This was better than anything, *anything* . . .

He had to slow down for the villages, but on the straights he let her fly . . . On and on, with no end to it.

The suburbs of Paris came too soon.

He felt a vague disappointment until he saw how people stared at the car. Then he began to enjoy himself again, pretending that he hadn't noticed their glances, looking as if he'd owned the car all his life.

He smiled to himself. Oh yes! It had been worth all the waiting.

And the price – that made it even better. What a bargain it had been. Vasson couldn't believe his luck. The stupid old count was typical of his class. Useless with money. His type didn't deserve to have it in the first place.

Eventually he slowed the Delage right down and guided it carefully through a narrow archway, into a cobblestone yard and up to some garage doors. He jumped out, opened the doors and drove the car slowly in.

He turned off the engine and sat for a moment in the silence, reluctant to leave the soft luxury of the leather seat. When he did get out it was to touch the long lines of the bonnet, to admire the four external exhausts which led out of the right-hand side of the engine-casing and into the wing, and to feel the fine elegant sweep of the rear, which seemed to go on for ever.

Eventually he stepped out into the courtyard and closed and locked the doors. He hated to go, but it wouldn't be for long. He'd be coming back the next day with a mechanic, to get the dynamo and battery problems sorted out.

Automatically he looked around to see if anyone was watching him, but the dirty windows overlooking the courtyard were blank and anonymous. He'd been rather careless, he decided, driving through the Paris streets with the top down. In time it wouldn't matter who saw him, but at the moment it was just a bit too soon after the Occupation to be affluent . . . Rather, he corrected himself, to be *seen* to be affluent.

Once he'd got the club going it would be different.

He walked the short distance to his apartment. It was the fourth he'd rented that year. It was as dingy and cheap as the others. Soon – within the year – there'd be a decent apartment. But not quite yet. Again, it would be too soon.

But then, as he'd discovered with the car, the waiting would make it all the better.

He changed out of his best clothes and put on something cheaper and more casual.

Then he went out again.

It was a long journey to the *dix-huitième* by Métro; he had to change trains twice. Immediately he came out into the daylight and saw Pigalle and the familiar streets leading up to Montmartre he felt at home.

He walked a short way up a side street until he came to an almost derelict building. There were many buildings in Paris like this at the moment, their leases unsold, their owners vanished, their occupants bankrupt. It was a perfect time to make a good deal.

Vasson had bought a forty-year lease on this property for almost nothing – but then he'd paid in gold, and gold was worth more to a seller than any amount of paper money.

He ran down the steps to the basement, found the door open and went in. The builders were there, tearing out the partition walls of what had once been a series of storerooms.

Vasson wandered around, exchanging a few words with the men. He wanted to get on friendly terms with them so that they'd work harder and finish the job on time, and more important, on budget.

He'd worked the figures out very carefully. He should get his money back within eighteen months.

He stood back and examined the scene as a whole. Already one could get an idea of how large the room would be once the partition walls had gone.

Just right. There'd be a bar in the far corner, a small dance floor, and plenty of small tables. Then, the special touch . . . A girl, dancing all by herself, high up in a golden cage. Gold! He liked the irony of it.

That was what he was going to call it.

The Golden Cage.

An English name. Very smart. The sign would be gold on black. He'd helped to design it himself.

He smiled. It was happening at last. And what made it so satisfying was that he'd earned it all himself. Every single penny.

Chapter 36

THE POLICE STATION was busy. People strode across the hall from one anonymous door to another, or from the main door to a sergeant sitting stoically at the front desk, and then back again. The waiting area was crowded, all the seats long taken. No-one looked at Julie. She sat very still, staring at the opposite wall, and, like everyone else, waited.

She'd been there for several hours, waiting at first, then giving her statement, and then waiting again. She would probably have to wait a while longer, but she didn't mind; she could stay for just as long as necessary.

It was almost midday. Her stomach was beginning to rumble. She ignored it for as long as possible then took a piece of bread out of her pocket and chewed on it. It would have to last until the evening: she could only afford one meal a day. She'd managed to save very little from the small pension the War Office had arranged for her, and most of that had gone on the train and ferry fare.

The sergeant at the desk was eyeing her with an expression of patience worn thin. He sighed heavily and beckoned to her. She put the bread back in her pocket and walked over.

'The commissaire's still tied up, madame. And probably will be all day. Look, we *have* all the details. Every single detail, every single word ... It's all in your statement. The matter will be looked into by the appropriate department—'

'But I still want to see the commissaire.'

'He won't see you, madame! He's too busy.'

'Then I'll wait until he *is* able to see me. Thank you.'

The sergeant shook his head and rolled his eyes.

As she returned to her seat and her bread-chewing, she felt the sergeant's despairing gaze drilling into her back. She knew what he must think of her, but the statement wasn't enough. She had to be *sure*.

She closed her eyes and tried to sleep, but it was difficult: the chair was narrow and uncomfortable. Finally she managed to doze a little, dreaming strange, disturbing dreams which blended in with the sounds in the hall so that she couldn't tell what was real any more.

Then she sat and thought about Peter and how he was getting on without her. Later, she dozed again. The hours were interminable.

When she next looked at her watch it was nine in the evening. It had been a long day. To get to Rennes by nine that morning she had left Madame Boulet's before dawn. Now she had missed the last bus back to Morlaix.

A door opened. Laughter came drifting through. That's all they were probably doing, Julie thought angrily, telling jokes!

She got up and strode over to the desk. The sergeant looked up wearily. She said, 'Please – ask again! Please!'

The sergeant made a face. 'They already know you're here. There's no point. Anyway—' He looked at a clock. '– the commissaire's hardly likely to see you now. He's had a long day.'

'But he's still here?'

The sergeant had been caught out and he didn't like it. He pressed his lips firmly together. Julie said, 'I'll wait then,' and went back towards the chair. It was a very hard chair indeed. She looked for other vacant chairs to pull together for a couch, but there were none. On an impulse she lay down on the floor, put her handbag under her head and closed her eyes. It was much more comfortable.

There was a hush. People paused in their journeys across the hall. Julie could hear their feet shuffling. She kept her eyes tightly closed and began to feel a little less comfortable.

Someone was approaching. 'Madame, get up please.' It was the sergeant's voice.

She didn't reply.

'Madame, do you want me to move you by force?'

She opened her eyes and said, 'No. But I must stay. I'm sorry.' Beyond the sergeant's legs she saw people staring and quickly closed her eyes again.

There was a pause then the footsteps receded. Julie relaxed a little and breathed deeply. She was beginning to regret her impulse. They'd probably throw her out.

After a while the footsteps came back. 'Madame, get up. Now, please.'

'No.' She could hardly believe she had said it.

He hissed. 'Come with me. *Please*.'

She held her breath.

The sergeant dropped his voice. 'To see the commissaire, madame. That's what you wanted, isn't it?'

Julie opened her eyes. He meant it. She got to her feet, triumphant. The sergeant was already walking towards one of the doors. She followed him hurriedly, her eyes on the floor to avoid the curious stares of the onlookers.

She was shown straight into an office marked 'Commissaire de Police'. Behind the desk sat a man in shirt sleeves, a cigarette in his mouth, a plump belly protruding towards the desk. For several moments he viewed Julie through heavy-lidded eyes. Julie stared back at him. Eventually the commissaire indicated that she should sit down. Then he said, 'Well, madame, I hear that you've been disrupting the entire police station. May I ask why?'

'I had to see you.'

'Yes?'

'It's about Michel Le Goff!'

The commissaire raised an eyebrow. 'What about him?'

'He's innocent. He was on our side. I can swear to that!'

'Indeed?' The tone was sardonic.

Julie paused, slightly nonplussed. She pressed on, 'He's not guilty of the crimes he's charged with. He must be freed!'

'Ah.' He glanced down at some papers on his desk. 'And this is the evidence you are presenting?'

She peered over the desk. 'Is that—'

'Your statement.'

So he had seen it after all. She had been certain it would get ignored or forgotten. She murmured, 'Yes. That's my evidence.'

'Would you like to go over it again? Now?'

She could hardly believe her luck. 'Yes!' She took a deep breath. 'I was a member of the *réseau* led by the agent known as Maurice, at Tregasnou. I interrogated the parcels – the airmen, I mean. And ... I did beach duty ... And, well, all kinds of jobs. I was with the group for over a year ...'

The commissaire said solemnly, 'You were very patriotic, madame. And very courageous.'

Julie blinked at the unexpected compliment. 'Anyway, Michel Le Goff helped us. A lot. He got this very important scientist out of a factory in Brest and delivered him to us and ... Then, when everything went wrong and the Boches closed in, then he helped us to escape—'

'Helped who exactly?'

'Me. And my son. And this scientist from the factory ...'

'No-one else?'

'Well – no. The others had already been caught.'

'Go on.'

Julie stared at him. 'Well ... That was it. I mean, he

was on our side. He helped us. His actions prove it . . . He gave us his boat, he risked his life . . . I know him. I don't believe he betrayed us!'

The commissaire said gently, 'Why not?'

'I'm sorry?'

'Why couldn't he have betrayed you? Or rather, the others?'

Julie thought hard. 'Because – because he saved us. He risked his life . . .'

'He saved *you*, madame.' The slightly mocking tone was back in his voice. 'Tell me, what was your relationship with Michel Le Goff?'

'He was – *is* – my cousin. A distant cousin by marriage, in fact. But that means nothing. Half the people in the village are related.'

'Nothing more, madame?'

Julie felt herself blushing. 'Certainly not! Whatever you're implying it wasn't like that! Not at all!'

The commissaire looked at her dispassionately. 'If you say so, madame.'

There was a knowing look on his face. Julie glared back at him, hating herself for blushing, hating him for not believing her.

She made an effort and said calmly, 'My evidence will go before the examining magistrate, won't it?'

'Yes. But there is a great weight of evidence against Le Goff. He will go on trial, I can assure you.'

'What evidence?'

The commissaire raised his eyebrows. 'People – reliable people – heard him swear to get his revenge on your *réseau*. Apparently he believed that they were responsible for his comrades getting caught in Brest – on that evening, when the scientist was being removed from the factory.

Julie frowned. He knew it all.

'Also, he was seen in the company of informers from time to time. Believe me, madame, he was trouble. Always.'

Julie said quickly, 'But what about the others – in my *réseau*? There were plenty of others who might have betrayed us. Have you looked into them? Have you *interrogated* them?'

The commissaire shook his head. 'Madame, the Germans left only six weeks ago. We've had very little time. We have dozens of people coming in every day. You saw them out there! All of them have so-called "information". Most of it's sour grapes and make-believe! There are hundreds of cases under investigation . . .'

He raised a finger. 'However, we *have* done some work on this particular case and we *have* followed up the obvious leads. Many of your *réseau* died, as we know. Here in Rennes. Others, we know from the Gestapo records, were sent to Germany.' He threw out his hands in an expansive gesture and shrugged. 'Whether they are still alive or not we do not know. We *cannot* know until Germany is defeated.'

'What about Fougères?' she demanded.

'Ah! The man you accuse.' He leant forward in his seat and said with emphasis, 'He died, madame. In Fresnes. Well over a year ago. We have confirmation from Paris.'

Julie stared in disbelief. 'There was no doubt it was him?'

Without a word the commissaire got up and went into an adjacent office. A few minutes later he came back with a file in his hand. He flicked through it. 'Fougères was seen by two other prisoners before he died. They were positive it was him.'

'When? When did the prisoners see him?'

The commissaire looked down the file. 'In approximately April last year.'

She frowned. It was about the time Jean and the others had died. It seemed to fit . . . 'But why was he taken to Paris when none of the others were?'

'Madame, I cannot say at this stage.' He started to

shuffle the papers on his desk. The interview was clearly over. 'I'm sorry, madame. Now if you'll excuse me, I have a lot of work to do.'

She stood up. 'But wait! Please – there's more. I must know if you have information about the British crew! The men off the boat, the ones who were captured at the same time—'

'British—?' He sucked in his breath and shook his head. 'No. The Germans left a few records behind, but foreign sailors – they would have been prisoners of war ... We don't deal with them. You should try the Americans. They might know.'

'But they were brought *here*, to Rennes. To the *prison*.'

'Sorry. Any records of foreign prisoners would be in the hands of the Americans. Really, you must go and see them.'

'I have.' And there had been nothing, no trace. It was as if Richard and his men had vanished.

'Ah.' The commissaire tapped his fingers on the desk. 'Well, I really must get on now. If you please, madame!'

'At least let me see my cousin!'

The policeman stood up, laughing. 'Quite impossible, madame! At least, not without permission from the examining magistrate. Applications take days and even then I doubt you'd be allowed to see him ... People charged with treason don't get visitors! Goodbye, madame.'

She lingered, reluctant to leave.

The policeman was getting impatient. 'I'll have you shown to the main hall.' He called to someone in the next office then sat down and studied the papers on his desk.

Julie said quickly, 'Monsieur ... Will you be interrogating him again?'

'What?' He looked up vacantly. 'Probably, yes.'

'Couldn't you face him with *me*? With someone from the group he is supposed to have betrayed? Wouldn't that be useful?'

The commissaire was way ahead of her. He shook his head. 'Madame, really—'

'But it might help your interrogation considerably!'

He looked at her quizzically. 'In what way?'

'He might talk freely!'

'You read too much fiction, madame!'

'But you have nothing to lose! *Please.*'

The commissaire shook his head and sighed deeply. 'Madame, I just cannot!'

But she nearly had him, she knew it. She leant over the desk and said passionately, 'He'll answer questions from me, I *know* he will!'

The commissaire regarded his hands, then shot a glance at her. He sighed and shook his head unhappily. 'You win. Be here at eight tomorrow morning.'

Julie clasped her hands together.

He added, 'But remember this! It's only because you were in the Resistance. No other reason! And whatever you do, don't tell anyone I let you see him. All right?'

'Yes, I promise!'

Julie closed the door behind her, pleased that she had achieved something at last.

Then she remembered it was a very small victory and there was still a long way to go.

The prison was large and sombre and forbidding, its high walls dotted with small barred windows from which escape was clearly impossible. Julie looked at it and felt sick at heart.

Inside it was worse. Dark and terrible, rank with the smell of humanity and suffering and untold horrors; yet hauntingly silent, as if empty of inhabitants.

A warder led the way down a series of long gloomy passages whose walls threw off a palpable cold. Julie shivered involuntarily.

'Not so good, eh?' remarked the commissaire. 'They haven't done much to it since the Germans left. But then most of the new inhabitants are collaborators and black marketeers . . . So—' He shrugged.

They came to a door. The warder unlocked it. The commissaire said, 'Wait here until you're called,' and disappeared.

Julie leant against the wall in despair. Her mind was full of terrible visions, of Jean and Maurice and Gérard and Jacques and the others.

Here.

The Gestapo had brought them *here.* She closed her eyes. She wanted to know nothing – no details. Not where their cells had been, nor the place where they'd been tortured, nor the courtyard somewhere just down *there* where they'd been taken to die.

The door was opening. 'Come in!'

She opened her eyes with relief. Then, hesitating slightly, stepped inside. The room was large and almost bare, and dimly lit by a single barred window. There was a table in the centre. Michel was sitting at the far side of it.

He looked up, startled. She thought: They didn't tell him I was here.

She smiled faintly. '*Salut*, Michel.'

He stared at her, confusion and amazement on his face. The commissaire said abruptly, 'Madame, can you identify this man?'

'Yes, he is Michel Le Goff.'

'And do you affirm that he arranged the escape of the scientist, Freymann, from the factory of Goulvent, Pescart et Cie in Brest?'

Julie sharpened her wits. She hadn't realised it was going to be like this. She looked at Michel for help, but he was still staring at her. As she brought her eyes back to the commissaire's, Julie noticed that there was a young man in the corner, taking notes on a shorthand pad. She would have to be careful.

She replied slowly, 'He was the contact – between his group and ours. I don't know if he actually arranged the escape.'

'But as contact man, he knew certain facts about your group? The mode of operation, the people involved?'

Julie said firmly, 'No! He knew nothing. Maurice was very careful!'

'Your leader?'

'Yes.'

'But perhaps you told Le Goff certain things?'

'What things do you mean?'

'Things about the group.'

'No!'

'Consider very carefully, madame ... I will ask you again. Perhaps Le Goff discovered certain facts about your group. Perhaps you mentioned certain things without realising—?'

'No!' Julie said angrily. 'I never told him anything! He knew nothing!'

'Then how did he know where to find you when you were hiding on the beach? How did he know *which* beach to go to?'

She hesitated. This was becoming a nightmare. 'It ... must have been through my uncle. Jean must have asked Michel for help and then told him where to find us. That must have been it!'

There was a pause. Julie looked to Michel for confirmation, but he was still staring at her and she had the feeling that he wasn't really listening.

The commissaire asked, 'After he'd collected you from the beach, he took you to a fishing boat that he kept hidden in Kernibon?'

'Yes.'

'And you escaped on it?'

'Yes.'

'Did he say why he had a fishing boat?'

Julie blinked. 'No. But – I supposed it was to escape if the Boches got onto him.'

'But suddenly he felt no need of it and gave it to you. I wonder why he should do that?'

'Because – we were in desperate need. The Gestapo were looking for us ... They would have killed us. He gave it to us because he was *kind*. He wanted to *help*.'

'Indeed ... Or perhaps because he had just done the Boches a favour and felt safe. So safe he wouldn't be needing the boat any more and could afford to be generous to his – friend?'

Julie felt herself turning scarlet. She wanted to step up to the commissaire and slap his big, fat face. She made an effort and said quietly, 'That is not true. None of it is! He wasn't the traitor! I've told you who was – it was the man Fougères.'

The commissaire ignored her remark. 'Is there any more evidence that you can offer?'

She wished there was. She said quietly, 'No.'

The commissaire looked at the warder. 'That will be all, thank you.'

Julie started in alarm. She caught hold of the commissaire's arm. 'Please,' she whispered, 'can I have a few words with him in private?'

The policeman's eyes were cold. 'No, madame.'

'Not in private, then. With *them* present.' She indicated the warder and the man with the pad.

The commissaire was considering. Eventually he said grudgingly, 'All right! But no more than five minutes.' He turned abruptly and the warder let him out of the door.

Quickly, Julie sat down at the table. 'How are you?'

Michel shook his head. 'You shouldn't have come.'

'But why not?'

'Because . . .' He shrugged. 'It won't do any good.'

'No! Don't say that! We'll—'

He interrupted, 'How's Tante Marie?'

Julie shook her head. 'Not – well. She hardly knew me.'

'And Peter?'

'Oh fine. I left him in the Scillies. But Michel we haven't much time. Please tell me how I can help you!'

'The boat. It got you to England all right then?'

'Not quite,' Julie said unhappily. 'It was wrecked.'

Michel nodded as if the news was to be expected.

She said, 'It was my fault.'

'You did well to get there at all.'

The time was slipping away. She said urgently, 'But what can I do to *help* you?'

'Help me? I think no-one can. They're out to get me, and they will. One way or the other.' He smiled but there was a hint of false bravado in it.

'But there must be evidence! Michel, who really did it, do you know?'

He laughed. 'You ask *me?*' He shook his head. 'How should I know? All I can say is it wasn't one of mine.'

She reached over and gripped his hand. 'I believe it was a man called Fougéres. A stranger in the line. He came from Paris and was meant to have survived the Meteor collapse. But I always distrusted him!'

'And what's happened to him, does anyone know?'

She paused and withdrew her hand. 'Well – they *say* he's dead. But—'

He nodded and gave a small shrug as if he'd expected it.

Julie said crossly, 'You've given up hope!'

'I'm a realist, that's all.'

She sighed deeply. 'Michel, what can I do for you when you won't give me any help!'

'Don't concern yourself, Julie. My friends are doing what they can. They're asking around . . .'

'Have they found out anything?'

'I'm not sure.'

'How do I find these friends?'

For a moment she thought he wasn't going to answer then he said, 'In Paris, a bar called Chez Alphonse. Ask for Pierre.'

She nodded. 'I'll do everything I can. Everything!'

There was a pause. He asked, 'Have you any money?'

Her face fell. 'Not much.'

'If you can get into my apartment you'll find some hidden under the bottom plate inside the oven. Just lever it up. All right?'

She nodded. 'I'll return any I don't need.'

He gave a bitter laugh. 'It's not important.' A strange look flashed into his eyes – a look of fear and despair. It sent a chill through Julie's heart.

The warder said, 'Time up!' and moved towards the door.

Hurriedly, she touched his hand. 'I've never really said thank you for what you did. The boat . . . and getting us from the beach . . .' She shook her head. 'You should have kept the boat and got away . . .'

'No, you needed it more.' He stood up and pushed the chair into the table. He smiled and his grave, lined face looked a little less severe. 'See you! Take care!'

'I'll do everything I can—'

'Sure.'

He turned quickly and walked to a door on the opposite side of the room. Though she waited an instant, he never looked back.

Chapter 37

IT WAS ALMOST as if there had never been a war. The city lay pale and gleaming under the late September sun, its long boulevards and elegant buildings apparently unscarred by bombs and bullets. Julie was faintly surprised: it was so different from the devastation of London.

When one looked closer, however, one could see signs of the long Occupation: years of stringency and neglect had left buildings in urgent need of repair; the streets were littered and uncleaned; and walls were daubed with slogans or, in some cases, with rough white crosses where people had died.

Nevertheless, the atmosphere was festive. Even the shabbiest buildings were draped with bright flags, many of them home-made. More than a month after the city's liberation the bright colours of the Stars and Stripes and the Union Jack still hung from dozens of balconies. But, brighter, taller, prouder than these was the *tricolore*, flying high above the rooftops of a hundred buildings, a symbol of many things, but to most Parisians a symbol, above all, of freedom.

Julie found a room at a small hotel in the *treizième*, then went in search of the place called Chez Alphonse. It wasn't listed in the telephone directory, but a shopkeeper knew it and gave her directions. It was a small bar, narrow and dim, its walls yellow with nicotine. When she asked for Pierre, the bartender told her Pierre might not be in for days, but it should be possible to send him a message. Julie

composed a short message on the back of an envelope and
left it with the bartender. He told her there was no point
in coming back until much later, at about nine.

It was only five. Julie went to a brasserie and ordered a
meal. It was difficult to make rabbit stew last four hours,
but she managed it by ordering coffee afterwards, then
water and then coffee again. The bread coupon she'd
proffered entitled her to a full three-course meal, but she
wanted to economise. She had money all right – she'd
taken Michel's from the hiding place in the oven and there
had been quite a bit – but she didn't want to squander it,
not only because it might have to last a long time, but
because it was Michel's.

To pass the time Julie watched the people in the street.
The Parisian women looked incredibly well dressed,
though how they managed it when materials were so short
amazed her. They made Julie feel inadequate and inelegant;
her frumpy, second-hand suit must look dowdy by comparison. She tried hard not to mind but failed.

At last it was almost nine and Julie headed back towards
the bar. The streets were busy. Everyone seemed to be out
for a stroll, talking in groups or wandering in and out of
cafés.

When she reached Chez Alphonse it was crowded and
noisy, and the atmosphere thick with smoke. The barman
was busy serving and it was some minutes before she
managed to catch his eye. He nodded and turned to speak
to a man at the far end of the bar. The man stood up and
came over to Julie.

He smiled and said, 'I'm Pierre.' He was about forty,
fair and boyish and jolly-looking: not at all how Julie had
imagined a hardcore communist to look. He took her
elbow and said above the noise, 'Come. We can't talk here.
Let's go for a stroll.'

He led the way out of the bar and waited for her to join

him on the pavement. They began to walk slowly up the street. Pierre said, 'So! They're still trying to hang everything on Michel, are they?'

'I'm afraid so.'

'Ha! He always made enemies, Michel. Always attracted trouble, even in the old days.'

'The old days?'

'At university. I was his tutor.'

Julie looked sideways at him. She asked, 'Have you found out anything? That might help Michel?'

He shook his head. 'Not directly. I've asked around – my friends in the police and so on. Nothing. No rumours, nothing. Mind you, they have a basinful at the moment, sorting out the black marketeers from the collaborators, and the collaborators from the informers.' He snorted. 'Most of the real villains will get clean away, of course!'

He made it sound hopeless. 'But why?' she asked.

'Oh, they'll have covered themselves well and in a little while they'll pop up as magistrates and bankers and swear they were never fascists . . .'

They came into a wide boulevard full of light and activity and crowded cafés.

Julie said, 'The traitor, the man I'm looking for, he came from Paris. At least I'm fairly sure he did. *Someone* must have known him . . . or seen him. His name was Fougères.'

'The name means nothing. He probably used a hundred different names. Do you have a photograph?'

Julie shook her head. She wished she had. But when she had prepared the identity cards she was always careful not to keep any spare photographs. It was maddening when she thought about it now.

'Never mind. Let's go and see what we can find.' He indicated with his head and quickened his pace.

'Find—? Where are we going?'

'I'm not promising *anything*, but there's someone you should see. Someone who might know something.' He emphasised, 'But I'm not promising a thing.'

Julie ran a little to keep up. 'Who? Who is this person?'

Suddenly Pierre gave a short laugh. 'Ah . . . Well, you see, we like to help the police out. In our own small way.'

She looked at him questioningly.

'We've caught ourselves someone. Someone who might otherwise have avoided the full force of justice.'

Julie tensed. 'Who—?'

'An informer.'

'And he might have known—'

Pierre said firmly, 'Not necessarily. But he knew the Gestapo well enough. He worked for them for at least two years. He might have heard something about your man, you never know. Anyway, let's go and see.'

Julie followed, trying to absorb the full meaning of what Pierre had said. This informer – would he have known about other informers? Would they have met? It seemed very unlikely. And would they have had the same contacts? Again, it seemed unlikely. She decided not to raise her hopes too high.

She found the idea of the captured informer rather disturbing; she couldn't help wondering what they would do with him afterwards. She thought of asking more, but in the glow of the occasional light Pierre's face looked stern and unboyish and she decided against it.

They walked in silence for ten minutes, into a darker quieter area with few cafés or restaurants. Julie had no idea where they were. Eventually they came to a tall, red-brick apartment building.

Pierre guided her into a narrow alleyway at the side and then to some steps which led down to a cellar. The alley was dark, filthy and oppressive. Julie hung back.

Pierre turned. 'It's all right. Just follow me.'

He led the way down the steps and knocked softly on a

door at the bottom. There was a long pause. Finally the door opened slightly. Pierre put his head to the crack, murmured a few words, and the door swung open.

Pierre stepped forward. Julie followed, half-impatient, half-frightened of what she might see.

It was a bare cellar, cold and damp, its floor scattered with rubbish. There was a blinding electric light hanging on a wire from the ceiling. It cast a pool of white over the centre of the room, leaving the walls in deep shadow.

Immediately under the light was a chair. A man was sitting on it. He was bound to the chair by rope which had been passed several times round his chest, pinning his arms to his sides. The front of his shirt was covered with blood which seemed to have come from his face, though it was impossible to be sure because his head was lying forward on his chest. He seemed to be asleep.

Pierre strode across and, grasping the man's hair, raised his head. Julie gasped. The face was a mess, the nose bloody and the eyes blackened.

She stared hard for several moments.

Then she exhaled.

She had never seen the man before in her life.

She kept looking, just to be sure. But there was no doubt.

'You don't recognise him?' Pierre asked.

'No.'

Pierre nodded. 'No reason why you should.' He let the head fall again.

There were two other men in the room, the one who had opened the door and another who came up to Pierre and said under his breath, 'I think we've got the lot. Shall we—?'

Then they were whispering and Julie didn't hear any more. Eventually the conversation finished and Pierre came back to her.

Julie began, 'What exactly—?'

Suddenly, the man in the chair jerked up his head and moaned. Julie held her breath. Then he slumped forward again.

She asked again, 'What exactly did he do?'

'Oh, he was a little sneak, a tell-tale ... He shopped people to the Gestapo. For money. Not much money, either! That's because he enjoyed doing it, you see.' He shouted, 'Didn't you, you *con*? Eh!'

The figure in the chair whimpered and began rocking his head from side to side.

'But he doesn't enjoy it so much now,' Pierre snorted contemptuously. 'His national socialist principles didn't last very long. In fact, he's prepared to swear to anything just at the moment.'

Suddenly the figure began to wail, a continuous whine that rose and fell like a dog howling in the night.

Pierre regarded the sight with distaste. 'Four of my comrades died because of him.'

'I'm sorry.'

'It's always the spineless little shits who do the damage. Look at him! He's frightened, the yellow-belly! Terrified of what we might do to him! Spineless little shits!'

She shook her head. 'Our traitor wasn't like that. He was clever ... hard ... and cunning. Not like that.'

'Ah. Well, let's find out what this creature knows.'

Pierre went up to the chair and pulled up the man's head again. There was a shriek and the man started sobbing and whimpering. 'No, no ... please ... please ...'

'Your masters sent someone to Brittany. Do you know who? *Do you know who?*'

The man shook his head from side to side, his eyes wide and staring. 'No ... No ... Brittany ... no!'

Julie stared, repulsed by the bloody face.

Pierre was getting impatient. He waved to one of the other men. 'Encourage him, Charles, will you?'

'No, please!' Julie exclaimed.

Pierre paused in surprise.

Finally he shrugged. 'All right. If you wish.' He said to the figure in the chair, 'The lady is kind. She doesn't want you to suffer. Tell her what she needs to know, eh? Otherwise we'll go back to the other way. Tell her! Who else did your masters use? Who was sent to Brittany? *Eh?*'

The wild eyes swivelled round and fastened on Julie's face. The mouth opened and closed, like a fish. Eventually the man whined to Julie, 'They're – going – to – kill me!' And started to cry. 'Please – stop them. *Please!*'

Julie looked to Pierre for help. He said roughly, '*Tell the lady what she wants to know.*'

The man's eyes were fastened on Julie. 'I know n-nothing! *Nothing!* I was innocent! The Gestapo blackmailed me. They forced me into it. Save me! *Please! Please!*'

She said quietly, 'If you could tell me what you know . . . I'd be grateful.'

The man gulped. '. . . I heard very little. They were *very* careful. They forced me to tell them things, then they made me go away. *Really.*' He was sobbing gently.

The sight was pathetic, cruel. Julie made herself remember that this man was a murderer, just like Fougères. She pressed, 'But gossip . . . rumours . . . there must have been *something.*'

He shook his head. 'I can't think . . . I can't think!'

Pierre said roughly, 'Who was in charge of informers?'

'Kloffer.'

Pierre said quickly, 'And did Kloffer ever talk about his – agents?'

'No! Kloffer was too grand for me. I never talked to Kloffer! Never! I wasn't important enough! I wasn't one of their informers. I only dealt with stockings, perfume – I was never an informer. Never!'

Pierre said to Julie, 'He's lying,' and made a sudden movement towards the chair. The man threw back his head in terror.

'Who *did* you deal with then?' Pierre demanded.

'There was a sergeant – and a junior officer. *Not* important people. They never told me *anything*!'

Pierre was getting impatient. '*Try harder*!'

The wretched man rocked his head slowly from side to side. 'Please . . . I was never told anything . . .'

'*Try harder.*'

'Oh please, oh *please*!' He was whining again. Suddenly he stopped. There was a long pause. He frowned with mental effort. Finally he gulped and said, 'The sergeant . . . he was in charge of false papers. I never had any, of course! I was only a black marketeer. I wasn't important enough. But . . . I know others did.'

Pierre urged, 'Others?'

'No names were ever mentioned. Never. But—' His bloodshot eyes fastened on Julie again and he spoke quickly through swollen lips. 'Once or twice I heard things. F-from the sergeant mainly. He'd talk about successes. Things they'd found out, groups they'd smashed, th-that sort of thing. There was one man I heard about, a t-top man, someone who w-worked for them all the time . . .'

Julie held her breath. '*Yes?*'

'. . . the tip of one of his fingers was m-missing! So the sergeant said . . .'

The man desperately searched Julie's face for a sign that he had said the right thing. She looked at Pierre and shook her head.

Pierre said coldly, 'No good, *con.*' He began to move away. 'That's it then.'

'No-o-o!' It was a great wail. 'Please, I *beg you.*' Then he was looking from her to Pierre and talking so fast that she missed the first few words. '. . . and there was another. Someone they gave false papers to all the time. He was important, I knew. He'd started as a dealer, like me. Usual things – petrol, stockings, perfume. Then he became an informer. The sergeant talked about him a couple of times.

I never heard a name, never a *name*. But they called him the Marseillais. Or the Man from Marseilles. Something like that.' He looked desperately up into their faces. 'He was important, I know that – but nothing else. They never told me anything else! *Believe me.*'

A Marseillais. Julie tried to recall Fougères's voice. It had been an educated voice without, as far as she could tell, any regional accent. Not very likely, then.

She asked, nevertheless, 'Did this sergeant ever say what this Marseillais had done exactly? What sort of jobs?'

The prisoner's head fell to one side and she thought he was going to faint. But he mumbled, 'Infiltration. His s-speciality. Very s-successful...' The puffed eyes re-opened. '*Réseaux* ... he got inside an escape line ... for airmen ...'

Julie stiffened and put her face up to the prisoner's. 'Yes—?'

'That's all I know. He was very important!' The man grimaced as if in pain.

'But which line?' Julie took him by the shoulder and shook him slightly. 'Which line?'

'I don't know ... I don't know!'

'Was it Meteor? Was it? Or ours in Brittany?'

The man threw his head from side to side and started to sob again. 'I don't know ...'

Julie stood for a while, watching him. Pierre took her aside. 'It's not much.'

'No.' It was almost nothing. She asked, 'What about this Kloffer? Was he captured?'

Pierre shook his head. 'No! The Gestapo were the first people to disappear. He'll be holed up in Germany by now, planning his excuses.'

A cry came from the figure in the chair. '*Please, lady* ... Please have mercy ... Please don't let them kill me. Please!' He was wailing again.

Julie looked back. 'What about him?'

Pierre murmured, 'We'll decide.'

'Are you sure he did it?'

'We're sure.' He went to the door. 'Here, I'll see you back.' As she stepped out into the cool night air a howl came floating through the door. Julie clenched her fists and walked quickly up the steps towards the street.

Pierre caught up with her and they walked in silence for a while.

Eventually he asked, 'What will you do now?'

'I don't know.'

'Will you go back to Brittany?'

She shook her head. 'There doesn't seem much point. Fougères wouldn't have gone back there.'

'So you'll stay in Paris?'

She sighed heavily. 'I suppose so.'

'Well, keep in touch. I might hear something. The police might come across your man, you never know. He probably shopped a lot of other people too. It's bound to catch up with him sooner or later. I'll leave messages at Chez Alphonse from time to time. Okay?'

'Yes.'

'I'm sorry there wasn't more. But one could hardly expect names.'

'No.'

'I'll ask about this Marseillais. Perhaps if he really *was* important he might be your man.'

'Yes—' She stopped and looked at him. 'The one back there. Couldn't you give him to the police? Couldn't you?'

Pierre's face was sad and cold. 'What would *you* do if he had killed *your* friends?'

Julie stared at him, then looked away. There was nothing to say.

They walked on and came to a street which she recognised. She said, 'I can find my way from here.'

They said brief goodbyes and separated. Julie walked

back to the hotel, deeply depressed. She went straight to bed and lay awake most of the night, thinking.

The next day she returned to Chez Alphonse. There was no message.

She returned every evening for a week, after long days spent at police stations, military headquarters, and obscure departments of the new French government.

Nothing. No information on the Marseillais. No information on someone who might, at one time or another, have called himself Fougères.

The other branches of the Resistance could not help either. Fougères? No, he had been one of their own. He had never betrayed anyone. Had someone impersonated him then? They didn't know. Fougères had disappeared when the Gestapo made it too hot for him in Paris. He'd phoned a friend and said he was going to Brittany. Description – Yes, tall and dark. Yes, that was Fougères. He was long dead now, taken from Fresnes and shot at Mont Valerion.

But they would make more enquiries. No traitor would stay alive and unavenged while they still lived. If she ever heard a whisper about the true identity of the Brittany traitor, she had only to contact them—

On the eighth day there was a message at Chez Alphonse. It said 'No trace of anyone known as the Marseillais. Nothing on any other informers. Sorry. Pierre.'

That night in bed she spent a long time thinking about the number of infiltrators the Gestapo might have used on a regular basis – was it a few? Or a dozen?

And what made one of those infiltrators really success-ful, so successful that he stood out from the rest?

By the morning she thought she knew, and then she made her decision.

*

The woman was leaning over him, her face leering and cruel. She laughed, loud and triumphant. He tried to move but she held him in a vice-like grip. He couldn't *believe* how strong she was.

It wasn't fair! He wanted to say it wasn't fair.

He tried to call out. But however hard he tried his lips wouldn't move. He couldn't believe it.

He made a superhuman effort to get free.

His limbs were heavy and useless. They wouldn't move either!

He begged, *Move!* Please *move!*

She was killing him now, slowly but surely. Covering his face, squeezing his neck . . . He gasped for air, craved for breath . . . *sucked* for the precious air . . .

But she squeezed tighter.

He was panicking now. The blood was roaring and singing in his head.

He was *desperate* for air . . .

Death rushed up to him, nearer and nearer. He *sensed* it coming . . .

And all he could think was: It's not *fair*.

Then she was laughing again, the sound fading and swirling in the distance. Everything was fading . . .

With a terrible shock he realised he had slipped over the edge of a precipice and was falling down and down . . .

Oh Christ! I'm so frightened. Maman, help!

Maman!

He woke up sweating and murmured, '*Merde!*'

He looked up at the ceiling, then closed his eyes again and tried to calm himself.

What a stupid thing. He hadn't had a dream like that for a long time.

He wondered vaguely why it should come back now.

There must be a reason.

He rolled over and, taking a cigarette from a packet

lying on the floor, lit it thoughtfully. He inhaled deeply and let the smoke take effect.

No, there was no reason for the dream.

It usually came when things were going badly. But nothing was going badly at the moment. In fact, everything was going rather well . . .

Perhaps he'd overlooked something. Quickly he went over everything in his mind: the club, the permits, the financial calculations, the details – always the details.

He'd forgotten nothing.

Stupid, stupid . . . that dream.

Still, it bothered him. He hated its power over him.

Angrily he stubbed out his cigarette. Immediately, he lit another one and inhaled deeply.

He closed his eyes and tried to think of all the good things that were happening, like the car and the new suit he had bought. Yes, there were *lots* of good things.

The dream meant nothing.

No-one would ever find him.

He was safe.

The dream belonged to the past. And the past was locked safely away.

The Man from Marseilles.

Julie looked at the people milling around the station and thought: But they're all from Marseilles!

She picked up her case and walked out of the station into the street. Though it was barely nine, the sun was blazing out of an empty sky. She hadn't realised it would be so warm in October. Her woollen suit felt rather hot.

She was standing in a wide boulevard, busy with cars and the occasional horse-drawn vehicle. She was struck immediately by the noise – the hooting of the cars and the loud conversations – and by the colour: the people seemed brighter, more exotic. It was partly their clothes and partly the different races – Arab, Senegalese and Asian.

She looked around blankly. She wasn't sure where to start.

She crossed the boulevard and began to wander down what seemed to be a main street. After a while she paused. This sort of wandering would do no good; she had to do something positive.

The police first, then. She stopped and asked a shop-keeper for directions to the nearest police station.

It was not far – five minutes away – but it was the wrong police station. She needed the *Police Judiciaire* – the criminal investigation branch. They redirected her. It was a long walk and her case began to feel heavy in her hand. She stopped and removed her jacket. She should have done it before: her blouse was damp with sweat.

It took half an hour to find a sufficiently senior officer and explain what she wanted.

Then they laughed at her as she had known they would. Not rudely or unkindly, but politely, with a shake of the head.

'A man called the Marseillais? Madame, have you any idea how many characters are called by that name?'

But they did let her look at the rogues' gallery. There were vast numbers of wanted men and ex-convicts. After three hours one face began to look much like another and Julie lost heart. Why should she find him there anyway? He probably had no criminal record. Nevertheless, before she left she arranged to come back the next day, just in case.

She ate a late lunch in a pavement café then, taking a slip of paper from her purse, made a telephone call. The number belonged to a friend of the Paris Resistance, a colleague of theirs, someone who might be able to help; a man called Alain.

The number rang. A woman's voice replied.

'I want to speak to Alain, please.'

'You mean Doctor Hubert? I'm afraid he is at the hospital at present. Please try later.'

Julie rang off. They hadn't told her he was a doctor. She decided to try again in the evening.

In the meantime she had the rest of the afternoon to spare. When the waiter brought coffee, she said, 'I'm a stranger to the city. Can you tell me where I am? In relation to the centre?'

'La Canebière is about five minutes away. Down there.' He indicated a direction with his hand.

'And that's the centre?'

'It's the main street.'

She nodded. 'And where would I find a reasonably-priced hotel. I mean – a cheap one?' She didn't want to waste money unnecessarily.

The waiter shrugged. 'All kinds of places. But try nearer the harbour. That's probably your best bet.'

'Where's that, please?'

'Turn right at La Canebière and you'll find it at the far end.'

She found La Canebière immediately, a wide street full of shops and restaurants. It looked a long way to the harbour and she hopped on a bus. After five minutes she glimpsed the water, got off and walked the last few yards, over the road ringing the harbour, to the quayside.

The harbour lay before her, its waters pale and tranquil, crowded with fishing boats and trading ships. To the left the city rose in an orderly jumble of multi-coloured buildings up the slope of a gentle hill to a magnificent church at the summit, the famous Notre-Dame de la Garde which Julie had seen in photographs.

To the right there was a quay . . . She frowned.

Then there was nothing. For quite a long way.

It looked like a giant demolition site.

Julie picked up her case and walked over, trying to imagine what could have happened to the place.

She climbed what had once been a narrow street of houses. Now there was little but a mass of masonry, splintered wood and the occasional door or window lying crushed and forlorn on its side. The place was disconcerting, like a graveyard. As she went further she saw that, here and there, there were makeshift stalls and shops constructed out of the ruins, where traders – Arabs mostly – were sitting waiting for business. There were shanties, too, with smoke coming from their roofs and washing hanging outside.

At the top of the street was a junction with a larger road. On the opposite side were buildings again, more people, and order.

She took a last look at the extraordinary derelict wasteland and crossed the street to the normality of the other side.

She began looking for a hotel, and not a moment too soon. She was hot and very tired; she'd hardly slept at all on the train. The first hotel she came to was run-down and dirty, the second had a girl standing provocatively on the doorstep, and the third looked rather dark and uninviting. She decided on the third because she couldn't face going any further; her arm was at breaking point. She should have left her case at the station.

The room they gave her was clean and tidy and perfectly adequate. She lay down and rested her aching feet until six, when she went down in search of a phone.

The doctor still wasn't in. Would she like to leave a message?

Julie hesitated, instinctively reticent. Then she remembered that the war in France was over and there was no more need for secrecy. She said, 'Tell him a friend from the

Resistance called.' She left her name and the number of the hotel.

The next morning there was a message. Doctor Hubert would come to the hotel at twelve.

She spent the morning with the *Police Judiciaire*, looking at more pages of photographs. Still nothing. It got to the point where she wondered if she'd recognise him even if she saw him.

She got back to the hotel breathless and fifteen minutes late. An elderly man who had been sitting in a chair beside the reception desk rose to his feet with some difficulty.

She asked in surprise, 'Doctor Hubert?'

He bowed slightly. He was at least sixty, probably more, and was painfully thin with a marked stoop. He was leaning heavily on a stick.

She said hurriedly, 'I'm sorry I'm late.'

'Not at all,' he said softly. 'It is a pleasure to meet anyone – who is a friend.' He blinked at her over his spectacles. 'Are you here on a visit? Or—?'

'I need some help.'

'Ah. In that case, perhaps you would care for some lunch?'

They found a brasserie a few streets away and ordered what seemed to Julie to be a rather extravagant meal of soupe de poisson, veal – when had she last had veal? – and wine.

As they talked, Julie decided that Alain Hubert was a remarkable man. Gentle and self-effacing, he seemed an unlikely Resistance hero. Perhaps that was why he'd never been caught.

When the food arrived, Julie ate heartily; she'd almost forgotten what good food tasted like.

'So this person might have come from Marseilles?' the doctor asked.

'Might, yes. It's not much to go on, is it?'

'Well, who can say? Maybe someone would recognise his description, you never know.'

'The police didn't.'

'Maybe he's not known to them.'

Julie sipped at the rich fruity Algerian wine. 'He's probably not known anywhere . . .'

'I'm sorry that I can't be of any help.'

She smiled. 'Not your fault.'

'The only thing I can suggest is the *milieu*.'

'Oh?'

'Most of the crime in Marseilles is highly controlled. There's an organisation which runs almost everything – black market, prostitution, and, of course, drugs. They must know a lot more about what goes on in this city than the police.'

He was describing a world that Julie didn't understand at all. She asked, 'It's possible they might know this man, then?'

'I really can't say. But if you have no luck with the police it's worth a try.'

'How do I find them?'

'Ahh, that I don't know.' He looked at her over his glasses, his eyes twinkling. 'I don't move in those circles actually.'

She grinned. 'No, of course not.'

'It would have been easier in the old days, before they demolished the Old Quarter. It was the centre of all that, it was the *bas-quartier*.'

'What happened to it? Why was it torn down?'

'The Germans decided it was undesirable and had it flattened. The real reason, I think, was that they couldn't control what went on inside.'

They finished their coffee and the doctor insisted on paying for lunch. 'It's my pleasure. Forgive me, but I have to go now.'

'Of course.'

He swivelled in his chair and reached for his stick. Julie
got up to help him. He said, 'There is just one thing . . .
There's an old friend of mine, a chap who's been in a little
trouble from time to time. He might know how to contact
the right people . . .'

'I thought you said you didn't mix with those sorts of
people,' Julie laughed.

'Ah, well, one's not so choosy about one's friends in
prison.'

'In prison?'

He got slowly and painfully to his feet, falling slightly
against the table as he did so. She held his arm until he had
regained his balance. 'This leg . . . Slow to mend . . . An
infernal nuisance . . . Yes, prison. We were lucky, he and I
. . . We were lucky . . .'

So the mild manner had not deceived the Gestapo after
all. It explained his frailty and the broken, badly-mended
leg.

He was holding out his hand. 'It was a great pleasure,
madame. Goodbye. I'll make enquiries of my friend. I'll
telephone. Goodbye.' He made his way slowly down the
street.

Six hours later there was a message. It read simply: Try
Chez Henri off the Rue Caisserie. Good luck.'

She had no trouble in finding Henri's Bar; the hotel
proprietor directed her straight to it. The place was
narrow-fronted and dark. She hesitated. Often bars were
combined with cafés or restaurants and a woman could go
in quite happily. But this was a bar, a drinking establishment pure and simple.

She drew a deep breath and marched straight in.

The interior was dimly lit and, seeing a vacant table
beside the door, she sank quickly into a chair. Then she
changed her mind. She might as well go the whole hog.
Getting up, she perched on a stool at the bar.

The place was, she imagined, typical. Dark polished

wood, yellow paint, and the odour of a thousand cigarettes. But there were exotic smells, too, of spices and
herbs and strange unfamiliar scents. A handful of regular
customers sat at the bar, well into café-cognac, pastis and
wine and cassis.

Behind the counter was a young man, busy serving
customers, and an older, plumper man, carefully adjusting
the rows of bottles that lined the back of the bar. The older
man was surreptitiously watching her in a mirror. She
guessed he was the proprietor.

The young man came by and she ordered coffee. As he
went to get it she saw two oranges behind the bar and
immediately wished she'd ordered *orange pressée*. Oranges
were virtually unobtainable in England.

The coffee was put in front of her. A moment later the
proprietor drifted past.

'Excuse me—' Julie asked quickly.

The proprietor continued as if he hadn't heard her, took
his time putting a bottle on a shelf, then slowly returned.
He said without looking at her, 'Yes.'

'I want information.'

'Oh yes?' He gave her a hard look. 'What kind of
information?'

'I'm looking for someone. Someone who might have
lived around here, or visited the Old Quarter . . .'

'His name?'

This was where it got difficult. But there was no way
round it. She said, 'That's the problem . . . I don't know
it.' She sighed and smiled a little. 'All I know is that he was
called the Marseillais.'

The proprietor looked at her from under his eyebrows.
'The Marseillais?' He nodded slowly, as if humouring an
idiot. 'The Marseillais? Madame, can you imagine how
many people are called that in the world? Eh? Every *mac*
in Marseilles! And whenever a Marseillais goes away, guess

what people call him! Why yes, madame!' He shook his head and sighed. 'They call him a Marseillais, that's what!'

Julie nodded. 'Yes, I know it sounds ridiculous but – he must have been known here. Before he went away. Known . . . in bars, around the place . . . He was the kind of person who might have been involved in – *le milieu* . . .'

'So—? Half the population of this place is involved in *something*!' He was glaring at her, hostile now.

Before Julie could say any more, he moved away and served another customer.

It was five minutes before he came her way again, hurrying past on the far side of the bar. She leaned over the counter and said, 'Please, another word—?'

He hesitated for a moment, poised to walk away again.

'Look . . . can you give me the name of someone who might know.'

'Who do you suggest?'

Julie began to get exasperated. 'Someone who can help. Look, this man – the one I'm looking for, he's wanted by—' She almost said the police, but realised it might count against her. 'By the Resistance. He was a traitor. He's responsible for people's deaths.'

She had him now: he was moving closer, his eyes curious. The rest of the bar was silent, too, and five pairs of eyes watched her intently.

Julie said, 'He worked for the Gestapo. He has to be found to save an injustice, an innocent man. And – for other reasons.'

The proprietor stared at her thoughtfully. 'Ahh. Well . . .' He nodded slowly. 'That's different. But – it won't exactly be easy.' He asked sceptically. 'What *do* you know about him? Did he have an accent? Did he speak like a Provençal? Like *me*?'

'No.'

'Mmm. An educated type, maybe?'

'Yes, very likely. I know it's not much to go on, but I could give you a description of what he looked like. And then – perhaps you could ask around? Perhaps you know someone—?'

He nodded. 'I'll ask the boys.' He used the slang word *malfrats* – good-for-nothings. Taking a pencil stub and an old till receipt, he painstakingly wrote down the details she gave him: dark hair, thin, about thirty, medium height, gold ring, no accent. It wasn't much. She made him add: clever, probably well-educated, dislikes women.

He said, 'I'll do what I can, but—' He shrugged. 'I can't promise anything.'

She pressed him, 'How long before you might get news—?'

'Ah!' He shrugged. 'Two hours? Two days? You come back from time to time, then I'll tell you how long it'll take!'

Three days later Julie thought: I'm wasting my time.

The proprietor – Henri – was earnest and well-meaning but she was beginning to wonder if he had all the contacts he'd hinted at. He didn't seem to be getting anywhere at all.

But then, she thought unhappily, perhaps there wasn't anywhere to get to. There was no proof – not even a shred of a suggestion – that the Marseillais and Fougères were one and the same man.

And yet Fougères had been so very *good* at deceit and treachery that he *must* have been important to the Boches. She couldn't believe he was just a casual informer. No – he was *experienced*.

And yet, she had to face the possibility that the two men weren't the same. And if so, where did that leave her? In a dead end. There were no more leads to follow.

That was really why she had come to Marseilles – because it *was* the only lead.

After an aimless walk around the harbour she went back to the bar, utterly dispirited. It would be the third time she'd looked in that morning. Doubtless she would hear the same thing again: no news. Henri's shrugs and 'Don't worry' and 'Be patient' were getting on her nerves.

But when she went in, something was different. Henri was smiling slyly, his eyes gleaming. *News.*

He ducked under the flap and, coming out from behind the bar, beckoned her to one side. 'Someone wants to see you. He's been away, that's why there's been a delay. He'll see you this afternoon.'

'But who?'

'Ahh,' he whispered conspiratorially, 'he's what you might call the *Patron* – with a capital "P", you understand.'

Julie didn't completely, but she nodded anyway.

'You're very lucky. He's interested in your story. And if anyone can help – well, *he* can!'

'Where do I find him?'

'No problem, just be here at three. It's all arranged!'

She was there at two-thirty because she had nothing better to do. She drank coffee nervously and, though she'd hardly ever smoked in her life, accepted two cigarettes from Henri.

By three her eyes were fastened to the door. By ten past three she was looking desperately at Henri. He said, 'Don't worry. We keep Marseillais time here. Nice and slow.'

At a quarter past three a long black car drew up outside. Henri led her to the door. 'Good luck!'

The driver was standing beside the car. He had a broken nose, large shoulders and a surly expression. He looked just like a criminal. It suddenly dawned on Julie that he probably *was* a criminal. As she approached he slid into the car.

Henri ushered Julie into the back, closed the door, and the car moved away. Julie sat stiffly in her seat. The back of the driver's head didn't invite conversation.

The car eased gently through the narrow streets until they reached a wide boulevard. Then they accelerated past the harbour, across several junctions and onto the hill topped by the magnificent church. After five minutes or so, the driver braked and turned the car into a street full of small shops. They stopped. The driver turned and swivelled his eyes in the direction of the pavement. Julie guessed she was meant to get out.

As she opened the door the driver murmured, 'In there,' and indicated with his finger. Julie looked: it was a restaurant. The driver added something in slang that she didn't understand. Then he translated. 'The waiter,' he explained, 'ask the waiter.'

She crossed the pavement and pushed open the door. It was very dark inside. She paused, trying to get her bearings.

Someone appeared from the shadows. 'Come this way.'

She followed the man to the back of the room and saw the figures of four men dimly visible at a table. As she approached, one of them rose to his feet and extended a hand. The conversation at the table petered out.

Julie shook the man's hand and sat in the chair he offered her. As her eyes got accustomed to the light she took a good look at him. He was well dressed in a conventional but slightly flashy way. His suit was obviously expensive, and there was a gold chain visible across the waistcoat and another round his wrist. Several rings glinted dully on his fingers. As he sat back in his seat she caught the whiff of liberally applied cologne.

He smiled. His face was pleasant, his eyes twinkling under a high forehead and receding hair line.

He enquired, 'Would you like some wine? Or a coffee?'

'Nothing, thank you.'

He said, 'My friend Henri tells me you're looking for

someone.' He had a strong Provençal accent, but the voice was soft and soothing.

'Yes. Someone who came from here. Probably a long time ago.'

He sipped some wine and smiled again. 'Tell me about him.'

'Everything?'

'As much as you know.'

She told him about Brittany and the escape line and the betrayal and how Michel had been accused; and she told him about the man from Paris, the outsider with the narrow face, the lanky hair, the dark almost black eyes, and the sallow skin. She finished, '. . . And he was cruel, that's what I remember most.'

The *Patron* frowned with concentration. 'And his manner?'

'Cold. Always – watchful. And underhand. Devious.'

'And – how did he speak?'

'He had no accent,' she admitted, 'not that one could catch anyway. Certainly nothing like—' She hesitated.

'Like mine?' He smiled again.

Julie nodded.

'And you said something about women. About him not liking women.'

'No . . . he hated them, I would say. And he was frightened of them – well, wary, anyway.'

The *Patron* sipped his wine again. 'No facial scars or anything like that?'

'No.'

There was the sound of the restaurant door opening and closing. The *Patron* looked up. 'Ah here we are!'

A man came up and put an envelope into the *Patron*'s hand. He opened it and shook out the contents. 'Some pictures for you to look at. Just a few ideas.' He placed them in a pile on the table and turned to one of the others. 'Throw some light on the scene, will you, Isso?'

A lamp was switched on and the table was flooded with sudden light. Blinking, Julie picked up the first photograph. It was a snapshot of a family group. There were five people: a middle-aged couple and three young men, presumably their sons. The faces were blurred but she knew immediately that none of them was Fougères. She put the picture back on the table.

The second was in fact two photographs: a front and side view of an unsmiling man with frightened eyes. The pictures looked like the police shots she'd seen at the *Police Judiciaire*. She didn't recognise the face.

She picked up the third picture and, as she did so, she caught sight of the one now visible on the top of the pile. It was of a formal group, a dozen or so young men standing stiffly in a garden with, at either side, four black-robed men: priests. The picture was blurred and indistinct and had been taken in strong sunlight, so that the participants were frowning against the glare. But there was something – *familiar*.

For a second she didn't move then, with a trembling hand, she reached for it. Very slowly.

But even before she picked it up she knew.

It was him.

It was him.

She looked closely. Very young, perhaps only fourteen, but the hair, the narrow face ... It was him all right. It was a moment before she could speak. Then she whispered. 'This one. This is the one.'

The *Patron* took the photograph gently from her hand and stared at it. He looked up at her. 'You're sure?'

'Yes. Positive!'

He shook his head and murmured, 'So! I knew the bastard would turn up again somewhere! Scum always do.'

'What's his name?' she demanded. 'Who is he?'

The *Patron* was staring at the photograph again. 'His name? Vasson. Paul Vasson.'

She said it over to herself. 'And what was he? Where did he come from?'

'He was the illegitimate son of a whore – a junkie whore at that. The authorities found him starving in a cupboard when he was about eight and handed him over to the Jesuits. The priests did what they could. They educated him well – Vasson was always a clever sod.' He paused. 'Later he became a small-time pimp with ambitions. He wanted to make the big time. He had expensive tastes . . .'

'And?'

'He disappeared in '35. No-one's seen him since. Not that we haven't been looking.' He laughed bitterly. 'We would love to find the cheap bastard again, believe me!'

She was gripped with excitement. 'But now we've got him, haven't we!'

He regarded her patiently. 'Got him? Listen, people have been looking for him for a long time . . . The police – *they* would like to find him. Me – *I've* had the word out for a long time now.' He shook his head. 'Nothing. Oh, once someone said they'd seen him in Toulon. But we never found him there. Another time someone saw him in Paris . . .' He shook his head. 'But never a real lead.'

He held up the photograph. 'Then I got hold of this. In about '40, it was. One of my men flogged it round. Thought I'd got the swine then. He'd been seen all right, in Paris, round the *dix-huitième*. Working in clubs, that kind of thing. Thought I'd got him. I put the word out. Then . . .'

'What happened?'

'He disappeared again. Vanished. Never a trace.'

Julie was crestfallen. 'Oh . . . I see.'

'We've tried, believe me. But he's a cunning little sod. He's kept out of sight.' He shrugged. 'He'll still be in a big city somewhere – Paris probably. With his liking for the big time he wouldn't be caught dead in a provincial town. But apart from that . . .'

Julie sighed heavily. 'Well . . . at least I know who he is, that Vasson was Fougères. That should be enough to free my cousin.'

'You don't seem very happy . . .'

She frowned and looked at her hands. 'I can't bear to think of Vasson not being caught.'

'Well . . .' he shrugged. 'Perhaps I'm wrong. Perhaps the *flics* will pick him up straight away . . .'

'Yes, but . . . suppose they don't?'

There was a silence.

'Where will you go now?' he asked.

She considered. 'To Rennes first to free my cousin, then – Paris.' She seemed to make up her mind. 'Yes. Paris.'

He watched her for a moment. 'And what are you going to do there?'

'See if I can help the police, identify him if necessary . . .

'You're going to look for him.'

She didn't know what to say. She wasn't sure what she was going to do herself. Eventually she murmured, 'If I have to.'

The *Patron* shook his head. 'He's a dangerous man – a lunatic!' He sighed and leant forward. 'Please, be very, very careful! Look – if you're really determined, then you'll need help. What about money?'

'I've got enough for the moment.'

'Well, if you need more, just phone this number in Paris.' He wrote it on one of the restaurant's cards. 'I'll tell them you're coming. They'll be able to help in other ways, too.'

'Other ways?'

'Manpower . . . That kind of thing.'

Julie nodded uncertainly.

The *Patron* tapped her hand. 'Look, if you *should* happen to find him, keep clear, won't you? And let my people know straight away – they'll be *neater* than the *flics*, you understand. Whatever you do, don't approach him yourself, will you? He'll kill you as soon as look at you. Just let my people know – they'll deal with him, eh?'

She had no doubt they would. She said, 'Thanks for your help. May I take the photograph?'

'I'd like it back when you've finished with it.' She nodded and put it carefully in her bag along with the telephone number. He got up and helped her to her feet. As they walked to the door she asked, 'What did he do? When he was in Marseilles, I mean?'

The *Patron* opened the door and the sounds of the street flooded in. He said quietly, 'He bought me three years inside, that's what he did.'

'Oh!' She didn't know what to say.

He looked thoughtfully out into the street. 'And ...' His face clouded. '... he killed a woman.' There was a pause. 'My woman.'

Julie stared, aghast. Eventually she stammered, 'I'm sorry ...'

He shrugged and said briskly, 'Now remember, if you *do* come across the bastard, whatever you do don't go anywhere near him. Just call that number and mention my name.'

She stretched out her hand. 'I don't know your name.'

'Jojo. Just say Jojo sent you.'

There was a midnight train to Paris. Julie packed her case, paid the outstanding money on the room, and, with plenty of time to spare, went to the bar to say goodbye to Henri.

He welcomed her effusively and pressed a drink on her. It was a cognac. She rather liked it. She liked it even more a few moments later when the alcohol sent a warm glow round her body. Suddenly she felt tremendously optimistic.

She knew almost everything about him, his name and his background. And most important of all, she had the photograph. What a bit of luck that was! Somebody somewhere must have seen him. Somebody somewhere would know where he was. The photograph *must* find him in the end. It would just be a question of looking hard enough and for long enough in the right places . . .

The telephone at the end of the bar rang. Henri answered it, put it down on the counter and came over to her. He indicated with his head. 'Telephone.'

'For me?'

He nodded. She went to the end of the bar and lifted the receiver cautiously. 'Yes?'

'Madame? It's me.' She recognised the *Patron*'s voice. 'I remembered something . . .'

Julie gripped the receiver. 'Yes?'

'It's not very much, but it might help?'

'Yes?'

'You remember I said he had expensive tastes? Well, he always longed for a fancy car. He was quite mad about it. Always had pictures of it in his room, even in his wallet . . . A Delage. He always wanted a Delage. Nothing else would do. You know the car I mean?'

Julie tried to hide her disappointment. 'Oh yes, I know.'

'Well, it's not much . . . But he really was mad about that car.'

'Thank you.'

'A Delage. Nothing else would do.'

'Thank you again.'

'Good luck.'

Julie put the receiver down.

A *car* . . . A Delage . . .

She shook her head. A long time had passed. Vasson had probably forgotten he had ever wanted a Delage – dreams didn't last. At sixteen she herself had wanted – what was it? – a fur coat. She never thought of having one now.

No, the car wouldn't lead her to Vasson.

But the photograph would. That was the key.

Chapter 38

'ARE THERE ANY further charges against Le Goff?' The examining magistrate peered at the commissaire.

'Not at the present time.'

'I order, then, that Le Goff be released forthwith.' The magistrate stood up and walked out. Julie got to her feet and stared blankly at the high ornate chair where the magistrate had been sitting. She should feel triumphant, or at least relieved. Instead she felt dissatisfied, almost cheated.

The commissaire was standing in the aisle, waiting for her. She made her way between the seats towards him. They walked towards the courtroom door.

'You were very certain in your identification of Vasson,' the commissaire said.

'Oh yes.'

'I wish all witnesses were as definite.'

They came out onto the front steps of the law-courts.

'You are a very determined woman, madame.'

'And what's wrong with that?' Julie demanded.

'Nothing – please don't misunderstand me!'

They began to walk down the steps. Julie asked. 'When will Michel be released?'

'Within the hour. One of my men can take you over there, if you like.'

'No, that won't be necessary, thank you.'

The commissaire looked surprised. 'You're not going to see him?'

She shook her head briefly.

'I thought—'

'You thought wrong, monsieur. I told you that before.'

'Ah. I stand corrected.'

They reached the pavement and paused. The commissaire said, 'We believe Vasson was involved in other crimes. We think he may have betrayed the Meteor line.'

Julie looked at him sharply. 'He was Lebrun?'

'Possibly. But it is difficult to find anyone who might identify him. They all died or got sent to Germany.' He added, 'Where can I contact you, madame – in case we have news?'

'England. I gave my address to your inspector. I'm going to Paris today, then on from there.' It was almost the truth. 'But – will there be any news?'

'In due course. His description will be everywhere by now. And his photograph. We'll find him.'

'But it's been two weeks.'

The commissaire threw up his hands. 'Two weeks. That's nothing, madame! He could be anywhere, hiding under an assumed name . . . It'll take time.'

'Yes.'

'We can only do our best.'

She stared thoughtfully at the sky, then said abruptly. 'Goodbye then, monsieur.'

'Goodbye, madame.'

The commissaire watched her slim figure walking briskly away and thought how deceptive appearances were. She may have soft, gentle looks, but she was like steel inside.

Julie sat in the train and read the letter again. It was from Peter, in his best rounded handwriting. He was very well, he said. He went to tea every day with John (his best friend) and on Saturday they had been fishing all day (this last part was underlined). He was glad about Michel. He sent her lots of love.

She put the letter away. He sounded happy enough. Julie had been away almost a month now. It was a long time to leave a child. But he was eight; quite old enough to look after himself.

She got out her purse and counted the money in it. Five hundred francs or thereabouts. A hundred of her own and four hundred which she had taken out of Michel's money. She had put the remainder of Michel's money in an envelope with a letter and left it with his *concierge*. In the letter she had explained how the money had been spent, wished him well and excused herself for not seeing him on his release.

She hadn't seen him, either, during the two weeks the police had been unravelling the Fougères identity. Instead she had gone to Tregasnou and arranged for the sale of the farm to provide money for the proper care of Tante Marie.

It was the end of her life at Tregasnou. Perhaps of her life in Brittany, too. Her debt to Michel had been repaid; she didn't want the embarrassment of his gratitude.

Five hundred francs . . .

She already had her train ticket back to England, so the cash should last three weeks. No, perhaps that was optimistic for Paris. Perhaps only two.

Two weeks, then. She would give herself two weeks.

She became a good walker. For eight days she walked all day – and a lot of the night, too. She tried a hundred places – cafés, restaurants, shops – in half a dozen different areas.

No-one had ever seen Vasson.

After the cafés, restaurants and shops she drew in her breath and tried the clubs. It took a lot to walk into a club, a woman alone, and ask for information. Sometimes she had to wait, standing conspicuously in a corner, while someone was fetched. Then people stared, wondering what a woman like her was doing in such a place. Even though she wore the darker and plainer of her two staid suits, she had to learn how to look unobtrusive and to turn down all kinds of propositions, some blunt and exotic. Once, a man actually stuffed a thousand francs into the neck of her blouse and started pulling her towards the door.

She hated everything about the clubs, the darkness, the stink of tobacco, the leering men. To keep sane, she forced herself to see the light side of it. It was there – if you looked hard enough.

But she didn't smile for long – the time was slipping away. Suddenly twelve days had passed, and no Vasson. No-one had seen him. No-one remembered him. It was as if he'd never been to Paris . . .

The clubs didn't open until nine-thirty or ten, so she spent the earlier part of the evening asking in restaurants and cafés. Then, once the doors of the clubs opened, she went in quickly, anxious to be away before too many customers arrived.

She completed the narrow streets of Montmartre, then started on the area around Pigalle.

One evening she managed three clubs before eleven. She came to a fourth club and, without bothering to examine the name on the neon light, went straight down the red-lit stairs. It was better going straight in – there wasn't so much time to hesitate.

There was no-one at the desk so, without slowing down, she walked across to the bar where a barman was polishing glasses. She pulled out the photograph, which she had masked with black paper to hide the other figures, and thrust it across the counter.

The barman looked at it then asked, 'So who's looking for him?' That was what they always asked. That, or, 'In trouble, is he?'

She replied, 'I'm looking for him. It's a personal matter.' It was the answer she always gave. It usually brought a knowing smile and a comment about all poor sods being on the run from some woman or another, and she wasn't going to give him a hard time when she found him, was she?

This time the barman said, 'You're looking for him, eh?' He eyed her thoughtfully. 'It doesn't seem very likely.'

Julie looked at him in surprise. 'No? Why not?'

'You don't look the sort to have mixed with him.'

Julie tensed. 'You know him?'

The barman took another look at the picture. 'Used to. Used to work here, the slob.'

'When? When was he here?'

'Ohhh. Must have been before the war. Yes, just before . . .'

'And since then?'

'He was around for a while at the beginning of the war, so I heard. Started dealing in specialities. You know, stockings, cigarettes, fancy underwear, that kind of thing . . .'

'Then?'

The barman shrugged. 'Don't know. He wasn't seen again.'

'You've heard nothing since?'

He shook his head. 'Nothing. Not that I've asked, you understand. And he wouldn't exactly be welcome in this place. He half-killed the boss.' He rolled his eyes.

'What did he call himself then?'

'Ah . . .' The barman frowned. 'Can't remember exactly . . . Wait a minute. Ah yes . . . Biolet. That was it. Biolet.'

Yet another name. Julie asked, 'Where did he live, do you know?'

'No. Never knew. Never cared. Always changing rooms, I believe.'

Julie racked her brain for more questions. 'Did he have money in those days?'

The barman laughed. 'Money! Never. Always broke, he

was. Tried to get into the big time, of course, but never made it. A real loser. Too clever-clever, see. No-one around here liked that, not one bit.'

And that was it. He knew nothing more.

Two days later Julie found another person who thought he recognised the photograph. A café proprietor up a steep hill above Pigalle. But he, too, hadn't seen Biolet for a long time. After some thought he remembered that the last time must have been '39 or '40 – before the Occupation. He, too, mentioned that Biolet had always been broke. But he couldn't remember any more.

After that – nothing.

She had been in Paris fifteen days. And she had nothing.

Wearily she went back to her cheap cheerless hotel in the *treizième* and fell on to the bed, exhausted.

Clubs, cafés ... Montmartre, Pigalle ... He'd been there all right *before* the war.

But after—? Nothing!

Had he gone away? To another large city?

Perhaps ...

Another area. Another name. Another job.

But would he *need* a job? The Germans must have paid him well; he was their most important informer. Yes, he *must* have money, and for the first time in his life!

She opened her eyes wide.

Of course. *That* was the difference. He had *money*.

The big time at last. All the things he'd ever dreamed about. She tried to imagine him with money ... dressing well, wearing gold jewellery. Indulging those expensive tastes ...

All the things he'd ever dreamed about.

She remembered what the *Patron* had said. Perhaps there had been something in it after all. It was worth a try—

Just one more day. She'd give it one more day.

*

Julie trudged along the Champs Elysées, looking for the right number. Most of the buildings didn't seem to have any numbers, but at last she spotted one in small figures high above a doorway; there was still quite a way to go. She eyed a passing bus longingly. It would be quicker and easier by bus, but they cost money and she was running dangerously short.

She was down to her last fifty francs and her train ticket home. In Paris fifty francs would last two days, maybe three if she really spun it out and cut down on her food.

She walked on, watching the numbers. Nearly there. It must be on the next corner . . .

There was a smart shop selling handbags, a cinema . . . It must be the next one.

She walked faster. The shop front was clearly visible now. She stopped in front of it and stared.

It was empty. Most of the windows were boarded up. Only one window still had glass in it and that was whitewashed on the inside.

She went up to the window, found a tiny gap in the whitewash, and peered through. There was a large empty showroom, littered with rubbish and a few posters of cars.

She stepped back and looked up. The sign, made of letters fastened on to a marble facia, had largely fallen off. But the shadow of the letters remained. The name of the agents. Then, in small letters: Delage.

She went round to the side. There was a side door, again firmly closed.

Dead end.

She leant against the wall. She'd got this address from a garage. Obviously their information had been a little out of date.

She should try another Delage dealer – if there was one.

She tramped along until she found a post office. She looked up Delage in the telephone directory. Not listed.

Next idea.

None. She felt weak and tired. The thought of pressing on was terribly depressing. She decided to go back to the hotel for a rest. It was a real indulgence: she'd never allowed herself that luxury before. She saw a bus stop and, weakening, caught a bus in the direction of the *treizième*. She began to plan what she'd do when she got there: she'd go mad and buy cheese, fruit *and* bread and take them back to the hotel and eat the lot.

She had to change buses twice. At the second change she was overcome by guilt at her extravagance and decided to walk the last mile or so.

On the way she looked up and saw a garage. Without hesitating she walked straight in. A mechanic was working on a car. She asked, 'Where would I buy a Delage if I wanted one?'

'A new one, impossible. They haven't been making them recently, or hadn't you noticed?' he said with heavy irony. 'A second-hand one . . .' He shrugged. 'Wherever you could find one. There must be plenty about if you have the money.'

She thought: A real help. 'What about servicing one, then. Where would I go?'

'Juno's. Juno's garage. They're the only ones who do them nowadays.' He gave her an address. It was on the other side of the city, near the Bois de Boulogne, back the way she'd come.

She hesitated, thinking of the cheese, fruit and bread, and the nice soft bed, then marched firmly back towards the bus stop.

Juno's was a large garage full of smart cars in various stages of repair. There was a sporty racing-type car, a limousine, and a long, sleek open-top – all magnificently expensive.

A fierce-looking woman was perched inside a glass

booth, guarding the working area. She raised a sliding window and asked sharply, 'Yes?'

'I'm looking for a Delage,' Julie asked.

'What do you mean *looking*?'

'I'm looking for someone who might have bought one recently.'

The woman looked Julie up and down and raised her eyebrows. 'We don't buy and sell.'

'I just wanted to ask if you knew of any Delages for sale – or recently sold, in the last few years'.

'We don't have records. Look, the answer's no, and that's all there is to it.' She slammed the window shut.

Julie went past her into the garage. The woman spotted her and, pushing up the window again, started yelling. Julie walked briskly on.

She found a mechanic who was working on a long silver touring car. She said, 'Hello.'

He looked up and smiled appreciatively. 'Hell-o!'

She admired the car. 'Lovely. I didn't know people could still afford things like this.'

'Not many can! This one's been locked away all through the war. Now we're trying to get it going again. Anyway – what can I do for you?' He had a friendly grin.

'I want to find someone who owns a Delage.'

The mechanic made an extravagant gesture. 'For you, I'd buy one myself!'

Julie smiled. 'If I wanted to buy a Delage where would I look? A second-hand one, I mean.'

'You want to *buy* one!' Wiping his hands on a dirty rag, he gave a long low whistle. 'Well, well . . .!'

'No, not me exactly,' Julie said hastily. 'In fact I want to trace someone who *may* have bought one. In the last few years.'

He shook his head. 'You ask a lot . . . My goodness, it would be difficult to know where to begin! And there aren't a lot about nowadays. Most of them are still off the road . . .' He looked over Julie's shoulder and made a face. 'Ooops!' Julie followed his gaze and saw the fierce-looking woman waddling aggressively in their direction.

Julie said hurriedly, 'Any ideas?'

'What about the police? They have a register of all owners.'

'No – this person wouldn't be using his own name, you see.'

The mechanic laughed. 'More and more mysterious!' The fierce woman panted up to them, prepared for a speech. The mechanic took Julie's arm and led her quickly away, back towards the main doors. 'There *is* something called the Delage Society. Well, there *used* to be anyway. I've got the address somewhere. Would that be of any use?'

'Yes please. Anything.'

He opened the door of the glass booth and riffled through some papers on a shelf. He came out with a slim magazine in his hand. 'Here. They used to send out these things every few months. The address of the organiser will be in there somewhere.'

The fierce woman had followed them and was standing a few feet away, hands on hips, eyes blazing.

The mechanic shrugged apologetically. 'Better get back to work. Good luck!' He grinned at her, his expression full of many meanings, all of them nice.

Julie smiled back. He had cheered her up.

A few yards along the street she paused and opening the magazine, glanced through it. On the first inside page there was the name of the publisher and further down, the editor, with an address in Paris.

The editor's address was on the other side of the city.

She sighed and looked for a bus.

*

It was an apartment building. There were two long rows of bells with names on them. Some of the names were very faded and she had trouble in reading them, but then she found the editor's name. He still lived there; it was something at least. She pressed the bell.

There was a buzz. She pressed against the street door and it opened. The apartment was on the fourth floor. When she arrived, breathless, at the head of the stairs a man was standing on the landing, waiting.

The editor of *La Société des Propriétaires de Delages* was a man of about sixty, who wore shabby clothes and smelled strongly of garlic and old vegetables. He welcomed her warmly. 'I don't get many visitors. Please come in. Come in!'

The apartment was none too clean and rather shabby, like its owner.

The editor bounced around like a small boy, offering her a seat and a cup of coffee. Then he sat absolutely still, listening to what she had to say.

He nodded slowly and promised to help all he could. But there was a problem. 'We had to cease publishing at the beginning of the war,' he explained. 'And even before the war, only about half the owners belonged ... As for finding out what's happened to the cars since then – new owner and so on ...' He shook his head. '... it would be *difficult* ...'

'This person *might* have been an owner before the war. It's just possible ...'

He shot out of his seat like a jack-in-a-box. 'Say no more!' He disappeared into another room and a few minutes later returned in triumph with a dusty box full of yellowing papers. He pulled out the papers and looked at her expectantly. 'Name?'

'Vasson. Or Fougères. Or Biolet.' Even as she said them Julie realised it was hopeless: he wouldn't be using any of those names nowadays.

As the editor started to leaf through the papers she began to feel a deep despondency. This would never lead anywhere.

After half an hour the editor was satisfied: none of those people had ever been members of his club. 'I'm sorry,' he said.

Julie sighed and tried to think. 'What about buying a second-hand Delage?' she asked. 'How would one find one?'

'Ah! Ahhh!' The editor looked earnestly at the ceiling as if that could give him the answer. 'Mmmm. A newspaper. Yes, through a newspaper! That's about all that's been published, you see. Though there is *Auto* – I believe that's kept going after a fashion. Yes, there's *Auto* too. Here, I'll give you the address.' He scampered into the other room and came back with a piece of paper.

Julie got up to go and said wearily, 'Thank you. You've been most helpful.' At the door she asked. 'Did you have a Delage yourself once?'

'Me!' He laughed heartily, throwing back his head in a great guffaw. 'Goodness gracious no! I could never have afforded even a twentieth of one. I was only an enthusiast! I just loved being *near* the lovely things, you understand. The most beautiful cars ever made . . .' He chuckled again. 'No! I just loved being *near* them.'

The *Auto* office was quite near, only twenty minutes' walk away. Although it was late – almost five – and the place likely to be closing, she decided to try anyway.

In the end it was further than she thought, a good twenty-five minutes away. By the time she found the right doorway she was so tired she could hardly climb the four flights of stairs. No energy: she hadn't eaten since breakfast.

Finally she arrived, panting and shaking slightly, in

front of a half-glazed door inscribed with the word *Auto* in scratched gold letters.

She knocked and someone called, 'Enter.'

The office was a single room with a large desk on which a lanky man of about thirty was sitting, speaking into a telephone. He waved her into a seat and continued his conversation, which mainly consisted of sighs and tuts and expressions of despondency.

Julie flopped down and closed her eyes for a moment. After a few minutes she opened them again and looked around her. She saw a copy of *Auto* on a side table and, picking it up, leafed through. Most of the magazine was made up of articles and photographs of racing cars, but at the back there were six pages of advertisements.

Julie scanned them quickly. There was a Delage for sale ... and a second and third. It looked quite promising. She looked for the date at the top of the page and felt a pang of disappointment. March 1938. Years ago.

The telephone receiver was clanged down into its cradle and the lanky young man said with a frown, 'How can I help you?' He was, he explained, the editor, sub-editor, secretary and sole reporter of *Auto* magazine. 'We've had to cut down a bit. We haven't been able to publish very often. No paper, you see! No money! Nothing much to report – no new cars, hardly any races...' He sighed heavily. 'But you never know, we might be able to manage three editions this year.' He added morosely, 'Better than nothing, I suppose.

A really cheerful fellow.

She asked to see some of the recent editions. 'Oh *those*!' he said heavily. 'They're *awful*. I was only allowed four pages and an edition of five thousand. Hardly worth printing!' He looked up. 'When you say recent, how recent?'

'Since the beginning of the war.'

He gave her the editions for the last three years. There

were a surprising number of advertisements. The editor commented sadly, 'It's everyone trying to sell cars they can't afford to run.' He pointed out the racing and sports types, the Bugattis, Maseratis, and Mercedes. Then there were the plush tourers, Delahayes, Bentleys – and Delages. Julie saw with relief that there weren't too many Delages advertised. She started making a list. With only three editions per year for the last three years, the total number of Delages advertised, when she added it up, was only twenty-four. Some of those were duplicates of previous advertisements and when those were eliminated she ended up with sixteen.

Some Delages had been advertised under box numbers. 'May I have the names and addresses of the sellers?' Julie asked.

'I'm not meant to . . .' the editor sighed. 'But . . . seeing as the whole world's gone mad and I don't much care . . .' He pulled a number of files out of a cabinet and threw them on the desk. 'Here! They're all in there somewhere.'

And they were – scribbled in almost illegible pencil or heavy black ink with the words half smudged. After forty minutes she had them all. 'Thank you. If I need to look at some more back copies, may I come and see you again?'

'Why not!' he exclaimed with a look of deepest depression. 'I'll still be sitting here, most likely. No events to cover, no new cars . . . God, yes! Why not! Come and cheer me up!'

It was only when Julie got back to her room and was eating great mouthfuls of bread and cheese – the fruit had been too expensive – that she looked at the list properly.

Her heart sank again. The Delage owners were spread all over the country, some as far away as Nice. Contacting them would be impossible: letters would take too long and telephone calls would be too difficult and expensive.

There were telegrams, of course. But sixteen . . . They would cost more, much more, than she could afford.

She lay back on the bed and, shaking off her shoes, examined a blister on her heel. The entire thing was hopeless. Why *should* Vasson have bought a car at all? Perhaps he'd hidden all his money and was lying low. Perhaps he'd squandered it years ago . . .

The big time . . .

What did it mean to him now?

It was hopeless. She should go home. She barely had enough money to feed herself on the train. Her shoes were worn out. She was tired, so tired.

She should give up.

But then she remembered the hard black eyes and the *coldness* of him, and she muttered, 'Merde.'

One more day. Just one more day.

She sat up and, reaching for her bag, searched in the zip compartment. The card was there, just where she'd put it all those weeks ago.

Jojo had offered help. Well she wasn't too shy to ask now. To use the language of the street, she needed the necessary. And the necessary was money.

The count heard the sound of crunching gravel on the drive and hid. He was quite an expert at hiding now; creditors and angry tradespeople arrived almost daily.

There were footsteps. The front bell jangling. The count peered through a crack in a shutter and saw a bicycle. It looked vaguely familiar. Of course – he had it now. It was the postman's.

Why should the postman be here in the afternoon? It must be bad news – a summons for a bad debt or something like that.

He chuckled. Only six more days and the château would be stripped of all its remaining valuables. Then he would disappear to Paris and they could send all the summonses they wanted.

The count watched the postman come into vision, mount his bicycle, and ride off down the drive. As soon as everything was quiet he hopped silently down the stairs to the main hall. He looked nervously towards the large double front doors. An envelope had been slipped underneath and lay invitingly on the stone floor.

Impatiently the count strode over, grabbed the envelope and tore it open.

'Good Lord!' he exclaimed.

It was a telegram. It read: INTERESTED IN BUYING DELAGE. IS YOURS STILL AVAILABLE?

It was signed LESCAUX, followed by a post office box number in Paris.

At the bottom the post office had stamped: ANSWER PREPAID.

The count said, 'Damn! Damn and blast!' He'd known it! That deal had been a disaster. People were queuing up to buy the blasted car and he'd thrown it away. God, what a waste!

'Damn!' He repeated, and stamped off in the direction of the cellars to see if he could find a last bottle of claret.

Later, he considered whether to reply. He decided against it. He didn't see the point. He'd sold the damned car, hadn't he?

Another telegram came four days later. It read: IF CAR SOLD, STILL INTERESTED. URGENTLY NEED INFORMATION. PLEASE USE PREPAID REPLY. LESCAUX.

The count took more interest. Whatever this was about, he could smell money in it. He slipped down to the village and sent a reply, saying that he'd sold the car recently and adding that he'd be in residence for only two more days.

The following day there was the sound of an approaching car on the drive. The count took cover on the first floor. Through the shutters he saw the village taxi draw up. Out of it stepped a girl. Even from this distance he could see that she was rather a honey.

He straightened his tie, walked down the stairs, and flung open the front door.

The girl said, 'I sent the telegram.'

'Come in! Come in!' He gestured her inside to the main salon, which was the only room still with any furniture in it. He offered her a Louis XV chair and apologised for the rickety legs. When they were seated, he smiled at her charmingly. 'And to what do I owe this singular pleasure?'

'*Auto* magazine. I've been contacting everyone who's advertised a Delage for sale in the last few years. You advertised, so here I am.'

The count smiled again, though he had the feeling his charm was wasted on this rather serious young lady. 'But why come to me when I've already sold my car?'

'*Because* you've sold it. Your car was one of the few that did sell.'

The count frowned. 'Ah. Not many have sold, then?'

'No. Apparently there's no market for them.'

The count tried to feel mollified about his deal with the scar-faced young man, but he failed. He couldn't believe he hadn't been cheated.

'But continue,' said the count. 'Why are you looking for a car that's already sold?'

'I want to contact someone, someone who may well have bought one.'

The count's curiosity was pricked. 'You mean a *particular* person?'

'Yes.'

'Someone you wish to trace?'

'Precisely.'

What a businesslike young woman this was, the count observed. Normally he didn't like that in a woman, but in this case it would be an advantage. When they got to the nub of the matter – the money – she would be easy to deal with.

'So – you wish to have details of the person who purchased my car.'

'Please. Perhaps I could show you a photograph, to see if you recognise him . . .' She dug into her handbag and passed him a small rather indistinct photograph. It showed a young man, no more than twenty, with a thin face and dark lanky hair.

The count swore under his breath. This wasn't the man. And if it wasn't the man then there couldn't be any financial negotiations. How annoying!

The count pretended to muse. 'Mmmmm. It's hard to tell. This is a young man . . . The person I sold to was older, definitely older . . .'

'In his thirties?'

'Mmm. Maybe. Maybe.'

The girl leant forward and peered anxiously at the picture. 'What about the eyes? Do they look familiar?'

'Maybe. Maybe.' The count pretended to examine the face, then focused more sharply. Yes, now she mentioned it, there *was* something familiar about them. Good Lord. Maybe it *was* him after all! He said, 'Yes, it definitely *could* be him. But the man I sold the car to was heavily scarred. His face was terrible, quite *unpleasant* to look at. He'd obviously been horribly injured in some way. What he looked like before . . . well, it's difficult to be *sure*. It *could* have been this fellow, but I honestly couldn't swear to it.' Which was true enough and it should keep her sufficiently interested to come up with the lucre, which was the important thing.

The girl's eyes were blazing with excitement. 'Heavily scarred . . .?' She paused, deep in thought, then asked, 'But medium height, dark haired and thin?'

'Yes.'

'And his manner? Was it—?'

'Hard. Unfriendly. Not a very nice fellow. Not a very nice fellow at all.'

The girl's look was triumphant and full of hope. 'It just might be him!' she breathed.

'You're obviously very keen to make contact.'

'Oh yes!' she exclaimed. 'You *do* have an address don't you? And a name?'

So she didn't even know his name. Better and better. 'Will – *might* – this information be of value?' the count began.

For the first time she faltered. 'Of value?'

The count smiled sweetly and lowered his voice. 'Will this information be of material value to anyone?'

'Well . . .' She was confused now. 'If you mean, will it be of financial value, the answer's no.'

'I meant, rather, of sufficient value to someone to enable them to see me right. You know, recompense me for my trouble and the inconvenience of looking out the paperwork.'

Her expression had hardened. 'The person concerned has very limited means, very limited indeed. This is a matter of honour, of justice, not – money!'

The count was unimpressed. Honour, justice, it was no matter: the price would be just the same. He'd learnt his lesson from the scar-faced young man. When the market was all in your favour you named your price.

'I see, I see,' said the count soothingly. 'In that case I'm sure a very small fee will be sufficient. Shall we say four thousand?'

'Four *thousand*!' she gasped. 'Out of the question. I don't have a tenth of that!'

The count made tutting noises. 'What a pity!' What a pity! There we are then.' He started to his feet.

She had gone quite pale, an expression of desperation on her face. She opened and closed her mouth a couple of times then whispered, 'One!'

'Three and a half!'

They settled on three. The girl looked as though she'd been hit over the head. She turned her back to take the money out of her purse and the count guessed her purse was rather full. He immediately regretted having let her beat him down. Why was it he always got cheated by people with lots of money?

He left her in the salon while he went to find the bill of sale. He copied the name and address of the young man on to some blank paper then put the bill of sale into his pocket. He took the piece of paper to the girl. 'There we are!'

She looked at the name and address as if she could devour it, 'Lelouche . . .'

He asked, 'Could I have your address – just in case I remember something . . .?'

She nodded and, reaching into her handbag, pulled out a scrap of paper and scribbled on it.

The count placed the paper carefully in his wallet. 'Did you keep your taxi?' he enquired.

'Oh . . . no. It's coming back in a few minutes.'

It couldn't be better. The count said gallantly, 'I'll go and see if it's on its way. Sometimes the fellow forgets.'

'That's not necessary.'

'No, I insist!'

Quickly he pulled on a coat, took his wallet and, leaving her pacing the hall, hurried down the drive.

He met the taxi a short distance down the main road. He flagged it down, told the driver that the visiting lady had already left, and asked to be taken to the station in her place.

A Paris train came in almost immediately. As the count got in he calculated that it would be a good two hours before the girl realised what had happened and walked to the station to find a train.

Two hours should give him plenty of time.

With a final lurch the cage rose to the ceiling. One of the workmen, balancing on a plank supported by scaffolding, leant across and guided the hook at the top of the cage into the massive eye which protruded from the ceiling.

'What I'd like to know,' one of the workmen mumbled, 'is how the girl's gonna get *in* there.'

'Rope ladder.'

At the sound of Vasson's voice the workmen fell back. Vasson stepped forward and eyed the cage critically. With the correct lighting it should look all right, he decided. The only disappointing thing was the height of the cage. He'd wanted it further away, more inaccessible. But the ceiling couldn't be raised any more, so this was it.

There was silence, the men waiting expectantly. Eventually Vasson said, 'Yes, that's fine.' He could almost hear the sigh of relief; this was one of the few jobs he hadn't asked them to re-do in some way.

But it had been worth it. Vasson looked around him. The group of storerooms had been completely transformed. There was now one large room, which, because of the lighting, managed to look pleasingly intimate. Around the sides there were booths with seating for between two and six people, while in the centre there were a dozen small tables. At one side there was a stage with room for a performer, an upright piano, drums and bass. On the other side of the room there was a bar.

The colour scheme was black, beige, and gold. Very striking. To soften the effect there were exotic plants everywhere, between the booths, hanging from the ceiling, around the light fittings. No-one had ever used plants before.

Vasson had overspent his budget, but it had been worth it.

Already everyone was talking about the place. At the opening the cage would be covered with a drape, then, accompanied by appropriate music, it was going to be unveiled to reveal a girl painted with gold. Her skin, that was. Apart from a G-string she'd be wearing nothing else at all. It would be a sensation.

He turned and hurried through the club into his office, a small room at the rear. There were still a thousand things to do before the opening, and there was only one day left.

Half an hour later there was a tap on the door.

'Yes.' Vasson barked impatiently.

The new barman poked his nose into the room. 'Someone to see you.'

'Who?'

'Wouldn't say. But something important.'

Vasson sighed. 'Very well.'

A minute later the barman showed someone in. Vasson looked up and stiffened.

It was the stupid old boy – the count.

Vasson swore to himself. He should never have put this address on the bill of sale; he had known it was a mistake when he did it. He said quietly, 'Whatever you want, forget it.'

The count smiled inanely. 'But I bring you good news.' He sat down in a brand new chair.

Vasson said quickly, 'I don't think so.' And, standing up, called for the barman again.

'I wouldn't be hasty if I were you. I bring you news from the past.'

Vasson suddenly felt cold. Slowly, he sat down again. 'The past?'

'Yes. I bring you information which I think you will be very happy to have.' The count grinned like a cat.

Vasson's mouth felt dry. Slowly, he licked his lips. 'Well? Go on.'

The count said triumphantly, 'Someone's looking for you!'

'Oh yes?'

'Someone who knew you some time ago.'

The fear clutched at Vasson's heart, but he kept his face impassive. He asked quietly, 'This person found me through the car?'

'Yes. Knew you'd bought it. Must have seen you at the wheel perhaps?'

'Perhaps. And who is this person?'

'Ahhh. That's the question, isn't it?'

The old bastard wanted money then. Vasson considered the alternatives. He could beat the information out of him, there was the gun of course, or . . .

'I don't think the information will be worth enough to pay for.'

'No?' enquired the count sweetly. 'But on the other hand, maybe it will.'

Vasson picked at his fingers. 'If I *was* interested, then what would you be able to tell me?'

'Name. Address.'

'How do I know the name and address would be real?'

'No assurance. But I think they would be.'

'Is it just the one person?'

The count considered. 'I think I can say it's probably only the one.'

Vasson nodded slowly. 'Did the person say he'd definitely seen me in the car?'

'Ahh. Really I feel unable to answer . . .' The count looked supercilious, like a complacent schoolmaster.

Sickening old sybarite. Vasson observed him with distaste. But the choices were limited. He *had* to know. 'I'll offer you five hundred.'

The count shook his head and laughed. 'Really! Really! Five thousand would be a little nearer, don't you think?'

It was more than the club would take in a good night. 'You're out of your mind!'

But he wasn't and Vasson knew it. Eventually they settled on four thousand.

Vasson handed over the cash and, his heart hammering, asked with difficulty, 'The information?'

'A girl. Named Lescaux. Dark hair. Mid- to late twenties. Her address is Hôtel Hortense. It's a cheap place in the *treizième*. She came to see me today. She had an old photograph of you. I didn't recognise you at first – the face was unmarked – but then I saw a similarity in the eyes and realised it must be you after all.' He paused, watching Vasson's reaction.

Eventually Vasson said, 'What ... What led her to you?'

'The advertisement.'

'So she never saw me at all ... in the car?'

'She didn't say.'

Vasson stood up stiffly and murmured, 'Get out and don't let me ever see your face in here again.'

The count needed no second invitation and disappeared rapidly out of the door.

Vasson thought carefully for five minutes, then, taking his coat from the peg, slipped out through the back door into the night.

Chapter 39

———

THE ADDRESS WAS somewhere near Pigalle; Julie had realised that the moment she'd read it.

The street, when she found it, looked familiar and she remembered that she'd walked down it a week or so before. It was narrow and very dark, except for the occasional blaze of light from a small bistro. She went slowly, keeping close to the side and pausing now and then to look for the indistinct, sometimes invisible, street numbers on the shopfronts and door frames.

When she was almost there she stopped in a doorway and checked the numbers again. It was just two away now. Her heart beating in her ears, she looked out along the street. Next door was a shop, closed and shuttered. Then, beyond, a dull gold pool of light spilling out of a doorway on to the pavement.

That must be it. She peered into the darkness. There was a sign hanging over the door. It wasn't illuminated, but she could just make out some sort of painting on it. Above, there was a name. She wasn't sure, but it looked like The Golden Cage. A club then? How strange. She could have sworn the place hadn't been there before.

She drew a deep breath and, crossing the street, walked past on the opposite side. Without being too obvious, she took a good look. It was definitely a club. But not, apparently, open for business. The door was open but there was a plank straddling the entrance and, just inside, some kind of notice on a board.

She went on walking, resisting the temptation to look back over her shoulder. She saw a deep doorway ahead and slipped quickly inside. She moistened her lips and waited for her heart to stop hammering. Then she peered back round the corner.

Nothing. No-one had seen her. She relaxed a little.

What next? It would be madness to go in, in case Vasson was there. So she must wait; wait and watch.

Assuming this *was* the right address.

The count's behaviour had been so extraordinary she still didn't know what to make of it. At first, when he didn't return, she'd given him the benefit of the doubt, but after trudging wearily into the railway station at the end of a long walk from the château she had found the taxi driver waiting there, and slowly, the truth had come out. The count had done it on purpose. But *why*? What could have made him want to run away like that? Perhaps, she thought wearily, he was Vasson's friend and partner. Or perhaps she'd got this far only to be tricked and sent on a wild goose chase. This club might be nothing to do with Vasson at all.

It was very worrying.

She moved to a corner of the doorway where she could watch the club while keeping in shadow. The street was getting busier now as the evening trade began to pick up. A man spotted her and came into the doorway to prop-osition her. Julie got rid of him quickly enough – he was as nervous as a mouse – but she knew she'd got away lightly. Next time it might not be so easy. She remembered she still had a lot of money on her – over two thousand from the money the *Patron*'s friends had given her. She wished now she'd left it at the hotel.

Someone was coming out of the club. Julie stared. It was a man dressed in baggy clothes with a beret on his head. He paused in the doorway, pulling on a jacket, then called over his shoulder. Another man appeared carrying a workman's bag, and the two of them walked off in the direction of Pigalle.

She relaxed again. Workmen. That would explain why the club wasn't open.

After that there was no-one for several hours. The time passed slowly. She was ravenously hungry; for once she'd forgotten to put any bread in her pockets.

By ten-thirty she was numb with cold. Then, just before eleven, there was a movement outside the club. She stiffened. Four or five people were coming out. She peered forward, trying to see their faces in the darkness.

Workmen again: most wore old clothes and carried tool bags. Another man appeared, well dressed and smoother looking than the others. He moved the plank, turned off the lights, closed the front door and locked up. He was very tall, with thick, rather bushy fair hair.

It wasn't Vasson. None of them was Vasson.

The men walked off. The club looked deserted; clearly, it was closed for the night.

She should go back to the hotel and get some sleep. There was no point in staying here.

She hesitated, then decided to take a quick look. It wouldn't take a minute and it couldn't possibly do any harm. She stepped out of the doorway and, looking quickly from left to right, crossed the street and walked up to the front of the club. She peered at the sign. Yes: The Golden Cage. Below, pasted on the door, was a notice. The club was opening on the 14th November. She realised with a slight shock that the 14th was the following night.

What a stroke of luck! If Vasson had any connection with the place, he was bound to be there ... She could stand in the shadows and watch until he arrived. But would she recognise him at a distance? From the count's description he was terribly scarred.

She tensed and looked quickly over her shoulder. The street was darker now, full of deep shadows. Apart from the faint drone of traffic the only sound was the distant beat of music. She started to walk. Suddenly her hackles rose and she shivered slightly. She walked faster, an uncomfortable feeling in her spine, until she was safely into the brightness of Place Pigalle.

She took the Métro across the city, thinking hard.

An idea came into her mind. She should get one of the *Patron*'s friends to take her to the opening. Yes! That would be perfect. She could imagine it all: arriving with all the other guests, looking into the scarred face, knowing immediately it was him, seeing the shock on his face . . .

In the next moment she knew it would never work. It would be madness to let Vasson see her.

No, the best thing would be to identify him from a position of safety, somewhere close enough but not too close. Then once she was certain that it *was* him she would tell – who? The *Patron*'s friends. Yes, or the Resistance. Either group would kill him straight away.

The police would be too kind – or would they? No, perhaps it would be better to let him sweat through a long trial and the fruitless pleas for clemency before he was taken out and shot in cold blood. That way he would have more time to think about what he had done.

It was a fifteen-minute walk from the Métro to the hotel. Tonight it seemed longer because she was dog tired, but finally its dreary façade came into view. The Hôtel Hortense was extremely modest, which was why she'd chosen it. It was so modest, in fact, that there was no night porter. The front door was locked at eleven, after which the guests were expected to let themselves in using a key for which they had to pay a generous deposit, in advance.

Julie trudged up to the door and fumbled in her bag. She swore quietly. The key wasn't in the bottom, nor in the side compartment. She looked nervously up and down the dark deserted street. Eventually she found the key wedged inside the pages of her pocket diary. She unlocked the door and went in, closing the door gratefully behind her.

The lobby was lit by a single white light, which cast a cold inhospitable glare over the floor and left the rest of the hall in shadow. Julie walked across to the stairs and started to climb. She'd taken a room on the fourth, topmost, floor because it was cheaper there. In the centre of the staircase there was an ancient cage lift in an open mesh shaft, but like most lifts in Paris at the moment it was usually out of order and she never bothered to try it any more.

The building was quiet. The only sound was the slight creaking of the boards under her feet. The hotel had very few guests – at least Julie hardly ever saw anybody.

She reached the first landing and paused. There was a sound; it was coming from the lobby. A gentle rattling. She realised that someone was trying to open the street door.

She went on, a little faster now, up towards the second floor.

From below there came a faint clang. Someone had closed the lift door. Julie reached the second landing and hurried on. Suddenly the lift machinery burst into action with a loud whine. Julie jumped. The lift wires started humming. The lift was coming up.

She reached the third floor and looked down the central well. The lift was rising steadily towards her, but the top was closed and it was impossible to see inside. She climbed on and, panting slightly, hurried across the top landing to her door. She opened her bag and started to look for the room key.

The lift mechanism whirred louder and louder. The key was nowhere to be found; Julie shook her bag impatiently.

There was a loud *Clunk!* and silence. The lift had stopped. There was a click as the gate was opened.

Julie thrust her hand into the outside compartment of her bag and at last her fingers closed over the large metal key tag. She raised the key to the lock but her hand was trembling slightly and she couldn't get it in.

A soft footstep fell on the thin carpet behind her.

She whirled round.

It was the tallest, blackest man she'd ever seen. Julie put her hand to her chest and laughed nervously. 'Oh, good evening! You startled me!'

The man was in French Army uniform. He was grinning from ear to ear, revealing an enormous row of white teeth which were in startling contrast to the blackness of his skin. Julie stared, fascinated. The soldier bowed low and straightened up again, swaying slightly. Julie realised he was rather drunk.

He said in a low booming voice, 'Mademoiselle, my sincere apologies!'

Julie nodded politely and quickly let herself into her room. As she closed the door, she saw he was still standing there, beaming happily. Drunk but quite harmless, she decided. She turned on the light and locked and bolted the door.

The room was quite simple: a bed, a rug on the floor, a chest of drawers and a narrow wardrobe. But it was clean and, most important, no-one in the hotel took any notice of her.

She threw herself straight on to the bed and lay there for a moment because it was so lovely to get her feet up. Then, reluctantly, she got up again and, opening the double windows, reached out to close the shutters. The window was a dormer, set into the roof behind a parapet. You couldn't see the street from there, but you could see an enormous amount of sky. It was very clear tonight and, above the faint glow of the city, Julie could see a thousand stars.

It had been a long time since she had seen a night sky.

For several moments she stood and watched and remembered Brittany a long time ago.

The night was cold. She fastened the shutters and closed the windows again.

Hastily slicing some cheese on to a slice of stale bread two days old, she ate ravenously. Then, gritting her teeth against the cold, she undressed as quickly as possible and pulled on her nightdress.

She didn't bother to wash, but hopped straight into bed, shivering violently. She spread her dressing gown over the thin blankets then pulled her coat off the chair and spread that over as well.

She wriggled down into the bed and curled herself up, wondering whether she'd ever feel warm again.

It was a bit of luck, the black soldier coming along like that. Vasson even helped him to find his key.

Vasson waited for the lift to disappear, then slipped quickly behind the reception desk and looked for the registration book. It wasn't there. He looked around. Immediately behind the desk was a door which probably led to an office. The registration book would be in there. He tried the door; it was locked. He cursed softly.

Then something caught his eye and he let out a small hiss of triumph. To the right of the door there was a notice board covered with yellowing fire regulations and taxi numbers – and a fresh white piece of paper with a list of room numbers and, where appropriate, names. He read it quickly. There weren't many guests – just six or so – and it took him only a second to find the name he wanted.

Lescaux. Room 25.

He took a swift look round the lobby, then tiptoed quickly across to the stairs. He ran lightly up to the first floor, checked the room numbers, and then continued up the building.

As he approached the fourth floor he slowed down and listened.

Silence.

He climbed the last few steps and paused again. Softly, he padded across the landing until he could see the numbers on the doors.

Room 25 was in the left-hand corner, at the front of the building. Vasson crept up to the door and listened. He stiffened. Someone was moving about inside. There was a click as if a window was being closed.

He looked round the landing. There were several other bedrooms, then, on the opposite side, a door marked '*Salle de Bain*' and another marked 'W.C.'. Beyond was a plain painted metal door. He ran across and tried it, but it was locked. He looked up. Above was a sign: *Sortie de Secours*. Beside it was a key hanging on a nail.

He took the key and tried it in the lock. At first it wouldn't move but then he pulled on the handle and the key turned quite easily. He opened the door and put his head out. He looked both ways then, satisfied, pulled his head back in and closed the door again without locking it.

He walked lightly across to the bathroom, which was open, and went in. He flicked on the light, locked the door carefully, and turned the light off again. Then he sat down on the floor to wait.

He fingered the gun in his pocket and decided against it. Far too noisy. No, it would have to be done quietly – the other way.

Damn the woman. She'd been trouble all along.

What really upset him was that she'd found out about the car. But how? He couldn't imagine and it was driving him mad. He'd never told anyone about it, he was certain, at least not for years and years . . .

Damn her. Was she alone? Had she told anyone else? He'd have to risk it. If he didn't deal with her he'd be a dead man anyway.

Damn her.

He leant his head against the bath and, looking unseeing at the night sky, waited impatiently for the minutes to pass.

She couldn't sleep. She kept thinking about the day's events and what they meant. Every time she started to drift off she woke up with a start and began to go through it all over again.

There was another thing keeping her awake: she needed to go to the lavatory. She should have gone before, of course, but the bed had been too inviting. Now it couldn't be put off any longer. With an exclamation of irritation, she got out of bed into the cold air and pulled on her dressing gown.

She unlocked the door, walked quickly across the landing and went into the W.C.

When she came out, she went towards the bathroom to wash. She tried the door but it wouldn't budge. She glanced up at the fanlight; there was no light showing through. She tried again, pushing hard against the door, but it was firmly locked. She stood still for a moment, then gave up and went back to her room.

She threw her dressing gown back over the covers and dived into the still warm bed. This time she was determined to get to sleep. She closed her eyes and concentrated on relaxing each part of her body, limb by limb.

Eventually she began to doze off, but then she thought of Richard and was immediately awake again. She often thought of him, but tonight the memories were particularly vivid. It was that lovely night sky. She could almost see the little attic room. She missed him terribly.

She relaxed her body again and tried counting sheep.

Bump!

She was wide awake instantly.

A sound. *Something nearby.*

She stayed perfectly still, listening to the roar of the silence. But nothing.

Perhaps the sound had come from further away after all, from the street . . .

She stiffened.

A sound. This time a faint scratching. *Close.*

She sat upright, her heart hammering in her ears, and strained to locate the origin of the noise.

At first she couldn't hear anything, then it came again, a soft, barely audible scratching. An animal? It must be . . . She tried to see, but with the shutters closed it was very dark; the only light came from a small gap under the door, and then it was the faintest sliver.

Very slowly, she pulled on her dressing gown and did up the cord. Then she swung her legs out of bed and, careful to make no noise, stood up. She listened again.

The scratching had stopped.

She felt her way slowly past the bed and across the room until she reached the door. She put her ear against it. Nothing. Automatically, she checked the key and the bolt to make sure the door was securely locked. She put her hand up to the light switch, then changed her mind and moved slowly back to the centre of the room. She stood absolutely still, straining her ears.

This time the scratching, when it came, was louder.

Now she'd placed the sound. It was coming from near the window. She crept forward and, stooping down, listened again. A mouse, probably . . .

The sound was muffled now and very soft again. She crept right up to the window and waited, completely still.

Nothing.

There was silence again. It lasted a long time. She almost gave up.

Click!

Julie jumped and looked up. There was a sudden

movement. A rectangle of light appeared in the window where the shutter had been.

Julie screamed.

The head and shoulders of a man were silhouetted against the light.

She cried, '*God!*' and staggered back against the bed.

The silhouette suddenly vanished. Julie stared in horror at the place where the man had been, the image of the crouching figure engraved on her mind. It was *him*, it had to be! *It was him*.

She couldn't move, she couldn't tear her eyes away from the window. *Was he still there?* She pressed the back of her knees against the bed and reached out for the bedpost.

Silence again.

She tried to gather her wits, but all she could think was: It's *him!* It's *him!*

The silence stretched on.

Suddenly, another movement.

She stifled a scream.

An arm. At the window. It had something in its hand. It was reaching for the latch.

She cried, '*No!*' and scrabbled around looking for something – *anything*. Desperately she lunged at the chest and pulled out a drawer. Raising it above her head, she ran to the window and rammed it against the frame.

She shouted, '*No-o-o!*' and pushed the drawer harder and harder against the window.

For a while she stayed there, her head against the drawer, murmuring 'God!' over and over again.

Then she moved her head away from the drawer and listened.

Not a sound.

She raised her head and looked. The arm had vanished.

She waited, frozen with indecision. He must have gone – *or had he?* For a moment she could have sworn he was still there, waiting under the window sill, poised to pop his head up like some ghastly jack-in-a-box ... The next minute, she was sure he wasn't there at all.

But if he wasn't there, *where had he gone?*

She knew one thing: *she had to get away!* With an enormous effort of will, she dodged to one side of the window and, shaking violently, put the drawer down on top of the chest. Then, with her eyes fastened on the window, she retreated to the bed and slipped off her dressing gown. She reached down for her coat and pulled it on over her nightdress. She fumbled with two buttons and gave up the rest.

Shoes ... God, where were her *shoes?* She felt around with her feet and touched one. She bent down and pulled it on. Crouching lower, she put a hand under the bed. Nothing. She almost cried out. She reached further. The second shoe was right under the bed. Panicking, she grabbed at it and pulled it hastily on.

All the time she watched the window. Nothing.

Slowly she stood upright and moved sideways towards the door. Quietly she did slid back the bolt and turned the key in the lock. She listened carefully. Silence.

She gripped the handle, turned it and opened the door a little. A beam of light darted in from the landing. She paused, suddenly full of doubt. Slowly she put her eye to the crack.

She could see the W.C. and the bathroom opposite, then the lift, and to the right, the beginnings of the stairs.

The landing – what she could see of it – was empty.

It was now or never.

She flung open the door, ran out and stopped dead.

A scream stuck in her throat.

He was standing against the wall at the top of the stairs, crouching slightly, poised like a cat.

She stared at him, horror-struck. The face was livid and ugly, the angry scars red against the pallor of his skin.

But it was Vasson all right. She recognised the eyes.

Hard. Dark. Glittering in the dim light. Watching her carefully.

For a moment they were both still, staring at one another.

Then he moved.

She cried out and went rapidly backwards, past the door of her room, along the landing. She looked wildly over her shoulder. *Where was the black soldier?*

She drew a deep breath and tried to shout. The *Help!* came out as a gurgle. Vasson was coming faster now, poising himself to spring. A wall came up against her back. She screamed at last.

Vasson sprang forward. She dodged sideways but he caught her hair and pulled her head back with a snap. She cried out in pain. He clamped his hand over her mouth, digging his fingers into her cheek. She kicked out and pushed him away with her arms. But his other hand closed firmly round the back of her neck.

She lashed out again with her feet and felt her shoes fly off. She tried to claw at his face but he was keeping her at arm's length, gripping her head tightly between his hands.

He started to drag her across the floor. Panic clutched her. She struggled, throwing herself desperately from side to side, trying to tear the hand away from her face.

God, where was the black soldier? Surely he'd heard!

Vasson was pulling her faster now. She tried to dig her heels into the thin carpet, but he yanked her off balance and her feet went from under her. Her legs cartwheeled as she tried to regain her grip.

He gave a final heave, something hard bumped against her side and then it went dark. *They were in her room.*

She heard the door close and struggled harder. She kicked viciously in all directions and heard him inhale sharply as her foot met his shin. Her next shot hit the bedpost and jarred her leg.

She aimed for his shin again but suddenly her head was

being jerked sideways, fast. There was a moment of dizziness, then a sickening thud as her skull hit something solid. She saw stars and stopped struggling.

Still dazed, it took her a moment to realise what was happening. He had pushed her down on to the bed and had moved his hand away from her mouth. She opened her mouth uncertainly, gathering strength to scream, then froze. *There was something tight on her throat. His hands* . . . round her neck. *Getting tighter.*

Cold terror gripped her. Then she really started to fight.

She tore at his hands, digging her nails deep into the skin. She kicked with her feet, great wheeling kicks that circled the air. She felt him shift his body over hers, to stop the kicking. She pulled up her knees in a quick movement. She got him in the groin, not very hard, but he pulled back slightly. She arched her back and wriggled sideways on to the floor. His hands loosened slightly as he followed her, then he gripped again, much tighter.

She couldn't breathe. She tore at his hands again. His hands were the only things that mattered. *His hands.* Then she remembered she *must kick too.* She thrashed her body from side to side, striking out with her feet. She felt something in her stomach – something heavy, squashing her – *a knee.*

She couldn't breathe.

Air. She must have *air.* She panicked completely. She kicked out again, wildly, twisting her body round, pushing against something solid, wrenching her hips out from under his knee, lashing out again. *Kick! Kick!*

There was a loud *crash!*

Then a splintering and breaking sound, followed by a muffled exclamation. The hands round her neck loosened. She opened her eyes. In the pale light she saw him pushing off a darker object – the wardrobe.

She scrabbled away like a crab and made for the window. She heard him get to his feet and start after her.

She threw herself at the window and wrestled with the latch. He was almost on her.

She ducked and screamed, really loudly this time. She screamed until he got her firmly by the throat again. This time he squeezed very tight straight away.

This was it. She couldn't struggle any more.

Breath, no breath. *G-o-d. Agony.*

Her ears were roaring and singing, her body was screaming . . .

She felt as if her head would burst . . .

G-o-d. I'm going to die . . .

A fog spread over her in a claustrophobic blanket.

Blackness.

Then a vague perception.

Awareness again.

I don't understand.

A voice, a movement, the weight lifting off her body. The hands leaving her throat. She drew in great gulps of air, enormous greedy gasps of air, and felt the coolness shoot down into her lungs.

She opened her eyes, bewildered, dazed. There was light, a yellow light from the door. *Someone else. A voice. A deep voice . . .*

Everything faded for a second. She made an enormous effort and opened her eyes again. A large shape was filling the doorway. Voices. *The black soldier.* 'Hey . . . Hey,' he was saying. 'What's happening, little lady?'

Julie blinked and sat up. Giddiness hit her in a wave.

Vasson was crouched, watching the soldier like a hawk.

Julie's head cleared. She looked from Vasson to the figure in the doorway. Realisation came. *This was her only chance.* She got uncertainly to her feet, her head splitting with pain, and staggered towards the door. Vasson sprang up and grabbed her arm.

Julie shouted at the soldier, 'Help me! *Help me!*'

The soldier swayed forward a little. Vasson dropped

Julie's arm. The soldier said, 'Hey! Hey! Let us all cool down now. Hey!' Julie dimly realised he was still very drunk.

She stumbled to the doorway and began to squeeze past the soldier. He swayed towards her and she caught the whiff of drink. He grasped her hand. 'Now, why don't we all relax, hey? What's the problem, little lady?'

She cried, '*Please! He's trying to kill me!* Please let me go, let me get away. *Please.*'

'Now, now . . . Why don't we all relax, hey?' He leered at her, his large face inches from hers.

She darted under his arm and staggered across the landing and down the stairs. She tried to run two steps at a time, but tripped and fell against the banisters. She took them singly then, her limbs shaking, her lungs gasping, *begging* for breath.

Faster, she had to go *faster*.

Third floor —

Above her she heard a voice raised in argument, then silence. Her leg gave way under her. She lurched to one side, grabbed the banister, and pushed herself forward.

Second floor —

She ran on, her legs wobbling terribly, half-listening for other sounds. All she could hear was the hammering of her heart and the rasping of her lungs.

First floor. Just one more. As she raced across the landing and launched herself at the last flight of stairs something caught her eye and she glanced hastily upwards.

Legs. Running legs, beyond the wire mesh of the lift-shaft. Above, but coming fast.

She gave a little cry and hurtled on. She jumped the last step into the lobby. The front door beckoned ahead. She ran for it.

She stopped dead.

No! He'd get her in the street.

She looked wildly about and darted sideways, past the

desk and down a dark passage. On one side, she knew, was the dining room. *Not in there! Nowhere to hide.*

On the other side was the kitchen. *Kitchens had back doors.* Still running, she took a quick look over her shoulder. No-one in sight. She pushed at the kitchen door. It was a swing door and opened easily. She fell in and, panting wildly, spun round to grip the door and close it slowly so it wouldn't swing back the other way. The door had a circular window in it. She peered through. Nothing.

It was dark in the kitchen but there was a large window along one side and by its pale light she could just make out the lines of the room. There was a large table in the centre. She shuffled round. *There must be a door.* She reached the far corner. A door. She opened it. Cupboard. She closed it again and looked over her shoulder.

God. He'd be here any moment . . . God.

She felt her way forward. A recess here . . . Behind it – a passageway! She stumbled down, the flagstones cold under her bare feet. Yes! A door! She gave a small sigh of relief.

She tried the door. It was locked. She found a key in the lock, turned it and tried again. Still locked. She gulped. *God, please let it open.*

Desperately, she felt the surface of the door with her hand. There must be a bolt. There was one at the bottom. She exhaled in triumph. It slid back quite easily. She tried the door again.

It still wouldn't move.

She imagined Vasson creeping along the passage towards the kitchen door. She muttered, 'Please, God, *please!*'

She felt the door again and guessed there must be another bolt right at the top out of her reach. She felt around for something to stand on. There was an object by the door. A fire extinguisher. She put her bare foot on it and, balancing precariously, reached up.

Her hand fell straight on to the top bolt and she tugged
at it quickly. It wouldn't budge. She made another effort
and tugged harder. At last it shifted, but slowly, the noise
rasping loudly in the stillness. At the same time her foot
slipped and she landed heavily on the flagstones. The fire
extinguisher clattered over, rolling noisily along the
passage.

She wanted to scream.

She held her breath and shivered violently. The
extinguisher stopped its roll and there was a terrible
silence.

She staggered to her feet, her hands shaking wildly.

She tried the door. This time it opened.

She closed it again and leant against it, trembling.

At the front door Vasson froze, his fingers on the handle.

It had sounded like something falling, a vague clattering.
From the back of the hotel somewhere.

He listened for a moment, but apart from the panting
of his own breath there was silence.

He decided to check the street anyway. If she'd gone
that way he'd still be able to see her.

He threw open the door and darted out. Nothing. No
running figure, no moving shadows. Just to be sure, he
sprinted to the other side of the street and looked wildly
up and down. But she wasn't there.

The hotel, then.

He ran softly back across the street and into the lobby,
closing the door quietly behind him.

There were several doors off the lobby and two passages.
Starting on the left he began trying the doors methodically,
one by one.

*

Silence.

Where was he? When he came for her what would she do? Run? *God, he'd catch her just like that!*

She thought for a moment, then made herself creep back towards the kitchen and peer in. The room was empty and quite still. She looked towards the far door. Its round window, faintly lit by the distant lobby light, stared back at her, blank and expressionless.

She forced herself to go right into the kitchen. She crept towards the table and felt along its length. There must be a drawer! There wasn't.

The hackles on her neck began to rise. He was getting nearer, she felt it . . .

I can't stand this!

Along one wall was a dresser. Lots of drawers here. Hurrying now she tried one. Papers, all papers . . . The next drawer, *better* . . . Spoons, large ones . . . Forks . . . *But no knives.* She fumbled with the last drawer.

Open! Damn you, open!

At last! . . . Knives, neither large nor sharp, but *knives.* She picked one up and, looking hastily over her shoulder, started for the back passageway. Something caught her eye. The cooking range. Something *behind.* She stopped.

Knives, lots of them. Long kitchen knives . . .

She threw the small knife aside and picked up a long one. She touched it: very sharp.

She looked over her shoulder and darted down the passageway. Weak with relief, she fell against the door. She thought for a moment and deliberately turned the key in the lock – he might come at her from the *outside.*

Then she waited, her fingers round the key. *Ready.*

She leant her head against the door and breathed deeply. Her neck was hurting horribly and her head was stabbing with pain. Worse, her legs were like jelly. She wouldn't be able to run . . .

She bit her lip. *Must hold on.*

The silence crept on endlessly.

She couldn't believe how long it was—

She wanted to fling open the door and *run*. But no. He might be outside . . . Better to *wait*.

Her shaking fingers slipped off the key. She gripped the key again, more firmly.

The silence was appalling now, pressing in on her, *roaring*.

She jumped.

The sound of a lorry echoed from the distant street.

That was all . . .

Her heart thudded in her ears. She felt incredibly weak.

She rested her head on the door again.

She stiffened. Was there another sound?

Dear God! Her heart missed a beat.

Her fingers tightened over the key. She stared up the passageway into the kitchen, peering into the darkness, *listening* . . .

A faint sound.

From the kitchen.

Her heart leapt into her mouth. Hastily, she turned the key, then the handle and started to pull the door open.

Something caught her eye. A *dark shadow was racing across the kitchen.*

She gasped and leapt out of the door. She ran, bicycling her legs, pumping her arms, pushing her bare feet painfully against the rough surface. The nightdress flapped around her legs – it was *tight, too tight*, she couldn't stride out—

She was in an alleyway, very dark. It seemed to have no end—

Suddenly she heard the padding of feet behind her.

She gasped and raced on, faster and faster, pushing until her breath came in great pants.

The footsteps were closer.

Dear God, give me strength.

The alley – *where did it go?* It went on for ever; dark and endless!

She stumbled and almost fell. She righted herself and tried to accelerate again.

She could hear his breath now. G-o-d.

Light, a glimmering of light.

She raced for it, came to a corner, swerved round.

The street. Some way ahead. The ground was rougher now . . . Suddenly she cried out. A terrible pain in her foot! Something sharp was in her foot! She tried to run on, but the thing was sticking *into* her foot!

She hobbled desperately for a couple of steps.

He was panting up behind her.

The panic was roaring in her ears. She gave a moan.

He was close now. *Close!*

She *wanted* to keep running, to run and run until her heart burst, to run and run – *for ever and ever.*

She let out an animal cry and spun round. She whirled round and faced him. She braced herself, the blood screaming in her ears. *Keep away, keep away from me!*

He was still running. He was trying to bring himself up short but his momentum was too great. He was cannoning into her.

She screamed, 'No!' And in the split second before he hit her she gripped the handle of the knife in both hands and, with a loud grunt, thrust it forward.

His body hit hers with a thud, carrying her backwards. She fought to keep her balance but staggered under his weight and fell. His body came down on top of her with enormous force, crushing the breath out of her.

His hand was on her neck and she felt an instant of blind terror.

Then his hand fell away and, by the light of the street lamp, she saw his mouth open in a ghastly grimace of pain. With a roar, he rolled off her and lay on his back. He clutched his belly and, raising his head, stared in blank amazement at the blood seeping out from beneath his hands.

His head fell back and he stared at Julie, pain and disbelief on the twisted scarred face.

Panting hard, Julie got unsteadily to her feet and looked down. The knife was still in her hand. Moaning quietly, she shook her head and walked backwards.

The sharpness stung into her foot. She cried out in pain and, dropping the knife, reached down. Glass. She got hold of it and pulled.

A movement.

She jumped.

He was getting up.

He had one hand on the ground, levering himself up, the other on his belly.

She growled, 'N-o-!'

The knife! *Dear God, where was the knife?*

He was on his feet now, swaying slightly, his eyes piercing into her, dagger-like.

She caught a gleam. The knife. At her feet.

He moved forward.

She grabbed for the knife. He was still coming. Her fingers gripped the handle and she held the knife out in front of her. *Keep away from me, keep away!*

He paused, wary this time, keeping his distance, arms out, ready to spring.

He began circling, panting slightly. Occasionally he put a hand to the wound in his stomach.

She thought: I didn't hurt you enough, *not enough.*

Then she saw that one hand was in his pocket, searching. He was pulling at something. It got caught in the pocket lining, but then it was in his hand, reflecting dully in the street light. A gun.

A gun. I can't fight that. Can't—

There was a faint roaring from the street: a lorry. The sound grew louder until it filled the alleyway.

Vasson's eyes flicked away, towards the street, and then down to the gun. Suddenly she realised he was fiddling with the mechanism, trying to make it work . . .

Now. It's now or never. Dear God, I feel so weak . . .

Wobbling violently, she gathered all her strength and lunged forward. She saw his eyes dart up, his hands rise in defence —

She raised the knife high above her shoulder and with a loud gasp plunged it forward and *down*, hard, *hard* at his chest.

The knife travelled forwards then stopped.

Was it in? Had she hurt him at all? She kept pushing, straining to push the handle in, sobbing, *'Keep away, keep away. Leave me alone. A-l-o-n-e!'*

At last she realised the knife was rigid, fixed in the man's body. She let go and fell back.

Vasson looked at the knife in amazement. It was sticking out of his chest. A sharp pain pierced through him, worse than anything he had ever imagined.

He couldn't believe it. She'd stabbed him again. *Hard.* She'd hurt him badly. *He couldn't believe it . . .*

He gasped for breath. There was a soft gurgling noise. His lungs drew in liquid.

Very slowly, he slid downwards, first to his knees, then on to his side.

Wet black blood trickled from his chest on to the ground.

He lay still in the hope that the terrible pain would go away, the bleeding stop . . .

He felt very heavy now, his limbs like lead. Liquid was rising in his throat. He choked a little.

What did I do? Dear God, what did I do? It's not fair, it's not fair.

His lungs expanded but found only blood. He panicked, gasping for breath. He felt as if he were drowning.

At last the realisation came – this horror would be the very last, this final prison the smallest, darkest room of all . . .

He wanted to cry out but the darkness was already closing in.

Why did you abandon me? Why?
Why are you abandoning me now?
I don't understand.

For a moment his face was contorted with pain and rage, then a look of shock and terrible sadness came over it. His eyes opened wider and wider. Blood trickled out of his mouth. Suddenly he gasped. The eyes rolled once, then were still, glazed and unblinking.

She stood, sobbing quietly, watching him. She stared at his eyes, horrified in case they should move again.

She shook her head slowly from side to side, moaning, 'N-o' over and over again.

There was a sound. A car in the distant street. She blinked and, looking hastily around her, hobbled back towards the darkness of the back alley. Her foot was still agony. She leant against a wall and felt the sole of her foot. There was still some glass in it. She pulled at it. A fragment came away. The foot was bleeding heavily; she was leaving a trail of blood. She tried to tear the bottom off her nightdress and make a bandage, but it wouldn't come. She found a handkerchief in her coat pocket and tied that round the foot instead.

She hopped and hobbled back round the corner and down the alley towards the hotel.

The door was still open. She closed and bolted it and hopped through the kitchen to the lobby. It was empty. She climbed the stairs as fast as she could, walking on the heel of her injured foot, and reached the top landing. She found her shoes lying on the floor where she'd kicked them, and picked them up. The door of her room was closed but not locked. She went in, switched on the light, and locked the door.

For a moment she stood perfectly still with her eyes closed, then, methodically, she started to do what had to be done. She made a mental list: clothes, wash, change. She took off her coat and nightdress, which were both bloody, and wrapped them neatly in a bundle. Then she put on her dressing gown and picked up some day clothes. She went across to the bathroom and, trembling wildly, stripped completely and washed herself all over. She dressed and went back to her room.

The trembling had become a violent shaking. She ignored it and, taking out her writing pad, picked up a pen and began to write. At first she couldn't keep her hand still, but she gripped the pen tighter and forced herself to concentrate. She wrote carefully, in plain block capitals. The first attempt wasn't right and she tore it up and started again. Finally she was satisfied. The message was simple, but it would do the job.

It read:

PAUL VASSON. ALIAS LEBRUN, ALIAS FOUGÈRES, ALIAS THE MAN FROM MARSEILLES. TRAITOR, COLLABORATOR, MURDERER. BETRAYER OF METEOR AND TREGASNOU RESEAUX.

JUSTICE!

She read it several times.

The way she had worded it, it shouldn't lead to her. It could have been someone from Meteor, *anyone* in the Resistance.

It was two-thirty. Before she lost her momentum, she went quickly down the stairs to the kitchen, unlocked the back door and, after looking carefully up and down the alley, limped along to the corner. She looked ahead. The distant street was deserted. The body was still there, lying heavy and inert like a sack of coal. She limped quickly up to it and, averting her gaze from the staring eyes, put the piece of paper beside it and weighted it down with a small stone.

She forced herself to look at the body. Swallowing hard, she leant down and gripped the knife handle protruding from Vasson's chest. She closed her eyes and pulled with all her might.

The knife shot out and she staggered slightly.

She looked over her shoulder and scurried back into the darkness, round the corner, and along the alley to the hotel.

She closed and locked the door, checked that she hadn't dripped blood on to the floor from her foot, and crept into the kitchen. Carefully, she washed the knife, dried it, and returned it to the rack where she'd found it. Then she climbed quickly back to the fourth floor.

As she reached for her door handle she heard loud snoring from the room next door. The black soldier. It had to be. Asleep. She listened to the steady rise and fall of the snores and felt a wave of despair. The black soldier could give her away.

She went into her room and locked the door behind her, then turned off the light and lay down on the bed, fully clothed.

She stared at the dark ceiling and it suddenly occurred to her that the black soldier would probably remember nothing of what had happened, nothing at all.

There was a glimmer of hope.

That left the blood-stained clothes – they would have to be disposed of. She would throw them in the river, weighted down with a stone.

Then there was the hotel register. Yet the body was some way away. There was no reason why they should look here.

Even if they did, who was Juliette Lescaux?

No! She was safe.

She closed her eyes.

Who was Juliette Lescaux? She didn't know any more.

She had been someone, a long time ago.

The shivering started again, first gently then violently until her teeth rattled.

She pulled the bedclothes over herself, and, curling up into a ball, closed her eyes tightly against the terror of the darkness, desperate for the oblivion of the sleep she knew would never come.

Epilogue

Summer, 1945.

There had been dancing and flag-waving on VE Day, cheering and hymn-singing on VJ Day, but for sheer uninhibited happiness there was nothing to beat the homecomings.

All over Britain there were joyous reunions, first in the privacy of homes and then outside in the streets and village lanes. People wept and laughed and hugged and shook hands, and realised that life would never be as sharp or intense again and weren't sure if they were sorry or glad that the war was over.

For those not welcoming sons, husbands and fathers it was still a good time because the festivities took their minds off the austerity and bleakness that seemed to have become a permanent part of British life.

In the main street of Hugh Town, St Mary's, a banner reading 'Welcome Home' was strung between two houses. The day before, no less than five men had returned: three soldiers, a sailor and a merchant seaman. It had been a day of great rejoicing.

Peter looked out of the window and giggled. 'Mummy, there's a soldier kissing Tommy Blair's sister! Mummy?'

Julie came in from the other room and went to a mirror on the wall. She patted her hair, put on some lipstick, and viewed herself critically. Older, of course. There were tiny lines at the corners of her eyes and the sides of her mouth.

Less young in other ways, too. The look in the eyes, mainly. She frowned and turned away.

Peter was still giggling. 'Mummy, he's hugging another girl!' He turned to see if she had heard. He gasped. 'Hey, Mummy, you *do* look smart!'

'Not really,' she said briskly. 'It's just my old suit remade, that's all. Now, are you ready? Have you combed your hair?'

Peter came closer and peered at her blouse. 'You've got Tante Marie's brooch on!'

'Yes, it seems a pity not to wear it.' Tante Marie had died at Christmas – a welcome release under the circumstances.

'And Mummy!' He was jumping up and down now. 'That smell! Have you put on *perfume?*'

'Shush!' Julie said impatiently. 'We should go soon. Are you ready?'

'Mmm.' Peter shuffled off in search of something. A moment later he wandered back and asked, 'Mummy, d'you think he'll be different? You know . . .'

'What do you mean?'

'Will he *look* different?'

'Good Lord, how should I know? Now hurry up and comb your hair. It looks terrible.'

The letter had been waiting for her when she returned from France in November. It came from Major Smithe-Webb at the War Office. It was brief and factual. Notification had been received from the Red Cross that Lieutenant Ashley was being held in a POW camp near Stuttgart in Germany.

She couldn't believe it. Alive! She had been bracing herself for bad news for so long that it took her entirely by surprise.

Alive! Her first reaction was joy and relief. For *him*. Because he had always been so full of life and optimism and burning energy, and it seemed only right that he *should* be alive. For *him*. Because by staying alive he had cheated Vasson and that was a victory.

She was happy for herself too – at first. Then she had doubts. In Brittany, in the old days, everything had seemed so simple, a matter of right or wrong, and black or white. She had loved him with all her heart. She still did. And yet . . .

Nothing would ever be straightforward again. The events in France weighed heavily on her mind. She dreamed terrible dreams not only of Jean and Tante Marie and Maurice, but of blackness and running feet and blood . . . She often woke in the night, gasping for breath, crying out. At those moments she felt unbearably lonely.

Life with someone like Richard would offer love and security. Perhaps even peace of mind if—

If everything was the same. If he still loved her. If they both hadn't changed too much.

You couldn't stop people changing, she decided. It just happened. It was a long time since Brittany – two years. For him, two years in a camp. Now he was back home. With his family, his own people, the old way of life.

'Mummy, I'm ready. Come on!'

She led the way out of the house and along the street towards the harbour, her face solemn and pale.

The boy danced along at her side. 'It's so exciting, isn't it, Mummy? Will we go and have tea later, at the hotel, like we do on birthdays?'

'I don't know. I don't know what we'll be doing yet.'

'But I thought—'

'Quiet!' she snapped. A moment later she sighed, 'Sorry. I didn't get to bed till late.' She'd been finishing a dress for someone. It was her trade now, remaking clothes into new styles.

They walked in silence for a while.

'Mummy, you *are* glad he's back, aren't you?'

'Of course, darling! Of course! I'm – delighted.' And

terrified, she thought, because in a way I'd rather remember everything – *him* – as it used to be.

They turned on to the mole that formed one arm of the shallow bay and walked past the inter-island boats waiting at the steps, towards the end, where the steamer berthed.

Halfway along she paused. 'Let's wait here.'

'But the ship stops up there!'

'I know, but – I'd rather we waited here.'

She wanted to avoid the group of people she saw gathering at the ship's berth.

She leant against the wall which ran the length of the mole and watched the boy standing on the edge of the quay throwing pebbles. She raised her face to the sun and tried to quell the fluttering in her stomach.

The *Scillonian* was late. She wandered slowly along the quay, back in the direction of the town. It was a balmy day, the breeze no more than a faint stir, and the light that strange translucent white which was peculiar to the islands. It was so very peaceful here, which was why she had grown to love it.

'Mummy! Here it is!'

She spun round. A trail of smoke showed above the high wall of the mole. A few minutes later the bow of the *Scillonian* appeared round the end of the wall, and the steamer began to manoeuvre slowly into her berth.

She walked back to Peter and took his hand.

After a while the lines were secured and the gangway lowered.

People started to come off in ones and twos. A couple of soldiers walked jauntily down the gangway, waving to some people on the quay.

Then Peter was pointing. 'There! Mummy, there he is! Look!'

She spotted him straight away. He was wearing naval uniform and carrying a bag. He looked taller than she remembered. As he came down the gangway he paused for a moment and she knew he was searching the knot of waiting people. He reached the quay and, looking round again, made his way clear of the onlookers.

She waved. He saw them almost immediately, and, waving back, started towards them.

Julie didn't move. The boy tugged at her hand. 'Come on, Mummy! Come on!'

'You go.'

The boy ran forward, a little shyly, and she heard him shout, 'Hello!'

Ashley stopped in front of him and, smiling, said, 'Hello, young man! How are you?' He reached out and tousled Peter's hair. 'You're a sight for sore eyes, I must say.'

He looked up to where Julie stood and came towards her.

'And you too.'

She smiled. He embraced her, gently, then bent and kissed her cheek and held her at arms' length, looking into her face. She stared up at him and was surprised. There were so many things she'd forgotten about him . . .

She said quickly, 'How marvellous that you're safe.'

'And you!' He was going to say more but changed his mind. She realised he was nervous too.

He tucked her arm in his and they began to walk slowly along the quay towards the town, Peter hopping up and down beside them.

She asked quickly, 'Will you be able to stay a while?'

'Several days, at least. Then I must go back and see my family for a while. Did you get my letters?'

'Yes. Thank you for writing. It was – lovely to hear so soon.'

He looked down at her for a long time. 'You look just the same.'

'Do I?' It wasn't true, but she smiled anyway. 'Well, it's very nice of you to say so.'

When he looked away she glanced up at him and noticed how thin he was and how pale his face. His eyes were the same, warm and caring, but she sensed a reserve behind them that hadn't been there before.

It was just as she'd thought. He'd changed.

A woman Julie knew slightly passed by and smiled. It was a knowing smile directed first at Julie then at Richard. It happened twice more and Julie quickly suggested they went and had some tea.

They chose the hotel on the harbour. Peter thought it was the best place in the world because it had scones and a sweet mixture that resembled jam. No cream, though; that was still unheard of.

Because of the boy, they talked lightly about school and homecomings and how difficult it was to find eggs and fruit and chocolate. Food, they decided, was not what it used to be.

Richard said, 'But it's a darn sight better than I've been used to, I can tell you.'

'Didn't you get anything to eat in the camp?' Peter asked. 'Was it awful?'

But Julie interrupted, 'Not now, Peter. Richard won't want to talk about that now.'

Richard nodded at the boy. 'Some other time, Peter.' He looked away and Julie saw that he was frowning.

Later they separated for a while, he to take a room in the hotel, she to put on her best dress and brush her hair and dab a little more perfume behind her ears.

'Can't I come too?' Peter asked hopefully.

'No, another time. You can come out to dinner another time, I promise. But not tonight.' She'd arranged for him to go next door to Mrs Trehearn's for the evening.

He stamped his feet a couple of times then accepted defeat gracefully and went off to find out what Mrs Trehearn was cooking for supper.

Julie was ready early and sat down by the window to

wait. Her stomach was still fluttering. Excitement. He still had that power over her. Yet in many ways he was a stranger. And she was a stranger to him . . .

Finally he arrived, looking handsome in his formal dark uniform. And attractive. Very. She decided she was rather pleased about that.

They walked slowly towards the hotel and talked about the Scillies and the sort of war the islands had had.

Richard stopped and pointed to the far side of St Mary's Sound. 'In the early days we used to take Concarneau trawlers there, to New Grimsby, and repaint them in their proper colours.'

'Yes, I know. Everyone guessed what was happening.'

He laughed. 'I should have known. There isn't much you locals don't know.'

They walked on a little way. Suddenly he said, 'It all seems a long time ago, doesn't it?'

'Yes.'

The dinner was execrable, but then everyone was used to that. However it was made more palatable by a bottle of wine which the hotel proprietor had been keeping for a celebration. It was a celebration, wasn't it? Julie said that yes it was, and Richard smiled. The wine, when it came, was not much better than the food, but they drank it anyway.

'Not a touch on your uncle's stuff.'

'No.'

He smiled briefly and looked at her over his glass and she knew he was remembering the evenings in the attic room.

There was a silence. Eventually he said, 'Smithe-Webb told me everything about what happened to the others. I never saw them, you know, after we were taken from the beach. Only my crew, and even then we got split up. I'm very, very sorry. And I'm sorry about your aunt.'

She nodded. 'It was a blessing. She wasn't very well . . .'

'But this traitor . . . Smithe-Webb told me you'd identified him and proved that someone else was innocent – your cousin, wasn't it? That was wonderful, Julie, a great achievement!'

She murmured, 'Thank you.'

'But how on earth did you do it? How did you find out who he really was?'

She hesitated. 'It's a long story . . . But it was the Resistance and other people – friends – who really found out who he was. Not me.'

'The Major thinks you're something of a heroine all the same.' He smiled warmly at her. 'But I knew that anyway.'

She dropped her eyes.

He went on, 'But this fellow Vasson . . . I gather the Resistance got him and executed him, didn't they? That's something. It won't bring the others back and it sure as hell won't make up for my two lost years. But . . . well, it's something. And I bet they made him go through it before they finished him off.' He laughed briefly. 'I bet the devil suffered!'

She stared at him. 'Yes, I suppose so . . .' She opened her mouth to say more, but couldn't. She wanted to tell him, to share the dreadful weight of it . . . But what would he think? How would he look at her once he knew, once he realised she was capable of such a thing?

Better not to tell, much better.

Perhaps one day . . . perhaps never.

Instead she asked him about the camp. Haltingly and a little unwillingly, he sketched out the story. With relief she realised that there were whole areas of his life that he, too, didn't want to talk about.

Finally he said, 'It drove me mad, being locked up. There were thousands in the same boat, of course. But even now I can't talk about it without . . .' He shook his head.

She reached over and gripped his hand. 'Then don't!'
He looked up in surprise.

She said, 'Let's talk about something else! Something
. . . *nice*!'

He laughed. 'What a marvellous idea.' Julie noticed that
the reserve had gone from his eyes.

They started to talk of less serious things and she felt
more at ease. She even found herself laughing, which she
hadn't done for a long time. She'd forgotten how funny he
was, how warm and vital. She began to remember other
things, forgotten words, small incidents . . .

Perhaps, she thought, he hasn't changed so much after all.

They talked a little about the future, though not too
much and not too deeply. He had lots of plans. She realised
that, for Richard, the future was everything. She was glad,
thankful – he made her feel optimistic again.

After a while he paused and asked, 'Do you remember
the holiday we were going to have?'

'You mean . . .'

'Here, in the Scillies. On *Dancer*.'

'Yes, of course I remember. Perfectly.'

'Well? Would you like that?'

She smiled slowly. 'Very much. I'd like that very much
indeed.'

Later, when the wine was finished and the meal cleared
away she watched him and thought: There's something
else I'd like very much too.

You.

In that respect nothing had changed at all.

And why not now, tonight?

Yes. Life was too short.

Yes, she would stay with him tonight, whatever . . .

Then, in time, maybe everything would be all right.
Maybe there would be love and security and a new life.
Perhaps the nightmares might eventually go away . . .

At least she'd be happy while she found out.

She smiled at him across the table.

'I'd love some fresh air. Shall we walk along the beach for a while, before we go home?'

Postscript

BY THE OUTBREAK of war, Germany had developed several successful early-warning radar systems to guard herself against air attack. These systems were large and land-based and worked on medium to long waves. Thus convinced of Germany's security, Goering ordered a halt to all long-term research. The many Jewish scientists and technicians involved in the work were sent to concentration camps.

Later, when it was realised that the British actually possessed radar, there was panic and the armed services, industry, and finally even the concentration camps were combed for technicians.

An electronics research laboratory was set up by the SS in Dachau. Eventually over a hundred skilled prisoners were employed on dismantling captured enemy equipment.

Right up till the moment in August 1943 when the captured Rotterdam Device (the British H_2S shortwave radar) was finally pieced together and made to function – it revealed a perfect 'picture' of Berlin – the German experts were convinced that shortwave radar was both impossible and impractical.

14 May 1943, Fuehrer Conference Minutes.

Admiral Doenitz's Report:
    We are at present facing the greatest crisis in submarine warfare, since the enemy is for the first time making

fighting impossible and causing us heavy losses, by means of new location devices.

Admiral Doenitz: Memoirs. January to March 1943, *Collapse of the U-Boat War*:

Radar, and particularly radar location by aircraft, had to all practical purposes robbed the U-boats of the power to fight on the surface. Wolf pack operations against convoys in the North Atlantic, the main theatre of operations . . . were no longer possible.

. . . I accordingly withdrew the boats from the North Atlantic. We had lost the Battle of the Atlantic . . .

Many, many brave men and women risked their lives to help Allied servicemen escape from Occupied Europe. Occasionally, an airman shot down over Belgium would find himself back with his squadron in England in just two to three days. The record was nine *hours*. Usually it took a little longer . . .

There were numerous escape lines operating through Belgium and France, most of them functioning on arms and money sent by MI9 in London.

One of the most successful lines was Comet which ran from Belgium through Paris to the Pyrénées and Spain.

In 1943 the Brussels end of the line was hit hard by the Gestapo and over a hundred people were arrested, many dying by firing squad or in the horrors of the concentration camps.

For a while the Paris branch of Comet continued to function until that, too, was hit by a terrible blow. This time the traitor was identified. He was a new courier by the name of Jean Masson. It was an assumed name, as were all the names he used in his long and terrible career.

His real name was Jacques Desoubrie.

Later Desoubrie penetrated another escape line, further to the west. As a result of this treachery seventy British and sixty American evaders were caught and sent to Buchenwald concentration camp.

There is evidence that, on the orders of his masters, the Gestapo, Desoubrie penetrated at least two other lines . . .

The French Resistance was at its strongest in Brittany.

However, early attempts to establish an escape line through Brittany met with difficulties, mainly organisational. Later in the war properly trained agents were sent in, and the Shelburne line was born. Motor gunboats, crewed with great bravery and daring by officers and men of the Royal Navy, made regular runs from Dartmouth across the Channel to rock-strewn beaches on the Brittany coast, right under the noses of the Germans. Knowing that coast as I do, I can only marvel at the incredible feats of navigation they displayed.

The Shelburne line was very successful; it transported 307 servicemen and agents to England in a single year.

Incidentally, when the Germans came sniffing round, the gunboats sometimes had to depart in rather a hurry. On more than one occasion some members of the gunboat's crew *did* get left on the beach.

The traitor Desoubrie continued his career of betrayal and treachery until the end of the war.

Then his luck ran out. He was, in fact, brought to justice and executed in Lille.

But it might have been different . . .